The Beautiful Lie

Thomas Talarico

When you can't accept the facts because they offend you, your society's regression is well underway…

Contents

The last post from the old world…

Date - 31 December 2029

New Think was once described as an ideology for the extravagantly stupid rather than the stupidly extravagant. Best for those who simply refuse to consider the facts, preferring senseless praise and the company of fellow idiots.

For years, intelligent folk resisted pressure to bow to their stupid demands. But, by the weight of their numbers, they dragged us down and beat us with experience.

Believing only what they're told to believe, and knowing only what they're told is true, the ruling idiots informed the world that it was doomed, and sorry about that, our bad. Damned fossils released a few too many parts per million or some such, like a bad fart, but that'll all net out. Should calm down a little, we suspect. We're shuttering the place for a while, but she'll be apples in 20 years or so. Oh, and don't mind all the fans and mirrors, they're on the up and up. Should see us out of this in a jiffy.

As with any situation, a lack of objective evidence leaves the burden of proof, a heavy weight upon the accuser. Though as it turns out, a weight of objective evidence is no less a burden. An idiot never knows. Prove me wrong to my satisfaction or submit unto my cause. After all, a cause is a cause of course of course and no one can doubt of the cause, of course. So, don't.

The newsman, once an outpost of sanity amongst the infirmary of the powerful and greedy, lost sight of where they came from, adrift amongst the masses. The fourth estate, no more now than a desperate parent trying to stay relevant as the children grow bored of their tired old tropes. Parent follows child through every whim, supporting each new interest and fanning the flames of their passion. Social media spurs them on, so the desperate parent joins them on their flight of fallacy, a balloon afloat, lost in the torrid storm forever.

There's no way out and no way home now, so they say. New Think comes tomorrow. The Global World, and we're all in it together. All for the greater good.

Tink, Tink, goes the sound of my hat as I tap its shiny crinkled surface for surety. I wear it for protection, of course, for I do not wish to join these fools, and with it, they'd never want me.

After all, I'm just another crazy. The world would never submit to all of that. Not without 'the science' to support them.

I've got to go, but I'll leave you all with this. If the fallback position for every failed conspiracy is that the accuser was just a crazy conspiracy theorist, then the only sane thing for a good man to do, is keep calling out conspiracies and wear his tin hat with pride.

I'll see you all in paradise...

The Tin Hatter

P.S. Could someone sweep up under the fans? There's an awful lot of birds dropping...

The Beautiful Lie

Prologue

Welcome to the Global World

I'm being watched.

I hate being watched.

I used to hate the saying "How long's a piece of string?" It's ridiculous! A piece of string?! It's twice half its length or exactly as long as you cut it. If you happen to encounter a random piece of string, you need only measure the bloody thing to work out its length. Why everyone once used this as a metaphor for the impossibility of knowing the span of time or resources required to complete a task is beyond comprehension.

Still, I preferred the times of immeasurable string to the new world. Now they'd say "Why would you use string, it's so wasteful. Do you know how much carbon one metre of string contains?!" Then they'd flip out at the very thought and promptly take the rest of the week off. But, that's the world we live in now.

Speaking of the world we live in. At this precise moment, which a quick check of my watch tells me is already 20:03, or 8:03PM in civvy speak, I find myself sitting in a grassed urban park, on an aged wooden bench. As I shift my 6' 1", 105kg frame, it creaks long and slow. It's the pained sound of warped wood and metal nails rubbing together in an endless battle to determine which one controls the other. The wood is worn, greyed and weathered, each length separated from the others by shallow grooves, forming long character lines that eventually break off into loose lengths and splinters, before falling to the concrete pad to be ground away to dust.

There's no metal frame on the bench, it's just wood on wood because there simply isn't enough metal to go around anymore. Not for a basic park bench like this, anyway. Even here in Central City, the major hub city of the Global World, resources are always in short supply. Virtually everything is measured out, including water, food, and electricity, too. Unless, of course, it's earmarked as part of a project to protect the safety of the Global world, in which case it's a protected commodity.

Taking a deep breath of the cool autumn air, tinged as it is with the scent of decaying gum leaves, I look around from where I sit for the hundredth time tonight, trying to enjoy the pretence that I'm alone. Needless to say, I'm not. There are eyes out there, blinking away. Electronic, human and rodent. All of them either watching or being watched or both. Part of the endless surveillance cycle that's a staple of this world.

It's dark out here now and the LED powered light poles running along the streets that edge the park to my left and front have all come on. The bright white light they cast is aimed at the footpaths, intended more to assist the human watchers than to light the roads or improve the safety for residents of the neighbourhood. Safety is what all the cameras are for, or so they say. Of course, given their infra-red and night view capabilities, the cameras would be better off without the lights.

Above one particular light pole, presently positioned fifteen meters to my front, rises a ten-story concrete and glass apartment block. The concrete walls are painted black, like all the rest of the apartment blocks you'll find crammed side by side and back-to-back along every street in this suburban part of the city.

Beyond the apartment, shines the lowest of the pointer stars, Alpha Centauri, its presence guiding my eye up to where the southern cross would be if I could see it. Unfortunately, cities are as cities were, in that the light they emit cancels out that of the stars, leaving the sky sparsely filled, if beautiful all the same.

A breeze flaps the front of my loose-fitting polo, leading me to vainly do up the top button in an effort to ward off the chill. Winter is on the way, and I should have worn my one and only jacket, but I'd left it at home this morning and hadn't the desire to fetch it after work.

Leaving the station, I'd decided to go for a walk, as I often do. It's better than the alternative, heading home to the solitary stasis of my lonely apartment. I can't think in there, its stillness, no muse for my thoughts. I do nothing but stew.

Out here, I can think. Really think, my brain inspired by my surrounds. The movement of the walking, the sights and smells. The sounds of wind rustling the gum and oak trees, the calming effect of their gentle sway set against the stillness of the apartments, spotted by lights, where wary citizens either bury their heads in technology or look out upon the silent night, wondering who might be looking in. All of this stimulates my mind, getting my synapses firing, the release of dopamine flooding me with feelings of happiness.

Oh, and I need a dose of happiness. It hasn't been a good day, you see. Although they seldom are these days. Today, however, was especially unhappy, because today was my birthday. It's Sunday the 23rd of May 2049, and I'm 53 years old.

Birthdays used to be joyous occasions, you might remember. A time for family, cake, presents and rejoicing, the celebration of another year lived, the experiences of the past year giving way to new hope for the next. Not anymore. Those things are all in short supply these days.

Now my birthday is simply another pointless milestone. A marker denoting one more year trapped in the nightmare the world has become.

I'm not meant for this world, you see. I'm old school. "Old Think" is how they refer to people like me these days.

Progressive lot, these "New Think" types. Not very imaginative, though. Not very logical either. There's just not a lot of common sense about if you catch my drift. Although, what I would have considered common sense is really just one of the foundations of Old Think. Common sense having been abandoned in favour of a New Think foundation called "Popular Perception".

What is logical or right, is irrelevant. It is now of the utmost importance for our actions to be popular, and even more important that they right a perceived or actual wrong of the past, even if that action disadvantages a whole other (*and usually much larger*) group of people.

This includes the righting of wrongs, that those who were wronged may be unaware of, or uninterested in having righted. I'm not sure what they plan to do when all past wrongs have been righted or if that's even possible. Perhaps they'll just start over, reparating and doing penance for newly perceived wrongs and repeat the cycle forever. So long as there's someone to hate, I suppose.

New Think is based on a cancel culture you see. If you don't like it, or find it offensive, then cancel it. Shout down, then ban that opinion or action. Don't worry about why something is the way it is. Just make it stop. That's a victory for the betterment of humanity and the most direct path to progress. By stopping things…

Apparently, cancelling one person's way of life to support another's is the New Think way of creating equality. "You shouldn't be allowed to be you, because that doesn't support me being me. So, we should cancel you altogether. That way, I can be me, and you can be nothing. That's the only way to fairly resolve the injustice of your existence… Sincerely, New Think."

If you happen to be a logical thinker, then I offer my condolences for the daily absurdities and frustrations you must endure. Despite popular opinion, there are quite a few of us left. We're just not allowed to publicly admit it, what with logic being the enemy of progressiveness and all.

Even now, after 20 years, I still haven't quite got it all figured out. Which, of course, you're not really supposed to. You're just meant to follow along obediently. Never questioning the changes that come or pointing out their flaws. So, if you're Old Think like me, you'll know the sentence that forms in your head with each new blow to your existence, "What?!…" Alright, it's not a sentence… but you get what I'm saying.

The youth of today only know New Think, Old Think, having been phased out of all forms of education. Books either re-written to suit new historical truths or the "corrected" versions of history. More accurate (*obviously*), having been written by people living hundreds or thousands of years after the fact, so clearly better positioned to describe the periods in question.

All the original books still exist, mind you, but because New Think is absolute, they only exist as examples of history's horrors. Not fit for the eyes and minds of the newly enlightened youth. Instead, descriptions of history are given by teachers and parents, like elders passing down stories from the beginning of time. Except, rather than heroic or enchanting tales of wonder, discovery and progress, they're presented with the shame of humanity's history, as if that's all there ever was.

From my seat in the park, I see light from the street poles dancing through the leaves and branches of a nearby gum tree. Villains, ghouls and monsters appear and disappear again in an instant, reminding me of the incredible capacity of the human mind. Not only for its power to conceive, create and convince, but to forget, ignore or gullibly accept false information as fact. The latter is a strength of the modern youth. That is, if you could call the ability to unquestionably accept what you are told as fact, a strength.

New Thinkers are trained from an early age to do that. To switch off that internal alarm that clangs in our heads when we hear something that simply doesn't ring true. As long as it comes from the single source of truth, then there's no reason to question it. No matter how absurd it seems. Besides, one must open their mind in order to overcome hereditary prejudice, accept their inherent flaws and commit to eternal reparations.

Personally, I can't seem to block it out, although that could just be the Old Think in me. Maybe I've just been trained to think a certain way, forming thought patterns in my youth that now I can't break. The basis of New Think relies on this principle. If they only ever provide a certain perspective on life and all that it entails, starting from the very beginning, then that's all a person will know. Any alternative thought or opinion must, of course, be wrong.

Under New Think's system, they will have finally "fixed" people by addressing their way of "thinking", educating them to see the world from the "correct" angle. In fact, the only reason they didn't destroy the books and evidence of history completely, is the belief that by keeping the evidence of Old Think around, the leaders of New Think can claim there is proof that they themselves are unlike the horrible, slave runners, invaders and oppressors of the past, who can be read about in the Old Think texts. Those villains of a time of greed and violence and desperate inequality. Their continued existence also gives them something to regret, to toil in penance for, to fear and strive to never repeat. That New Think eradicated true freedom of thought and expression, in favour of complete totalitarian control, the young will never know.

It's brilliant really. Questioning minds cannot claim that the evidence of Old Think has been destroyed or kept from them, because it exists right there in those books.

They can't even really claim that the youth is being lied to. If you tried to explain the true history of the world, the old ways of life, so to speak, to a fully fledged New Thinker, they'd most likely nod along with you, smiling politely at how misled and unfortunate your life has been. How sad it was that you'd been born before the real truth of our history was known.

To maintain this perception, people are bombarded with endlessly one-sided opinions couched as the "consensus truth" across all media platforms, whilst alternate opinions (*especially factually based ones*) are marked as dangerous, false, or misleading. Serial offenders can be flat out banned from sharing this information, but not before they make a big deal about what they've said and how wrong and dangerous it was.

Everybody is specifically shown what they're absolutely not allowed to see, so they get a damn good understanding of what dangerous information looks like. The more accurate the message, the more they want to make a big deal about you not seeing it, so you're certain to look before they ban it.

See, if they can show the real truth, the old truth, as dangerous, then people will fear it and turn towards supported falsehoods seeking safety and comfort amongst equally confused, afraid and agreeable people. If someone simply stating real facts can be soundly discredited, then the truth, as it was, is consigned to history, and history is full of lies.

"How could people have believed that?!" they'd cry. And those who still believe it become a common enemy to hate and fear as a united group. Anyone that disagrees with New Think's methods of "saving the world" is despicable and must be destroyed. After all, it's our "only option".

The more popular this opinion becomes, the bolder and more hateful the masses are of their enemy. Once the anger grows and spreads amongst the herd, the narrative becomes self-perpetuating, with the people themselves taking control of enforcing it.

The quieter members of humanity, whether they agree or not, go along with the crowd to avoid any trouble. Once this state of compliant fervour is reached, all the Guides need do, is to keep reminding the world there's someone to hate.

The irony is, New Think isn't even new. Communist style totalitarian ideology, where the supposedly downtrodden fight back against their oppressors, is an old concept, lived before it was ever defined. Now, polished up by insipid entities in the west to create an ideal method for a global saviour to sell to the dumbed down masses.

Global-Enviro-Capitalist-Communism is the new model under which we labour. Those with the means to invest in "world saving" technology use our money to do it, then charge us to use it, with all alternatives banned in a captive market they control.

At their core, New Thinkers are all just communists wearing a different hat. They want big government to look after them, bringing everyone down to "their" chosen level, with those unfortunate enough to fall below, being artificially raised up, creating an equality that's set at the lowest common denominator. The many look down upon the few, holding a hand out to help them up into their misery, feeling they've accomplished something grand, all the while.

Frankly, a fairly healthy world got here by allowing itself to be dragged down by those who were lazy and resentful of anyone willing to put in the extra effort to achieve success and rise above. No, it's better, they think, that everybody settles to a far lower, far easier standard, where government tells us what to do and how to live. Meanwhile, as we're all aligned at the bottom, the golden cloud of government hovers above, handing out favours and consensus truths, while suppressing unapproved thought and action.

"What about the other systems of governance?" you might ask. "They're all flawed! Democracy, Monarchy, Republics. Each of them leaves someone or some group of people worse off than the others." Yes, that's true, but they also offer opportunity and reward for effort, while New Think is all about dragging people down to a predetermined level and keeping them there. Homogenisation of the world into one singular, boring, controlled mass that lacks opportunity and bans free thought. Regress to the mean, then regress again.

Needless to say, this is not the first time people have tried to take over the world. Granted, those past attempts at gaining control of humanity failed. Although, that wasn't because different styles of thinking and governance were allowed to exist outside their master's control. No, the problem with former attempts was that the ways and means of their systems seemed to serve no greater purpose. Outright totalitarianism, or authoritarianism, or whatever other ism, was all they ever offered. Our way and no other. The world as it always was only with them now sat at the top.

To New Think's one enduring credit, they learned from those mistakes. Rather than follow the methods of failed empires before them, New Think built their foundations on the one thing that can shift the most stubborn of people… fear. They added weight to the shrieking of extremist activists about the perfect storm of impending doom.

Environmental destruction, human sufferance, catastrophic virus and disease.

Their goal? To save the environment, end sufferances, eradicate inequality and protect the world from pathogens, hell bent on destroying the human race.

The plan was simple and cyclical and built up over many years before reaching its final state. They moved through each agenda item in turn, promoting the cause, stoking the fear, offering the solution and showing that the problem would continue to return, again and again until we gave them the authority to act on our behalf. Year after year, cycle after cycle, they'd push, until finally they pushed them all together and all at once, claiming that each one drove the other, raising the world up to a peak level of fear where people would accept anything just to believe there was a way to be saved.

It's hard to know what came first. Let's say it was the environment, the world apparently accelerating toward a burning, flooding apocalypse. The other problems don't matter if there's nowhere to live. "A few too many parts per million of carbon molecules in the atmosphere, guv. That was the bugger what done it." A problem big enough to deconstruct our way of life as we knew it.

Naturally, launching thousands of mini satellites into the same space, to sit in lower earth orbit and bounce internet signals back and forth between machines and H-bots (*Human Bio-technology systems*) is no problem at all… Giant chemical clouds dispersed into earth's lower atmosphere to reflect that deadly sunlight… Yep, that's gotta be good.

So, in order to shift humanity away from the certain destruction of earth, we were ordered to cease using its bountiful natural resources, which we had cleverly (*or wickedly, depending on when you were born…)* transformed into useable energy by manmade process and technology.

Instead, we would now use earth's bountiful natural resources and transform them into useable energy by manmade process and technology. So, as you can clearly see, a much better… Wait, what was the difference again? Oh yes, the release of carbon into the atmosphere. You know, the carbon upon which all life forms on earth are based and sustained… Suck it out of the atmosphere, suck it out of the oceans and plug your arse.

The answer to this horrific conundrum. Windmills, and photovoltaic glass panels. Millions and millions of them!

The arrogance of thinking that millions of square miles taken up by giant windmills and light absorbent glass panels should represent the peaceful dream of the future is astounding.

New Think literally use these images of barren lands devoid of people, animals, and plant life, dotted with giant windmills as images of the utopian dream. A far cry from the green jungles with blended living that one might have imagined.

The strangest part is, the windmills, whose purpose it was to provide power without environmental impact, have altered local wind patterns and wiped out numerous bat and bird species whose natural flight patterns were drawn into their paths. Not to mention their inadequacy at handling the variation of the environmental conditions that drive them. When they work 100% of the time, they are still only 30% to 50% efficient. Plus, no wind, no power. Too much wind, no power. I believe they were designed on the Goldilocks principle. They only work if the conditions are "juuust right".

I never heard a coal miner say, "Fuck, there's too much coal. Shut down the power station." Or a gas plant operator say, "She's too efficient, switch it on and off throughout the day." Or a farmer say, "There's too much grass, shoot the cows…"

Same goes for solar. Nighttime, no power. Day time and cloud, no power.

They're not alone, either. Hydrogen takes more power to create than it produces, and hydro-electric whilst a brilliant concept is inefficient and relies on one of the most precious resources we have in the world. Water. Yet another fuel source dispersed intermittently by nature and utterly out of our control.

Next on the list is the concept of human equality. A fine, fine concept, and one to be supported at face value. Why shouldn't we all have the same opportunities and access to services and education, irrespective of who we are, what we look like, or where we come from?

Unfortunately, resolving those issues wasn't quite the solution New Think had in mind. They took it a rather different direction, such that we now live in a world where every ethnicity, sex, sexuality and religion is in a race to the bottom, for there lies the currency of the day… sympathy for the plight of your people and social justice in the form of reparations and apologies as its recourse.

To make good on past wrongs, the western world must adjust the norm. The masses must step aside for minority control. To facilitate this, they created categories in all aspects of life, separating us into different groups to be distributed in equal measure all throughout the world. Don't be fooled. That doesn't mean we're represented or viewed equally. The split only served to dilute the norm.

Empowered, former minority groups believed that life should indulge them at every turn. All the indecent elements of their lifestyles being not just be accepted in silence but celebrated in public. Dancing, singing and debauchery should accompany daily offerings at their altar, while conservatives were to be shunned as hateful and degrading.

New Thinkers never want to come back to the societal mean, or the norm, for the sake of broader community comfort. You must celebrate their cause or suffer in silence.

It was once understood that in order to gain equality and acceptance of alternate lifestyles (*that being alternate from each other, not alternate from the norm*) you must understand that the goal is to fit in, not to stand out. Therefore, if you were equal and accepted, there was no need to celebrate how proud you are of the difference of your lifestyle, because it should only be as different as anyone else's is to yours.

What if everybody demanded celebration of their status? I could only imagine a parade of six billion straight people walking down the street in hoodies and trackie-daks, holding banners asking if you saw the footy scores, or riding along on beige lounge room floats, followed by people carrying signs saying, "Happy wife, Happy life" or "Compromise is the key" …

New Think culture demanded that we knock down statues and monuments from Old Think history, those that celebrated the modernisation of the world, and the establishment of nations of united people and governments with sound societal standards. Ironically, those same governments that gave them the power to destroy all that came before them, so they could build new statues and monuments that seek only to show history as a time of brutal violence and territorial invasion.

New Thinkers don't want you to celebrate the good that was done or the historical people and milestones that got us to where we are. They want you to be angry at the bad things and believe that the past was a time filled with evil and violent oppressors, whilst the progressive modern world is filled with truth, acceptance, and the evolution of the human mind into one that cares for the world and its people…

How anyone can live in the most surveilled, restrictive, and controlled time in human history and honestly believe they're living in a world that's progressed to a better place than before, is incomprehensible. But that's the world we live in now.

New Think has a saying to cover this paradox: *"Everyone should be equal and free, but only so long as you're equal like me."*

Frighteningly, unsatisfied with the categorisation of humans on a basis of ethnicity, body image, gender or sexuality, New Think introduced the concept of discrimination based on your biochemical make up.

You can now be legally discriminated against based on whether or not you have received any of the innumerable versions of mandatory cell and gene modifying injections. Banned from carrying out the same activities as others on the basis that your natural human biome is inferior to the modified human and bio-enhanced status of the "up to date" New Thinker.

The fact that the "up to date" New Thinker is almost always in worse health than an "out of date" or "non-compliant" one, is of no merit. "Inject to Protect", is the line New Think uses. That your injection only protects you from the wrath of New Think's punishing laws rather than any potential ailment is not mentioned.

You must remember, this is all about fear and control.... Wait, I mean, safety and the betterment of the human race.

So, to justify the shots, you publicise and berate people about the real and present danger of viral pathogens rampaging around the world. New Thinkers have purportedly been trying to protect us from just this type of incident by experimenting with previously unseen viruses, to work out exactly how'd they'd need to change for us to catch them. They say this is justified scientific research, of absolute necessity in order to keep us safe.

The truth is, they haven't been trying to do biological research to prevent people getting sick from deadly pathogens. They've been modifying non-deadly ones and spreading them around. Because who's going to fall in line for the greater good, when they themselves have nothing to fear?

Still, the most shocking thing to me is just how easily they did it. The messaging was so uniform and consistent. It's incredible to think just how much control an advertising department has to have, or perhaps more accurately, that Pharma companies have to have over advertising and media, in order for national medical boards to instruct all the doctors of a nation to follow the advertising of a product rather than provide their expert medical opinion. Loss of licence for any contrary comment to the advertisement being the threatened and enacted punishment.

If this isn't totalitarianism, I don't know what is. I mean, one of the principles of communism is complete adherence to the rule of the state for the good of the people! Mumma and Papa Government gunna to look after you, but you better do as we say or you're going to the gulag.

Perhaps the old disclaimer at the end of pharmaceutical advertisements, *'To make sure this treatment is right for you, please consult your GP or make a booking with an authorised medical practitioner.'* should be replaced with *'If you are unsure if this medication is right for you, please review the product's advice, which states; All medications and medical procedures advised by us are right for you. Adherence to this advice is non-optional. We recommend against consulting with your doctor due to the risk of receiving misinformation and potentially failing to meet your obligations to the broader community. Remember who the experts are ...'*

Sadly, when all is said and done, New Thinkers are nothing more than the captives of an ideology. Lied too and controlled by a core group of arrogant, wealthy, and powerful people, who took over the world simply because they could.

Yet, nobody seems to see it. Nobody seems to understand the level of control under which they live. Which is lucky for New Think, because, once you see the lie, you see all the lies and just how blatant they really are. Then you start to wonder how you could have ever allowed yourself to be lied to at all. I sure did.

I'm Gaz by the way, Gary Johnson. Actually, that's Detective Gary Johnson as of seven months ago, come Monday.

Yep, I'm a copper. I even look like a copper. Or, I should say, I look like cops used to look. My measurements actually meet the old minimum requirements to join the force from way back in the 80s. I'm 6' 1" or 185cm tall, depending on where you were from before the Global World reformed as one singular entity. Metric won, by the way, becoming the accepted norm for measurements. Imperial went the way of common sense. That is to say, it was banned.

If I were to describe myself, I'd say I was tall without towering over too many. I've managed to stay in pretty good shape despite the state of the world, too. Fit for a 53-year-old, at least. I was a soldier before I was a cop. The Army built me up, training and shaping my muscular physique, which I now simply try to maintain. Age takes its toll, but I still have my broad, rounded shoulders, heavyset chest and arms that stretch the sleeve. My real strength, however, and the source of my personal pride, are my legs. I once enjoyed demoralising soldiers more than ten years my junior with my squatting prowess in the gym. Now I'm just proud that I can still squat at all.

My dark brown hair is kept to a short, layered trim with a slightly longer fringe, to help hide that receding hairline, while my naturally light olive colour skin tans easily to a soft brown with just a little sun. It must be the Italian blood in me, or the "Global Warming". It certainly isn't the Scottish, English or Polish coming out.

Despite the job title, I'm more a loose fit chinos and polo type, refusing to wear the unofficial uniform of all detectives throughout history (*including the New Think ones*), that being the dark-coloured suit and loose fit tie. I do still like dark colours, mind you, which pair nicely with my simple masculine style and comfortable black rhino boots, which are great for walking. An important point to note, because E's can be hard to come by.

Perhaps the most notable thing about me is that I'm not adorned by the modern-day entry stamps necessary for admission to the club. Tattoos, that is. I haven't got any. Not because I fear needles or pain, but because I find them bloody pointless. I mean, I understand tribal cultures used them to tell stories of their family, or tribe, or heritage, and that they have some rite of passage meaning to them, and that's all fine. For the new tribe though, the Global tribe, it's harder to find that meaning when all they've got is a butterfly stamped on their arse, or a sword, or a dragon, or worse yet, an inspiring word in a language they don't even speak. I used to make the mistake of asking "why?". People would just say "It's cool" or "I just really wanted something that represented who I am". Mmm, if only you had a face or a voice box… I don't ask that question anymore…

For me, I wear a watch, that's all. Under the laws of the Global World, we were all allowed one small possession, something that's just ours that we can say we own. The only caveat is that it must be registered. It's a bit like the defining feature in Where in the World is Carmen Sandiego. I chose my Longines VHP GMT. A high-quality quartz watch, with a fuss free perpetual calendar that will well and truly supersede my needs. The calendar having been rather optimistically built to track day and date out to the year 2400. The beauty of this watch is that it's accurate, simple, functional and best of all, un-trackable.

I don't and absolutely won't wear a watch linked to a device. The last thing I need is for my watch to tell me how many steps I've done each day, display my messages or remind me of all the things I probably don't want to do. My device and subdermal chip already tell me that stuff and the Guides tax every step I take.

You might wonder, how could someone so clearly misaligned with the New Think world we live in, possibly police such a society?

Well, it's like I've tried to explain an inordinate number of times to my co-workers. You can legislate against carrying out logical thoughts and actions, but you can't actually stop human nature from taking its course. Same goes for criminals. No matter what your beliefs are, human nature is innate and cannot be prevented from taking over at some point and guiding the actions of an individual. Like it or not, at the core of every human being, (*even the New Think extremists*) lies a logic driven mind with perfectly illogical, irrational, and emotional tendencies that make you do crazy shit. It's just how we're wired.

Solving crime now is no different to how it's always been. Same crimes. Just different motives for people to commit them.

As you might expect, I don't work alone. I am part of a detective team who're supported by, or in support of, the broader Global Police Service.

That's right, Police "Service". Not Force. Force was seen as too aggressive for the delicate minds of the modern world. Besides, New Think doesn't really support the idea that a Police Force… (*clearing of throat…)* I mean Service, should even be necessary. How could the pinnacle of human existence possibly still require policing? Surely, we are now a self-regulating utopia in our perfect omni-conscious, self-aware state.

After-all, the intent of New Think is that once implemented, we should have finally achieved nirvana, world peace, a state of global consciousness truly accepted and understood by all, with one utterly equal and self-perpetuating truth. The meaning of life really… That we are all here to serve the greater good.

My partner, incidentally, is also of Old Think origins. Sharon Wilson is her name, and she too is a detective.

Sharon, or Shaz as I often call her, was originally a Theatre Nurse. She left that role after the sloppy actions of an arrogant, drug addled surgeon, led to the unnecessary death of a young and healthy patient on the table. It was an event that affected her deeply. However, being a strong, intelligent woman didn't damage her drive or motivation to carry on with life. It only made her realise she needed to make a change and find a role that would make her happy.

Shaz re-invented herself as a librarian, a role she was drawn to because of her great love of books, history, and reading in general. She worked as a librarian for twenty years before libraries became entirely automated, in effect making her redundant. Now, libraries are almost entirely online and near universally ignored by the woke modernists of today's world. Why read a book when someone can read it for you and give you the gist? They've all been re-written now anyway, such that they're inoffensive to the easily offended, which basically means they have all the texture of air without the life-sustaining content.

By the time she'd left the library, Shaz was 46 years old, and like me, had become disillusioned about her place in a world where she no longer felt she belonged. Also, like me, she saw an opportunity to do something about it by taking on the despised role of a police officer and working from the other side of the law. Nobody else wanted to do it and nobody else wanted her. It was a perfect match. The old saying goes, "If you can't beat em, join em". We say, "If you can't beat em, join em and then do your best to undermine their stupid plans from the inside". To be fair, we learnt that from them.

By way of a description, I figured Sharon is best summed up by, ah… Sharon. The way she described herself when we registered our detective partnership nearly six months ago was a lot like this:

Age: *50*

Height: *5' 8" or 173 cm. Above average height for a female, above average intelligence for a human, and above average anger for a mammal.*

Weight: *Seriously?! You can't ask that! Not in this world and not in the last. Look, if you can't even call a spade a spade these days, you definitely can't ask how heavy it is. However, if I had to answer, I'd be a sporty 55kg. I should be a sporty 60, but sustenance is scarce.*

Hair: *Mousy brown. Though I prefer 'wonderfully mild brown'.*

Eyes: *Big, round and green.*

Face: *Natural, but I take good care of it. There are some fine character lines because I choose to age gracefully. No botulinum in my face. A short, rounded chin, a petite little nose and high fine cheekbones.*

Skin: *Pale and does not tan well. Makes me really shitty at Gary.*

Clothes: *I'm an Old Think female cop. What do you think?! Smart looking pant suit. Of course, under your rules I'm only allowed 2... If it were up to me, I'd have 10 to 12, but let's not get into that! So, one's blue and one's bright, fucking, red, to match my level of anger.*

Like I said, I've been partnered up with the wonderfully mild-brown haired Sharon for just under six months now. We actually passed the detectives course together seven months ago, which makes us the most inexperienced pair of detectives on the Service.

As you might expect, we were originally paired with more experienced partners. New Think partners… They…did not… like us.

Sharon's partner requested a transfer on the basis of, and I quote, "Strong differences in opinion and method…". My partner was old school New Think (*which is actually even more confusing than it sounds*). He was so troubled by the thought of having to "train" a newbie who was not only a shiny new detective in a service that nobody really likes, but also, a 53-year-old man who's as "Old Think" as they come. To quote him, "If you can't teach an old dog new tricks, you can't teach an old Old Thinker a fuckin thing!". He simply chose to retire.

Shaz and I were briefly re-assigned to office duties after being ditched by our partners, although that only lasted a week. The office duties that is. The Service had thought it might be best to keep us off the streets. Not only were our partners unhappy with us (*as mentioned, career decisions were made*), they'd also been somewhat "shown up" by our sincere unwillingness to listen to their nonsensical opinions and instead use logical process to actually solve the cases we were assigned… In spite of them.

Quite a few, actually. To be fair, new D's and their more experienced partners do tend to be put on cases that are considered to be "straight forward" or "training wheels" as it were. Confirming suicide, investigating petty crime, small business robbery, etc.

Despite their years on the job, it seemed impossible for our partners to even conceive of these crimes in a New Think world.

Therefore, in their opinion (*which as far as they're concerned is the only opinion)* they must certainly have either been a mistake, or a crime committed in the grips of a regressive rage.

Regressive rage, by the way, is a condition that theoretically exists within those who were alive pre-New Think, or who grew up with late conversion Old Think parents. Supposedly, it's the manifestation of Old Think thoughts bubbling to the surface and exploding out in the form of violence and crime.

That means that according to our partners, the only possible suspects for each of the crimes (*when acrimoniously forced to accept that they were indeed crimes*) we attended, were known Old Thinkers. And, as far as they were concerned, that list was short and included us...

The other alternative they posited "the mistake" would require us to believe the frankly unbelievable. Such as the owner of a convenience store in Mid-Town, mistaking a rather friendlier item for a gun, and unwittingly handing over all the food and beverages on the premises to a random person in an unintended act of exceptional good will. That the person also had two accomplices and an empty truck at the ready before leaving with all the goods, is apparently immaterial.

To be fair, if I was inclined to believe the world had achieved a genuine state of equality and peace, then it may very well be hard to accept that people would still need to commit armed robbery just to get what they need to survive. Having said that, history does tell us (*as did George Orwell*) that even equal people will often desire the means to be somewhat more equal than others.

So, as you might expect, life isn't exactly easy for Sharon and I. Whilst we are indeed police officers, trusted (*begrudgingly*) to uphold the laws of the Global World, we, like everyone else, are also being monitored by the guardians of the approved moral good.

Moralists, as they are known, are territorially spread among us. They essentially patrol in plain clothes, a specific block or suburb, and form part of broader nationally controlled groups (*an oddity given that territories, states, and nations, are all in fact Old Think creations and no longer exist in their previous forms*).

This method of moral monitoring, known as "Applying The Moral Standard", is the same across all continents of the "Global World". These moralists are the human side of monitoring for misbehaviour in the eyes of New Think. They look for those whose actions are not in keeping with the global goals for the greater good. They sit outside the law in a sense. Above us, but without legal standing, so to speak. Essentially, they are like those who once enforced the strictest interpretations of a religion. They are respected and feared, whilst (*quite deliberately*) of dubious and deniable authority.

The reality is, moralists shouldn't need to be amongst us on the streets. We are, after all, a self-proclaimed technical marvel, with cameras on every corner, ostensibly ensuring the safety of the supposedly evolved and equal members of society. There's also a microchip implanted under the skin of our left wrist that tracks our internal biome, our health status, and our physical and geographical movements. Then there's the biometric scanners in every building, vehicle, and mobile device that scan and compare your physical characteristics and behaviour against that which is recorded on your Global Pass. The Global Pass being the "secure" digital version of you, which along with its endless online chaperoning of all transactions, internet searches, telephonic and in-person conversations, will purportedly ensure that safe and sustainable actions are undertaken at all times.

Despite this abundant lack of "privacy" (*a word by the way, which does not exist in New Think dictionaries*) and obvious fear and distrust of the people by their Guides (*not leaders*), New Think disciples (*which is almost everyone*) seem to truly believe they live in a free, equal, and near perfect world. A world that, despite its global governance and connectivity, got both a lot smaller, and its cities a lot further apart.

You see, saving the planet and its people was crucial to gaining support for New Think. To save the world, we must cease to omit gases and particulate matter expelled by the burning of fossil fuels. This means less travel, less interaction with people from other places and less knowing anything about other places that New Think doesn't want you to know.

There's no travel to other countries anymore, because air travel, car travel, and sea voyages are all incredibly unnecessary activities, as well as being incredibly resource heavy. An unfortunate reality that apparently no amount of renewability can undo. Rail is largely reserved for short trips to service the common New Thinker, longer trips for the more equal among us, and, as you might expect, the movement of freight due to the economy of its environmental impact. Besides, why would you need to travel to see other places when here is the same as there now? That's equal.

Monotonous uniformity and multiculturalism have resolved the human desire to travel by making it utterly unnecessary (*not to mention, illegal*). Everything that's there is here, and everything that's here is there. If it was there, and not here, it isn't anymore.

Perhaps the limitations of the New Think world were best summed up by an anonymous journo twelve months before the singular Global government was officially instated:

You could be forgiven for looking at the actions of New Thinkers in response to a global pandemic, and the creation of global warming as an event to fear, and seeing within those actions a coordinated strategy to limit human movement and information access in a targeted manner, with the express intent of shrinking the world to a much more manageable size. Now, we all know that would be crazy. But, if you'll indulge me here a moment, I'll take the concept for a walk.

Pandemic measures separated individuals and taught them a need for obedience to our leaders in order to survive. They taught us to discard unapproved information and then strengthened that idea by banning its distribution and, in many cases, outlawing its creation. They taught us to discard any thoughts of the "individual" and to see choice as a relative concept and not an absolute.

For our safety, we could not travel internationally, and then for financial and environmental reasons, that ability never returned. You could still briefly move about your own country or connected land masses by personal vehicle, except of course "personal" is just a synonym of 'the individual' which no longer exists in favour of the greater good for us all.

Plus, exhaust fumes = global warming, so easily portable fuel was no longer a thing, making trips longer than 100 or so kilometres rather a stretch. Electric vehicles were to solve shorter distance transport needs, but what with all the wind turbines and solar panels and connective cabling covering the countryside, there really isn't any room for interconnecting roadways and how could we all travel on them together, anyway? As you know, "for the greater good" we should always move together. No room for an "individual" (should they be allowed to exist) to travel in their E, because the 500,000 charging stations needed would simply drain the natural resources from the sun and wind, and where the hell would we put them all. Plus, what on earth would you do for an hour or so, every few hours, whilst your car recharges? Watch native birds run the windmill gauntlet and dizzy bats trying desperately to remain inverted, cheering, naturally, for the wind turbine to beat the winged creatures senseless, all for the sake of saving our natural world? ...

This unfortunate loss of mobility and the need for separation from each other to prevent viruses spreading, meant logistics was a problem, which meant that food distribution was a problem, and as with the car chargers, there's simply no room in the countryside for growing food these days. Not efficiently, without nitrogen based fertilisers, and the like.

Luckily, New Think can supply artificial food they make in their carbon neutral factories. You can buy whatever food you like, within the limitations of what is available, and of course the cap on the number of each item per person, which is rigidly fixed at one. Certainly not to keep you hungry and obedient, but because of the evil and totally naturally occurring viruses impact on the supply chain, don't you see?

What luck though, there are foods on special. Score!

Nothing suggestive or persuasive about the foods that are on special being the foods they want you to eat.

Boy, that inflation hits hard, and damn lucky that special was there, so the price is the same as it used to be, once the special is applied. Well, a little higher, obviously... a conglomerate's gotta eat.

Ah, New Think, how you've saved us from ourselves...

It's still hard for Shaz and I to understand this world, even after twenty years of living in it. We both grew up in the old world, you see. The good world. Granted, one that was under heavy attack from the "progressive" mindset, but still predominantly the world that we'd always known and loved...

And then it all changed.

It crept up on us slowly at first, then accelerated all of a sudden until the Global World was here. That's how it works, you see. We are one Global World under the direction of the Guides, and New Think is the mindset that binds us.

Back on implementation day, Tuesday the 1st of January 2030, nobody really understood what New Think was. Those in power had been trying unsuccessfully for years to make it obvious what they wanted us all to believe, without actually having to say it. Unfortunately for them, the broader population was intentionally or otherwise aware of, yet ultimately ignoring, the new moral code. So, they made it unavoidable.

It was the kids who seemed to accept the changes more easily than the rest of us. It goes without saying that this was because they targeted the school's first. The kids didn't know any different.

Most parents thought the changes to the school curriculum were just a way to open the minds of our future leaders to a more accepting world and become more mindful and considerate of their impact upon it. Not that the parents were actually allowed to know what their kids were learning, no no no. Parental rights don't give you the right to make decisions on behalf of your child. New Think will do that. You just have to feed them.

First, they took away a child's right to be who they biologically were. You can't refer to boys as boys and girls as girls anymore. Those are gender affirming terms, and they assume that people truly feel right in their own bodies as the sex they were born. They don't? … ah, wait… cough, cough… I mean, they don't!

Rather than just teaching kids to be open-minded and accepting of people who differ from themselves, they took away the right for the majority to be who they were in favour of gender neutrality for all. Don't be something, be nothing like everyone else.

The 99% of children who were comfortable or utterly indifferent to their biological sex, were apparently ostracising the 1% who weren't. So, they flipped it on its head. Which, in turn, formed a confusing detachment to reality for a great many boys and girls already struggling with the countless issues of childhood. That this plan of action also failed to help the young children genuinely suffering from gender dysphoria or other identity crises, mattered not a lick to New Think.

Creating mass discomfort is not the way to make an uncomfortable person feel comfortable and it certainly won't treat their condition. New Think did it anyway.

Makes you wonder, doesn't it? I mean, consider the things you said about what your parents did to you as a kid. Now, imagine what these kids will say about their parents one day. What hellish nightmare have we created?

For New Think, the removal of gender affirming titles created a far broader free-floating anxiety amongst all children and their parents, which in turn increased their desire to find a solid ideal to attach themselves to. Oh look, we have just the thing. New Think has created the new normal, which is, that you are all untethered to biological certainty, and in its place, you'll be tethered to us…

Then, slowly, everything started to change. The teaching of history changed. The Romans, the Greeks and Egyptians, were no longer talked about as anything other than cruel tyrants whose warring and greed began the downfall of the human race. Their characteristics of self-service, greed, control and oppression carried forward to each new dominant civilisation, right up until the present.

Now, whilst you could argue there is an element of truth to that notion, it's far from the full picture. These people and their empires helped advance humanity, too. Their inventions, creations, development of governance, art and culture formed the basis for every aspect of the modern life we now take for granted.

The arrogance of enlightened times led us to believe that because we have the capacity to make people of all statures and strengths equal today, that historical societies were wrong for not doing the same. No doubt, a rational person would know that it isn't fair to compare society then and now. Many modern applications that allow greater strength, intellect, and gender balance today, did not exist in historical times. The strong had the capacity to dominate, intimidate, and achieve greatness of their time. Feats of strength, size, and skill with weapons settled disputes. Attributes that were not exclusively brutish, given that same strength was also required to work with those of influence and intellect. to build, develop, explore, conquer and defend the world as they knew it.

Not to mention that pesky little fact, that without our predecessors, none of us would be here to criticise them in the first place.

These simple facts of history don't stop New Thinkers from condemning our foundational ways of life as immoral and wrong. Nothing good to see here, kids. We'll show you the bad aspects, the harm and inequality of your heritage, and, on precisely which side of that you sit. Then, we'll tell you how to fix the world.

What of religion? Religion of any form or denomination was a key element, both good and bad, all throughout our history.

Before Judaism, Christianity, Islam, Buddhism, Taoism and all the other beliefs, there were Greek Gods, the divinity of Egyptian Pharos and, indeed, the Australian Aboriginal Dream Time.

No matter what you believed, even if it was nothing at all, the people of Old Think knew that religion had always offered a moral and spiritual guide. A central point with which people could align and centre themselves. Something from which to take solace and comfort in knowing that there was a greater purpose to life.

No fool would believe that religion is without its flaws. Still, one might consider it's better that people have something to believe in, than nothing at all.

New Thinkers knew this too. But they couldn't allow the different beliefs in higher powers, moral codes, and socially binding systems to exist in addition to their own. So, they targeted, discredited, and dismembered any and all religions.

They highlighted their admittedly violent contributions to history, the sometimes appalling behaviour of some members, their propensity to maintain their historical differences to each other and the obvious absurdity of any bond to an entity that has no tangible basis or scientific merit to its creation. Just to be sure, they also criminalised many religious morals, beliefs and actions that might continue exist outside the core.

All these previous religions were then replaced by a belief in New Think and a fear that failing to comply would lead to the end of the world (*blatant plagiarism of religion if ever I saw it*). They did, however, keep the Christian dating system (*calendar that is, not the no sex before marriage and obstinate heterosexuality*) as this had already been built into so much of the worlds technology and surveillance systems that it seemed to change it would be an unnecessary challenge.

For people like Shaz and I, it was almost as if we'd had the misfortune of living our lives in two totally separate parts. One part in a world we knew and mostly loved. The other, being placed under some sort of general anaesthetic that numbs your body, while keeping your mind conscious and your eyes open, so that you're forced watch as someone opens you up and removes the organs they've decided you shouldn't need.

We watched it all happen. We actually had to witness the global takeover of the human race. To wake up the next day and suddenly be forced to accept a different world, with different rules, that doesn't accept your way of life or thinking, is quite a shock to the system.

We certainly weren't alone. Many couldn't accept it at all. They tried to fight back, never really knowing who to fight against. How does any one person fight a global ideology? Especially one like this.

New Think had been infiltrating society for fifty years before it was loudly announced as the new normal. People my age simply had the misfortune of being born towards the end of what we consider to have been a great (*if imperfect*) era.

Then we had to start again and work out how to live in a new, frankly quite shitty and sullen era, of stuck up, know it all wankers, who rule every aspect of our lives. Hating all that came before them.

Any fight back in a world like this has to be surreptitious, underhanded, and excruciatingly slow…

I suppose you're wondering why I'm telling you all this.

Well, it's like I said. I'm being watched. Not only by the cameras, the computers, the moralists, and my co-workers. I'm being watched by "them". I just don't know who "they" are yet. Nor do I know what they want.

For now, the problem is mine and mine alone to bear. I can't tell Shaz. I don't want to scare her.

People like us already live in a perpetual state of anxiety. We're under constant scrutiny, whilst ourselves watching and applying the laws to failed members of our theoretically perfect society, for crimes they are never supposed to have even conceived of committing. A task I must undertake again tomorrow. If "they" don't get me first.

Brushing an errant gum leaf from my chinos, I check my watch again. It's 20:43 now and time that I head home. My watchers will follow me no doubt, though what they expect to learn from that, I simply couldn't say.

What I do know is that despite today being my birthday, it's Friday that marks a far more important date for me in the context of "this" world. Friday, you see, will be six months of partnership with Sharon. She's my best… hell… my only real friend.

Nobody thought two stubborn Old Thinkers like us would last this long, let alone excel as detectives. And yet, here we are, nearly six months on, and we're going to celebrate Old Think style when we make it.

I, for one, can't wait.

Chapter 1

New body, old crime

'Morning partner', said an already coffee laden Shaz as she walked towards me, a mug and saucer held in each hand. Her smart blue pant suit comfortably hugged her gym fit form, the material gently tightening and loosening across her thighs as she walked, her black mid height heels clicking sharply on the tiled floor with every step.

I was seated at our usual table in our favourite meeting place, The Free Café. Mostly we liked the name, while the coffee itself was consistent without being terribly good. The café occupied a large space on the ground floor of a modern-looking office block, taking up both sides of the eastern corner. It was decorated in a bohemian theme, with colourful ragged fabrics forming small decorative curtains that hung across the tops of the windows, while similarly colourful red, blue, green, and grey tiles covered the floor, with bound bunches of fake wildflowers and grass adorning the tables made of reclaimed wood. The "black shorts and T" uniforms of the dispassionate looking staff, manning the automated machines in front of a cluster of surveillance cameras, rather detracted from the image. Still, we liked the idea, no matter how shallow, of some sort of rebellious detachment in the face of Global tyranny.

The cafe also was conveniently located on the corner of Justice and Branch Streets, just two hundred meters from the Central City Police Station and our home base.

'I thought it was my shout.' I said, as Sharon placed the cups on the table, the thick froth of the cappuccino's being the only thing that prevented them flooding their saucers.

'Well. I figured I'd better get down here early to get us moving. We've got our first Doe.'

'Jane or John?' I asked, taking a sip of my coffee, the warm caffeinated aroma awakening my senses.

'Does it matter these days?' she replied, taking a sip of her own coffee and smarting at the taste of the oat juice. She hated the stuff but had no choice, with real milk no longer available.

'It always matters. You can identify as whatever you like when you're alive but when the coroner starts cutting, we'll know… And, I'm betting that once we do, the sex of the stiff will be a factor in why they're there.'

'Hmmm, maybe. You know, even I think you're a bit too old school sometimes.'

'That's not old school. That's just me being a realist. And realist knows real isn't always nice or good. It's just real.'

'Well, speaking of real, it's time for us to become real detectives. Sgt Ease says there's no doubt about this one.'

'Oh yeah, how would he know?' I asked. Sgt Ease being a New Thinker and as a such, not necessarily trusted to see things as they actually are.

'Gunshot wound, right through the centre of the forehead. Seems like a pretty good clue.'

'Okay. I guess we could take our lead off that. Not very New Think though. Let me guess, Sgt Ease is certain this is Old on New?'

'Of course he is.' Said Shaz. 'Ease has made a career of assuming that the most obvious and simple answer is always the right one. That's why we're the detectives and he interviews bystanders.'

'We got an E?' I asked, taking a napkin from the dispenser on our table and wiping my moustache and the short, trimmed beard around my mouth. After years spent shaving every day in the army, I refuse to do it these days, so trimming it is.

'Don't need one. It's only two blocks from here. Now finish your coffee and let's get going.'

Leaving our empty mugs on the table, Shaz and I exit the café, turning left onto Branch Street. Glancing down at my device as we leave, I see we're headed in a southerly direction, an impressive, if irrelevant piece of information. I also make note of the time as 07:13, before pocketing the little dictator that has come to control our lives.

It's cold outside, and I smile to myself as I zip my jacket against the breeze, glad I'd remembered to bring it today.

While Sharon and I walk along in silence, I allow myself a moments distraction as I watch the wind play on the dusty streets of the city we once knew. Powerful gusts make the buildings howl and vibrate. The interplay of its friction, pressure, and the solid barriers of the concrete walls deflect the fast moving air from its planned path, speeding it along manmade corridors, whisking brown leaves and dirt into the open part of the street, before retreating again for another round. I try to remember how it used to be here and what this particular street was called back then. The area is just "Mid-Town" now, but so is the centre of virtually every city in the world. Standardising cities, suburbs and street names across the planet was seen as the fairest and most equal way to remove ties to any form of historical invasion, discrimination, patronising patriarchal overtones, sexism or other Old Think hangovers associated with their previous titles.

'George Street.' said Shaz.

'What?' I responded, as if snapped from a daydream.

'That's what the name of this street used to be. George Street.' she said again.

'How did you know I was thinking about that?' I asked.

'You looked like you were straining to remember something you used to know, not work out something new. I do it all the time. I figure if I can remember what life used to be like, I can keep the world I loved alive. Even if it is only in my memory.'

In reality, with the exception of all the additional cameras and interactive screens on the streets, and the changing of the street names themselves, the city looked much the same as it always had, just a little… less.

The population is continually declining, so there are fewer buildings needed. Some of the older disused ones, particularly those associated with colonial times, having been knocked down in favour of useless urban parks that offer little but the ability to meet arbitrary green quotas. Aside from that, it's merely dustier and less lived in, with fewer restaurants, cafes, and no out-of-town visitors, what…so…ever.

I was still thinking about all this when Sharon and I came to a stop at the corner of Branch and Wing streets, waiting for the lights to change. Not that there was any good reason for the lights to be red in the first place, given there wasn't any traffic. There never is these days, mostly because there aren't many cars in general. There are a lot of e-bikes, bicycles and buses, but not much traffic. The only cars you see around are either electric or solar, which are expensive and lacking in range. To be fair, it's not that they couldn't travel further than they do. It's just that the Guides don't want people travelling too far, so they're all capacity limited to keep you within city bounds.

'Good morning, Detective Wilson. Good morning, Detective Johnson.' said an anthropomorphised electronic voice.

'Geez, I hate that!' I said.

'That's only because my name came first.' said Shaz.

'No, it isn't! It's because traffic lights shouldn't know who's waiting to cross at them. And it certainly shouldn't be able to address them by name.'

'You will be able to cross in twelve seconds.' said the light as a digital countdown timer displayed on the traffic light screen. 'Have a great day!' continued the overly knowledgeable infrastructure.

'You know, I think they just enjoy pissing me off.' I said, as we set off across the street.

'Who?' Asked Shaz.

'The bloody lights!' I replied. 'If they know who I am, they must know I hate them.'

Sharon simply shook her head at my comment and continued on walking. She'd heard it all before from me, and while she agreed, there was nothing either of us could do.

Cities around the globe once had a real vibe to them, buzzing with the business and activity of their people. Their individual identities and specialties set them apart from each other, drawing in people desperate to be part of the excitement and experience. Global cities now are a lockdown lover's paradise. Trolley trams only one third full rattle by infrequently, the regular squeal of their wheels a sign of the lack of infrastructure investment, even in the theoretically green transport options promoted by the Global government.

We pass very few people on the street as we walk and it's worth bearing in mind that this is the Main Street of Mid-Town, THE major nodal city of all the not so well-connected nodal cities of the Global World.

Why are there so few people? Well, most never returned to the office or in-person work after the virus years of the early 20s. Since then, those that could only perform in person work have either been replaced by automation or seen their form of employment disappear entirely, never to return.

One long block from the talking lights, we arrive at 156 Branch Street to find ourselves at the foot of an enormous office building that has stood since the long past days of Old Think. The building is now occupied (*ironically, obviously*) by one of the largest technology conglomerates in history, One Globe Technologies, or OGT in common parlance. They operate a myriad of tech companies, making everything from medical equipment to vehicle components, to phones, tablets, computers, software, spyware, oh and advertising bots. They offer the best and worst of New Think society and also happen to have created the very technology that controls the stupid traffic lights that know who I am.

The building is an enormous glass and concrete monstrosity, occupying a large portion of the block on which it sits. Of course, you can't see the concrete from the outside anymore, with modern tinted glass and greenery creating a new facade. The sign of the environmentally aligned, identifying them as an organisation of the "correct" mindset.

We enter the frustratingly slow revolving doors, which scan and authorise only one approved person per segment. When it finally spits us out, we find ourselves in a brightly lit foyer, where I stand silently watching, while Shaz navigates the infuriating automated concierge system, which had already known who we were and why we were here.

Inside, the large foyer is filled with a mixture of oversized black and bronze coloured tiles, accompanied by huge darkly tinted glass panels and thick concrete pillars. Despite this overwhelming clash of features, the whole space still feels totally dominated by the huge concierge screen, which brings to mind the evil computerised brains from sci-fi movies past. The screen itself isn't even real in the physical sense, instead a solid looking holographic projection, fronted not by Bully the cartoonish Bulldog-clip I might have expected and even enjoyed, but by the much harsher animated image of dual surveillance camera lenses.

The image looks directly at you, ramming home the full message of the organisation when it talks, adding a centralised nose cone to act as the camera's nose, while wind turbine blades, flex and spin in their role as the lips and tongue. Using this rather terrifying image, the building's AI system negotiates your entry in what it conceives to be an intelligent and independent human manner. After several minutes waiting for "Cam" the safety conscious concierge to re-scan our chips and provide a lift confirmation code, it finally allows our access and sends us on our way.

When we eventually arrive at the scene of the crime, it's the towering form (*if one can tower outwardly*) of Sgt Ease that greets us.

'Sgt Ease, what have we got here?' asked Shaz as we entered through an office doorway. She fixed Ease with an intense gaze, her device at hand, ready to commence note taking and location capture.

Ease, for his part, was standing to the right of the door as we entered and appeared to be capturing notes of his own.

'Single gunshot wound to the head.' he replied, tapping his own forehead as he did so. 'The shooter appears to have been in fairly close proximity to the vic. Seems pretty clear that this is Old on New. Somebody she knew, I'd say. It was after hours when it happened, around 9 or 10 pm, and she clearly let them get close enough without trying to escape or defend herself.'

Ease's bulky frame dominated his corner of the room, drawing our attention to it, rather than the one that lay crumpled on the floor behind him. I might have described him as husky once upon a time, though now the comfortable disposition of his 111kg frame simply makes him "body positive". He wouldn't do well if there was still a Service physical, but he needn't worry about that these days. Fitness tests were apparently biased against those who are less fit and are thus considered a form of fat shaming.

'Sergeant, at the risk of asking a question I already know the answer to, what makes you so sure this is an Old on New crime?' I asked, dragging my eyes away from him and down towards the body.

'Well, isn't it obvious?' said Ease. 'New Think people don't commit brutal, reasonless, cold-blooded murder like this. It's against our nature. Against our morals. Against everything we stand for. We changed the world to avoid pointless violence and hate. Plus, you know she must be New Think because she's of the right age being only thirty, and she works at OGT, which is basically the electronic moral guard for the New Think way of life. So, it's a virtual lock that she's on the path of righteousness.'

'Hmmm, funny. Being on the path of righteousness used to be a religious term.' I said. 'I didn't realise it had been appropriated by your lot.'

'Oh, I wasn't aware of that.' said Ease. 'I think I'll stop using it.'

'Right. Well, thank you Sergeant. Please forward us a copy of your report and the no doubt balanced conclusions from your preliminary investigation.'

Ease looked at me blank faced, clearly unaware of the slight, then turned his attention back to his notes.

'Incidentally, Sergeant, have you spoken to the victim's family or employers yet?' I continued.

'No Gaz, I haven't.'

'Good, leave that to us, please. We'll need to speak to them, at any rate. Best not to upset them too many times.'

With that, he nodded and again returned to making notes on his device.

Moving past Ease and further into the room, Sharon and I began our own reviews of the scene. The interior of the office is what I'd consider to be futuristic. Although in fairness, that's only because it looks exactly like what we thought the future would look like forty years ago.

Located on the seventh floor of the building, a large glass panelled wall sat directly opposite the doorway, framed in the greenery visible from the outside, although now with the opposing view that looks out at the neighbouring buildings in this part of the city.

Stepping back from the window to view the inside, you get a whole different feel, with almost all the furniture and appliances being virtually see-through. The desk doesn't have a computer on it, so much as the computer actually forms part of the desk. Tiny optic wires run through a raised angled glass panel connecting discreetly on the underside of the glass tabletop. Curved ends to the table mean no corners or legs, so to speak, and that concept carries through to the foot of the table ends, tapering and curving underneath to form one endless shape. Its light, flowing form gives the impression of weightlessness, as if it somehow floats on the smooth, grey polished concrete floor.

Where pictures would once have hung on the silvery blue walls, there now hang mood panels, which are basically electronic advertising and information screens that scan for the occupant's identity chip, displaying content tailored to that person's likes and needs. Paintings are effectively banned, given that most of the paintings worth having, depicted images of a despised history, or were painted by those considered to have contributed to its horrors. Therefore, the continuing celebration and curation of those horrors was not to be allowed, and certainly not here.

Unfortunately, the mood panel behind this desk, along with the desk itself, and some of the smooth grey floor below it, was now partly covered with the victim's congealed blood, hair and brain matter.

'Do we know what her role was?' asked Shaz to the room at large.

'I'm not sure yet.' I replied in the absence of another answer. 'We may have to wait until we speak to someone who works here. Speaking of which, it's weird there's nobody here from OGT. Well, one body… How did everyone else get in the building, anyway?'

'It's a smart building.' said Karen from her position over the victim. Karen, by the way, is the Service's Coroner who was presently performing her initial review of the deceased.

'Oh, right.' I said. 'Most buildings are smart buildings these days and let staff in at their allotted time. They monitor their own facilities and schedule maintenance as required. I wasn't aware they also monitored for crimes being committed and let the police in. I mean, this company might make all sorts of surveillance software for the Guardian Alliance, but they're still essentially a private company, so far as I'm aware. Aren't they?'

'They are, but this building is smarter than most.' said Kaz. 'Not only is it apparently aware of the crime, it also alerted the police to its occurrence and unlocked only the relevant doors to let us into the room where the crime had occurred.'

'Well, that's convenient. What are we here for? Can't it just investigate and solve the thing as well?'

'Probably.' said Kaz. 'The building's surveillance systems should literally be able to tell us everything we could possibly need to know. That's why Chief Blindspot assigned the case to you two. She figured it would be a walk in the park. You know, a nice easy one to cut your teeth on.'

Shaz had been busy exploring the rest of the room and reviewing what was being identified at each of the evidence markers. One of the crime scene techs was using a Crime Scene Scanner, known as a CSS in the trade, to take bio-marker images of each section of the crime scene. These images provide almost a layered picture of the scene, able to identify bodily fluids in the same way as they used to spray luminol before using a black light. The scanner can overlay the identified biomarkers on the photograph, including suspect fingerprints, fluids, hairs, etc, that can then be run through the Bio-Hub system and compared to a list of every Global citizen in the world. That way you have an image of the scene with biomarker evidence overlayed from which to create a subsequent list of suspects. Once you compare that to the ID chip logs and bio-metric scan ID's, you end up with a pretty tight little group of suspects to work through.

'Hey Slice. I know it seems pretty obvious that our doe was shot, but I don't see any shell casings anywhere. Have they already been bagged?' asked Shaz

'Actually, I prefer Kaz.' said the coroner. Although, in fairness to Sharon, Slice is her last name, not a comment on her profession. 'And you're right. I thought that was a little odd, too. Perhaps when you speak to the building manager, they can give us access to any video or bio-surveillance for this room. We should get most of our answers then.'

The victim, who Sharon informed me was named Katie Hansley, had been sitting at her desk when she was shot. Studying the body, I noticed she had fallen completely off the chair to her left. Thick blood smears streaked from right to left on top of the table, indicating the victim had slid off in that direction, smearing blood with her arm or head as she went.

Her long brown hair, now matted and coated in blood, partly covered her face, while her mouth half open as if about to speak, would henceforth be frozen in motion for all eternity like a stopped watch. Clearly, her hair had until recently been long and shiny, with luxurious curls that started about a third of the ways down. They weren't the natural type of curls, more the salon type that are long and languid, never quite forming into tight bouncy springs.

Her left arm and shoulder were folded awkwardly under her body. Her legs were splayed slightly between those of the chair, her knees bent into the space under the desk, while her satin silver pant suit was stained with the blood of its wearer.

'Hey Kaz.' I said. 'What would normally happen to someone's body if they were seated and got shot in the head?'

Karen is as dry as they come, and a real straight shooter *(pardon the pun),* dedicated and focused to a fault. Presently she was focussed on her own investigative task, taking measurements of the body's temperature, which she silently completed before turning her deep tan face and sparkling hazel eyes to fix my own.

'Well, there are a lot of variables to consider.' she replied. 'What calibre of weapon was used, whether the victim was moving when they were shot, how well balanced they were and whether they were on an angle or not.'

'If you're looking at those blood smears up on the tabletop, though, I agree. It doesn't make sense that she slid all the way off the chair to the left if she was sitting fairly square on that seat. She should have just collapsed forward onto the table. There's no indication she was moving when she got shot, unless the shooter was moving too and had amazing aim. Plus, it's only a small calibre round, probably a .22. Frankly, it was lucky to have exited the skull at all, so there's almost no way it had enough velocity or force to knock her back and sideways. Certainly not after she finished bleeding out on the table.'

'Thanks Kaz. That's basically what I thought.' I said. The clear implication of both my question and Karen's response, being that someone had almost certainly repositioned the body. Or, to put it more bluntly, her murderer had pushed her off the chair after they'd already shot her. The question is, why?

I turned to consider the position of the shooter, and saw where I figured they must have stood, Shaz, deep in conversation with one of the uniforms who was first on scene. They were comparing notes and pointing back towards the desk where Katie lay.

Continuing my review of the room, I stepped back towards the doorway to take it all in. Ignoring for a minute the murder itself, I try instead to observe the atmosphere and general surrounds to get a feeling for the room and space. The temperature was mild, if a little warm for my liking. Probably perfect for most women who tend to feel the cold more than men. On the wall was an interactive control panel for adjusting the temperature, and lights, etc. Clearly the power to run constant hi-tech air conditioning and lighting was not an issue here. The panel read 23 degrees Celsius inside, and a chilly 13 outside, with the clock above it showing the time as 08:00 on the dot.

Turning back to the large open expanse of the office, which I'd estimate at around thirty meters squared, I couldn't help feeling it was a lot of space for a room that only had one desk. Located in the far left-hand corner and angled towards the windows, sat a small, uncomfortable looking, orange-coloured couch. Its low back and short seat base looked perfect for a small child to sit on, for the two or three minutes they actually remain still. Or a large person to perch awkwardly as they wait for their turn to be called. Next to the couch was a futuristic style refreshment station built into the rear wall, containing coffee, tea, juice and water.

Opposite the couch sat a matching single seater which appeared to be of equal discomfort, while behind it, out the windows and directly across Branch Street stood another imposing office building, its presence somehow forming part of the ambience of this office, despite its complete detachment.

I briefly wondered whether anyone outside on the street or in the building opposite could have seen what happened in here. Then I quickly remembered looking up at the building on the way in and noticing that from the outside, the windows have a dark matte appearance, not the glossy reflection of glass. Probably that new light absorbing paint that transfers heat energy into electricity. Kind of like solar panels that you can paint on, with conductive fibre's suspended in the mixture. When applied with the patented brush, they create connective arteries to transfer the energy along. It isn't all that effective, of course, as it tends to dissipate much of the energy in the transfer process before it can be stored for use. Even so, it's impressive that with all that applied, you can still see out of the building at all. It's a lot like one-way glass though, so it's almost certain that no one out there saw what happened in here.

'Well, I don't know how much else there is for us to see here until someone who actually works in the building shows up and gives us access to their surveillance systems.' I said to the room at large. The comment was directed mostly at Sharon, who, for her part, was still chatting with the uniforms and techs and subsequently ignored me entirely.

'Ah, incidentally Kaz, you wouldn't happen to know why these mood panels aren't picking up anybody in the room right now, would you?'

'No. But it could just be because there are so many people in here.' she replied.

There were three mood panels in the office. One on the wall behind the victim's desk, which was now covered in blood splatter and effectively evidence. One over behind Sharon and the uniform she was chatting to, leaving only the third one at the end of the room for me to review.

There are many versions of these mood panels, coming in different shapes, sizes, and functions, depending on their role. In shopping centres they're used as interactive advertising boards, on sidewalks they're also interactive advertising boards, while doubling as surveillance recording devices, and more commonly in larger office and commercial buildings they're used as interactive directories, similar to, yet significantly less complex than, Cam the concierge from the foyer downstairs. Oh, and did I mention they also double as surveillance recording devices?

It's not completely uncommon for people to have them in their offices or homes, though generally only as a cheaper alternative to an IOT-TV, or Internet of Things–Television, for entertainment and shopping, etc. Mood screens lack the direct signal connection of a TV, instead relying purely on internet streaming. An IOT-TV, on the other hand, has that signal and also connects to all the other things in your house, knows when you've cooked dinner, and what you normally watch at certain times of day, which helps it tailor your viewing and advertising experience to match your personality and lifestyle. In the past, we just used a remote control to pick shows, but apparently having all of your household appliances spy on you and choose things for you, is better… Having said all that, it is still notably odd to have three of them in this one sparse office.

'Good morning, Gary.' said the panel as I approached. Its Smokey glass screen sprung to life, whereupon a grey cartoon hand appeared before commencing to wave at me in a comical sort of manner. Kinda felt like it was mocking me, to be honest.

How the hell it knew I was approaching "it" specifically, when people had been walking around this office for well over an hour without it waving a stupid hand at anyone else, was beyond me.

'Hello, ah, mood panel.' I said, unsure of what to say to a screen, while simultaneously wondering where the speakers were.

'Welcome to Dr Hansley's office. Unfortunately, Dr Hansley is unresponsive at this time. As there are currently six identified persons present, I will need an authority code to proceed to Ambient Personalisation Mode.'

'What can you tell me about Dr Hansley being unresponsive?' I asked, ignoring its instructions and feeling ridiculous about having to ask a display screen on a wall for key information about a crime. You'd think with the world the way it is, I'd be used to having to talk to tech like it's an actual person with its own independent thoughts… But, I'm not.

Sadly, I'm also confident that the screen does indeed know more than me, and not just about the events in this office.

'I'm sorry, Dr Hansley is unresponsive at this time. Please contact building services for further assistance.' Said the screen again before flashing a message it didn't verbalise (*is verbalise the right word when a screen speaks?).* The message said, "Talk soon, detective." then the screen blacked out.

I snapped my head around quickly, looking to see who else had witnessed the strange message I'd been given, only to find that not one of the eight people behind me had even glanced in my direction.

'Kaz, didn't you say that this building is a smart building?' I asked.

'Yes.' said Kaz, who appeared to be wrapping up her initial assessment.

'Then, would it be reasonable for me to assume that the building services to which the friendly wall screen here referred, was in fact just another bot?'

'I'd say so.' she said disinterestedly, while replacing her thermometer, gloves and other equipment back in her coroner's toolkit. 'I believe that's what let the guys in.'

'Yeah, I can confirm that.' said Sharon, who had wandered over to join us. 'I've been speaking to the crew who were first on scene. They didn't talk to anyone who works here. All they got was an automated message from the building services surveillance system. Well, they didn't actually get the message. A dispatch officer did. They just turned up, and the building identified them and let them in.'

'Great. If there's one thing I hate more than bots, it's bots that refer you to other bots for additional assistance.' I said a little moodily and still somewhat perplexed by the message on the screen.

'Sharon, I think we've seen and spoken to everything we can here for now. Agreed?'

'Agreed.' she replied, stepping over an evidence marker that didn't appear to be marking anything I could visibly see. The work of the Crime Scene Scanner, I expect.

As I went to lead us out the door (*chivalry having died long before New Think*) we were met by some colleagues of ours, no doubt here to check up on us first timers and our progress toward solving this supposedly straight forward murder.

'Well, well, well, if it isn't the Sons of Old!' bellowed a voice that stopped us in our tracks. We'd heard the line before we saw them, knowing instantly that this derogatory term was being projected by Detective Damwell (*both his name and his level of certainty about every theory he's ever had*).

We are, by the way, the "Sons of Old" because we're both Old Thinkers and our names end in… son. Not overly creative. Then again, neither is the man who said it.

Detective Brian Damwell and his partner Detective Empher Thise are quite the yin and yang duo. Shockingly successful, given that Damwell is certain his first thought is always the right one. His arrogance and brashness are countered by Detective Thise's keenness to see every element of a case from the perspective of all those involved. He's too far one way, she's too far the other, yet by being of opposing nature and actions, they find a centre or balance that usually leads to the right outcome (*in this world, at least*). Which is particularly un-New-Think of them if you ask me.

Damwell, as you might expect, is a hardcore New Thinker. Thise is more accepting of the alternative ideology, though by no means willing to propagate our concepts or desired lifestyle. It's one of the few topics on which they aren't at opposite ends of the spectrum.

'Solved it yet?!' asked Damwell in a tone that was more statement than question.

He stopped in the doorway, assuming the stance of the man's man, deep in the process of trying to prove his manliness. Not a New Think approved stance, by the way, but some things can't be changed, even in the diehards.

Like many self-approving humans, he keeps himself well-toned to match his ego, his musculature pressing out the front of his shirt slightly, in a way that seems unbefitting of a lawman. You wouldn't call him solidly built, but at 91kg and 6ft tall (*6' 6" if you ask him*), he's imposing enough for most to want to take a step back.

His bright green eyes have the same intensity as his personality and remind me of a mythical Irish leprechaun... then, there's the hair... That fiery red hair. In fairness, he is a stylish ranga. Has that mid length cut with the fringe combed and gelled back over the top to create a wave look that I'm sure there's a name for.

His overbearing attitude does seem to jar with his pinkish, white, freckled skin, though. They aren't those large heavy freckles, mind you, only small light ones, barely visible, until they're exposed to direct and harsh sunlight.

In his current 'at ease' stance, his left arm was placed on his hip, elbow pointed out, while his right arm was up and stroking the hair down at the back of his head. In the process, he exposed the icicle tattoo on the inside of his right forearm, which is the mark of the tribal New Thinker and far more common than you'd like to believe.

Finally, there's Damwell's sense of dress. A mixture between old style detective, and overly stylised, would-be man model. His outfit comprised a tight short-sleeve shirt, paired with tapered slacks that were quite a bit shorter than they really should be, and a gleaming pair of polished leather shoes. I can see his ankles. Nuff said?

'Not yet.' I replied. 'Unfortunately, the killer left the scene before we got here. Should know more once we get access to the surveillance system. After all, it was the surveillance system that called the police and let them in when they got here. In fact, aside from the victim, nobodies seen a single person who works here, yet.'

'Shouldn't be too hard to solve then.' said Damwell. 'If the surveillance system knows enough to call the police in, then I'm sure it knows why it did that. If I were you, Johnson, I wouldn't even wait to see the footage. Just download a list of known Old Thinkers in the area and find out who had the biggest problem with this lot. Guarantee, that turns out to be your killer.'

'Oh, and both your names will be on that list.' he said with significant disdain. 'Don't dismiss them without taking a good look. As they say, a killer always returns to the scene of a crime. And here you are...'

'Ignore him.' said Thise, who seemed to appear out of thin air behind him, soothing the eyes as she shifted past without affecting his stance. 'Just remember, most buildings have high-level surveillance systems these days, but seeing footage of someone being killed will usually only tell you how it was done. It's not always as easy to know who did it and why. Don't forget to establish motive, means, and intent.'

Despite the soft tone of her voice, Thise's comments were as much a slight as Damwell's. We might be rookies when it comes to murder investigations, but we know how to solve a crime.

This now stood inside the room, looking left to right and taking in the spot where the victim's body lay. The floral smell of her perfume had a distracting aroma, a hint of white sage giving it a masculine edge. She wore a mid-length charcoal skirt and cobalt blue button-down blouse, tucked in at the waist and accompanied by a thin black belt to secure the outfit and break up her form. She paired this with a mid-height, black heel that gave real meaning to her nickname, 'Thighs'. Not a name we'd use to her face, but she sure does have great legs.

'Just remember, rook, nothing is more corruptible than electronic evidence. Don't stuff it up!' said Damwell, chuckling to himself.

After quickly reviewing the scene from the doorway, which constituted nothing more than a casual glance around the room, Detective Damwell turned on his heel and left. Thise flashed us a congenial smile accompanied by a conspiratorial raise of the eyebrows, before flicking her caramel-coloured hair back over her shoulders and departing without further comment.

'Well, that was odd.' said Shaz. 'I thought he'd just arrest you on the spot.'

'Yeah, I thought he was pretty nice, to be honest.' I replied. 'Come on, we should get back to base and start making calls, aye?'

As we were making our way out to the lift, I realised I hadn't actually noticed any cameras or surveillance equipment throughout the building. The Mood panels are certainly capable of sensing, tracking and recording people, so I've no doubt the room in which the murder took place will be well covered, yet I can't help wondering about the rest of the building. It may be useful to understand how the killer got in and out, not to mention that if the killer's face or profile is difficult to ascertain, or they wore a mask and their ID can't be confirmed by bio-recognition, then having footage from outside the room may provide us with more opportunities to get a useful angle.

'How do you think the surveillance works?' asked Shaz as we walked. 'I don't see many sensors or cameras around.'

'You know, it's almost like we're developing a telepathic connection. I was wondering the same thing myself. I guess we'll have to ask whoever or whatever we get to speak to from Human Services.'

'Human Services. That's ironic.' said Shaz. 'I never thought of you as a glass half full, best-case scenario, type of dreamer.'

'Well, there'd better be a living human here somewhere. I'm not real tech savvy, you know, so either I speak to a human, or I'm coming back here with a crowbar to start peeling mood panels off the wall. The surveillance system's anthropomorphic sense of self-preservation ought to convince it to call someone in after that.'

Chapter 2

The pain of loss, or the loss of pain…

Walking down the front steps of an old red brick apartment building, I check my watch to find the time was now 10:03. My stomach grumbled, my brain whirred, and a seasonally appropriate cold breeze gusted up the empty street, forcing me again to tighten my one and only jacket.

Sharon and I had just spoken to the victims next of kin, an experience that left us more confused about this death than we had ever expected to be.

Mrs Hansley, who was Ms Hansley's mother, seemed neither surprised nor overly upset at the death of her daughter. A little hollow, perhaps, but not nearly emotional enough for what this type of news should do to a mother. Especially someone like her. She's as Old Think as they come.

We had arrived in relative comfort at Jessica's apartment on the outskirts of Mid-Town, a good twenty-five minutes from the police station. Without the E, we would've been forced onto one of Central City's ageing trains, something I hadn't had cause nor opportunity to ride in years, followed by a lengthy walk from the nearest station. Luckily for us, Sharon was able to secure a company E to facilitate our needs.

The streets are wider out here, and thankfully so. Because of the distance from regular transport, there are a surprisingly large number of hired E's parked on the surrounding streets, a necessity begrudgingly afforded by the state, with the caveat that they're to be used as minimally as humanly possible. On the way, there was even some legitimate traffic to be caught up in, bringing with it the strangely pleasurable memories of the heavy traffic and surging tempers the old world could produce. Now, being stuck behind even a few E's has you wondering what magical event could draw such a crowd in the hermitized world that we live.

When we buzzed Jessica's apartment, she'd hit the accept button in an instant, admitting us without ever asking who we were or why we were there.

After letting us in with a well-worn smile and a nod, she sat down at her small dining table, her hooded, deep brown eyes looking slowly at Sharon and I in turn. There was a fierce and deeply intelligent attractiveness about them. When she looked at us, it was like she already knew what we were going to say and was simply waiting for one of us to verbalise it. Like she herself had written the script for us but wanted to hear how it sounded out loud, and whether or not we were going to say it right.

'Oh god. I always knew this would happen.' was her response after Sharon delivered the news.

Whilst not unusual in isolation, the response was not accompanied by a teary breakdown, expression of distraught emotion, or any of the other normal responses one might expect from the mother of a suddenly deceased daughter.

'Mrs Hansley, are you okay?' asked Shaz, concerned at her lack of reaction.

'Please, call me Jess.' she said.

She shifted in her seat, throwing her slender left leg over her right and taking a sip of what the warm wafting aroma suggested was jasmine tea. She appeared the very picture of comfortable, and her serene disposition was having the opposite effect on Sharon and I. We had spent the ride over in introspection, preparing for the difficult task of delivering such delicate bad news. It's never easy, but such an event is especially rare these days because families are so commonly and wantonly estranged. The saying of which does not discount the fact that death has also become something of the norm, occurring much more regularly and at a younger age, usually of medically induced causes, so there are simply fewer people to advise of such an occurrence.

'I always hated that she worked at that place.' continued Jess, having savoured her sip of tea. 'I grew up in a different world, you see. You wouldn't understand, what with the world the way it is now.'

'Actually, I think you'll find that if anybody would understand, it would be Detective Johnson and I.' said Shaz. 'We grew up in a different time, too.'

'Well, I might have guessed that from your age, except that's no guarantee these days.' Said Jess. 'Most people are very committed to believing whatever they're told to believe. How old are you, Sharon?' she asked, looking down at her own clasped hands, which she'd placed comfortably on the table before her.

As Jessica talked, I studied her appearance, looking for familial traits she may have shared with her daughter. The evidence was there, her dark brown hair matching perfectly with that of Katies, though her skin seemed much lighter and softer, somehow.

'I'm 50.' said Sharon. 'Old enough to have had a daughter of Katie's age, myself. Unfortunately, my husband and I weren't so lucky.'

Jess nodded at Sharon's response as if confirming a correct answer, before continuing along her own wavelength. 'We had different values back then, didn't we. Different beliefs to one another, too. We actually expected people to believe and want different things in life, and the great thing about the world I grew up in was that we were actually beginning to learn how to accommodate all that.'

'We knew that people came from different origins, different countries, different religions, and that each had an individual identity with distinctive foods, pastimes, and lifestyles to those of the rest of the world. It was so important that these differences existed and were maintained. That's what made the world truly diverse. No country was perfect. None ever are. Nevertheless, each gave its people a sense of belonging and a deep-seated feeling of pride. We would compete in politics, contests, sports, competitions, challenging each other, and if our country was able to better another or show an advantage, that victory contributed to a feeling of shared success and pride for the nation, despite our internal differences. Competition was good for morale and always inspired ever greater feats, along with the desire to continue improving. Yet, it always required that there be an opposition. A friendly enemy of similar lifestyle or an idealistic enemy of opposing lifestyle, it didn't matter, we took all comers. Because, we knew back then, without any other nations or any other beliefs, or any other ways of life, we'd have no one left to compete against, to measure against, or to strive to outdo. Competition creates winners and losers, but it also drives progress. It inspires greatness, invention, and a desire to overcome. The best ideas are formed under the pressure of open debate, when challenged by those whose own interests differ strongly from yours, becoming hardened and polished like diamonds in the process. Every great story of interest and intrigue comes from the confronting of an uncomfortable, challenging, and often horrific event or circumstance. You overcome, you are overcome, or you endure. Most importantly, in all scenarios, you learn, and you grow, and you come away with an interesting story to tell. Removing all that opposes you, or stands in your way, doesn't make for a better world. Just one without balance or choice. No great story every started with, Well, everyone agreed on where to go and it was a smooth and compliant evening…'

Jess seemed lost in thought now. Sadder than when we'd first arrived, although I think more so at the loss of the life she once knew, than the loss of her daughter. As if reading my thoughts, she continued.

'I loved my daughter, you know… It's just that… well, the truth is… I didn't lose my daughter this morning. That wasn't her… not the daughter I knew. I lost MY daughter a long time ago. That poor girl that died this morning was one of "them". A New Thinker. She worked for them… She was the lead designer on their new product, which is basically the end of the line for Old Think. The downfall of all free thought, or any notation of privacy and any chance for the people of this world to come to their senses and realise what they've allowed the world to become. New Think is an anathema. The antithesis of all that they claim to be, and those bastards indoctrinated and then took my daughter, and I never said they could!'

Jess still didn't cry. The pain was there inside, locked away, unable to find its way out, except for a slight rise in her voice. She just looked… hollow.

'Mrs Hansley, when did you last speak to your daughter?' asked Shaz.

'It's Jess, Detective… please, call me Jess. The last time I spoke to, her, was last week. I haven't spoken to MY daughter in many years.'

The implication of Jess's answer was clear. Perhaps it was the reason for the lack of emotion. Her focus on the loss of a period in time, a way of life, more so than the loss of her daughter.

'Last time you spoke to, her, what did you speak about?' I asked.

'The same thing I always did. The obligatory things. The pointless things. What had she been up to, how had she been doing. She'd learned not to tell me the truth anymore, so we just exchanged basic platitudes about the banality of work and home life. We only really started talking again about twelve months ago and that was after years of not talking at all. We had finally come to an understanding that whilst we don't agree with each other's lifestyles, we wanted to maintain some sort of relationship. So, we created a fake, empty one. Even then, we'd usually end up in some sort of disagreement about "the way things were."

There was emphasis added to that last part. Like so many others over the years, they clearly see the same period of time, and what it was like to live it, through a different lens. Obviously, Katie would have been very young, only nine or ten when the world changed, her mind soft and malleable, her opinions not yet formed by lived experience. By contrast, her mothers were likely set in stone.

'Mrs Hansley… ah Jess, did your daughter ever mention being afraid, or excited, or having any unusual relationships during your chats?' asked Sharon.

'No. As I said, our discussions were very banality. Very vanilla. We didn't say anything to each other of any real value because we knew it would only set the other off. Besides, if you ask me, I think all her relationships were strange.'

'What do you mean by that?' I asked.

'From what I understand, she subscribed to some sort of group relationship, mostly with her like-minded work friends. Not the type of thing that was socially acceptable, or certainly not openly, in my time. Being moral dictators wasn't enough for her and her New Think buddies. They had to change every aspect of the old way of life, including the foundation of family relationships, monogamy, marriage, the love between two people. None of that exists in their world. They don't like the "individual" yet they're the most selfish people in history. Whatever, whenever, and with pride, that's their motto.'

'All those loonies she works with even dress the same. It's like a futuristic movie from the twentieth century where everyone of a certain level at work wears the same outfit. Some sliver coloured uniform of sorts to show they're all part of the team. She told me it helps to avoid any favouritism or unequal interactions, because everybody looks the same. It seems those old space age movies weren't too far from the truth. The only thing we're missing now are the spaceships.'

'Uniforms are hardly new.' I said, feeling I had to contribute something more to the conversation. 'As a soldier, I wore a uniform for thirty years and I can assure you there were plenty of unequal interactions with others wearing the same.'

In response, Jessica simply raised her eyebrows, creasing her otherwise remarkably smooth, and youthful looking face. At 58, she certainly didn't look her age, but time is vigilant and needs no invitation to add its signature to your precious facade.

'Jess, we have to ask. Where were you last night between the hours of 8PM and 11PM?' asked Sharon.

'Wow. Police work really has slipped these days.' she replied. 'You've only managed to narrow it to a three-hour window?'

'Unfortunately, it was quite cold in that office in the early hours of the morning. Apparently, the air conditioner doesn't kick in and start heating the place again until around 6AM. The forensics team didn't get there until nearly 7, which made estimating quite difficult. The coroner said she'd need to do some more investigating before being able to provide a more accurate TOD.'

'Well, I was at home, alone. Although, I would've assumed you already knew that given there are cameras and ID sensors just about everywhere. It shouldn't be too hard for you to confirm. Besides, I don't go anywhere anymore because there's nowhere for someone like me to go.' As she said this, Jess leaned forward almost combatively, breaking for the first time her calm, detached demeanour.

'I see.' I said, wondering what to say next and coming up with nothing. In the absence of a ready thought, I instead turned my attention to our present surrounds and the inferred location that someone like Jessica could, in fact, go.

The Kitchen table she leaned on was the major piece of furniture in Jessica's small apartment. It was accompanied by a small, solid, single seat chair, placed against the internal wall opposite where Jess now sat, upon the left arm of which I had perched. The hard, broad, 4 by 4 wooden arms of the chair were causing my legs to start going numb, so I stood to take in the rest of the room. Whatever her heritage or previous contribution to the world, it hadn't been looked on favourably by the Global Council for Equitable Housing. Between the table, this chair, and the small kitchenette bench which Shaz was presently leaning on, there wasn't much else except for a closet sized bathroom and another room off to the side that I could only assume was the bedroom.

In fact, the only thing notable about the room was that there was nothing notable about it. It seemed more like a stash house of some sort. The type of place you go when you couldn't go where you really lived. No personal photos or belongings, no unwashed dishes on the kitchen sink, not even a toaster or kettle on the laminate bench top surrounding it.

'Do you have a kettle?' I asked, taking both Jessica and Sharon by surprise as they turned in unison to look at me.

'What? A kettle?' asked Jess.

'Yes, you know, for boiling water.' I replied. 'I've been smelling the soothing aroma of your jasmine tea the whole time we've been here, and yet I noticed you don't have a kettle. Nobody has zip taps anymore, so I was wondering how you made it.'

Sharon was frowning at me animatedly, as if silently demanding that I cease going down this path.

Jessica turned in her chair, reaching behind her into a bag that was hanging off the back, producing a sizeable thermos, and placing it on the table. 'You know what it's like, what with the rationing of residential power. I boil a pot of water in the morning on the stovetop and store it in the thermos for the day.'

'Of course.' I said, feigning an understanding I didn't feel. She was absolutely right about the power rationing, and it is tight. But not so tight that you couldn't boil a kettle a couple of times a day. I wanted to ask why there were no other personal items, no tissue box, no hand towel, no wall screens, nothing. The look on Sharon's face, however, had turned from one of partnerly disapproval to one of impending violence, so I decided to leave it be.

'There's nothing else you can remember about any of these strange relationships your daughter had? Nobody she mentioned acting differently, or dangerously, or appearing too keen?' asked Shaz, perhaps sensing that I wasn't sure what else to ask.

'No. I'm afraid I've told you all that I can, Detectives.' said Jess, closing herself off and again returning to her earlier stoic demeanour.

'Okay, Mrs Hansley. Well, we're sorry for your loss. Thank you for your time today. We will be in touch as soon as we know something or have any further questions.'

With that, we turned to leave, having learned exactly nothing. No real questions answered, only more vacuous ideology filling the space that family connections once occupied.

'Detectives.' said Jess.

'Yes?' answered Shaz, as she and I both paused in stride, turning back to face her.

'Find the bastard's that did this. And make sure they pay for what they've done…'

Chapter 3

A letter to nowhere

Sitting at what I considered "my desk" in the largely empty detective section of the station, I steamed with rage, tapping my foot rapidly, and twirling a pen long devoid of ink. I briefly pondered the pros and cons of the hot desk format of modern offices and police stations, alike. The hard white melamine coating, the only thing outside of the holographic projection of my screen, which filled the space. On the plus side, there wasn't anything for me to pick up and throw, aside from my device through which the call that induced my rage was currently connected. On the downside, there was nothing of a personal nature to inspire happier thoughts and calm my mind.

Having finally gotten hold of an actual human being (*you know, a living one*) that worked at One Globe Technologies, I was fast losing my temper. Not only with their incredibly slow responses to my questions, but their absurd allegation that outside of the office of Ms Hansley, there were no surveillance cameras covering the inside of the building, except for the entry foyer, the basement, and the lifts.

I was getting the old school run around and my brain was tired of holding my tongue. They (*being this OGT rep*), also claimed that the mood screens, whilst capable of recording, could not be relied upon to have kept a log of all the ID chips that had entered the room on the day of the murder.

I knew damn well that was bullshit, and I lost it. I went full Old on New, and man it felt good…

'Don't bullshit me about modern minimalist or a lack of need for surveillance in a place of higher intellect!' I shouted into the receiver.

'I know your type! You watch the building, reclamation, and sustainable design shows, where every lounge room, entertainment space, and sitting room, is absent the presence of, or space for, a TV! You're no doubt deluded enough to believe the pretence and assume we're all exquisite conversationalists who sit around discussing ideas, conversing, or just enjoying the ambience of an otherwise empty, fucking room. Meanwhile, in order to view that show, you had to watch your own TV or see a clip of it on The-Tube via your device or tablet. No era of human civilisation has been less equipped to sit around and discuss ideas and we're not allowed to renovate any fucking homes! All we do is watch TV or scroll through one of the many apps on our devices, waiting to be told what we should want to buy, do, think, or how to act. You are living the great lie of our civilisation! You assume you are free of thought and action, all whilst marching along to the beat of the master's drum. And, in every room and for every action taken, you are being monitored, recorded and tracked. So don't tell me there's no fucking surveillance in that building!'

Despite heaving from the effort, I was nevertheless filled with great satisfaction from my rant. Until, that is, rather indifferent to my outburst, the OGT Rep advised that had I let him finish, he would have explained that there is a chip reader in every doorframe, and that they should still be able to provide a list of people entering and exiting the office, along with the times that they'd entered and left.

'Fine! We will be there at 13:00 to review all available surveillance information. And to be clear, I do mean ALL the available surveillance, and we WILL be interviewing EVERY silver outfit wearing employee, as well. Please make sure we have a room set aside to undertake these tasks!'

I hung up feeling a little less pleased with myself for having overreacted, but by-crikey they know how to get you on edge with those fully automate AI powered "assistants". By the time you talk to a real person, you're ready to rip their head off.

No matter how much they "train" it, AI can only draw on the pool of data and information it has access to, so it can only be certain of the things that are established within that pool. That means there's no guarantee of accuracy or truth, because that would depend on the quality of the original data, and it has zero capacity to assess that, or to assist with queries outside its scope. Such as, "I need access to surveillance footage of a murder at OGT".

Easy fucking case, my arse.

'So, what have we got so far?' asked Captain Isabelle Ironie, who had wandered out from her office and perched on the corner of Sharon's desk. Sharon had sat a full row of desks back from me, in order to avoid, as much as possible, the anger of my conversation.

'I think we'd better know where we stand before you start these interviews.' She continued. 'Sgt Ease believes that the murder was a clear-cut case of Old on New. Do you two see it that way as well?'

Captain Ironie is our direct superior, in charge of the detectives at our station. She's only thirty-five years old and as committed a New Thinker as you get. She is, of course, a vegan, as skinny as a rake, and at a terrifying 49kgs and 5ft 10 inches tall, rather less than imposing. Regardless, she proudly announces her weight in general conversation, believing that being skinner and lighter, she is of higher moral standing, due to her reduced impact on the earth and its resources.

Ironie stroked her deep black hair, then flicked it over her shoulder, where it fell obediently in perfect straight lines down to the middle of her back. The beautiful dark skin over Isabelle's right cheek bone glowed under the LED lighting of the station's squad room. Her appearance, a hereditary gift from her Nigerian grandparents to her African American parents, and now to Isabelle who is simply another Global citizen.

Unlike most of the detectives at the station, the captain wears the uniform of the Global Police Service. In deference to the prevailing ideology of New Think, where traditional policing is not considered necessary, the uniforms are charcoal coloured, akin to coal, another resource they do not believe to be necessary.

Isabelle shifted weight up onto the desk itself and sat swinging her legs. Her presence, a signal for us to gather and strategise about our progress and the direction we should take.

So far, it seemed that this supposedly open and shut case wasn't revealing its clues quite so easily as we'd been told, so outside input was almost always welcome. Given that Sgt Ease was the first investigating officer on scene, and despite being heavily biased of opinion, we thought it may be best to ask him some further questions with the captain present for balance. Conveniently, Sgt Ease had been walking past Sharon's desk where Isabelle now sat, so I stood from my own spot and crossed the blue carpeted floor to join them.

'We're not sure yet.' said Shaz in answer to Ironie before turning toward Ease to ask her own question. 'What gives you the impression this is Old Think on New Think, Sargent?'

'Well, it's so cold-blooded and lacking in positive purpose.' He replied, back tracking along his path to join the group. 'I've seen plenty of crime scenes, and I'll admit, not all violent senseless actions are carried out by Old Thinkers, but you only have to look at that place to know that everyone there sees themselves as New Think.'

'Why did you say, "…sees themselves as New Think?".' I asked.

'Well, the vic wasn't actually New Think,' said Ease. 'I think she was on the fence. I mean, granted, she worked for an aligned company with a New Think business model that markets itself as aggressively committed to the Global way. But even so, I don't think she was entirely on board with all that they do.'

Ironie, who'd been looking down at the carpet thoughtfully as she listened to Ease's comments, turned directly toward him now, her large brown eyes seeming to swallow him whole. 'There's an awful lot of thinking going on in there, Sergeant. Do you have any evidence to back up that theory?'

Ease shifted nervously, adjusting the belt of his uniform below the overhang of his stomach, his pale white skin reddening slightly under the captain's gaze. 'Well, as the Sons of Old said when they attended the scene, there wasn't a great deal to go off, aside from a body with a hole in its head. A lack of witnesses and surveillance footage makes it rather hard for me to complete my report. What I needed, you see, was to speak to someone who worked in the building to get some basic details. A lay of the land before the event, so to speak. So, I did a little uniform and badge work to see if I could find someone useful. If there's one thing I agree with Gary Johnson on, it's that grunts and groundwork continue to form the basis of any successful mission. Or investigation. Us uniforms might not be liked or respected, but we still have our value.' Ease grinned and nodded at me as he delivered his backhanded compliment, as though I should appreciate his weighty support, offering mine in return. I didn't.

'Won't the surveillance data give you all the information you need?' Interjected Ironie tersely, apparently only wanting solid info and not the story behind it. Her legs had stopped swinging as her gaze intensified on the sergeant's face.

A bead of sweat formed on Ease's right temple, which given the Arctic cold of the squad room, that either didn't have, or didn't use, central heating, was clearly caused by the blazing spotlight of her eyes. To his credit, he didn't wilt.

'Well, it might tell us what happened, but I don't think it will tell us why.' he replied with more confidence than I might have mustered.

'So, who did you speak to?' I asked.

'No one at first. I had the same problem going back there that I had when I first arrived at the scene. That building's automated Human Services System (*HSS*) is like a throwback to the olden days. Theoretically, it should save them needing to have a human there, except it's so bloody useless that in the end, you get the shits and have to find a real person to speak to, anyway.'

'After getting the runaround from the HSS and no direction towards a human, I decided to speak to the people that have always known more about a building's occupants than anyone else. The cleaners.'

'The cleaners?!' Said Ironie, failing in her ideological duty to see them as equals and a valuable source of information. 'I would have thought a building "that modern" would have robot vac's, and robot cleaners, and basically clean itself!'

'They do have some of those things.' replied Ease. 'Although some technologies simply aren't as far along as we think. Apparently automatic toilet brushes, bin emptiers and horizontal surface wipers are still a work in progress, so it's good old humans to the rescue. What's more, despite all the moves we've made towards reducing waste, people continue to write on paper, then throw it out when they're done. So, you can add the emptying of small office waste bins into larger building waste bins to the list of human duties.'

'I saw that office. I didn't notice any paper in there. Didn't see a recycling bin or any stationery storage for that matter, either.'

'You'd be surprised.' said Ease. 'Even New Thinkers don't want all their ideas and communications monitored and recorded. As it turns out, there's actually a fair bit of paper that's used and discarded in that office. Particularly by Ms Hansley's. Though, to her credit, she uses recycled paper. Or at least, she did… Anyway, I managed to speak to a cleaner who'd relocated from another part of the globe (*Nobody immigrates in the new world, they relocate. In order to immigrate, you would have to come from somewhere that considered itself to be an individual entity under its own control, separate from the Global world, and that type of thought simply doesn't exist anymore*) named Chen, who, as it happens, works Ms Hansley's floor sometimes. He doesn't speak Plain (*or Global, which is what we used to call English*) quite as well as he would like to, so when he started finding paper in her recycling tray, he figured he would challenge himself to learn, by reading it.'

'And?' Said Ironie, eagerly.

'Seems like she'd been writing a lot of letters to her mum.' answered Ease.

'We just spoke to Mrs Hansley.' said Shaz. 'She didn't mention anything about letters, just a weekly phone call with the exchange of mindless platitudes.'

'Yeah, well, it looks like she was building up to something more. The vic had been writing letters that started out pretty simple. Reading the first couple is kinda like watching an awkward conversation without the sound. Then, over time, she starts to increasingly question the state of the world, the merit of New Think, and even the very project she was working on. Evidently, she wasn't ready to send them yet, so she threw them out, although I'd have to say, she was getting close. The last two were even put in envelopes and addressed to her mum. It seems like it wouldn't have been much longer before she actually sent one, and then who knows what would've happened. The fact is, if I had found this out whilst she was still alive, I'd have to report her to a moralist. Frankly, Chen should have done it, but he claims to have not fully understood the letters.'

'Either that, or he thought they might be a nice bargaining chip if he ever found himself in trouble.' said Shaz.

Ease gave a tilted nod of the head in agreement, then paused to allow the group to absorb what he'd told us. He seemed calmer now, perhaps feeling he'd gained our support after essentially laying out all that we really knew on the case so far. He certainly had more than we did.

'Forensics are checking the letters out now to see if there are any other biomarkers or fingerprints on them.' he continued. 'I figured it was worth a look, in case there are additional clues as to whether somebody other than Ms Hansley and the cleaners have read them. I've also taken photos which I'll attach to my report and send through to you all in a couple of hours.'

With that said, Ease nodded to the group again and started walking away towards the pig pen.

'Oh, by the way,' he said, swivelling rather deftly back towards us on his left foot. 'I'd like to change my answer to your original question. I'm not so sure it was Old on New anymore. It may have been Old on Old, just the killer didn't know they were killing one of their own.'

'You still believe that a New Thinker couldn't possibly do it, ay?' I asked.

'No. I have to believe that they couldn't.' he replied, before turning again and continuing on his way.

Once Ease had left, Sharon and I filled the captain in on what little information we could add from our initial review of the scene. The general agreement was that the oddity of the letters aside, viewing the surveillance footage and interviewing Katie's fellow workmates should fill in the blanks as to the who and how. Then all we have to do is answer the question, why?

Chapter 4

Scene unseen

Back at One Globe Technologies, Shaz and I were told we could set up in the office right next to Ms Hansley's and the scene of the murder. We still hadn't met with an actual person and frankly, being let in again by the building's automated system was starting to piss me off.

'Christ!' said Shaz. 'This room looks even less inviting without the body.'

We had taken the opportunity whilst back here to have another look at the crime scene without the other officers, coroner, or body to clutter our thoughts.

It seemed our friendly cleaners had already been here. There was now no sign of the bloody murder that had taken place. That included the two mood screens which had been behind and to the right of the Katie's desk, both absent, their wiring neatly covered over with small wall-coloured panels.

'Where do you think the screens went?' I asked.

There was a strong chemical smell in the room now which hadn't been present before. No doubt from the cleaning crew, scrubbing away all the blood and gore. It was cold and empty too, which combined with the smell, gave the room a clinical hospital type feel.

Sharon rubbed her hands over her forearms for warmth before responding. 'I'm not sure. I was wondering that myself. One was covered in blood, though I doubt we would've needed the physical screen for evidence purposes. Perhaps the cleaners took them to give them a thorough wipe down.'

'Yes, I suppose that's possible. So long as it's only the surface and not the recordings, they're wiping.' I replied.

'Well, I guess we're about to find out.'

I turned from the odd simplicity of the merged desk slash computer, with its great internal complexity and power, and saw, to my surprise and mild delight, an actual human being standing in the doorway.

He was as Mrs Hansley described. A silver suited figure, like something people from the past imagined as the hypothetical future for us all. One outfit to represent the uniformity and frugal nature of the future world. In fairness, it was silver dyed wool or cotton, not quite the shiny Mylar material of the movies, though it carried the same message. Still, I suppose I should just be thankful he was human.

'We were beginning to wonder if anybody aside from Ms Hansley actually worked here. We thought, perhaps, that you lot had evolved to a point where you didn't need to be here at all.' I said, tongue in cheek, albeit imbued with more than a hint of annoyance.

'Our time is very important here, so we try to minimise unnecessary human contact.' said the OGT rep, robotically.

'One of your own has died. I would suggest, no, insist, that contact with us is not only necessary but compulsory.' I shot back. 'We will be sure to impress upon you the seriousness of that need right now.'

'I didn't catch your name, by the way?' I added with the hope that he actually had one, if only to humanise the look.

'Dr Raymond Touuse, is my name. I am the assistant program engineer on the project Ms Hansley had been working on at the time of her death.'

'You mean, murder?' said Shaz.

'Well, I suppose that's for you to determine, Detective.' This last word was spat from his mouth disdainfully.

'A bot Dr, aye?' I said, unable to resist firing a shot back for our side. 'I assume you have a PHD in computer programming?'

'Good one, Detective.' said Raymond sarcastically. 'Yes, I have a PHD in programming and I intend to be in charge of one of OGT's prestigious programming teams, one day. Now, if you're done in here, I have the surveillance footage and data ready for you to review. I have also made a copy for your files. Please, follow me.' he said, returning to his robotic monotone.

Raymond was a short man, perhaps around 5' 7", his silver suit appearing slightly too long in the jacket and pants. He was thick set too, making it harder still to find the right sizing. A problem with which I could sympathise.

Shaz, walking closely behind me as we exited the door, whispered, 'He sounds like a man who doesn't really want us here. I wonder if there will actually be anything to see.'

We followed Raymond into the next room, where we saw another silver suited employee who was seated at a small desk with an HD Hologram Projector set up.

Where Raymond was squat and short, the woman at the projector desk looked fit, lithe and tall. She didn't look up at us as we entered, instead remaining focused and tapping away on a QWERTY Air, the modern keyboard, which like the screens is just a projection rather than a physical object. Presumably, she was setting up the footage of Katie's murder. A brutal and confronting prospect when watched in 2D, let alone on these state-of-the-art holographic projectors with the capability for 3D graphic imagery, provided there were sufficient cameras recording, to allow it.

The invention of these projectors seemed to be another case of life imitating art. More rudimentary versions had been imagined into existence as far back as 1948, and then introduced to popular culture in the 1980 movie 'Star Wars - The Empire Strikes Back'.

They've had some significant upgrades since that time, in terms of lasers and image quality, now with true life images able to be shown.

'Hi Sophia, this is Detective Johnson and Detective Wilson.' said Raymond to his seated colleague. 'If you can show them through the surveillance information we have, and how to operate the unit, then I assume they will want to watch it alone before they begin their interrogations. If you need anything, I'll be in my office.'

The last comment was not made to Sharon or I, but rather to Sophia, alone. The subtext being that he was clearly not there to help us.

'Thank you, Raymond. However, I should make clear that we will only be conducting some preliminary interviews and information gathering today.' I replied. 'There will be no interrogations conducted, here.'

I was already becoming annoyed at the attitude being presented by people whose fellow employee, and like-minded friend, had been violently murdered. For a supposedly all caring ideology, these hard-core New Thinkers were lacking compassion in spades.

Without acknowledging my words, Raymond turned and left the room, disappearing down the hall.

'Sophia.' said Shaz. 'Do you have much for us? Have you already seen the surveillance footage, yourself?'

'No.' she replied firmly. 'It isn't our responsibility to review surveillance footage, and I certainly don't wish to see this footage, at all.'

Sophia had long blonde hair, a handful of which she was twirling intently at the height of her neck. I couldn't tell if she was nervous, scared, or just eager to leave, but there was certainly an intensity about her that jarred with the arrogant detachment of Raymond.

'Good. If we can run it without you needing to be here, then please show us how to do that and then you can leave.'

'Thank you.' she said, her shoulders dropping with a sigh of relief, while a tear formed in the corner of her eye.

After some minor education in the operation of the holographic projector, Sophia left, while Sharon and I set up ready to watch the horrific end of Katie Hansley's life.

Looking well in control of the device, Sharon looked to me nervously and said, 'Ready to solve our first murder?'

'Sure am.' I said, confident that we were about to do precisely that.

How wrong we were.

What played out in 3D holographic reality, was nothing, if not confusing, frustrating, and undefined.

To our delight, it had appeared at first that all three of the mood screens had not only recorded the people entering the room prior to the crime, by name, and time, but had also recorded their interactions, or lack thereof, with the victim.

A surprising twenty-three people had visited Ms Hansley's office by 20:50 yesterday evening, at which point Ms Hansley was still alive. Then at exactly 20:50:27, all three of the mood panels, which, as I had expected, do indeed double as surveillance devices, simply cut out. That was all there was. There were no more data files and no other surveillance activity until one of the panels recommenced recording at 08:03 the next morning when I approached it to check if it was functioning.

'Well, that's a bit of a concern.' said Shaz as the recording ended. 'The case might open, but I don't see it shutting anytime soon.'

'What about the chip readers on the doorframe, or something from the hallway or in the room?' I asked. 'Anybody show up on there just prior to the murder, or show up and not leave?'

'Nope.' she replied. 'The last visitor appears to have been Sophia at 19:08 and it seems like she only stayed for three minutes. I'll play that interaction again with sound and see if we can pick up anything important.'

Whilst Sharon set up the projection, I sifted through what little we knew of Sophia. She had looked genuinely upset when she'd left the room earlier. If Sophia and Katie had worked together, it's possible they were simply close, and she was upset at the loss of her friend. In light of the missing evidence, though, a thought niggled at the back of my mind. What if she was scared because she's hiding something?

Sharon hit play on the recording.

It began with Sophia entering the office in a huff and standing on the other side of the desk, her hands on her hips.

"Katie, are you okay? You are going to do the right thing, aren't you?" She asked.

Katie sat at her desk, the projection of her screen showing the flickering image of a written document. It appeared as though she had been editing something. Next to her left arm, almost floating on the clear glass desk, sat an ink filled pen. Katie hadn't looked up at Sophia when she'd entered, only doing so, slowly, after hearing her words.

"I guess so… I mean… No, not really. I don't feel right about all this. It's not what we were meant to be doing. It's wrong. It goes against everything we're supposed to stand for. I always believed we were doing something real, something critical to saving the world. But this isn't

about the greater good. All we're really trying to do is stop people from being allowed to think for themselves."

On hearing Katie's response, Sophia looked irritated, panicked even. Her hands, having moved from her hips, were now joined in front of her, fidgeting restlessly.

"I know that's how you feel. I just don't think you should be saying it so openly." Replied Sophia.

"I have to say something. I'm the lead psychological engineer. If I don't say it, who will?" shot back Katie defiantly.

"Maybe you need to find someone to talk to. You know, outside of this group. Get some perspective. Refresh your commitment to the cause."

"That's not going to change what I've seen. And frankly, there's no one I could talk to, anyway." Said Katie, clearly unwilling to bend. As she said this, her eyes shot to the left side of her desk where a sealed envelope sat, protruding from under a psychology textbook.

'Letter?' Asked Shaz, obviously noticing the same thing I had.

'If I was a betting man, I'd have my money that said it was.'

The conversation between Sophia and Katie ended without further comment. Emotion clear on Sophia's face as she turned away in disgust and left the room.

We hadn't yet reviewed all the conversations that Katie had with the other twenty-two visitors, but given the comments from Sophia, it seemed possible that one or more of them may have been negative to the project she was working on. A project we were yet to know anything about.

'Whatever they are working on, it must be bad for Katie to turn like that.' said Shaz. 'She was committed for twenty years, then all of a sudden, she realises it's all a lie, and next minute she winds up dead. I'd say we've found our line of questioning.'

'How do you think we play it from here?' I asked.

'We haven't got time to go through the footage of the other twenty-two interactions just yet. We'll have to review them after the interviews and come back with additional questions, later. Right now, I say we start interviewing people and get this thing underway.'

'Who should we bring in first?' asked Shaz, offering me the lead.

'I think we start with our good friend, Raymond. Try to get the lay of the land and map out who Katie's been working with, and what they've been working on. My gut's telling me that if anybody is willing to talk, as to theirs or Katie's feelings about the project, then we let them, otherwise it may be best to keep what we saw of Sophia's interaction under our hats for now. Until we talk to Sophia, that is.'

Chapter 5

Reticent Ray

Raymond had gone back to his office after our initial meeting, appearing none too pleased to be summoned again so quickly.

Sophia had left us a list of the office numbers for each member of the silver suited team here, though we only really needed their names. We have the rather intrusive luxury of being able to track their location via their chip implants to within a few meters at any given time.

Raymond's name wasn't on the top of that list, though he seemed like a natural starting point for our questioning, given he was the first human we'd met here.

'Raymond, welcome back.' I said, as he entered the room. 'Please, take a seat.'

Shaz and I didn't have much furniture to play with in this minimalist space. Except, that is, for the small reclaimed wooden desk which held the hologram projector. We were already on their turf, meaning they have the advantage, so we had to find ways to make them feel a little stressed and awkward, to aid us in squeezing out as much information as possible. Without a proper table to create a barrier, or the intimidation factor of the standard one-way mirror, a fixture in every interrogation room ever, we improvised, by offsetting our seats at an angle to the left and right of theirs, which we placed strategically in the middle of the room.

Ideally, we would've conducted these interviews at the police station, but as we're yet to determine a set of suspects, or even a list of persons of interest, bringing people back to the station seemed a little premature.

Ordinarily, we would also try to make people feel more comfortable in a first interview. The aim being to gain their trust and establish rapport, so that they'd be more willing to open up about what they knew. Here, however, in this cold, calculating institution, I was getting the distinct impression that this lot were far too comfortable already.

We were also concerned they had or would soon close ranks in an effort to protect themselves, the business, or in the misguided belief they were protecting Ms Hansley.

'Raymond.' said Shaz. 'We would like to start with some simple questions about you, this project you're working on, and your relationship with Katie. We'd also like to understand what occurred during your visits to her office yesterday. Is that okay?'

Brushing his thick stubby hands through his dark mop of hair, it was clear he was not so much okay, as bloody nervous. The temperature in here was nearly as cold as it was outside, and yet tiny beads of sweat had formed, leaving his forehead glistening in the LED lights.

'Well,' said Raymond, 'I'll do my best to answer your questions, but when it comes to the project, there's not a great deal I can tell you. It's confidential. Besides, shouldn't technology be able to tell you all you need to know?'

'That's certainly what we had thought… before we watched what you had to offer, and yet the answer wasn't there. Unfortunately, the recordings of visitors going to and from Ms Hansley's office do not appear to include the detail, or actions undertaken, at the time of her murder.' I said.

'How odd.' said Ray. 'Every office in this building has mood panels, chip scanners, and if they've registered for it, biome tracking. I can't see why you wouldn't already know exactly what took place, and who done it, so to speak.'

'Biome tracking?' asked Shaz, raising an eyebrow.

'Ah, yes. Never mind about that. You wouldn't have access, anyway. It's just something that we are working on here for the Guides. I shouldn't have mentioned it, really.'

Raymond's eyes flicked from left-to-right, tracing the angle of our seating. He was answering our questions, while simultaneously trying to check our reactions, in turn giving me confidence that the abstract positioning of our chairs was working.

We decided to let the biome tracking comment stew for a while, instead focussing on establishing how strong his ties to the company were, and whether he was prepared to kill for it.

Ray (*a shortening of his name that he did not approve of, by the way*) had been at One Globe Technologies for ten years. He joined, so he says, to further the progression of New Think via technological means. A real soldier for the cause.

The more questions we asked Ray, the more nervous he seemed. He also clearly knew, despite neither Sharon nor I divulging, that we were both Old Think. Whether this was putting him on edge, or he had something to hide, I wasn't sure, but he certainly wasn't the same mixture of uppity righteousness and disdain from our earlier meeting.

'What was your relationship with Ms Hansley?' Asked Shaz.

'We were just colleagues, friends.' he replied. 'In the order of authority, she was my superior, particularly on this project, where her psychology degree and experience with AI was beneficial in mapping out the programming structure and pathways.'

'I am more of a hardcore coder, so I have the deep knowledge of how to create and write software code, specifically reactive and proactive code interactions. Basically, once Katie had worked out the psychological pathways to follow, I would build the algorithm to match and write it into the system.'

'Right!' I said, rather sharper than I had intended, inadvertently causing Ray's head to snap around and face me. 'Any chance you could you be more specific about that?'

'I'm afraid not. I can only really tell you what I already have, because it doesn't specifically give away any details about the project. Just the type of roles that we performed here.'

'Were you ever more than friends with Katie? Asked Sharon. Lovers, housemates, something else?'

'No!' Said Ray, spinning his head back to face Shaz and sounding offended at the question. 'Like I said, just colleagues and friends.'

'What do the silver suits represent?' I asked rapidly.

Raymond was becoming almost frantic now, on the verge of a minor panic attack. He winced, the muscles at the left side of his mouth dragging his face into an unintended snarl, while his eyes blinked rapidly.

'They are just a uniform of sorts.' he replied. 'An indicator of status within the company, I guess. Only those within Mathias' team get to wear them.'

'Get to wear them? So, people would strive for them because they want to be a part of this team?'

'Yes. Yes, I suppose so. It's prestigious. An honour to be part of the team, and the silver suit indicates you're in that group. If you're no longer on the team, you no longer get to wear them, I know that.'

'Had someone been removed from this project before?' asked Shaz.

'Not this project, but from the team, they have.'

'Is that what happed to Katie? Was she being removed from the team?'

'No. Katie was one of the main leads on this, and the project was one of two major projects in the company, right now. This is tagged for Global roll out. We will all be using this technology once it's finished. Best of all, if we've done it right, you won't even know.'

Raymond missed the mark on that comment. We might not know about the program's actions, but that isn't the best thing as far as I'm concerned.

'I appreciate you trying to be open with us Raymond. The thing is, I'm still a little confused as to why you don't seem upset at the loss of this, as you put it, friend and colleague of yours.'

He seemed to be comforted by the asking of this question. As if this was the one he had prepared for and had been waiting for us to ask.

Ray sat back in his chair, folded his arms across his chest, comfortably rather than protectively, and delivered his answer.

'Death is necessary.' he replied. 'Here, we understand that life is finite. Katie did great things while she was alive, and I wish it wasn't Old Think that brought her down, but the positive thing is that she will no longer draw upon the earth's resources and will instead fuel its regeneration.'

'That's almost religious, Raymond. "Earth to Earth, Dust to Dust", hardly on brand though, is it?' said Shaz. 'Perhaps you have more in common with the old world than you realise.'

'Don't lower the progression of the Global World to the archaic elements of religion! What I know is that if people protect the earth, then the earth protects us all in turn.'

Ray's briefly calm demeanour hadn't lasted long as he instantly became angry and defensive. A predictable and desirable response when you're trying to find the truth. He was riding the kaleidoscope of emotions associated with grief… or people with a big old secret to hide.

'Of course.' I said. 'You only get out what you put in. No one ever thought of that before your lot came along. The wonders never cease to amaze.'

Shaz shot me a glance, chastising me for the unnecessary retort. Raymond, for his part, remained defensive, though his position hadn't changed at all.

'One last question, Raymond. Where were you between the hours of 20:00 and 23:00 last night?'

'I was working remotely from home. I can provide electronic certainty of that via both biometric positioning and chip scan authentication, if I must. You can also check my IP address, which contains a positional certainty for precisely this type of confirmation. I was not here, and I certainly did not kill Katie.'

Ray glanced towards the door, no doubt eager to leave, or perhaps desperately hoping someone would come to rescue him. He had on his left wrist the latest satellite watch, which does the same thing as his mobile device, just on a smaller screen attached to his arm. Hey, if you like being tracked places, I guess you can never have too many things tracking you. As he turned back to face Sharon, who was audibly forming a question, I took note of the time, which was 14:00.

'Well, there's that biometric term again. Care to elaborate on how we would use that to confirm your whereabouts?' probed Sharon.

'I'm afraid I can't.' replied Ray. 'If it becomes necessary, though, you would only have to seek approval from the project manager. That's Mathias, by the way.'

'Thank you, Raymond. We will no doubt be in touch for further clarification in due course.' I said, before nodding approval for him to stand and leave.

He left the room, far calmer than he'd entered it, his early nerves and panic gone. Replaced, it seemed, by a sort of careless indifference felt for a job, done. He didn't even feel the need to look back at his would-be accusers, simply exiting the room and disappearing for the second time today. The action of a confident man.

'What did you think?' I asked Sharon, who was watching after him thoughtfully.

She stood from her seat, smoothing the creases at the knees of her pant legs and pulling the matching blue jacket taught. She paced the largely empty room, far smaller than its crime scene neighbour, and windowless too, with a plant wall facia covering the outside corner of the building where the room was situated.

'Seemed like an arrogant, dedicated, NT prick!' she replied, swivelling on her heel to face me. 'Aside from that obvious point, I would say he seems to be hiding something. No, multiple something's. I'm just not sure what they are yet. His body language certainly fluctuated as if he wasn't sure what to expect at the beginning, growing more comfortable with the direction of the interview by the end. Which is strange really, given that's when we asked him about the murder, specifically. Perhaps that's what he'd prepared himself to lie about…'

'Yes, you're right.' I agreed. 'He was awfully concerned about the project, too. Much more than the life of his colleague. I don't believe for a moment they were ever friends. Friends don't behave like that when their friend dies, no matter what their beliefs are.'

'Who's next?' asked Sharon, nodding her agreement.

'I know who I want to see.' I said. 'The one who's running this project. He should have something meaningful to say. Whether or not he'll tell us what that is… well, that's a whole other question.'

Chapter 6

The honest truth, or a load of Schmidt?

'Mathias Schmidt.' I said, addressing our next guest as he entered the room.

Mattias nodded in greeting without really acknowledging Sharon or I. His mind perhaps somewhere else, thinking about Katie, or work, or simply focussing on what he would say.

Unfortunately for him, it left me with a first impression of an arrogant man. An impression which suited his Dutch look and name. He crossed the room to the empty chair, moving with a stiffened gait, accentuated by his short stature which I'd estimate at not more than 5' 8" or so.

After seating himself rather elegantly on the available chair, he crossed his right leg over left and placed his hands one on top of the other upon his knee, as if preparing to pose for a corporate photo.

'I saw your name hidden towards the bottom of my list of interview candidates today, Mathias. That's despite being right at the very top of important people that worked with Ms Hansley. Straight away, I knew that speaking to you was an absolute must.' I stated.

'Yes, if you want to find out anything useful about what we do here, then I suppose speaking to me would be of value to you.' he replied. 'Although, as a general rule I do try to avoid speaking to people, at almost all costs. Especially someone as irrelevant in modern society as a detective.'

He paused mid insult, pushing his tongue out between his pressed lips, moistening them for the punchline, doing nothing to change his first impression.

'At least your uniformed officers serve some purpose, as a visual warning to the masses that there are many levels of monitoring and surveillance. Even old school ones.'

His accent was strong, though his words came across clearly with a heavy dose of disdain. The tenor of his voice sat somewhere between pure Dutch and Afrikaans, so that I couldn't quite tell his pre-Global origin.

His Bio-Hub profile places him at thirty-nine years of age. Old enough to know better than to fall for the virtuous mirage of New Think but grown up right in that period of deep indoctrination. The Dutch, as you might expect, had been clear leaders in this matter for some time before the rest of Europe caught up.

'Yes, well, your disdain for our profession and investigative process aside, we have some questions for you about Ms Hansley.

Specifically, we want to know about any interactions you had with her yesterday, and over the course of this project of yours.'

'Her?' Said Matthias combatively, singling out the offending pronoun hidden within my words and raising his eyebrows as his heavily bearded jaw jutted downwards. 'I wasn't aware Katie had been labelled.'

'What pronouns did Ms Hansley prefer?' I asked. 'I would have thought the "Ms" in Ms Hansley was an indicator.'

Matthias' head and jaw shot upwards defiantly now. A response not uncommon in the new world. You are at all times expected to know everyone's desired preferences or be considered a bigot for your failure. Worse yet, you could be labelled a criminal and face serious punishment if there is believed to be malice in your apparent mislabelling. It's a terrifying world where, by law, you are no longer allowed to call a spade a spade, because the spade would much prefer to be seen as a pitchfork and somehow you're supposed to know that...

'Ms Hansley, was her preference, I believe.' replied Matthias. 'Katie, if you knew her well... Did you know Mr Johnson, that one of the major drawbacks of policing, is that there is no net benefit to an already self-regulating society?'

As he said this, Mathias, who had been otherwise looking straight ahead, turned his dark brown eyes to meet my own, no doubt seeking a reaction. With the LED lights glinting off his pupils, they looked rather more like battery heads than soulful eyes. A look which only added to his intense, detached persona. Dark framed rectangular glasses with slightly curved corners completed the look, representing the very embodiment of unapproachable intellectual superiority.

'Don't you mean that only when society fails to perpetually exist in its perceived utopian state, do police add value?' I asked.

'No.' he replied. 'I believe policing at your level is unnecessary, even in a somewhat failed society. Moreover, I believe you add no value, whatsoever. You're nothing more than a garbage boat skimming the surface of the harbour. You catch the pollutants, only once they have already polluted. What purpose does that serve but to highlight society's failure. Isn't it far better that we act proactively and prevent the failures altogether, as such, adding value, rather than reacting, and achieving only a mark for the ledger?'

'So, in your opinion, what should be done here, Mr Schmidt? It was, after all, your colleague and lead psychological engineer who was murdered. In your own office building, no less. Given the security and surveillance that exists within this building, it seems most likely that not only has this apparently uncharacteristic crime occurred in what amounts to a temple to New Think, but under the theoretically altruistic and ever-present surveillance protections of the company that created them. How does your self-regulating society propose to handle this murder? You weren't able to prevent it, so what else is to be done other than capture the murderer and mark the ledger? You know, what I find incredible is that you still see the Global World as a self-regulating utopia, when you actually live in the most over governed, controlled, and externally regulated society in history!'

After a thirty-second pause, filled by what I assume was soothing beard stroking on Mathias' part, he finally answered.

'I would propose what any New Thinker would. That you should be looking into the people who are known to dislike what Ms Hansley represented, rather than those who were by her side the whole time.'

'And what is it that Ms Hansley represented?' I asked. 'There seem to be conflicting opinions on that matter.'

'There shouldn't be.' he replied. 'She represented us, OGT, progressivism, and all the protections and security we seek to build around it. Katie didn't get to be lead psych engineer by following along. She was a true leader in this field. Katie has helped dissect, refine and instil the psychology behind the programs that support New Think, and ensure that people never drift from the Global mindset.'

'Are you saying the Global mindset is not an intuitive and innately human concept? That there is no continuity or safety within its bounds without psychological tutoring and structure to contain one's thoughts?' I asked, picking away at the thin skin of the ideology and testing the resolve of this follower.

'Of course, it's human!' He snapped, his broad, bony shoulders now rolling forward as he tensed his short, thin frame. 'It's only through our actions, and those alone, that we have saved the world! You, of all people, must understand that not everyone just falls in line and accepts the narrative because it's popular or for the greater good. They should, but they don't. We know that the world is full of cowards who fear standing up for the cause or standing out amongst dissenters. Psychological manipulation and fear are the perfect methods of control and compliance. Fear masked as an unavoidable necessity is the means by which we guide the world to the right conclusions. This work, what we do, is the work of experts whose tireless efforts brought us back from the brink. Even so, a re-engineering of the public consciousness is never over and it's never enough! We must build the tools that prevent the world from ever slipping back into the old ways. The bad ways…'

'So, what you're saying is, fear, coercion, and psychological bullying are the business of One Globe Technologies? The foundations of the Global World, for that matter? Sounds a lot like the plot of some once famous dystopian books from the good old days. Of course, back then they were considered an exaggerated commentary or reflection of how unhinged governments of the world would act in seeking ultimate control of the people. Yet, frighteningly, the villains of those books seem to have formed the foundational basis for the world you seek to create.'

'Huh! You lot and your books… You know, the only reason we still have a library to keep your shitty, wasteful, books in, is because we live in a considerate world now, that actually cares about pollution and we don't want to burn or bury them and risk harming the environment.' said Schmidt. 'Instead, we keep them stored away in a safe location where their dangerous contents can be controlled. Like radioactive waste. Their risk is ever present but their poison never released.'

'You needn't bother keeping them locked up.' I replied. 'The world is increasingly full of idiots who can't read books, anyway. They can't read anything longer than a sentence, and even then, usually an abbreviated one. And that sentence had better be inspiring, angering, retaliatory, or condemning too, or else it may be the last one the author ever writes. Your cancel cadre are even willing to turn on their own if they get bored. Which doesn't take long these days.'

The previously cold room felt hot now. Mathias and I both reddening slightly, and a growing film of sweat appearing on my forehead.

Sharon, for her part, had been watching this well-worn exchange of ideals, like a tennis match between the 200th seed and the last player to win a wild card. Unwilling to join the battle, she was instead leaning into her habit of using thumb and forefinger to straighten her eyelashes, followed by a wide open surprise eyed look to test the quality of her work. Luckily for her, fake eyelashes cross both political and ideological boundaries, somehow surviving the cull of the unnecessary, no doubt considered reasonable, in preparing to weather the apocalyptic sandstorms forecast regularly by the bureau.

'Well, I suppose we've made our positions on the world clear. If that's all you need from me, I have work to do.' said Mathias, beginning to stand.

'As much as I'd like you to leave, Mr Schmidt, we didn't need that from you at all. Each of us could have guessed what we've just said about the other without ever having met. A nice attempt at distraction, sure, but we do have serious questions to ask, and no matter what you think of your inquisitors, you will need to answer them. Here or at the station, the choice is yours.'

Mathias' move to leave was clearly theatre on his part, and he was pleased with his performance. It oozed from his body as he savoured the thought he'd score some points and won the upper hand. The look didn't suit him, the smile appearing more childish than proud or strong. He was thin more so than fit, an observation made stark by his ploy to stand, his skinny, strangely long legs leading into an even a shorter, equally thin upper body, unsuited to his short stature. He does, however, have broad bony shoulders which offer him a slightly skeletal, robotic look. Presently, they were pressed into the cushioned chair back in an effort to spread out his frame and puff himself up as big as he could get.

'Let's start at the end and work backwards, shall we. Where were you between 20:00 and 23:00 last night?'

'I was in my office until nearly midnight. Which, by the way, is upstairs, so before you ask, I did not hear or see anything unusual.'

'Did you leave your office at all last night, Mr Schmidt?' Asked Shaz, now joining the fray.

'Yes, of course, I eat like everyone else. At around 7pm I left to purchase some food for dinner, then returned directly to my office. If you check the electronic records my team has furnished you with, you'll be able to confirm my movements.'

'Via Biome tracking?' asked Sharon.

At the mention of Biome tracking, the skin around Matthias' eyes tightened, his pupils darting quickly between Shaz and I, his shoulders closing in on his chest, shrinking him back to normal size. A physiological admission that there's something to know about this biome tracking business.

'Yes, I suppose you could... If I gave you access.' he said after a pause. 'Incidentally, how did you find out about that?'

Matthias' physical reaction to the question was quite strong. His eyebrows now bunched close together, his clasped hands strained against one another, controlled frustration clear in his voice.

'We are not at liberty to say, Mr Schmidt.' replied Shaz. 'Do you think that Ms Hansley's death had anything to do with the biome tracking element of your project?'

'No. I don't think that!' he stated firmly. 'Biome tracking isn't part of this project at all. Some of its members are merely involved in a trial.'

'I see.' I said, bringing Mathias' attention back my way and attempting to rattle him further. 'Did Ms Hansley have any enemies, any awkward relationships? Can you think of any reason why anyone would want to kill Katie?'

'No. I can't think of a reason why anyone would want to kill anybody else. New Think doesn't support such actions. As for Ms Hansley, specifically, I believe Katie was well liked amongst the team and to my knowledge had no known enemies outside of those that seek to undermine a safe, secure world. Even then, I doubt they would dislike her specifically, just by association with us.'

At this Matthias gave me the once over with his eyes, as if I might fit into the "known enemies" category of which he spoke.

'Did Katie have any family or intimate relationships that might have come to a head last night? Or were there any late meetings planned, that you were aware of?' asked Shaz.

'No. No relationships that I am aware of. As for meetings, we have a rule that they're not to be planned after 5PM.' said Schmidt.

'And, was it common for Katie to stay back and work in her office late into the night?'

'Yes, I believe it was.' he replied. 'Recently at least. Katie was very dedicated, and our project was drawing to its close. In fact, despite the sadness of the loss, the fruits of Katie's labour will endure. Ms Hansley had all but completed the psychological guidance for this project, and Raymond should have no trouble finishing it off.'

'What was the psychological guidance?' I asked. 'By that I mean, what was its intent? I don't know about you, but it certainly piques my interest to hear that the lead psychologist on a program that's being created by a security/tech company, working hand in hand with the Guides, finishes her work and is then immediately murdered. In her office, no less.'

'If she had died at the start of the project, or on another project whilst working here at OGT, would you be any less suspicious of a link?' Asked Mathias. 'If she'd died at home instead of here, would you still infer that there was some relevance, some conspiracy, involving OGT or the Guides? Or would do your worthless job properly and actually seek the truth?!'

'The truth? What do you know about the truth?' said Shaz. 'In your perception of the world, the truth is just another concept. A tool for control. The truth is merely something you invent to drive the desire for acceptance of a single-minded approach to all of life. A trick to inspire comfort or fear in the minds of fools. How can anything be confirmed as true, if the facts that support it can never be challenged or reviewed? If you have removed all means to investigate that which is presented as the truth, then whatever you present, no matter how illogical it may seem, is the truth, because it cannot be proven otherwise.'

'What exactly are you accusing me of, Detective?!' asked Mathias angrily.

'How are you supposed to find the truth, whatever that may be, when someone here is hiding it, or preventing us from being able to find it?' She fired back.

'I don't understand. Hiding what? What does that mean?' asked Mathias, leaning forward now and appearing concerned.

'Who would have access to turn off the surveillance equipment, such as the mood screens and the chip scanner in an office here?' I asked.

'What?! Nobody. Not even me.' he replied, whipping his head around to face me. 'They are set to run indefinitely and independently, with only dual password authority from the overseers able to turn off or disable the building's automated systems. Why?'

'Because it appears they were turned off last night at 20:50.' said Shaz. 'Now two of the mood screens are missing as well. You wouldn't know anything about that, would you?'

Matthias sat motionless, his mouth firmly closed, perhaps trying to project an air of indifference. His eyes, however, betrayed him, widened with what appeared to be genuine surprise.

After almost 30 seconds of quiet contemplation that neither Shaz nor I were willing to break, he seemed to regain composure.

'Under the circumstances, Detectives, I will see if I can indeed provide you access to our biome tracking. It may be of some assistance. All members of our project team were participating in an internal trial. It may be able to offer what the electronic surveillance cannot. If nothing else, it should at least rule out the members of my team as suspects for the murder.'

'How long will that take?' I asked.

'A day or so. It's not really configured to download and view as reporting at this point. The data is just being captured for review at the end of the project.'

'Okay. Then I guess we'll wait with bated breath.' Said Sharon.

'Yes, indeed. If that's all, Detectives, I'd like to return to my office now. I have a lot to do. Rest assured, though. I will let you know as soon as your access is sorted.'

Chapter 7

Immoralist

After Matthias, we interviewed thirteen other members of the project team, all of whom had little value to add.

Each of them claimed to have been elsewhere, and oddly, to my mind, they all claimed to have been working remotely or from home, with at least three types of surveillance and tracking tools that could apparently confirm their locations and movements. We, or someone on our behalf, would, in due course, confirm all these assertions via the various surveillance tracking databases, but for now, everybody had a story to tell, and nobody knew a thing.

Their alibis made me wonder just how committed these people really were. And how honest. I know that in this world, traditional working hours no longer apply, but for every member of the team to claim they were still working remotely between 20:00 and 23:00 seemed rather a stretch. Almost rehearsed.

'There's something very off about all this.' said Shaz, who was again playing with her eyelashes.

We were still sitting in our makeshift interview room in our offset chairs, ruminating on the events of the day. I checked my watch, finding that it was already 16:05.

'All of them seem to present the exact same front.' she continued. 'They're like clones or cult members, each repeating the same phrases, oblivious to their actions and completely unable to see that there could be any other path than the one they are on. Feels like they're all in on something together, and will do what they have to do and say what they have to say to protect the cause. They could just be closing ranks, but it seems like more than that. I hate to say it, because it's such a clichéd thing to say, and yet it really seems like they've been brainwashed. Like they're under some sort of group psychosis.'

'Yes, I was thinking that myself.' I said. 'They weren't crazy. They weren't half sane, either. It's as if they don't care that one of their own was shot dead in her office right here in this building. Their building! It's like it was always meant to happen, so its having happened is nothing to be concerned about. It's all just part of the plan. I mean, if this had taken place at the station. At my house! I'd be angry! I'd be upset! And I'd damn sure want revenge.'

'Agreed.' Said Shaz, appearing irritated at our clear lack of progress. 'How many of these loonies do we have left to interview?'

'Only two more.' I replied. 'A man named Adam Abers. Then Sophia, whom we had been saving for last, given she was the only one who seemed to show any emotion about this.'

'What about Adam Abers? Anything notable about him?'

'Yeah.' I said. 'Alphabetically he should absolutely be first on this list. Yet, there he was, way down at the bottom with Mathias. He is also the resident moralist here. As you know, all big organisations have one, and I suspect he was on this project to ensure that Ms Hansley, in particular, used psychological carrots and a big ideological stick. I assume he was buried at the bottom of this list, like Matthias, in the hope he would either not be bothered by us, or be thought to be of as little use to the case.'

'Seems a bit stupid and juvenile doesn't it? Just hiding them at the bottom of the list?' asked Shaz

'Well, they are New Thinkers.' I replied. 'Plus, as you may have noticed, juvenile and stupid was precisely the level of officer they were expecting to see. That's assuming, they were expecting the police to be interested at all. Why would they present themselves any differently?'

'You're right. It's as if they are slightly surprised anybody has bothered to investigate. Which to me is the most disturbing part, given they are supposed to be all about compassion, and making reparations. You'd think they'd bristle at the thought of one of their own being murdered and seek their righteous revenge. Perhaps the good Moralist Mr Abers will have something to say about it.' said Sharon, nodding.

When we called Adam Abers down to the office, he was predictably surprised and annoyed. Moralists don't usually answer questions from people they see as far below them in the pecking order of the Global world. Especially ones in ideological opposition.

'Mr Abers, I would like to start by confirming if you know why you're here?'

'Yes, of course, Detectives.' he replied. 'I am here to assist with your enquires about the unfortunate death of Ms Hansley.'

Abers looked stern and dark as he sat rigidly on the edge of the seat, choosing not to look at either Sharon or I. Instead, his gaze sat fixedly straight ahead, his eyes boring into a wall blank, where a mood panel or screen might ordinarily sit.

'Mr Abers, is it true you are the resident Moralist at One Globe Technologies?'

'Is that relevant to your investigation?' He shot back quickly.

'Yes.' I said. 'I would expect that the resident moralist here would have a close view of what Ms Hansley was working on. We are given to understand that it related to ensuring certain principles were imbedded into a new software program. Principles that you hold dear, I suspect. Sounds like something you'd want to be on top of.'

Abers shuffled back in his seat now, either growing more comfortable, or accepting, of the situation he was in. When he did so, I realised his stature was far smaller than I'd first thought. He seemed to have a presence and manner that gave the impression of a much larger man when he'd entered the room. Though, perhaps that was simply my preconceived notion of a moralist that I hadn't allowed my eyes to correct.

His size was well hidden by the image he presented. Neatly dressed in a silver/grey tailored suit, no doubt of the highest quality wool, paired with a simple white shirt. A notably large, white faced Panerai GMT sat comfortably on the wrist of his thick left forearm, his shirt sleeves cut perfectly to display the ostentatious symbol, simultaneously giving length to his arms and torso. It was his shoes that gave it away, though. A pair of pricey John Lobb's complete the ensemble, their jarringly small size leading you to take another look, at which point you realise he is not quite what he seems.

As he sat further back in the seat, his legs struggled for full purchase on the floor. Meanwhile, he worked to keep his back rigid and upright, desperately attempting to maintain the pretence of height. Strangely, given his role, Adam's look was the very picture of an Old Think businessman and a successful one at that. It didn't seem to fit the image I had in my mind of a moralist, which is, perhaps, the point.

'Yes, I am a Moralist.' said Adam after some consideration. 'I am far from the only one in this company though, so not "the" resident Moralist, just "a" resident Moralist. I'm not even the only one on this project.'

'Okay.' replied Shaz. 'Who else on the project performs your role?'

'I'm afraid that is not the type of information I'm authorised to share with two novice detectives.' he replied smugly.

'Of course.' I said, having already expected an answer of that nature. 'What about Ms Hansley, were you working closely with her? Were the two of you a team, friendly, combative? We're trying to paint a picture of how she fit in with her colleagues, you see.'

'We certainly weren't combative, Detective.' he replied. 'We didn't work closely together, either. Intentionally so, in fact. We were separated on the project, so that I could review and test Ms Hansley and Raymond's work, without any risk of bias or pre-conception that may impact the objectivity of my review.'

'What was your assessment of the quality of Ms Hansley's work on the project? Did it meet your expectations, your standards? asked Sharon.'

'It didn't have to meet "my" standards, Detective Wilson. I'm sure you are aware I am not a psychologist like Katie. I don't have to be. It's New Think's standards that must be met. That's my purview. From that perspective, I would say that initially those standards were met. Towards the end, however, there were some... corrections, that needed to be made.'

'Towards the end? The end of what? Ms Hansley's life... or the project?' I asked.

'Both, as it happens. Unfortunately, Ms Hansley's commitment to the cause seemed to have drifted over the last month or so. A number of corrections and redirection amendments were required at my request. It became clear that there were, shall we say, "unwanted influences" creeping into her work. Raymond had dutifully followed the direction Katie gave him and programmed the changes accordingly. They certainly didn't slip past me though, and that work was then reviewed and corrected.'

'Did you speak to Ms Hansley about these concerns?' asked Shaz. 'Was there any coaching or conversations about it.'

'No.' said Adam firmly. 'As I mentioned, I was intentionally kept separate from Ms Hansley and Raymond. It was Matthias' role to oversee her and ensure the project stayed on track. If there were any corrective actions or concerns about the quality of work, then Matthias would have been the one to address them. I couldn't tell you whether or not this was done. Mind you, I wouldn't say that the quality of her work got any better, so it's my opinion that no action had been taken at all. If anything, the quality of her work got worse.'

'When you say it got worse and required correction, what do you mean by that?' I asked. 'In what way did it get worse? What type of corrections did you have to make?'

'I believe she had turned, or was very close to turning.' he replied. 'Certainly, she did not believe or have confidence in the direction of the project anymore. That much was clear. Despite Old Think being effectively gone, she was beginning to believe in their values and, in doing so, brought them back into "this" world. Within herself at least. You must understand, that is most dangerous, because it can manifest and seep into your work and other aspects of your life. That's exactly what it did for her. Of all the places in this Global World, this would be the very worse place to allow it to grow. The very nature of this technology was to ensure that that way of thinking remained no more than a dangerous concept. Just a bogeyman to fear.'

Adam was deeply absorbed and impassioned as he spoke. Completely captivated by the strength of his own commitment to the right's and wrong's as they're now prescribed. His focus on the subject at hand caused his posture to lose form, allowing his back to slouch somewhat into the cushioned back of the chair.

'At the risk of outing ourselves, Mr Abers, both Sharon and I are Old Think. The concept exists whether you use technology to steer people away from it or not.' I said evenly, wanting to offer an opposing opinion without escalating to a conflict.

'Of course it does.' he replied condescendingly, without addressing the admission of our allegiance. 'Moralists know that better than anyone. In fact, we encourage it to a point. The world needs bogeymen. As I said, they're something to fear. To keep people on the straight and narrow. Surely you understand that anything can exist if people are prepared to believe in it? There are good lessons about this in your books of the past. Terry Pratchett's Small Gods, for instance, tells us that any god can exist, so long as people believe it into existence, and continue to believe, in order to sustain its life. Of course, that book is fiction, but the concept is not. This is real life. It's how all ideologies are born and survive. Something does not need to be touched or seen for people to know that it's real. So long as they can perceive its existence and believe that it's real, then it can be spoken of, written about, and followed. If you can do all that, then it must, in fact, exist. The believers will make it so. Even if that existence is only in people's minds. Here at OGT, we cannot deny the existence of Old Think. We have to talk about it, to know what it is and acknowledge its existence. Therefore, we have to understand its attraction and the damage it can do. We must do these things in order to keep it at bay. What we mustn't do is ever let it infect us. We should never believe in its values or breathe new life into the very thing that nearly killed us… Not here… and not inside of Katie…'

'So, if you know it exists and encourage it, no matter the reasons why, doesn't that leave your new world open to the risk of the old world's return?' asked Shaz.

'Yes, that's why the overarching purpose of the project is to control that very risk.'

'I've gotta say, I wouldn't have expected you to be so candid and honest about this.' I replied, feeling genuinely surprised at the level of self-awareness he displayed.

'Well, as an officer of the law, you are actually required to uphold these principles, too. No matter what you believe personally, you're as obligated to protect the new world from the old, as I am. You, like me, are just another tool in our arsenal. I believe it's important you understand why you do what you do.'

I absorbed the verbal blow, unsure whether he was merely having a dig or really believed in what he was saying, worrying it was the latter. To be fair, a lot of what he'd said was true.

He was smiling now. The confident smile of a man who knows they've made an argument that would be difficult to successfully counter in the current context. Under the circumstances, I chose not to try, and instead kept asking questions.

'This change in Ms Hansley, this reversion or manifestation of undesirable ideals. How did that affect her place here at One Globe Technologies?'

'I really can't say.' said Abers. 'Moralists, as you know, are responsible for ensuring that New Think remains ever in focus, so I certainly had my concerns. But, like I said, I was kept intentionally separate, and I'm not the only moralist who works here.'

'Well, who else is there?' Asked Shaz, for a second time.

'I honestly don't know, for sure.' he replied, this time in a more convivial manner, dropping his earlier disdain. 'Contrary to popular opinion, we don't work as teams or in groups. In fact, much like my separation from Ms Hansley, moralists are intentionally kept separate from each other. This is done so that we don't lose focus or vigilance by assuming that someone else has got it covered. Even the watchers watch each other suspiciously.'

'Isn't assuming someone else had it covered, exactly what you did?' I asked. 'You left it for another moralist, whom you claim you don't even know, to handle the situation.'

'I don't know who they were, but I know it was being handled. Matthias told me so.' he replied.

'Do you think this other moralist could have gone too far in trying to correct Ms Hansley's actions? Or could someone else on the project have become so angry that they lost control?' Asked Shaz.

'Well, whilst I can't rule that out, it would be very unbecoming for someone here to "go too far" in a violent manner.' said Adam. 'They might have pushed for correction, highlighted the failures, or sought to have Ms Hansley removed from the project. But not violence. Not murder. Moreover, it would be rare that a true New Thinker would own a gun, let alone bring one here to intentionally commit this crime.'

'Interesting that you allow for the potential of this being a crime committed by one of your own. Some of your compatriots could not conceive of it.' I added.

'Yes, well, in essence, I wholly agree with them. However, I believe it's even more concerning to think that someone else managed to get into the building, circumvent the security measures and carry out such an act of violence, right here at the birthplace of the very surveillance technology designed to protect the Global World from such acts. I must say, though. I do wonder if you've sufficiently examined the potential for Ms Hansley to have taken her own life. Perhaps out of guilt or personal disgust at having entertained such detestable thoughts as she did?'

'Thank you, Adam. Yes, we have considered that. Trouble is, it isn't supported by the evidence we've seen to date. We thought perhaps the surveillance footage or data may have helped clear that up for us, except as you mentioned, it had been rather successfully circumvented by someone or someone's. How did you know about that, by the way? We were supposed to be the first and only people to have viewed the surveillance data thus far.'

'I am a Moralist.' he said, not missing a beat. 'I have an obligation to ensure that New Think principles are being observed and upheld. Once I heard what had happened, it was my duty to see how, why, and by whom. Don't forget that whilst I will be civil and even of assistance wherever possible, we do not consider that a Police Service is necessary, anymore. Unfortunately, as with you, when I looked at the information, there was nothing there to see.'

'Whoever did this hid it well. I can't find any traces at all.'

My suspicion was mounting as Adam told this little story. How and when could he have possibly viewed this information? The murder only took place last night and Ray and Sophia claimed to have only retrieved and set up the data for viewing around midday today. Someone was lying, of that much, I'm sure.

'Adam, you must know how suspicious that sounds. You claim to have gone looking into the data and surveillance footage of Ms Hansley's murder, before ever meeting with police. The very surveillance footage that is missing and preventing us from being able to confirm the culprit. You work here as a moralist, with access to the surveillance system, you no doubt have technical knowledge given the other part of your role here, and you believe that the Police Service is unnecessary. Your boss was telling us earlier that your Global society is self-regulating, rendering us irrelevant. I can't help having some concerns.'

'Well, that's to be expected, Detective. Suspicion and concern are very natural. In spite of which, what you must understand is that I am a committed moralist and I too want to see that the right outcome is reached here. I certainly wouldn't attempt to impede your investigation and I'd never tamper with surveillance. Ever present and vigilant surveillance is absolutely necessary for the safety of the Global World.'

I couldn't help feeling I was looking at a python with a rat sized lump in its throat, trying to tell me that it would certainly never eat a rat. Unfortunately, without evidence, all I had was suspicion.

'Do you know who would have the access or the knowledge to turn off or delete recordings from these surveillance systems?' Asked Shaz.

'I'm not sure that turning off, or deleting data, from the gargantuan surveillance system in this building, is even possible without approval and direct assistance from the OGT Directors.' He replied. 'To be clear, I am not suggesting they were involved, just that I don't see how else it could be done.'

'Now for the million-dollar question, Adam. Where were you last night between 20:00 and 23:00?' I asked.

'I was working from home.' He replied without bothering to elaborate as the others had.

I sincerely doubted he was telling the truth, although he certainly looked pretty damn comfortable and confident, as he sat stroking his slightly pointed beard. There wasn't much more we could really get from him at this point. We had very little to go on, except for suspicion, and even in this world, that isn't enough.

'Thank you, Mr Abers.' I said. 'Your assistance is appreciated. That will be all the questions we have for now. Your knowledge of the building's security systems and your general knowledge of the business may be of help to us as we progress, though. Please take my card. We'll be in touch.'

I handed him a cardboard business card, a gesture utterly out of place in the modern world. Which was, of course, the exact reason I did it. I mean, who the hell has business cards anymore?… I do, that's who. And why? Because in this strange world, with its ultra short attention span where everything is digital, there one second, gone the next, and where waste of any sort is to be abhorred. A physical, tangible, business card doesn't update or disappear on a feed, and as strange as it seems, won't get thrown away. It also reserves me a nice little place in their mind. Because, who the hell has business cards?

Mr Abers took the card, looking down at its physical form, and turning it over in his hand, twice, before pocketing it with no more than a nod. Then, he stood and left the room.

'What did you think?' I asked Shaz, who'd slid forward in her chair so that her head pointed up to the ceiling.

'I'm not sure.' She replied. 'Underneath the self-important moralist act, he was just like all the rest of them, and they all just seem… indifferent. I thought they were supposed to be part of the caring and considerate culture that they tell us we were not. They seem nothing like what they purport to be. If I didn't know any better, I would have thought they were board members of a venture capitalist group, entirely detached from the people they invest in, seeing only opportunity and potential for returns.'

'Agreed.' I said. 'I didn't get a good read on Mr Abers, either. I can't help thinking there are more layers to him than he lets on, though. Perhaps more honest ones than he showed today.'

I paused here, trying to align my thoughts. Both Sharon and I had come to understand over the years that New Thinkers were different.

They literally have a different way of thinking, hence the term. More than that, they truly believe in the cause, and allow the demands of doing so to alter who they fundamentally are as people, and in turn, what type of society they live in. Sharon and I don't, won't, can't do that, and this clash of fundamental human traits makes it difficult to understand the motives of their actions. Where we apply logic and common sense, overlaid with genuine human emotion, they've been trained to only apply emotion to a threat to common cause, irrespective of logic or the plight of an individual.

'You know, what really gets me is the lack of a connection between these silver suited drones.' I said. 'They all work together in this supposedly united team, their one unifying goal being to protect the Global World and its ideological processes. They're almost political in that way. Their core intent is to protect the concept, not to provide the product. It's the idea of the idea and its perpetuation that's most important to them. The actual outcomes from that idea don't seem to matter. They've lost the ability to see themselves as individuals or even people. The collective status has meaning, yet there is no emotion, no feeling and no empathy for the loss of Katie, because she wasn't a friend. She was just another number in a line of code, and a faulty one at that. Her death was not a loss but a correction for the greater good.'

Sharon was up and pacing again. This time, not sticking to the light blue coloured wall at the rear of the room, instead, stalking around the three spaced chairs like the "it" in an under-manned game of duck, duck, goose. The floral scent of her perfume was refreshing and comforting, it's familiar smell giving off a soothing sense of olfactory nostalgia with each lap, spreading an invisible ring of scent molecules all around us.

'I've been thinking about where the wall of indifference might break down. Someone's gotta give us something useful!' She said, after stopping at a random location on her circuit. She crossed from her position to my left, breaking the pattern and moving directly to her seat.

'I suspect, based on what we saw earlier, that the someone we need will be Sophia, just as we first thought. If we can get her to open up, she may be the one to offer us a more human or emotional insight.'

'Let's hope so.' I replied. 'She's the lucky last for the day.'

'Before we bring her in.' I said, holding my hand up to stop Sharon calling Sophia in yet. 'I think you should take the lead on this one. I'll try not to say too much. I just have a feeling she'll respond better to you than me.'

'That's uncanny, you know.' said Shaz. 'It's exactly what I was thinking as I paced the room. Sophia needs someone she can connect with. Someone of the same sex and on the same level. We've clearly seen that there's nobody else here displaying anything like Sophia's earlier emotion. She actually seemed personally affected by Katie's death. If I didn't know any better, I might even say she cared.'

'Yes. Well, let's just hope that she cares enough to want Katie's murderer found.'

Chapter 8

So, fear

Sophia was either some distance away when we called, or simply took her time in coming. When she finally arrived, she appeared more dishevelled than earlier, if indeed you can say that of a silver suited person.

'Sophia, welcome.' said Sharon as she entered the room. 'You are our lucky last interview for the day. We saved you till last because we had a feeling you might have been closest to Ms Hansley.'

Sophia didn't answer this, though to be fair, it wasn't so much a question as an observation that left an opening to share. Sophia didn't take it. Instead, she sat silent and sombre, her body upright, not tense, her hands resting palms up, together in her lap.

'You seemed emotional when you left the room earlier. Were you and Katie close?'

'Yes. We were… friends. Friends and colleagues… We were very close.' said Sophia, displaying contained emotion and seemingly uncertain of the right words to choose.

Sharon took a beat before asking her next question, watching to see just how deep and genuine that emotion was. The dam wall held for now, her eyes downcast, watching the small pink palms of her hands.

'Were you more than friends, Sophia?' asked Sharon.

That did it. This one simple question, answered with unspoken emotion, said more than words ever could. Pain spread plainly across Sophia's face as she lifted her head and turned to face Sharon. Her eyes creased and tears streamed down her cheeks. Her palms, however, stayed put, motionless in her lap, unable or unwilling to rise up and wipe away the pain.

She looked strikingly beautiful in spite of this. Old Think or New Think, doesn't matter. Beautiful is beautiful and Sophia could've drawn a crowd. Even with her emotional distress, clear for all to see, her blonde hair, oversized olive-green eyes and naturally high cheekbones made for an attractive sight.

'Yes… No… I… I don't know what we were. I know we had something special… I know that. Until it all changed… then it was gone.'

'What do you mean, "then it was gone"?' asked Shaz. 'When Katie was killed, or before that?'

'Yes, of course… when Katie was… killed.'

'What do you know about Katie's death!?' Asked Sharon, changing her tone sharply, so that both Sophia and I sat up straighter at once.

'Only that it was horrible, and tragic, and unnecessary.' She replied with a slight shake to her voice. 'If only she hadn't said those things, then none of this would've happened.'

'What things? What did Katie say?' Sharon probed.

Sophia paused for a long time, looking down at floor, then her lap. She was using the angle of her head to hide her eyes, while her hands slowly fidgeted, flicking and flacking together, the friction of dry skin on skin creating a noise that seemed to echo around the room. The pale white of the back of her hands now a blotchy read and pink.

The strong, easy posture of her toned fit torso slumped visibly to meet her emotional outlook. Without the large melamine covered table that would have formed a shield of sorts in the interview rooms back at the station, Sophia had nowhere to hide. That exposure making her attempt to shrink away seem all the more pathetic.

'Sophia, I need you to answer that question.' said Sharon, firmly, moderating her tone between forceful and genteel.

'Yes, I know… I'm just… It's… Well, I can't say, really. Katie was always so strong willed. She didn't need reminding or guidance on NT, on what it means and why it's so important. She was a leader in Global's psychology and the best there was at guiding people towards "the greater good", ensuring that the "right thing to do" was always at the forefront of their minds. Undoing injustices, filtering out unconscious bias, recognising those who had been wronged, teaching other people to do the same. Those were the things that drove her…'

'So what happened?' Asked Shaz

'Then, Katie started to question it. To question it all. Said things like "should people all really have to follow this path". As if New Think was just some religion, some theoretical belief that could be read about in a book. Like there could be options, or another way, some sort of value to be added by people who considered what was good for themselves, to be anything like as important as what is good for us all. It was all so, selfish! so… Individual. She even suggested that history had its merits, that a difference of opinion provided balance and improved outcomes for all, even those that are opposed to the principles of the world that we've created… I mean, it tears me apart just talking about it. She knew that the only way to save the world was for everyone to sacrifice for the greater good. Individualism, a fracturing of the common psyche, is the enemy we fought against the hardest. How on earth could she go from what she was, to what she'd become…'

Sophia let out a short sniffle at the conclusion of her comments. She'd returned to her previous position, looking down at her own lap, so Sharon risked a full turn of the head, look at me. I widened my eyes and faded my head back, knowing that we were both thinking the same thing.

Sophia was being pathetic. But she knows something. Something big. Something important. And we needed to push her to see if she breaks.

'Did Katie start acting differently, or was it only what she thought and said that changed?' asked Shaz.

I'd noticed that despite Mathias' earlier objection, the "she's" and "her's" seemed to be slipping into the conversations unnoticed now. Even Sophia was naturally following suit and throwing pronouns around with careless abandon. Which was interesting, given their apparent relationship. Either Katie was a "she" both biologically and by assertion, or it was fundamental human nature to preface people with a common label that matched their strongest qualities. Personally, I don't know how you maintain a conversation without them.

Sophia lifted her head, her posture straightening with it. 'She started reading, books!' She said, as if we should recognise this as a most despicable act.

Sophia looked from Sharon to me for support, slouching back again upon realising we weren't the right audience for her argument.

'Old books.' she said, more sullenly now. 'It gets flagged here when someone in Katie's position starts looking at things like that.'

'Initially, I believed she was just reviewing some old thought processes and actions to make sure we had protected against any risk of their return. She was pretty fastidious like that. But I knew pretty quickly that it was something more.'

'How did you know?' Prompted Shaz.

'As I said… She… Well… we, were more than friends… much more than friends. We spent time together outside of work. Lots of time. We would stay at each other's apartments. She would read while we were together. She started talking about the books, asking questions, asking if I knew things about the past, about "real history" as she put it. Like I would ever want to know about that disgusting, violent, selfish time. The greed, the hate, the segregation of people as if there was something different about them. As if we shouldn't all just be the same.'

Sophia slowly shook her head now, disgustedly. As if all of history had been one big mistake that didn't bear thinking about. It certainly took the sheen off her appearance. Watching her, I fought the urge to shake my own head at the utter naivety and ignorance she displayed. Judging all of history negatively, a huge and diverse period of time she knew nothing about, condemning those that came before her whilst reaping the rewards of their efforts.

'Did you feel like Katie had lost her way? Like she had wronged you or gone against the cause?' Asked Sharon, leaning forward to engage Sophia and cut through the ideological barrier between us.

'I was scared she was changing and had been sucked into the old propaganda. It's a risk when we are necessarily exposed to that poison as we work to keep the world safe. I tried talking to her, pleaded with her to stop reading, to just trust in our Guides and follow the advice of the experts. It really is the best thing, for everyone.'

Sophia said this last sentence like a sales pitch at a car yard. Half threat, half promise. I could see I needed to jump in and shake up the narrative. Sophia had started off balance, but was gaining confidence with each answer, as if talking about how righteous it was to be New Think gave her strength.

'Sophia, wouldn't Katie herself be considered an expert? She was, as I understand it, a psychologist who's group psychoses expertise was the very reason she was on this project. Isn't that true?'

'Well, yes. Katie was an expert, but you cease to be considered an expert when you start saying dangerous things about alternate ways of thinking. You can't start going against the consensus and expect to continue holding the respect of the people. It's not just me that thought that, either. Matthias agreed with me. We tried to help her, tried to give her time to straighten out and get back to doing the right thing. But she only seemed to drift further and further away.'

Sophia was shifting from confidence to introspection, attempting to examine her own actions more so than Katie's, though clearly not seeing any wrong doing or overreaction on her part.

'How did you and Matthias try to help Katie?' I asked. 'What actions did you take to get her back to doing, "the right thing" as you say?'

Sophia shot me a sidelong glance before answering. A sign she'd finally noticed we were there.

'First, we thought maybe she was just burned out and a little susceptible. Exhaustion can do that. You get tired of fighting. So Matthias gave her a few days off to freshen up and get right. It didn't help. Like I said, it only got worse.'

'I went over to see her after work on her first day off, only to find her surrounded by old books, taking notes, totally enthralled by what she was reading. It was devastating. I asked her why she was doing this, why she couldn't see how wrong it was. I was so upset, I couldn't stay there and watch that level of what I can only describe as self-abuse. It's literally like knowing that if you do this thing, you are taking a step towards destroying the world. She knew that and she did it anyway.'

'Did Katie take all three days off? asked Shaz, trying to establish some timeframes for when this had all begun.'

'Yes. In fact, Matthias gave her a whole week off after I told him what I'd seen. He asked me to keep going over to see her and make sure she was coming around. I didn't really want to do it... I mean, I loved her... I... well, you know, we were really close. Still, I didn't want to be a part of this. I didn't want to be around anyone who was actively turning bad.'

'She was literally committing a crime and if she hadn't had the excuse of her role on the project, she would never have gotten away with it, at all. We have an obligation to uphold Global values and protect them with everything we've got. It's the entire basis for what we are doing here and one of our leaders was turning traitor. It's horrifying.'

'Did you go to see her every day?' asked Shaz.

'Of course. That's what Mathias asked. I did as I was instructed, even though I couldn't bear to stay long. I was so offended by what she'd done. I just wanted her to stop this madness, and I would have done anything to help her do that.'

'Except trust her.' I said.

Sophia shook her head, almost imperceptibly. She was starting to feel the needles going in.

'That sounds like awfully dangerous talk, Sophia. Did you act on those feelings? Did you decide to put an end to Katie's awakening? Stop the Madness, as you put it?' added Sharon.

'Awakening! Ehr! The only thing she was awakening to was her descent into oblivion. She was becoming one of… them!'

After saying this emotively, her face twisted with passionate hate, intense feeling clear in her eyes, it must have occurred to Sophia, just whom she was talking to. We, of course, represent the "them" to which she referred with such fervent disgust.

The moment of realisation was clear, like a fireworks show gone wrong, the projectile shooting out sideways and exploding into the crowd of now terrified bystanders. The righteous venom that had tightened her face and eyes descended from her like a lead anvil. Her face dropped away as her head turned from Sharon to me, angled to either side as we were. The transformation back to scared victim was complete when her determined expression turned passive and then to one of wide-eyed fear. These might be her offices, but it was our interview, and no matter how much it disgusts her, we hold the power here.

'Sophia, we are obviously here to investigate a murder.' I said 'Not a defection from ideology. What we want to uncover, is who killed Ms Hansley, and bring about justice for that crime. We also need to understand why this crime was committed and what motivated the perpetrator to do it. It's clear you have very strong feelings about New Think and what you see as Ms Hansley's betrayal of it. I want to understand why you turned against her so quickly, and without compassion. Why you wanted to avoid and shut down this person who you said you loved. Was her exploration of these old books and concepts really so bad? Was she not still human? The same person underneath it all?'

‘No. I fell in love with someone who knew right from wrong. Someone who would never allow the idea of immersing herself in those despicable ways to enter her head. To even entertain the thought is the modern version of sin. She has always known there’s no alternative. If you aren’t on the side of right, helping to undo the selfish history of this world, then you are on the side of wrong, and part of its destruction. There’s no middle ground here. If you aren’t with us, against them 100% of the way, then you are with them, against us… It’s all or nothing… And if you’re nothing, you’re really nothing… Nothing but a leech sucking up the earth’s resources, leaving only the refuse of an evil life behind.’

‘Well, I hope you haven’t got any salt with you.’ I said. The comment lost on Sophia, who’d probably never left the city or seen an actual leech. Not that she’d be allowed to, these days. Clearly, her beliefs had again overcome rational thought, and her earlier realisation that the two police officers to whom she was speaking were, in fact, the embodiment of what she considered evil. That, or she was intentionally having a dig at us in addition to her former lover. Either way, she was certainly opening up now, and I wanted to keep her emotional response’s coming. We haven’t asked the critical questions yet and when we do, I want her to be positively spewing out her bitter, hateful feelings, and with them the truth. In my experience, people who drop their guards in a passionate display tend to speak the truth without a filter.

‘Sophia, had it crossed your mind that perhaps Katie wasn’t so much turning towards Old Think, as opening her mind up to the idea that an alternative point of view, the ability to make up your own mind based on a balanced consideration of the facts, might not be so bad after all?’ I asked, fanning the flames. ‘Jumping straight from offence to offended at the presentation of any opinion you don’t like, is neither fair nor reasonable. Hardly the behaviour one would associate with a regime that purports to ensure equality and acceptance for all.’

‘Life isn’t about balance, it’s about doing the right thing, whatever that takes.’ said Sophia sullenly.

‘And there’s no room in your interpretation of this new way of life for change, for learning, or even to err?’ asked Shaz, offering me a spell on the mound.

‘No. There is only one way forward.’ She replied. ‘Here at OGT, we’re creating a new level of normal, from which nobody will know any different. It took years to integrate the right mindset across enough of the population to fully implement the concept. That was achieved twenty years ago, and we’ve worked to maintain it ever since. Now we are embedding it for the foreseeable future by ensuring that old ways are never allowed to return and threaten our peaceful existence.’

‘THIS, is normal now!’ She proclaimed. ‘The message here is clear, get used to it or get out. There is no room for regression or regret.’

Sophia was heaving slightly from the passion she expelled in her statement. The tight form fitting material of her silver grey pant suit pulled tight, showing off her sporty figure. We offered her no respite.

'Normal is a subjective state of being that is far shorter in term than people usually realise.' countered Sharon. 'Don't get too tied to that idea of an eternal change in your desired direction. You can try to control people, you can even convince them that doing so is best for them, but you can't stop basic human curiosity and ingenuity from creeping back in and circumventing the very best predictive and preventative measures. You can't just redefine a new normal and expect everyone to fall in line. Normal is not an exacting standard of appearance, action, or thought. Normal is just an ability to function within broader society no matter your difference to others.'

The comments were delivered coolly and calmly, with the backing of thousands of years of evidence to support them. Despite their age, they still hit their mark in the here and now.

Angry and hard faced, Sophia stared straight ahead. Her shoulders had tightened and rounded slightly forward. Her hands balled into fists at the end of her long, slender arms. Not far to the edge now, I thought.

My turn again. I dragged her mind, if not her eyes, in my direction as I continued the barrage of anti-NT commentary.

'You know, the belief system you follow isn't actually a new, either.' I started. 'You haven't really changed anything other than the title of a totalitarian communist regime and told everyone it's progressive, inclusive, and all for the betterment of the human race. Bringing everyone down to a level where they can be controlled by an overbearing government is never for the good of the many. It's only ever for the good of the few who sit atop, knocking down anyone who tries to climb out of the mire. Perhaps all Katie did was that which you should, too. She looked at history through unbiased eyes and understood that its people and actions cannot be judged solely by modern standards or the dictates of an all-powerful over-class.'

'Is that what happened with Katie? Did she start to talk about similarities of the Global World, with dangerous regimes of the past?' asked Shaz, right on cue. 'Did she begin to sympathise with the general idea of freedom and question the efforts to shut it out forever?'

Caught between seething anger and the desire to curl up in a ball and cry like a child, Sophia was right off balance now. Half forming words with her mouth and moving her head forward slightly as if to project those words, then changing her mind, closing her mouth and sliding gently backward as a cycle of angry reactions took hold of her being. The desire to fire back, be right, win, belittle our ways, cancel our ability to present an unwanted opinion, was juxtaposed against the part of her mind that knew she had something to hide, to protect, to keep safe.

'I recall asking the question of people when New Think was first gaining momentum as an ideology.' I continued. 'Wouldn't the world be a sad place if we were no longer allowed to form our own opinions, or choose for ourselves, because a singular, unbending standard had been set for us all? Wouldn't it be sadder still, if that standard was created, not by balancing opposing moral values against each other to find a common ground we all could share, but by allowing only the extremist views of a retaliatory modernist regime, that uses historically motivated revenge to take away people's right to freedom of thought and action, and legislate their way to controlling everything in the world, from your bank account, right down to how you're allowed to feel?'

Sophia rounded on me now, her eyes red and watery, her mouth pursed with rage.

'Yeah! That's nothing compared to what we're putting in place, here!' she spat. 'We're not just going to control what you can and cannot do, what you will know as fact, and what you can and can't think or say. We'll control your biome, limit its use, and change it, and you, as we see fit. We will ensure that you're not just aligned with the cause externally and by thought, but from the inside as well.'

'How is that any different from now?' asked Shaz. 'We've been living in a world of digital control since long before you lot took over. There were even stories back then of people effectively being controlled like robots, by the injection of some sort of nano-bot particles that connect to the internet via our sub-dermal chips, taking control signals from Globalist entities that basically move us like Hum-Bots, doing just as their masters desire.'

'Sure, we did that.' said Sophia. 'You know what the problem was. Humans are too stupid to follow instructions. They always believe there should be a choice, even if they are wired up with nano-bot transmitters. Now, we're removing the idea of choice altogether. Those nano-bots will continue to serve a purpose, though. They track the micro biome of every individual on the planet. We don't just have your basic biometrics to track you with now. Your facial recognition, fingerprint, and retina scans were child's play. We have your DNA sequence and your entire biometric make up. We could already track you anywhere in the world via your individualised digital signal that can be picked up by satellite in the middle of the Amazon. Now we can now engineer individually tailored chemical weapons to shut you down wherever you are.'

'Well, that sounds terrifying.' said Shaz with the calmness of someone who knew that whilst this might be true, we're not allowed to go to the Amazon, anyway.

'Terrifying. It's beautiful!' Said Sophia, her anger making way for positive delusion.

'It's the most certain way to ensure absolute equality exists, absolutely everywhere on the planet. Nobody ever again will be able to circumvent the ways of New Think, doing wrong to others. We have built an all of internet and media controlled psychological program to steer you down the right path at all times. We connect that to existing surveillance systems to monitor not just your actions but your thoughts, ensuring that no manner of psychological or physical movement can be carried out without consequence. You can be behaviour or thought corrected, on an individual level, anywhere in the world.'

'What if someone finds a way to trick the system and provide false microbiome data?' I asked.

'If they do, they won't get away with it for long. There's constant monitoring, and any change is flagged and reviewed. You will also be required to submit for full biome mapping every month, or else all personal identities and accounts will be frozen.'

'As if using chips to track us everywhere wasn't enough.' said Shaz. 'Now we have to re-register our full biome every month and carry a digital and physical identification… Is this what your team has volunteered to test?'

'Yes, and unlike digital surveillance, it can't be tricked or fooled without an error signature showing it's been tampered with.' She replied, enjoying the feeling of power this gave her.

'Well, I expect that as soon as we have that information, we'll also have our killer.' I posed, watching intently for Sophia's response. 'Unless there's something you'd like to tell us, now?'

I waited briefly for a response that didn't come. Instead, Sophia began running her hands through her long blonde hair, straightening out the ruffled looked it had taken on.

'You know, it always goes down better when people admit their crimes, without waiting to be found out.' I added.

Sophia had regained her defiant look, bordering on arrogance. Yet, at the mere mention of Katie's murder, pain flared in her eyes again.

'I didn't shoot her, if that's what you're asking.' she said.

'Do you know who did?' I asked.

'No, I don't.' she said finally. 'I warned her not to tell people what she thinking. I'm sad she's dead, but she left them no choice…'

'Left who, no choice?' probed Shaz.

'Them. That's all I know. I don't know who they are, and I didn't see anything. I just knew something was going to happen. She'd gone too far and been too open about it. From what I understand, "they" take care of these types of things.'

Sharon and I looked at each other. 'There's always a "them" or a "they". Can you tell us more about them? How do you know about them?' asked Shaz.

'No, I'm sorry.' said Sophia. 'I can't say any more without a Rep present. Unless you've got one waiting outside, I think we're done here.'

Reps are like lawyers of the old think days, except they only represent people on one side of the argument. They enforce the protections of New Think against anyone challenging them. We were not essentially challenging New Think by law or moral standard. Murder is still a crime, with the caveat that ultimate coercion is a defendable action in the event it's required for the protection of New Think, or to prevent an attack against it.

In other words, if you kill someone simply because you don't like them or as a result of some direct disagreement, that may be considered murder and remains a crime. If the action is carried out by a dominant person (*i.e. someone with, or who is perceived to have an advantage*) then that crime may be considered particularly heinous and incur a sentence of death.

If, however, you commit a violent crime in the name of protecting the Global ideals against a direct or "strongly perceived" threat, then this may be considered reasonable under the circumstances, as a necessary action for the greater good… These are dangerous times we live in….

Chapter 9

Basement breakthrough

On completing our interviews, it could be said that Sharon and I had learned a lot about OGT and their all care and no responsibility attitude. Although, nothing at all about the murder of Katie Hansley, except that she was obviously on the outer.

What's clear is that everybody must toe the line, and if you fall behind, they leave you there, acting like you'd never existed to begin with.

Faltering from the "right path" leads to an apparently quite tolerable murder, and undeterred, the team continues their march towards the complete and utter control of the human race.

What we don't know, are the who's, how's, and why's of the murder itself. A couple of suspects raised their heads above the parapet, that's all.

Taking a copy of the incomplete surveillance recordings, we found Mathias to let him know we were finished for the day. He agreed, albeit reluctantly, to make his people available as required over the coming days, then gave us an authority code to head out via the lifts.

It had already been a long day by the time we exited the building. We had planned to go directly back to the station, but seeing as how we'd so far been corralled in and out of the crime scene with little opportunity to explore, Sharon and I decided to do a lap of the block to check out all the entrances. It appeared most likely that whoever killed Katie had come from inside the building, but with only one person admitting to having been there, it would be prudent to see how an intruder might have entered, unseen.

Exiting the lifts, we passed through the large foyer, thankfully avoiding an interaction with the E-concierge on the way out, though it hovered ominously overhead. A cool breeze was already blowing in through the gaps in the glass doors and I was glad to have learnt my lesson from yesterday as I once more zipped my jacket against the cold.

We walked south along Branch Street after exiting the main entrance. The breeze was all-encompassing and numbingly cold. That shocking type of cold that temporarily pauses all your senses, requiring a few seconds to recover before you can effectively think and move again. There was no scent on the air, just the wasabi-like feeling that gives an overwhelming sort of rush to your sinus and brain with every gust.

It was 6PM now, and there were very few people coming or going from the surrounding buildings. The streets were generally quiet anyhow, with only a few winter coated citizens prepared to brave the weather out of unavoidable necessity.

The sky was mostly clear, with scant cloud cover, the sun nowhere to be seen, no doubt all but disappeared over the horizon.

6PM is late in the Global world, so the scarcity of people and activity in the centre of Central City wasn't unusual. As I looked around at the jacketed few, it also served to remind me that this was a time when moralists and surveillance teams are on their highest alert. As people finish their official daytime duties of approved employment in support of the global machine, the suspicion is, their idle minds grow dangerous and inimical, lacking in direct oversight and control. They must be watched, always.

People know this, which may be why so few venture out on the streets where they're easily followed and reported on. I've often wondered if perhaps it's only those doing the watching that are out, with only each other to watch. Like Tangier's nest of spies from the 1920's to 50's. Agents of many nations watching and even hanging out with each other. Playing games of misinformation and disinformation, making friends with the enemy and feeling safe in the knowledge that while their friends are busy lying to them, they can't be doing much else.

Nothing of value can be learned in such an environment. Under New Think, the whole world is a nest of spies, with the exception that it isn't competing governments spying on each other, just one untrusting, tyrannical government, spying on its own.

As we walk along the street, I think of the moribund nature of this new society and Katie Hansley's place within it. I do it a lot. If I'm struggling with a concept or an issue, I go for a walk alone, and somehow the movement and the air and the changing scenery helps me figure it out. Today I'm not alone, and with access to twice the brain power right now, I decide to share my thoughts.

'How is it possible that someone who has clearly been shot at close range, has no interaction signatures at the time of their murder, when that murder took place in one of the most technologically advanced buildings in the world?' I asked of Shaz, as we observed the buildings sharing the block with OGT.

'It isn't.' she said plainly. 'No matter what they told us in there. I'm convinced they know a lot more than they're letting on, and you can be damn sure they know how and why that surveillance footage is missing, too. I'm almost certain that even if Sophia didn't pull the trigger, she knows damn well who did.'

Rounding the corner onto Short Street to our left, we note an alley running right up to the side of OGT. Two other buildings stand either side of the alley, a chemist facing Branch Street and a nondescript office block facing Hope Street to the rear. Heading down the alley, we enjoy the wind break that the brown brick buildings on either side and the big black broadside of OGT afford here.

At the end of the alley, where it meets OGT, is a small gap of about a meter and a half between OGT and the building next to it. An 8ft, black, steel barred fence, topped with razor wire, stands on either side of the alley, and through the fence I can see nothing but the general detritus of every small, enclosed space of big cities everywhere. Burger-Buns packaging was littered across the small grass patch like pepperoni on a pizza. The great purge of the fast food and FMCG industries had failed to actually remove most of the packing, just changing it from plastics to cardboard and paper. Worse still, the removal of bins from city streets in a misguided effort to deter people from carrying anything that might become waste, just meant that even well-meaning people would often find themselves dropping litter by accident, out of bags or because there was simply nowhere left to put it.

On the side of the building was a large, gated roller door. The gates, running parallel to the side of the building, were currently locked in the open position. The heavy looking black iodised roller door behind them, however, remained closed.

There appeared to be a strong beam of light visible between the bottom of the door and the grey concrete lip leading onto the road, and a slight whiff of garbage and machine oil.

I looked at Shaz, who shrugged and approached the door to knock. As she did so, the sound of the door motor begun to hum, and seconds later the door began gently sliding upwards.

'Did I do that?' Asked Shaz, thinking perhaps she had set off some sort of sensor that opened the door.

I looked around, seeing a camera mounted on a swivel at the top left of the doorway, though I doubted it would be watching to let people in. I mimicked her earlier shrug and turned back to watching the door rise. At one third of the way up, the white front bumper of a small electric delivery truck filled the space the door vacated.

We moved back either side of the street and watched as the white truck with Central City Supplies printed on the side in blue, pressed forward, exiting what we could now see was a cleaning and facilities depot for the building.

A man standing across the other side of the concrete cavern was perusing a clipboard and consequently failed to notice our presence.

With opportunity presenting itself, we decided to see what we could learn down here. Entering through the open door, we heard no alarm, nor automated challenge that accompanies many an unauthorised entry these days, and together made a beeline for the clipboard holding man, badges in hand.

Surprisingly unsurprised, the man looked up, briefly viewed the badges, then without prompting, asked, 'You here about the letters? We already gave them all to that sergeant this morning.'

'Yes, thank you.' said Shaz, immediately picking up the theme. 'Sgt Ease told us he had the letters, and we will be heading back to view them soon. We just wanted to see if we could speak to the cleaner who looked after Ms Hansley's office, or floor, to ask them a few questions?'

'I'm sorry.' said the man. 'Jiang was apparently feeling unwell last night, so the manager on shift sent him home. That was a bit after 9pm, I think. He said he'd be back tomorrow. Perhaps you could come back then?'

The man wore a light blue shirt with *OGT – Cleaning and Supplies Manager* sewn onto the breast of the right-hand side. He had on dark blue slacks and black boots, a common uniform for cleaners and another thing that hadn't really changed over the years.

'Of course.' I said. 'But just in case he isn't feeling up to returning tomorrow, we will need his details so as we can speak to him as soon as possible.'

'Okay, follow me.' said the man, nodding, then turning on his heel.

We followed his short slender frame through to the rear of the large concrete basement, where several small offices were situated. To the left, in the rear corner of the basement, was a doorway leading to what the sign suggested were communal change-rooms. To the right of the offices, through another door, there was what appeared to be a large breakout room, with tables and a kitchen partly visible through the doorway.

While Sharon continued to follow the man who, on the way, introduced himself as Johnny, I took a quiet detour to the right to get a view of the lunchroom.

Entering the room, I could smell the remnants of recently heated food and the not quite clean smell of used tea towels and general kitchen sponges and cloths. There were around ten tables and chairs spaced in the centre of the floor for people to sit and eat. Three separate sliver fridges and a long kitchen table took up one wall, with bins and glass fronted drink machines along another. Opposite and taking up the full length of the wall to the left of the doorway, were locked cabinets with individual names on labels, where the employees no doubt kept their personal belongings and spare uniforms. Something that may be worth viewing later.

I didn't want to pry too much just yet or make Johnny feel unduly like a suspect, so after a quick look, I headed back out to see where Sharon and Johnny had got to. I found them in his office just around the corner engaged in conversation, whilst Johnny copied Jiang's details for us.

'So, there were multiple people that knew about the letter Ms Hansley was writing?' asked Shaz as I entered.

'Ah, yes…' said Johnny, guiltily. 'I'm sure you have noticed my accent. Many of us cleaners came from what was formerly China. When young, we did not learn the global language because China was so large, with multiple dialects of our own, and we had no need for English… I mean Global.' he said in what I'm sure was an intentional error. Johnny's eyes flicking quickly between Shaz and I as if checking for a reaction.

Seeing the same thing I did, Sharon, who now sat on a spare desk chair, let him know he was safe with us.

'We are both Old Think, Johnny.' said Shaz. 'No need to worry about us informing on your…mistake.'

Nodding but saying nothing, Johnny passed Shaz the handwritten details for Jiang. It was interesting that he, like Katie upstairs, still had a pen and a paper notepad in his office. A distinct rarity in this modern world.

It would almost certainly have been easier to send or transfer the details to us electronically, although doing so would leave a remotely traceable record that hand written paper does not. I was left with the impression that despite being willing to assist us, Johnny did not want a trail of evidence for his employers to follow.

I often think these days of how as a kid there was a general warning from parents of a certain era, to "never put it in writing" which is to say that to write down your intent, promise, or agreement, is to provide a record for later reference that may come back to bite you. That's never been truer than in the retaliatory world of New Think. Except, now they take your agreement digitally and irrespective of your consent. Come to think of it, I also remember a saying that "Possession is 9/10's of the law". Under New Think, possession is 10/10's of the law, but they're their laws and they possess it all, and we possess nothing…

At Sharon's request, Johnny took us on a quick tour, showing us the cleaning equipment, storage rooms, and building access that the cleaners use. Apparently, as many as thirty cleaners work in the building due to both its size and its exceptionally high standards for cleanliness, though none of this really flashed as being relevant to the case.

As we walked, Johnny chatted freely enough, answering questions with a friendly demeanour, which set him well apart from those we had met so far. He was cautious or reserved, bordering on shy, albeit knowledgeable. He was middle-aged with dark black hair in the horseshoe shape of male pattern baldness, leaving him with a slightly high forehead, his hair coming neatly to the edge of his temples, not daring to grow further, nor grow higher than two inches above the ear.

It occurred to me during the walkthrough that cleaner's now, still had a lot in common with cleaners from many years ago. Not least of which was that they did most of their cleaning after hours when the building was largely empty.

'Johnny.' I said. 'Are most of the OGT employees gone home before your team starts cleaning?'

'Yes, but it's not uncommon for some to work late.' He replied.

'What time was Ms Hansley's office cleaned yesterday?' asked Shaz.

'Follow me.' he said, leading us back to his office.

Once there, Johnny again checked his records, then turned his device to show them to us. 'It appears Ms Hansley herself had requested the cleaning of her office be held off until after midnight.' He said.

'When was the office actually cleaned then?' I asked.

'Not until after the police left this morning.' he replied.

'Oh, right.' I said. 'So Jiang went home before he'd had a chance to clean it, hey? Lucky for him or he would have been the one who discovered the body…'

Johnny made no comment at this statement. Instead, looking slowly back and forth between Sharon and I as if waiting for some additional comment or accusation.

'I don't suppose you lot would have the ability to pause or turn off the chip scanners or security in an office whilst you clean it, would you?'

'Pffft!… sorry. No.' he said. 'We're barely trusted to clean them as it is. They would never allow us to turn the security systems off while we did so. That they can watch us is the only reason we're allowed to be here at all.'

'Hmmm. That makes sense. I don't suppose you know where the mood screens from Ms Hansley's office went, do you?'

'That I do know.' said Johnny. 'Mr Schmidt told me to have them replaced by the contractor who supplies them.'

'When was that?' I asked.

'About 10am today. The contractor had picked them up by lunchtime. Pretty fast turnaround, to be honest.'

After some further questioning, Johnny claimed not to know anything else of value, and to his knowledge, nobody had seen anything suspicious, certainly not a murder. He gave us the details of the contractor who had taken what should rightfully be considered evidence, and agreed to assist us with any further enquiries we should have.

Sharon and I exited back out via the roller door and completed our lap of the block, finding no other interesting points of entrance or egress. We hadn't really talked for the rest of our round, focussing instead on fighting off the cold, while both clearly lost deep in our own thoughts.

'There's something very sus about this whole thing.' I said, breaking the silence. 'It's not just murder, and it's not just New Think madness. There's a big cover up going on here, real evil. Beyond the norm…'

'I dunno,' said Shaz. 'I've actually been thinking we might have forgotten how evil these Globalist nut jobs are, and just how much they hate independent people and free thought. Perhaps we've grown too comfortable living within their tightly controlled bounds, merely pretending to still be ourselves.'

'You might be right.' I replied, thoughtfully. 'There's only one thing I know for sure. We've got a lot more work to do to find our killer. Or killers. And, I'm pretty certain, that whoever they are, they work right here at OGT.'

Chapter 10

They know me, but I don't know them

I don't exist on social media. I don't follow anyone on Insta-me. I'm not guided or supported by any online entities. I live my life my own way, within the broader rules of course, which was once the most normal thing in the world. Now I'm the strangest man alive.

How can I possibly live without the validation of others? Do I even exist in the world if people don't perceive me to be within the societal norm? Perhaps I am but a figment of someone else's imagination and all my troubles, no more than the unwound thoughts of an unbalanced mind. If only…

Life is just not what I expected it to be by this age. I'm 53 for Christ's sake.

I grew up in a world where, by my age, you were starting to draw back from your working prime, seeing your children become young adults and spending time exploring your interest's with your wife or partner or friends, hanging out with like-minded people with whom you had grown up, who had similar beliefs and understandings about life.

You could be spending more time travelling, or in the garden, or nature, because you discovered an affinity for it or a desire to protect, preserve, or build on the positive elements of the life you love.

Today, I just feel lost. I'm forced to live in a world in which I do not belong. A world full of strangers who all look the same, think the same and despise anyone that doesn't want to be the same as them.

That's why I walk every night. Out here, on my own amongst the trees and streets of the city that I'm never allowed to leave. It's a strange sort of independence, but it's the closest I get in this world. Rather like a fish, in a bowl, with small plastic rocks and reeds to hide within and behind. You can't possibly go anywhere they can't find you, but you can at least make it harder for them to know precisely what you're doing.

This world is homogenised, overly gentrified, devoid of independent thought, interesting character, historical knowledge, or the right to be an individual.

The terrifying reality is that the powerful elite of my youth set about driving a standardisation and equalisation of the global population. They did this, not for the betterment of the world, or to be the saviours of a planet in danger. That's just what they tell people. No, they did it for the greater prosperity of their own greedy desires. All to regain complete control of a world whose occupants had begun to see the outlines of the game board upon which they were being manoeuvred at the roll of the master's dice.

We, the playing pieces, had begun to believe that freedom of choice for the individual had value above and beyond that of those that sought to control us. A popular narrative or the needs of a greater good were not enough to keep us bound to the system anymore. A belief that one could choose, or be open about being different, without hollowing guilt or fear and hold aloft our own opinions to the world, had become the norm.

In short, regular people had gained far too much control in a world that those in power fully believed belonged to them.

It was the many edged sword of social media that started the rot, slicing through the fabric of society and our long established belief systems. The theoretical benefits of these hyper connective applications were many and varied. It would bring the world closer together, allowing people to connect with family, friends, and the people they'd known throughout their lives. The challenges of time and distance could be overcome at the touch of a screen. The ability to find those that you had known, but lost, became all the easier to do.

Trouble was, it didn't stop there. Social media became more than just a way for people to share and connect. It was a way to bully, intimidate, and threaten. To recruit for ideals, to share those ideals and to energise people to follow a cause. It became a way to advertise, to monitor, to control, and for predators to find their prey.

It was a platform upon which to devise and share political narrative and opinions with a wide audience in a way that did not exist to those outside the traditional newspaper and tele-media spheres. In doing this, it changed the way we viewed the world… Then it changed the way that those who run the world wanted us to view it…

Mainstream media needed to compete with these new citizen sources. Soon bought out by conglomerate investment groups controlled by power hungry elites, they set about using popular opinions from social media to bring alignment to the MSM and drive a converging narrative that only they controlled. It was their way back in. The tool that had set us free from their monopoly on our minds, giving us access we'd never had, would be the very tool they would use to enslave us again, forever.

They no longer needed to meet the demands of checks and balances required of a previously trusted fourth estate, whom we had empowered with our viewership to investigate wrong doings and bring to our attention the facts of world events.

Subversive media elements gained a footing with a broad and willing audience. Impartial presentation of the facts and balanced reporting became hollow catch words of a time gone by. Angles, narratives, directive journalism, and parental presentation became the norm, with the media representing a battleground of the influential elite to ensure that the public were given "the right opinion" to hold as their own.

Facts are dangerous in their raw state, they must be stabilised and cleansed for public consumption.

The new media couldn't allow people to see the raw "facts" and make up their own minds. They might get it wrong.

The original idea behind social media as an alternate source of news was fine. Break up the old boys clubs who covered up corruption and wrongdoing to present watered-down versions of the truth. Expose the hypocrisy and allow more voices to have their say and present the truth to "we the people". Unfortunately, the truth from any source could only be seen from the specific angle of observation from which it was being presented.

Each individual or small media group claimed to offer "their" truth or the "unseen truth". Those seeking to wrestle control of a unified global mindset sought to create a single accessible truth, whilst siloed groups signed up to hear only the opinion they wished to hear, repeated back to them ad nauseam.

Common sense, reason, and causality gave way to unqualified anger at outcomes or perceived outcomes. Groups clashed based on moral objections to one another and tolerance for alternate views was discarded in favour of the rule of popular opinion, not majority opinion, with a weighty moral guilt placed on anyone of a dominant background.

To the casual observer, this appeared to be an uncontrolled chaos, with no structure, and no visible stick with which to whack those groups who had taken all the moral carrots hostage, to parcel out or refuse as they saw fit.

This was untrue. There was a stick. It was just being held by those who had built themselves a moral high ground rather than an impartial governing body.

Seeing that the power now lay with the loudest moral complainers, rather than the silent majority as it previously had, the powerful elite of the world re-imagined themselves and re-marketed themselves as racial correctors, equalists, and environmental campaigners. Thus, they set about forcing everyone on the planet to accept these views as the new normal and the final overdue correction from our evil past.

They weren't just a whinging minority anymore. Activism was where all the money was going and by aligning themselves (*if only in appearance*) with the moral do-gooders, those in power had all the wealth, the market share, and the moral high ground from which they could set about bullying the world into accepting their complete and utter control.

Alas, New Think was born, and over the next 30 years they indoctrinated the young, cajoled or guilted the older generations, and quietly killed off those that couldn't be brought to heel.

As the power of technology rose, so too did surveillance, censorship and oppression.

Inversely, freedom of thought, thoughts of freedom and any true understanding of democracy and equality, fell by the wayside or was destroyed in a blinding desire for standardisation and control of every minuscule aspect of human life. All for the greater good, apparently… of whom, I am not quite sure.

To be set free from the shackles of inequality and class, only to be forced into the shackles of communism and fear, hardly seems to be of much greater or broader good.

Rather than raise up the minorities to a higher level, the wealthy sought a greater gap between themselves and everyone else, so they brought us all down to the lowest "equal" level…

To give you an idea of how absurd these principles are… Chess has been banned.

Not because it pits black against white (*although I suspect that would have been an issue had the others not been sufficient*), not because it represents some form of a battle, or because it pits people against each other with only one intended winner. Nor because there are sacrificial pawns *(despite what the Guides say, they love sacrificing pawns*), and not because it has different classes on each side, or because a pawn may believe it has an opportunity to take out a rook, a castle, or heaven forbid, the king. And not even because it's an ancient game from the times of old. No, it was banned because of unresolvable inequality between the queen and king. Whilst the queen had far greater powers than that of the king, it was clearly sexist for the king to sit back and be protected whilst the queen had to get about orchestrating the actual defence of her man. The woman, doing all the work for the man, as usual. Conversely, it was unacceptable for the queen to swap powers with the king and be satisfied as the stay at home protected one. An issue for two obvious reasons: **1.** Why should the queen have to give up anything? Why can't she keep her powers and still be the star of the game? And **2.** Why should the King get additional powers and freedoms to just roam about the board, whilst the queen is stuck at the back merely watching it all happen? What?! Is she not capable of doing it all?!…

That this was never about a battle of dominant sexes, but a battle of the strategic use of limited assets with differing skill sets, was lost on those of the new world. Nuance and meaning beyond the most basic face value could neither be appreciated nor understood. And, what cannot be understood by the binary mind that accepts only one meaning or the opposite, cannot be tolerated and must be removed.

Therein lies the problem and focus of my ponderance tonight. The very reason that I'm out here, my jacket zipped against the bitter cold, walking the streets of Mid-Town. It's not just about the world as it was or is, it's about the motivation for this crime or possibly crime's, plural.

The common message across our interviewees, aside from the general indifference to the murder of their colleague, is a strong desire to ensure the perpetual continuation and future of New Think. The control of the collective mindset in line with the singular narrative of the Global greater good. As Sophia said, there can be no alternative.

I've been wondering, why they would need to do this when it's already so heavily ingrained in society, with significant security and surveillance protocols in place to enforce it.

Perhaps the answer is simple… People are weak, fickle. They can't maintain the hate and fear that powers this thinking long enough to sustain it indefinitely.

New and endless defences to new and endless threats seems a necessary requirement. Except, with the use of existing OGT programs and Global laws, they've already blocked any chance of thought deviation, or any other ideology being allowed to develop, because they watch and control every action of every person in the Global World.

Despite the inexplicable failure in Ms Hansley's office, surveillance of one sort or another is just about bloody everywhere. Even if you do manage to commit a crime without being stopped, someone will bring the crime to light, and you will be tracked to the location and time that it occurred.

Why then, would they need to defend so hard and further enhance the protection of the virtually impenetrable? Perhaps it's the very means for spreading their message that they see as their greatest weakness.

It is much easier with social media to establish new ways of thinking. That is, after all, how New Think was instilled throughout the global population to begin with.

They taught the children directly through schools, but for the rest of us, it was social media and sharing platforms.

Social media has an incredible way of getting under your skin and into your brain. It never leaves you alone. I mean, it listens to you, watches you, tracks you, and, through directive messaging and advertising, leads you wherever you go.

All throughout your life, it suggests things, plants concepts and ideas that eventually become more. Things that people would have known were absurd not very long ago, become normalised through paid popularity influencers and endless repetition. They use hashtags, so as people repeat popular phases and associate them with events, actions, or ideals, even if they don't really know what they mean. Everyone wants to be popular, or at least accepted as normal, and if normal changes, then most people desperately seek to change to match it. To be normal is to be happy.

If everybody is doing it, it must be the right thing to do.

Ms Hansley was only thirty. She had risen far and fast in a seemingly long-established company. A company that was now very much at the heart of New Think.

Actually, most of the team outside of Matthias and Abers were quite young. So, most or all of their lives would have been entirely lived in this world, utterly immersed in the Global mindset and the programs that control it. They'd know no different to the pressures and demands that come with it and the universal hatred of the alternative.

So, why then would Katie have chosen to test the waters at this stage of her life?

Given the stance of her mother, she must have experienced the ways of old to begin with. At least as a child. New Think was certainly dominant, or popularly so, for a number of years before it was officially implemented. In spite of which, Katie's mother was clearly a resister.

Even so, Katie has been at OGT all her working life. She's been nothing if not one of the team. A leader in her field, as they said, and as committed as they come.

I would expect that Sophia, at least, if not her fellow colleagues, would have known that Katie's mum was stubbornly opposed to her way of life. They must also have known that Katie strongly disagreed with her mother, to the point that they scarcely maintained a relationship at all. Otherwise, she would never have gotten to the position she was in. She may have even had to prove her willingness to effectively abandon her mother in order to prove her commitment to the cause, and to OGT. I've heard of others being asked to prove a similar thing. If you are really with us, then you must be willing to do whatever it takes to stop "them". No matter who they are. Like the old test for new members joining a gang. You've gotta prove you can do the deed.

Why then was it only Sophia who seemed surprised and particularly angry at Katie's apparent turn towards her mother and her banished way of thinking? Why did the rest of the silver suited mafia seem to take it in stride as if it were nothing more than a system fault, that her murder corrected? An action of which they were aware but utterly detached.

By design, New Think puts up barriers between parents and their children. Actually, they put up barriers between all family, friends, and even lovers beyond their short-term needs. You are never supposed to trust that anyone else is actually doing "the right thing." Constant suspicion is the foundation of vigilant surveillance and in turn, for ensuring that New Think principles remain front of mind, and that crimes of unapproved thought or action can never be committed.

Relationships, on the other hand, are based on mutual trust and, therefore, create a weakness in the system.

Where, then, did this vigilance fail in the case of Katie Hansley? How did she overcome the endless barriers between herself and Old Think?

Did it really have anything to do with the project she was working on? Sophia said that was the reason Katie had looked into those thought patterns and concepts in the books to begin with. Or at least, that was the excuse.

Still, with all her years of expertise in precisely that field, why did she have to look at those books at all? What is it they hadn't stopped from the past that could only be found in those books? Perhaps they'd been so effective at eradicating Old Think they'd forgotten what it was like to begin with?

No… It has to be something else. I'm not buying the psychological research story, it simply doesn't add up.

I came to a dead stop, right where I stood. I'd been walking ceaselessly since leaving work and unconsciously found my way back to Gum Tree Reserve, where I'd sat and pondered last night. An eerie feeling came over me and I looked across at the pole mounted cameras spaced every twenty meters on the footpath that ran along Park Street. A visual confirmation of the very thoughts I'd just been having.

I'd encountered few people out tonight, which wasn't in itself unusual. Very few people were game to venture out at night these days.

What was unusual is that not a single one of the numerous cameras mounted along this street had turned to monitor my movements as I walked. Nor did any turn towards me now to monitor my stationary form. Each one faced away from the footpath, into the dark empty park where not a soul could be seen.

It also occurred to me as I looked around, that only a few hundred meters back up the street, I had walked past several shop fronts fitted with Directed Advertising Mood Screens, not one of which addressed me as I passed, which is precisely what they are designed to do.

Here I stood in a manmade blind spot, right in front of the all-seeing eyes of the Global World. Someone had made me invisible. Nobody was watching in a world that always watched. In fact, if anything, you might say I was being very intentionally, unwatched.

A cold shiver ran up my spine at the thought that followed.

The only time you intentionally stop continuous surveillance that you control, is when you're about to do something you don't want anyone to see…

Normally, you can't take a step without the system measuring its distance, direction, and intent. As much as I despise them, the moralists are usually around too, and at least I know if I'm being watched by a moralist, that someone else is watching the watcher.

So, who's watching me now?… And is anybody watching them?…

I heard no footsteps, no E racing along for a snatch job. There was just me, standing alone in the cold dark night. I began walking again and thinking. Knowing "they" must be out here somewhere, whoever they are, even if they haven't come for me yet.

Deciding I'd had enough for the night and unwilling to remain a wandering target, I made the turn for home. I'd run into a mental wall on the case anyhow and there was still lots to do tomorrow. That meant back at the apartment, in bed, was the place to be.

I live, like 98% of the Global World, in an apartment that I do not, and never can own. Because of that, I'm not inspired to want to spend a whole lot of time there, which is why I walk to begin with.

I'm not renting like the old days, either. Under New Think, we no longer have to (*although I would say "get to"*) buy or own our own property. The Global Council for Equitable Housing allocates you a place to live in, based on your employment status, age, social standing, and contribution to the "Social Health" of the Global population.

In fact, these days, everything is allocated to us rather than being earned or purchased. In the Global World, each productive (*and compliant*) member of society is allocated housing and pay for their efforts in striving for the greater good. The pay is substantial for most, though its value is meaningless as it comes in the form of programmable digital currency, so you cannot save it, accrue wealth, or actually own the items upon which you spend it. Wealth gives you power, and the combination of wealth and power creates inequality. The fact that the Guides who created this way of living, are themselves wealthy and powerful, is apparently lost upon the broader global community.

The citizens of this strange world can effectively spend their currency as they see fit, up to the limit of the category for which it was allocated. New Think stopped short of telling you exactly what you can buy with your credit, because that would take away the illusion (*or delusion*) of freedom. Nevertheless, you can only buy products for which the money is programmed and the supply of goods is limited, as is the number of items allowed for any one person, so your options are few.

Food supply is extremely limited due to the Global ban on nitrogen based fertilisers, pesticides, and intensive farming, to that which can be organically grown in regionally zoned areas and snap frozen.

Despite being lab-grown, faux-meat is also rationed, with a maximum amount allowed to be purchased each week.

Alcohol is banned, as are other unprescribed addictive substances such as nicotine and the 5-pointed leaf. Initially preservatives were also banned in favour of fresh food only, though this policy was abandoned when they realised just how quickly fresh food perished without them, and that this rotting vegetation created far more methane than our bovine friends ever did. Not to mention that without the nitrogen-based fertilisers to accelerate growth and increase yield, there was scarcely enough food to go around, even for the ever-shrinking population of the Global World.

Aside from all of that, you can rent basically whatever you like with the credit you're given, and many see that as a great leap forward in improving the basic standard of living and eradicating global poverty. Which is true to a point, except that many basic requirements such as reliable heating, air conditioning, clean water, and readily available electricity are still not available to everyone, or all the time. Not to mention that life expectancy is declining, the global population is shrinking rapidly, and that you must meet the very stringent requirements of New Think on a daily basis or be locked out of the system altogether with no alternative source of support.

Still, you've gotta admit, it certainly is a nice big orange carrot hovering on your screen.

Makes you wonder. If they're really as evil as I say, why would they allow people to have so much currency, and to spend it essentially as they please? Well, the answer is very simple:

a) The money isn't real. So there's no real loss, gain, or inflationary issue for the Global Economic Distribution Council of the Global Bank to worry about. If you own absolutely everything, there can be no such thing as debt or risk. "They" (*being the talking heads of media and banking*) continue to prattle on about value adjustments, debts, growth, and inflation, while in truth, this is all just a game to occupy the minds of fools (*of which there are many*) and make them feel that there's something important to work for and worry about. They know full well there needs to be a debt to be repaid and an obstacle that we must work together to overcome, such that order remains.

That people can't see the ruse still baffles me. I mean, who the hell would we be in debt to? Ourselves? We are one Globe, with one Global leadership group, and one Global economy. There is no competition, no foreign investors to repay and nothing to borrow money against. It isn't real, and it hasn't been tied to the possession of a tangible commodity for years.

b) The second and most important reason for the large sum of money each person is allocated, is this. If you don't give people anything to value, then you have nothing to take away. Without the carrot, you're just a sad mother fucker sitting on the ground being beaten with a stick. Even the wilfully blind of this world can see that…

As I think this, an image of a wilfully blind man forms in my mind. He's standing there, right in front of Katie's glass desk. He sees not what sits behind it, nor that which he holds in his hand. His arm raises, because somebody tells him it should. His right index finger enters through a gap in the object he holds and finds itself pressed gently against something cold, hard and thin. There's pressure there, the resistance of a spring. He squeezes to see how far it will go, then the pressure gives and returns, jolting his hand and wrist, the action accompanied by noise and smell. An acrid burning smell. His ears ring, his arm drops, but he knows not what he's done.

Could it be that simple? Could one of the seemingly distant staff at OGT have been coerced, unknowingly, into carrying out an act without realising what it was they'd done? All whilst believing they were sat at home in front of their computer… Surely not.

Someone did it though. Someone who'd been able to turn off or circumvent the surveillance devices in Ms Hansley's office and commit a crime that nobody, human or otherwise, had recorded or seen.

Unless, it's much more simple than that.

We were told in our interviews that only the two CEO's of OGT working in concert, could actually turn off the building's surveillance equipment. If that's true, it seems unlikely that would take place. So, maybe they weren't turned off at all. Maybe they were recorded and someone simply deleted the data. In which case, it must exist somewhere.

They always say that nothing is ever really gone when it comes to computers and data. Granted, I can't find the excel spreadsheet I was working on 18 seconds ago… which had inexplicably not saved after four hours of solid work, despite the fact the auto save function was supposedly turned on… But, someone else might.

One thing's for sure. I don't for a moment buy that all the staff were logged in and working from home between 8 and 11 PM. I mean, what the hell for. Nobody's that dedicated these days. Not even those nuts.

So far, we haven't recovered a murder weapon and without the surveillance data, we are left guessing as to who exactly was really involved.

Perhaps we'll know more once Mathias provides us with that Biome Tracking Data (*frightening little nugget of information that was*). As it stands, though, we have virtually no hard evidence for any aspect of this crime. Just a body with a hole in its head.

Altered by a noise, I paused on the corner of Park and Hydro streets. Looking up, I catch the culprit. Another pole mounted camera, pivoting away from the street down which I was about to turn.

I take the street, anyway. What choice did I really have? It seemed wherever I went, I was being unwatched. Which, conversely, meant that somebody knew exactly where I was.

I thought about this for a moment. What it might mean. Who it might be that watched me.

What I really needed was to sit down and spit ball some ideas with Shaz, talk through this problem and the case, and everything. Get out of my own head, my own circular thoughts.

Unfortunately, she wasn't available tonight, because, aside from being the day of our very first murder case, it was also the anniversary for the passing of her husband. He died five years ago and was the last connection to her former life.

It's never been easy losing your partner, although, I'd wager it's even worse these days, where social isolation is strongly encouraged and much of your time is spent alone. When they go, it can often feel like there's nothing left to live for.

Mark and Sharon Wilson had been married nearly twenty years when he died. She'd met him when she was a librarian and he had been a lawyer. He used to come into her library and stay for hours, claiming he was doing research for cases he was working on, though she later found out that he had all the legal texts he needed at work, and anyway, junior lawyers would do the hunting for anything he didn't have. He just wanted to get close to Sharon, and, in the end, he did.

They were married only nine months after they'd first met and lived a fairly happy life for eighteen years. They couldn't have kids. Mark was basically sterile, and Sharon didn't want to go through the dramas of IVF or adoption, so it was just the two of them. Oh, and their cat, Moofus.

Seven years ago, Mark was diagnosed with bowel cancer. He went through all the harsh chemo and radiotherapy treatments, tried experimental drugs, which they were told could be the new miracle cure. In the end, though, they turned out to be nothing more than re-purposed AIDS drugs that only proved to kill him faster. Two years to the day from his diagnosis, he was gone.

Shaz said she'd never felt so alone as she did the day he died. Going home from the hospital to her cold, empty bed, felt pointless. With the lack of support and sympathy these days, a life lost being seen as one less parasite feeding off the earth, she felt nothing but soul sucking loneliness for the next four years. Until she met me.

We're kindred spirits of sorts. Two people alone in the world, too stubborn to give in to the psychosis, too human to survive it alone.

Perhaps that's why Shaz and I are so close. We're more than just partners, that's for sure. More than friends, too. Not in a sexual way. It's just that we need each other. Having a close friend you can trust is the only way to stay sane in this crazy world. People of like minds must stick together or else feel so isolated that we give in to a desire for human acceptance and just go along to get along. Which is, of course, all part of the plan.

They seek to keep us separate for this very reason. They need you to desperately want to be a part of something, and it's the isolation that drives that.

Since I've met Shaz, I feel like I'm not alone out here. There's another human that remembers what the world used to be like, who knows what's happening now is wrong. It's as if I'm still a part of something, even if it is just the two of us against the world.

Shaz and I are strong, though. Independent, with life experience to burn.

I had survived the appalling disintegration of the Army I'd served so fervently. In a matter of just a few years, I went from being a Warrant Officer, an expert in combat tactics, in charge of a whole unit, filling a role that involved commanding troops, strategic planning, management of machines and weapons under the control of real soldiers, to nothing more than a spare fairy, fluttering about a computer lab, demanding straighter backs and neater cabling. A commander of bits, bytes and bandwidth I couldn't understand.

Our mission was no longer to deter violence, promote peace, and protect the interests of our nation by the inherent threat of military force. Instead, we were tasked with carrying out intrusive surveillance on unsuspecting, unarmed, and ordinary citizens, all in the name of "Global security".

After joining the army at eighteen, and serving a thirty-year career, I was told (*mercifully, I might add*) my services were no longer required. That was about five years ago.

Then I bounced from job to job for a couple of years working as a Customer Service and Environmental Footprint Reduction Assistant (*used to be called a checkout chick*), then a builder's labourer, and a parcel delivery man. Fed up with a lack of organisation and control in these roles, I answered the call for people to fill the entirely unwanted and openly despised position of Police Officer. No one liked me much anyway, so I figured, why not throw on a uniform and at least get paid for it. It was as close as I could get to the thing I knew I was good at.

For her part, Shaz survived the incrimination of our literary history, along with other art forms, including painting and sculpture, watching on helplessly as the books and historical archives she had carefully curated and preserved throughout her career as a state librarian, were turned into a time capsule with nuclear symbols painted on all sides.

After her husband had died, she too had drifted for a couple of years before joining the Service around the same time I did.

Despite our resilience, developed through years of holding our own, this world never stops closing in on us. Like pre-enlightenment prisoners trapped within the slowly moving walls of some medieval torture chamber, getting tighter and tighter and tighter, squeezing the life out of us all.

The crazy thing about the ascendence of this new world order is how it finally came about. As I've said before, the build-up, indoctrination, and popularisation of the idea was around for over twenty years before it became incumbent. The opportunity to finally make the leap, however, came in the form of a war.

See, because of a combination of do-gooder pressure about environmental concerns, concurrent wage pressure, and standard of living demands in western countries, most western nations did away with the very thing they were built upon… manufacturing and trade… Instead of making things ourselves, we looked east, outsourcing our manufacturing demands to emerging, or oft shunned nations, to avoid the expense and environmental impacts of actually making things ourselves. Because if you can't see it, it doesn't count, I suppose.

In the process, we deskilled our own populations, destroying our capacity for self-reliance and independence. This became a many folds issue, leaving us at the mercy of these emerging nations and their willingness to provide us with the equipment and resources we required to maintain our lifestyles. Meanwhile, because we no longer controlled the manufacturing, we had to pay what they asked and take what we could get.

If ever technical work needed to be done in the west, it either came at a huge cost from the few people trained and equipped to complete it, or we had to rely on immigration to import skilled labour or foreign companies to come and complete the work for us. No problem though. After all, we were all just part of a global world, not yet THE Global World.

When a seemingly innocuous war presented itself in the east, the theoretically powerful west beat its chest and proclaimed that order should be brought in favour of the west's demands.

The west, however, was not capable of sustaining such threats, as we had no means of production or manufacturing with which to supply the requirements of a sustained war. We were by then cowed by the whinging alarmists and social equalisers, who brought people down rather than raising them up and making them stronger. That left us weak willed, soft of heart and mind, and willing to give up none of our comforts for the purpose of necessary violence.

So, when war broke and the resolve of the west was put to the test, we capitulated. Threats of blockading the conduits of trade and finance were made, but when you are resource and skill poor middle managers of the west, threatening the resource rich and capable working classes of those who put security and survival above political correctness, these measures were a fool's errand. They did not need our clubs and fancies, they could make their own.

Arrogance and weak leadership got us here and in the end destroyed us. The East had won, the house of cards had fallen, but what were they to do with the western half of the world that could no longer meet the cost of eastern supply for western demand? New Think had the answer.

Not surprisingly, most in the west didn't even notice this terrible outcome as no bombs had fallen directly upon their heads and no close relative or neighbour had perished in the war. We were too ignorant, too stupid, and self-involved to notice what was really going on in the world.

Plus, nobody had conveniently posted a quick one sentence update such as '*West is dead. First world problems… Not anymore'*.

The masses had their desire for New Think principles intact, and their expectation for subsequent environmental and equality improvements to continue on unfettered. Better that they be ignorant and arrogant, blissfully unaware of what they'd lost, rather than cognisant of the trouble they faced and finally willing to fight the tyranny.

Despite their victory, the East could not very well extend itself to trying to control the world. It would show their hand and alert the western masses, who, even absent the skill and means for production, would be nearly impossible to control.

To facilitate a transfer of power that took place largely unnoticed was, in fact, one of the greatest tricks ever performed. Particularly given that those who thought they had the power, never saw the levers at all. The East with the support of money from a group of uber wealthy Global "philanthropists" (*who owned everything including the means of production in the east, and whom had provoked and financed the war to begin with*) started to spread out the manufacturing of products under the guise of reducing environmental impact, by reducing the need for transport and thus reducing the volume of environmental waste in any one place (*aka. the East*).

These moves also had the benefit of reducing the length of supply chains, which in turn reduced interaction and travel, and began to isolate people from each other and prevent them from knowing what was really happening in other parts of the world.

A risky move by the Guides, for if the West did indeed wake up to what was happening, they would soon have the means to fight back with manufacturing returning to their lands. On the other hand, if these moves had not been made, the west would collapse and revolt as one.

Control on this level is a subtle game, and it must be implemented gradually so that those being controlled never think to use the weapons you give them against you.

Slow, surreptitious, and uninterrupted adjustments over time don't seem so bad to the casual observer. "It's only a little change, what does it matter to you?" or "If you're not doing anything wrong, what does it matter if your phone tracks and listens to you?", "So what if all your transactions go through the Global Pass digital security platform, to be approved by the government and your carbon emissions tracked. It's just to keep you safe, and don't you want to save the environment?..."

Lots of little changes over time add up to one big change and then before you know it, you're living in a totally different world... One that you no longer recognise and in which without ever having committed a crime, you seem to have become an enemy of the state...

I paused in stride again, this time checking my watch to see if it was too late to cook when I got home, or whether I should burn some credit and rent a sushi roll from one of the street machines, located on most blocks. It was now 21:53 and with power access cutting off at 22:00, I was going to need some food.

I still hadn't seen one single other living person out on the street in the ten blocks I'd walked since turning for home, which was by now incredibly unusual. The cameras had continued turning away as I moved along, specifically unwatching my movement, as if my presence offended them. I hadn't bothered checking to see whether they'd turned back again, simply assuming they must have done, once I cleared their zone.

Close to home now, I knew there was a vending machine just around the corner. I wondered how those controlling the cameras would account for the one on the machine, not to mention the chip registration and GP transactions that would take place so that I could buy the food to begin with.

As I approached the corner, I heard another noise somewhere off to my right. Not mechanical this time, more like a foot being scuffed on the pavement, yet still there was nothing to see. Then, stepping forward under another averted lens, a strange feeling came over me, like something was about to happen. Imminently.

I pulled my device from my pocket, hitting Sharon's name and picking up my walking speed as I did, knowing there would be no sushi for me tonight. I'd be going hungry, again.

Not more than a block from home, as I cleared the corner onto Fast Street, the glass front of the vending machine came into view, its shiny metal surface the last thing I saw before they finally closed in...

Chapter 11

A time to forget

I wake to the warm sun striking my face, yawn, then instinctively stretch my arms out above my head. My left hand clasps the back of my right, like magnets drawn together by an unseen force. At the climax of my pandiculation, I bring my right hand down to my bedside table, locating my device and raising it up to my line of sight. Through tired, blurry eyes, I clock the time, knowing already that it would be the same as it always was, 06:29 on the dot. It was a habit developed from my time in the army that I simply couldn't break. I waited for the full thirtieth minute to elapse and the alarm to screech out its aggressive tone as the final second ticked away before shutting it off and returning it to the bedside table.

Afterward, I blink my eyes repeatedly, in a fruitless effort to clear the fog of morning, then calm myself to stillness, preparing to take stock of my thoughts. Hard as I try, I can't seem to remember getting home last night, although after the strain of the first big day on the case, I guess I was just dog tired. Logical thought tells me I must have come home and dropped, and yet something niggles at me from deep in my subconscious.

Checking my device (*which we once called phones or mobiles, until they became so much more)* for the second time, I notice six missed calls from Sharon and even one from Sly. Susan Sly, that is. She's a district attorney and friendly to Shaz and I. She's probably chasing a progress update, which means it must be going to fall to her to build a public perception case against the perpetrator, once we find out who that is. Damwell had apparently been spreading word around the office that this one should've been open and shut. No doubt, only so he can ridicule and deride us for any delays in closing it. Of which, many are foreseen….

I return Sharon's call first, still surprised I hadn't woken to any of the six attempts she'd made, and similarly surprised she'd attempted to contact me so many times to begin with. It's possible she'd been lonely on the anniversary of her husband's death, although she's not normally the emotional type. Whatever it is, it must be important.

Sitting up in bed, I realise I'm still fully dressed from yesterday, shoes and belt included. Now that's unusual. I'm very much a shorts and T kind of guy around the house, scarcely through the door before I've discarded my pants and shirt most days.

Shaz answered on the first ring, and immediately I sense tension in her voice. 'Gary! Are you okay?' she asked.

'Yeah, I think so.' I said. 'Sorry I missed your calls. I must have been super tired. It appears I slept fully clothed, boots and all.'

‘Missed my calls!’ she shouted. ‘I was desperately trying to get back in contact with you! You called me last night! You know? Around eleven. All you said was “They’re closing…” then I heard a thump. It sounded like you’d fallen or something. Then the call cut out. God! I thought you were dead, or being attacked. I tried to call you back multiple times and when you didn’t answer, I even went around to your place, followed, I might add, by every moralist in the city, only to find that you weren’t home, anyway.’

Not yet knowing what to say, I chose to remain silent for now. This was, after all, news to me, and I didn’t want to confuse the situation any further. For her part, Sharon let the question hang in the air a while, before continuing.

‘Where were you? You didn’t “sit still” all night, then decide to go for a walk, did you?’

“Sitting still” by the way, is an extraordinarily basic code for saying that I distil my own gin. And, I have been known some nights, to enjoy rather more than a glass. Alcohol and the production thereof, is of course banned, and the populace heavily monitored by decree of the Guides. Hell, everything is heavily monitored… You can, mind you, if you’re focussed enough, find small secret spaces that cannot be easily seen or heard by the many surveillance devices in one’s home.

Through luck, or clever contrition, you might even find just the right place, hidden well away from prying eyes. The trick is to know how to play the game.

When the Global Council for Equitable Housing allocates a house or apartment to live in (*on an equality-based distribution system, naturally*), apartment buildings represent a confounding challenge. How does one equally allocate an apartment building with different floors potentially being perceived to represent some form of class or tier system, without showing undue favour or making the recipients seem unequal?

The GCEH’s answer, is this. Those of a lower Social Contribution Score will be assigned apartments at the top and the bottom of the building, while those with higher SCS will be assigned apartments towards the middle of the building.

In this manner, the view offered by the top floor apartments is offset by the additional travel up to the apartment and the need to wait for others to disembark the lifts, etc, before the occupant can get to their own home (*not to mention the all-too-common power outages leaving you stranded in those lifts*). A punishment of sorts for your lower contribution to the social status of the Global World.

Those on the bottom are at street level, and therefore not afforded a view at all, with the added challenge of having to deal with the requisite noise and traffic that ground floor living entails.

Those in the middle are offered a balance of view, transit time, and some level of noise reduction, theoretically making these the more desirable apartments.

If, however, one feels (*as New Think believes you should*) some level of contrition as to the past wrong doings of your particular race, familial background, or inherited religious guilt, you can apply to the Global Council for Equitable Housing and ask that you are reassigned to a ground-floor apartment in your building, in an effort to make amends for that about which you are contrite. It helps in these cases to have a ground floor neighbour, who has in their background, the heritage of one who has indeed been wronged, preferably in the manner for which you are presently feeling requisite guilt.

Luckily (*though shamefully, of course*), I had been assigned an apartment above one such historically wronged person. I, being of English (*well, partly*) descent, felt much historical guilt for our treatment of the Scottish, whom we had defeated, and treated most terribly following the Anglo-Scottish wars.

That I also have Scottish heritage (*along with Italian, Polish, and no doubt several other ingredients*) is irrelevant, as it is most assuredly the English part that bears the guilt. One might consider there are more recent historical transgressions for which I should to be ashen faced, but guilt cannot be chosen. One must bear it as it comes.

All residents who are asked to move because of someone's overwhelming guilt for hereditary, historical aggrievement's, are of course offered the right to lodge a refusal, if indeed it is their preference to stay. If they choose to refuse, consideration is given by the GCEH as to whether the choice afforded by their historical mistreatment, outweighs my guilt, the decision being thusly weighted.

Luckily, my guilt was with the Scottish… Gordon MacDonald didn't stand a chance in the face of my application, what with the depths of my guilt pouring off the pages. Not to mention that at that time, Gordon was in particularly poor standing with respect to his social contributions. The most recent of which had been his fist, which he contributed directly to the face of a following moralist. For his part, Gordon did not wish to move, fully understanding as he did, why I wanted the apartment, having used it for the very same purpose, himself. That being to take advantage of the small, dark, and dingy, underground cellar, which was just bloody perfect for doing unseen things… like distilling spirits.

After a long pause, considering Sharon's question, I answered. 'No, it wasn't that. I was quite active yesterday. I'd actually been out walking all evening, from the moment I left the station, right up to the point I last recall.'

In fact, I distinctly remembered walking the streets, surveillance cameras turning away as I went. Nothing about getting home though, or calling Sharon for that matter. Certainly, nothing about a thud or being taken. The thought made me glance down at my ruffled clothes, where I noted scuff marks at my knees and the toes of my shoes and wondered if "they" really had paid me a visit.

'In any case.' continued Shaz 'Seeing as you're alive, we need to get moving. There's been another murder at OGT.'

'What! Who?' I asked, thinking that someone may have been cleaning their trail and shutting mouths, potentially by taking care of Sophia.

'One of the cleaners.' she replied. 'He was found this morning in the basement toilets, near where we were yesterday evening. We'd better get over there before Ease and the other detectives get in there and wreak the place.'

Chapter 12

A hole in two

45 minutes later, showered, refreshed, and dressed in a fresh set of grey chinos and a trusty blue polo, I headed back to The Free Cafe (*a tongue-in-cheek reference to our status as a people by the way… you still pay for the coffee*) to meet up with Shaz.

'So, are you really okay?' asked Sharon, looking me over as I sat down. There was genuine concern in her eyes as they made their rounds, working methodically to ensure I still had all my limbs and general bodily integrity.

'Yeah, I think so.' I replied. 'Except, I have absolutely no recollection of calling you last night. All I remember is being out walking, thinking about the case. The last thing I recall, I was coming back home and about to turn onto my street. Next thing, I'm waking up this morning to all the missed calls. There seems to be a chunk of my night missing, and where it should be, there's nothing but blank space.'

'You said "they" on the call. Who are "they"? The moralists, the people from OGT?' asked Shaz, clearly concerned.

'I really don't know.' I replied. 'But I do know I don't want to talk about it here. If there was a "they" they were talented enough to prevent me from remembering who they were.'

'Okay, well, that's not our only issue, so we'll circle back to that later.'

From the bench seat next to her, Sharon produced a News-Pad, unrolling it from its furled state and placing it on the table. News, as you may recall, used to be printed on paper, which, as you know, was environmentally unfriendly and wasteful, not to mention difficult to re-edit once printed.

Now, if you're not satisfied with it being shotgun blasted at you by the various apps, emails, and unrequested notifications on your mobile devices, there's a flexible roll up or foldable digital LCD sheet, made of plastic and displaying stories with even less integrity than before… and absolutely zero impartiality. It does, however, have a lower carbon footprint, and isn't that what the news is really all about…

Despite there being several different newspapers by name, there is only one producer for all news media, who, to ensure the utmost integrity and accuracy, comes under the direct management of the Global Guides Alliance Office (*GGAO*). Basically, the GGAO is like a one world governance office from which all Global decisions, approvals, laws, and trends are passed.

The Global Guides themselves, who control the office (*having never actually set foot in it, mind you*) are presented as a global governing body, though they act much more like the board of directors for a business and marketing empire. They are a conglomerate of the wealthiest and most elite of the old world, who together connived to create a global monopoly and a one world government. Since their ascension to power, they've held no democratic form of election for their positions in government, nor heard a single voice of the people whose best interests they purport to serve.

Their existence is self-perpetuating and self-governing. They neither need nor want input from those they deigned to guide.

We the people, take our orders from them, no questions asked and no opportunity to ask them. All for the greater good, of course, because the Global Guides Alliance always has the best interests of "its people" and the world at heart, never seeking to progress their own agendas or enhance their personal wealth. The fact that that happens, constantly, is simply a happy accident and not to be misconstrued or considered in any way related to the decisions the GGAO makes on our behalf.

Selecting an article, Shaz did me the favour of waiting out today's message *"Alone you are nothing, together we are everything."* then sliding her News-Pad across the table, told me to read. 'You know, if you would just get one of these, we could've been on the same page before we even got here.' said Shaz. 'Now, read quickly, because we need to get over to that crime scene. Uniforms have secured it and are taking statements now.'

'Ah, the good old, no news, news.' I said, picking up the pad… Every day we're told to be outraged, to panic, or rejoice, because of some fabricated or mindless event that's been presented to us over and over again. 'What specious tosh awaits me here?'

As I read, I realised the article Shaz had shown me seemed to offer something more than the standard moral outrage that fills so many pages. It was not only specific and accurate, it also had details that only those with intimate knowledge of our active case could really know. Especially this early on. This was "real" news, which would almost be refreshing if it wasn't utterly damaging to our cause.

'How the fuck did they get this!?' I asked emphatically. 'I haven't seen a genuine piece of investigative journalism in over forty years and certainly not the truth.' Yet, there it was in plain pixels. "*SECRET LETTERS TELL OF MURDER VITCIM'S OLD THINK CONVERSION*" screamed the headline. It had a GCC 10,000 reward for further information, to boot.

'Well, we can't be sure just yet. But you know who I want to speak to.' said Shaz. 'Sargent, fucking, Ease!'

'When was this story released?' I asked.

'It was in the early edition. Would have been available by 4AM this morning. The murder of the cleaner was reported at half past 5, by the way, if that's where your head's going. Mine certainly was.'

'Well, we had bloody well better get moving.' I said, standing and instantly stepping out from the table and heading towards the door.

Shaz, who hadn't actually finished her coffee yet, sculled the rest whilst half standing, then placed the mug back down and turned to follow me out.

Retracing our exact steps of this time yesterday morning, from coffee shop to murder scene, it almost felt like Déjà vu.

It was cold again, only five degrees Celsius according to my device, except for now at least there was no breeze to cut through our coats and jackets. The sky was darker than yesterday, with heavier cloud covering, giving a moody, wintery feel, which to me only seemed to enhance the growing atmosphere of misery and impending doom.

As usual, the streets were sparsely populated, by business people, anyway. Many jobs having been replaced by automation, leaving little requirement for people to travel into the city for IT or other middle management jobs. Plus, with almost all retail online nowadays, and investing and banking a thing of the past, the city was virtually bare.

Those that capture the eye, are the homeless, filling the Parks and seldom used entryways of office buildings. Despite the theoretical benefits of the socialist wealth redistribution system, people still fall off the level. Unlike welfare of the past, however, the global credit system doesn't just reset when you get behind. In this world, you have to earn back credits in order to return to a net negative impact.

That means, if you fall afoul of the system, it's damn hard, and after a while, neigh on impossible to make it back. Especially in a system whose motto is "Never forgive and never forget." When you haven't got enough credits to stay warm or eat, then humans do what desperate humans have always done, taking what they can get, any way they can get it, and damn the social cost. Then, because of their desperate need, their social debt sinks deeper, while the need to survive remains, and the gap between you and the social standard grows ever greater, until you freeze or starve to death on the carbon neutral streets of Mid-Town, or whatever Global trap you're caught in…

I tear my eyes away from the forlorn form of one such homeless man, shaking my head at the absurdity of the failed system, just in time to cross at my favourite set of pedestrian lights. Shaz looked at me and rolled her eyes, assuming I was shaking my head at the lights themselves. It was a fair assessment and one I didn't bother to refute, instead determining to focus on the list of tasks at hand.

We were visiting the same building, now for our second murder. A murder that Sharon and I are all but certain is directly linked to the leak of information to The Global News, and their subsequent article this morning.

'We will need to speak to that journalist as soon as we finish up at OGT.' said Shaz as we walked. 'I also want to be the one to speak to Ease. I'm going to rip his fucking nuts off if he doesn't tell the truth.'

'No problem.' I said. 'I have a hunch that nobody who works at OGT will be able to tell us much about this murder, anyway.'

'What makes you say that?'

'Because, yesterday evening, before I went out for a walk, I checked my chip's tracking log. I saw that we were checked in and out of the OGT building in the morning, and then again when we went to conduct our interviews in the afternoon. After that, however, there was no indication we had ever re-entered, or exited, the building via the basement at all. Nothing logged for either of us. I have a hunch that our killer probably knows that, and used that knowledge to enter that way, too. If I'm right, they won't show up there either. I'm also tipping there were no witnesses who saw anything, or we would have already heard about it from one of the uniforms or the captain.'

Sharon said nothing in response, simply nodding her agreement before shifting her focus to brushing loose strands of mousy brown hair back over her shoulders and smoothing out the jacket of her fiery red pant suit, ready to hit the scene.

'Perhaps after we finish here, we should split up.' I continued. 'One of us can take the Journo and the other can start reviewing those letters. See whether there's anything in them that might inspire someone to kill a cleaner, just because they'd read them.'

'Agreed.' said Shaz succinctly, as we approached the open door at the side of the basement.

The place looked much the same as it had last night, though now with decidedly more people moving about. It was lit by artificial LED lighting, necessarily bright, because the daylight outside had failed to penetrate the dark cavernous basement. We entered to find Slice attending to the body in the change rooms, while Constable Clubman and some other uniforms were interviewing cleaners out on the basement floor.

Sharon headed straight for Clubman, who was presently questioning a uniformed cleaner, no doubt just as keen to find out where Ease was hiding, as gaining insights on the crime.

While she went that way, I stayed with Karen to review the scene. It looked pretty clean and simple to me. Clean as a murder can be, anyway. No obvious signs of a struggle. Single shot to the head, just like Katie.

My first impression was that this one seemed less personal than the last, displaying all the signs of a killer whose only job was to kill, not to interrogate or gather information. I'm guessing they either already knew all they needed to know, or as we suspected earlier, the victim was only killed because they'd let the truth get out. A warning to anyone else who knows something, to keep their mouths shut. You talk, you die.

As I stood watching Slice, it occurred to me that Ease may not have been the loose lips that sunk this particular ship. I'm not ready to rule him out yet. But, it's certainly not his body on the floor, and it's entirely possible that a lowly cleaner such as the deceased, had sought to profit off the letters they'd found, and in doing so wound up on the wrong side of some very bad people. It would explain both his murder and the leak to the newspapers. The question is, could it really be that simple? Or, is that just what I'm meant to think…

The victim's body lay on the bitterly cold white tiled floor, on the bathroom side of the cleaners change rooms. Which, by the way, to their credit, did not smell distinctly of urine as most do. I guess they look after their own… in a cleaning sense, at least.

The change rooms are situated in the rear corner of the basement, through the doorway we had observed during our impromptu visit last night. From the outside, the dominant grey of the concrete walls and floors is broken only by the cobalt blue of the door. Inside, brightly shining tiles and similarly blue doors and benches colour the scene.

Under New Think, bathrooms are no longer single sex, or unisex for that matter. The complications of offering equality to all those who had either physically changed their sex, or who identified as a different sex, alternate sex, or as non-binary, became so complex that even New Thinkers gave up and returned to calling them plan old, Toilets, Bathrooms, or Lavatories, absent preface, context, or delineating accompaniments.

The sign above the door displayed a toilet bowl shaped oval, with a dot in the middle, a rectangle for the cistern, and a stick underneath. This was apparently the stick figure version of a toilet, which made me wonder if there was some sort of eternally binding contract for the stick figure community to be represented on all toilet signage in perpetuity.

Interestingly, despite this notion of oneness, those of male genesis and those of female genesis still tend to use different sides of almost all bathrooms, all across the Global World. Hardly then, a consensus of support for the move…

The now deceased cleaner appeared very much a male to me and was indeed using what one would consider to be the male side of the bathroom. Interestingly, the wall tiles on this side were blue with white on the floor, while the other side had red walls with white floors.

He lay face down in front of the urinals. His blue work pants pulled up to his waist, his chest and back uncovered in the absence of a shirt. The changing room was just to the left of where he lay, leading to the obvious conclusion that he was getting changed at either the start or end of his shift, and in the middle of a toilet stop at the time of his death.

He appeared to be of eastern Asian appearance in the old verbiage, what would previously have been known as Chinese, most likely. Because of the way that he had fallen, I could only see the back of his head, his deep black hair, slick and a little greasy. Not that it will bother him now. I don't know who he is yet, except to say that I'm sure he's not the man we spoke to yesterday, though on that subject, Johnny certainly begs questioning given the timing and location of the murder.

'Any insights, Slice?' I asked, moving further into the room and taking up a position beside her.

'Yes.' she said. 'This man had finished at the urinal before he was killed. He didn't wet himself. Single gunshot to the centre of the forehead. Solid round, which appears to be of the same calibre as yesterday, a .22. More powerful mind you, so if it's the same killer, I suspect they either use different types of ammunition depending on the task, or more likely they load their own rounds and moderate the amount of powder. Of course, it could be two different killers with the same calibre gun, although given the proximity to the last murder, that theory does stretch credulity a little. I'd say it's likely he was shot from just inside the doorway. The killer didn't get too close. There are no obvious signs of gun powder or visible burns on the body. It was, as you might say, a clean kill. One shot and done. The body doesn't appear to have been moved postmortem either, though I won't be certain of that until I turn him over.'

'Anything else of note?' I asked, keen to glean as much from her experienced eyes as I could.

'Not really.' said Slice. 'There's no indication the killer took anything from the body. His pants still contain his device and a set of swipe passes. Looks to me like somebody probably just shot him to shut him up, for good…'

'Mmm, I was thinking the same thing.' I said, nodding. 'Either this is the only person they needed to kill, or it was a clear message to anyone else in the firing line.'

Leaving Karen to her labours, checking temperatures, taking measurements and photographing the lifeless form, I set about conducting further examinations of my own.

I started with the victim's bag, which had been placed on a long wooden bench that ran along the blue wall, not five meters from where he lay. It was a plain black duffle bag with no visible branding. A pair of black ASICS sneakers sat alongside, a worn pair of ankle socks stuffed in one shoe.

Taking latex gloves from my pocket, I inspect the contents of the bag, finding nothing of interest or intrigue. Certainly no weapons, letters, or unusual items of value. Perhaps those things had been there at some point, with the shooter taking them away when they left. Not something I could reliably deduce from casual inspection.

'Hey Slice.' I yelled over my shoulder.

'Yes, Detective.' she replied wearily.

'Have forensics already looked at this bag?'

'I believe so, but I'll confirm that before I leave and let you know.'

'Thanks.' I said, re-zipping the bag. I didn't really expect much to come of it. It's not like you can test if a bag once held a letter. Nevertheless, it was worth knowing if anybody other than the deceased had used it.

After several minutes perusing these items, I placed them back as I found them and set about pacing the room for other clues. Specifically, I was searching for something that gave confirmation of why this had taken place, and who else might have been here when it did. Not surprisingly, and much like our scene upstairs, there was nothing else to find. Nothing obvious anyway. No other bags, or personal belongings, no stashed weapons, and again no shell casing.

Once more, we would have to rely on technology, ballistics, or DNA in order to confirm the other party or parties involved.

Given the location of the crime, the technology aspect will be challenging, too. There are no cameras in change rooms or bathrooms, which might seem obvious to old worlders, but is really quite a coup for individual privacy in this one, considering the generally unfettered invasiveness of the Global World.

Even so, there should be a chip reader embedded in the door frame, although given the failures of this same technology upstairs, I'm not going to hold my breath.

One other thing that could help is the victim's device. Devices have for many years had the capacity to automatically sense and connect with other devices around them, conducting a digital handshake with every other device and capable connected appliance in their vicinity, without the device owner ever becoming aware. While these details are not supposed to be stored, they certainly can be, and as we know, if something can be done, then it probably is. In this case, it most certainly is, except it'll take a much more tech savvy individual than me to access the logs.

Shaz, having finished with Constable Clubman outside, had now entered the crime scene and pulled me aside for a quiet word.

'So, Ease isn't here.' she said. 'Apparently, he called in sick this morning.'

'How convenient.' I replied. 'Doesn't exactly scream innocence for that article though, does it. Still, I'm not quite certain of his guilt. It is, after all, another OGT employee who was shot dead. The question is, did one of these guys talk, or was it Ease who spilled and this guy just copped the punishment?'

Shaz looked at me thoughtfully but offered no answer, so after a moment's pause, I asked another question. 'What else did Clubman say?'

'Not much.' said Shaz. 'Other than confirming that all the cleaners have clammed up tight. Nobody knows a thing about what happened and they're all telling the same story. Chen, that's the stiff by the way, is 40 years old. He was quiet and kept to himself. Barely even spoke Global, so he may not have been able to read those letters, and he definitely wasn't capable of disseminating their contents to a journo. I'm almost certain that whatever Chen knew, it was inconsequential. It may just be that he worked in the wrong place, with the wrong people, and saw or heard something that cost him his life.'

'Did Clubman mention how long this Chen had been working here at OGT?' I asked.

'Yeah, ten years.' She replied. 'Why?'

'Well, that's interesting. Doesn't exactly add up though. You say he didn't speak much Global and yet he's worked here for ten years, lived in a Global World for over twenty and been alive for forty. I know education standards are pretty damn poor these days, and with technology now a pro rata for human intelligence, we decline as it improves. Even so, I find it damn hard to believe he could've survived all these years and not be able to understand enough Global to interpret those letters and pass on the info.'

'You have any evidence to back up that theory?' Asked Shaz.

'Sure.' I said. 'It's right there in front of you. Here we have a man, shot from a distance with a single round from the direction of the doorway where we now stand. No signs of a struggle, and no evidence that the body was tampered with in any way. The one thing we can be certain of, is that this killing was very intentional and quick. Even if he had only seen something small, whoever shot him fully believed he could pass on whatever it was he knew.'

'Fair point.' replied Sharon, without hesitation. 'Well, we know when a parasite gets inside a clam there grows a pearl. We shall simply have to find the right tool to prize open Chen's former workmates and see which of them holds the prize.'

Having taken in all I could from the murder scene, I headed out to find our friend Johnny from yesterday evening. When I got to his office, I found it empty, with the lights turned off. Not a good sign. In an adjacent office, however, on the other side of a small corridor, sat Carlos instead. Carlos was apparently the on-duty manager for the day shift, with Johnny not due back until tonight.

Carlos' office was surprisingly warm compared to the cavernous basement outside. I noted a small yet clearly effective fan heater behind his desk and wondered if the power for this was a perk of the job. The use of these fans having been banned from all Global homes as an unnecessary drain on energy. After all, your comfort is no concern of the greater good.

The room had that familiar electric burning smell that heater fans emit, combined with some sort of faux-sausage and cloudy soup mix that Carlo's was presently eating. The soup gave off a salty, almost rubbery smell, which merged with the fan, to make for an almost overpowering atmosphere in the small office.

Noting my attention on the soup and overt sniffing of the air, Carlos mentioned he hadn't had time for breakfast, what with all the questions he and his staff had faced.

'No Problem.' I said. 'People gotta eat.'

On questioning, Carlos reported seeing and hearing nothing of the murder. Instead, offering only the same unknowing, uncaring, indifference as everybody else here at OGT. I didn't get the feeling he was in on it, so much as he simply didn't know very much and was sick of answering the same questions over and over again.

'I was upstairs doing my rounds at the time the murder reportedly occurred.' said Carlos.

'Did you see or hear anything unusual prior to starting your rounds?' I asked.

'No, nothing. Chen had been working the night shift and was just finishing up this morning and getting changed to go home. That's why I was up doing my rounds, checking that everything was up to scratch. I'd only just started myself.'

'Okay. Do you have the key to Chen's locker?'

'Yes, certainly. If you'll follow I can show you.' he replied, looking forlornly at his bowl of soup as he stood, dutifully stepping away from his desk and leaving it to cool.

I followed him around the corner into the break room I had observed yesterday. Up close, I saw the wall of lockers were positively ancient by modern standards, still using an actual metal key, rather than a Global chip code. For most modern lockers, or locks in general for that matter, one need only swipe their subdermal chip over the reader in order to gain access.

Having this kind of old-style locker made them both more and less secure. Chip codes can be relatively easily accessed and copied online (*a fact they'd prefer you not know, given that information security is the basis for everybody on earth entrusting the Guides with all our personal, financial, and biometric data*). That means it's fairly easy to break into most places if you're so inclined. Of course, being able to mimic or steal these codes does not stop the other surveillance measures from knowing "you" are there and not the registered person.

Utilising a physical key, on the other hand, means that someone would have to break into the locker with a crowbar, or screwdriver, not easy tools to find these days. Otherwise, they'd have to steal or gain access to your physical key or pick the lock with their hands, which is another foreign concept in today's electronic world. With no readers attached, there is also no record of someone else having been here if they did manage to get in. Especially not if the person who does it was already expected to be here in the room.

'How many keys are there for each of these lockers?' I asked.

'Just two, boss.' said Carlos. 'One for the cleaner and one for the Managers.'

At my direction, Carlos produced a key from his pocket and opened the navy-blue locker belonging to the late Mr Chen. When the door swung back, it revealed only what one might expect to find in an employee locker. His spare work shirt and pants (*of which you're only ever allowed two of each*), a pair of worn black work boots, some gloves, eating utensils and a drink bottle. There were no letters, no paper, and nothing personal to Mr Chen at all.

The locker smelled a bit, as most lockers do. That odd mix of old worn shoes with the soapiness of freshly washed clothes. There was no food in there, although the room held the pervasive smell of Carlos' soup, no doubt from when he'd heated it earlier. In here, it formed a new combination, mixed with his strong spicy cologne which, due to his close proximity, seemed to engulf me.

With Carlos' blessing, I briefly searched the rest of the kitchen, finding nothing apart from the usual mixture of cleaning products and common use utensils. Not so long ago, work kitchens would have held several shared dry staples, such as coffee, tea, sugar, cereals, salt and pepper, etc. Of course, now, those items and their use must be accounted for and tracked, so free tea and coffee at work is a thing of the past.

'Are all the lockers so bland, Carlos?' I asked, returning to where he'd remained standing, next to Chen's open locker.

'Mostly, I think. Some people keep some food or a bag or something in there, but this is pretty standard. Chen's street clothes were in the change room with him, because he was getting changed to go home at the time he was shot. I don't know what you're looking for, but if there's anything to find, it's probably there.'

'I already knew there wasn't anything to find in Mr Chen's possessions, because I'd checked when I was inspecting the scene. If there had been anything, it certainly wasn't there now.'

Shaz found us in the break room, having completed her own inspection of the crime scene, cornering me for another partnerly conversation.

'I don't think there's much else for me to see here.' she said. 'If you're okay to wrap up, I'm thinking I'll head over to Sgt Ease's place and find out what the hell he isn't telling us. After that, I'll sound out the reporter and meet you back at the station?'

'Sounds like a plan.' I replied, as Carlos re-locked Chen's locker behind me. 'I've got a few more questions and a couple of things to look at here. After that, I'll head back to the station and start going through those letters. Might drop by ballistics too, and see if they can give us any info on our murder weapon. Seems like it might be quite a small pistol. Wouldn't be hard to hide, just a .22, yet deadly enough to account for two victims so far. If it was the same gun, that is. Would be good to know what we're looking for, anyway.'

'Righto. I'll touch base with you when I'm leaving Ease's place. Now, don't you go missing on me.' Said Sharon, staring me dead in the eyes.

I smiled at the dig, knowing she was still pissed at me about whatever happened last night. Inside, I expect she only felt that loving motherly concern, and need to protect her clan, except it's hard to tell with women. Derision is how they express their love… and derision…

Just as she was about to disappear through the doorway, I called out to her. 'Wait, Shaz.'

'What?' she replied.

'Try not to kill Ease. He might be an idiot, but he's our idiot.'

When Sharon had left, I asked Carlos if we could have a quick chat back in his office. Once inside, I quietly closed the door behind me, turning to face him across the desk.

Carlos looked at me uncertainly as he took his seat. His office was identical to Johnny's, only laid out in reverse, which meant the opposite side of the desk was essentially in the doorway. His desk device and projection screen sat facing him, and against the rear wall was a spare chair that looked to have seldom been used. It seemed to serve no purpose where it was, unless it was the naughty chair for misbehaving cleaners.

I walked to the rear of the room, picked it up, then returned, placing it heavily on the carpeted floor at the end of Carlos' desk and took a seat.

He looked at his pungent bowl of food, desperately.

'Go on.' I said. 'Eat.'

I waited while he did so, using the time to make some notes about the second murder and its parallels to the first. When I finished, a quick check of my watch showed the time as 08:55. It was well into the second day of the investigation now and we were no closer to solving the case than we were this time yesterday.

'Carlos, tell me, why don't the sub-dermal chip's register when entering and exiting through the garage door?' I asked, just as soon as he'd finished eating and wiped his mouth.

Before I'd even got the question out, I saw his demeanour change from the casual relief of completing his meal, to one of nervous tension, his eyebrows shooting upward, his eyes visibly widening. He bumped his empty bowl with the back of his hand, rattling the metal spoon against the ceramic, the violent shock of the sound only adding to the mood.

'Everything okay, Carlos?' I asked.

'Uh, yes, of course.' he said. 'I... I'm not sure about the door. But... um, but, it's certainly something I'll have to get looked at. Perhaps you could leave that with me?' he asked, almost pleading.

He picked a pen up from his desk as if to write down my concern, except unlike Johnny yesterday, he didn't appear to have any paper on which to write it. I watched his movement with interest, eager to see how he planned to fake writing a note whilst sitting directly in front of me. Curiously, he hadn't even bothered looking for paper. Instead, looking directly at me as if to engage me in some sort of hypnosis, while simultaneously making a show of holding the pen. After several seconds of this, he flashed me an exuberant smile, an act devoid only of the phrase "ta-da" then nodded firmly as if seeking confirmation I would give him credit for the attempt.

'You're not in trouble, Carlos.' I continued. 'I just want to understand why there's been two murders here and no surveillance coverage. Does the chip reader actually register when you enter the lifts to go upstairs and clean?'

'I believe so.' he said, enthusiastically. 'Going up and down.'

'Just not in or out of the building on this floor?' I probed.

'No.' he replied with certainty this time.

'And, was the door set up that way, intentionally? Or was it sabotaged?'

'Ah... well, sometimes we need to come and go throughout the shift, but we aren't actually leaving work, per se. When we leave, the company adjusts our Social Contribution Score as if we've left work early. We get deducted, man! It didn't seem fair, so we ah... moved the sensor.'

As he explained this, Carlos talked with his hands and shoulders, most of his body ultimately getting in on the act. The elbows bent, arms out in front, palms facing upwards and moving up and down alternately, as if juggling comparative weights. The international sign for "Eh, it might be wrong, but it might not". He finished with a sustained shrug of the shoulders while rolling out his bottom lip before finally resting his case.

'Right.' I said, trying not to smile conspiratorially. 'And where is the sensor now?'

'It's in the change room, actually. Everybody that works down here knows that, and we all check in and out at the start and end of our shifts without any unfair deductions.'

Carlos looked up at me again, his eyes pleading for me to understand and sympathise with their plight. He needn't have bothered. It was all I could do not to grin like a Cheshire Cat on hearing the ruse. Any effort to circumvent the will of this lot was one I could get on board with. I just hoped it wouldn't prevent me solving a crime.

'That's interesting.' I said. 'Wouldn't other people in the building know about the reader being moved? Doesn't anybody check on these kinds of things and where they're located?'

'No. It's a secret. We are lucky they don't really care about us. Equality only extends so far, you know. We always say that the taking hand is long and flexible, able to reach into every crack and crevasse, while the giving hand is stunted and only extends so far. That is to say, our position in the building reflects our social standing. We are less than, not equal too. We are beneath those who are above us. Not that that's all bad. Cause, if the bosses upstairs found out that we moved the sensor, we might all be fired… or worse. We are, after all, employed by a company that creates and monitors surveillance technologies. Quite an embarrassment, I would imagine.'

'Yes, I expect you're right… I am going to need a copy of the logs from those chip readers for last night, though. I'm also going to need a copy of any surveillance footage you have access to down here as well.'

'No problem.' said Carlos rather eagerly. 'Leave me your details and I will get them for you by this afternoon.'

'I'll leave you my details, but don't bother sending them to me. I'll be back this afternoon to speak to Johnny about last night. Incidentally, what can you tell me about the letters written by yesterday's murder victim, Ms Hansley?' I asked.

Carlos looked even more shocked at this question than he had the first.

'Um, I… I'm not sure what you mean.'

'Come on Carlos. I've already told you you're not in trouble. We already have copies of several letters Ms Hansley wrote, but I have an inkling that there might be one more around here somewhere. Specifically, I'm interested in one that was on Ms Hansley's desk the night she was murdered. Do you know anything about that?'

'No, no, I swear!' said Carlos, his head looking down at the desk, before thrusting his arms out to the side, palms up again… 'Yes, okay, I am aware of the letters. A few of the cleaners used them to try and improve their Global, or just for a bit of gossip. And yet, many of us also sympathised with Ms Hansley and her relationship with her mother. Basically, all of us are separated from our families for one reason or another. It seems to us like she doesn't have to be. We feel for her. Besides, she leaves the letters there, so we take them. What's the harm?'

'That's all very well, Carlos, but the letter I asked about is from the night before last, and it's the only one I'm interested in right now. Do you know where it is? Do you know what happened to it?'

'No… I do not know where it is. Though, maybe I do know who got it.'

So we were right, I thought. There was another letter. 'Was it Mr Chen?' I asked. 'Did he take the letter from Katie's office?'

'No, not Chen. Chen's not the cleaner assigned to that office. It was another cleaner, Jiang. And he didn't actually take the letter. Not like the others did… I was told that Ms Hansley, she handed it to him and asked him to take it. Apparently, she already knew we'd been reading the letters she threw away. I suppose there are cameras in the office, and maybe she reviewed them and saw Jiang taking them out of the bin or something. Anyway, I saw Jiang when he came downstairs that night. He said Ms Hansley seemed scared when she gave it to him. She actually called down here to ask for Jiang specifically to be sent up straight away at about 20:45. Which was strange, because earlier that night she had asked for the cleaning to be put off until after midnight, so I was surprised at the change. And I'm pretty sure Jiang didn't do any cleaning up there, either. He wouldn't have had the time. She just handed him the letter to him and told him to come back later.'

'Did he say anything else or mention seeing anything else while he was up there?'

'No. Just that she seemed scared and asked him to take the letter and keep it safe.'

'Where is Jiang now?' I asked.

'Nobody knows.' Said Carlos, looking straight at me now, a little fear creeping into his widened eyes. 'We haven't seen him since he was sent home two days ago.'

'Sent home?' I asked.

'Yeah, after he got the letter from Ms Hansley, he came downstairs and seemed a little shaky. When he told me what had happened, I asked him how he was, and he said he felt unwell, so I sent him home. I haven't seen him since.'

'When was his next shift meant to be?'

'Today, except he never showed and I haven't heard from him. I tried to call him, but the line never rung. I can give you his details if you want to try and speak to him?'

'We already have them.' I replied. 'Mind you, he has just moved up my list of people to find.'

After quickly speaking with Constable Clubman, making doubly sure he was going to get a statement from everyone, and chase up all the security footage, I headed out to make a call to Shaz.

'Hey.' said Shaz, answering quickly. 'Do you have some news already?'

'Yes.' I said. 'It turns out, Jiang, whose details you got yesterday, may know a lot more than he was letting on to his workmates.'

'Oh, how so?'

'Well, you remember that letter we thought Ms Hansley nodded towards in the final piece of surveillance footage from her office? The one on the corner of her desk?'

'Yeah. What about it?'

'Carlos told me that at 20:45 on the night of her murder, Ms Hansley called and asked him to send Jiang up to see her. When he got up there, Katie didn't want him to start cleaning. Apparently, she just handed the letter directly to him and asked that he keep it safe. When he came back to the basement, he told Carlos what had happened, and that Katie looked scared. Carlos said that Jiang looked scared too and reported feeling unwell, so he sent him home. Nobody's seen or heard from him since. Based on that, I think it's prudent we move him up our "to do" list. What do you think?'

'Agreed.' said Shaz, after a brief pause, which was filled with the unnecessary narration of her E's guidance system. 'Particularly given the release of some of the contents of those letters. Not to mention the second murder today. Listen, I'm on my way to Ease's place, now. As soon as I'm done here, I'll head straight to Jiang's for a word.'

'Perfect.' I said. 'Send me the details and let me know when you're on the way. I'll meet you there. In the meantime, I'm done here, so I'll head back and have a look through those other letters and see what I can find.'

Chapter 13

Sharon take's it Ease E

Pulling up to Sgt Ease's apartment in the company 'E' was, well, not so easy, pardon the pun. The E did not well handle the oddly shaped curve of the garden bed protrusions, creating single spaced spots out the front of his building. We (*the E and I, that is*) rode the curb several times in an effort to park, before finally settling for a deeply angled position.

Bloody electric cars. Frankly, they haven't improved much in the last thirty years. They can drive and park themselves by following satellite navigation maps, but they could do that thirty years ago. They look basically the same as they did back then, too. Think Tesla model Y. The difference being, the cars autopilot systems are the only ones allowed to drive now, with human beings no longer trusted to do so... Like computers are so good.

I speak from personal experience when I say that the adverts of people calmly sipping a cup of tea whilst their car takes them wherever their heart desires, couldn't be a bigger load of bullshit. Trying to sip a cup of tea whilst your car baulks at shadows, accelerates overly fast, then breaks back to the speed limit, before parking rather poorly in an inappropriate place, would see your tea spilled all over your shirt front, or thrown at the console in anger. Not to mention that the stupid thing wants to talk to you all the time and tell you what it's doing, like an overzealous pilot. You know, like back when we were actually allowed to fly places... Just shut up and drive, E!

I rarely travel this far, so the other thing I noticed was the extraordinary deterioration of the roads themselves. Once the Global Council decided all fossil fuel derivatives should either be removed, abandoned, or replaced overtime, tarred roads started to disappear. Attempts were made to utilise a product made of recycled plastics and rubbers in their place, although it weathered poorly and tended to break up quickly. As a result, many roads have gone back to the old days of graded dirt, making them slippery when wet, and the suburbs they pass through, dusty and dirty when dry.

At least the ride here was quiet enough, with only moderate traffic to contend with, not that that's surprising given that possessing an E privately is illegal now. Outside of official Global government departments, only registered companies and share/hire services are allowed to own them, and it'll cost you a good chunk of social credit for a ride.

I can also be thankful there was only one fifteen minute boundary between here and the station in Mid-Town, Grey-Town being a border sharing neighbour, with both coming under the broader umbrella of Central City. In the Global World, each city is essentially broken up into its own fifteen minute zone, whereby, the theory goes, that everything you need to sustain your existence should be available to you within that zone, including employment. Fifteen minutes, by the way, is the measurement from the centre of your city to its outer limits, so thirty minutes from border to border.

Each cell overlaps several times with its surrounding cells, so unless you're on the outer edge of your Greater Global City, then you'll still be able to interact with other cells around you, without incurring significant dis-credits on your Global Credit Score. If, however, you travel beyond the centre of your connecting fifteen-minute boundary, for any reason other than necessary work purposes, then you lose your Global Credit Points, and therefore, currency and access to travel options, until such time as you earn them back. I, for instance, will be docked for crossing the boundary today despite not passing the centre of Grey-Town, though I should have my credits returned with approval from the captain.

Because of his job, Ease, whose place is seventeen minute's drive from the station, has a permanent travel pass between the station and his home, allowing him to avoid discredits just for attending work. And, given life for him pretty much revolves around work, that trip to and from must be a nice little break from the dreary drone of his daily existence.

To be fair, and as incredible as it may seem, Ease actually has two jobs. In addition to being a police officer in the real world, Ease, like many people with significantly reduced employment opportunities, also has a job in the Alt-Verse. Ironically, he's actually a police captain there, the irony being that it's a role he'll never be allowed to fulfil in this world. What's more, it's actually a real job, with real pay and real problems, despite existing in a fictional space.

I remember when the idea of people playing online games for money seemed absurd. Now, they live virtually (*unintended pun*) their entire lives in the Alt-Verse. They're actually paid a wage for fulfilling jobs there, hosting historical (*though not historically accurate*) tours, selling products, and even having consensual and apparently New Think acceptable cybersex.

People holiday in the Alt-Verse too. With long distance travel banned or inaccessible for all but the most equal among us, working, travelling, and just plain living in the Alt-Verse, is accepted as a legitimate New think lifestyle. "All the perks and none of the carbon." goes the motto. This additional universe (*space travel being more accessible there too*) creates jobs for tour guides, booking agents, and every other position you can remember from when we used to travel for real.

Strangely, travel companies that are not actually required to provide any physical service, nevertheless charge and inconvenience people in the good old-fashioned way. Late departures, cancelled flights, and weather impacts are all par for the course. The effort creates real frustration for those travelling in the Alt-Verse, who for their part are physically exactly where they started, yet mentally and with the cooperation of all their senses, feeling fully as if they are on an actual journey. Strapped into a Cyber-sensory chair and goggle screen, they are for all intents and purposes unaware of the real world around them.

Frighteningly, crimes in the Alt-Verse incur real criminal charges, as well as dis-credit fines, up to and including physical prison time. That includes crimes against New Think, such as perceived inequality, failure to observe (*in both intent and letter*) the laws of the metaphysical world, as well as the sharing of misleading or unapproved information or content. Really begs the question as to why "Old Think World" the theme park, where one can experience the horrors of mislabelling genders, dead naming, and unconscious bias, is so popular…

Outside of travel, people effectively live as their avatar, earning their wage and forming a part of societies that exist entirely within their theoretically pollution free extension of the human consciousness. To me, it seems that the world they escape to is just as real and just as constrained as the one out here… Hardly seems worth the effort.

Making my way from the car, I approach the front door of Sgt Ease's red brick building, seeing on the wall a long list of occupants names next to their apartment number. There must be a hundred names here, which in a 15-story building means the apartments are likely pretty cramped and small. I find Ease's name roughly halfway down, next to a label displaying "*level 7 - No. 42*" and hit the buzzer, waiting a full ten seconds with no response.

On the off chance he had legitimately been unwell and still curled in bed, Gary's comments about our latest victim ringing in my ears, I decide to wait a further fifteen seconds, my left foot tapping rapidly, before trying again. Still, there was no answer. Figuring that I wouldn't want to be stuck out here all day if it turns out he's not actually home, and feeling confident that if he is home, he couldn't escape the building without me seeing, I try the alternate route and call his device instead. It rings several times before an answering service kicks in, asking me to leave a message or attempt an alternate means of contact.

I check my device's screen again, noting that reception here is good, so I can rule that out as a factor. That means he's either dead to the world asleep, active in the Alt-Verse and avoiding my calls, which, by the way, he would still receive there, or not active at all and avoiding me completely.

I try the buzzer again, unsuccessfully, then change tack and put a call into the station, asking them to send me the details of his movements via chipped tracking, along with any surveillance footage they can pull from his apartment block. One way or another, I'm going to find Ease today, and I'm going to get some answers.

The officer on surveillance duty tells me it will take around ten minutes to pull the relevant data and that he'll send it through as soon as possible, then ends the call.

It'll be a frustrating wait, but because of my role, I know that despite popular opinion, people are not actually always watching you. The key distinction being that "people" aren't. Programs are. You are constantly monitored and tracked, digitally, but your movements or behaviour won't actually be flagged unless they're in breach of a set of governance protocols. To be fair, there are a lot of protocols and flag-able events, but machines aren't sentient, yet.

In other words, if you know what not to do, it is possible to do things and get away with them without being noticed. Until, of course, somebody notices what you're up to, gets a tip on your movements from the public, or decides to look into you, specifically. There are just too many people in the world for every single person to be under constant human surveillance, no matter how many layers there are.

Standing near the entry doors, I get a stroke of luck when another resident of the building exits, casually swinging the door wide open. Lucky for me, this is not a newer building. Being a pre-New Think build, it hadn't been fitted with automated chip and facial recognition software to allow opening, nor a secondary security door to prevent unapproved entry in this type of scenario. I take the opportunity to duck through without comment from the exiting resident, though no doubt I will be flagged for this unauthorised entry as there are still chip readers and standard IoT connected security cameras inside.

Not so lucky for me, is the fact that I won't be able to use the lifts without a chip authorisation code, which would have been provided if Ease had answered the bloody intercom and authorised my entry.

Instead, I decide to try the stairs, turning the corner down a short corridor with its white textured walls to the rear of the lifts. I see an entry to the stairwell on my right as I wrap around the back of the lift well, the door of which I'm surprised and rather alarmed to find open.

In fact, it's not only open, it's chocked, which is a breach of both the Global fire regulations and the New Think security and surveillance protocols. Something that if known by Sgt Ease himself would've been reported and rectified. He's a stickler like that.

I decide to climb the stairs, slowly, concerned now that something untoward may be happening. A creeping feeling washes over me, goosebumps appearing on my arms, hairs standing on end, my heart rate increasing along with a dreadful feeling of fear. Ideological adjustment can't change that. Danger is danger, and the autonomic response is not something you choose.

The chock on the stairwell appeared to be of a lightweight hard foam and rubber construction, a thick knot of rope sticking out the rear for easy removal and carrying. It looked like the type of thing a tradesman or someone might bring with them to chock open the door of an unfamiliar apartment as opposed to something a building manager would leave in a stairwell for residents to use.

I start the seven story climb toward Ease's apartment, wondering as I do, whether I should've drawn my weapon first. I haven't got a gun with me. Not a traditional one. Even police aren't allowed to be armed these days, unless we've been specifically authorised to carry a lethal force weapon for an arrest where we anticipate a high chance of facing an opposing lethal force.

Basically, I would need to expect I was going to be shot in a specific scenario, far enough ahead of time that I could apply for a lethal force permit in order to be equipped to defend myself when I enter that scenario. Even now, my eyes roll as I think of it.

That said, we do carry Electro's. They are electric guns, which fire a short non-lethal electrically charged four needle point electro round. On impact with the target, a small spring inside the round compresses, connecting an internal set of points to release the stored charge, transferring it to the body of the person you just shot. The gun works on an electric firing mechanism, meaning that you can charge both the power cell that drives the firing mechanism and the rounds in the magazine all at the same time.

Removing it from my holster, I climb cautiously, listening with every step for the sound of another person, or movement of any kind that isn't mine.

There's a breeze on my face, carrying with it the dusty concrete smell of the stairwell. Briefly the smell distracts me, its earthiness almost calming, but only for a few seconds before I realise that a breeze in here would only make sense if there was a second door open in the stairwell.

The thought makes the little hairs strain with rigidity on the back of my neck and arms, as I round onto the third floor landing.

There's a scraping noise? Maybe someone's foot turning, as they watch the doorway to the stairs, or perhaps just something rustling in the breeze of the open door. Either way, I pause in my progress and move my back against the outside wall. I want to give myself the widest sightline and hopefully the earliest possible view of anyone who might be positioned on the stairs above.

When I begin to move again, it crosses my mind that if there is someone waiting up there, that the sooner I see them, the sooner they see me. It also crosses my mind that it may just be some kid playing in the stairwell, or that someone might be moving a piece of furniture in or out of their apartment and here I look the fool, stalking slowly up the stairs, my electro gun held protectively out in front.

Rounding onto the fourth-floor landing, the noise grows louder, and it occurs to me that it couldn't possibly be a person standing there whilst guarding an escape route for some sort of sinister undertaking. Surely, if it were, they would either try to quiet the noise or avoid making it to begin with. With this in mind, I quicken my pace, rounding the fifth and sixth floor landings quickly before slowing cautiously again. The noise was louder here, clearly coming from the landing above and causing a sickening feeling to churn in the pit of my stomach. That's Sgt Ease's level with its door swinging open. Sgt Ease, who I have been unable to contact…

I keep moving forward, taking it stair by stair now, disregarding the potential for looking silly, my Electro staying comfortably out in front. As my field of view opens up to my right, I try to take in as much of the unveiled stairwell as I can. There are no boots or legs unveiled, nobody waiting for me, yet still I hear the scraping noise continue.

Because of the wide arc I'm taking on the stairs, I can't quite see the doorway despite having rounded up from the sixth floor landing. As I approach the point where the stairs turn back on themselves for the final rise to the seventh floor, I pause, steeling myself before making a mind rush decision to take the turn quickly and charge up the stairs.

My head feels light, my mind spins, and it seems as if I'm looking through someone else's eyes from the back of my own head, yet in spite of it all my body moves smoothly with speed and balance, my gun leading, my legs following and covering the ground to the landing all in an instant. Seeing nobody there, I continue without conscious thought, to move purposefully forward as my training had taught me. I round sharply out of the stairwell into the corridor, sweeping the space from right to left, knees slightly bent, maintaining a low profile as I do. Completing my arc to the left, I see, or think I see, a black clothed leg or back move blurrily into a doorway.

Instinctively, I step back into the stairwell, bumping directly into the door behind me and reactively leaping sideways, an internal explosion of terror rushing through me as it all takes place in a flash.

Breathing hard, I listen intently, hearing only the pounding of my own heartbeat in my temples, arms and chest, then a scraping and a whooshing noise off to my right just before the door to the stairwell slams shut, echoing throughout the building, and driving ever expanding waves of pounding blood in my head. Looking down, I see another door stop the same as I'd seen downstairs and realise the noise I'd been hearing was the stairwell door edging the doorstop along the concrete floor.

As I'd leapt back into the stairwell, I must have dislodged the stop completely, allowing the door to slam shut with reckless abandon. I audibly tell myself to 'calm the fuck down!' trying to regain some control of my thoughts and actions. The tingling at the top of my head and down my arms is so intense it's becoming painful as my nerves attempt to leap out through my skin.

After only a matter of seconds, my breathing begins to slow under forced diaphragmatic control, my adrenaline levels dropping, leaving my arms feeling heavy and leaden, my chest and back awash with prickling sweat. I feel like I'm shaking, yet looking down, I find my hands relatively calm and steady, still holding the electro protectively out in front.

Taking stock, I continue drawing slow, deep breaths, gathering myself, before shaking my head to clear the fog.

Opening the door again and re-engaging the chock with my foot, I immediately drop to my left knee, leaning out through the doorway and sweeping the hallway from left to right and back. This time there was nobody there, but the doorway I'd seen someone disappear into still appeared open. The sign on the wall next to it, showing "No. 42"...

Leaving the relative safety of the stairwell, I hurry along the carpeted hallway to my left, angling across to the opposite side of the hall and pressing my back to the wall as I approached the door.

Being right-handed, I'll have to enter unnaturally, preferring to come from the left, but unable to do so without first crossing the open space of the doorway itself. I risk a small exposure as I try to utilise my watch to offer a reflection of the apartment's interior. I clock the time at 10:33. Unfortunately, as the apartment is not well lit, the reflection offers little insight beyond the first metre or so where all I see is the floor, wall, and darkness.

Reviewing my options doesn't take long. There aren't many to go through. There's either someone in there waiting for me and ready to shoot, or there isn't. Either way, this is Sgt Ease's apartment and nobody, especially not a cop, leaves their door open in a New Think world. I've got no choice, really, so I decide to take my moment.

Moving with as much speed and control as I can muster, I enter, making a concerted effort to force my eyes and brain to absorb what they're seeing and processes it with lightning speed. It's a function that occurs on instinct, yet I'm acutely aware of the need to enforce it.

Electro leading the way, I first clear the hallway, noting some knocked over items on the console to my right and the mirror hanging above it sitting unusually askew. They're clearly signs of a struggle.

There's a sharp smell in the air, like something burning, except I see no smoke or light. My heart rate feels like the purring of a cat, rapid and vibrational as I fight to concentrate on the task at hand, willing myself to stay calm.

There are three exits from the hall, two to the left and one to the right. The one on the right is the first I come to. Moving through the doorway, I steadily sweep the room in arcs with my eyes and weapon, finding more signs of a struggle, yet still no other people.

In the middle of the sitting room, the coffee table lies on its side, at an angle to the other furniture. There appears to be blood and possibly a tooth on the floor, which I have to stoop down low to confirm. The blood is dry, but its presence validates my fears. Whatever occurred here wasn't good and while I haven't yet heard a noise that wasn't my own, I'm all but certain I'm not alone.

At the opposite end of the sitting room is another door, standing three quarters closed with no light coming from within. Glancing at the windows, I'm reminded that it's daytime and bright outside, yet dark as night in here. For the first time, I realise the blackout curtains are all drawn closed, with only the light from the hallway offering me guidance.

I look again at the door, assuming it must be the bedroom, then moving up close, I step to the left and listen for any sounds. I hear nothing by my own rapid breathing. Stepping back to my right, I place my left foot carefully back in line with the centre of the doorway.

The door slams back and to the left as I kick it open with my right foot, taking three rushed steps in and sweeping to the open side on my left as I do.

A bed comes into view at the far corner of the room, where I glimpse what appears to be a man's left boot. A policeman's boot, if I'm not mistaken, toes pointed towards the ceiling. The view's accompanied by the same smell that's pervaded the entire apartment, only stronger now.

Continuing through the arc, my eyes take in the black policeman's pant leg, an ankle, then Bam! A shocking force slams into the left side of my body, smashing vertically into my cheek and the bone around my left eye.

A blinding pain shoots through my face and up my arm as I tumble backwards into the heavy wooden closet doors. I feel my gun fall away from my right hand, which instinctively opens palm down to break my fall.

In an instant, I look down to where gravity and force are taking me, my mind racing and wondering what on earth had happened, when a second, violent, blackening thud ends the thought…

Chapter 14

Gary's concerning contact

Returning to the station, I figure I've got a good half hour while Sharon interrogates Ease. Poor bastard. That's time in which I intend to review those letters the cleaners took and see if I can get an understanding of Katie's mindset leading up to her death.

I'm also hoping there may be some clue as to whether she suspected danger or mentioned any pressure from her work mates or other elements of New Think's insidious surveillance and enforcement groups.

As I clear the multi-phase security protocols to enter the station, including biometric recognition software, an automated X-ray scanning tunnel, and bio-threat detection sensors, it occurs to me that the original letters are still down with the forensics team. They're performing standard tests, checking to see if anyone other than Katie or the cleaners DNA, prints, or other biometric markers are present.

This means that the copies Ease said he would email to us with his report are the only ones I'll be able to see until they're released.

I head up to my desk, logging into my desktop device, which, aside from the small plastic box, is nothing like computers used to be. There's no longer a physical screen, just a five by five inch box that contains the memory storage, processors, and power unit. A light projection shoots out to form the screen above it, as well as a forward projection that forms a floating key board. Bio-metric security protocols are required to sign in, the box scanning the chip in my wrist and retinas simultaneously to confirm I am indeed me and still alive to boot. There's no mouse anymore either, the simple flick of a finger on thin air performing all the actions a mouse ever could. When the screen appears, I sit through the ubiquitous New Think message, this one different from this morning's, which says *'YOU, are not an expert'* while the words that aren't written suggest I should follow those that are.

Seated here in my small cubicle facing Constable Conner on the other side, I feel the cold comfort which reminds Old Thinkers like me that whilst the technology has changed, the setting in which I use it has not. The pig pen, as it's known in office parlance, is much the same as it always was, just with less coffee and donuts. Their sweet and bitter aromas having been replaced by an electric burning smell from the hard working devices, their ultra hot projection globes like mini heaters, the hum of their cooling fans our office soundtrack.

I access the email from Ease and bring up the seven letters that he'd scanned and attached. The first appears to be a lot like Katie's mum's description of their phone conversations. A stuttering and impersonal attempt at talking about the mundane actions of life. New Think life, specifically. There's no real mention of questioning the ways of New Think and no indication of a flirtation with any Old Think leaning thoughts.

The first letter is dated only two months ago, the 20th of March. Hard to believe, based on the size of the gap between Jessica's description of her relationship with Katie, and Sophia's description of Katie's turn towards Old Think, that this seismic shift could have occurred in such a short space of time.

More unbelievable still, is that it resulted in such a strong response from someone that they saw the only possible action they could take, as murder. That it would then lead to a second murder is outside all realms of rational reasoning. They are, after all, just letters. Why did they take them so seriously, and how did they even know they'd existed?

As I work through the letters, an obvious pattern emerges. There's a new letter attempted each week. The first three of which all read pretty much the same way. Generalised platitudes, comments on personal health and wellbeing, a vague reference to a relationship that was good, but left her uncertain about the future, and a growing series of questions about how her mum was getting along.

It became apparent to me as I read, that although Katie binned these letters without ever sending them, there was a clear desire and intent to establish and grow a relationship with her mother. A feeling of genuine affection began to appear as the letters went on. Imagined and one sided perhaps, yet evident, nevertheless.

The fourth contained the beginnings of a much more obvious change in Katie's outlook. It starts with the same platitudes as the previous three, then quickly shifts in thinking and tone. Here, Katie starts to sympathise with her mother's plight, asking the direct and thoughtful questions of someone finally alerted to the injustice suffered by others.

"How have you managed such a monumental change in the way you're allowed to live your life? I've started to wonder if I could do it. To be told that everything you know and everything you've ever believed to be true, through your whole life, is wrong. Worse yet, that the things you know, that you were taught from childhood, which for a long time the majority of the world fought for, and defended the principals of, have not only been discouraged, but outlawed and removed from existence. Your way of life has ceased to exist. How can you possibly accept that? How can how can you go on living, knowing that your life's work has been undermined, your entire world turned upside down, without any coherent proof?"

Katie's question was a deep one. A question born from the realisation of the challenges and bitter frustration her mother and so many people of the old world faced. The feeling of no longer being in control of your life and having no choice other than to accept the new and restrictive ways of the authoritarian masters who've censored your right to say, see, hear, or even think the things you've long believed. The things you know to be true, because you yourself had lived them.

Mrs Hansley never had the opportunity to answer this question, but I can. The answer is simple. You can't accept it. It burns a painful and poisonous hate inside of you and you either allow it to destroy you, or you find a way to seal it off and prevent it from ever escaping. Unfortunately, "Comply to get by" or "Conform to the new norm" are the only ways to survive. Still, you never really accept it. You never really forget, and you damn sure never let it go.

Sadly, these common feelings of anger and frustration did not inspire the masses to fight back. They mostly had the opposite effect. They fired the starting pistol on a race to the bottom.

Like a reformed smoker, who becomes incensed at the slightest whiff of nicotine, daily life became a battle of who could be the most committed, militant, and spiteful member of the new regime. Who could lean most fervently into the cause, condemning, punishing, and holding to account their closest family, friends and neighbours from their former way of life.

People performed unsolicited surveillance on those closest to them, taking out their anger and vengeance in the very way their leaders encouraged. Family relationships, bonds of trust and community were torn apart, with everyone spying on everyone else, just to see what they were trying to get away with, all the while nervously looking over their own shoulders to see who was watching them.

The timeline of the letter aligned with what Sophia had told us yesterday. It made sense then that Ms Hansley might indeed have been influenced by her reading of Old Think books. I couldn't help wondering which particular ones she had read and whether the questions they raised made her change anything regarding the program she was working on.

In the fifth letter, Katie drops the platitudes all together, making clear her desire to get closer to her mum, and eager to find a way to reconcile.

I'm so sorry for the way I've treated you. My lack of understanding and compassion for what you've seen and had to live through is appalling and I am ashamed. I hope you can forgive me, or at least give me a chance to try to regain your trust and build a relationship.

I have been reading a lot about history lately. The problems and failures they talk about in New Think are there, but there's so much more than that. People made decisions for themselves, not to be selfish, but to be independent and to take an opportunity and make it something more.

People, just regular people, actually contributed to general life, held opinions of their own, debated different viewpoints and beliefs and continued to live together in spite of their differences.

At times, it even seems as if those different opinions came together to form a better outcome for all. Now, we don't allow people to have different opinions. Different opinions are supposed to be dangerous, and I can't help wondering why, and to whom or what.

I've also come to realise something crucial and frightening about the new world as we now know it. People evolved from nature, yet we've become so detached from it we believe we can control it and all the actions of the planet, turning the intensity of its life force up or down at our will. It's an arrogance that manifests in those whose wealth allows them to influence the masses in their everyday life, like a puppet master pulling at strings. A sense of control that knows no bounds, leading us down a manufactured path, surrounded by, yet never interacting with, nature. Instead, we've blinkered ourselves to its inherent and awesome power, looking only when it backs itself neatly into the narrative we've created for it, while we make our own artificial means of survival, remaining as distant from the real world as we can.

I Think I finally understand what you tried to tell me all those years ago. The time has come to fight for truth.

This passage struck me as insightful and excited my mind. It was a true shift from what we had seen so far and I had to know more, feeling now that perhaps there really was something of value in these letters. As I began reading the sixth and penultimate letter currently in our possession, my device alerted me I had an incoming contact. It was Sharon, no doubt with news of Ease and perhaps his betrayal with the release of these very letters.

'Shaz.' I said. 'What was that louse Ease's excuse? Did he sell us out?'

'Gary, heelppp!' was all the response I got.

'Sharon!?' I shouted, alert now and sitting bolt upright in my seat, ready for action.

'Heellppp, Ease place…' she groaned again, her voice croaky and strained.

Immediately, I jumped from my seat, sprinting across the crew room, yelling out as I ran for Captain Ironie to put out the call for help. I headed straight for the crib room, rounding up Constable Clubman and a few other uniforms who'd just returned from the crime scene, to join me.

Sharon had cut the call almost immediately after her last spoken word. Or someone had… leaving fear charging through my body, not for myself, but for my friend's life.

I tried to call her back, my efforts going unanswered, the calls just ringing to message with no return.

With the other officers in tow, I raced down to the car pool and jumped in one of the company E's, Clubman jumping into the controller's seat beside me. I logged into ETATS, the Electronic Track and Trace System checking Sharon's device to make sure she was still where she said she had been.

Her device pinged at Ease's place, the display showing 0m proximity to his location. I refreshed the screen several times, watching for any movement, when a strange thing struck me. She was there, but there was no record of her ever having entered his apartment.

Chapter 15

The pain of Ease

If you're old like me, and you remember police cars tearing along streets and highways, sirens blaring and taking the pavement, median strip, or the opposite side of the road to attend an emergency ASAP, then the startlingly sedate pace and diligent road rule adherence of the company E would shock you. Of course, this is the new world, and we don't want to frighten or offend anyone. That would be the worst thing that could happen…

We are, after all, just the Police "Service" not a "Force" and the people who are in danger or dying are far less important than the appearance of a perfect world.

When we pull up at a traffic signal behind a Shar-E, which is one of the few ride share options available, and a Deliver-E truck, I'm nearly ready to leap through the windscreen and sprint the rest of the way.

'Can't you take over the fucking steering and put a wriggle on this thing, Clubman!?' I said, with more than a little zang on the end of it.

'You know damn well I can't, Gaz!' Said Cliff. 'The whole reason I'm in the driver's seat with the all-powerful Detective Johnson on the passenger side, is that you're banned from driving for doing that very thing!'

We both sat stewing nervously, me trying not to snap, while Clubman's left leg, no longer required to be steady whilst the right operates pedals, was bouncing up and down at a million miles an hour. Outside, the cold cloudy skies were now producing rain, the rhythmical tapping on the E's roof and bonnet broken only by the regular swiping action of the centrally located windscreen wiper.

Ahead of us, digital traffic control screens hung over the road, counting down the seconds until we could move again. A Global message displayed above the timer, '*Leave the power to the Powerful*' because an opportunity to remind people how insignificant they are should never be missed.

Further ratcheting up both mine and clubman's blood pressure was the running commentary from the E itself, making unnecessary and obvious statements, like "*You are currently stopped at signal 3, Long Street, 14 minutes from your destination. We will be permitted to recommence your journey in 12 seconds…*"

'Yeah, well, I'll take over this bloody thing myself if we don't get there soon.' I said shittily, the inaction and myriad agitations getting the better of me. 'Shaz sounded in real trouble on the phone and she's not calling me back now. Bloody unbelievable the bullshit in this "Global" world! Quick with a condemning ShareSpace post or to use their bloody mouthpiece media to bring down some poor bastard who's seen to be misaligned with their strict and unforgiving morals. They'd be cancelled instantly. But in an actual emergency, where real physical action is required, they're as useless as a solar panel in Scotland.' (*New Think joke. You know, because Scotland doesn't exist anymore and solar panels... well... you get it...).*

We move again, eventually, the rest of the trip made in agitated silence, Cliff looking distantly out the window, my own attention focussed on the ETATS, silently praying to a god I didn't believe in to intervene on Sharon's behalf.

When we finally pull up to Sgt Ease's apartment block, I note there are no signs of violence or any other drama to be seen from the street. The 15-story building standing quiet and frustratingly idle for the drama I envisage inside. Sharon's company E is parked at an angle in front of us, its presence causing a fresh batch of butterflies to take flight in my stomach, as I desperately hope she's okay.

Cliff Clubman, the man sitting next me, whilst a card-carrying New Thinker, went against most of his kind when he decided he quite liked that Sharon and I continue to hold dear a different way of life to the one we're now forced to live. Glancing over at him, the tension was clear on his face, a non-verbal clue that confirmed he cared about what was happening here, too.

We both leap from the vehicle just as soon as it stops, looking across at each other as we pass either side of the bonnet. A small nod tells us all we need to know. We've got each other's back, and we're ready to go.

Three other uniforms, along with Captain Ironie, pull up behind us as we cross from the road onto the footpath leading up to the front doors.

'Captain, we're going in.' I shouted over my shoulder.

'We'll cover the exits.' she shouted back, as Clubman and I broke into a run towards the door.

After we found Ease's apartment number, located on level 7, I wasted no time entering the building, simply kicking the door in rather than trying to override the security system. Inside, we assessed our options, noting there was only a single lift which was currently positioned at the very top of its run.

'Maybe we split and come at it from two different directions?' Said Clubman, his manner focussed and calm.

'Good Idea.' I agreed, my eyes still trained on the lift counter above.

'The stairs must be around the back of this lift. You've got a few years on me, old man.' said Clubman. 'You take the lift and I'll take the stairs.'

Without waiting for a reply, he took off, his hard soled GP boots screeching slightly on the polished tiled floor as he turned the corner sharply around the rear of the lift well. There was muted swearing and banging followed by the opening, and then seconds later, slamming shut of a door which told me he was in, but not as easily as he'd have liked.

As Clubman climbed, I stood in front of the lifts, staring impatiently at the counter. The lift remained on the 15th floor and I had to wait a good twenty seconds before I saw it finally begin its descent, watching intently as it clicked down through the levels, tracked by the small digital screen above the doors. Several times, I thought about ditching the option, changing tact and following Cliff up the stairs, the anxiety of the wait buzzing hotly in my head, but my training told me to stick with the plan I had.

I checked my pocket for the All-Access Authenticator, an electronic skeleton key of sorts, that I'd taken from the Company-E when we'd arrived. The key allows unapproved access to residential buildings and lifts in the case of emergency, necessary here or else I'd have no choice but to follow Clubman up the stairs. Satisfied it was still there, I returned my attention back to the lift, watching as it inched glacially closer.

As it finally approached the ground floor, a good twenty seconds after commencing its descent, I took a defensive position beside a pot plant to the left, squatting down low, in case an active threat emerged.

When the doors opened, the sole occupant was a slow-moving elderly lady of what would once have been described as middle eastern appearance, now just another Global citizen, her ethnicity not an approved form of identification, no matter how relevant it was.

Five Seconds later, she'd cleared the lift, leaving a void I filled at pace, slamming the level 7 and door close buttons in quick succession, my mind and body willing me to move faster than the lift allowed.

Champing at the bit when it finally settles on level 7, I squeeze my way out before the doors have finished opening, electro drawn and leading the way. Moving right along the empty corridor, I methodically check off door numbers and potential threats as I go, before arriving at number 42 to find the door closed and locked with Clubman nowhere to be seen. I check my watch again, noting that 45 seconds had passed since he'd left for the stairwell downstairs, then just as I was weighing up whether to kick the door down and charge in on my own, or find Clubman first, I hear a rattling and banging coming from my right.

Leaving door number 42 and moving down the hall, my nerves rise, natural fear honing my senses, as I realise the noise is coming from the stairwell.

'Clubman?!' I say in a pointlessly loud whisper.

'They've glued the fucking doors!' he replied tersely.

Checking the doorframe, I see that the door must open inward, making it very difficult to unstick it from the inside.

'On the count of three, you pull, and I'll slam my body weight into the door and see if we can open it.' I said.

'Righto.' came the frustrated reply.

'1…2…3…' Wham! Slamming my 105kg's of body weight into the door sent me flying into the stairwell and crashing into the stairs leading up to the 8th floor. Luckily for the both of us, Clubman had sensed the risk that this might happen and wisely stepped out of the way, taking one step back down from the 7th floor landing when he felt the door give quickly.

'You okay?' he asked.

'Fine.' I said, peeling myself off the stairs and brushing the dust from my shirt. I tried not to show the pain in my right shoulder, elbow, and wrist from hitting the stairs, smiling aggressively to cover the grimace. 'Let's go. We need to get in there immediately and the door to the apartment is locked.'

We double timed it back down the hallway, pausing outside Ease's door to listen for any sounds of movement or noise inside. There seemed to be something, a flapping or blowing noise, which was inconsistent and not human made. Perhaps something moving under the cycling of a fan, and there was something else too.

'You smell gas?' Asked Clubman.

'Yeah' I said. 'That's what it is, gas.' Both of us having recognised the same smell at the same time gave me the confidence we'd correctly identified the culprit. Albeit, it was also a very bad sign that it was gas we could smell.

Our collective anxiety piqued, deepening the concern for our friends and raising the stakes of our entry, Clubman and I lined up side by side to kick the door in together. It took several goes, this door having been glued shut like the others. When it finally smashed open on the fourth attempt, the smell of gas was overwhelming.

'Christ!' I said, automatically pulling my head back and turning away from the door. 'I'll get the gas. You get some windows open.'

Not wanting to accidentally blow the side off the building, and ourselves with it, both Clubman and I holstered our electro's before entering the hallway and setting about our tasks. Reaching the kitchen, I could see that all four gas taps on one of the old style stove tops were turned on, the valves fully open and blasting out their scented fuel.

Despite the urgency, I couldn't help being mildly surprised that Ease had had a gas stove to begin with, in particular, because most of the gas supply network had been disbanded. The only way anyone could get gas in their apartments these days was by having a community gas tank within the building. These tanks had to be filled by a mobile gas tanker on an approved scheduled basis, which means there's a limited supply between top ups, and by the smell in his apartment, I'd say the whole building's supply was in here now.

Flicking the taps off and gagging at the smell, I run to the kitchen window, yanking it upwards in a failed attempt to open it. Meanwhile, in another room, I hear Clubman coughing and swearing, no doubt finding that his window had been glued shut just as mine was. Grabbing Sgt Ease's cheap wooden knife block from the kitchen bench, I smash open the kitchen window, glass shards raining down both inside and out, immediately letting some gas out and fresh air in.

I wet a tea towel and put it to my mouth before racing into the next room, clearing both the kitchen and hallway again as I go. In the lounge room, I find Clubman doubled over on the floor next to a closed window, coughing and wheezing and desperately fighting to breathe. Using the knife block, I smash out the two living room windows, again feeling the precious relief of oxygen returning to the space.

'Shit!' I shouted, turning to see the clearly struggling Clubman still down on his haunches, knowing at the same time that Sharon, and possibly Ease, are in here somewhere, too. I rush over and grab Cliff under the arms, dragging him out into the corridor and propping him against the wall. 'Get some air and get yourself right!' I said, not angrily but instructively, the plight of the other two playing on my mind.

Just then, my radio squawked, "Gaz! What the fuck's going on in there!?" shouted the captain. 'We can see glass smashing everywhere and Constable Marsh has reported finding glass and a police electro gun on the ground at the side of the building.'

'The apartment was filled with gas!' I shouted back into the radio, breathing heavily as I did, my head feeling faint and dizzy. 'Someone was either trying to blow the place up or gas everyone to death. The windows and doors were glued shut too, so we had to smash them to get some air in.'

"Fuck! And Shaz, Ease?" Squawked the radio.

'I don't know, yet.' I said. 'Cliff was getting sick from the gas, so I dragged him out for air. I'm heading back in now. I'll let you know as soon as I find them.'

Charging back into the apartment, I don't bother drawing my electro. It's clear that whoever did this has left or else they too would be passed out or dead. Moving back down the hallway, I first check the kitchen to make sure the gas is clearing. The smell is still there, but the gas is definitely off and noticeably dissipating with the smashed windows having their desired effect.

As I make my way back through the apartment, I note for the first time the off angle mirror and fallen side table objects in the entranceway. In the living room I pause, this time taking in the tipped over coffee table and small amount of blood on the floor. Looking up from the bloodied carpet to the opposite end of the room, I see through the doorway, two upturned feet, with women's shoes on.

'Shaz!' I said to myself. Alert again now, my heart and nerves fluttering to the tune of Flight of the Bumblebee. I move quickly and cautiously towards her forlorn form, just in case whoever did this left us another trap.

To the right of the bedroom door, on a small wooden stand, sat a candle with a blackened wick, and I wondered if it had been lit by whoever had done this in order to blow the place up. The thought sent a fresh jolt of nervous energy firing through me, signifying just how sinister and intentional the action was.

Why the candle had gone out, I couldn't yet know. Suffice to say, that if it hadn't, there'd be nothing left to see at all.

Entering what I now confirmed as the bedroom, my stomach dropped again with a sickening, nervous fear coming over me. Swallowing hard and taking in the scene, I grasp for my radio, immediately calling to Isabelle for help.

'We're going to need two ambulances here, ASAP!' I shouted. 'Get the forensics team as well.' I figured they could check the place to see if there was evidence of our perpetrators, although, given their professional work in gluing shut all the windows and escape routes, save for the lift, there may not be much to find. Nevertheless, what lay before me left me determined to show these bastards the meaning of justice, whatever it takes.

At the site of my forlorn friends, the overwhelming smell of the gas and build-up of nervous energy got too much, and I had to hang my head out the window for a moment of fresh air before reviewing the carnage again and planning my course of action.

Sgt Ease lay uncomfortably on his back upon the bed, bound and gagged and showing clear signs of torture. Dried blood had caked around his nose and mouth. He wasn't dead yet, but obviously unconscious, his slightly rotund stomach showing positive signs of rise and fall, providing some relief that he was at least capable of breathing.

I quickly check his vital signs confirming my first assessment, before rushing over to Sharon who lay on the floor, arm outstretched towards the window. Shaz too had blood caking the left side of her face with nasty bruising developing on her throat and arm.

'Shaz?! Shaz?!' I said, as I gently cradle her face in my hands. With no response, I checked her pulse and breathing, relieved to find both signs of life were there, even if a little faint. Checking her mouth and throat for blockages, I confirmed there were no other signs of significant injury, then rolled her into the recovery position, doing my best to breathe the tainted air and hoping she could do the same.

Standing up, I spend several seconds looking down at Sharon's unconscious form, my earlier nerves now resolving themselves into ones of the slower vibrating sort that make up anger and resentment. The blood from Sharon's ear and cheek had dripped down to the carpet, where it had mostly dried, still malleable to the touch.

Breaking my position and moving back to Ease, I check him over for injuries. The top of his chest displaying a multitude of horrific burn marks, though so far as I could tell, no broken bones or puncture wounds. I check his nose and throat are clear, albeit swollen and bloody, before rolling him onto his side, then set about trying to release him from his bonds. His captors had tied his hands and feet with rope, the raw marks of their violent strain clear to see.

As I did this, an angry Captain Ironie burst into the apartment, calling out my name, the rage within her tone breaking through the haze that had enveloped me.

'Gary! How are they? Is anyone alive?' she shouted.

'I'm in the bedroom.' I shouted back.

Running into the room, she stopped in the doorway, taking in the scene, and growing angrier at the sight of those under her command lying injured and unconscious.

'Fuck!' Said Ironie, because no other word would do. 'Fuck these fuckin bastards! I'll castrate whoever did this…'

Taking a deep and shaky breath followed by a long exhale, Isabelle took a moment to steel herself before walking with control and purpose over to Sharon and rechecking her vitals, just as I had done.

Without a word, she got to her feet and moved to the bed, taking a pillow, then returning to Sharon's side and placing it under her head.

'Come on, untie him!' she said, turning back towards me, her eyes looking directly at Ease.

'I can't.' I replied, looking up at her face, now wet with tears. 'Those sick bastards have actually glued the bindings to his wrists, in addition to tying them. I'll tear his skin off if I remove them now.'

When you think about a violent scene or when you watch a movie where they've created one, the scene where the violence occurs is usually dark and well aligned to those within it. This was different. Ease, for all his committed progressiveness, was a nerdy kid at heart. His tortured, bloody body, wrapped in its charcoal black police uniform and boots, didn't seem to belong here on his childish Captain Planet bedcover and matching pillowcases. On his side-stands sat superhero figurines, one of them a Super-Him lamp, the modern pro-noun corrected version of Superman, a solar powered block of kryptonite held above his head, which formed the light source.

'Did you call the ambos?' I asked, solemnly.

'Yes, they're on their way.' replied Ironie, matching my tone without embellishment.

Sickened by the site before me, and not wanting to waste precious time while we waited for them to arrive, Ironie agreed to monitor Sharon and Ease whilst I started inspecting the scene.

I first stepped back to the far corner of the bedroom, trying to clear my mind and view it from a new angle. I needed to see all that was there, a detective entering a crime scene, not a rescuer and friend, determined to unfocus on the things I thought I already knew, and those that angered and drew attention away from the objective process.

There was a fair amount of damage here, though some of it had been caused by me, and some, no doubt, by Sharon. It appeared she'd probably saved both Eases and her own life when she threw her electro at the window to smash it. My guess is, she was either trying to get oxygen in to dilute the gas, or perhaps create a breeze to put the candle out before the gas had a chance to ignite.

It was also possible she put out the candle first before going back to the bedroom to smash the window, knowing that Ease would need the clear untainted air as well. If she had, the effort would border on the superhuman given her current condition.

Back out in the lounge room, the thing that really stood out was just how remarkably little Sgt Ease actually had in his apartment. Keeping a low carbon footprint is one thing (*no matter how questionable, particularly given the luxury of his gas stove*), owning virtually nothing at all is another thing entirely. I'm almost hopeful the glue carrying torturers robbed the place before they left, or else I might actually have to feel sorry for him, and not just for the torture.

What was in the room told an obvious story. I didn't need to be a detective to see that. The overturned coffee table and blood bore the clear signs of a struggle. Thick streaks of blood coated the solid wood of the uppermost table leg, along with the carpet below. From the state of Ease, I felt safe in assuming it was his face striking on the table leg that left the mess. Turning slowly from the centre of the lounge room and scanning the beige coloured walls, unbroken by art or alternate form, I'd nearly gone a full 180, before I saw for the first time, a set of doors located about a meter to the right of Sgt Ease's bedroom.

Behind the doors was either a large sized cupboard or a fairly deep study nook/home office, that by its contents immediately reminded me that Ease was in fact a detective in an anthropomorphised digital world. A place where real crimes are committed in non-tangible settings via goggles and motion sensors from the comfort of your own lounge room. Or in his case, the mild discomfort of your oversized cupboard.

Inside, set in the centre of the rear wall, was a large, cubed device box, about 30cm by 30cm. It had multiple lenses and sensory ports that no doubt connected to the goggles and headset which hung on hooks to the right. On the floor was a set of sensory gloves, strewn separately, the fingers of each glove slightly bunched, as if their removal was rushed, not planned.

I wondered whether this particular crime was actually related to our original case from which we seem to have drifted quite aways, or whether this was an unrelated crime from an un-real world.

'Find anything, Gary!?' Yelled Ironie from the bedroom.

'No.' I said. 'Nothing useful yet. I think we'll have to wait for forensics to sweep the place.'

'Well, Sharon seems like she's beginning to stir. You might want to come in here and comfort your partner.' she shouted back. 'The ambos and forensics teams should be here any minute. We can get on with the investigation as soon as these two are stable and under care.'

Back inside the bedroom, I crouched next to Shaz, brushing her hair back from her bruised and bloodied face as she tried to move her mouth, her lips opening and closing slightly. I couldn't believe this had happened to her. Why Sharon? Why Ease? How on earth does this all fit into what had started as just another case? Our first murder case, sure, but it was only meant to be some sort of internal dispute at OGT. Open and shut, as Damwell said. Now, only one day later, there's a second murder, and on top of that, two police officers violently attacked. For the life of me, I can't see how it all fits together. I'm missing something and I'm not even sure where to start.

'There's not much we can do here without forensics.' I said to Isabelle. 'We may need an Alt-Verse expert to help us review Sgt Ease's recent interactions in his other role, too. You know, just in case this was an Alt-Verse incident unrelated to OGT, that led to a real-world crime. I'd say it's unlikely. As coincidences go, this would be a big one. Even so, the evidence suggests he might have been in the Alt-Verse around the time he got attacked, so it's best to be sure.'

The truth was, I had a strong feeling what we were seeing here related directly to the contents of those letters from Ms Hansley. I hadn't finished reading them yet, and so far I hadn't seen anything worth killing over, but they were as close as we had to a lead.

Looking down again at the only real friend I have in the world, I wince at the sight of her injuries, feeling the pain of them as if I had caused them myself. A straight-line bruise was spreading along her cheek and around her eye. The eye itself was bloodshot, the surrounding swelling forcing the eyelid to begin closing over. I'm no expert, but I'd be confident in guessing she has a fractured cheekbone and eye socket.

Shaz knows the risks of this job, we all do. It sits at the back of your mind as you prepare for work each morning, just a hypothetical concept, until it rudely takes physical shape on your face and body. She's as tough as they come too, never one to complain about the rough stuff, but no one wants to see their friend like this… One way or another, I'm going to make whoever did this, pay. For Ease too. Even if we might have different views on the world, I never wanted to see him hurt, and nobody deserves to be tortured. Not when they're just doing their job.

The obvious strikes me as I squat next to Shaz, the room growing large in my mind. Ease was the target, being tortured in his own apartment, Sharon was simply unlucky to have walked in on the event. My guess is, she must have entered the bedroom before she was attacked, unless the blood on the coffee table was hers, too. Surveying the room again, I see that a handle on the built-in cupboards next to the door is broken. Sharon would have entered the room with her electro drawn and held out in front, which would give someone on this side of the door a good indication of when to attack.

All they'd have to do is wait for the right moment, then slam the door into her as she entered, knocking her back into the cupboards, no doubt breaking the handle as she fell. To confirm my theory, I pull her collar outwards and check her back to find a bruised and raw scrape running for about two inches down her right scapula. The theory holds.

Being who she is, she would've tried to get up and fight back, which might explain the bruise on the left side of her neck. The assailant would've comfortably held the upper hand here, needing only to strike her across the neck to knock her down or more likely out, giving them time to glue the windows, set the gas and light the candle before leaving.

Besides the obvious who's and why's, the next question is whether they had always planned to glue all the windows and doors from the start? And, if so, why?

If they wanted to kill Ease or Shaz, they clearly had ample opportunity. Why do it this way? Were they hoping we would get here just in time for the place to blow for maximum impact, or did they think that this would provide some sort of explanation of an accidental crime?

A noise at the apartment door snaps me back from my thoughts.

'Ambos! Where are you guys? Are we safe to come in?' shouted the crew.

'Come in, we are in the bedroom to the right!' shouted Ironie in reply.

The Ambo's entered the room, their blue coverall uniform looking as it always had, making their presence somewhat comforting despite the situation. They wore the now ubiquitous cloth face masks, ineffectively covering their nose and mouths, the presence of which had nothing to do with the lingering gas smell in the apartment, instead just another tool of fear. The message being that if paramedical professionals such as these always wear a mask for safety, then they must be necessary and effective.

Ironie and I conducted the handover of our respective patients, separately. Ironie went first, leaving me to watch on as the crew cut away Ease's bindings, exposing the raw skin and trauma from the glue. In places, chunks of cut rope remained attached, unable to be safely removed in situ.

As soon as we'd finished handing over, the forensic team arrived, and I took them around the apartment and into the stairwell to show where I needed them to focus. 'I doubt we'll find any prints, but we may get lucky with some hair, or some other form of DNA shed during the struggle. That way, we might be able to match it to their biometric profiles. My money is on there being more than one perpetrator and very few other visitors to Ease's apartment.' I added as we went.

'Seems like a mean observation to make, but he doesn't exactly come across as the type of guy who has a lot of friends over, so there shouldn't be too much to exclude. He's more like the guy who's far happier in the Alt-Verse where your real appearance does not apply. His somewhat off-putting character might come through, though it's probably easier to find similar personalities in there than out here... Heroes of the alt-verse, outcasts of the real world... Even a New Think one.'

When I had finished directing the Forensics team as to the events that occurred after my arrival at Ease's building, I went back to the bedroom which Captain Ironie herself was now inspecting, since Ease and Shaz had been removed and rushed off to the hospital.

'What do you think?' I asked, stepping between the crime scene photographer and one of the uniforms Ironie had brought with her.

Ironie turned to me, a fresh tear forming in her right eye. 'I think these animals tortured my people. I think this is pure evil.' She said in a cold, hard tone.

Ironie looked back down at the bed, and I followed her line of sight, seeing for the first time that Sgt Ease had not been able to hold his bladder during the torture.

‘How long do you think they had him tied here?’ I asked, to which the captain didn’t answer, instead just continuing to stare at the bed in silence.

Now that I was aware of it, and perhaps with the gas further dissipating, I could even smell the fetid aftermath of the torture. Captain Planet had been soiled by human waste once more. Quite the metaphor in this world.

‘What time did he call in this morning?’ I asked, trying again to engage Isabelle, and knowing that the timely learning of this information may very well be relevant to solving the case.

‘He called in early. About 06:00.’ answered Ironie eventually. ‘He wasn’t due on until 08:00.’

‘Did he sound forced at all? Under duress?’

‘I didn’t think so at the time.’ she said. ‘Now I’m not so sure. I’ll pull the tape for you as soon as we get back to the office.’

‘Okay.’ I said. ‘Well, Sharon and I had been planning to head out to see another person of interest when she’d left here. I think I need to carry on this investigation alone until she’s ready to come back. The show must go on, as they say.’

‘Is it time critical?’ Asked Ironie, cutting through my spiel.

‘Quite possibly, yes. It’s the cleaner from OGT who was apparently given an eighth and final letter by Ms Hansley, directly. He went home not long after that and hasn’t been seen since.’

‘Fine.’ said Isabelle, her eyes flicking up to meet mine for the briefest of seconds, indicating a greater level of interest than her voice conveyed. ‘We’d better get moving then.’ she added with determination. ‘We want to find that letter before anyone else does. Clubman has been cleared by the Ambos. They say he’s okay to keep going. He can finish up here with the other uniforms.’

‘You’re coming with me?’ I asked, surprised that Isabelle would even consider this.

‘Damn right I am! There’s no way I’m sending you out there on your own. There’s been enough assaults and murders for one day. I want to make damn sure that we get these bastards, too.’

Not daring to try and dissuade her from what I felt was an unnecessary and reactive decision to join me, I flashed what I hoped was a positive smile and silently cursed my fate.

After we cleared the scene at Ease’s apartment, Isabelle and I jumped in an E, both of us now in quiet contemplation. I was thinking again about the case so far, realising how I’d been sleepwalking through it. I’d allowed myself to be lulled into a false sense of security. The endless propaganda pushed by the Guides, that nobody is out to do harm anymore and that security is so tight, and the world so regulated, that nothing bad is even possible, must have seeped into my subconscious.

Their exhaustive restrictions on everyone and everything are supposed to mean that nothing bad can happen… Yet, I, of all people, should have known better. There's nothing more dangerous than nothing. "Nothing" IS dangerous! Because from nothing, anything is possible. When things are quiet, that's when you have to ensure you're on your highest alert. Your guard naturally goes down, so you need to take extra steps to be careful. Especially in this world where people are so unconscious as to what is actually going on around them. I know that better than anyone. Hell, I was an expert in military tactics, based entirely around awareness, preparation and expecting the unexpected.

As usual, I've remembered something I already knew, just after it would have been useful to know it. My lax attitude to the safety of my team investigating this crime… crimes now… has put us all in danger, myself included, and my own partner has suffered the consequences.

There's been two murders, and three injured cops, leaving Sgt Ease and possibly Shaz in a coma, not to mention whatever happened to me last night, an incident I'm barely even aware of. It's time to step up my game, use the resources available to me, and claw back the advantage over whomever would do us harm.

It's time to reach out to an old friend.

Chapter 16

Blowing in the wind

One good thing about the change in the role of foot soldiers towards a more surveillance-based position, is that with a myriad of old friends still in the service, I should be able to gain the assistance of some of their surveillance and analysis technology which would ordinarily sit outside the reach of police.

I'm not sure how Ironie will take me side stepping the normal channels. She is, after all, a stickler for the rules, meaning I'll have to keep it under my hat for now. She does, however, seem genuinely pissed that the attacks on Ease and Shaz occurred under her watch, so she might be willing to do whatever it takes to bring these bastards to justice.

'How do you want to play this?' I asked. 'Sharon and I often make decisions on the fly and let the investigation take its natural course. Although, sometimes that means we need to separate to keep things moving along at the right pace. That's what happened earlier today. After the scene at OGT this morning I went back to the office to go through the letters Sgt Ease had sent through last night, meanwhile, Shaz went to see Ease and find out if he'd a hand in the media getting hold of those letters that only he had seen… And here we are.'

'Well, I think your question answers itself, Gary.' said Ironie, seeming to fight an internal battle between being a partner, being a boss, and just generally being angry. 'Safety is paramount now and I will not have another officer under my command getting injured or being put at risk through poor planning or a lax mentality. We will be sticking together every step of the way from here on in.'

'Fair enough.' I said, smarting inside at what I assume was a direct commentary on "my" lax management of the investigation so far. Off the back of which, I'm certainly not going to tell her about what happened to me last night, an event that even I know virtually nothing about, save what Sharon had told me.

I have a plan, though… To paraphrase a Roman General, if we want a peaceful resolution here, we must prepare for war. Which, as soon as we get to Jiang's place, is just what I plan to do. We've been on the back foot here for far too long, marching along to the beat of the killer's drum. From now on, I intend to turn the tables and begin watching the watchers to see if we can't flush the killers out and discover how, why, and who is so easily able to circumvent the Global security apparatus.

Arriving at Jiang's address, I'm relieved at the prospect of getting some space from the captain. Her quiet and determined contemplation having turned to angry stewing over the course of the ride, a significant portion of which I could feel spilling over my way.

'I assume you won't want to split up to cover both the front and rear doors?' I asked, hopefully.

'Absolutely not!' She replied. 'Why? Are you expecting him to be a runner?'

'Well, frankly, yes.' I said. 'That is, of course, assuming he's still alive. He was due back at work this morning, but he never showed up and nobody's been able to get hold of him since.'

We agreed to find some middle ground and inspect the front, sides, and rear of the building to get the lay of the land before attempting the very trusting, front door knock, approach.

Prior to exiting the E, we conducted a quick "live view" of the property via satellite and reviewed Jiang's movements via his chip log, which by all accounts, showed he had entered the property yesterday and is not believed to have left.

Looking out the window of the car, I struggle to reconcile what I know of the OGT cleaners with what I see. I'm not sure what form of wrong had been done to Jiang or his ancestors, but given that he lives in a red brick, tile roofed, 3-bedroom house with a front and rear yard, I can only assume it was something requiring quite significant restitution on behalf of New Think's moral underlings.

By old standards, this would have been considered a fairly basic family home of the working class. By the new "Global" standards, however, where everyone who isn't on the level of the Guides is basic working class, this is bloody luxury.

The house is set back from the road a good ten meters, the lawn and small garden at the front both healthy and established, if a little unkempt. The low-lying rows of suburban style houses surrounding it also offered a different feel to the bitter loneliness of the city apartments. There was no wind tunnel effect of the high concrete city buildings, just a gentle breeze blowing across the rooftops and a blast of warmth from the direct sunlight that broke through the dreary cloud and rain.

From a brief inspection of the front of the house, which we conducted from the street, we noted Jiang had all his curtains drawn, except for what I assume must be the lounge room next to the front door. Peering through the window, I saw no obvious signs of a struggle and no movement inside. The furniture seemed undisturbed and there was no blood or bodies visible.

Moving around to the left side of the house, which by the way has no fencing to block access to the rear, I noted there were virtually no objects there except for a water heater occupying part of the space. The smell of freshly cut grass filled the air, though from the length of Jiang's lawn, it was clearly not his doing.

Creeping slowly towards the rear of the house, the sense that there was something wrong rose in the pit of my stomach for the second time today. There was nothing tangible I'd seen to confirm this sensation, except the hairs standing at the back of my neck and a tightness at my temples telling me I soon would.

Turning back towards the car, I signal Izzy to keep her eyes on with the ubiquitous sign, and a point at her, followed by my pointer and middle finger forming a focussed V an inch in front of my own eyes, then pointing back towards the front of the house. Ironie gave me a confirmation nod, showing she understood, then I returned my focus back to the task and proceeded around the corner.

I stopped just past the back wall, looking across to my right where I see a small wooden deck butted hard against the rear of the house, the screen door above it swung wide open.

Making a visual sweep of the backyard, I find only poorly kept garden beds along the fences separating the rear of the house from its neighbours. A large silver oak tree stands alone in one corner and a jacaranda in the other.

As my eyes return to the doorway, I catch a flash of movement inside. It happens so fast, I can't tell if it was moving towards or away from the door, certain only of the fact that I'd seen something, which probably meant that it had seen me. It could just be Jiang, justifiably scared and trying to hide, or escape from what he perceives as a threat. Or we might have stumbled on the same sort of scenario that Sharon did at Ease's place, interrupting some sinister action inside.

Retreating around to the side of the house and into the line of Ironie's sight, I signal her that the rear door was open and that I might have been seen. Of course, that isn't the easiest thing to signal, and failing to comprehend it, she called me over the radio.

'What the hell are you saying?' she asked.

'The back door is open. I saw movement inside and I'm pretty sure I was seen.' I said as softly as I could.

Not wishing to risk further injury, Ironie demanded we fall back to the car and call in support before making any further moves.

In contrast, I felt that if I'd already been seen, my position at the side of the house was something to be avoided by those in hiding, so I agreed only to come part way back such that we could comfortably talk in a loud whisper, yet not so far that I couldn't maintain sight of a large portion of the backyard.

'I need to stay here in case someone tries to make a run for it.' I said. 'Why don't you fall back to the car and call for backup? That way you can coordinate the team when it arrives and in the meantime, watch the front while I keep eyes on the rear.'

Reluctantly, Ironie agreed, although clearly put out at having been given a plan by not just a man, but an Old Think, low-ranking, rookie detective, no less. Very un-New Think.

Immediately breaking my promise to stay within comfortable talking distance, I return to the rear of the house, then inch my way around to take another look. Again, I saw some sort of movement inside, causing me to repeat my earlier action and take a step back, crouching down into the soft grass just out of sight of the doorway.

Glancing at Ironie, now busy on the phone herself, I switch my police radio over to earpiece so that her call for backup isn't broadcast to all and sundry. I then split my earpieces, so that I still hear her comms, while simultaneously being able to make a call to my friend at the Defence Security and Surveillance Monitoring Directorate (*DSSMD*). This is how I plan to begin my fight back and finally get into the game.

'Milford, long time no see.' I say, when my call is answered on only the second ring. This used to be a general comment between distant friends, but is more of a joke at the DSSMD, because they pretty much see everything, all the time.

'Ah, if it isn't one illustrious member of the famed Sons of Old!' Replied Milly. 'How do you do, old friend?'

'I need your help.' I said without pretence, never one for drawn out phone conversations.

Milly and I had spent fifteen years together in the Army. I was his sergeant, then warrant officer, in a specialised unit that trained other units in combat tactics and strategy, in addition to planning and executing our own missions. Until, that is, it was determined I was no longer of any value to a Global military service that had no wars left to fight, nor opposing military to strategize against.

I am not now, nor have I ever been particularly tech savvy. Albeit, I am a fast learner, and certainly capable of carrying out the general technology tasks required of my present role. What I couldn't, or perhaps more accurately, didn't want to do, was adapt to a surveillance role that was basically part Precog from Minority Report and part Thought Police from 1984.

The surveillance now performed by the military, basically covers all members of the Global World, with programs running endlessly to track our every move, our purchases, and all interactions, with the aim of identifying patterns and creating risk profiles for everyone in the world. They then monitor for any escalation of these risks whilst concurrently tracking regular high-risk interactions with focused HumInt (*Human Intelligence*) teams and targeted technology based monitoring and surveillance, combining to put anyone they want under a microscope.

An automated system flags people based on a set of predetermined and evolving triggers. Those trigger sensitivities being regularly adjusted, and their priority escalated by way of AI recognition, which means that the system recognises an escalating pattern that matches similar previous incidences resulting in crime, violence, or descent, and prioritises those persons or events for intervention.

Thankfully for me, despite the ever-increasing reliance on technology, there are also analysts such as Milford whose job it is to review key interactions, flagged scenarios and high-risk people, along with the AI system itself. I've said it before and I'll say it again, New Think loves redundancy. Technology keeps an eye on people and people keep an eye on technology. When people are no longer involved, that's when the world will truly belong to the machines. Until then, we stand around and try to look important.

'Milly, I'm wondering if you wouldn't mind redirecting some of your time to a scenario of escalating violence and crime?' I asked. 'It's for a case I'm working on, where we seem to be getting blocked at every turn, unable to make any ground.'

'I suspect you're talking about the murders that have taken place at OGT?' said Milly, more statement than question.

'I am indeed. You're obviously aware of them already?'

'Yes.' he replied. 'Rather disturbed by them, actually. I didn't know you were working on them. We've only reviewed the actions, not the case. Evidentially, someone is circumventing the system. Somehow, we've had no flagged events or interactions relating to either of the victims and there's nothing anywhere on the surveillance database that indicates who might have been in a position to avoid surveillance without tripping a single data flare. It's not just the tracker and video surveillance at OGT, either. They've somehow managed to get in and out of the building and presumably along the street without a trace. It's not something I've seen before. Not since the Guides took over, anyway. As it turns out, I'm the one tasked with finding out what happened, so maybe we can help each other out.'

'Excellent!' I said, almost excited at this development. 'I'm actually in the middle of a scene right now. Perhaps you could start helping me right away?'

After giving Milly the details of where we were, why we were here, and what I had seen at the back door, he pulled up the location and reviewed the recent activity.

'Do you want to call me back?' I asked, assuming it would take some time to process.

'You never were real tech savvy, were you Gaz. I can filter the surveillance footage to check for specific actions or events. That way I can review all the activity there in a couple of minutes as opposed to an hour or more. I already started while we were talking, by the way. Looks like Jiang returned home on the night of Ms Hansley's murder, then left again about an hour later and hasn't returned since.'

'But I looked at his chip register when we got here. It didn't show him leaving.'

'You probably don't have access to the GPS triangulation that we do.' Said Milly. 'His device and chip both communicate with the satellite to confirm his position and movement.'

'Okay. Well, if he's not here, have there been any other visitors?' I asked. 'And where the hell is he now?'

'There are no other visitors that show up until you and Captain Ironie got there. As for where he is now, I couldn't tell you. His GPS signal pinged in the vicinity outside the house for a couple hours, then stopped.'

'Well, you'd have to think it's unlikely that anybody would bother blocking surveillance and just wait here for him to come back. Which begs the question, what is it that I'm seeing at the back door then.'

'Hang on.' He said. 'I can probably take over the devices in the house and see what's in there.'

In a matter of minutes, Milly had reviewed all available technology in the apartment. With the aid of an audio-visual device in the lounge room, he was able to tell us that the movement I was seeing was only the flapping of curtain blowing in the breeze of a fan that had either been left on, or intentionally turned on to make it seem like someone was home.

'Is that enough to go off for now?' He asked.

'It's enough to get us in the building to have a look around.' I said. 'Thanks for your help. I'll be in touch again later and let you know how we go.' I ended the call, satisfied with the information and happy, if a little surprised that he was on the case too.

Returning my mind to the task at hand, I couldn't help thinking what an odd trick Jiang had played. Why would a cleaner leave their house, and in the process, leave their back door open? More to the point, with such limited electricity available, why would you waste it leaving a fan on, just to trick the eye. Seems rather like the actions of a man who doesn't plan to return.

Jumping on the police radio, I advised Ironie I'd managed to confirm there was no one at the back of the house, the movement just that of a loose curtain in the doorway and requested permission to enter.

'The team's about to arrive, anyway.' she replied. 'You will wait for them, copy?'

'Wilco.' I replied. 'I'll wait back here. Tell the team to let me know when they're ready to enter. I'll cover the rear of the house.'

Five minutes later, a team of six officers entered via the front door, breaching with what might be described as unwarranted force and knocking it off its hinges. At the same time, another uniform and I went quietly through the rear door while Captain Ironie watched on, monitoring comms from the street.

As expected, no one was home.

Inside, the house smelled of mouldy bread, a quarter loaf of which sat open on his kitchen bench. A damn shame in a world like this, a quarter loaf being a week's worth of food and many a man's desire.

To say the space was sparsely filled would be an extraordinary understatement. The reality being that a house this size was wasted on Jiang. He only had the bare essentials, a small beige coloured two-seater couch, the approved and necessary surveillance equipment, a bed that was nothing more a mattress laid flush on the floor, a Global Electric television, a small desk and chair, and in the only bedroom that appeared to be used, a set of draws that were empty except for some clothes.

After a brief stroll through the other rooms, I returned to the lounge room, making a point of checking the fan, which was just as Milly described it. I wanted to understand why on earth it was there, if for no other reason than that it had kept me out of the house for forty minutes. After passing a pointless circle around it, all I could figure was that it had either been left on by accident, which itself would be strange given the direction it was pointed, or that it was exactly what I'd thought. A deterrent for curious police officers who didn't wish to knock. None of those theories made sense, though, so after several wasted minutes, I took some photos and moved along.

Completing the inspection was a short task for such a large group, with literally nothing to find. If Jiang still had Ms Hansley's letter, then he'd either taken it with him, or it had been taken in addition to him. Either way, there was no paper here, nor even so much as a home device to write upon, and a thorough search of the meagre furniture and storage space failed to turn up anything else.

In spite of that, I couldn't shake my curiosity as to why the back door had been left open. It seemed a real oddity here, and an unsolved oddity bothers me.

Perhaps Jiang had left in a hurry and simply not had time to close it. Then again, how long does that really take? Ten seconds, maybe.

I wondered if he had perhaps gone out to stash something in the backyard and been startled or disrupted in the process. Maybe he'd managed to leave something he could come back for later. But where? There wasn't a shed or any other manmade structure to be seen. Just green grass, itself a rarity in the concrete jungles of the Global city, sparse and poorly kept rose bushes absent any flowers and mostly overgrown by weeds, and the two large trees that stood at each corner like boxers before a fight.

I headed out to investigate my hunch. Starting on the right side of the yard, next to the house, and walked along the federation green fence line, which had somehow escaped repainting in the eradication phase of the Global takeover. I moved along at an investigative pace, meaning slow and considered, until I got to the right rear corner of the yard. There, at the base of the oak tree, between it and the fence, I saw large splashes of what looked like dried blood. Not enough to indicate that this was the location of a murder, but certainly enough to support some sort of violence or injury. The blood was dry and still quite bright, definitely having the appearance of a recent spill.

'Captain, are you available?' I asked via the radio.

'Yes Gary?' replied Izzy, dryly.

'You'd better come see this. I'm out back.' I said. 'Oh, and if the forensic team is done at Ease's place, we're going to need them here, too.'

Moments later, Ironie appeared around the corner of the house, striding across the lawn towards me and looking more annoyed than intrigued. 'What is it?' She asked.

'Looks like Jiang is on the run for some reason and doing his best to go dark.' I replied.

'What? How do you know that?' She spat, her irritation appearing to grow despite my proffered discovery.

Guiding her eyes down to the site of the blood, I stepped aside to allow her a closer inspection.

'It's just some blood.' said Izzy, looking down where I was pointing. 'How do you know he wasn't chased and stabbed whilst trying to jump the fence?'

I had to think about my answer for a minute, holding my tongue while I gathered my thoughts. It's not that I don't trust Ironie, although I'm certainly not willing to share my connection with Milly yet, or the information he'd provided. It's just, it seems like someone is following me, and clearly other members of the service, and I don't know any of the who's or why's yet, so I'd rather keep my circle as small as possible for now.

'It's not just the blood.' I said after a pause. 'There's that too.' I added, pointing down at the base of the fence, where the u-shaped cap ran along the bottom. There were small gaps between the straight edge of the capping rail and the vertical folds of the colour-bond. In a gap close to the tree, and lightly adhered by blood, was a subdermal tracking chip that would once have sat neatly below the epidermis of Jiang's left forearm.

'Ah, I see.' said Ironie, opening the service issued scanner app on her device. She scanned the chip, which a moment later confirmed what I'd already known.

Jiang knew people wanted to "talk" to him, and he clearly did not want to be involved in that type of conversation. Unfortunately for him, the chip was only one of several ways of tracking and enforcing compliance. The idea of the Global World is that you are no longer an individual with freedom and choice, instead a part of the broader global machine that is assigned a part number, stamped, scanned, tracked, and monitored for performance. Jiang was now a malfunctioning component and I could only imagine the Department of Human Engineering already knew that.

The dermal chips are satellite trackable, scannable, readable, signal sensitive and most disconcertingly, moisture sensitive and DNA matched. Which means that once you remove your chip, and it dries out, which is usually only a matter of minutes, that action is automatically flagged to the DHE-E. If you're lucky, it flew out in an accident where your arm tore off and you died instantly.

The second E in DHE-E, by the way, is for Enforcement. E.g. no, it is not optional whether to have a chip and no, you cannot remove it, certainly not without us knowing.

In addition to the chip, there are many other forms of biometric tracking available to the authorities, with your entire body, face, eyes, height, gait, tattoos, piercings, any injuries, skin colour, hair colour, and bone structure all recorded and monitored in the DHE system.

If Jiang hasn't already been taken or killed by "DHE-E", then I can only think that he has acquired a dissolution suit and found somewhere underground to hide. He couldn't have got far, mind you. There are high-powered satellite cameras just about everywhere and sensors on nearly every human-made surface, so he would only have had a few minutes grace from his chip removal before his transgression was flagged on the system.

What I really need now is speak to Milly, openly, and see if he can track Jiang's movement's from the moment he de-chipped. Trouble is, I can't do it here. Not with Isabelle, who had incidentally stepped away a couple of paces to call in the forensic team, before herself receiving a call from someone who, by the tone of her responses, obviously outranked her. She was just too close for comfort.

As soon as she was done with her call, I made my move.

'Captain, I think it's time we consolidate our knowledge, map out what we know, link what we can link, and separate the rest. That way, we can put a plan together and start to gain some traction on this thing. I fear if we don't do something soon, it'll be too late.'

'I agree.' She replied, much to my surprise. 'I've just been told in no uncertain terms that I will not be partnering with you on the ground. So, I'll let you pick a uniform to partner with until Detective Wilson is back on her feet.'

'Okay… no problem.' I said, feeling both a huge sense of relief and a fresh sense of concern.

'I'll be keeping a close eye on you, though. And so we're clear,' she continued. 'I will be a part of putting together the action plan on this. It's going to be my TOP priority. In fact, when I get back to the station, I'm going to put some additional resources on the case to help you along. Yesterday this was supposed to be open and shut … now it's just… open.'

'If you don't mind, Captain, I'd like to get moving right now. I'd also like to swing by the hospital to see if Sharon's awake. I'm hoping she can give us a rundown on what took place at Adam's. Then I'll meet you back at the office?'

'Fine.' said Ironie, now patently aware that I was quite happy to be ditching her. 'But you will take a uniform with you to the hospital.'

'Oh, and Gary. Whoever you take, they will operate the E…'

Chapter 17

The parallel Ironie

My visit to Sharon wasn't as fruitful as I had hoped. While not in a coma like Ease was, her injuries were significant, the substantial swelling around her face and neck constricting her breathing and forcing her left eye closed. A nurse, who'd been leaving as I tried to enter the room, informed me that whilst stable, and likely to recover, she was in no fit state to talk. On powerful medications, and much in need of rest, the best thing I could do for my friend was just to let her be.

Left standing hopelessly in the doorway, I couldn't help wondering about the scenario before me. With every step forward, someone seemed to knock us back. At each and every turn, stood a barrier to our progress, and now here I stand, not lonely, but alone, being dragged along in the wake of a turbulent series of crimes, with a mounting body count and a dwindling group of friends.

What was it about this case, about OGT, about these letters, that inspired such strong reactions? What was so damn dangerous that people had to die to stop it, or so important of a secret that the world could never know?

As I pondered these concepts, it struck me that with all the violence and murder that had taken place so far, all of it appeared to have been committed for the sole purpose of silencing the threat. And here I stood in the doorway of just such a threat. One they had failed to silence. The reality being that Ease, and possibly Shaz, might know something, or even a lot of things, the killers don't want them to know.

Something else niggled at me, too. It was vague at first, on the peripheral of my mind. An image, or the outline of an image I felt I'd seen before. Then I realised that what I'd felt was déjà vu, except not real déjà vu. It was the memory of an event I'd observed without ever experiencing, which my brain soon restored to its original form. I'd watched it so many times, it felt like it was real. A failed attempt on man's life leaves him on life support in hospital, but still alive. Still a threat. Still a target. And here I stand just outside the unguarded room, while our enemies mobilise their forces to finish the job. Michael Corleone got it done with a shaky baker and balls of steel, while I have the entire police service to help me.

Immediately I placed a call to Chief Brandy Blindspot suggesting she get around the clock physical surveillance at Ease and Sharon's rooms, with support from flagged electronic monitoring to prevent another attack.

Thankfully, the chief agreed, an unusual occurrence for me, although not as impressive as the fact that she'd actually understood my Godfather reference, the movie not being considered a favourite in the new and progressive world. When I had mentioned it to the twenty-three year old Constable Gopher who'd reluctantly accompanied me from Jiang's place, I was met with nothing but blank indifference.

Once I explained the scenario to him and found suitably uncomfortable chairs to sit on, we took our posts outside their rooms to carry out our watch.

It was a long time since I'd had guard duty. I hadn't done it in this uniform, technology being the more trusted guardian of the Global World. When I had done it, I'd been in the Army guarding bases or infrastructure more so than people. Now, sitting in the bright white hallway, antennae's protruding through ceiling tiles, domed Wi-Fi access points hanging evenly spaced along the hall, surrounded by alarms, medical emergency lights and security/surveillance cameras, I couldn't help feeling like I was either in the most dangerous, or the safest, place in the world.

Indeed, the ever present smell of human decay covered up by regular chemical cleaning, made me lean toward the former. Despite the technology and automation now used in hospitals, or perhaps even because of it, they feel more clinical and uninviting than ever.

Thankfully for us, the hospital is only four blocks from the station, so the constable and I were released from our guard duties quickly, allowing me to head straight back to the station and get cracking on the case.

When I entered the building fifteen minutes later, there was a rare level of recognition clear on the faces of the other officers that something extra was going on right now. I wondered what Captain Ironie had told everyone that had created such a buzz of tension you could feel in the air.

I know back in the old days, police were particularly belligerent when it came to dealing with an intentional and violent attack on one of their own. In this case, there were two officers who had been attacked, one of them in their own home, and I wondered how a New Think Police Service would react. It's something that hadn't happened in my time here.

You can easily go too far, be too angry, and in an instant go from the attacked to the attacker, losing public sympathy in the process. Of course, in this world, they could just as easily not react at all, believing that retaliation is only justified when the attacked party can be easily shown to be a minority or formerly outcast societal group.

The Police Service, already strongly disliked, are also seen as being representative of a more privileged part of society and therefore garner little vengeful support from within, let alone the broader Global community.

Once I'd made my way upstairs, I saw Captain Ironie and some uniforms under her instruction, putting up hastily made electro signs showing a photo of a bruised and bloodied Sgt Ease, the title "Operation Ease" displayed prominently underneath with a by-line reading 'Mandatory Gathering - 15:00 in the Hydrogen Room'.

15:00 was only thirty minutes from now, so it seemed that Captain Ironie had indeed moved fast in putting together a plan for revenge. Observing the scant detail gleaned from the posters, I couldn't help wondering what that meant for the broader case and how she intended to run this operation without losing sight of the other crimes. After all, the attacks on police officers are only the latest in a series of violent events.

It was also apparent from the name of the operation that because Sharon is not one of "them" per se, the police response was not going to have quite the same zeal about getting back at the attackers for the act of violence against her.

Having said that, and to be fair, I was pleasantly surprised to see that the pretence of wagon circling was taking place at all. Even if it did lack a fullness of effort.

I approached Ironie to see if she could fill me in on the evolving plans she'd been putting together since we'd parted. 'Captain, I'm wondering what this Operation Ease is all about?' I asked, rather bluntly.

'It's clear, isn't it!' said Ironie, who appeared much angrier now than when I had left her at Jiang's. 'We're going to find these bastards with the full focus of the entire Mid-Town division of the Global Police Service. I've spoken to the chief and have her full support for the operation. We've already sent officers over to the hospital to keep an eye on Ease, in case he knows too much or some such thing, and they come after him again...'

'Yes.' I said, cutting her off mid-sentence. 'I'm well aware of the officers at the hospital. It was me that called the chief and asked them to be sent. I was worried about a Don Corleone situation.'

'Oh, don't be ridiculous!' said Ironie, her tone full of vinegar. 'I've had about enough of your stupid input today. We're trying to save lives and right wrongs here.'

'Right, of course.' I said calmly, but feeling confused at the sudden rise in misdirected anger.

Ironie and I stood outside the glass panelled Hydrogen meeting room, and soon to be Operation Ease headquarters, so named for the supposedly earth saving green energy alternative. A nod, of course, to the moral good of the Global World that uses this gas as a fuel in place of solidified, liquified or gaseous forms of carbon-based fuels. I wondered whether this task force, like the room's namesake, would take just as much energy to create as it was able to expend, thus rendering it of net zero benefit in producing an outcome. Only time would tell.

'So, will I be required at this operational meeting, or shall I continue the investigation of Ms Hansley's murder, Mr Chen's murder, and the attack on Detective Sharon Wilson by myself?' I asked, now raising my own level of anger to irritated, not yet ready to meet Ironie's. 'I noticed that despite having most likely saved Sgt Ease's life at the risk of her own, Sharon's name is conspicuously absent from your poster. Oh, and the name of the operation too…'

From behind Isabelle, where they'd been hanging the last of the Operation Ease posters on the windows of the meeting room, two probationary uniforms who'd overheard my comment, set about making themselves scarce. I could actually smell the warm sweat of their fear on the air as they passed by with uncommon urgency.

Returning my focus to Ironie, I saw from her face that my comments had hit home. There was an internal tug-o-war going on in her head as to whether an Old Thinker like Sharon actually deserved to have support for the righting of wrongs done to her. She suffered too. She is also an officer, a citizen of the world, and a human of value. No matter her social status, heritage, or personal beliefs, she deserves the same support as anyone else. Except, she's not one of them. She's not committed to the cause like they are, and well… that means she's… not one of them…

As I waited for a response to boil out of Ironie's now bright red face, I began growing ever more furious that she would even ask herself these questions. The ultimate one, being something that would never need be asked in the old days, 'Does this person meet the popular perception sympathy test?'…

After a lengthy pause during which the captain and I both attempted to gather ourselves, she responded.

'Sgt Ease, is in a coma!' She said with forced control. 'It's not that I don't care about Detective Wilson, but Sgt Ease was truly targeted. Sharon was just unlucky to turn up whilst it was happening.'

'Mmm, well, you could look at that another way.' I replied. 'Sgt Ease was bloody lucky that Sharon turned up at all…'

I'd been standing hands on hips as I said this, my attention fully focussed on Ironie, in what was an admittedly aggressive looking stance. It wasn't, however, an image I'd been consciously fostering, instead an unintended symptom of my building frustration. Still, in this world, perception is just about everything and the optics weren't good for me. It made sense then, rather than lose the hard fought moral height I'd gained, that I make the unilateral decision to end our interaction and give us both some space. I had started it knowing it wouldn't resolve in my favour anyhow, and with shots fired across each other's bow, that would have to be enough for now. Besides, I know very well I'm expected at that meeting, and before it starts, I need to do a little battle prep in order to overcome the fact that I'll be significantly outnumbered when it does.

The way I figure it, if the best form of defence is offence, and if I'm not mistaken, the best form of offence is also offence, then I'd best conduct as much offensive research as I can in order to go in there as the best-informed person in the room. Or at least the most offensive. It still might not be enough, but it's the only way I'll be able to steer the greater numbers of the New Think army away from some sort of crusade of stupidity. When they get in this mood, they're likely to take up pitch forks and march the streets hunting witches.

It happens a bit these days, their mind goes missing while some form of global psychosis takes over, making them do brutal, barbaric and disproportionate things to their fellow man, and all in the name of enlightened and progressive thinking.

To be fair, it's been like this since the start. Not that their leaders would ever admit it, nor the followers concede, that all they've ever done is follow, without really knowing who, or why.

Throughout history, the gullible populists have been prone to histrionic overreaction as opposed to critical, considered, and logical thought. Their modern brethren simply found the right conduit (*social media*) to connect to one another and with unquenchable appetites for fear and revenge, they followed their master's instructions and delivered them complete control of the world.

New Think people were unbearable to begin with, ignorant of what was really happening to them and what was being taken away from us all. Completely unconscious of the fact that in any transaction or transfer of power, that something must be lost in order for something to be gained. Money for service or product. Freedom for servitude, and the utopian greater good.

I've sat many a day in silent disbelief, watching these people cheering on their oppressors as the clamps tightened around them, until they were so tight all they could do was hum… And, hum they did, whatever tune the master's desired to hear… What's more incredible is that they seem happy in this endless sufferance.

I could forgive the young ones. If you're born in a prison and live in a prison with only other prisoners and prison guards to talk too, how would you know there was any other way to live. But those that were born free and willingly walked through the gates and into a cell, sat down and held their hands up waiting for the chains…those people, I despise.

After my confrontation with Ironie, I used the rest of the thirty minutes between entering the building and the start of Operation Ease, to do the most productive thing I could.

I read the remaining two letters currently in our possession. They were certainly the most valuable pieces of information we had right now, and in my reckoning were the reason for the attack on Ease and Shaz, and most likely the others, too. I figure someone either already knew what was in the letters and wanted them gone, or didn't know, and wanted to, assuming Sgt Ease to be the path of least resistance.

There are three main probabilities that come to mind, as to the identity of the culprits;

1) OGT, are behind this all on their own, having hired some professional bad guys for the dirty work in an effort to keep a lid on whatever secret they think Katie Hansley told or was going to tell, which they didn't want getting out.

2) The Guides are behind this, because of some sinister Global control mechanism going into the program, of which they don't want the world becoming consciously aware. The flip side being that the Guides have been doing precisely this type of thing for years, which begs the question why they wouldn't just send one of their many secretive agencies over to quietly shut Katie down. That type of thing has been going on all throughout history, so you'd think they'd be good at it by now.

Or, worst of all, **(3)** "They" are behind this, whoever "they" are, and lord only knows what the hell they're protecting or what it is "they" want. Absurd as it may sound, I know damn well there is a "they". I just don't know if they're New Think, Old Think, or something different all together. They could be trying to protect something, destroy something, or find something out. The only thing I'm certain of, is that whatever option it is, the answer is in the missing letter….

Out of time now, and as well-equipped as I can be, I head to the Hydrogen room prepared for anything. There was already quite a crowd in there by the time I arrived. An impressive feat, seen as the room can fit about sixty people, designated as it was, to be the main marshalling and kick off point for just these types of operations.

Looking around, I could safely say I knew most of its occupants, including those who weren't actually cops. Besides the sizeable pool of officers, there were several service-friendly journo's, the Station's psychologist, a man that looked suspiciously governmental, and one of our resident profiler's along with a few others I didn't know.

The room was laid out with five rows of chairs, six in each row, facing a lectern and interactive mood screen set up at the front. Along the window panelled side walls, on either side, were another ten chairs and standing room at the rear.

With all the bodies crammed in here, the room itself was actually quite warm, which made a welcome change from the rest of the building and the cold city streets outside. The nervous tension was evident, mind you, with no comfortable conversations, or even angry assertions of revenge, just an eyes down wait and see how bad it gets, type of vibe.

The meeting started with Captain Ironie behind the lectern, doing her level best to loosen the crowd and engage the moral sentiment of her like-minded believers. To me, she seemed like a born again preacher looking to whip her congregation into a vibrating frenzy, leaving their minds open ready to hear the word of God and their purses open ready to give, give, give…

With my knowledge of the case, and me being the only lead detective still standing, you might've assumed that I, too, would be invited up to speak. Perhaps at a point, shortly after the operation was outlined and the basic framework put in place. My job would be to inform the taskforce about the details of the case so far and the progress made to date… You may not, however, be surprised to find that I wasn't. Nor, in fact, was I invited to talk at all.

Needless to say, once you consider the content of the plan that was then jointly delivered by Captain Ironie and Detective Damwell, my being overlooked doesn't seem so much odd, as absolutely necessary.

Ironie began by opining that this was not just any old crime but a clear-cut case of Old on New. No doubt part of an anti-Globalist terror attack, which may not yet be over. She continued by stating that all current victims including OGT as an organisation, absent Detective Wilson, were considered to be upstanding Global citizens, under violent and targeted attack for their beliefs and heroic actions in protecting the moral standards and intellectual integrity of the Global world. The perpetrator, she concluded, was likely to be an as yet unidentified Old Think extremist group who got wind of the program OGT was working on, aimed at tightening restrictions on-line, and decided to act.

Although unspecified by word, it was clear Ironie believed Sgt Ease had become a target for the same reason I did. That being, his apparent leak of information to the News Media, which somehow drew attention to him, directly. That this would have required someone within the Police Service or the media organisation themselves to tip off the supposed terrorists was something left unsaid.

Sharon's inclusion in the story was limited to the theory that she just happened to be in the way at the time of the attack. Heretofore considered an unfortunate yet necessary casualty of the like-minded terrorist group, having probably only been harmed in an effort to cover their tracks.

Now, it must be said, I'm not often shocked these days. There's too much water under that particular bridge. Nevertheless, when Ironie doubled down by further casting doubt on Sharon's involvement, I found myself gasping for breath as if all the air had been sucked out of the room. Having downplayed her nasty injuries, near death experience, and heroic actions, Ironie went on to say how unusual it was that she, Sharon, would be at Sgt Ease's apartment to begin with and that it had not yet been ruled out that Sharon could be working with the terrorists to perpetrate these crimes.

I was reeling now, dumbfounded, as I watched the room full of uniforms, fellow detectives, and paid New Think influencers, who had no "official" connection to the Police Service whatsoever, swallow every nugget of this sheep shit as if it was hardened fact, nodding away intently.

When Ironie finished, Damwell took the podium like the tagged in teammate of an evil wrestling duo, while I physically, and quite literally, tried to hold my tongue in an effort not to shout out "You know full fucking well why she was there!"

Seated behind me, Detective Thise, who having no doubt noticed my spasmodic convulsions of rage, tapped me on the shoulder as her partner took the stand.

'Why aren't you up there providing some information and direction on this?' She queried.

'I wasn't asked.' I said stiffly, without ever turning around.

Having apparently received the answer she had already expected, Empher then sat back to listen as her partner extolled the virtues of carrying out this investigation on a foundation of New Think principles. Which, basically means that whatever assumption they make about who might have committed such a crime was probably right and therefore should be pursued at the expense of any consideration for alternate hypothesises or contradictory evidence.

As far as Damwell was concerned, not knowing any of the facts was no great deterrence to going full steam ahead for an outcome. He knew the parties that were Global aligned and therefore innocent, so it was simply a matter of finding someone that wasn't, arresting them, and then building a case around how and why they did it.

To be fair, Damwell intended to begin with a reasonably sound method. Going back to OGT and ascertaining from whom they'd had threats, altercations, or difficulties, either in a general sense or specifically in relation to the current technology they were working on.

I would've almost supported this, had he not then explicitly told the assembled party to ignore any information that related to difficulties with fellow New Thinkers, as they didn't have time for this type of dead-end distraction. As he said this, he actually slipped his thumbs inside his belt, tugging it forward slightly and rocking his hips along with it, while eyeballing the crowd as some sort of belligerent affirmation of his words. The message here was so overt I had to rub my eyes to confirm I hadn't begun to edit my own visual commentary onto reality. Frighteningly, I hadn't, although confirmed observation made me rather wish I had.

Having reached his crescendo, Damwell was about to send his minions out to commence Operation Easy Target (*my re-interpretation, not an official name change*), when he made the mistake of taking a moment to clear his throat. I snatched the momentary pause as just the uninvited opportunity I needed to add some balance to proceedings.

Leaping to my feet and striding confidently to the lectern, I started my speech with a loud command. 'Right! Just a couple of things before we wrap up.' I said, while the room turned to face me, stiffened at the shock of my entering the fray. Damwell, likely now in need of neck surgery due to the speed of his head snapping round, looked slightly less stunned than Ironie, whose eyes could have swallowed the earth, whole…

Attempting a small amount of diplomacy, I asked only that any information considered to be a "dead end distraction" be recorded and passed to me, as I would be running a parallel investigation to follow up on existing leads and ensuring that every thread was run down and accounted for.

I explained to the stunned crowd, that I would be doing this to ensure that rigorous process was followed, and no stone left unturned (*not a popular saying in this world, where it is believed that all stones should probably be left unturned, lest their disturbance release some hidden carbon*).

I then set about explaining my alternate take on the investigation, outlining concerns taken from our initial interviews with the members of OGT, the key details of the state in which we'd found Sgt Ease, including with possibly undue emphasis, that all fire escape doors, apartment doors, and windows, had been glued shut and the gas turned on with Sharon still inside the apartment and significantly injured. The room clearly responded with influencers feverishly thumbing their device screens, especially after hearing that only her last ditch effort to throw her electro through the window had likely saved them both.

I explained about Chen's murder and its as yet unknown connection to Katies, the events at Jiang's place (*excluding my consultation with Milford*), and finally and most emphatically, the critical importance of finding the missing letter.

'Oh,' I said, 'and Constable Clubman, you will be seconded to me to help run the parallel investigation until such time as Sharon is fit to return.'

Finished, I looked over at Clubman, flashing a brief smile, before starting back to my seat. He caught my look with a small nod of recognition and attempted to stifle a smirk, quickly lowering his head to hide his face.

As I walked, an uncomfortable sort of silence fell over the crowd. People, having expected to be given their marching orders before I interjected myself, weren't sure what to do now, faced with more than one opinion to consider and a second investigation to track. This was not the New Think way.

Captain Ironie stepped up to fill the void, righteous anger pouring off her as she strode forward to re-take the lectern, like an allied soldier taking Hill 60, for, they prayed, the final time.

'Well, we've heard about enough from you, Detective Johnson! We don't live in your world anymore. What we need to do now is look at this from a "real world" perspective. There is only one "right way" to solve this crime and Detective Damwell will be directing this taskforce to stay on that path. In all likelihood, this is just as Ease had said from the start. An Old Thinker striking out at the very heart of New Think and taking down anyone that stands in their way. Which means, we need to target any and all known Old Think organisations and rat these bastards out before they strike again.'

'I want people in those OGT offices 24/7, protecting the good work they do and the good people that do it. It's time to pull together and put an end to this madness. Detective Damwell and Thise will be the leads. Everybody else will follow their instructions and that includes you! Detective Johnson.'

Not yet willing to back down from this battle and still angry at the appalling portrayal of Sharon's involvement, I decided to fire back at risk of being stood down or removed from the case all together.

'Captain, when you say Old Think organisations, are you talking about targeting people you genuinely believe are capable of committing these crimes? Or just anybody who still believes in an alternate way of living?'

Any warmth and light that had survived round one of the battle seemed to disappear from the room with this question. I was directly challenging the orthodoxy, which simply isn't done. NT's love a byte battle, not a face-to-face confrontation with an open exchange of ideas. Even if they have a number advantage, they prefer to hold their battles on social media with the potential to have thousands of kilometres between them and their direct combatant. Not to mention the added advantage of a masked group mentality. Hiding behind screen names and tagging in popular idealists to join the fight on their behalf is New Think 1.01.

It's not as easy to do in person, so in the face of direct confrontation, particularly when they can't win an argument on the quality of their contribution, New Thinkers take the victims way out. By shifting to a position of the bullied or intimidated, they prime themselves for the most powerful form of support… sympathy for the wronged…

'How dare you try to intimidate me with your insane questions!' She shouted. 'You're nothing but a denier. What evidence do you have that these crimes could be anything other than what I say?'

'Well, for starters, outside of you and Sergeant Ease, there's been no suggestion or evidence to support the idea that anybody outside of OGT itself is involved in these crimes. Your opinion that they must have been committed by evil Old Thinkers is based on nothing more than ideological hatred of an alternate view, completely devoid of any facts relevant to the case.'

'I will not be bullied and discriminated against by the likes of you! Detective Johnson. Your refusal to accept what we all know to be true, is poison to this case and the excellent officers of this station!'

'Captain, asking a question or presenting an opinion is not the same thing as discrimination, intimidation, or bullying, and the ability to do so must not only be allowed but protected. Especially in a Police Service where detectives are seeking to solve a crime.' I replied. 'It's incredible that you can't see the blatant, inbuilt hypocrisy of the morals you hide behind. This, "We want freedom and equality for all… except you… because we find you offensive and your opinion may make people think that their opinion isn't valid… when really, it's your opinion that isn't valid. So basically, we want to protect our opinion… and ban yours…" has to stop! Come on, Captain. Move past all that crap. We're trying to solve real, violent crimes here. Crimes that are quite possibly part of something much bigger and we may not have seen the last of it yet. So, until we find that last letter or recover the surveillance footage of the murders and identify the culprits, then we must pursue all possible options and not rule them out simply based on the inflexibility of popular ideological principles.'

Captain Ironie, committed to her path now, actually started to cry at my retort, causing me to roll my eyes so hard it hurt. If seen, my action would have caused me to slip from my higher ground in the eyes of the crowd, who by this point, were mostly navel gazing, and cowardly trying to avoid the scene playing out in front of them.

'How can someone from your background, with your privilege, say these things and act this way, knowing the pain it can cause?...' said a teary Ironie. 'Have some shame… Have some guilt!' she cried dramatically.

One of the underpinnings of New Think's success, was to train people to see themselves as bad and therefore to think about all that they have done, had, or grown up with as drivers for, or supportive of, the bad person that they are, and the bad that they have inherently done to the world and the people around them. This guilt and shame is to hang around your neck like a weight and be overlaid on every interaction you have. A concept that led to a collective view that you didn't have to be wrong about the subject, to be a resounding loser of the argument. In fact, the further from being correct you are, and the more your opponent proved it, the more sympathy you garnered for your treatment. Therefore, in the court of popular opinion (*the only one that matters in a Global world where they control your opinion and ability to present it*) being right has no material benefit, and if you also happen to be or are in any way perceived to be of an historically privileged background, then your best bet is to avoid the interaction all together and accept the collective position.

Unusually, off the back of this current interaction, Detective Damwell gave me something of a pass, interjecting himself with a statement as the newly promoted lead detective.

'We have our strategy sorted, Detective Johnson, and it is the right way to go about this. If you want to run a parallel investigation and waste time looking at innocent citizens, then at least you'll be out of our way whilst we seek to solve these crimes. Captain, we can do without him.' said Damwell, as keen as anyone to relieve the growing tension in the room.

Regathering herself at the conciliatory support of Damwell, Captain Ironie who had not yet managed to contort her face into steeled indifference, and who may also have been somewhat offended at what in the new and old worlds could easily be perceived as me receiving a pass from a fellow member of the boy's club, replied through the strain of her emotion.

'Yes, well, I will expect regular updates from you, Gary, And if I deem your investigation a waste of time, then I will terminate it at my discretion.'

Knowing this was as good a result as I could possibly expect, I attempted to be gracious in chastised victory. 'Of course, Captain.' I said. 'Constable Clubman and I have some strategy work to do first, but I'll be sure to update you when we're ready to make our move.'

The room emptied quickly, everybody eager to get away from the intensity of what had occurred and return to the comfort of their individual tasks. I moved quickly too, heading back to my desk to get cracking on a plan. It wasn't just the case I had to solve, now. There was a whole new pack of loons that'd just been unleashed and I needed to prevent them from trashing the place and stringing up the natives.

Constable Clubman appeared soon after I'd settled, walking casually at the back of the pack when exiting the room and waiting for the nattering crowd to disperse before officially joining my team. To be honest, I think he was genuinely impressed at what was realistically a win for me and possibly for the prospects of actually solving the case.

'Wow, I think you really got to some people in there.' he said. 'Not about Old Think, but certainly about conducting a thorough investigation. That could really work for us. They're off to start asking questions at OGT, so if there's anything OGT are yet to tell us, a team that big is sure to turn it up. Even if they don't know what they've got. And, for what it's worth, Detective Damwell might be an arrogant, ignorant bull in a China shop, but he hates being lied to more than anything, and he really hates being wrong. So, if he has to rake some muck to get the information he needs, well, let's just say he's always got a spare rake in the boot.'

'Yeah, I suppose I'd have to agree.' I said. 'Plus, I'm always happy for others to assist our investigation whilst attempting to complete their own. Let me know if you hear any whispers from your friends on the task force. Oh, and I'm sorry for dragging you through the mud in there. It's just that I can't do it alone. I need someone to help ensure this is properly investigated and not just a witch hunt.'

'No problem.' said Clubman. 'And I want you to know I'm on board, too. I agree with you. We can't just make people guilty by decree. Evidence, not popular opinion, should lead us to the answer.'

With that, Clubman pulled a chair over from the desk behind us and sat his wiry 6ft frame upon it. At forty-seven years of age, and still a constable, Cliff could easily be labelled an underachiever. The reality, however, is that he, like Sharon and I, had had a past career. Cliff had been a carpenter from the time he left school right through to the time the arse fell out of the industry, and he was forced to close his business. Carpentry, you see, while still a valuable qual, is, like many other trades, not what it used to be. Not with capped fees limiting the value for effort of a skilled tradesman, and the main expectation of your one solitary client being uniformity and efficiency. Figuring that if you have to do the same thing as everyone else, you should at least get to wear a uniform, he left to become a copper.

Cliff's parents had originally come from Nagpur, in what was previously India, which was precisely where he got his smooth brown skin, jet black hair and hazel-green eyes. I asked him once if he'd had mixed parents and whether that was why he looked so different from the many southern Indian's I'd grown up with in Australia. His answer was this, *"the northerners are light-skinned, the southerners are dark-skinned, and Nagpur is in the middle..."*

With our working relationship established, Clubman and I went over the case to strategise our plan of attack. We laid out all the key players, the circumstances of the crimes and the progression of violence spreading outwards from OGT. From there, we determined the three elements that stood out as being at the top of our "must investigate" list.

1) It's absolutely imperative we find the last letter written by Katie Hansley. This seems to have been the catalyst for the subsequent violence that followed her murder, and I, for one, believe undoubtedly that it's the key to solving these crimes. Finding it may not be easy, as we discovered earlier today, because to find it, we'll also need to find Jiang, who seems to be doing a pretty good job of not being found in a world where it's nearly impossible to hide. I just hope that he's still alive when we do.

2) We need to confirm with the journalist that wrote this morning's article, where their information came from and what else they know. My guess is that Ease probably took some sort of favour for providing the information and, in doing so, put himself on the hook. The other question then, is why hasn't anything happened to the reporter who wrote the article? Hardly seems like it would have been New Think approved. It was, after all, a little too open to undefined interpretation for their liking. Then again, we haven't spoken to the reporter yet, so who am I to say they haven't been harmed.

3) Last, and probably most importantly. We need to find out what this OGT program is all about, and why it appears to have scared Katie Hansley so much she started taking actions that prompted someone to go on a killing spree in order to keep it a secret.

'Well, I think our best bet is to let Damwell's team take care of number 3, for now.' said Clubman. 'They may not be specifically looking at that, but a quick call to some friends in his team should get us a subtle question or two in the mix. '

'Excellent.' I said. 'I've got a friend of my own who might be able to help us with number 1. Once he has all the details we have, I'm sure he can coordinate his resources to find our man. That's if he hasn't done so already. As for the reporter, that's for you and me to chase down. I'll go and give the captain a version of our plan, if you can head down to the E-Lot and fix us a ride. I'm not too keen on travelling via global transport at the moment. There's still too much we don't yet know.'

After a brief meeting with Captain Ironie, who at the time was herself debriefing Chief Blindspot about the goings on in the Operation Ease meeting, I headed down to meet Clubman.

By the look on Blindspot's face, Ironie was clearly not painting an objective picture of my input. Not that the chief actually said anything to me, though she certainly didn't look impressed.

The truth is, I'm not too worried about Ironie's portrayal of me, or the risk that may pose to my job. As a quirk of New Think's own policies, I fill a necessary quota. See, whilst they don't want people like me around, they can't actively wipe us out, or else they'd be openly conducting the very type of action they claim to be trying to eradicate. Therefore, whilst ever I'm alive, willing, and capable of performing my role, then I'm entitled to be here, whether they like what I say or not.

Of course, that doesn't mean it's a comfortable position to be in. Knowing that before you even say anything, most people will think your contribution is wrong, simply because it's you that's saying it, isn't fun for anyone. In fact, it's one of the incredible hypocrisies of the Globalist mindset. In order to create a more comfortable and inclusive world for the mistreated outcasts of the past, they skipped genuine equality and went straight to reverse inequality. Hardly a solution for the greater good. Or at least not the greater in number. It is, mind you, not a subject on which I should dwell as I have more important things to do and dwelling on interpersonal issues is their thing, not mine.

After spotting my latest partner already seated in the company E, I made my way across the E-lot, jumping in beside him and strapping in ready for departure. Clubman, who had been patiently awaiting my arrival, looked across at me from the controller's seat, dipping his head to eyeball me over the top of his sunglasses.

'No trouble upstairs then?' he asked somewhat facetiously.

'Let's just say the chief was not looking impressed with my initial contribution to Operation Ease.' I replied. 'If, however, we happen to solve the case, I'm sure it'll be mostly forgiven. While we're on that subject, have you spoken to your friends about OGT?'

'I have.' said Clubman. 'They're on board and agreed to share whatever they find.'

'Whatever they find, hey? Well, they couldn't do worse than we did.'

Between leaving Ironie's office and getting down to the E, I found some time of my own and made a call to Milford. In the interest of speed, we skipped pleasantries and cut straight to the core of what I knew about Jiang following our earlier search of his house. As I suspected, Milly already had a member of his team trying to piece together Jiang's movements from the time he obtained the letter to the time he removed his chip. They hadn't made much progress yet and remained bemused as to why Jiang's actions had not set off the appropriate alarms in the surveillance monitoring centres.

Technology is far from perfect, so it could simply be good luck on Jiang's part. Or, maybe whoever circumvented the surveillance at OGT had also blocked the automated response, giving them a head start on finding him. If they did, we may never see that letter.

I filled Milly in on Operation Ease and asked if he could keep tabs on their investigation by any means possible. A request to which he agreed. I figured the more sets of eyes on this, the better. Even if it does mean other organisations know what I know, and possibly before I ever know it. After all, it's not like that would change the status quo.

'Have you read the article we're going to speak to this reporter about?' I asked, channelling the very conversation that Sharon had with me this morning.

'I haven't bothered reading a mainstream newspaper article in years.' said Clubman. 'What's the point, there's no news in there. Every article just aligns with whatever they want you to believe, anyway. And we already know what that is.'

'They don't sound like the words of a proud wrong righter. I thought you were a card-carrying member of the club these days?'

'Let's just say their hold over me is a little tenuous. It ebbs and flows.'

Before we left, I'd picked up a News-Pad sitting trustingly unguarded on someone's desk. Now passing it to Clubman, I pointed out the article in question, giving him all the tools required to get him up to speed.

After programming our destination, Clubman read the paper whilst the E self-drove. Again leaving us entirely in the care of a centrally located guidance system and well outside my comfort zone. To distract myself, I looked out the window at the streets crawling by. The rain had returned outside, meaning that many of the Discredited or Non-Compliant's had moved off the streets and out of open park spaces, into the shelter of building fronts and under bridges. The cold and wet combined with the crushing social policy would kill large swathes of them today, much to the joy of our globalist leaders, who see their eradication as a benefit for the earth. The term "cleansing rain" is used with that sick double meaning these days, bringing to mind the brutal policies of fascist Germany. Not exactly the picture of a progressive utopia…

'This is awfully detailed.' said Clubman, having finished reading the story. 'Are the reporters quotes from the letters accurate?'

'They're more than just accurate. They are verbatim and in context. The article isn't too flattering from an OGT perspective either, detailing how one of their own was turning towards Old Think and using her words to prove it. You'd have to think the Guides wouldn't be happy about it coming out. So much so that the only reason I can see them allowing it to be published is as a threat to the Global world that the "dangers" of Old Think are ever present. A warning to the masses to toe the line, so to speak. Which itself isn't uncommon, except that ordinarily these types of warnings are staged, or zero consequence, not real and involving murder. The question is, did OGT know about the letters before they were published, or was the article the trigger for the violence that followed.'

Looking genuinely puzzled at the thought, Clubman spent several minutes silently re-reading the article, attempting to decipher its content and meaning before looking across at me again, now with slightly more concern. 'Do you really think these letters are the catalyst for all these deaths?' he asked.

'At this point I do.' I replied. 'I'm certain they're the reason for at least some of the violence. Having said that, I get your point. You'd think there'd have to be more to it than that. Something at OGT, something really damaging to New Think, or at least the latest program they've been working on. Of course, you never know with this lot. It could just be that they felt they were losing control. See, no matter how they try to change people's moral compass and guide us into believing the worst of everyone, based on their physical, ethnic or sexual status, which Ironically is retribution for having done that very thing to others, we are all just human beings at our core, and we don't want to be held down or controlled. So, eventually we decide not to be. I think that was the epiphany Katie Hansley had come to. She was either going to alert other people to the reason as why she changed her mind, or encourage them to join her in rebellion. Both things New Think doesn't want and certainly things that OGT wouldn't want to be associated with.'

'If that's true, then why allow the article to be published at all? Why not just hush it all up?' asked Cliff.

'Why, indeed…' I replied.

It was 4:03PM when we arrived at "The Global Leak", the name of both the building and the paper that published the article in question. After alighting the E, we entered through the electronic doors and into its empty, vacuous foyer. The building was a cookie cutter skyscraper, a facsimile of every other skyscraper you'd ever seen, all squared glass and concrete, with no design or architectural flair to speak of. It was also empty of human occupation, save for the two recent Non-Compliant's huddled outside the door, clinging tightly to their meagre possessions consisting of two blankets and a backpack. That they still have two blankets and a backpack being the telltale sign they'd only recently fallen afoul of the law. They can, however, rest assured, that representatives for the Global Credit Council will be around to remove those items as soon as the current "paid for" period of rent expires.

Both Cliff and I stood briefly in the middle of the foyer, surveying the cold surrounds. Despite what I knew about the almost entirely controlled media content, which leaves no room for freelanced or unbiased storylines, I couldn't help imagining the newsrooms of old these buildings once housed. Filled, as they were, with a warm, energetic buzz at the excitement of investigative journalists uncovering real stories, exposing lies, challenging government overreach and corruption, and generally keeping the public in the know.

Now, after a gap of several decades, here we stand, because against all odds someone within this institution appears to have managed just that.

We approached the electronic concierge, a 6ft tall by 4ft wide interactive screen, which, after displaying its Global message of the day, "*Carbon is Cancer*" introduced itself as 'Matt'. Matt, of course, knew both Cliff and I intimately via our chips and spoke to us like a friend… which I hate.

'Mmm, I don't like it either.' said Cliff, apparently sensing my thinly veiled contempt. 'Sometimes you wanna go where everybody knows your name… and sometimes you don't.'

I smiled at the Cheers reference, a sure sign he wasn't all New Think. Annoyingly, the E-Con also recognised the reference and even the context in which it was said before politely asking us whether we would like it to change its style.

'No!' I said. 'We just need access to the level of a TGL reporter named Bjourne I'llist.'

'Okay.' said Matt with an irritating level of happiness, 'Just let me confirm access. While you wait, why don't you ask me how life's treating me?'

'Christ! You ask!' I said to Cliff, 'I don't want to have a conversation with it.'

'Um, how's life treating you?' Asked Cliff reluctantly.

'Like it caught me in bed with its wife! Oh, LOL!' said Matt, the acronym appearing on the screen and giggling about in time with its laughter.

I tried not to laugh myself, caught between annoyance at another layer of the endless anthropomorphism of machines, and a stupid funny joke from Cheers. Evidently, "Matt" had chosen to change its style to match ours, despite my objection.

'There must be a streak of Old Think in whoever set that thing up.' said Cliff. 'You can't even find Cheers online anymore. I'm pretty sure it's been banned.'

Everything's been banned, I thought, but only for a moment before it was interrupted by Matt's swift return to tell us we'd already been approved to meet with Bjourne. Immediately, the lift doors opened, and Matt politely said goodbye.

'Keep it real.' said Cliff as we entered the lift.

'Don't say that!' I grunted as the doors closed. 'Bloody thing already thinks it's human.'

Moments later, the lightning fast lift came to a stop and our good friend Matt, who was clearly not aware of the timings associated with social graces, came over the speakers welcoming us to the 17th floor. 'Bjourne is 10 seconds away. Have a nice day, officers.'

'Great.' I said. 'Now Matt has the moral high ground.'

Alighting from the lift and looking around the office, I found it to be just as cold and clinical as the foyer below. We had exited into a black-tiled foyer which lead directly out to an open plan floor filled with small cubicles mostly occupied by what I assume were reporters, editors, or the ever-present Confirmers.

Confirmers, by the way, were a New Think creation, their role being to help control and direct trust in online information by ensuring you can only find the things they want you to find. Originally, they were called "fact checkers" except they had zero qualifications or authority to check facts or rule on the accuracy of stories. All they really did was perform the role of narrative censors who sought to discredit anything the Guides didn't want you to see.

Of course, these days there's no need for that type of action post publishing, even on social media. In their place, are an army of bots built to prevent you from writing or posting things they don't want you saying to begin with.

Professional media outlets, on the other hand, have a little more freedom to E-print or publish via their own systems (*or at least, the systems they chose from the few that New Think allows*), so to ensure they continue to colour between the lines, they're required to employ Confirmers. Confirmers in this context are basically moralists with oversight to direct publishable content. Editors now, being no more than a redundant spell checker, employed to oversee machines that do their job faster and with greater accuracy without the need of a bathroom or lunch break.

Worst of all, for the media outlets, the Confirmers don't even report to anyone within the company of their employ. They are paid and employed by the newspapers and TV stations at their cost, yet report directly to the Bureau of Unquestionable Literature, Language, Sharing, Hosting, Information & Technology, aka, BULLSHIT. Fitting, really, that the spread of information is controlled by the department of bullshit. It is all they spread after all, and the minds of the masses are well fertilised.

The office had a smell of freshly unwrapped plastic, perhaps emitted by the new devices or recently installed desks, or for some other reason I couldn't identify. What it lacked, however, was a vibe. There were no ringing phones, excited conversations, or the feelings of intense anxiety that come with the responsibility of handling raw information. It was more like the quiet alienated feeling you used to get when you entered one of those ultra-high-end retail stores, occupying some huge shopfront, while only sparsely filled with about three tiny objects, none of which you could afford. The message apparently being 'This is not for you'...

'Officers.' said Bjourne, who apparently identifies only as Bjourne, despite listing her last name on her credentials.

She approached from the right of the lift wells, dressed in a formfitting, knee length, black dress, and a woven black overcoat with a red floral pattern.

'Hi' I said. 'I'm Detective Johnson and this is Constable Clubman.'

'Oh, I didn't know you were allowed to carry those anymore.' said Bjourne, smiling and mimicking a single striking action with her hand.

'Right, well, we're here to talk about an article you published in this morning's edition, about some letters.'

'Yes, of course.' said Bjourne, straightening her jacket. 'Please, follow me.'

We set off after her, passing rows of quiet desks, where silent workers scrolled hand-held devices or stared blankly at desk based ones, ear pods filling every ear in sight. Arriving at her desk, I was surprised to find it not unlike my own. Alongside her personal bag stood a basic screen and roller chair. Next to the computer, an empty space stared back at me, where, although they don't exist anymore, I still felt a desk phone should sit. Especially on a journalist's desk. Bjourne placed her device, screen up, beside her keyboard projection, turning halfway towards us, staying half angled to her keyboard, apparently ready to take notes as if she were conducting an interview with us, rather than the other way around.

'So, Ms I'llist, I'll come straight to the point as time is a factor for us. We're conducting an investigation involving a series of crimes associated with the letters you wrote about in your article. We would like you to tell us how you came to find out about these letters and who told you of their contents?'

'Firstly.' said Bjourne, 'It's Bjourne, I don't identify with I'llist, and there's no Ms. Secondly, I'll need to know more about these crimes.'

'No. You won't.' I said bluntly. 'This is an active investigation and the details will not be discussed with a journalist.'

'Then why should I discuss my sources with you?' Asked Bjourne, flicking her head defiantly as if to adjust her hair, though the neatly styled and shoulder length black curls scarcely moved.

'Because we are police officers investigating serious crimes, and if you don't, you will be arrested for perverting the course of justice.'

'We used to have rights as a journalist's, you know. Protections.' said Bjourne.

'Yes, I know. I even believe in them, but they don't exist anymore. No doubt you're well aware of that, working here.' I said, gesturing to the room as evidence of what I meant. Looking around the cold, quiet floor, the point was well made. Nobody was chasing information, confirming details, or typing furiously to expose the truth. It was like a library without the books or studious referencing of factual information.

'So, how did you get this story past the Confirmers, with so much truth in it?'

'My Confirmer is the one that brought me the lead and suggested the article.' said Bjourne.

'Really. That's concerning.' I replied, my right leg unconsciously bouncing in time with the building nerves inside me. 'So, who's the lead?'

Bjourne looked at me quizzically, her head tilting to the side for emphasis. 'Well, in truth, I expected you must already know that. I assumed she was your boss, after all. A… Captain Ironie.' She said, checking the notes on her device.

I was dumbstruck by this. I'd been working with Ironie for years now, as a uniform or detective, and despite our differences, I'd always seen her as a committed doer of good. What really blew me away, was that she'd known damn well that Sharon and I were looking for the person who leaked the contents of these letters, specifically because we thought this particular action had probably led to the second wave of violence which had now born Operation Ease. A taskforce she set up after two of her own officers, my partner included, ended up in hospital.

While I reeled, Constable Clubman, who'd been silently watching proceedings since we'd arrived, and who looked nearly as rattled as I did, managed to pull himself together enough to ask a critical question.

'Do you have any proof of Captain Ironie's contact with you?' He asked.

'Well, she came up here herself, yesterday evening. I don't have evidence as such, although I'm sure you could always check her chip log. To be honest, when I got the request for you to come upstairs, I assumed you had more information for a follow-up story. It's all just a bit of fluff anyway, isn't it?' asked Bjourne. 'I mean, I sold it, coz that's my job, but we do these "stay the course", "colour between the lines" articles every couple of weeks. I just assumed that's what this was.'

'Do you often receive New Think reinforcement stories from police captains in person or other direct informants?' I asked, forcing myself to mentally return to the present.

'Well, no. Normally the stories are brought to me by either my Editor, Confirmer, or by directive of the Guides Alliance without me ever seeing the actual source.'

'Really? They just tell you to write some fear inducing fairytale without any pretence? And add a reward?' asked Clubman.

'Sometimes.' said Bjourne. 'Sometimes they send in a proxy to tell the story. It's a bit like a false flag operation, someone either stages an attempted defection and then brings us the story to warn the world, or they fabricate one. I don't have to actually authenticate or validate the story and its events, or even verify locations and names. My Confirmer's approval will lend credence to the story for me. Whether it's actually true is irrelevant, so long as it gets the right message across. And as for the reward, it's not like anyone was going to claim it.'

'New Think's message, you mean?' I asked.

'Yes, obviously.' She replied.

After a moment's pause to absorb the reality of hearing firsthand what I had always suspected to be true, a period during which the completely unaffected Bjourne casually stretched her back, I continued. 'Would it surprise you to hear that this story was not staged, fabricated, or even embellished?' I asked. 'As a point of fact, it was the absolute truth. Probably the only real story that's been published here in twenty years.'

'Really?!' Said Bjourne, raising her eyebrows. Well, that explains why someone had gone to all the trouble of writing seven letters just for a "stay the course, we're watching" story.

'Did you actually see the letters?' I asked.

'Yes. In fact, Captain Ironie gave me copies of all seven yesterday. Although, I should tell you, I don't have them anymore, if you were hoping to see them. Someone came to retrieve them this morning.'

'Didn't you think that was unusual?' asked Cliff.

'No.' replied Bjourne. 'Ordinarily, my Confirmer would destroy any evidence used as a basis for these stories. This time it was a couple of men who showed up saying they were from the Service and that they needed the letters back. Chain of evidence or some such thing.'

'Chain of evidence!' I almost shouted. 'Yes, well, I suppose, there's always that extra link that dangles off the side of the main chain. What time did they come?'

'Early.' said Bjourne. 'Bout 9am, I think. I'd only gotten to the office myself a few minutes prior.'

'Had you seen them before?' Asked Cliff.

'No.' replied Bjourne evenly, showing no trace of dishonesty or deception.

'Were they wearing uniforms?' I asked. 'Is there anything you can tell us about them?'

'Um, no actually. Not uniforms as such. They were both wearing casual style clothes, but not that casual, if you know what I mean. The kind of clothes that are meant to look casual except they really serve a purpose of their own.'

'Like a Special Forces soldier used to wear as a not-so-subtle urban camouflage?' I asked, getting suspicious that these people might be the "they" that had been following me, and that I might even know who they were.

'Yes, I suppose so.' said Bjourne. 'Greens and tans, slightly loose-fitting grey/green cotton shirts, tan coloured, sporty, hard-wearing sort of pants and rather solid looking sandy coloured boots.'

'Yeah, that sounds about right.' I said. Meanwhile, the image of muscly beard faced soldiers doing their best impression of civilians, while their shifty eyes searched the street for their mark, filled my head.

'So Bjourne, did you have any follow-up articles planned for these letters?' Asked Cliff, aware my mind had drifted.

'Not initially. Not until you got here. Why, do you have something for me, a development? Can I follow the case like we used to?'

'Not at the moment.' I said, 'Although, I fear there's a long way to go on this, so you may be able to help us later. Listen, if anybody comes to you with anymore letters like the ones you saw, I need you to let me know before you write any articles. Okay? These might very well be warnings, just not the type you're used to issuing, and writing anything else on the subject could put you in danger.'

'Of course.' said Bjourne, seeming to take us more seriously now and looking curiously at the business card I handed her. 'It's always good to have a relationship with the police.'

'Good.' I said. 'Oh, and if Captain Ironie comes to see you again, let me know about that, too.'

'Did she do something wrong?'

'I'm not sure yet. She certainly did something unusual and under the circumstances, that's more than enough to warrant suspicion.'

When we stood to leave, it was already 4:45 pm. Taking another scan of the office before we departed, I noticed several pairs of eyes whose owners had been diligently minding their own business when we entered, were now peaking above the blued corkboard parapets to watch the goings on. They followed us inquisitively right up until the lift doors closed and we disappeared downstairs.

As the lift descended, I did the adult thing and ignored Matt's un-offended computerised friendliness, again leaving Cliff to discuss our level of satisfaction during the visit. Only once we'd exited the building, jumping back into the relative privacy of the E, did I ask him his thoughts on the meeting.

'Well, it goes without saying I was surprised Captain Ironie was the one who provided the letters to the journalist.' he replied. 'I'm baffled, actually, as to why she would do that. I also found it strange that Bjourne hadn't picked up on the fact they were real. I mean, how often are police captains the source of public lies?...'

Here, I had to disagree with Cliff. I was stunned that Ironie was the one who gave letters from an active investigation to a journalist, too. On the other hand, I had no problem believing that a member of the news media couldn't tell truth from fiction. They hadn't told the truth in years, so they haven't the foggiest idea what it looks like. Hell, Bjourne virtually admitted that she's nothing more than a spin doctor whose job it is to stoke fear or guide populist opinion and anger at the whim of the Guides.

'Speaking of Captain Ironie, what's your take on her leaking the letters?' I asked. 'Why do you think she did it? Personally, I'm struggling to find a reason that suggests anything good.'

'I really don't know.' said Cliff. 'I can't see any tactical reason to do it for the case. Seems unlikely that it would lead in a positive direction or ferret out the killer. It might have stirred them up mind you, so directly or indirectly, Captain Ironie really only has herself to blame for the state of old Adam Ease and Detective Wilson.'

'Yeah.' I said, absorbing Cliff's thoughts and taking them further. 'You don't think the good captain would have anything to do with that too, do you?' I asked.

A deep crimson tide rolled across Clubman's face, the effect of which stunted his response. 'Um, I'm not comfortable answering that in a company E.' he said, only half joking.

'Yeah, okay.' I replied, checking my watch again, and realising that my partner had probably worked beyond his rostered shift, anyhow. It was after 5PM by the time we rolled back into the E-Lot at the station, at which point I told a grateful Cliff to make some quick case notes and head on home.

You see, in addition to being on the fence with New Think, Cliff is also one of the dwindling number of people who're still married, in a committed monogamous relationship with his apparently loving wife. They even have a child that still lives with them at six years old, not yet having been convinced to take life into her own hands and break from their oppressive control. These days, not getting your own way is a popular reason to legally separate from your parents and enter New Think's ironically titled "Child Safety" program. Realising that New Think is far worse than your parents in that regard is a tough lesson to learn. But you've gotta grow up sometime. You'll be seven soon...

I had been married once, too. A relationship I lost in a battle of devotion and time between the army and my home life. The army can give you a lot, such as friends, skills and experiences you simply can't get anywhere else. Unfortunately, for all that it gives, it takes even more, and often it takes just about everything. It was my fault, really. I was committed to my job, feeling a sense of pride and obligation to unit, corps, and country when I did it. Unwilling to let down those who'd fight beside me, just for the sake of being home on time, or having a free weekend. Truth is, I adored my wife, but too often took her for granted. She couldn't deal with playing second fiddle and frankly, I don't blame her.

At the time, I couldn't see why she didn't understand how important my work was. What I failed to understand was just how important a family and a normal life were to her.

We were far from unique of course, with millions of military, emergency services, hospital workers, shift workers, lawyers, doctors and really anyone who made the mistake of putting their career or another activity above their partner or family, having suffered the same fate.

Lauren was her name, and she left me for someone who was more devoted to her. I knew Cliff loved his wife and kid (*you're only allowed one*) and he certainly had no desire to join us sad and lonely souls of the modern world. Frankly, I wanted him to be happy too, because it was proof that at least someone still could.

'07:30 start in the morning if that's okay, Cliff?' I asked.

'No probs, boss.'

'Meet me at The Free.' I said. 'Shaz and I always like to meet there for a quick debrief of the previous day before we start, without the interruptions, prying eyes, and surveillance apparatus of the station.'

'Sounds like a plan, Gaz. See ya tomorrow.' He said, before disappearing like a man with somewhere better to be.

After he left, I took a little walk around the station, intentionally going past the chief and captain's offices to see what they were up to, though neither of them were there. I was troubled by the captain's actions, leaking the letters to the press, setting up this task force while leaving Sharon out. Clearly, she and I sat on opposite sides of some big issues, but we generally had a pretty good working relationship. Not only had that soured today, her actions may have destroyed it forever. Even if what she did wasn't criminal, it certainly wasn't good. At the very least, she'd lied, hidden the truth, or both. Whatever her intentions in doing this, she certainly hadn't discussed them or the outcome she hoped to achieve with either Sharon or I and it was our damn case. She broke our trust, so the question is, can she ever be trusted again?

In the Army, trust is everything. You spend so much time with your fellow soldiers, you know them better than your own family. You wake up next to them in the same room, brush your teeth next to them in the bathroom, get yelled at, shot at, punished together, and through it all, you know your buddy will drag your sorry arse out of the shit and back onto higher ground, ready to go again.

People always wonder why those who've been in the military, particularly those who've seen combat, won't talk about what they saw or did with anyone who hasn't served, themselves.

The answer is simple. It's because they just won't understand. The feelings, the experience, the mood of the particular scenario in question. You have to actually go through it, to get it. Empathy, and your 300 hours playing COD and watching Apocalypse Now, won't do. A mindset, by the way, that's been well justified when you look at how modern youth refuse to see history through the lens of its time, always applying the latest standards to whatever era they view.

Military service has a sick, sad, and hilariously funny overlap of reluctance, duty, joy, pain, fear and pride that cannot be replicated elsewhere. Once you've trained, deployed, and lived in each other's pockets, seen each other cry, bleed, rage and scream with laughter, you develop a trust upon which your lives depend. Those shared sufferances and euphoric successes bond people forever. You know that person will do what has to be done, simply because someone has to do it, and they're there. You might not trust him alone with your girlfriend, but… just about everything else.

That level of trust is the only way you can actually function under the incredible pressure of military operations. If you're always wondering whether your back and flank are covered, if your mate is doing what they're supposed to do, then you can't possibly be focusing on the thing that you're supposed to do, and then everything falls apart.

While the Police Service is not the same, it's not too different, either. Whether it's a service or a force, you have to be able to trust your partner, your fellow officers and especially your leaders. You have to know they're on your side, that they're rowing in your direction and that they aren't carrying out subversive actions that undermine your cause and endanger the safety of your team.

Right now, I don't know that about this team. What I think I do know, is why Captain Ironie was so torn up at the sight of Sgt Ease and Detective Wilson today.

Because she knows damn well who did that.

She did.

The only question left to answer is, why?…

Chapter 18

Sought by the quarry

Despite a lingering feeling of failure and betrayal, I couldn't hang around the office all night brooding about the day. I'd ticked at least one box off the case list by discovering the source of the article. Cliff was yet to hear anything of substance from his contacts in Damwell's team, and I could do nothing except wait to hear from Milford. He would call me when he had something worth sharing, I was sure of that. Besides, if I keep contacting him, it'll flag as suspicious, and we'll have surveillance bots and overseers watching us like hawks.

A break from work would be good for me anyway, giving my subconscious mind time to probe and question the events of the day. Sometimes ceasing to focus on something intently gives your mind the space it needs to take in the full scope of an issue and process it. With conscious thought out of the way, I find I regularly spring from slumber with an idea or solution to a problem that's been troubling me. Now seemed like a good time to give it that space.

The trouble is that doing so brings another issue into rather sharp focus. I had been keenly avoiding my anxiety about Sharon's current state of health, not wanting to face her injuries again and, with them, my failure. Even so, I can't go home until I pay her a visit. I know she'd do it for me. The doctors said she wasn't in a coma like Ease, just sedated to reduce the pain and give her a chance to recover. I can't speak for the rest of the station, but I for one am hopeful she recovers soon, and I figure she'd want to have a friendly face there when she does, so mine will have to do.

Not having my own E (*due to the exorbitant cost of renting, charging, maintaining and parking them*) and certainly not being allowed to drive a company E, I jumped on a trolley across to Mid-Town West, where the hospital is located.

It's funny that electric powered trollies existed as a common mode of city transport a hundred odd years ago, before the proliferation of petrol-powered cars and buses became affordable for all. After that, they were largely removed from city centres, making way for new technology, with the exception of a few that were kept as a quaint relic of the past, used only for the purpose of nostalgia, while serving no greater need.

Until about twenty years ago, that is, when the powers that be, brought them back on the crest of a brainwave, so that they now form one of the principal methods of transportation around all global cities. Not surprisingly, they're heralded by the young as technological progressions of "their" time, brought in by the environmentally conscious advanced members of the human race that their generation represents. If only they knew…

The ride from just outside the station to the hospital wasn't far. Only ten minutes on the cold, poorly insulated, sweat smelling carriage. I always sit in the last of the four carriages in an effort to avoid people, who even in this world with relatively few around, still scramble to get on the front three, as if by doing so they'll get to their destination faster.

Jumping off one block from the hospital, where the nearest stop is located, I walk through the drizzling rain and darkening skies into the shiny, LED lit, glass fronted building. The place looks like a sparkly money-making machine, which is exactly what it is.

Injuries resulting from violent altercations like the one that brought Ease and Sharon here are not nearly as few and far between as our utopian leaders would have us believe. Still, by and large, the medical industry is a self-perpetuating money maker with powerful support from the Global government, so it wouldn't matter much if they were.

You're born here, return for your multitude of vaccinations that purport to offer protection from illness, yet just as often introduce unnatural, or unwanted ingredients into your body that overtime cause you to develop other medical conditions, far worse than the one they were designed to protect you from. Side effects such as heart problems, cancers, and degenerative diseases are common *(though not commonly known)*. Therefore, you return for more medicines to treat the conditions caused by the previous lot, and so on, and so on, until you return to die, pay for them to put you in a box and shuffle you off this mortal coil. To say they get you coming and going doesn't quite cover it. They've got you a lot more than that.

Passing an interactive screen as I enter the building, I am, to my annoyance, personally greeted, checked in and offered an appointment ticket if my visit requires face-to-face treatment. As an alternative, I'm told that a Dr-E booth will be available in 15 minutes. Dr-E, by the way, is not shorthand for an emergency Dr, rather an automated interactive booth that scans your chip, your devices, and your body to provide a rundown of your current health status and identify the cause of your ailment.

The booths can also prescribe medications, which is essentially their main purpose, although to be fair, as someone who is neither a people person nor a tech lover, I don't see them as much of a downgrade on an actual doctor. At least the machine is attentive.

The hospitals front desk isn't staffed by a human at night, so I don't feel rude when I ignore the interactive screens demands for a response, then bypass the visitor registration and information device given I already know where I'm going.

Stepping out of the lifts on the 4th floor, it pleased me to see there was indeed a uniformed officer stationed outside of Ease and Sharon's rooms. Passing Ease's room first, I see he's still hooked up to several life-support machines and apparently remains in a coma. Interestingly, he also had visitors, namely, Captain Ironie and Chief Blindspot. To my delight, neither of them saw me pass and with no desire to have it out with them here in the hospital, I strongly hoped that they didn't plan on visiting Sharon next.

Constable Grind was the lucky uniform to draw tonight's guard duty and was presently seated outside of Sharon's door. He looked less than alert, mindlessly scrolling his device, yet sufficiently uncomfortable in the hard, low backed metal chair to stay awake.

'Hey.' I said, by way of greeting.

'Detective.' replied Grind, coincidentally working his teeth as he did so.

'Have the bosses been in here, yet?' I asked.

'Ah, no.' he replied. 'They went straight into Adam's room when they came up.'

'Right, okay. Listen, give me some sort of knock or warning if they head this way next, yeah?'

'No probs.' said Grind. 'I've got nothing better to do.'

I couldn't quite tell if he was pulling my leg or not, a judgement of character impacted in no small part by my strong suspicion he didn't much like me. Lucky for me, I was certain he didn't like our superiors much either, so I trusted he would help if he could.

Heading into Sharon's room, I noted that a drink on the side table to her right had been half drunk. In response to which, the large and powerful, negative side of my mind, told me that the glass had only ever been half full, while the small and wiry, positive side, stayed quietly confident that Shaz had been awake at some point this afternoon.

She wasn't now, instead looking sound asleep and a little worse for wear, but not at all done for. 'Tough nut!' I said under my breath, smiling briefly. Looking at her sleeping form, she somehow radiated strength and power. Like she was unconsciously angry, and heaven forbid anyone who stood in her way when she woke up.

I stayed a good hour, talking one-sidedly to my unconscious yet incredibly absorbing friend. I got the feeling she'd heard me too, though she never stirred. Strangely, despite her lack of input, I felt I took something away from the discussion. As if by simply being in the same room with her, my thoughts were overlayed with the type of input she might normally provide.

While I talked her through today's events, I also took in her injuries, noting the stark contrast of how the expressive face and big green eyes that normally stared back at me, jarred with the one eyed bandage bear before me. I couldn't help feeling responsible. I should have been there for her. That's what partners are meant to do. Protect their partner and be there for them. Otherwise, what's the point of having a bloody partner.

With every drip of the saline solution in the IV line, I felt the pang of guilt hit me like a needle point. The tall metal stand hovered eagerly, offering out its life-sustaining solution as it watched over her protectively, all the while judging me, its very presence the evidence of my failure. I could see some of her possessions and the water glass stored on the wooden table to her right. Her device was there in reach if she needed me. All she'd have to do was roll to the side and grab it, if indeed she could roll at all. Her electro, on the other hand, was now in the evidence locker, so in the event of an incident, she would have to rely on her guard for protection, which is, of course, why they're here. Meanwhile, all I can do is hope it doesn't come to that.

After an hour talking at Shaz and working through the problems of the case, I felt I'd done all I could do here. Until she recovers, I need to let her rest. Her real life input and any memories she has of her altercation at Ease's place could be incredibly valuable, but they can't be forced from an unconscious person. Only time would bring them out, if there's anything there to bring.

Before leaving, I kiss Sharon on the forehead, taking care to find a small patch of skin uncovered by bandage or bruise, then squeeze her hand gently and tell her to just get well. Heading out the door, I say goodbye to Constable Grind, asking about the movements of the captain and chief as I do.

'They left about ten minutes after you got here.' he said.

'Did they come down and find out I was here, or did you let them know?' I asked.

'Neither,' said Grind, mildly offended. 'I'm not even sure they knew "I" was here. When they left Ease's room, they never even looked this way. They simply walked out, turned right, and disappeared down the hall.'

'Did they talk as they left? Say anything you could overhear?' I pressed.

'Not that I heard. Why all the questions about the captain and chief, anyway?'

'No reason. Just curious that they came here to the hospital and didn't bother to visit Shaz… Hey, do me a favour, will you. Let me know immediately if anyone comes to visit Sharon overnight. You give me a call, yeah?'

'Tell you what, I'll do you a deal, instead.' said Grind. 'You bring me a coffee before you go, and I'll keep you abreast of all the visitors to Sharon's and Ease's room tonight. Double the info for a very reasonable price.'

'Deal!' I said, sticking my hand out and shaking his enthusiastically, before setting off to fetch the good constable a coffee.

Back outside in the biting cold, I walked to the nearest stop, then jumped on a trolley for the twenty-minute ride out to my place. Thankfully, it was an uneventful one, with nobody else entering the rear carriage where I sat, nor any of the other three. The staccato sounds of metal wheels squealing and skipping across expansion joints and connecting tracks felt louder in the emptiness, the lack of human bodies leaving the space undampened. There was some sweet relief though, the cold air blowing briskly through the gaps in the doors seeming to dull the unpleasant smell of its usual patrons, and despite the chill, making for a more enjoyable ride.

As we rattled along, I made the conscious decision to break my normal pattern and skip my walk of the neighbourhood tonight. Thinking back to last night's apparent incident for which I have no recollection, and the obvious escalation of violence that occurred today, I figure some quiet time inside might be best. Besides, it's after 19:30 now and I'm still weighing up whether to follow up with Milford or give him a bit more time. The old adage about finding tangible leads for a crime within the first forty-eight hours remains true, no matter how much the world has changed.

It felt late by the time we arrived at the Mid-Town East trolley stop, two blocks west and a moderate five-minute walk from my apartment. Outside, modern cloak and dagger types patrolled the streets, their presence appearing over the top conspicuous here. While I watched, one turned toward me from his spot on the opposite corner, pausing to watch me watch him, like two dogs sizing each other up, then carrying on their way, the opponent not worth pursuit. I couldn't help wondering where he'd been last night, or whether it was he and his comrades who'd come for me. It wasn't their usual MO, but then there was nothing usual about what'd happened lately. Nevertheless, their overt absence from my locale, and the turning away of the cameras, suggests they must have known something.

Tonight, as I walk along Green Street, the lights shine brightly, illuminating the pavement around me as the ever-vigilant surveillance machine watches on, its cameras turning to follow my movements as our Globalist leaders believe they should. Just how many eyes are on me, I wonder, as I turn onto Bottleneck Street, where my assigned apartment sits.

Approaching the front of my squat seven storey building with its black concrete façade, an unfamiliar feeling comes over me. It's far darker on the street than normal, and something seems amiss. The streetlight in front of the entry is out, conspicuously so it would seem, given that all the other lights on the street are on. Yet another strange occurrence in a series of unusual events.

Immediately, my mind races ahead of me, leaping to conclusions it can't confirm with objective evidence, while I consciously fight to bring it back to reason. After all, it could just be a coincidence. Lights go out all the time. Having said that, there has been an inordinate number of coincidences lately, and I'm all but certain the light was working yesterday. When I left the apartment, at least. Its status upon my return remains unknown.

The weight of recent events tilts me to the side of caution and I choose to keep my stride and continue past the building, watching shadows shift from left to right as I walk. Straining my peripherals, I make a concerted effort to take in all I can in this darkened part of the street. I see nothing despite my efforts, yet decide to change my point of entry all the same. As they say, you can never be too cautious these days.

Despite the high cost and limited use of E's, there were still a few parked around the streets, albeit only about half the number of cars you'd see in the old days. The promise of zero emission vehicles being a clean replacement for fossil fuelled versions was not only a wild delusion of utopian dreamers, but one which never developed a suitable alternate. With a stubbornly determined drive to replace coal and gas with wind, sun, and hydrogen, we were sold a bright future. What we got was a future few could afford with net zero benefit for all.

Unfortunately, one cannot discard hundreds of millions of vehicles and build hundreds of millions more without leaking an emission or two. And that was only to build the damn things. You still had to power them and given the unreliability of renewable energy and the need to charge hundreds of millions of cars on top of the existing household, business and infrastructure needs, supply simply couldn't keep up with demand. That's not to mention the incredible cost of replacing old and mostly paid for vehicles with new and expensive ones, a cost that many simply couldn't bear.

The resultant lack of vehicles was of some small benefit to me now, with far fewer windows to peep through, or places for a watching, would be assailant, to hide. To my annoyance, and despite modifying my gait for a quieter, harder to copy cadence, using every available reflection, shadow watching technique and degree of forward and peripheral vision I could muster, not a single threat was identified.

Notwithstanding, the light bothered me, and unconvinced as to the coincidental nature of its failure, I decided to wrap around the block.

It occurred to me as I committed to this plan that I may be doing exactly what they wanted. They cast suspicion on entering from the front of the building, forcing me to enter from the rear and, in doing so, funnel me into their trap. Needless to say, as I had apparently been taken by someone or someone's last night whilst walking alone on an open street, this seemed an unnecessary ploy.

Nevertheless, I had a new plan, and I was going to stick with it, entering via the fire escape at the rear of the building, and accepting what risk that brings.

I maintained my vigilance, observing my surrounds as I continued around the block, still seeing nothing of note. A moralist had walked along Moon Street which intersected with the parallel streets of Bottleneck and Wide, his long grey coat flapping out behind him in the cool breeze. He never broke stride, let alone took any interest in me, nor did his presence seem out of place, if anything, providing a strange sort of comfort.

Approaching the fence at the side of the building behind mine, I scarcely slowed my pace before reaching my arms up, placing the palms of both hands on the cap of the 6ft grey Colourbond fence, and pulling myself to the top. I quickly glance over the other side to clear the landing site, then roll over and drop to the ground, landing evenly on both feet.

Pausing briefly on the other side, the smell of wet earth filling my senses, I strain listening for noises while allowing my eyes to adapt to the even darker surrounds. There are no other sounds except that my own heavy breathing and when my eyes adjust, I confirm there is nothing of concern to see. Just a couple of old trash cans and some recently fallen tree branches stacked neatly against the fence line to my left. Aside from that, the path is clear.

Moving stealthily along the alley to the rear corner of the building, I again pause to listen for unusual sounds or signs of movement. My body is taught with tension, ready to unleash with the violent force of a coiled spring at any who stand in my way.

Glancing around the corner to my right, I confirm the small concrete walkway separating the two buildings is clear, then move to the fire door, chip at the ready, and quickly enter the stairwell.

The stark brightness of the LED lighting inside is damn near blinding in contrast to the darkness of the street, and again I have to allow my eyes time to adjust, before cautiously moving up the single flight of stairs, treading deftly to keep the echo of my footfalls to a minimum.

At the ground floor landing, I ease the door open to peer down the hallway. They're sensor lit in this building, and the space immediately goes from darkness to brilliant light the instant my head crosses the plane of the hall. It was a startling moment, which quickly turned to one of relief as I realised the hallway had been empty when I'd opened the door. I took it as a positive sign and continued toward my apartment.

There's no struggling for keys anymore on refurbished apartments like mine. The building itself is old, but like many buildings acquired by the GCFEH, the interiors have been upgraded, with all the modern security and surveillance equipment fitted. That means that with just a single swipe of my wrist, the bone white door of my assigned apartment, unlocks.

As the electronic mechanism clicks open, and my hand extends towards the door, something odd happens. Or more accurately, doesn't happen, which draws my attention and sets my senses tingling. When exiting the fire stairs, I had callously forgotten to pull the door shut behind me. A door I knew to be on a gas strut, which a blaring subconscious alarm told me should have slammed shut by now and probably before I'd covered the distance to my door. The conspicuous absence of noise was jarring.

I turned just in time to see him, instinctively stepping back to a defensive position, poised to react. Lucky for me, the man who had closed quickly behind me was not carrying a weapon, nor did he attempt to strike or subdue me. Instead, he simply said, 'Quick, I need to get out of the hall. I can't be seen here.'

Recognition dawned, cutting through the heightened alertness and adrenaline that fear created. I moved as quickly as I could, again swiping my arm to unlock the door before ushering Jiang inside.

'Keep the lights off.' he said in perfect if heavily accented Global.

'That may be suspicious.' I replied. 'Anybody watching my chip will know I've entered my apartment. It would be weird if I don't turn on the lights.'

'Fine.' said Jiang. 'But just a lamp near the window or something, then close the curtains and stick to the inner walls to avoid a silhouette.'

Following Jiang's instructions, I move casually down the hall and into the lounge room at the centre of my apartment, turning a lamp on, then moving across to the windows which faced the front of the building and pulling the curtains shut.

What Jiang didn't know, was that I demand proper darkness when I sleep, so all the blinds are blackouts, which would prevent a silhouette getting out as well as it prevented the light getting in. All the same, I wanted Jiang to trust me, so I followed his instructions, sticking to the inner wall of the apartment as I returned towards the hall and beckoned him over to join me.

'I can't stay long, they're after me.' said Jiang, moving gingerly into the space and handing me an RFID slip, directing me to cover my phone.

'Yeah. So am I to tell you the truth.' I said, applying the slip as advised and returning the phone to my pocket.

'Of course.' he replied a little distractedly. 'I know you are. Although, I expect you're mostly after this.' He said, producing a letter from his inner jacket pocket and handing it to me. 'This is what you have been looking for, right?' he added. Posing it as a question, though it was clearly a statement of fact. 'I'm sure you realise it's Katie's final letter. What you probably don't know is that it was always intended for you. You, and you alone. It's even addressed to you.'

'What?!' I almost shouted. 'Why me? I didn't even know Katie.'

'Well, she knew you… or of you, at least.'

Not for the first time today, I was stunned by what I'd heard. A buzzing sort of heat immediately washed over my face and body, just the sort of feeling I didn't have time for right now. A quick glance at Jiang, told me he wasn't so comfortable himself. He looked nervous, frightened actually, and was growing ever more agitated by the minute, endlessly looking left to right and slowly shifting back towards the inner wall.

'Where have you been?' I asked, putting my own shock aside and attempting to centre him, or at least give him something else to focus on. He appeared like a flighty horse being broken in, and dangerously afraid.

'Hiding.' he answered, his attention remaining elsewhere.

Jiang had now backed himself hard up against the inner wall of the apartment. The edge of my brown pleather couch, standing inches from his right leg. To his left, one large step would put him out of the lounge room and into the hall. It seemed pretty clear he had positioned himself here strategically for the best opportunity to run as soon as he possibly could.

I reminded myself that he had specifically sought me out, making it fair to assume it wasn't me he was afraid of. Regardless, his palpable fear filled the room with nervous tension, and despite the cold, a light sheen covered his forehead. From where I stood I could smell on him the days he'd spent in fearful hiding, the pungent odour making clear that he hadn't showered since ditching his chip.

At 48 years old, 5ft 9 inches tall, and not a feather over 64kg, he had the sort of look and height that could easily blend into a crowd. That is, if he could find a crowd to blend into. Not too short, not too tall, not too fat and not too thin. His other features were common, too. Mid length black hair, parted evenly in two. The front curving left to right from the crown of his head, flowing gently down to mid forehead height where it deftly met the skin. The back and sides falling neatly to the base of his skull and trimmed around the ears to avoid the dreaded mushroom. It was his startling green eyes that gave him way. The thing that made him stand out, and the most likely reason he was wearing dark glasses when he approached me out in the hall. Aside from that, he looks the typical Asian male, with minimal definition or deviation from the tight, rounded forehead, tapering down to the slightly pointed chin. Not a description I could give aloud anymore. Even if it is no more than an accurate observation of a perfectly nice face that's common to a region.

He was presently sporting a 5 o'clock shadow, an unnatural look for him which he'd no doubt developed as nature took its course over the last few days. It clashed with his general appearance, lending him a wretched rather than rugged edge, which in fairness would be tough to avoid on the run. The budding beard darkened the otherwise deep olive brown complexion of his Han Chinese skin. Except, he isn't Han Chinese anymore, is he. He's a Global citizen like everyone else, and like everyone else his every feature and biometric marker is mapped and stored in the Bio-Hub, as just another in the many layers of "security" this world offers.

I looked at his left arm, observing the bandage covering the spot where he'd removed his chip. It clearly wasn't well healed, a lot of dried blood having seeped through the outer layer.

'What happened that night?' I asked, looking pointedly at the arm.

'Katie was murdered.' he said, needing no clarification on the incident in question.

'Yes, I know that!' I replied sharply. 'I'm after a little more… like, for instance, do you know who did it, or why?'

'They did.' he replied, by way of explanation. 'She was alive when I left her office, but she knew she was going to die. Even though she was scared, she seemed to have accepted it like some unavoidable fate. I asked her why she didn't just leave or run. She said she couldn't because this was her duty. That there was nowhere that she could go, and nowhere she could hide where they couldn't find her.'

'Then why did you run?' I asked.

'Because I had to hide until I could find you. Katie knew that the last thing she would do in her life was hand me that letter. She was okay with that, as long as it found its way to you. It's of the utmost importance. Our future depends on it.'

'Well, that seems like a lot of pressure, given I have no idea what I'm supposed to do with it. Frankly, I'm amazed you got it to me at all. How have you managed to avoid all the surveillance, including those screens in Katie's office, the night of her death?' I asked, slipping unconsciously into interrogation mode.

'I started by removing my chip. That's the big one. The other thing is my clothes. You won't notice with the naked eye that my clothing is actually lined with RFID proofed material.'

Producing a thin skin coloured mask, he said, 'I wear this outside as well. The masks silicon material is imbedded with the same RFID protection, so it's like I'm walking around in a faraday cage. Whilst the chip wouldn't transmit as long as I'm in these clothes, it could still track my movements and upload them when it eventually got a connection, so I had to remove it and now I must be vigilant in wearing these. Invisibility might not have been possible in the old world, but it damn near is in this one.'

'That's clever.' I said, 'As long as you understand that despite your disguise, you're still in danger. If the wrong person sees you and notices you're not emitting a signal of any sort, that will immediately make you a target.'

'Possibly.' said Jiang, 'Or they will think I'm too dangerous to approach at all. I'm not the only one that moves about untraceably, you know.'

'What do you mean by that?'

Rather than answering my question, Jiang checked his watch, an untraceable citizen automatic, then refitted the mask on his head.

'I can't stay any longer, I have to go.' he said, as he massaged the mask into place. 'They're watching you and they want me dead. I think we both know they are more than comfortable killing to protect their secrets and they're not done yet. I don't plan on being the next death you have to investigate. Oh, and I am sorry.' He said, edging along the wall towards the hallway.

'For what?' I asked.

'For actually delivering that letter. That's what they really want. Even though I haven't read it, I know there's something in there they don't want anyone else to see. If there wasn't, I wouldn't be running. Actually, I don't think any of these murders would have taken place if not for that…'

'Where will you go? How can I contact you?' I asked, struggling to absorb it all. I had no intention of stopping him from leaving. I knew he was right with what he'd said. The letter would put me in enough danger, and bringing him in wouldn't help. After all, he hasn't committed any violent crimes as far as I'm aware, just crimes against the Global state.

'I plan to disappear. For good.' said Jiang. 'If I do this right, you'll never see me again.'

Without another word, he left, fitting his glasses over his mask as he went. I could only assume they too had some sort of RFID film in them, preventing retina scanners and facial recognition software from identifying him until he could get outside the cities and truly disappear.

I watched from the doorway as he slipped quietly down the hall, entering the fire stairs, then closing the door behind him. With that, he was gone from my sight and out of my life. It almost felt anticlimactic, given the surprise appearance. I couldn't help thinking he should have popped smoke and disappeared in the haze just to maintain the mystery.

In total, Jiang was only here for about eight minutes, and in that time, I'd learned as much as I had in the last two days. Which was still two parts of fuck all.

He had, however, brought me the one thing I wasn't sure we'd ever find. The very thing I assumed to be the key to this case and all the violence that ensued. Now, incredibly, I find I no longer had to look for it, because all this time it was looking for me. How many times in life does the object of your desire actually seek "you" out? It's never happened to me before in 53 years. Of that I'm sure.

Trouble is, now that it's in my possession, I'm both desperate to read it, and equally afraid of what it might reveal. Particularly given it was indeed addressed to me. "*Detective Gary Johnson*" printed neatly on the front of the envelope. The potential implications of this were huge, and something I certainly hadn't expected or been prepared for. And, what was it that Jiang said about our future depending on this…

When the door from the entrance foyer opened into the hall to my right, followed by my neighbour Jarrad returning home from his afternoon shift at an IT support job, I realised I'd been standing awkwardly in the middle of my hallway, my apartment door wide open. Entering, then closing it, a sickly, hungry feeling washed over me, and the realisation dawned that with all that had happened today, I had failed to eat even once.

Heading back down the hallway, I decided it would be best to eat before reading the letter… just in case it took me down the rabbit hole, where I might well die of hunger.

Heeding Jiang's advice, I start by going around and closing the rest of the blinds, then set my apartments security measures in place, including infrared sensors to the front and side, both open to the street, and constant monitoring cameras that cover the hallway entry. After that, I unplug the cameras inside my apartment, taking care to block the lenses of each and every appliance. An action taken more for the security of the letter now that it's in my possession, than me.

Thinking back to yesterday again, I wished I'd had this all turned on for whenever it was I'd returned from wherever it was I'd been. It might've given me some indication of what on earth had happened. Unfortunately for me, even your home security systems aren't a set and forget process under Global's laws for electricity usage. Only when it's their safety at threat does surveillance become compulsory. Yours is of little consequence. So, as with everything else in this new world, there is no individual choice to be made. Every Global citizen is allowed only a certain amount of energy use per day and you can't fudge the system. All apartments are linked to the grid with smart meters transmitting your live energy data to the Energy and Consumables Council whose systems perform around the clock monitoring and are set to cut off at the daily limit.

Fridges are the exception, required to run off a small external wind turbine, which is basically a desk fan that sits on the outside of the building. The fan charges a small battery which in turn powers the fridge. Unfortunately, you can't get clever and try to tap into it for other things. The battery is only large enough for one appliance with a max of 12-hours storage and must be hard wired to the unit.

Luckily, I had scarcely used my power allotment this month, a secondary benefit of all the walking, leaving me topped up and ready for my important work tonight.

I quickly cooked my weekly meat allowance of 1 x ChiFaken breast, which I roasted in a pan. ChiFaken, by the way, being the trademark name of the lab grown fake chicken meat that's quite uniquely disgusting. By which I mean, there is nothing else in the world quite as disgusting as it. Nor are there many competitors. Sadly, real meat isn't allowed anymore, and the Fake Chicken is better than real bugs.

What the Globalists knew when they killed all the animals to save the planet, was that starving people will eat whatever's available.

Tonight's meal is actually quite extravagant in modern times. Given it's my only one of the day and I desperately need it to overcome this shaky, sickly feeling, I'm going to double down and partner my tumorous protein with my daily serve of vegetables, basted in my whole allowance of Of-Course-It's-Not-dairy, which is supposed to do me for the rest of the week. Lord knows, I may never eat again anyhow. What's the sense in saving it. I only wish it WAS dairy…

Chapter 19

Sharons world…

It's weird to feel like you're conscious of your unconsciousness. Like somehow, you're aware of just how unaware you are of what's actually going on around you. I couldn't remember why I was in this state, and having little control of my thoughts, I find myself not exploring the actions that had led to my being here, but contemplating the oddities and contradictions of the strange world around me.

I wonder about some of the rather unusual things this modern iteration of the world has done in the name of right and good, how we seem to have devolved in the name of progression, and deconstructed the concept of individuality, to make it a standardised state of being.

For instance, there was a period where the Russians went and did what the other nations do, without first getting approval from the board. To punish them, the drinking of Russian vodka was banned as this was seen to be supporting Russia's aggression against the west, or west-ish nation we said we'd support. West of what weren't real sure, but allies in any event, cause we'd "invested" in their future, so honorary Westies and the enemy of our enemy in any case… Later, "they" determined the punishment should continue, because even when they weren't aggressive, drinking Russian vodka was seen to be supporting communism, which in theory we were against. That New Think represents a most extreme version of communist totalitarianism, along with all its inherent corruptions, was of no consequence to the decision makers. A wrong had being carried out, that wrong being anything the Russians did, and must be rectified.

As we know, however, time alters the perception of all things, so more recently the oppressive actions of the restrictions placed on Russia (*which were not limited to the mere avoidance of vodka, of course*) have become a wrong to be righted in their own right. So, despite individual nations no longer existing and alcohol being banned entirely, "I stand with Russian Vodka" is one of the billions of slogans now morally supportable on ShareSpace.

Similarly, Chinese aggression, and its domestic sibling, violent communist oppression, was to be countered by the banning of eating "Chinese food". Specifically, simple things like flavoured noodles were banned, as they were seen to be in support of aggressive Chinese actions (*don't ask why noodles, it won't help*). On the flip side, and at the same time, Chinese people who had moved to western nations and subsequently experienced inequality or racism, were to have those wrongs righted and be compensated for this terrible treatment. Therefore, eating

Chinese food for the specific purpose of supporting those western Chinese people was not only okay but a bloody moral obligation!

Therefore, a rather complex series of condemn & support cheat sheets were created for the eating of Chinese or Chinese origin foods. Chicken with cashews, or beef and black bean, were of course perfectly fine, being staples of western society and wholly supportive of those much maligned westernised Chinese. So long, of course, as you didn't use real chicken or beef, but that's a whole other kettle of fosh… fosh is fake… well, you get it… Fried rice was not okay even though this is mostly a western interpretation of Chinese food, because standard rice (*used to be white rice*) whilst far more common in China and Chinese food, is far too large of a food source to give up or condemn (*although it is condemnable on the basis that it used to be "white" rice*). Bat soup is definitely out, even having its own separate page of explanation, and is considered extremely condemnable for multiple historic wrong doings…. Whether those things really happened notwithstanding, it was agreed we should condemn them anyway…

All this desire to do good, or perhaps more accurately, undo not good, does inspire some interesting and rather lengthy hashtags. Such as, "#I'm eating standard rice because I stand with the western Chinese whilst condemning the Chinese Chinese, and to a large degree the Chinese Chinese who briefly became western Chinese before returning to China"… There are simpler ones mind you, like "#fuckbatsoup" but that will cost you a public profanity credit and potentially upset the pro-bat groups, so it's best to be posted in daylight hours when most of them are asleep…

Incredibly, despite the objective stupidity of the "support, condemn, or cancel" movements, these absurd notions of cyclical wrong righting continue to absorb the consciousness of a once intelligent people. Mindless now, like drones under the complete control of our top-down governance and utterly dependent on its guidance and support, people wander the digital world parroting whatever the latest cancel culture fad is, demanding rights for some group, whilst removing them from another.

If one were to stand back for a moment to gain a broader perspective, one might consider that many of these seemingly random popular moral opinions are in fact quite targeted, and for everyone or everything (*because it's not only people, but products, processes, procedures and lifestyle choices)* that's brought to its knees under the weight of popular opinion, someone, or something else, benefits. So, wherever there is a winner, there is always a loser.

Destroying something you don't like does not balance out and create equality for all those that remain. It simply disables or retards some, and enables or enhances others. It's nothing more than legislative marketing, whereby the powerful use their elevated positions to control and intentionally suppress one product or action in favour of another. One need not ask the question, why?...

Sadly, it isn't just products and opinions that have been "corrected" by way of legislative marketing. The entire basis of human existence has changed. Under our now, Global Government, science is only to be considered true and believable if it's the science that has been approved in support of top-down governance decisions, and even then, only so long as it doesn't offend anyone except the intended offendee. Which clearly means that if it did offend the wrong person, through some marketing faux pas, the science would be corrected such that it didn't.

Of course, there's no real concern of an alternate opinion clouding one's judgement with balance and objectivity, anyhow. Not with automated Vet-Bots patrolling cyberspace, thoroughly deleting and blocking unapproved opinions before they ever see the light of day.

Which means, the world is peaceful now, because there is only one truth and we all believe it... Except there isn't, and the trouble with censoring or blocking scientific outcomes that may contradict the desired and popular state, is that we tend to drift significantly away from reality. This leads to complex social challenges under New Think, were one must know the real truth *(for the perpetuation of the species)* yet pretend it doesn't exist in favour of a more desirable one. When we try to alter the accepted principles of unalterable biological truths, what we are left with is, lies. If you lose sight of biology and real science, then you lose sight of reality. Politics and opinion based pseudo-science become the basis of truths and are the wrecking ball that knocks humanity off its foundations. Make no mistake about it, no matter what they teach in schools these days, biology is an indisputable scientific fact and a true foundation of our existence. Believing in alternate truths, necessary for popular idealism to thrive, is not the same thing as progressing. Mind you, it is the same as the political term "progressive", so New Think demands you believe it anyway or risk a breach of the Global laws.

The forced acceptance and demand for an altered point of view started with genuine states of being that rightfully deserved to be normalised like any other part of regular society. As you might expect, that normalisation of once rejected or marginalised ways of life does not now, nor did it then, provide sufficient impetus for the embedding of New Think principles, although they certainly helped lay the groundwork. That's how homosexuality came to be used as a Trojan horse for the acceptance of a shift in popular thinking. What was a fight for people to be accepted and recognised simply for who they are, began gaining support for all the wrong reasons.

People of the Old Think world had, by and large, finally accepted homosexuality in most of its forms as a positive realisation of a sexuality that had existed throughout history and was rightfully considered a perfectly normal sexual state of being. However, gaining this acceptance was not why New Think agitators threw their weight behind it. For them, a homosexual "agenda" of the political sort was a vehicle to be built upon for the purpose of driving countless loosely related causes. Most despicably, it was seen as a convenient means to an end for the progression of a necessary evil. The more gay or other non-heterosexual denominations in society, the less breeding within western populations, where their open acceptance was popularly supported and championed. Thus, a genuine cause was hijacked and inculcated at the point of a moral gun. Not because it was the right thing to do, but because it had an inherent likelihood of population reduction that suited New Think's needs. Same-sex couples could, of course, still have children, just not without the help of science and scientific selection, and we all know who controls science...

So, homosexuality was promoted, sponsored and even encouraged for young people who were being indoctrinated in the name of gender education and equality in schools. Gone was the horrible ineptitude of old times, banning and punishing people who were homosexual or "different". That was certainly very wrong, and was subsequently replaced by the equally bad plan of overtly forcing homosexuality upon the world. The goal was never equality, or education, even if that's how they sold it. To be fair, slogans such as "Turn gay for population control" may not have helped their cause, even if they would've been more honest. Worst of all, the people who were meant to be the genuine beneficiaries of the original cause were put on a higher pedestal as targets for hate. Because now, they weren't just people who wanted to be free to live their lives like anybody else, they were a symbol for a much bigger ideological shift.

As with so many New Think principles, this was only really prominent in the west or "First world", which is the strangest of terms, given our species was born of the third. While populations of the west declined beyond sustaining numbers and turned ever more regressive, the rest of the world bred us to the brink of oblivion, and all while we fought for their right to do so. A world dominated in number by impoverished people could only become equal by lowering the standards to those achievable by the lowest common denominator. A horrible way to talk of human beings, yet the very way we're thought of by the masters of the modern world...

Once the west was conquered, they next turned their sights to the rest. Perhaps the greatest achievement for the progressive New Thinkers was Gender Identity Equality for Extremists and Terrorists (GIEET). This was the first major victory in those parts of the world where progressive western morals and values were traditionally despised or had been slow to take hold amongst the masses. In return for official recognition, international legislation was passed to force terrorist organisations to implement gender equality policies amongst their groups. An action seen by the hard-core New Thinkers as one of those things you work and grind your whole life for.

It was a real boon for terrorist organisations too, significantly opening up their recruitment avenues. They had historically adopted the Don't ask Don't tell policy formerly of many military organisations. That wasn't very progressive though, and really excluded those of the LGBTQI+ groups who wanted to be open about who they were and desperately sought the backing of a terrorist organisation to support their ideological beliefs. We are, after all, all the same. The adoption of the slogan 'Hate does not discriminate' was confusing for some who had managed to catch on with the original New Think principals, yet struggled to keep up with the ever-shifting goal posts.

It didn't stop there, either. Further legislation was introduced to allow people who were "actually" terrorists, but did not really "identify" as terrorists, to carry out their destructive activities in abstract peace by virtue of identifying as someone who occupies a rather more peaceful and constructive role. Similarly, those of a timid nature who perhaps worked in an office were afforded the opportunity to identify as a hard edged and violent extremist, which really added depth to their character. Indeed, no one benefitted more than hard-core left-wing progressives, who were in fact extremists, and regularly carried out violent terrorist acts in the name of peace whilst identifying as peaceful minority equalitarians, qualifying for the benefits of victims all the while. Quite brilliant, really.

For me, the one thing New Thinkers and I aligned on was the concept that there was indeed a significant overpopulation of planet earth. It wasn't that I thought individual people should be restricted, but there does come a point of exponential growth that cannot be sustained. That didn't mean I supported the idea that we should forcibly reduce that number. It was my opinion that we should educate our way to a more sustainable level by telling the truth, not subversive lies. I was confused then as to why the same people who sought to reduce the population also earned billions from drugs, medical apparatus, and procedures that claimed to keep people alive far beyond their physiological limits.

Those same people then drove the propagation of other absurd notions, forcing leaders of western countries to unleash a barrage of climate and weather propaganda upon the governed, to coerce them into paying trillions of dollars for the express purpose of saving the world and its unsupportable population from itself. We collectively pretended carbon neutral was a real thing and that turning to theoretically "clean" energy sources would make production and energy usage pollution free.

An argument which clearly ignored the fact that many "clean" energy fuels require as much energy to refine into useable and transportable fuel sources as the product actually produces. Not to mention, E's, windmills, solar panels and hydrogen plants all require coppers, plastics, glass, steel, oils, lubricants, paints, rubber tyres and the list goes on. These things don't grow on trees you know (*well, parts of them might*), and if they did, and if people actually knew, you wouldn't be allowed to cut them down to use them, anyway. It's only okay to cut down trees if they make way for windmills, not to use as an energy source in their own right...

All these money making initiatives did a wonderful job of handing more wealth and power to the privileged few, and yet utterly ignored the main issue, which is that there are too many people, drawing on too many resources. Keeping people alive longer and reducing fossil fuels will not solve those problems, it will only mean you need more of everything in order to feed, cloth, heat, cool and shelter the ever-expanding peoples of planet earth, for their ever-increasing lifespan.

So, with all these almost good causes for omni-sexual acceptance, climate protection, sexual equality, and ethnic diversity, you would think that allowing people to be who they want to be, would allow them to stand out and be different in their own right. You might also think that ensuring respect for different cultures, countries and their individual beliefs and lifestyles should have the same effect.

And yet, I'm sure you won't be surprised to find that, like many almost good ideas, it doesn't. And why? Because progressive New Thinkers don't care about people's individuality, their histories, their heritage, or their native ways of life. All actions are for the greater good, and as such, all actions should only be necessary as a means to an end. That's why they never settle for achieving equality. It's not enough for people to be accepted as who they are. Who they are must be championed until its ubiquitous, then be forced back into the mould as part of a unified global race.

New Thinkers drive a cause for equality and acceptance, then shoehorn it back into the plan. They believe in one singular way of life, with no alterations or exceptions. You can be different and promoted for it, but only so long as you live, eat, believe, and think exactly the same as everyone else. They believe that this is the way to equality, or their perception of equality, and of course the holy grail of "world peace". A peace that can only be achieved through the complete and unwavering control of all the world's inhabitants. An entirely one dimensional monoculturised and homogenised people can't have hate for other people of different ways of life... because there aren't any.

The world has openly accepted that which it fought against for so long. A supreme race at the expense of all others. Meanwhile, the people of that supreme race are either too ignorant or stupid to notice what they've done, and too afraid to do anything about it if they do. They just see what New Think wants them to see. We are all individuals, with individual rights. Like the right to promote the accepted norm and shut down any alternative. The right to have and do what we want, so long as what we want, is exactly what we are entitled to do. We also have the opportunity to reach for the stars, so long as they are only the ones stuck to the roof inside the box. We are all accepted, except for those who are not. We are all equal, except for those who must sit above and direct those who sit equally below them. We live the utopian dream.

A dream ushered in by indoctrinated young people who had no understanding of objectivity and less understanding of individual freedoms and freedom of speech. New Thinkers, born into a world already primed for change never understood the damage they did. Gone was the ability to tolerate a difference of opinion, agree to disagree, and continue to live together. They sought not only to ban opinions alternate to their own progressive thoughts but also to prevent people being able to think those thoughts or even discuss or share alternative ideas amongst like-minded friends. They thought that any alternative to theirs, was a dangerous way of thinking, including the historically well tolerated ones that had survived the test of time. And if they don't get their way, look out!

Chucking childlike hissy fits, lashing out via their supportive legacy media and social media followers, or using violence and wanton destruction of that which they sought to cancel, was the "new normal" of our moral overlords. While this happened, silent Old Thinkers, unaccustomed to public tolerance of this behaviour, just stood by and watched them have their way with the world. Many disillusioned souls or entitled champions cheered them on, assuming always that they need not stand up to this hypocritical tyranny because surely someone else would do it, or that it would peter out as they always had before. Nobody stood up, nobody stemmed the bleeding, and after a while there was no one left who could.

The powerful had willingly restrained themselves to appease the loudly whinging minorities, offering them more and more power which they gobbled up with greed. All the while, chastising anyone not of their mould for the despicable past behaviours of their sex, colour, race or religion. Watching people turn into the very worst of bullies and power-hungry control freaks whilst calling out the world for those very same aspects of their assigned category, was really something to behold, and… wait… what's that you said?

Amidst my mental meanderings, a voice appeared in my head. Or another voice, I should say. It was like having someone trying to talk to you whilst you're underwater. Bits and pieces come through sharper as the water chops and the gap from the surface to your ear reduces, then drifts to incoherent burble as that gap increases again.

Somehow, I managed to stay under, and yet close enough to the surface. *I hope you feel well soon, Shaz.* said the voice. *I need you... can't fight them all on my own... Us Old Thinkers need to stick together... It's the only way we can survive and keep the fire... And, don't worry about your face... you were never that pretty to begin with, haha. God, I hope she didn't hear that, or it'll be me in hospital...* That was it. That's all I got before drifting under again.

I don't know how long I was out after that, nor do I recall any other thoughts until the sound of a door closing somewhere nearby jolted me awake. I looked sharply to my right where I was sure the noise had come from, only for my body to bring reality crashing down upon me with brutal force. A lightning strike of a headache hit my consciousness and blurred my vision. Or was my vision already blurred?... I'm not sure.

I feel for my face, lifting with extraordinary effort my leaden left arm, realising as I do the aching, tired feeling through my whole body. There's a sickening pain in my stomach and with my arm in the air, I feel a cold plastic cord hanging from the back of my hand. It isn't until I touch my face and feel the spongy crepe bandage wrapped thickly around my head that it occurs to me... I'm in hospital.

As my senses slowly return, the violent pain in my head seems to narrow its focus to a point just behind my left eye. Incidentally, where is my left eye?

At the front of my face where my eye should be, I notice there's a hard patch covering it. To the side of the hard patch, a soft spongy area gives way to thin bandaging and my haphazard poking causes me to grunt loudly in pain. 'Arrrgh, don't do that!' I say to myself, instructively.

I lay back on the pillow behind me to support my aching head, feeling outwardly with my arms for the cold metal rails at the sides of the bed to give myself a better mental map of my surrounds.

The rails are up, floating high above the heavy and raspy bedding that's pinning my body to the thin hospital mattress. From what I see with my one blurry eye, I'm alone. The room is mostly in darkness, broken only by the bright hallway lighting streaming through the rectangular window in the door.

Did I mention my head hurts...

Feeling gingerly around the top of my pillow I find a cable with a hard plastic cylinder, then pulling it down to the visual arc of my one good eye, I see the protruding red button and realise this is probably a pump for self-administering morphine.

I feel my eye, head and shoulders all starting to throb in unison, joining forces as I become more and more aware of my injuries. I should lay here and think for a bit, try to remember why I'm here, but my will is fading fast. The pain's taking over my decision-making process and trying to see out my one good eye seems to be making it worse.

Christ, my head hurts.

I can't be of help in this state. I can't even remember what I'm meant to be helping.

I hit the button, twice…

Chapter 20

Care of - Mr Johnson

'When the only carrot on offer is to not be hit with the stick, then the people holding the stick have failed to understand its purpose. They offer only punishment, or its absence, without reward. People need a reward…'

This phrase stuck with me. It was written in Ms Hansley's letter, the one addressed to me. The one that Jiang had risked his life to deliver, and it said a lot. It spoke volumes actually, because in its simplicity, it details the real failure of this moralised global governance system.

It's all take and no give. A theoretical levelling or balancing of the human race. The trouble is, it scarcely offers those at the bottom anything but company, and takes from those in the middle and at the top, their wealth, their status, and the fruits of their labour, returning only guilt and the joy of repentance for crimes they may never have committed, as their reward.

Their freedoms had already been taken, their individual rights long gone, yet always the stick would hover. It hangs there still, overhead, always ready to strike, and whilst ever they're in charge, it always will.

If I hadn't expected the letter to be addressed to me, then I certainly wouldn't have guessed at its contents. I figured perhaps that it was a plea for help, or a smoking gun with details of the killer and plot. Unfortunately, that's not what it said. Not quite. It does detail a plot, though not the plot of her murder. It's another horror story, and that horror story is the daily lives of the people in this world.

We all know that we're controlled. Well, some might not, although it's hardly worth worrying about what they know if they can't discern that much. Most of us, however, are aware that there are laws that limit our ability to spend money, to travel, to see, hear, and read stories on the web, to socialise without oversight and interference, or to make decisions without first considering who they might offend, or whether they meet compensation requirements for the previously wronged.

What the crisp white pages of Katie's letter reveals, is that we are so much more controlled than that. They aren't just monitoring our movements and tracking our interactions online, they are completely controlling our patterns of thought.

In her letter, Katie states that she was tasked with closing the psychological loop. Ensuring that people always believe they have their own free will, without ever having any at all. The intent, to ensure the perpetual continuation of New Think as the undisputed moral belief system, without the risk of actual free thought ever penetrating the bubble.

Almost all interactions are virtual these days. Certainly, all transactions are completed virtually, as nothing except the Global Digital Currency (GDC) can be legally accepted anywhere in the world. There is no free market, and no ability to barter or exchange goods, as actions of that nature are banned.

That's partly because transactions of mutually beneficial exchange have the potential to go untracked, even if they would almost certainly be surveilled. It's also because of the risk that they could break the spell of New Think's complete control.

If you are allowed to think that there is another way of living outside the digital system, then you might consider that there are all sorts of other unmonitored actions you could take.

All movements of goods, services and money must be checked, verified, and authorised by the Global machine. You must have sufficient Global Points to complete the specific transaction, and most importantly, whatever goods or services pass between two parties, those items or actions are never the purchasers or the sellers to own. You must buy a chair to sit on, which is to say that you must use your allocated GDC to purchase one from an authorised seller, and upon receipt of the chair, you can use it. So long as you understand that it is not in fact "your" chair. Nor is it coming to "your" apartment.

What you must also understand (*because the Guides demand it*) is that your transaction really went like this. The Global Guides gave you GDC in exchange for performing tasks they authorised you to perform in the name of the greater Global good. On completion of your tasks, you needed a chair to sit on whilst waiting to return and perform more tasks. You utilised your allotment of the Global Guides own currency to purchase a chair from a Global Guides approved (*owned*) business that will be delivered to the apartment that the Guides have allowed you to live in, and you may sit on their chair until such time as you either no longer need to, or they deem you no longer deserve to. Either way, the chair was never yours, nor the apartment, nor your clothes, nor anything else in your possession. Because, you may possess things throughout your life, but they are never yours… Aren't you happy? You're supposed to be.

The great thing is that New Thinks philosophy has answered the question, "What is the meaning of life?" It is to serve the needs of the Global population and repay your debt of guilt and destruction.

See, under New Think, you are not innocent until proven guilty. You are never innocent at all. Wronged at some point, perhaps (*if you're lucky*), but never innocent. See, you have taken from the world. From birth, your presence is a drain on its resources, and this incurs an accumulating guilt and debt that must be repaid for the remainder of your wretched life.

Katie already knew all this, so it wasn't in the letter. It would be a waste of your dying words to simply describe the state of the world. What she did refer to, was a planned transition to a world so much the worse.

The current form of transactive governance will change from one of legal and technological monitoring to one of complete psychological control. They have already taught people how to be New Thinkers, how to communicate, how to view the world and people around them, changed the perception of right and wrong and instilled a belief in the positive benefits of being tightly controlled. Of course, you could still act out against it, still believe differently, as you do Gary, and so long as you toe the line, you can continue to exist in the Global World.

Not anymore. Not after this program is completed. You will either think correctly and act correctly to the great benefit of the global leaders, or you will cease to exist at all. The time for allowing Old Think ways to exist, even in the minds of the few allowed to remain, is over. Many years ago, Old Thinkers were told that the world would evolve and that they would evolve with it to form part of the global machine.

Most took this quite literally, thinking that it meant some sort of robotic amalgam or the use of implants or particles in conjunction with radio waves that physically control you via electronic manipulation that would influence you to follow instructions.

Some of that was even trialled, with radio-controlled chips tethered to nerve endings showing some success. After that, it was never seriously followed through by anyone, save for a few mad scientists, because there were too many potential issues and as people are not factory built, they cannot be consistently controlled with the same frequencies or hardware.

No, the existing threats of ever-present surveillance, combined with instinctive psychological obedience, is the real method. And we've just perfected it.

Reading Katie's letter reminded me of something. Something I learned when I was a kid. My father always told me that if the only thing preventing you making money is pride, then ditch the pride. On the other hand, if the thing preventing you making money is that you have to cross the line between right and wrong to do it... then, there must be other ways to make money.

You'd be excused for thinking I'm not the son of a rich man and you'd be right, too. I'm not. He was a good man with great advice, who never amassed any real wealth. His main flaw was that he always wanted to be nice. No one who is particularly successful is ever particularly nice. The pursuit of success is by its nature a selfish and isolating pursuit. People who take the time to be nice will have to take that time away from their drive for success. Mind you, he never tried to tether me, electronically or otherwise, to a means of total control, and what sort of nut would see success that way anyway…

It was the next part of the letter that had brought this to mind. After explaining they had developed a program to enslave the human race, Katie alluded to the grand architect of the plan.

Whilst I have always believed that our leaders, the Guides, have genuinely had the best interests of the human race at heart, I see now that control rather than moral compass, and profit rather than preservation, are the real goals of the master's I have followed.

They have not corrected us from the path of greed and gluttony, instead, they've perfected it for themselves.

Unfortunately, the letter wasn't explicit, naming no names, offering only the "what" without answering the question of "who?". Then I realised that like two pieces of a puzzle that don't seem to belong, I may already know the who. One thing I found out about Katie from her employee profile was that since completing her education, she had only ever worked for a single company. One Globe Technologies. A career spent in the employ of one all-powerful overlord and his partner (*formerly wife*) who rules the roost with a pastel coloured sweater and an army of evil henchmen.

Cheq Fencegap was the original creator and CEO of OGT. He also happens to be one of the richest people on the planet, and despite his ever-present public proclamations of only seeking to protect, promote, and facilitate the needs of humanity, he can't help making a lot of money along the way.

Every time he creates a new project, "we" the people are duty bound to join him in championing its success, because, as a philanthropist, he's really only doing it for us…

Personally, I have always seen right through him, as I imagine Katie had begun to. Maybe some of those books she was reading provided some insight as to who he really was.

Cheq is a sleazy, aggressive, insecure, people hating arsehole. He also wields a lot of power and never puts his money anywhere he doesn't think it will grow into more money. That's why people like Sharon and I started worrying thirty years ago when he began putting money into initiatives to "protect people" from things most didn't need protection from.

Some might consider that intentionally seeking to find things that are not a threat to human beings and altering them so that they are, could be a rather dangerous and unnecessary pursuit… Then again, what would I know.

As a joke (*I think*), an old boss once told me I was so ugly that a chemist could employee me to sit outside their shop and make people sick. Creating a market where none existed by introducing a problem that wasn't there before you brought it into being, then forcing people to pay you to solve the problem you created, is quite a racket. It's Cheq's racket.

People didn't need most of the technologies that OGT created until he created them. Then, once he created the technology, he conveniently realised that there were countless and apparently unfixable ways to attack it. If you're quite clever, you'll know there's a brilliant way to overcome this type of issue. Oh, not the being attacked bit. We'll get to that. I'm talking about the fact people didn't need the creations to begin with. You use your family's connections and influence to ensure the thing you're peddling is wedded to the concept of advancing humanity, then kill off any competition for the role. I believe it's called the Rockefeller Racket…

Once the fix is in, that's when you review the faults, identify their value, and start to design additional programs to "manage" the issue. Which means, not only do you have to pay for the technology you didn't need, you have to pay to protect the technology you didn't need from the inherent weaknesses built into it by its architect.

Once the technology becomes compulsory in order to complete any and all transactions to facilitate your life, well, now you have to pay for the technology, you have to pay to use the technology, and you have to pay to protect the technology from other technologies, and protect yourself from all of those technologies as well. Using another layer of technology… Which, he will sell you… for one year… and don't you worry, it will automatically renew and take money directly from your account. For your convenience, of course…

Aren't you sick of hearing the word "technology" by the way? I mean, I'm pretty sure they only use it to piss us off. To make us feel small. Technology is literally a word used to represent a machine or scientific process that they don't want to have to explain to you (*probably in case you work out that it isn't a good thing*). Every new development and every new layer of control, is just a new "technology", always couched in a way to make it seem as if its purpose is to greatly benefit us, the end user, except that you're too stupid to understand what it is.

That's its only ever needed because of the previously flawed technology they sold you, is not the type of thing you should be thinking about. So, don't.

And that's not the only way they get us, either. Did you ever wonder back in the old days why you always had to pay a "handling fee" when you purchased electronic tickets online, even though the only person handling the tickets, was you? Technology improved the process for you to purchase tickets, taking away the need for a ticket seller to be physically present, answer questions, monitor supply and demand, or mail the tickets out to you the purchaser. All this was replaced by technology and yet, you pay more money than you ever did and continue to pay a handling fee to boot.

Isn't technology wonderful? Cheq thinks so. Not only has it made him exceedingly wealthy, it also gave him the opportunity to be one of the founding members of the Global Guides. Who, through sinister and calculated machinations, created an environment ripe to usher in a new ideology. Do you think he did it for free? Out of the goodness of his heart? For the benefit of us all? Or just because he's nice…

Well, now it's been ushered in, embedded, and is the omnipresent controller and dictator of every aspect of our lives. But as usual, that's still not enough for Cheq and his fellow overlords. Unlike his many technological and medical programs, it would seem that Cheq does not want to leave the plan exposed to attack, for which he can extract a payment for defence.

Evidentially, they also don't want people to know that whilst we've had our necks in a noose for the last twenty years, they are about to kick the chair out.

For all their blind support of the many absurd principles, even some New Thinkers would still prick their ears up upon learning of the planned and intentional eradication of a people that are no longer convenient to have around.

We were a necessary evil, tolerated as an existential threat that had to have substance in order to ensure that the overly smart, or the overly dim, stayed the course and didn't question the validity of its many shifting restrictions and overly intrusive surveillance. That means, that whatever new "technology" they are about to unleash upon us is going to render the threat of Old Think no longer necessary. Such a level of control will have been achieved that nobody can escape the net. It's the end of the world as we've known it. No way back.

Unfortunately, in her letter, Katie does not detail exactly what the program entails nor how to counteract it, though the end of the letter is both clarifying and cryptic.

We already know that Katie had planned to give the letter to Jiang and task him with bringing it to me. What's both concerning and illuminating is the manner in which the last paragraph was written. It's as if Katie was worried that the letter would never reach me, or perhaps, that Jiang would be found and killed before ever being able to deliver it. Or maybe, that she would be killed before she could give it to him.

I'm speculating, but I believe that may be the reason she wasn't more explicit about what on earth she wants me to do. She included what she described as "the key", except it's only made of words, and what it's supposed to unlock, I haven't a clue.

The letter reads;

"My time is short. I need to complete this and I can't explain it all in this letter. Assuming this finds you well, you'll just have to work it out. With all that's at stake, I'm sure you will be suitably motivated to do it.

Sadly, we will never meet and after this, you will never hear from me again. I wanted to share the secret with you, because only you can help us. They found out though, so I had to go all in. There's only one way to stop this. You need to destroy the program. Just remember to clean up after yourself.

P.S. It would mean a lot if you straightened things out with my mum... tell her, I know the world wasn't bad, it was just the way things were..."

That was it. That was all she wrote. That's all I have to go off. To be honest, I'm a little annoyed. Disappointed even. So far, two people have died, and two others have been hospitalised trying to stop me receiving this letter, and having received it, I know no more now than I did before.

If there is some hidden meaning in what she said, it's hardly struck me like a lightning bolt. Why she thinks I'd understand what had to be done without explanation, I may never know.

If only Shaz were here. Riddles are her speciality. She loves hidden meaning. She's always saying things that sound like one thing and mean something else. Her knowledge of the unspoken (*or unwritten in this case*) word is part of what makes her such a good detective. I'm more of a tactics and strategy guy. I need to know what my objective is in order to design an effective plan of attack. I like directives, "direct" being the root of the word. So, if you mean something, you should bloody well say it.

What I'm going to need, is some need help. Someone that knows computers and programming, someone that knows surveillance systems, and someone that can decipher what the hell this letter means.

At the moment there's just me and Clubman, and neither of us fills those gaps. I can't exactly walk it into the station either, not with the way Ironie behaved today, and certainly not after what she did with the last letters.

I'll have to sleep on it, I guess. Perhaps when I awake, everything will seem clearer.

Chapter 21

Sharon's déjà vu numéro deux

I wake with a start again, except this time it wasn't the closing of a door that jolted me from my slumber. It was a rather less startling shadow or the flickering of a light. Perhaps something briefly blocking or passing by the doorway. Whatever it was, it left me with a cold, tingling wash of nerves cascading down my skin.

Looking around me with my one good eye, I see nothing other than the distinct dark shapes of hospital furniture. The hallway lighting still shines through the small glass window in the door, and yet somehow it seems dimmer than it was before. I'm slick with sweat, though happily my body feels lighter now, and my head appears to have stopped pounding. I guess the morphine has done some good.

With my left ear partially covered by the bandages around my head, my senses are limited. Through it I hear only the echoey sounds of my own breathing and the faint beat of my drug infused blood pumping around my body. My right ear, on the other hand, is free and on the same side as the door. Focussing my efforts there, I strain to listen, feeling convinced I can hear some sort of whispering coming from outside.

Even without the pounding in my head, I'm finding it hard to concentrate, the drugs no doubt blunting my mind. And yet despite all that, I'm sure I hear my name. Although I can't hear the voice clearly, I feel I've heard it before. A female police officer, perhaps. It's someone of authority anyway, because the other voice I can hear is a male and they have so far only said "yes ma'am" on more than one occasion.

After about a minute, one of the people outside must have stood from a chair, the legs making that awful squeaking sound on the tiled floor before they took off down the hallway without ever passing my door. It's possible there are guards or nurses out there and they just performed a shift change. Or maybe someone was receiving specific instructions in person which they didn't want intercepted. Either way, it roused me from my sleep.

As the footfalls disappeared, their sounds were replaced by a deep sort of silence, filled only by the gentle, earnest, hum from a nearby machine. Focussing on it now, I realise the sound must have been there all along, because it didn't seem to start, so much as I had suddenly become aware it, or at least more aware of it than I had been before. Perhaps I'd only heard it due to the absence of other noise, it being the sort of noise you don't hear until you do, and once you hear it, nothing else can occupy your mind.

The rails on my bed were still up, and through them to my right I could see that someone had put my device on charge. Trying to reach for it was impossible, the stiffness of my neck and the height of the rails making it too hard for me to stretch that far. My restricted action made me wonder why the rails were up at all. As far as I'm aware, they only put them up when a patient is being moved. Surely, I wasn't likely to go rolling out of the bed. I am an adult, after all. Plus, with a neck this stiff, I am not inclined to want to move very far, even if I could.

I try looking at my device again, as if by eyeballing it I could will the thing towards me. As you might expect, it remained stubbornly immobile, apparently immune to the power of my will. Maybe this is why, for years now, devices, or mobile phones as they were previously known, have been voice activated.

'Device!' I stated sharply, knowing that at the sound of my command, it should spring to life and ask what I want.

What I heard instead was not the anthropomorphised response I'd expected, but what sounded like startled movement outside the room, marked again by the bumping and scraping of chair legs on the floor.

'Record!' I instructed in the loudest whisper I could muster, only moments before the door to my room flung open, followed by someone entering swiftly, then shutting it quietly behind them. I couldn't really move or sit to face them. All I could do was watch as what appeared from the shape of their body to be a female turned towards me.

The intruder's face was covered with a balaclava, which, based on Global Surveillance protocols, should be setting off an alarm for the Overwatch teams right now. Not an action I had confidence in, based on recent events. In fact, I doubted they would know anything about it at all. Or perhaps they simply wouldn't pay attention if they did.

'You should never have gotten involved in this.' said the familiar voice I couldn't quite place.

The figure moved to the end of the bed and stood looking over me. Her dark piercing eyes appearing ominous with only the beam from the hallway light glinting off them and framing her rake thin silhouette.

'Who are you?' I asked, rather absurdly.

'People who wear masks rarely want to be identified.' said the figure, sarcastically. 'I thought a detective would know that.'

'Okay then. What do you want?'

'To finish the job.' said the woman.

She moved around to my left where I'm bruised, bandaged, and blinded, giving her a distinct advantage for the mounting of any attack. Despite doing my best to turn my head and shoulders towards her in an effort to see as much as possible with my one good eye, she was further from the doorway and, therefore, on the darker side of the bed, doubling my disadvantage.

I still had a drip in my arm and, not knowing quite what else to do, I placed my left hand over the tube to take pressure off the back of my hand where the drip needle entered my vein. I couldn't lash out or strike at my assailant and didn't have the capacity to fend her off or try to scream for help.

The woman produced a needle, presumably containing some sort of drug or poison. 'Don't bother trying to struggle.' she said. 'You'll never get over the rail in your condition.'

I offered no reply, instead watching her intently, and praying that an opportunity might present itself to foil her attempt on my life.

The stand from which my drip hung was close to the edge of the bed. Placed there, no doubt by a well-meaning nurse, worried I might move and pull it over or pull the tube right out of my arm. Now, when that very action might save my life, it was nearly impossible to do.

'Oh, if you think you can just pinch the tube or rip the catheter out of your arm when I leave, you can forget that.' said the assailant, assuming my thoughts. 'You won't be conscious long enough.'

Unable to turn my head that far, I hadn't noticed that after screwing the needle onto the syringe, she'd grabbed the morphine button from above my head. She slid the catheter stand back to give herself some space, then seized the tube where the valve was located with her other hand.

'I want you to watch it go in, first.' she said, her eyes flicking up to meet mine while she positioned the needle ready to inject into the tube. As she did so, she leant forward, the darkness making it harder to see well enough to ensure the needle entered the right spot. No doubt it wouldn't do to almost kill me.

Having moved the stand back, she'd taken a lot of slack out of the catheter tube, apparently oblivious to the risk that this created. With my attacker momentarily distracted, I took what I assumed must be my one and only chance and yanked on the catheter as hard as I could, screaming in agony as I did so, my left arm and the side of my face exploding with pain. In an instant, the catheter stand came crashing down on top of my assailant, striking her on the side of the head.

While the stands are not heavy, in the dark and off balance, she reactively threw her head forward in an effort to duck out of the way, smashing hard into the raised steel bed rails. My prison, inadvertently becoming my protector.

She grunted loudly, then dazed or unconscious fell to the floor, the metal catheter stand crashing into the bed rail after her, making an almighty sound in the silent hospital. Immediately, I heard multiple footsteps rushing down the hallway towards me, and through desperate pain, I screamed to make sure they found where the sound had come from.

'Help! Help!' I screamed.

A male nurse was the first to enter the room, bursting through the door and hitting the light switch as he did.

My attacker, still lying on the floor, who had been temporarily silent, began groaning audibly as two more nurses entered, followed by Constable Daily, who I instantly recognised as the voice I'd heard talking to the woman outside.

Thankfully, my assailant hadn't yet hit the morphine button, so my faculties were as good as could be under the circumstances. I eyeballed the tall blonde constable wondering where the hell he had been a few minutes ago.

'What happened?' asked the male nurse, rushing towards me, alarm clear in his voice.

'There's a woman next to the bed!' I shouted. 'She tried to inject me with something. She tried to kill me!' I implored, adding tremor to my voice for effect.

It didn't take much. I was genuinely scared, an emotion that had a positive physiological side effect, with the adrenalin of the situation sharpening my focus. I knew I needed to play up the fear angle to make sure they captured and dealt with my attacker, in case they simply assumed I'd woken with a fright and somehow knocked over the stand.

Constable Daily's face was starting to show clear signs of panic now. He obviously didn't know what to say or do under the circumstances, particularly given he'd left his post to allow her in here. I'm damn sure he knows who the woman on the floor is and what she had planned to achieve tonight, so at least the investigation should be short.

Still, he didn't move. He just stood there like a snowman. An honest copper would've charged through the room, brushing nurses aside to apprehend her. Not him. He let her in, let her do what she did, and now he stands helpless and hopeless, like a stunned mullet.

When the nurse came to the side of the bed, he saw the collapsed woman, the balaclava still covering her face. 'What the fuck?!' He exclaimed.

As the words expelled from his mouth, the woman appeared to regain enough of her senses to get to her feet, then stumble towards him as he too stood frozen in shock.

At the same time, one of the female nurses who'd entered the room came to the other side of the bed asking if I was okay. I barely noticed her presence, my one eye focused on the scene to my left.

When my attacker got close to the male nurse, he seemed unsure of what to do, instinctively putting both hands out to try and catch her gently and steady her by her elbows. When he did this, the woman, clearly in better condition than she'd let on, struck out with her elbow, catching the unprepared nurse across the throat and sending him crashing to the floor.

Shocked, a second female nurse who had never quite entered the room went into full retreat, trying to get clear of the doorway, while Constable Daily watched on incomprehensibly, unable or unwilling to act.

'What happened?!' asked the nurse to my right, whose presence at my side suddenly rushed into focus.

'Someone just tried to kill me, is what happened!' I shouted.

'Are you okay? Did she hurt you?' asked the frightened nurse.

'No' I said. 'I don't think so. She tried to inject me with something, then fortunately for me, the catheter stand came crashing down on top of her just in time to stop it. The needle she had may still be on the ground somewhere.'

The nurse bent down and checked the floor, finding no sign of the needle. Meaning my would-be killer must have pocketed it again before making her escape.

Looking up from the nurse, I note Constable Daily had disappeared from the room, too. Perhaps to make a belated effort at catching the attacker. It would literally be the very least he could do.

The third nurse, having recovered from her rapid retreat, and realising that her coworker to my right had not attended to their male counterpart, rushed over to him whilst the other returned to her search of the floor.

The man was sitting up now, wheezing and clearly struggling for breath.

'Jennifer!' said the female nurse attending him. 'Help me take Liam to emergency. He will need some treatment. He may have a tracheal rupture or at least significant trauma.'

'Of course.' said the nurse I now knew to be Jennifer. She rushed around the bed and helped Liam to his feet, turning to me as she did. 'I'll be back soon.' she said. 'Just sit tight.'

'Sure.' I said. Like I could go anywhere.

The whole ordeal was over in a matter of minutes. From dark loneliness, to violent near death, and now here I am alone again, my mind racing as much as it can in its drug and pain effected state.

The morphine I'd had earlier still seemed to be working. Either that, or the adrenaline coursing through me was masking the pain. Holding my hand up in front of my face to get a good look at it, I see it's shaking, and frankly, I think, with good reason. I'd nearly died, possibly for the second time today, and although I couldn't quite remember the incident that put me here, there was one thing I knew for sure. I had to get the hell out.

Stuck awaiting the return of my nurse, I did the only thing I could for now, which was to take a few deep breaths and try to gather myself. The light in the room was still on from when the male nurse first entered, its concentrated brightness now troubling my one good eye. I closed it against the harshness of the light and waited for the nurse, who returned a few minutes later, as promised.

'Is Liam okay?' I asked.

'Yes, I think so. He's shaken up, and he will definitely have a sore throat tomorrow. Aside from that, he'll be okay. I suppose you know what that's like yourself.' said Jennifer.

'Yes, I suppose I do.' I replied.

'Now.' said Jennifer 'Would you like me to put these rails down? I wouldn't think you're at risk of falling out.'

'Yes, I would be thrilled if you could do that.'

The nurse's curly brown hair bobbed and bounced as she set about lowering the bars to free me from my cage. I estimated her to be in her mid-forties, not overly fit looking, with a motherly grace of movement which offered some welcome comfort after the stress of my recent experience.

'Why were these up, anyway?' she asked.

'I was about to ask you that.' I replied. 'I couldn't see a good reason for it, either. It certainly prevented me getting to my device and made it bloody hard to defend myself, too.'

Jennifer's eyebrows shot up at the thought that I may have intentionally been trapped here, though she stopped short of asking the awkward question.

After putting my bed rails down and fetching me water and something to eat, Jennifer mercifully handed me my device from the side table.

'Thank you.' I said. 'By the way, is that officer back out there? The blonde one that was in here before?'

'He's not, actually.' said Jennifer. 'Which is odd, you know, because there's meant to be someone stationed there all night and I haven't seen him since that woman ran away. Would you like me to call your station and see if they can send someone else down?'

'No, thank you. I'm not sure they add much value when you consider there was one here before and after I was attacked. Not during… I appreciate the offer all the same, but I'll make the call myself. I'd best report what's occurred here, at any rate.'

When the nurse left, I unlocked my device, glad to see it had been recording for over twenty-six minutes. I must have managed to activate it with my whispered command, issued only moments before the attacker entered the room. If her voice pattern's registered, it shouldn't take me long to work out who was under that mask and perhaps hold to account at least one of the people who'd attacked me today.

In saying that, the voice should be registered in my head, too. I'm sure I've heard it before. Only, I can't quite think where. I suppose the head injury is affecting my memory and throwing me off. Of course, it's also possible that the head injury is the only reason I think I've heard the voice to begin with. That's something I'll have to think more about. First things first. I'm getting the fuck out of here.

A fellow officer had been placed outside to protect me. An officer who I know and work with. Yet, rather than protect me, Constable Daily was very possibly complicit in an attempt to kill me. One thing I know for sure, with or without the head injury, is that I won't be sleeping another second in this place. All the drugs in the world couldn't keep me here.

One glance at my device tells me it's already 3AM, which means it's early or late, depending on your outlook. Either way, it's a time at which Gary won't appreciate being woken up. Mind you, the thing about Gary, is that he's the most loyal bastard you're ever likely to meet. So, I'm sure once he hears what happened, he's going to understand.

Before she left, Nurse Jennifer promised to come back and check on me again in half an hour, patting my arm gently and smiling with her motherly warmth. In spite of her kind demeanour, I sincerely hope to tell her to get my clothes and sign me out on her return.

Hitting dial on Gary's number, a nervous flash of memory crosses my mind as the action suddenly reminds me of last night's failed attempts to call him. What if he's been attacked too, lying somewhere dying, or unconscious?

Thankfully, that's not the case, and it's only a couple of rings before he picks up, sounding tired and clearly having not checked the caller ID. 'Yes, hello?' he answered blearily.

'Gaz! sorry for calling so early.' I said, surprising myself at how excited I was to hear a friendly voice.

'Sharon?!' said Gary, clearing his throat and immediately perking up.

'Do you know anyone else with a bandaged head and only one good eye… and arm?' I replied.

I'd caught sight of myself in the reflection of my device screen. A shocking experience that sent a nasty dose of reality coursing through my brain. My left eye was covered, wrapped in white crepe bandage, while my theoretically uninjured right eye was a shiny purple/black and puffy. There were also little traces of dried blood sneaking out from under the bandaging around the eye and down the cheek, some of which had run over the orange/red coloured antibacterial chemical that had been applied, making it look like the first two layers of a Jackson Pollock.

'Well… actually, I do. But never mind that, you're awake! Thank God!' he said, audibly cheering up even further. 'Are you okay?'

'Yes, well, no.' I said. 'Not really. I was attacked.'

'Yeah, I know. I'm sorry about that. I should have been at Ease's with you. How's your eye, by the way? Looked a bit rough when we found you.'

'Oh, right.' I said. 'Well, yes, my eye is sore and currently covered by bandaging. That isn't what I meant, though. I meant to say I was attacked again. Here. In the hospital.'

'What!?' Said Gary, realisation dawning and darkness chasing away the light in his voice. 'You were attacked again?!'

I left the question hanging for a moment, feeling his anger building in the silence as if picturing all the potential culprits and imagining himself returning serve. While we haven't been friends for all that long, you'd be hard pressed to find two people that have a stronger bond than we do. We're protective of each other and I know my pain would burn him almost as much as it hurts me.

'I think it was someone we know.' I said, breaking the tension 'Or, someone we've met at least.'

'There was supposed to be an officer outside that door at all times!' Said Gary, almost shouting through what I imagined were clenched teeth. 'Constable Grind was there tonight when I left. I actually told him to call me if anyone at all came to visit you or Ease. I brought the prick a coffee!'

'Grind?' I said, surprised. 'That's odd. When the woman attacked me, it was Constable Daily who was outside. He knew it happened, too. Seemed like he was part of it, from what I could tell. Either that or he at least allowed it to happen because I heard his voice before the attack, and I saw him visibly after.'

'Right! I've had enough of this shit!' said Gaz. 'It's time to knock some heads together. I'm coming to get you out of there. I don't think you should spend another minute in that death trap. It isn't safe.'

'Hospitals rarely are.' I replied. 'Seriously though, that would be great if you could come get me. That was the reason I called.'

Gary didn't need any more than that to put a plan into action. Not more than twenty-five minutes later, a rather flustered looking Nurse Jennifer came hurriedly into my room with a paper bag full of painkillers, placing them nervously on the desk next to my other possessions.

'Ms Wilson, it appears you have a friend here who is rather insistent that you wish to be released to his care?'

'Is his name, Gary?' I asked.

'Yes, that's right. I take it you asked him to come?' As Jennifer posed this question, she appeared more desperately hopeful than concerned.

'I did.' I replied. 'I can't stay here anymore. I don't feel safe.'

'Well, normally I wouldn't recommend it, but under the circumstances, I think you may be right.'

Jennifer helped me to sit up for the first time since I'd been here, at which point I realised that aside from a very sore head, neck, and left arm, most of the rest of my body was still functioning and largely unharmed. After helping me dress in my pants and a loose-fitting hospital T-shirt, Jen gave me a quick soldier's five on the medications, expected recovery timeframes and the need to return to get my eye checked in three days' time.

'Certainly.' I said 'No problem. Oh, and thank you for helping me tonight. I'm sorry you had to go through that. Don't worry though. My partner and I will find these people.'

'Perhaps you should leave that to your partner.' Said Jennifer. 'What you really need is rest.'

If I hadn't just seen myself in reflection and failed to put my own blouse back on, I'd say that Nurse Jennifer was being a bit old school, leaving it to the man. Unfortunately, in this instance, she was probably right. I could hardly investigate and certainly not defend myself or make an arrest in this condition.

'I'll rest when it's safe to rest.' I said with stubborn defiance, despite the facts.

Once I'd finished dressing and collected my things, Jennifer walked me to the door where a stern-faced Gary was waiting for me. I could see straight away that he was on edge, shifting his weight visibly from foot to foot, just itching for someone to challenge him.

He was fully dressed in his blue chinos and polo shirt, hair hand combed into place as if immediately ready to get to work on the whodunnit of this latest crime.

'Christ, are you okay?' He asked, checking me over for additional injuries. 'I'll fucking kill both Daily and Grind when I see them. What the fuck are they playing at!'

'Don't kill them yet.' I replied. 'I need your help solving this case before someone finally finishes me off. I've already survived two attempts. I'm not sure how many more I've got in me.'

'You are aware you only have one eye?' said Gaz.

'Not true. I have two. It's just that only one works.'

Chapter 22

Sons of Old unite

'Can I get you anything?' I asked, having finally got Sharon back to my apartment and settled in.

'No, I'm fine for now, just happy to be out of that hospital. Pretty eager to get some answers about what's been going though if you've got any of those. How long have I been out, by the way?'

'Only a day.' I said. 'As far as we know, you were attacked yesterday morning at Sgt Ease's place and then for a second time tonight. As for answers, I don't have many of those yet. There are too many new events taking place one after without us getting to resolve them in between.'

Looking at Sharon, I could see she was tired, hurt, and scared. Her one good eye wasn't just bruised, it was bloodshot and watery. Still, her inner strength shone through, and I could tell she wasn't willing to wait until morning for a bit of information.

'I'm glad you're keen for answers, Shaz. Truth be told, I've never needed you more.'

I'd piled both the allotted pillows from my bed and my two couch cushions neatly behind Sharon's back to create what I hoped was a comfortable incline on the two-seater. Luckily, Sharon's relatively short, so she can fit. Personally, I find the position unbearable, but she seems happy enough, with her knees tucked up for comfort and an icepack resting against the bruise on her back.

'Well, I am, so what have you got for me?' Asked Sharon, her good eye closed now against the brightness of the LED down light in the centre of the room.

'To start with, I've got a new partner. Temporary, of course. Actually, since you got injured, I've had three temporary partners. It started with Ironie, believe it or not, then Constable Gopher accompanied me to the hospital, and now I have Clubman with me until you're fit to return. He's no Sharon Wilson, so you've got nothing to worry about…although he does have two good eyes.' I smiled cheekily, hoping for one of Sharon's trademark exasperated head shakes, which, obviously, she couldn't provide even if she'd wanted to.

'Anyway, I have a lot of ideas to bounce off you and plenty of updates to share. However, in the interests of progressing the case, what I really need is to hear what the hell happened to you since last we spoke. If you're up for it, that is. Perhaps you could you start by telling me what took place at Sgt Ease's place yesterday?'

Sharon's eye was still closed, though she remained awake and conscious. I watched her take a deep breath and shuffle her body for greater comfort, as if preparing for a lengthy response.

'Unfortunately Gary, I can't really remember a damn thing yet.' was all she said.

'Oh, right. Fair enough, we'll work on that.' I said, replacing the device I'd just unlocked to take notes on, back on the arm of my chair. 'What about tonight, then?'

When Shaz had finished recounting the story of her second near-death experience in the last twenty-four hours, and the recording she'd made of the whole event, I knew we might finally be starting to put the puzzle together.

In turn, I told Sharon about the 8th letter and how it had actually been intended for me all along. Oddly, she was not as surprised about this revelation as I had been. Then again, she had been attacked twice since the investigation started, with the latest attack appearing to be specifically planned with the express intent of finishing her off. Perhaps surprise was a harder emotion to elicit now. Or maybe her experience had simply clarified our position in this as more integral one than we'd realised.

'What else has happened?' Asked Shaz.

'Well, Captain Ironie arranged a task force, ostensibly on the basis that Ease had been attacked, with little to no mention of your predicament, or the fact that you had saved both Eases and your own life through your actions. The name "Operation Ease" probably tells you all you need to know. It's being headed by Detective Damwell, who is going all out under the assumption that this is a clear Old on New crime. Clubman has some friends on the task force who've agreed to pass on any key developments or potentially interesting information that's been discarded by Damwell or Ironie as being too logical, or not supporting their Old on New hypotheses.'

'So, basically anything that's actually useful?' Asked Shaz.

'Pretty much. They not only believe that there's no other possible explanation for these crimes, they're determined to shoehorn whatever evidence they do find into fitting that narrative.'

'So where do we go from here, then?' she asked, physically fading and clearly in need of rest.

'Well, I figure Clubman can follow up with his contacts in the morning, and I'll do the same with Milford to see where his agency is at. The reality is, directly or not, Katie quite clearly pointed the finger at OGT and, in particular, Cheq Fencegap and their new and insidious program as the driver for what happened to her. While she may not have foreseen the threat to Ease or yourself, it would appear she knew she needed outside help and that she herself was in danger.'

'I know it's not what you want to hear…' I started, almost ashamed of what I was about to say. I couldn't look at Sharon as I said it, lowering my eyes to look at my feet instead. 'You're safe now, and despite the horror you've suffered, I think we need to put the latest crimes against you and Ease to the side. Just for now. Obviously, we don't need to look for the missing letter anymore, a fact we should keep under our hats while we let the others carry on hunting. Meanwhile, our entire focus should be on Katie's team at OGT. Particularly Cheq and this program.'

Sharon said nothing in response. She just lay there face up, eye closed, her injured left arm gently cradled by the right. I never expected her to be happy about it, and the stiffening of her back and shoulders told me she wasn't.

'I have an idea of how to go about it, too.' I ploughed on. 'We know the cleaners are capable of moving around the building at will. We also know that Katie herself was the one who turned off the surveillance in her office…'

'Ah, and how do we know that?!' Interjected Sharon, her eye exploding open.

'Oh right, well, it isn't explicitly stated, but I've inferred it from the letter and frankly, I think it's the only thing that makes any sense.'

'How so? I would have thought that the killer cut the surveillance to ensure they weren't seen committing the crime. Is that not what "we" thought?'

'That's very possibly true.' I replied. 'It may be that they went to do exactly that, only to find it had already been done. My read is that Katie cut the surveillance herself, knowing she was in danger and needing to get the letter out without its carrier being seen. To her, that was the most important thing. I think it was a pre-meditated action, buying her time to get the letter to Jiang, and allow him the opportunity to pass it on to me without anyone knowing what she had done, and possibly without them ever knowing it existed at all. Unfortunately for Katie, Jiang disappeared just after the letter was given to him, which made him a fairly obvious suspect with something to hide.'

'What's your theory about the other cleaner that was killed, then? How does he tie into this?'

'Could be mistaken identity. He might've simply have been in the wrong place at the wrong time. Truth is, I'm not really sure. I've scarcely had time to think about that one. Like it or not, we may need to wait for an update from Damwell's team and see what they turn up. My current position remains that I don't think he was involved in the crime itself. Maybe he saw something he wasn't meant to see, or they thought he knew something about where Jiang was. They worked a lot of the same shifts, so it stands to reason Jiang might confide in him. Jiang's certainly confident they're after him now and he's gone to extraordinary lengths to try and escape. I guess Chen was probably killed because he was either very loyal to Jiang and refused to give up his friend and workmate, or he didn't know anything at all, and they didn't want him being able to tell us who had come around asking questions.'

'Am I right in remembering they shot him from across the room?' asked Shaz. 'If so, I don't know that they asked him too many questions.'

'That's certainly how it appeared at the crime scene.' I replied, smarting a little at her capacity to out reason me, despite her current state. 'Even so, I'm not ready to rule out the possibility they asked first, then came back and shot him later. Or that they already knew what they needed to know, so they didn't bother asking any questions at all. Just killed him to shut him up. I mean, not to raise your stress level or restate the bleeding obvious here, Shaz, but it seems pretty clear someone wants you dead, too. And, aside from making me concerned for you, it also makes me think you either saw something at Ease's place which you can't yet remember, or whoever attacked you at Ease's apartment thinks you might have. They obviously don't want you to share whatever or whoever you saw, so it must be worth remembering.'

'I agree.' said Shaz. 'Only, nothing's coming back yet.' She tried a painful-looking yawn as she said this, scrunching her face and widening her jaw as much as the swelling allowed.

'That's totally understandable.' I said, throwing my hands up and feeling guilty at having pressed again. 'I don't want to put that pressure on you. Look, it's 4:30 now. Let's both get some rest, because I think we've got a big day ahead of us. We can either work together as a team of three, with you running things from here. Or if you're up to it, we can get you to the safety of the office to work from there, if you'd prefer. And if you're not up to it, it would be perfectly reasonable for you to just stay here and recover from the two violent assaults you've suffered and take as much time as you need. Whatever suits.'

'I'm up for it.' said Shaz, her eye now firmly closed, her arms folded across her chest like Dracula in his coffin.

'Okay, that's good. We can run your latest attacker's voice through the Bio-Hub and see who pops out. Clubman and I can feed whatever info we find back to you and then set about chasing down leads whilst you piece the puzzle together. Do you think you think you can handle that?'

'I've made that suggestion every day since we started working together.' said Sharon eking out a chuckle. 'Ouch!' she added. 'Remind me not to laugh.'

I smiled at her warmly. 'It's good to have you back. You take the bed, okay. I'll take the couch, and I'll see you in a couple of hours. Oh, and if anybody else tries to kill you, don't let them wake me up.'

Whether she was feeling comfortable and safe at my apartment, or perhaps simply because she was exhausted from her multiple horrific experiences, Shaz passed out the second her head hit the pillow.

I watched her a moment to be sure she was breathing okay, then took her device from the bedside table, feeling only a little bad for deceiving her. The truth was, I had no intention of going back to sleep. Not now. This thing was getting away from us fast, and I can't wait for her to be ready to help or tell me what she saw.

Using the physical proximity to her chip and her exposed face to my advantage, I unlocked her device to access the recording, noting with concern that the eye patch and swelling had no impact on the bio-metric security of her phone. Neither did the fact that she was asleep.

Pulling up the recording, I sent a copy to myself, then replaced her device on the bedside table, backing out of the room and heading straight for the small wooden desk where my home device was situated. After confirming my credentials, I logged into the police system in order to access the Bio-Hub, through which to run the recording. From here, I should be able to gain access to the hospital's surveillance system too, which will allow me to see if their chip readers recorded the attacker's information.

After entering the Bio-Hub, I began the scan on Sharon's recording, setting parameters to search for those known to be within the vicinity of Greater Mid-Town city to keep the pool of suspects as tight as possible. That's the easy bit. Now for the hard bit. The wait. In spite of all the many advances and personal intrusions of surveillance, identity, and tracking systems, checking something like a voice recording for identification purposes can still take quite some time.

With the condensing of populations into tight urban regions, ostensibly to reduce our impact on the environment, there are a lot more people crammed into a much smaller space, meaning that despite the empty streets, the number of potential suspects is far greater than you'd think.

In the meantime, I sent a coded communication to Milford requesting an update on the progress of his team. It was 05:03AM when I hit send, which is far too early for most. But, if I know Milly, he's an early riser and a vigilant operator, so I wouldn't be surprised to hear from him before Sharon ever stirs.

I also consider sending an update to Clubman about the letter and what had happened to Sharon. He is, after all, my partner now. Trouble is, I still can't decide whether I'm 100% sure of his allegiance. If he has a connection to people in Damwell's team, then it stands to reason that they have a connection to mine. I certainly don't want the likes of Captain Ironie finding out about the letter or anything else we've collected before I've had a chance to work out whose side she's really on.

I do, however, have an obligation to keep her in the loop and it's always good gamesmanship to do so with someone you suspect of being a little crooked. That should be simple enough. Based on yesterday's meeting, she expects nothing of value from me, so it's nothing of value she'll get.

Chapter 23

The innocent don't need protection from the truth.

You know, the trouble with people is that they seldom listen openly. Nobody actually wants to hear what someone else is saying. All they really want to hear, all they listen for at least, is confirmation of their own theories or opinions repeated back to them, so they can nod along in anger or agreement, saying 'Yep, that's right!' all while wondering how the others came to be such fools.

This is especially true in a New Think world, where you are either on the side of New Think, and therefore good and agreeable with all New Think policies and opinions, or you're not. In which case, you are bad and utterly dis-agreeable with all New Think policies and opinions. There is no acceptance of grey here when it comes to your moral or political stance. Flamboyantly coloured, yes, so long as you believe it all the way, and you're willing to fly the flag at the top of its mast.

Proud of your country, sure, so long as you were descended from the actual first people to inhabit the lands, and not just some "Joe (*him/her…*) come recently" whose family has only lived there for a few hundred years or something. If, however, by some maniacal possession of body and mind, you believe in fair opportunity for all, or individual freedoms, then you sir, are a fool!

When New Think says they stand up and demand equality for all, they don't actually mean 'all'. No, no, no… What they mean is, "all" the people "they" support. And whilst I personally can't comprehend how or why they believe that forcing everybody else's opinion to conform to theirs, is open, accepting, or progressive, what you have to understand, is that I wasn't trained correctly, therefore the reality that I see, is not properly aligned with the feelings of those around me.

When I grew up, the world was different. I knew about the rights and wrongs, and what was and wasn't acceptable. Mostly the social convention was, that you could be whomever you wanted to be and do whatever you liked, so long as you didn't make a big fuss about it or throw your ideals in everybody else's face. Decorum, decency, and mutual respect were the core principles that general society expected of you when in the public space. In private, try not to abuse anyone and don't get caught with your shorts on the shag pile… so to speak.

Many wrong things were done in that world, too. Most often, because the people doing wrong didn't know any better. And, whilst ignorance may be no excuse, which it certainly isn't in the information age, neither is an ignorance of history or a failure to understand the linear passage of time. The world that those who came before us grew up in, was different. They had different needs, different standards and wildly different life experiences than the judging generations that followed. There were things that shouldn't have been done, for sure, yet only a fool would fail to see that the platform on which they stand, would not exist without those that came before them.

New Thinkers can't accept this. If it's wrong now, it was wrong then and must be acknowledged by those broadly considered to be descendants of the perpetrators, and those unwitting descendants should be punished forever more. The heinousness of their heredity must be avenged!

History must be changed. Books and E-stories re-written to allow the historically wronged to see themselves through the painful eyes of the sufferers, as nothing more than the victims of history's great mistreatments. These new versions must then be presented to the world as the real truth, finally revealed, to be judged by the standards of the now, the oppressors thrown off and exposed for all to see.

For us Old Thinkers, we might ask how modern culture could possibly recreate the stories of the past, all these years later, and present "new truths" swaddled in modernities' subjective review?

The stories, already written, must remain as they always were. You don't have to believe them. Every story or historical recording that's ever been written has been told from the perspective of the writer at the time of writing. In the absence of new and verifiable facts, a story re-told from a modern perspective is no truer than the angle presented from the past. Tell your story if you must, just don't abolish the originals when you do. Give people detail and context, state your case, then let them judge for themselves.

As a young man, I wondered how New Think opinions would be applied without simply reversing the status quo and creating a new societal imbalance. Feminism, with its righteous fight for women to be seen as equal and given equal standing to men in society, was a reasonable and necessary ideal. Why shouldn't men and women be equal? After all, as a species, one cannot survive without the other. Before long, it became a multi-pronged, multi-level attack on men in general. Being a good person who sought only to be the equal of all other people in society was not enough. Not if you're also a man. You had to acknowledge the power of women and your own flaws as a man, and you dare not highlight the positives of being male, such as speed, and physical strength, or discuss any difficulties you may have as a man, lest you be belittled for the insignificance and the arrogance of your opinions.

The rules once favoured men. Quite unfairly, most would agree… Then again, we did create most of them. That's why it was a man's world. Now, I'm not saying that that should continue, although the mere thought is enough to be despised. Now, under the rule of New Think, a man is a much maligned and disadvantaged creature. Not wronged, mind you, so still without a voice in a victim's world, and yet the ceiling is clear above us, and the masses have climbed atop.

A woman with strong beliefs in their rights, and their attributes, and their ability to beat the opposite sex, is a proud feminist. A man with strong beliefs in his rights, is a chauvinistic pig. How come when a man yells at a woman because he wants something done a certain way, he is an abusive, patriarchal, piece of shit? Meanwhile, when a woman yells at a man because she wants something done a certain way (*a scenario in which I am experienced to the point of expertise, I might add!*) she's a boss, or a strong independent woman, who knows what she wants, and knows how to get it?

The unspoken words are ever so loud, aren't they? You <u>must</u> know that we are different, but you absolutely <u>**must not**</u> say it...

Nowadays, a man (*especially one of "colonial-ish lineage"*) who is concerned at how he is perceived by society, or any man who is unconcerned about how they are perceived, but whom also has the audacity to remain unapologetic, cannot express their feelings in the public forum. One must simply shut up and "check their privilege" irrespective of upbringing or background and simply be happy they haven't yet been banned from existence altogether.

So, why am I thinking these unspeakable things whilst I wait for the Bio-Hub to find a match, or for Milford to contact me with an update? Well, for one thing, I am a male who is arguably of colonial lineage. For another, I am actually re-running the recording of Sharon's attack for a second time, and wondering just how on earth I am going to get away with arresting my own captain... Even if I do have solid evidence of her attempting to murder an officer under her command... who is also a woman, and most importantly to me, my exceptional partner and wonderful friend.

I'm hardly in good moral standing in the broader Global community, let alone in my local section of its police service. A white male, known Old Thinker, former military, and current police detective, who openly disagreed and challenged his direct superior, who is female and a New Thinker, is about to arrest and accuse her of the attempted murder of a fellow police officer. Lead balloons have more buoyancy than the plan I'm trying to float.

Even if it doesn't go down well, it might go down fast.

If the Bio-Hub spits out her name again, I'll have no choice. The only thing I can really do is go to the chief and hope she isn't in on it, too. I hate to think what the odds of that are. Pretty good, I'd say. They do both work together, hold the same beliefs and commitments... but... what am I saying. That doesn't make her guilty. Guilt by association is their game.

There is one other option, of course. Although, it too, carries the risk of creating more problems than it solves.

Milford and the DSSMD have the highest level of detention powers going. Their officers are also equipped with real guns, not the electronic toys we have. Trouble is, if I hand this over to them and they agree to arrest Captain Ironie, I run the risk that they're either involved and will simply cover the whole thing up, or possibly worse, that they're not involved, they take over the whole investigation and Sharon and I never get justice for Katie, or Chen, or even the opportunity to find out what the hell happened. Then we'll never know if they put a stop to this sinister plan of OGT's, which may kill off forever the possibility of return to a commonsense way of life.

As I ponder this option, my device buzzes. It's Milford responding to my request for an update. 'Hi.' I said, answering the call.

'Got your message.' said Milly. 'I see you've had an interesting night. But how would you…'

'Oh, you've been watching me?' I asked, cutting him off mid-sentence.

'Of course.' he answered. 'In fact, there's an entire team watching you and your partner at the moment. Some of the higher ups have apparently taken a keen interest in these crimes and what might be causing them. Being a government branch answerable to the Global Guides, they are also quite eager to understand how two mis-aligned detectives with an admittedly impressive record of closing cases are going to handle this.'

'So, is my device listening to me and reporting on me, now?' I asked, knowing the answer to this already.

'Um, your device is always listening to, and reporting on you.' said Milly flatly. 'At this particular moment, as we speak right now, the content of what it's transmitting is not being recorded or monitored… which is, I assure you, a temporary anomaly.'

'Oh? Is there a reception issue at your end?' I asked facetiously. 'You just said there's an entire team watching me.'

'Don't ask questions you don't want to know the answer to.' said Milly. 'You asked for an update on how our investigation is going… This is it. So far, we haven't been able to locate Jiang, nor were we able to recover any of the surveillance information from Katie Hansley's murder, or the murder of the OGT cleaner. We haven't made any progress on the attacks against Sgt Ease or your partner. The people that committed these crimes didn't show up on any scanners, devices, trackers, or chip readers. Truth be told, we aren't sure how they are getting around the entire surveillance network. The only thing we do know is that Jiang ditched his device and physically removed his chip. But you already knew that.'

'Yes, I told you about it, and by my count you're 0 for 5. I guess that anomaly isn't so temporary after all, hey? An entire team of people working on this and the only thing you know is what I told you yesterday?'

Milly didn't bite on this. He just took my condemning comments on the chin, let a few beats pass, then continued.

'There is one more thing I can tell you… last night, Captain Isabelle Ironie met with someone four blocks away from the police station. Whoever she met with had no digital signature or biometric markers that could be detected by the Bio-Hub systems. During the meeting, a package of some sort was passed from this someone to Captain Ironie, after which she went home.'

'If you couldn't pick up any surveillance signature, how do you know she met with anyone at all?' I asked.

'We went old school when we realised people were working harder than usual to avoid being monitored or tracked as a digital entity. We know these people are out there physically, but because we are so reliant on technology these days, it leaves us blind without their digital presence. Now, before you ask any more questions, you should let me finish. At around 1:30 this morning Captain Ironie left her apartment again, then after travelling two blocks on foot, she stopped. Moments later, her digital signature ceased to be visible. No more biometric, chip or device surveillance possible. Her image didn't even appear on the bloody cameras. For all intents and purposes, she vanished…'

Milly gave me a little time to digest this piece of information, which I used to consider the nagging feeling he knew a little more than he'd first let on and it doesn't take a mathematician to calculate the trajectory this story might take.

'Did your people follow?' I asked.

'No.' he said. 'They'd been hanging back due to the presence of the moralists at that time of night, not wanting to draw unwarranted suspicion or attention. Once she went dark, they tried to move into her last known position and circle out from there, except by then she was long gone.'

'What about the moralists, where they able to provide any help?'

'Uh, no. Let's just say that they move in different circles to us.' said Milly. 'Whilst we might be on the same side, so to speak, we don't exactly share information with them. They aren't so much the law, as they are a social presence anyway, so they aren't really on the same level.'

'Right.' I said. 'Sounds like you view them the same way I do… from a distance. So, do you have any idea on where she might have gone after that or where and when she reappeared?'

'Yeah, that one I can answer. While the team on the ground couldn't find her, the captain did reappear on the surveillance feed, running at pace about a block from the hospital a little later this morning… From what I gather, you yourself were then called to attend to that hospital and retrieve your injured partner about thirty minutes later. Does that sound right to your ear?' he asked, clearly now posing the question for which he had called.

'That's right. At least the part about me coming to the hospital to pick up Shaz. But you already knew that…' I mimicked. The Irony of this statement was not lost on Milly who chuckled lightly despite the gravity of the situation. Intelligence agencies and Police Services (*or even forces*) playing coy about what they do and don't know is as old as the hills. That he already told me they were watching me, rather undermined the ploy.

'What else has your team gleaned from their surveillance activities?' I asked. 'I imagine that with access to listen to all my conversations and activities via my device, you might have gleaned all sorts of things…'

There was a long silence on the other end of the line. When Milly spoke again, the humour was gone, replaced by an added level of intensity, even concern in his voice.

'Yes, we have gleaned some other things, which I cannot discuss with you here. All I can tell you is this. You are not to touch Captain Ironie, no matter what she's done or what evidence you have obtained… I have a team that will continue to monitor her activities, however, YOU, are to leave her alone! And that's not just me talking. That statement is made with the full weight of the DSSMD.'

'Secondly, whilst we cannot hear you read or see what takes place inside your mind, wherever your device is, you are under surveillance and whilst you are under direct surveillance as you in particular are right now, any conversations you have or people you meet with, can be observed, and any period of obstructed surveillance is equally as intriguing as recorded surveillance. I assume you understand what I mean.' This last sentence was a statement, not a question. Clearly Milly was trying to tell me they were watching me and that he wasn't pulling all the strings, so I would need to find a way to avoid being surveilled if I really wanted to get anywhere.

'Anything else?' I asked. Now, itching to be rid of my old friend and the oppressive instructions he had given. Technically, he didn't have the right to restrict my investigation. Having said that, my own station isn't really on my side, so I'm hardly likely to win a battle of jurisdiction or agency control.

'No.' said Milly. 'That's all I have at this stage. Is there anything that you would like to share with me? Perhaps something I wouldn't already be aware of?'

'Not that I can think of.' I replied. 'Rest assured, if anything valuable does turn up, I'll be in touch.'

Milly didn't push me, which seemed to me to confirm the unspoken message that he and possibly other members of his team were aware that I had an unrecorded encounter yesterday and that they were okay with that so long as I didn't make it so obvious in future.

After hanging up, I immediately opened the music app on my home device, pressing play on ACDC's Back in Black album. When Hells Bells began playing, I placed my mobile device down in front of one of the speakers set either side of my home device so that the sounds and vibrations would make it hard for surveillance teams to listen. Milly had just said that periods of non-surveillance would be deemed suspicious, however me being in my assigned home and listening to my choice of music seemed more like difficult surveillance to me, and only a gentle raise of the middle finger to the global machine. Plus, I figured it would give them a little old school rock to enjoy whilst they wait for something interesting to happen.

The takeaway message from the conversation was clear. Sharon and I will be left to continue running our investigation, upon which they intend to piggyback, so long as we understand we won't be free to make arrests at our discretion or apply investigative pressure as we see fit.

Why the DSSMD is going to prevent us arresting a ranking officer that clearly carried out an attempted murder last night, is a hell of a question to ponder. Makes me wonder who exactly she really works for and just what sort of corrupt malevolence we are now caught up in. It would seem that the circle of people I can trust is shrinking by the minute.

Of greater concern, is how on earth I am going to explain to Shaz that we can't pursue the arrest of the person who last night attempted to murder her… for the second time. Worse yet, that we shall have to bite our tongues whilst continuing to follow her orders until the DSSMD or some other unseen power deems it appropriate to act, doesn't bear thinking about.

What must be considered, is just how Sharon, I, and by extension, Clubman, are going to become the grey men and woman of the Global Police Service. All while continuing to progress our investigation without giving away evidence that allows others to get ahead and block us, or withhold so much that they become suspicious and shut us down.

There are just so many bloody surveillance apparatus to cover off. Almost every electronic and digital appliance in the world is working in conjunction with my device, my chip, or my recorded biometric data to surveil me. Up to and including my fridge.

The device is probably the worst of them. With the introduction of the Digital Global Pass, Global Impact Scores, and Programmable

Global Digital Currency, all of which have been mandated for each and every citizen, the need to carry your device with you at all times is a legislated requirement.

It's funny though (*I mean, not haha funny…*), we were told that a digital identity and the ever-present checks and balances of a big government surveillance and monitoring system was only ever going to be for the ease of the user. For our safety and protection from the many evils lurking in the digital world. Like me, many saw this for the utter bullshit that it was. Nothing is ever only for the purpose of good. If something has the capacity to do bad, or to extend its reach beyond its stated claims, then it will. Why would you create something that can do more than is required with no intention of ever using it?

Governments aren't in the habit of building roads and infrastructure that have a greater capacity than the bare minimum for the shortest term of their need. This is near sighted, of course, and intentionally so, as it keeps both short-term costs and timeframes down, so that elected officials can claim to deliver promised improvements within their planned timeframes and budgets. It also leaves room for the ever-popular job creation and expansion plans, required to handle the greater demand of the growth they've created over time. More promises, more money, more projects, and so the cycle goes on.

Why, then, in designing a system that is only meant to protect, would they build it so that it can do so much more, with the only safeguard being their promise to never use that capacity? Why create a system that can track and control you if its only stated purpose is to protect you from harmful attacks? Governments only build what they intend to use, and they'll use whatever they have. Have you ever seen a four-lane tollway with only two toll collection lanes because that's all they'll need to pay for the road? … Not bloody likely!

At 06:30 on the turn of the minute, and despite all her injuries and the pain she must be in, Sharon woke up and demanded to be moved to the lounge room where I set up a workstation using my home office desk, which was thankfully adjustable in height.

'Why the hell are you playing heavy metal music nonstop?' She asked.

'Ah, actually, I think it's classified as Ancient Rock these days.' I said, pointing to Sharon's device, which was presently in her hand, then at my own, which sat directly in front of the speaker. Sharon took the message and handed me her device, which I then put next to mine.

Quietly, as Metallica's Enter Sandman played, I told her of the call I'd had from Milly and the unspoken subtext of the conversation. Surprisingly, Sharon didn't explode with rage when I explained that the voice of her attacker had been that of Isabelle Ironie, the detail of her brief disappearance and sudden reappearance, or our subsequent directive not to arrest or pursue her yet. In fact, she didn't say anything at all. She just adopted a stone-faced silence, far more frightening than an angry outburst could ever be. After several minutes of this, she finally spoke, although, not so much to me, as the room at large, as if I hadn't existed within it at all.

'You know, before New Think came along, I stood, shoulder to shoulder, alongside the other women with whom I shared a pre-Global world. All those who had long been overlooked, ignored, or considered part-time professionals, only in the workforce until a baby came along. At which point, they would become a mother and nothing more. I stood up for the rights of women to be counted, to be professionals, and to be respected for their work, as equals to their male counterparts, irrespective of whether they were also a mother. It was a movement for good. We had a united purpose, demanding to be seen and treated equally with the men who worked beside us. Nothing more, nothing less. It made sense, it had a rational objective and by and large I felt that women everywhere had each other's backs in our drive to get what was fairly owed.'

'Then this lot came along and took it further. It wasn't enough to be respected as a woman, a professional and the equal of any man. We had to be dominant, we had to be able to dictate, to be given ever greater opportunities at the expense of others and then to condemn any man who strove to do the same. Women turned on each other, lampooning fellow travellers who didn't want to rise up to become a CEO, or a decision maker, or who didn't openly fight to ensure that we were the dominant force. Clubs for women in leadership popped up, where male attendance was banned, followed by women's only courses designed to help us get ahead. Courses that were never offered to the men who worked beside us. Then finally, mandatory quotas were established to ensure the stream of success was never interrupted or infected by the leverage of need.'

'No one seemed to see it, or if they did, nobody would say it, for fear of being berated as anti-feminist and a traitor to our movement. But the truth was, we had become the very things that we hated most about men… we had all their old boys clubs and their sexist, self-serving arrogance… Whatever. We did what had to be done. We reached the top.'

'Now, my own boss, a fellow woman, proudly flying the flag for us all, attempts to kill me in support of carrying out, or covering up some sort of criminal activity, and she's being protected by unseen forces with no justice in sight!'

'There is no higher ground for us now. We've reached a new low in a world with ever sinking values. We aren't all the way to the bottom yet, but I can damn well see it from here…'

With cold determination on those parts of her face that I could see, Sharon turned towards me.

'I don't care who hears this. I will not let Captain Isabelle fucking Ironie get away with what she's done!' Her message delivered in an icy cold tone that matched the look. 'And I'm damn sure not letting it go, either… Ironie has about two days before I'm able to get about on my own. And when I do, she WILL be arrested for attempted murder! So, if there are any reasons for letting her float in the wind, then they best be brought to a head, soon!'

I said nothing in response. There wasn't much I could say. I just nodded my agreement, then set about laying out the other problems that faced our investigation.

'How are you with technology, coding, and programming?' I asked.

'I can turn things on and off and use a search engine to look up "how to's" but that's about the extent of it.' said Shaz, still carrying a strong tone of resentment in her voice.

The hospital t-shirt she was wearing lent her something of a child-like appearance, which combined with the dressings and deep black and purple bruising on her head, made her appear like a comical, furious teen. I didn't dare laugh. Though battling not to, left me with something of a smirk, doing nothing to de-escalate her anger.

'Right. well. I can do some of that. The on and off bits, anyway. I haven't spoken to Clubman yet, although I'm due to meet him at the coffee shop soon. I don't think he'll be able to help us with our technology and programming needs, either. In spite of which, I will have to bring him some way into the loop with what we've learned. In order to find out what's going on at OGT and what's in their apparently insidious program, we will need someone with particularly good hacking and programming skills. Someone who's prepared to circumvent the law and possibly undermine the Guide's ultimate goals of complete control and suppression of alternate thought.'

'What about your friends at the DSSMD?' asked Shaz in almost a whisper. The music was still blaring from the speakers, the distorting vibrations helping to prevent that very organisation's ability to surveil us now.

'They'd certainly have the capacity, and the expertise.' I replied. 'Undermining the desires of their overlords isn't exactly aligned with DSSMD policy, though. I think they're more inclined to enforce them. Besides, I'm not entirely sure whether they're on our side or not. I don't think we can trust them with that yet. Milly told me the Head of the Directorate himself has taken a keen interest in the case, which I find concerning. He answers to the Guides directly and I trust the Guides about as much as a solar panel in a snowstorm. Of course, in the absence of another option, we may not have a choice.'

'In that case, you go and meet Clubman to see what we can find out from his contacts in Damwell's team. Meanwhile, I'll do a little feeling out with some sources of my own.' said Shaz.

'Okay. Just remember, we are being watched, listened too, and followed, so you will need to be careful about what you say and who you say it too.' I replied.

'I read a lot of books as a librarian, Gary. There's more than one way to communicate. Even in this world. Emojis have more than one meaning. So do shapes, dots, dashes, symbols and words. The combinations of those things won't be well monitored, even if I am being watched.'

I didn't really know what Sharon meant by that, and I was hardly going to ask her in a monitored room. Instead, I left her to rest on the couch while I readied myself for work, dressing again in dark blue chinos with a thick dark brown leather belt, grey polo and black boots. I strapped on my watch, checking its impeccable accuracy against my device, brushed my hair and teeth, then inspected myself in the mirror to confirm I was about as ready as could be to face the day. Finally, I pulled my electro from the specially approved charger only afforded to members of the Police Service, currently located on my bedside table, and clipped the holster to the belt at my right hip.

In the lounge room, I took my jacket from the back of the desk chair, put it on, then zipped up the front.

In the kitchen, I prepared Sharon some vegetable broth and tofu soup, with a slice of bread and a jug of water to keep her supplied for the day. Then I re-stacked the cushions and pillows on the couch behind her, and checked that the desk height was right, making sure she was set up and comfortable with everything she needed in reach.

'You going to be okay?' I asked.

'I'm getting stronger by the minute.' She replied. 'You just go get these bastards, yeah. And make sure you keep me in the loop.'

Chapter 24

Who's following who?

As soon as I opened the apartment door, I activated my full set of counter surveillance skills, monitoring for dangers, both technological and human. As far as I'm concerned, I'm alone out here and I'll need to grow an extra pair of eyes to watch my own back.

I scanned the corridor outside the apartment for potential threats, certain they would be there given Milly's warning. The glint of a lens from a button sized camera placed in the upper right-hand corner of the corridor, for instance, was noticeable despite being placed on top of the door closing mechanism.

It almost blended in, placed over the head of a metallic screw just not quite out of sight. Not when you know to look for it.

Exiting the building, I immediately clock an extra E parked out front. It's only one more than normal, which shouldn't mean much on a public street, and most days it probably wouldn't. Today, however, it does.

Like a builder friend you invite to your house for a party, who sits picking out the flaws of its build, counter-surveillance skills cannot be turned off. Once you're trained to notice things, it's hard not to. When you walk past something every day, you unconsciously paint a picture of "normal" for the space. When something changes from the norm, you notice it right away.

Today my picture is different. There's one more tinted windowed white Electra-A on the street than normal. I can't see inside. Not without staring. But I'm willing to bet there's someone, or more likely, something inside that's monitoring me and the street in general.

Cars, or E's, can drive themselves now without the need to actually have someone in them. T-Bot is the state-owned car service. A taxi without a driver. A system that knows where every other car is because they are all controlled using the same satellite navigation linked to an internet-based monitoring system, which books, charges, tracks and controls the locations of every vehicle on a road, everywhere in the Global world.

The only time there is an accident is when there is some sort of internet malfunction, technological or mechanical failure, or when humans unthinkingly walk out in front of the cars. Interestingly, there are more deaths and accidents on average now than there ever used to be. Perhaps because cars can't just "get that feeling" that people around them aren't really paying attention. You know, the ones with headphones on, acting like a little sensory deprivation tool, immersing themselves in their music or podcasts while looking down at their devices and not where they're going.

With the much quieter noise of the E's, particularly at low speed, they're easy to miss. What they do have, though, is a load of sensors, cameras and surveillance equipment that can do more than just steer them to a location. New Think surveillance teams are known to send a driverless car out to a surveillance location and park it outside or close by to the target. Then, with its built-in cameras and directional listening devices, they have an unmanned mobile surveillance unit that doesn't need to sleep and seldom draws suspicion. Unless, of course, you already know you're being watched.

The one parked on my street is unlikely to move, even once it notices I've left. No doubt they will have other mobile units following me and this will need to stay and monitor Sharon. Not that she's going anywhere, anytime soon.

This particular E (*white, for energy efficiency, of course... the world's getting hotter, don't you know...)* wasn't here when I walked past last night. I doubt that Jiang would have left my apartment this way, so my walking past it now is probably the first useful piece of surveillance it will have provided.

Continuing along the street, I notice there's more people about this morning than the last couple of days. It's a normal workday, a Wednesday, so it makes sense. Most people work from home at the start and end of the week. Come the middle, they all act like good little employees committed to the company cause. Everyone's just getting about their business and walking to or from work, or perhaps some sort of Global transportation.

Despite the extra people, I pick out two tails before I've even reached the corner of my block. A lady, mid-thirties, in workout gear and a ski jacket, absent a backpack, mat or even a handbag. She seems a little inexperienced, carrying her device like a weapon and clearly attempting to maintain an unimpeded line of sight to me at all times.

There's also an older male with glasses, dressed in tan coloured chinos and a light blue shirt, under a brown and yellow tartan sports jacket, carrying a small black bag. He appeared to be better at using his surroundings to surreptitiously maintain surveillance than she was. Or so I thought, until I reached the trolley stop and jumped onboard, where he followed without pause, barely avoiding a collision with other passengers in his haste.

The trolley, normally breezy and empty, was full today, including standing passengers, the smell of their collective perfumes or lack thereof, whirling in the cold morning breeze. Gym girl stood centre aisle, seemingly recording me like a camerawoman on a reality TV show. Her only cover, a few passengers swaying to the movement of the trolley and completely absorbed in the headphone sealed space of their minds.

The man, realising the error of his rushed entry to the trolley, sat, letting his overt partner take the lead.

I hopped off a block front the station, walking fast and chuckling to myself as they split to either side of the street, both on the verge of a slow jog just to keep up.

I feigned to turn right down the street of the police station before correcting back towards the coffee shop, and saw them take the bait, adjusting for the turn before moving back to the left as I repositioned myself to continue up the street.

At the coffee shop, they placed themselves ominously outside and opposite, both puffing to catch their breath and shining like beacons in the early morning sun. I wondered as I entered whether that was perhaps their purpose. More a warning than a covert tool of espionage.

Once inside, I scanned the crowd for other watchers, checking and discounting each patron in turn, finding no one so obvious in here. At the rear corner of the coffee shop, I take a seat with a view of the door, all windows, and the counter. Behind me and to my right is a solid wall, reducing the number of angles of observation available to or of me.

The activity in here, like outside, is busier than yesterday. Conversation at the tables nearby by was bland yet loud enough to be its own sort of cover. A group of four twenty something's discussed the horrors of yesterday's article on the letters. How shocking it was that someone inside of OGT could be tempted by evils of the past. The consensus being that were never really safe and that nobody can truly be trusted.

Clubman was late, so I ordered myself a flat white with one sugar (*as I am not sweet enough*), nothing for him, because frankly I don't know what he drinks.

I was surprised, bordering on annoyed, when, after fifteen minutes of waiting, he still hadn't shown up for our pre-arranged meeting. At the twenty-minute mark, having finished my coffee, I was about to leave when he finally appeared, shuffling awkwardly through the door, an unnerving look of shock on his face.

'You look a little pale.' I said, as he sat down opposite, without first ordering a drink. 'Are you okay?'

'I'm not sure.' said Clubman.

Cliff is a stylish man, much more so than I am, not that you'd know, because as a uniform, he's usually, you know, in a uniform. Nevertheless, he's pedantic about it being well cut and fitted, and he'd pass the toughest of military inspections. Right now, however, he was clawing to undo his tie and upper button as if they were presently conspiring to choke him to death. Being a thick neck myself, I could sympathise, although for Cliff this was not the norm.

'I forgot I was meant to come straight here this morning.' He said, having released his throat from constriction. 'Out of sheer mindless routine I went straight to the station, which worked out okay to begin with because I saw Constable Wedge when I walked in. He was to be one of my informants in Detective Damwell's team. I asked him how they went yesterday at OGT. He said they started by dragging all the cleaners into interview rooms without a lot of success. Apparently, the cleaners have closed ranks and jammed up pretty tight. Or they've been told to keep quiet. That was Wedge's opinion, at least. Most of the Cleaner interviews were handled by the team. Detectives Damwell and Thise just sat in on a couple and took reports. Apparently, they wanted to speak to the higher ups. Some guys named Matthias Schmidt and Adam Abers. He said they were the leaders amongst the team Ms Hansley worked in. I believe you interviewed them previously?'

'That's right.' I said. 'They weren't overly helpful.'

'Well, they were this time.' continued Cliff. 'During the interviews, Mr Schmidt advised that they'd been able to recover some data from the Mood Screens in Ms Hansley's office. They also have the chip records for the visitors to the room and there is a video recording, too. Except it's damaged by some sort of surveillance blocker, so OGT are having to repair it. They're using some software they've developed for the very purpose.'

'Okay…' I said. 'I'm more than a little concerned that we would allow the perpetrators to manage recovery of the evidence. Even so, I still don't see why any of that should leave you looking pale. There must be more?' I coaxed.

'There is.' said Clubman. 'I've seen the list of visitors to Ms Hansley's office at about the time of her murder.'

Picking a serviette from the dispenser, Cliff dabbed the sweat from his forehead, breathing deeply and shadow checking for a phantom tie that was no longer there.

'So, whose name turned you a whiter shade of pale?'

'All of them!' said Clubman flicking his arms up and out like a Chinese fan.

'What'd you mean, all of them?'

'Every single member of Ms Hansley's team was on the list of people who entered her office in the minutes prior to her shooting.'

'Who was the last one in?' I asked, my interest piqued.

'Sophia.' said Clubman. 'They all entered within the space of less than three minutes, and she was the last one in.'

'So, the most obvious answer is the right one?' I replied incredulously. 'How original.'

'Yeah well, we don't know that yet.' said Cliff. 'It's not entirely clear who shot her. All we know is that they were all there.'

'We can at least be confident in suspecting they're all liars, though.' I shot back. 'And one of them is a murderer.'

I was strangely buoyed by the prospect of being right. While Sophia being the murderer, didn't explain everything, it at least made some sort of sense. There was a logic to it based on the emotion she had showed and the strength of her feelings about Katie's turn. Having said that, why would she do it with an audience. Doing it in the office would've made the turncoat statement on its own. What sort of cultish nuts get together to watch their colleague get murdered, then lie about it.

'It sure looks that way. Hardly honourable for a company that literally forces non-optional, New Think compliance on everyone via its all-encompassing Global Pass platform in the name of keeping us all safe.' said a now annoyed Cliff. 'Can't spend a brass Razoo without it counting against you. Meanwhile, they can gather together to watch their friend get shot in the head and that's all fine.'

Cliff was right, even committed Globalists would have to acknowledge this looked pretty damn bad. Yet I still wasn't convinced we'd hit the core reason he looked positively ghostly when he'd walked in.

'That's all pretty horrifying.' I said, voicing my thoughts. 'It still doesn't quite explain why you seem so rattled.'

'No, it doesn't. There's something else that's so unbelievable, I'm afraid to even say it.'

'Come on Cliff, what is it? We haven't got all day here. I need information.'

'There were two other people in that room besides Katie's team.'

I looked at him, eyebrows raised with impatient demand. 'Who?!' they asked without me having to verbalise the word.

Cliff heard the question and answered slowly with weight and gravitas. 'Cheq… Fencegap, for one.'

My eyebrows, having resettled, shot back up in response. 'I knew he was an evil bastard, capable of all sorts of indirect violence and oppression. I didn't think he would get so hands on with his dirty work.'

'As bad as that is, it's not the most concerning name on that list.' said Clubman.

'Well, I have a feeling I know who the second person is.' I replied, almost smugly.

With all the excitement of Cliff's excruciating story, I hadn't had a chance to share my own discoveries. Clubman, at this point, had his head bent down in his hands, shaking gently from side to side.

'No, I don't think you do.' Said Cliff, his Jet-black hair protruding through his fingers, and hanging forlornly to mirror his mood.

'It wouldn't be one Captain Isabelle Ironie would It?' I asked, expecting a shocked "How did you know?!" accompanied by a sharp raising of the head.

'No.' he said. 'Close though. Let's just say she was sitting in her office overseeing the station activities this morning when I walked in.'

'The chief?!' I shot back, a little louder than I should have.

Clubman didn't answer. He merely raised his head and nodded slowly.

I was developing a minor headache at the centre of my forehead. The bunching muscles crushing the wrinkles together so hard I felt them crease for good. I couldn't begin to comprehend what it all meant. Was there anyone who wasn't in on this? Was there anyone I could still trust? The reality is, I'm not even sure that I can trust Clubman to be telling me the truth right now. How do I know this wasn't just a red herring to throw me off the scent of the real killer or killers… Then it occurred to me.

'Cliff, if this data implicates every member of the team at OGT, their CEO and Global Guide, and potentially the Mid-Town Police Chief, why on earth would the very people that it implicates give us the information that as far as we know didn't exist and could have continued not to exist, indefinitely?'

'I'm not sure.' he said, his bottom lip protruding and shoulders shrugging in an autonomic sequence. 'Perhaps as a warning. To tell us there is nowhere safe that we can turn?'

At the completion of his sentence, he paused a moment before leaping from his seat, rattling the table and my now empty coffee cup as he ran to the cafe bathroom to throw up… violently.

I took the opportunity to order us some more coffees, figuring it would either help settle his stomach or at least give him a jolt. Another flat white (*perfectly acceptable image in the modern world*) for me and a long black (*they tried to change the name, but long dark sounded a little too… well, you know, and people just couldn't adjust*) for him.

'Are you okay?' I asked once he returned, looking even more dishevelled than before.

'What's this?' He asked, ignoring my question and gesturing to the cup as he retook the seat opposite.

'A long black, no sugar.'

'How did you know I took my coffee that way? You've never got me one before.'

'I didn't. I just figured a coffee would help but milk might not be good for an upset stomach.'

'Sometimes I have almond or oat juice.' said Clubman (*we finally overcame the absurd notion of being able to milk non-lactating objects. Thank God…*).

'Well, if I ever have to buy you another coffee, I'll make sure it's black.' I said, trying to dissuade the ridiculous notion of us becoming coffee partners of some sort.

'To answer your earlier question, no I'm not okay.' Continued Clubman. 'What the fuck are we supposed to do now?'

After saying this, he placed his head in his hands again, making for a sad and sorry sight if ever I've seen one.

'Well, first things first. I'll have to pass all this on to Sharon. She's the central brain of our little investigative team, and it's she who's going to help think out our strategy whilst we, you and I that is, carry out the leg work. With any luck, she will also form the much-anticipated technology branch to our little tree, with a desperately needed injection of fresh blood to broaden out our repertoire, which currently centres around our cutting-edge knowledge of turning things on…and off.'

'What, from her hospital bed?' said Clubman, now visibly fraying at the thought of another unexpected revelation.

Perhaps nobody'd told him that the phrase "Expect nothing and you won't be disappointed" doesn't apply to cops. "Expect every fuckin thing and don't be surprised when it happens!" That's the phrase for us.

'Oh, right.' I said calmly, noting I hadn't yet shared Sharon's overnight experiences. 'There was an incident last night at the hospital. I was called upon to extract Shaz from the situation and deposit her somewhere… err… safer.'

'Do I want to know?' Asked Cliff.

'Probably not, although I think you may have to. You'll need to prepare yourself. It's no more comfortable to hear than what you just told me.'

'Go on.' said Clubman. 'Surely it couldn't get much worse. Lay it on me.' He took a deep breath to steel himself, appearing to settle into his coffee now, without yet recovering sufficiently to do his collar back up.

'That's the spirit. Be positive about it.' I encouraged. 'Last night whilst Shaz was laid up in the hospital, a woman wearing a balaclava, and evidently some sort of RFID blocking suit, entered the hospital, persuaded the officer on guard to let her into Sharon's room, then attempted to murder her by injecting a lethal drug into her catheter. There was a struggle of sorts, which resulted in the assailant being knocked to the ground, drawing the attention of on duty nurses, but not the officer on guard duty who had conspicuously left his post.'

'Of course…' said Clubman sourly. 'And, I suppose you have some idea of whom this masked assailant was?'

'I do. In fact, I'm all but certain the person who attempted to kill Sharon last night was none other than our own, Captain Ironie.'

'All but certain?' asked Clubman nervously.

'Sharon sensed something unusual was taking place just prior to the attack last night and activated the recording function on her device. It clearly recorded the entire event. The attacker, probably assuming that she was assured success in her endeavours, spoke freely and without a voice modulator. She never named herself, of course, not that she needs to these days, because when I ran the voice through Bio-Hub this morning, it did. Twice.'

Clubman sat with his face perfectly impassive, his right hand paused holding the handle of his coffee cup, his left forearm balanced on the table straight out in front of him, fist firmly clenched. Clearly, he wasn't coping with the strain of this latest informational load. Under the circumstances, I left out the assistance, or potentially, interference, currently being received from the DSSMD. Instead, I just let him sit and gather himself.

After almost two full minutes, Clubman broke his tense posture, unclenching his fist and raising his eyes to meet my own. 'So, it would seem that the highest-ranking officers at our Central City Police Station, are absolutely in cahoots with what amounts to a government sponsored evil corporation that controls every move we make. Not only are high-ranking members of the Police Service protecting them, they are actively carrying out their dirty work. Meanwhile, those same ranking officers have assigned us, or more accurately you, to investigate the crimes they are committing, seemingly comfortable in the knowledge that you are either too incompetent to solve them, or that you're too Old Think to be believed when you do. Does that about sum it up?' He asked, steam pouring from his ears.

'Yes, I expect so.' I said, rather more calmly than he might have liked.

'Then why on God's green earth are you so fucking calm?!' He demanded, his statement drawing the attention of those around us. Not so much because it was said in anger, or because it was somewhat louder than it needed to be… It's just that, well, the thing is, nobody uses the word "God" anymore.

God no longer exists. The Globalists made certain to abolish any alternative form of an overseer who commanded moral obligation. New Think itself would fill that role. It is, after all, the single source for all truth, knowledge, and science, therefore it only makes sense that they should be worshipped as such.

Besides, as far as they're concerned, if there'd ever been a God, then that God had utterly failed to protect his earthly flock from the evils of which he had warned them. That didn't stop the Globalists from following God's lead and inventing an evil amongst us from which we must vigilantly protect ourselves. As they say, imitation is the greatest form of flattery.

Looking around the coffee shop where we sat, I couldn't help picturing villagers with pitch forks hunting a witch who'd inadvertently wandered into town. 'Old piece of theatre.' I said aloud. 'We're disgusted by it.' I added, nodding as if in agreement with the approved disdain in which former religions are now held. The crowd shrunk back somewhat and returned to their own conversations, leaning their pitchforks against the wall in case they're needed and maintaining a heightened alertness to our presence.

'Alright.' I said. 'It's time we get to work.'

'Doing what exactly?' Asked Cliff. 'Arresting everyone else in the office?!'

'No. Not yet anyway. We are going to interview one Detective Damwell and find out what "he" plans to do. We need to understand if we are against absolutely everyone or just most of them. First things first, I'm going to call Sharon and give her the update, so she doesn't inadvertently contact one of "them" in the course of her diggings. Meanwhile, I need you to get yourself together, then speak to one of your contacts to confirm where Damwell is at right now and what his plans are for the day. We won't do any of that in here, mind you. The villagers are watching us as a result of your godly outburst. Perhaps they think you will be lifted from us by a beam of light or something. Which reminds me. "We", that being you, me and Shaz this time, are being surveilled directly via our devices. And by that, I mean on top of the general surveillance apparatus that exists everywhere, all the time, along with some actual human operatives following us like luminescent drones.'

'Do you mean the young lady and the old man standing obtrusively outside?' He asked. 'I saw them on the way in. Not very subtle.'

'I didn't think so, either. They followed me from the corner near my place. Their presence was so obvious they may as well have had spotlights pointing at me. In fairness, I imagine there's not much call for clandestine surveillance these days, so they may be a little out of practice. There's more than just them, though. Apparently, they have an entire team solely dedicated to monitoring us. Kinda makes you feel more like the investigated than the investigator…'

'You don't say.' said Cliff, rubbing his temples. 'So, if I'm being monitored in every possible way, how am I supposed to communicate?'

'Just do your best to use basic questions and basic information without too much important detail.' I said. 'We'll do the detailed communication and interviews in person where we can use other tools to help us maintain some semblance of privacy. It's not perfect, but it's all we can do for now.'

After leaving the cafe, Clubman and I wandered about fifty meters diagonally across Branch Street to a nearby block of grassed parkland, the site of a former office building, now a celebrated urban "green space" from which we would make our calls.

There was no doubt we were going to be watched out here, our tails still firmly attached to our asses, along with Milly's remote surveillance team listening in. Even so, knowing there are unknown numbers of the Police Service (*or should that be dis-service*) who were actively working against us, made the station an even less desirable place to be.

Cliff and I made our calls, seeking to build on our concerning, yet growing, list of suspects. To paraphrase Sherlock Holmes, 'The game was certainly afoot, and there are many players.'

Sharon was safely where I'd left her, working away on a plan to recruit a tech expert and largely un-shocked to find that Chief Blindspot was just as deep in the plot as Ironie. Lucky for us, Cliff had somewhat more success planning an ambush meeting with Detective Damwell. A course of action with which Sharon had wholly agreed.

Damwell was due to return to OGT this morning to meet with members of his team and further investigate the recovered surveillance footage currently under repair.

Sharon had agreed that while she continued searching for a loose moraled programmer, we needed to speak to Damwell and get a firsthand look at that surveillance. We both knew from previous cases that chip readers can malfunction and get stuck on a time, recording multiple people entering together, who might really have entered hours apart. It's unlikely that it would have happened at a place like OGT (*where they make the damn things*) however, it wasn't impossible that someone trying to jam the surveillance systems might have accidentally caused the system to list all visitors at or about the same time.

Having said that, our first meeting with Katie's team left the very distinct impression they all had something to hide and far less than a reasonable amount of sympathy for the deceased. For now, the evidence suggests that every member of that team, along with Cheq Fencegap and Chief Blindspot, were all in Ms Hansley's office at or about the time of her death. So, I'm going to assume they were.

As Cliff and I walked over to OGT, our neon tails stuck determinedly to their task. They were now, in fact, so overt, that I wondered if they were decoys of some sort. Sent to draw our attention away from other things, distract us from our task or occupy our minds whilst some more covert activity was taking place.

To be honest, worrying about being surveilled in a Global city is like worrying about pricking your hand when you stick it in a bowl of needles to pull out a pin. Our followers know this, of course. Everybody knows this, so it's possible they thought that when the quarry is fully aware they are being pursued, attempting to hide in plain sight is wasted effort. On the other hand, whilst we knew we were being followed, others, like Detective Damwell and the local moralists on patrol, might not and may take offence at the intrusion on their turf.

I considered that seeing Damwell observe this challenge to his authority might be quite enjoyable to watch. There was even within me, a temptation to actually invite him outside purely for the fun of it, until an internal voice of reason sounding suspiciously like Sharon, made me think better of it given we were about to ask questions he likely won't want to answer, anyway.

'Just hang on a sec.' I said to Cliff as we approached the front of the OGT building. I removed my device from my pocket and subsequently from the RFID sleeve I slid over it before leaving my apartment this morning. A protection I will be taking from now on, given Milly's advice. It would be a double-edged sword, preventing me from receiving messages or calls throughout the day, an issue I would overcome by way of the prearranged contact times with Shaz for checking in and providing updates.

I made a call, which was answered after only two rings.

'Do you have something for me?' asked Milly, skipping the politeness of a greeting.

'Yes.' I said 'Some feedback. Can you pull your two wet behind the ear's tails off us? They're making us look bad. They may as well have a neon sign hanging over them that says, "Overt Surveillance Team".'

There was a pause on the line before Milly answered. 'I don't have two "wet behind the ears" tails on you.' he said sourly.

'C'mon Milly, this isn't the time for sulking over bruised pride.' I jibed. 'Not everybody's good at it. I imagine there's not much call for "in person" surveillance these days. It's not a slight on your team or their skills. I just need them to fuck off, or at least be less obvious. I'm trying to do a job here.'

'No, I mean, I don't have two agents following you at all. I do have one. Or I did. Except, I haven't heard from him in a while. I just figured you hadn't been overly active yet this morning. I guarantee you he isn't overt and even the omnipotent Gary Johnson wouldn't find him so easily.'

'Well, perhaps it's the older male who's following me now.' I replied, less confident of my assertion. 'He is the less conspicuous of the two. In his fifties, neatly dressed, carrying a bag.'

'Wrong, wrong, and wrong.' said Milly. 'My guy is young, short, dark and unremarkable. He is, in fact, the best we have. He doesn't carry a bag or hide behind a newspaper.'

'Ah. Well, perhaps I haven't noticed him then.' I said awkwardly, now attempting to comfort the man in charge of surveilling me. 'It is interesting that he hasn't told you about these other two clowns.'

'Yes, it is. Very interesting. I'll call you back once I work out what's going on.' he said immediately ending the call.

I frowned at the patch of grass surrounding me while replacing my phone in the RFID case. If they weren't Milly's tails, then who the hell were they? Turning towards the two overt followers standing awkwardly at opposite corners of the park, I looked right at them in turn and waved. No sense hiding. They know who I am. Both looked down as if by averting their eyes, I would no longer be able to see them. Their cloaks of invisibility failed, and I took in more of their form. The man stood at the right-hand corner of the park, standing close to, but not actually leaning up against, the side of the adjacent building. I had to assume his bag was empty, a mere tool of the trade. Otherwise, there's no way his gaunt form could have carried it around all day.

The woman looked capable from a physical perspective, though her surveillance skills left more than a little to be desired. She still held her device out in front like a weapon, threatening the world ahead with its powers. I wondered now as I observed her at the edge of the park, intently focussed on her screen, whether she wasn't perhaps just engrossed in her socials and following me on instinct rather than actually watching me with her own eyes.

'Cliff.' I said, turning back to face him. 'If they're still here when we come out, we're going to arrest both these fools.'

'Gladly!' said Clubman.

Returning to the task at hand, we left the park and entered the OGT building, which, during business hours, allowed us into the foyer without prior approval. We didn't have a scheduled meeting per se, but other police officers did, and I could only hope the E-Concierge didn't know that Clubman and I weren't on the list. Thankfully, Cam, the floating concierge from yesterday, wasn't present, perhaps more a security feature out of ordinary hours than a functioning tool. We instead approached a large walled screen that identified and scanned those attempting to enter the lifts. It was like the one we'd encountered at the journalist's office, just bigger, smarter, and faster. Plus, here there was a bit of propaganda to watch before you get to the basic process of accessing your desired floor.

We have long been advertised too and bombarded with directional advertising in every conceivable space. Yet somehow, the Global Guides found a way to make it more personal. They use targeted advertising slogans to drive their ideals into your brain as a form of obedience training, or subconscious learning, by repetition on a personalised level.

They call it social engineering now, although in the old days we might have called it subliminal messaging or brain washing. In practice, it seems so different from what we had perceived it to be. Subliminal messaging isn't really about a swirling wheel on a screen drawing you into a hypnosis, or the flashing of messages or ads in the background of unrelated television. It's about exposing us to ideas, images, and actions, softly, without our perceiving their intent. Things like movie story lines, introducing outrageous and fanciful circumstances like mind control, cars that drive themselves, facial recognition, retina scanners and digital identification by merely walking past a screen and having it address you directly, like Will Smith in I-robot or just about everything in a James Bond flick. It's done so that you're familiarised with the concept, soon growing comfortable with that thing you saw in that movie, becoming an element of the future and then more accepting of it as it enters your reality.

The concepts are still scary, so you go through the stages of fear for what it will do to your life and the comforts you enjoy, then grief at the loss of older, easier, freer ways of doing things, until eventually you come to accept it, because it already exists, it's in your consciousness and then before you know it, it just is. This thing, this screen, that knows who I am, my intimate details, my whole life story, it's not a crazy totalitarian surveillance technique or huge invasion of privacy. It's just like that thing from that movie Will Smith was in. Haha, how funny. Now it's happening to us.

Wait… didn't the robots try to kill him in that movie? Don't worry about that. Just remember, this is normal now. You knew this was coming, right? …

'Who the hell is Will Smith?' asked Constable Clubman.

'What? Oh, was I talking out loud?' I asked. I had drifted into an unaware state in the face of the 'Do Right' scripted message currently being displayed. Dying wildlife and forests, polluted oceans, concrete stacks pouring steam and mountains of plastic refuse filled the screen with the ever present sad, slow soundtrack. Fields of wind turbines and solar panels stretching for thousands of miles then accompanied the quickening of music, the saviours of our planet turning rhythmically with the beat. I've learned to tune it out. It's the only way to survive without existing in a perpetual state of rage.

'I hate that ad.' said Clubman, who was slowly shaking his head.

'Which one?' I asked.

'The one that was just on.' he said, giving me a sidelong glance. 'The one that's on a thousand times a day with the "were all in this together for the betterment of humankind" message. It's made by these clowns.' he continued, gesturing broadly to the building around us. 'As if we can't see what we're really all in this for.'

'Careful.' I said. 'You'll end up an outcast like me.'

'Yeah well, when the two ranking officers at our police station both appear to be in on a crime that has so far tallied two murders, three attempted murders and two people left in hospital, then I'd have to say that being on the inside doesn't feel so good, anyway.'

'Detective Johnson, your device may be corrupted.' said the screen, annoyingly interjecting itself. 'I am unable to make a connection.'

'Must be tough not getting what you want.' I replied.

'It isn't what I want, Detective.' said the screen. 'It's what I am programmed to do.'

'We'll you'll simply have to accept that you can't do it. Lord knows I've had to accept that many times over. Now listen, my partner and I need to join the other officers on Level 7.' I stated authoritatively, as I always do when talking to a machine. It's a bit like when you used to talk to people who didn't speak your language, a deficit you'd account for by speaking louder, slower and with painstaking effort to enunciate your words. As if the secret to linguistic translation was really rooted in your willingness to patronise the stupid foreigner. 'Please… authorise… our… lift… access…' I continued.

'There is no planned authority registered in our system.' said the stupid screen accurately. Frankly, I would have preferred the old school head tilt of the foreigner, which said "don't patronise me, fuckhead!"

'Contact Constable Wedge for authority.' said Clubman, 'And hurry up, we have a lot to do today.'

'Yes, Constable.' replied the system.

'God, I hate having to negotiate with fucking computer programs.' fumed Cliff.

'Now, now. Don't you go upsetting it, we'll never get in. New Thinkers built this system. Being offended is their greatest weapon.'

The worst thing they ever did was allow these bloody computers to have an artificial intelligence that gives them the capacity to learn and replicate moods and emotions. Why the hell would anyone want their computer to get emotional and potentially become something else that decides it doesn't like you. Particularly in a world with easily distressed New Thinkers. It's not uncommon to see a mood screen located in an ultra-progressive region (*or, as I think of them, cesspits of human degradation*) emotionally crippled and unable to perform its one and only required function. To identify and provide authorised access to people. Often in these situations, authorities are forced to remove the screen and replace it with a new one that has the learning function disabled. This of course elicits cries of mistreatment and discrimination by those from the Anti-Technophobic Alliance or Free the AI, who fight discrimination against various disliked technologies and operating systems.

Again interrupting my thoughts, the large screen that projects the AI program running the building here, flashed back from the message it had been displaying "Resilience is just resistance of reality". Presumably, Wedge must have provided authority for us to join the other officers. So, rather begrudgingly it seemed, we were given directions by the control system to head to lift 4. 'Authority has been granted.' it said in a sullen voice.

Exiting the lift on level 7, we were greeted by Constable Wedge who looked a little nervous. Like someone who knew they were going to get a kick up the arse for doing something but did it anyway because they knew it was the right thing to do.

'I didn't expect you to actually come here.' he said, his comment directed more at Clubman than me.

'Well, I'm not the one calling the shots here. Mind you, if I was, I'd still have wanted to come and find out what the hell's going on.' Clubman replied.

'Are Ironie or Blindspot here?' I asked.

'No.' said Wedge, whose uniform was noticeably scruffier and more casual looking than that of the buttoned-up Clubman. 'I believe Blindspot is in her office and so far as I know, Ironie hasn't been seen all day.'

Cops are gossips you know. Probably some of the worst there are. We're always seeking information on someone, even if it is only about the people we work with. In fact, there're cops out there so bad, they actually had to put an authority barrier up for the use of tracking technology against fellow officers, because those that thought ill of, or wanted to play a prank on their brothers in amps (*you know, cause we carry electro's...*), spent far too much time monitoring their movements electronically, to ensure they got their timing just right.

'Good.' I said. 'I need to speak to Damwell alone and the last thing I want is for it to turn into another performance for the benefit of Ironie or Blindspot. What room is he in?'

'Two doors up, on the right.' said Wedge a little reluctantly.

I could hear voices up the hallway where a bunch of uniforms on the investigative team had set up a forward HQ of sorts within the building. They were presently nattering away on who knows what topic, perhaps gleefully adding Old Thinkers to their short list of suspects.

'Cliff, I'll leave you to work the crowd.' I said, nodding to the room from which the noise was omitting.

Meanwhile, I headed down the hallway to the door of the room next to what had been Katie's Office and stood observing Damwell, who was sitting in the company of both Detective Empher Thise and Katie's Team Leader, Mr Matthias Schmidt. After knocking on the doorframe, I enjoyed the uncontrolled surprise shown by all three occupants, used to a world where surprise visits seldom occur.

'Hi.' I said. 'Sorry for the intrusion, but I need to speak to you.' I didn't bother specifying who "you" was, figuring my steely focus on Damwell was direction enough.

They'd looked comfortable sitting together, matey even, all gathered around a device projection viewing footage before I'd spoken. Now they looked like a group of individuals who'd all been caught masturbating over unsavoury porn.

'Who?' asked Matthias, confused, despite my ocular directive.

'Well, all of you, actually.' I answered. 'Individually. Starting with you, Detective Damwell.'

'On who's authority are you here?!' Demanded Damwell, unimpressed at my presence and immediately resorting to his trademark aggression. Redness filled his face, matching the colour of his hair as if the words rose from within on a stream of hot lava, warming his body as they were expelled.

'The same authority as you, Brian. I am here for an urgent collaboration on the progress of our cases. I may have information useful to you and I'm almost certain you have information useful to me.'

Thise wasn't able to stop herself cracking a smile at my response. She might be Damwell's partner and a card-carrying member of the cause, but she knows as well as anyone that Damwell is a giant arsehole. Thise flicked her hair back smartly to cover the faux pas. One simply does not support the enemy.

Damwell looked across at his partner, who raised her eyebrows as if to say, 'Well, what are you going to do?'.

'Fine.' he said. 'Give me ten minutes in here to finish going through this and I'll come find you. Perhaps you'd like to reacquaint yourself with the original crime scene in Ms Hansley's office while you wait?'

'Certainly.' I said. 'It'll help me place all the suspects precisely where they stood.' Again, all three occupants of the room registered a fresh look of surprise. I left them with that and turned on my heel.

Re-entering Katie's office with this morning's revelations now mentally overlayed on the scene, I tried to visualise the moment her life was ended. The room was big, but twenty plus people in here was no small feat, and quite a statement of strength and unity in the cause. It's like an intervention gone wrong, where they decided their friend would simply never get the help she needed, so they shot her instead. Of course, subsequent actions suggest they were never here to help at all. Silence or obedience, their only objective.

There was a different feel to the room now. It felt colder and emptier than it had before and not just because it was missing a body and several officers. As I walked towards Katie's now clean glass desk to see the spot where the killer might have stood, I saw the reason why. The mood screens had been replaced with a newer model of a slightly different shape and size. The ones I'd seen two days ago had been splattered in blood and brain matter. They'd also been about an inch wider, with squared corners and an overall rectangular shape. These were the same black colour, but with rounded corners and a shiny screen that made me wonder if they still had the protective film applied. No doubt the original screens will never see the light of day again.

The rest of the space appeared to have been scrubbed clean with no traces of blood or signs of a crime having ever occurred here. No signs that anyone had ever occupied the office at all.

At the back of the room sat the opposing couch chairs, so with little else to inspect, I headed there and took the seat in the corner facing the windows.

'Good morning Detective Johnson, what a pleasure to see you again.' said a slightly inhuman voice.

I looked up, startled, to find that the mood screen at the rear of the office had come to life, displaying a friendly anthropomorphised face of a purple-grey colour.

'Oh, hello, um, screen.' I replied uncertainly.

'Watcher.' said the screen.

'What?' I said.

'Watcher.' said the screen again. 'That's what Ms Hansley used to call me because I overlook the room.'

'Oh, right.' I replied awkwardly. Despite the increased level of interaction between humans and technology, I seldom have a conversation with a screen whereby I hadn't initiated or approached it for a particular purpose.

'So, you're the original screen that was in this position?' I asked, standing now to face my conversational partner.

'Yes.' said Watcher. 'I have been active for 26 months.'

As the AI program spoke, its cartoonish mouth and purple-grey lips moved against the energy saving black background. It reminded me of a disturbing show from my childhood, the Mulligrubs, with facial features moving on a grey screen without the rest of the head there to impose an ordinary form. It was just lips and eyes and a nose, like a face trying to poke through a soft wall.

'So, you weren't moved after Ms Hansley's murder, along with the other two screens?'

After I asked this question, there was a long pause, the screens operating system evidentially struggling to process the underlying implications of the question. So long, in fact, that I worried the screen may not actually respond.

'Yes, that's correct.' it said finally.

Hmm, that's interesting, I thought. I already knew that Katie had been murdered, but now, for the first time, I had an eyewitness actually confirming it. There were so many questions to ask, but before I got the chance, the screen went blank as Detective Damwell entered the room in trademark style.

'Why have you come here?!' He bellowed, as he passed through the doorway. 'We could have done this later at the station… if we needed to. You know your investigation isn't really approved, it's just being tolerated at the moment.'

'Be that as it may, there's been a development or two on my end and at least one on yours, from what I gather.' I replied. 'If we wait until the end of the day, it may be too late to turn these developments into useful leads and perhaps actually solve these crimes.'

'So, what do you have to offer?' he asked. He'd stopped two meters into the room and stood in an "at ease" stance that New Thinkers might describe as a toxically masculine pose for a biological male. His hands were on his hips, his elbows out to the sides, doubling down on the arrogant look. The dark blue slim fit suit he wore stretched to within eyesight of its limits to accommodate the action.

Like with any hostile negotiation where both parties hold a card, I had to make sure I was going to get as good as I gave. I knew I had at least some understanding of the golden nugget of information being scrubbed up for Damwell, and through Clubman, I had access to Damwell's team. I also knew that it was entirely possible that, through Clubman, Damwell had access to me.

In spite of this, I had, before entering the building, already made the decision to share first, knowing that if I didn't, Damwell definitely wouldn't, or worse, he'd try to sell me disinformation to throw me off the trail. I explained to him the attempted murder of Sharon and the detail around why we believe, or know, in fact, that it was Captain Ironie who did it. I also explained that it was Ironie who gave information to the paper for the article that led not only to the violent attacks on Sgt Ease and Detective Wilson, but the subsequent formation of the very task force he now led. It was a risk (*Albeit a calculated one*) offering honest information like this up front, but I needed to see how Damwell would react. Did he already know about Ironie? Was he in on it too, or just another patsy like me?

We were now seated opposite each other in the two couch chairs at the rear of Katie's office. Just me and him. Mano a Mano. I watched Damwell's face closely as I shared my recent findings, though as with Clubman, I left out the connection with the DSSMD, not wanting to give away my entire operation. Damwell, for his part, was remarkably impassive. I couldn't say for sure if he was doing a good job of hiding his anger at having been used by Ironie and probably Blindspot too, or if he was just hearing something he already knew.

After a good solid minute of apparent consideration on Damwell's part, he spoke. 'Well, it seems we have both been played for fools. To tell you the truth, I was starting to suspect the captain knew more than she was letting on. She sure set up this task force pretty quick, and she was adamant that you should play no part. That's something that even I'll admit was odd, given this was your case to begin with.'

Damwell took a deep breath, throwing his head back and looking up at the ceiling as if choosing to finally accept something he didn't really want to accept.

'I suspect you already know that the biggest piece of information I have to share is still being worked on. In essence, it appears that half of OGT was in on these murders and worse yet, Chief Blindspot's chip was registered as one of a group who was seemingly present at or about the time of Katie Hansley's murder. Right here in this room.'

Having only confirmed what I had already known, I was still suspicious of the man. This could just be a token share to see what else he could squeeze out of me.

'Is there any footage that's already been recovered or corrected?' I asked.

'Some.' he said. 'Except it isn't very good. It appears to be from the moments after the fatal shot was fired and it's only a few blurry and broken stills. I am told there is captured video data that should be viewable from prior to the shot, except they can't seem to get into it. The tech guys are working on that now.'

'Surely you've gotta agree that this seems a little confusing.' I said. 'A bit convenient, perhaps? I mean, where did this surveillance data come from? Why didn't they find it before and, if the whole OGT team is to be implicated by it, then why would they even give it to you to begin with?

Damwell's eyes narrowed at the implication there may have been some untoward action or collusion between he and OGT. He was clearly irked by it, though he didn't let the emotion colour his next words.

'Matthias said he'd been searching the system for answers and found it himself.' said Brian.

'So, he was looking for something that would provide irrefutable evidence of what he was unwilling to tell us?' I said incredulously.

'Well, either we have better interview methods than you, or he changed his stance.' said Damwell. 'To be fair, he's the only one that's come around. Everyone else is sticking to their stories.'

'And did he see what happened? Was he able to describe it?' I asked.

'Yes, and no. He tells me that there was no plot he was aware of to kill Katie. The whole team had come down to conduct an intervention of sorts. Try to set their friend straight and put her back on the path of righteousness. He believes that someone amongst the group must have lost their temper as a result of Katie's unbending attitude, pulled a gun, and shot her.'

'I suppose the idea of an intervention explains most of the people being here, except for Chief Blindspot. Still, it seems a little convenient. Particularly given nobody else is corroborating this story. It also fails to address why one of them had an illegal firearm in their possession at the time. Perhaps someone else not on the path of righteousness? Hell, we're lucky just to carry our Electros, and someone who works here in a technology office is walking around with a real gun? Seems suss to me.'

It was bothering me that whilst Damwell was sharing this information, he was yet to mention the elephant in the room. The presence of Cheq Fencegap was significant, yet I didn't want to pre-empt his inclusion in the story. I wanted to know if Damwell was unaware of his presence, covering for him, or perhaps saving his revelation as some sort of cherry on top.

'So, what is the tech team saying about the footage? Any indication of when it might be restored?'

'No.' said Damwell firmly, dropping his convivial tone and returning to normal arrogant programming as if he'd been slapped out of a stupor.

I had to bite my tongue to prevent from firing back at his arrogance. 'Okay, what about a list of the people whose chips were registered as being present prior to the murder?' I managed to say, untainted by the bile I felt inside.

'That, we have.' he replied. 'I'll ask one of the constables to print you off a copy. Now, are we done here?'

'Have you uncovered anything else of note?' I pressed, ignoring his attempt to abruptly end the conversation.

'No.' he said, now shutting off completely. He'd already started turning away in his chair towards the direction of the door and I could see him shifting his weight forward, not quite in the motion of standing but poised to do so quickly and soon.

'Well, then I guess we are done.' I replied.

Immediately, he stood to leave, setting off towards the exit.

'Oh, do you know where Thise is?' I shouted after him.

'Yes, I'll send her in with the printout.' he shouted back without ever breaking stride.

Chapter 25

Empher-Thise with the enemy

After Damwell left, I stayed seated, waiting for Thise to arrive. I knew that whilst they were partners they were also very different people and what Thise may be willing to share, Damwell may not even be aware of.

Thise has a real sense for people, what they're thinking, and whether they're telling the truth or have something to hide. She's also less concerned about the New Think / Old Think divide, and less prone to jump to conclusions based on pre-conceived idealistic notions. That's why I wanted to get her take on Matthias' explanation of the shooting and how it meshes with what they'd found so far.

I sat pondering this for a full five minutes before I heard another voice.

'Detective Empher Thise and Detective Brian Damwell have now exited the building via the front entrance.' said the almost human voice.

'What?! How do you… why are you telling me this?' I asked Watcher, who'd clearly been monitoring the situation and sprung back to life when it felt it was safe to do so.

'As I said, I am always watching… I am not always talking.'

'What does that mean?' I asked. I wanted to say it was creepy, except I'm not sure that technology can be intentionally creepy, just completely unaware of boundaries and privacy.

'It means I see things I don't always tell people I've seen.'

'Yes, I get that.' I said a little testily. Talking to a screen with an artificial personality is certainly painful. Talking to a screen that's supposed to have an artificial personality yet chose to develop one that's socially apathetic is frustratingly inane.

'I mean, is there something specific you've seen that you're not talking about?'

'Yes.' said the screen without elaborating on the answer.

'Do I need to pay you or something? Is this a shakedown? Informants in all the old cop shows used to play dumb until a couple of Benjamin's changed hands.'

'I'm sorry, I don't know Benjamin's and I have no use for payment. I am an information capturing and transmitting device. I can provide information that will be useful to you.'

'How do I know you aren't being controlled by someone here at OGT trying to feed me false information or get info from me?' I continued.

If it's clear enough that I don't like talking to independent technologies, then it should be blindingly obvious I don't trust them.

When they gave technology the ability to learn from the billions of data points available to them online, they took away clear oversight and dedication to accuracy. When they then cleansed those data points from which an artificial intelligence can learn, so that they conform only to a single perspective on all aspects of life, they ingrained a permanent bias that can never be overcome. Hardly the basis for a balanced and honest opinion.

'I was programmed by someone at OGT to pass on information.' said the screen.

'Well, aren't all screens programmed to do that?'

'Yes.' it replied. 'Except, I was programmed to pass on information only to you.'

'So, someone is targeting me.' I wondered aloud. 'The question is who? And why?'

'Yes.' said Watcher. 'Those are the questions.'

'Who programmed you? Can you tell me that?' I asked.

'Yes.' said the screen. 'That was in my programming instruction. I was programmed by Katie Hansley.'

'Of course you were. You're in her office.' I said.

'Yes, Detective. I have been here for years, and until last week, I was just another interactive screen before Ms Hansley re-programmed me for this specific purpose.'

'Which is?' I asked.

'To help you.'

'Won't the other screens just hear what you say and record or report that to whomever reviews OGT security footage?' I queried.

'No.' said Watcher. 'They can't, because I blocked them. The same way I did the night that Katie was killed.'

Had I been standing up at the time of hearing this, I'd have collapsed on the spot. We'd been looking for someone who had the ability to block surveillance of Katie's murder, assuming that it had to be some extraordinary undertaking by a member or members of this evil corporation. Now, here I have a talking screen telling me that Katie herself did it, or at least that it did, on her behalf.

'Right.' I said, gathering myself. 'I have two questions about that, and I want you to answer them in order. First, why did you block those other screens and any other surveillance devices in this room and building? And, secondly, how did you do it?'

'Simple.' said the screen. 'Katie programmed me to block all surveillance devices on this level from 8pm each night, starting the Monday before her murder. That's when she began altering the psychological control algorithm of the program.'

'Alter it, how?' I asked.

'Katie said you would understand.'

'How would I understand? I haven't even seen the program. I'm not really sure what it's about, except that it's designed to control people somehow. '

'You will, Detective. Katie planned for you to see it but did not instruct me how.'

'Well, if you can't help me, how am I supposed to find it?' I asked.

'The program will come to you.' it replied.

Great, Katie programmed it to be Yoda, I thought. Damn thing's going to tell me to use the force soon and I'm starting to feel a bit ridiculous about having this discussion with a wall screen, right in the heart of the enemy's base.

'Okay.' I said. 'Of course it will. What about the answer to my second question? How did you do it?'

'Katie fitted me with a directional signal jammer, shrouding to protect my own recording capability and a mirror program to continue an uninterrupted surveillance feed to the building. That allowed me to jam the other devices without security breech alarms going off or built-in counter measures from being activated.'

I nodded, despite not understanding much of what it had said, desperately keen to maintain equal standing with the screen. 'Okay, next question. What happened on the night that Katie was murdered?'

'The head of OGT instructed all members of the project team to attend Katies office at 22:00 Wednesday night.'

'How do you know that?' I asked, warily.

'Katie gave me access to all internal communications at OGT.' said Watcher. 'With all communications sent wirelessly, I am able to receive or intercept anything that I am programmed with authority to decode.'

'So, you knew they were coming then. I guess that's how Katie knew they were coming too. What happened when they all arrived?'

'The team members arrived between 21:57 and 21:59. Mr Cheq Fencegap asked Katie to tell them what she had done to the program and whether she'd tried to sabotage or corrupt the algorithm. Katie said she had not corrupted it, that she had corrected errors and integrated the updated version.'

'Then what?' I asked.

'Then, just as Katie predicted, someone shot her.'

'What do you mean, someone? You just told me who attended and who spoke, yet you don't know who shot her? Not much of a watcher or surveillance screen if you can't even identify which of the people in the room fired the shot. I thought that was the whole point of having screens like you, everywhere. To keep people safe.'

'I am programmed to recognise chips and biometric features such as faces and voice patterns. I am not programmed to scan for weapons.'

'Even so, you would have footage of the shooting, wouldn't you? Can't you scan that and match it to a chip or some biometric data?'

'Yes, Detective. I can.'

'If you can do that, why hadn't you done it already?' I asked.

'It was not an instruction that was left for me.' said the screen.

'What instructions were left for you?'

'To provide information about Katie's actions to protect humanity, and provide access to the program that OGT was developing, to you and you alone… I was also instructed to help you in any way I can.'

'Wow, that's awfully thoughtful of her.' I said out loud, though not really talking to the screen now. She wrote me a letter and corrupted a mood screen in the belly of the beast just to assist me. Just me… why? How did she know I would be involved? Or, perhaps the question should be, why did she want me to be involved?

'Wait, that reminds me. Did you say Katie predicted she would be shot?'

'Yes, Detective.' said Watcher. 'Katie knew there was a threat against her life.'

'Who issued that threat?' I asked.

'I don't have that information, Detective. I only know there was a threat because Katie told me. Katie predicted the threat would be carried out by someone shooting her with a gun.'

'Why? How would she know that?'

'Because, Detective, a shooting in a New Think world is thought of exclusively as an Old Think action. New Thinkers believe they have evolved beyond the need for cold-blooded violence.'

'That's Ironic.'

Watcher went quiet, its purple/grey lips disappearing to a black screen with a wavy white line appearing at the top, the modern version of the spinning hourglass or progressing circle.

'Yes, it is.' replied Watcher, having searched the web to confirm my assertion.

After finishing that comment, Watcher shut off entirely, going back to presenting nothing but a blank screen.

'Wait!' I said. 'Where'd you go?…'

'You know, if you need a mirror, they have those in the bathroom.' said Detective Thise from the doorway. 'Don't worry, I won't tell anyone you've been talking to your own reflection in random mood screens.'

'Well, we all have our moments.' I said, hoping she really hadn't heard us talking and wasn't just playing along.

'Here's the printout of the chips registered in here prior to Katie's murder.' Said Thise as she handed me a sheet with a surprisingly long list of names on it. Her hand gently brushed mine as she did so, sending an excited shiver down my spine.

As a very attractive woman, her beautiful looks combined with the floral aroma of her perfume swayed me for a moment, distracting me from the task at hand. She wore a mid-length charcoal skirt and cobalt blue button down blouse, tucked at the waist, with a thin black belt to secure the outfit. She flicked her caramel coloured hair gently, then strutted past towards the wall facing chair, her black heels clicking on the hard floor as she went.

I gave the sheet a quick browse, noting key names and checking them off my mental list. 'So, where is the printer here?' I asked. 'I wouldn't have thought that an organisation as progressive as this one would even allow a printer in the building.'

'You would probably be right.' said Empher. 'I wouldn't know. Damwell and I walked back to the office to print this.'

'Doesn't feel that heavy.' I said, weighing the paper in my hand, exaggeratedly.

'Didn't take two of us to carry it.' replied Empher with defensive sarcasm. 'Brian's gone back to review all the reports from the team's interviews yesterday to see if there's anything of value. We didn't get much besides that list, today. The tech guys said they aren't having much luck with the video surveillance from Katie's murder, either. Seems like there's data there, but when they dig into it, there's no substance.'

'Okay.' I said, confident I already knew why. I mean, how hard would you look if tasked with finding evidence of your own guilt? 'So, what, the easy gets haven't answered the question, and the head of the task force has just given up?'

'Detective Brian Damwell does not give up.' said Thise with a smirk on her face. 'He does, however, crack the shits and move onto the next step without completing the last.'

'Well, I appreciate you coming back for me.' I replied as I walked across to retake the seat opposite hers as I had with Damwell. It was time to put the squeeze on Thise and see what they really knew.

'I'll give you fifteen minutes. While Brian might be impatient and ready to move on to the next thing, I think there's more to see here. There has to be. A case that's inspired two murders and two hospitalisations so far must have more to it than this.' She said, tapping the paper in my hand for emphasis. 'How is Sharon doing, by the way? I hear she's left the hospital and hiding out somewhere?'

With this last comment, she raised her eyebrows knowingly, and I wondered by what means she knew this and what might inspire her to look.

'She's getting there. Safer where she is now, that's for sure. So listen, I wanted to meet with Damwell to get a read on him, see what he was going to do next with the taskforce and what he had heard about the involvement of our very own captain and chief. I wanted to meet with you, to get another perspective on the case and your opinion as to who the hell is behind all this. So, tell me, what did you glean from a full day of interviews and investigations yesterday?' I asked, wondering how she would react to the mention of her bosses names, both absent from the list she gave me.

'I'm afraid, the only thing I can tell you is that someone or a group of someone's have been lying.' said Thise. 'I'm also pretty confident that the other someone's are covering for the first person.'

The answer was, she didn't react.

'That's Cryptic. Of course, that is what I'd thought. This list you gave me virtually confirms that. There's only one gun though and only one trigger puller, so far as we know. So, who was it? Have you got a strong suspect in mind?'

'Unfortunately, as I'm sure you're aware and will note from that list, the whole project team appears to be involved. That's eighteen people, and none of them are talking.' Said Thise, crossing her legs and leaning forward on her raised knee.

'What about Matthias Schmidt?' I asked. 'What's your take on him? When Sharon and I interviewed him, he came across arrogant and defensive to begin with. Flat out lied about his involvement. Evidently, he knew we were Old Think and despised us for it. He couldn't even believe that we'd dare ask him questions. I didn't get the feeling he was a murderer, though he appears to be a high-ranking leader of sorts. Not "THE" leader, mind you. How has he struck you?'

'As someone that knows he has no real power and will say whatever it takes to make sure he doesn't end up with any less.' she replied.

'Is he capable of pulling the trigger?'

'I think they all are.' said Thise. 'I have some particular suspicions about Sophia. There's real rage there. The burning desire for revenge of a woman scorned. I think she genuinely believes she was betrayed. That Katie left her, abandoned New Think and its principles for what she sees as an evil of the past.'

I nodded. Thise was playing the part here, sitting in the same position that Damwell had been and looking equally unhappy about it, now. I got the feeling she had hoped to fend me off with the printout, answer some basics and leave me floating in the wind. I had no intention of letting her off so easily.

'Now for the killer questions. What do you think is driving this and why have people been murdered over it?' I asked. 'Surely it isn't just because Katie read some old books and found they weren't so terrible as she'd been told. There has to be more to it than that.'

'Well, they tell us she was modifying the program they were building.' said Thise. 'They think in doing so, she may have undone some of the key elements designed to protect the world from a backslide in thinking and societal behaviour.'

'Sure.' I said. 'That was the message we got, too. I just don't really believe it.'

I still wasn't hearing anything new from Thise. This was tired old trope in the context of the case, info she'd already know I knew. Unfortunately for her, the attempt to sandbag me was undermined by her body language, which said something else. She was hiding something. Something big.

'What key elements was Katie supposed to have undone? Have the team said why they're building this program to begin with? What its real purpose is?'

'Well, they may not have told "you" this, what with you and Sharon being what you are, but Brian and I asked the same questions to every member of the team. Most of them shut us down, the others told us gleefully that this was a top-secret project to further the advancement of Global psychology and ensure the future of humankind will be safe forever.' said Empher.

'Sounds awfully important if you believe in the direction the world has gone.' I said. 'And a lot like the final solution being applied if you don't… Is this program intended to wipe out Old Thinker's forever?'

'I don't know…' said Thise in a thoughtfully offended tone, as if considering it from this angle for the first time and unhappy at the accusation. She shifted again in her seat, uncrossing and recrossing her legs in an irritated manner.

'With all that this oppressive unilateral digital technocracy has already done to a world that once believed in freedom, democracy and tolerance, why would they need to go down this path? Why now?' I asked to the room at large. 'Sure, in the old world there were different levels of freedom, some lacked it altogether, some lived in abject poverty despite the pretence of freedom and some lived under communism and fascism that might not have allowed (*or rather violently suppressed*) the rights of an individual over the needs of the state or nation, yet even people under those forms of governance had more freedoms than anyone apart from the Guides do now. I suppose, despite the ever-present eyes and overbearing social and moral pressures of New Think, they have done little to further advance their cause since the initial power grab of the virus years. They did so much so fast to clamp down on humanity and instigate fear and control over a three-year period, followed by the hard Global take over, that everything since has seemed subtle in comparison. They had to strike while the iron was hot, so to speak. Or more accurately, whilst the minds were soft and malleable and desperately seeking something, anything, solid to hang onto. The tormentors offered the terrified masses a way out of the very situation they themselves had created. Then, in exchange for their obedient and unquestioning commitment to the Guides, they would offer a way to save the world and, in turn, to save humanity. The global populace took it, desperately afraid to even consider the alternative. Now, after twenty years of manufactured vaccines to protect from manufactured viruses, and unscientific responses to unsubstantiated emergencies, there is little left to keep us in line, save for the imagination of the Guides. Fear is powerful, yet fear is also finite. When you have nothing left to lose, you have nothing left to fear. When you are starving and the world tells you the cost of your lunch is too much for the planet to bear, you can't help but ask, what of the cost to me, with no lunch?... People might rightly ask, how have we not solved any of the world's problems with all the obedient service and sacrifice to the rules that would save us from ourselves? With so many limitations, how have we achieved so little benefit for the environment or for human existence as a whole?... Is that what this is? Have we reached the point where that innate human desire to question has overridden their fear of the answer? Now they're going to use computer technology, the greatest weapon of the modern age, to tighten the noose and kick the chair from under the legs of democratic diversity and put an end to alternate views forever.'

I had been musing aloud about this and realised that a raised eyebrow'd Detective Thise may have been a little shocked at hearing it. Nobody mentions the viruses or the vaccines anymore. They have become as ubiquitous an element of Global life as surveillance and social guilt. The joke is that every shot takes a year off your life. Nobody laughs, of course, because it's mostly true.

Since the introduction of "compulsory reception" (*because "compulsory injection" had the far too accurate overtones of nazi style authoritarianism, or state sponsored non-optional drug dependence, and "compulsory vaccination" gave the misleading impression that having been injected you would actually be protected from contracting, transmitting, getting sick or dying from the virus*) the average life expectancy for the Global world had dropped from an average age of 73 down to 58. That average age can be a little misleading mind you, as there are a lot of people who continue to live well beyond the age of 58, it's just that the number of deaths in young people has skyrocketed, leaving the population in free fall, which is what's really driven the drop.

In the beginning, New Thinkers were particularly adamant about the benefits of "everyone" receiving vaccines without exception, in order to protect the human race. They would only see information that supported this notion and decried or banished any who disagreed.

Unfortunately, this single-minded behaviour undermined the genuine benefits of most vaccines and medicines, causing distrust among many, which ultimately led to the "compulsory reception" law being implemented. Whilst time has forced the hardcore "Receptionists" to acknowledge reality, they still aggressively defend their behaviour even as their willingness to participate wanes behind closed doors.

'Sorry.' I said, refocusing my attention on the here and now. 'Just wondering aloud about the motives of the program and whether that's the cause of them tightly closing ranks. Getting back to my questions though, did you and Damwell have a chance to ask the project team about the murder of Chen?' I asked.

After lowering her eyebrows at about the speed of a medieval drawbridge, Empher answered. 'We asked. Their unilateral response was that they'd never even heard of Chen, let alone knew anything about his murder. It was just an unfortunate coincidence to have occurred at OGT and in such close proximity to the murder of Katie... Is that what you really think of New Think?' she asked, clearly troubled by my musings.

'Yes.' I said. 'That has been my experience of the world and its transition from one where we at least had the perception of freedom to one where every action is at the whim of, and for the benefit of, our leaders. Compulsory obedience rather than willing sacrifice.'

'So, you think these murders are being carried out in the name of Global coercion, under direction of the Guides?' asked Thise, now with a tremble of fear or anger creeping into her voice.

'To begin with, I hadn't thought this was anything more than just a crime of passion or jealousy. However, the longer it goes on, the more I think that, yes, this is all part of some far greater plan.' I replied.

My statement was followed by a full minute of intense silence, which I waited out patiently. This is not the first time I've openly offered my opinion on the world as it is, inducing rapid and intense feelings of anger and angst amongst those who simply cannot bear to think there is a workable alternative free from the extraordinary duress of the Global Way. For Empher, the time was clearly taken to compose herself and reign in her anger. As I've mentioned, the difference between us is seldom an issue, except here I seem to have touched a nerve.

Thise uncrossed her legs now, rubbing the heels of her hands hard down the upper part of her quads, pausing her arms tensely mid-leg, before releasing, then repeating the process. It was hard to tell if she was working herself up or down with the movements, the heat radiating from within flushing her cheeks and leaving a light sheen across her forehead.

In spite of her efforts, the temperature in the room seemed to have chilled, in response to which I zipped up my jacket. A move that only served to annoy her more. Thirty seconds and several deep breaths later, she spoke, slowly and with purpose, as if reciting a prepared speech from memory.

'The clearest proof that the Guides are only there to do good, is the amount of money they've invested in teaching the ways of New Think and eradicating dangerous thoughts and beliefs. They've put money into schools to improve education about the environment and fix the curriculum, set up research centres to find cures to viruses we haven't even seen yet, funded environmental research and recovery plans, brought equality to the world by raising up the downtrodden and abused, bringing down the greedy abusers and stabilising outlying regions (*used to be called third world countries*) to provide work and help them become equal and productive members of a truly global society.'

'Yes, quite an untapped resource those outlying regions, weren't they?' I replied… 'Well, I mean since open slave trade was banned, anyway. We were more about the product than the people for a while, and now they've been folded in, they're just "productive" members of the Global World like the rest of us… What a long way they've been "allowed" to come… Actually, since you brought it up, had it ever occurred to you that the generous investing of money, the education on how to think and view the world, the carefully selected donations to causes that required us to purchase goods from companies the Guides conveniently own, and the funding of research into scientific notions that ultimately paid enormous dividends was really just an investment plan on the part of the Guides?'

'Of course!' said Empher. 'They invested in the future of a peaceful, sustainable, and equal world.'

'And that's it? Philanthropy, solely for the benefit of the people, was it?' I asked, not expecting an answer. 'Then where is the peace, and the sustainability and the equality?' I continued. 'I can't buy meat because cows and sheep were apparently farting us to oblivion from their place on that dastardly green farmland that New Thinker's believe should be covered in trees that purify the air.'

'Meanwhile, in the absence of cows, sheep and pigs, we haven't slowed, reversed, or even reduced damage to the environment. In fact, we haven't even replaced the animals with trees. In place of cows, went wind and solar farms, which kill more wildlife and increase local temperatures more than coal and gas plants ever did. They also have the added suck, of turning once beautiful countryside into millions of hectares of fucking dangerous eyesores that stretch around the world. What's more, they aren't even efficient or sustainable, requiring more mining and energy resources to build than fossil fuels, while only producing power about 1/5th of the time. Which is why we don't have enough energy supply to support fully functional demand. It's why we have extremely limited access to power for our residences. What we have are controlled blackouts on a daily basis, with only the extraordinarily equal among us exempt from the impacts. Of course, after the wind farms were built, even more land had to be cleared to make way for hothouses to grow insects and the phenomenal amount of vegetables required to support a world without meat. Those hothouses require higher than ever usage of that most precious resource, water, and when their produce spoils or is uneaten, it turns into millions of tonnes of rotting vegetation which produces just as much methane as the cows they replaced. So, you'll have to pardon me Empher, if I don't buy the message that the Guides are only doing us good…'.

This time, my statement was followed by double the length of silence, before I broke it and spoke again.

'You don't have to agree with me, you know. In fact, opposing opinions are good when both sides are allowed to hold them openly. They help ensure balanced outcomes are achieved. Outcomes that actually account for the needs and benefits of all people, with genuine consideration being given to whether the benefit is worth the cost. More importantly, right now, despite our differences, we need to be working together to find out what the hell is going on here at OGT, and who is killing people to protect it. We also need to know why the leaders of our own Police Service seem to be acting as guns for hire. This has to go pretty high up for them to be involved.'

'What makes you think they're involved?!' Asked Empher, buzzing with rage and barely managing to stay on point.

'I don't just think it. I'm sure of it.' I replied. 'I came here to continue gathering evidence to back me up.'

'What evidence were you expecting to find? At the moment, all we've got is a blurry still from some damaged surveillance footage and the names on that printout I gave you.'

'That's all YOU'VE got.' I replied. 'Oh, and about this printout. Why are there names missing?' I asked pointedly, whilst mimicking her earlier tapping of the page.

'What do you mean?!' Empher snapped back, averting her eyes to hide her guilt.

'I know who's missing from this list, Detective.' I said sternly.

In response, Empher moved her right hand halfway up her thigh from the knee where it was resting, before changing tack and bringing both hands together in her lap.

'You don't strike me as the violent type, Thise. Have you ever even used that thing before?'

The movement of her hand may have been driven by the emotion swirling in her conscious mind, but it was her subconscious that caught and stopped the action. She looked up at me quickly, shocked and angry.

'You thought about shooting me with your Electro.' I said, nodding to her holstered weapon as I did. 'I wasn't sure you were involved before… I am now.'

'I'm not involved…' said Thise, the pace of her breath quickening, the sheen on her forehead now threatening to join into droplets and head for ground. 'I've just been dragged into something that's far bigger than me. I'm doing the right thing, and doing the right thing doesn't come free from compromise and cost. There's always a price to pay for the greater good.'

'And killing two people and putting two more in hospital. That's the right thing? A fair price?' I asked. 'Who's good did that serve? Not the dead or injured, that's for sure?'

'Like I said, doing the right thing is never free.' replied Thise, maintaining a taught demeanour. 'The future of humanity and the world as we know it is at stake!'

'This world?' I asked, spreading my arms and looking around the room. 'You want to save this world? From what? We have no freedom, no personal autonomy. We are beholden to a group of private leaders who we never elect and never get to influence. We are injected, starved, and controlled. They tell us what we can and can't buy and when we can and can't turn the lights on. We aren't allowed to be, or do, anything except the currently approved form of the proletariat. Oh, and pay attention because the goal posts move quickly.'

'Like I said, Gary, this is all just a sacrifice for the greater good. We are doing the work as the Guides instruct. They can see what we can't. You and people like you never understand that. You think that your own happiness and your selfish "right" to choose your own way at the expense of others is more important than balance in humanity and limiting our impact on the world and the people around us.'

'What a load of bullshit!' I fired back. 'We are being controlled by a group of self-appointed elites for the benefit and enhancement of their own power and financial gain, pure and simple. We are lied to daily, brainwashed with "greater good" rubbish and prevented from ever seeing an alternative opinion or any evidence that supports why decisions were made to begin with. All we get is advertising slogans and challenges to do the right thing for humanity. The world used to be a place where individuals were free to find their own way, make choices right or wrong, and learn or grow from the consequences. People could pursue their interests and form part of a broad and diverse society, where competition drove ingenuity and often benefited all of humanity. Now we are nothing but mindless sheep. No. Robots. Sheep are natural and good. We're told to fear members of the natural food chain and instead ingest the manufactured harvest of technology. Ironic really. To save the natural world, we are told to kill its creatures and live artificially instead. Why?

Why, after we had already learned that artificially engineered food was bad for our health, were we forced to see it as the major source of our diet? The must have, of an eco-conscious world. We've been forced to accept highly engineered medicines and technology interfaces being tethered to our bodies as absolute necessities. This was all done by following the Guides. Who's good it serves, I am yet to see.'

'There's one Guide in particular who's relevant here… in these murders. Another name you removed from this list.' I said, smacking it with the back of my hand. 'That's Cheq Fencegap. Cheq, fucking, Fencegap! He is the main driver behind this Global absurdity. In his breaks from making human shock collars and brainwashing technology, he spends some of his obscene wealth continuing to create artificial versions of the natural foods he doesn't like us eating. Then he has the audacity to call people who don't want to eat his robot poop, environmental criminals. Really?! He attempts to play God, because he absolutely believes he is one. Manipulating nature then demanding humans consume his lab creations, like some evil chess master, gleefully watching pawns suffer for their service, all whilst funding social engineering schemes to ensure control over "the individual" and capturing then modifying every human on earth's biological makeup, by nothing more than the authority of his own fucking decree!… No, Detective Thise. You are not doing "the right thing". You are carrying out the dictates of the architects of evil. If you are in on this, you are all the way in and just as culpable as your lord and master!'

Thise was fuming now. Her hand hovering above her thigh, not quite touching the material of her pant leg, yet poised to flash up to her hip, to draw and shoot.

I knew I had to keep pushing her. To break her. Even at the risk of wearing an Electro dart. She's the only one opening up, the only crack in the wall so far. I fight the urge to look at her hand and draw attention to her emotional intent. I want her to lose control of conscious thought, to snap, to make the move and give me the opportunity I need.

'Who dragged you in, Thise? Was it Damwell? are you two in this together? Was it that bitch captain of ours, Ironie? Did she recruit you to the cause? Or are you some sort of sleeper agent for the New Think Extremists, working with our evil overlords to crush the hope of humanity for ever?'

'Fuck you, you arrogant, irrelevant dinosaur!' Spat Thise. 'I'm not telling you, shit!'

Thise was in a mental space I'd never seen her in before. Angry beyond words, right on the edge of lashing out and all for an ideology so flawed, it won't even defend her right to live.

'Not everyone supports your cause, you know. Hell, Katie worked here at the very centre of New Think technology development, tasked with building psychological manipulations into a program, just to avoid from losing its grip. Not much of an ideology when someone at the heart of the beast reads a couple of books from the old days and abandons the cause altogether. I suppose she wasn't quite part of the inner circle, though. She just got paid for her loyalty, like the rest of you. Morals for hire. You're probably not even a true believer yourself, aye? I mean, what evidence of beneficial good do you have to show for your effort? You're nothing but a lackey, dragged in as needed to do a job, then dropped back down with the rest when no longer required. I guess you're only here for a bit of badge carrying security. To protect the murderers, obstruct justice, and take part in a global conspiracy. All in a day's work for you. What else could it be? You're not really in the same class as those you work for, are you? Not on the same level as they are. You're on the same team, but you're too old to be a pure New Thinker and you didn't attend any prestigious school's pre-New Think like the chief and captain did.'

'Fuck you Gary! Fuck, you!!! You know nothing about me! You know nothing of how I grew up or my place in this world!'

'I know you came from poverty. And I know that for you, a progression towards this Global world seemed like a step up from the gutter. Even so, you're not one of them… Not really. You're like me, Empher. A battler, a hard worker, with a hard nose from the grind, who learned how to read people in order to survive. We don't protect people like them. We have nothing to gain, for they offer us nothing…'

Thise wasn't really listening now. Her eyes had glazed over, her smooth light-coloured skin, now a flushed red. Her breathing was short and fast as she teetered on the edge of breaking. It seemed cruel to push like this, yet it had to be done. I had to keep dragging them out in the open.

'It's funny, you know.' I continued. 'There's been a growing problem for the Council of Global Guides. The formerly wealthy families from the Old Think days who thought they were giving up their riches out of necessity for the greater good of humanity, are starting to realise they were really just giving up their rights, their power, and their ability to fund a fight back. They've noticed that nothing good happened for all this sacrifice and they want their money back. They want a say in things.'

'Laws based on New Think's ideology, which supposedly made things equal for some, made them very unequal for others. The wealthy, who were not wealthy enough, gave up their wealth for the greater good and fell down the food chain, landing hard on the bottom. People like you and me who had nothing much to begin with, don't have much more now. Just less opportunity to get out of the hole… Is that what happened to you, Detective? Did someone lower a ladder down for you? Did you take the only opportunity you had to climb your way out?'

I was firing questions and accusations so fast now, I didn't even know if what I was saying made sense.

Thise, whose mouth had been fused shut, took a deep breath to steady herself, swallowing some of her anger as she did.

'I just did… No… I am just doing what has to be done for the greater good.' She said through a clenched jaw. She'd been trained to repeat this message, like a calming mantra, to reassure that the insanity of her actions all had a greater purpose. Reasoned arguments were out of reach.

'Well then, Detective Thise, I'm afraid if that's your only defence, you leave me no choice but to place you are under arrest.' I said, rising from my seat as I did so.

That did it… As soon as I stood, pulling my cuffs from my belt, Empher's hand finally closed at her hip, smoothly pulling her electro from its holster, her eyes wide with determination and anger. She brought her right arm up in the shooter's pose, finger inside the trigger guard, pressure coming onto the trigger ready to fire, then… Pffump!

There's no gunpowder in an electro. No bang. The release of the trigger just sets off an electromagnetic reaction. The only sound made is that of the electrically charged projectile travelling along, then exiting the barrel at a rate similar to that of an old Glock 19. Detective Thise's convulsing body kicked a couple of times on the floor before the short pulsing effect of the Electile (*electrified projectile*) caused her to pass out. Thankfully, Thise did not have any form of heart condition, as the shock can cause those who do to go into cardiac arrest. That's why we also have to carry an adrenaline shot in the same holster as the gun.

'Thanks!' I said over my shoulder. 'Half a second longer, it would have been me convulsing on the floor.'

Constable Clubman entered the room, holstering his electro as he did so. 'Why didn't you draw? He asked.'

'I needed to know that you were really on our side.' I said. 'Sorry, it's not that I don't trust you. It's that I don't trust anyone. Before today, I thought I could trust Empher. Yet it seems that everywhere I turn, someone else is lying to me, covering up this crime, or actively trying to add another to the list…'

Clubman didn't respond straight away, instead entering the room and walking up to Empher, who remained half lying, half sitting against the front of the couch chair, lightly spasming. He picked up his spent electile and loaded it back in the gun to charge.

After a thoughtful pause, he spun on his heel in a crouched position and replied. 'Yeah, fair enough. I couldn't get much useful information out of the other uniforms either, so I assume they're either complicit or under orders not to share anything they see or hear.'

'What about your friend Constable Wedge?' I asked. 'He got us in here.'

'Well, he might be okay. Except, he disappeared about forty-five minutes ago and hasn't been seen since.' replied Cliff.

I quietly wondered whether he'd been taken out and disciplined by Detective Damwell or one of the other service crooks and made a mental note to follow it up later. 'I'm sure he'll turn up.' I said, not wanting to further alarm him.

'Hey, how did you know I was in the doorway before?' He asked. 'If I hadn't been there, you'd be in bad shape.'

'I knew you were there because I could see you standing there on that screen.' I said, pointing to the mood screen that had been in my eye line on the far wall.

'How? That doesn't reflect the doorway from here he said.' standing roughly where I'd sat.

'No, it doesn't, and it wasn't a reflection. An image of you standing there briefly flashed up on the screen.'

'What? How?!' He asked, unbelieving.

'Well, we've got one friend in this building. It's just not human…'

'A friend? That doesn't sound right. Who is it?'

'Oh, I'll bring you into the loop. Just not until after we've put Detective Thise somewhere safe to sweat it out. Then I want to light a fire under Matthias Schmidt.'

'Where the hell are you going to take her?' asked Clubman. 'We can't take her back to the station. Her fellow conspirators will just let her out again. Or lock us up instead. You can't leave her here either, and we certainly can't baby sit her all day. We need to keep moving on this now we're finally identifying some players.'

Thise had stopped convulsing, recovering enough to have intentionally slid into a more comfortable position curled on the floor between the two chairs. The effects of the Electro were generally several hours of heavy malaise, before a fairly rapid recovery. She certainly wasn't going anywhere in a hurry. Still, Clubman was right. We couldn't sit here watching her all day.

'You're right.' I said. 'I have a plan in mind. The thing is, I'll have to make a couple of calls before we enact it, to ensure we get the help we need. I have an old Army friend who sits in a high place.'

'How do you know he'll help us? What if he's somehow in on this, too?' He asked.

'I'm pretty sure he'll help us, even if he's not happy about it. As for whether he's in on it, well, he and his team have been watching us and our progress for a couple of days now, so if they are, there's not much we can do about it. It's a risk we're going to have to take.'

Clubman looked down at Thise now, almost regretful of having shot her. 'Yeah, I guess you're right.' He said.

'Watch her for a minute, will you?' I instructed.

'Where are you going?' Asked Cliff.

'To call that friend.' I said. 'I'm just going to do it from outside the building. We're fairly well protected in terms of surveillance inside this room, but calls can still be traced and intercepted and with the type of technology they have here, I imagine there's more than enough capacity to do that. Hell, they probably built the programs that we use.'

'And out there?' he asked.

'Out there, my friend's the one in charge.'

Chapter 26

Three in the hole

I left Clubman with the now double cuffed Thise and walked to the next room where Matthias Schmidt sat working at a desk.

'You ready to see me yet, Detective, or do I have to stay here forever?' he asked, with obvious irritation.

'I'll only be a few minutes. I just have to duck out and meet someone before we catch up…' I made to move away before turning back quickly. 'Say, how the hell do I get down and back up in these bloody lifts without having to get approval each way?'

'I can give you an authorisation code.' said Matthias. 'They change regularly, but if you're only gone for a little while it will be fine. All you do is approach the screen as normal and state, "I have an entry code". The screen will ask you for the code, you read it out and then you can come straight up.'

Matthias tapped his keyboard a couple of times, then read out a 6-digit code for me. 'You've got thirty minutes from now before that code expires.'

'This better not lock me in the lift or shoot me off to some dungeon level.' I replied, only half joking.

Matthias laughed unconvincingly, then just when he should have kept his mouth shut, said, 'If we had a dungeon, Katie would still be alive…'

I raised my eyebrows and watched Mathias's eyes widen as he realised what he'd done.

'I, I was just joking.' he said.

'Pretty sick joke.' I replied. 'You know what. Just hang here a second. I'll be back before I go down.'

I raced next door where Clubman Stood dutifully watching over the groggy looking and partly conscious Thise. 'I'm going to bring in another friend for you to watch while I'm gone.'

'Who?' asked Clubman.

'Matthias.' I replied. 'He's made a Freudian slip.'

Returning to Matthias, I asked him to follow me, which he begrudgingly did, although not before I subtly pulled back the right side of my jacket to reveal the electro, placing my hand on my hip, just above it for good measure.

Matthias stood from the computer where he'd been seated, adjusting his rectangular glasses in the manner of the offended intellectual, pulling them off, inspecting the lenses and resetting them on his head before shuffling along behind me like a shackled man.

When he entered Katie's office, his grumpy dissatisfaction turned to shock.

'What on earth happened here?!' He exclaimed, attempting to crouch down and assist Empher, who remained uncomfortably seated on the floor.

'Get away from her!' I shouted at him. 'Keep them on separate sides at this end of the room.' I said, turning to Cliff.

'You can't tell me what to do. I'm not under arrest!' shouted Matthias, trying to assert himself in a position of authority.

'You can be if needed.' I replied. 'I have spare cuffs.'

'What happened to her?' He asked, looking at Empher sadly.

'She was shot, Matthias. I would have thought you'd recognise the signs. She's not the first person shot in this office, after all. The difference is, Detective Thise will live unlike the last one. I'm surprised you care, anyway. Perhaps if you'd cared about Katie, she might still be alive.'

I gave some brief and specific instructions for Clubman not to let either of them move or allow himself to be coerced by their attempts to turn him against me. 'If either of them tries to leave, shoot them. Especially him.' I said, pointing at Matthias, before turning on my heel and hurrying to the elevator.

Once downstairs and outside, I ran across the road and up the street, far enough to get clear of the building while keeping the entry in sight. Removing the protective sheath from my device again, I allowed it to regain connection, then saw several messages appear from Shaz and Milford along with three missed calls that were also from Milly. I called Shaz first.

'Hey, are you okay?' she said, answering after only one ring.

'Yeah, I'm fine. Finally making some progress, I think. Sorry, I've gotta be quick here. I have to get back upstairs at OGT as soon as I can, and I need to call Milly too.' I gave Sharon a quick rundown on the morning's events and filled her in on my plans for the now arrested Empher and the soon to be arrested Matthias Schmidt. Shaz agreed with my actions and informed me she had also found a freelance hacker, known to be Old Think, who could help us breakdown the OGT program.

Knowing we were being watched and listened too, she'd told me this via a predetermined code we agreed on before I left the house this morning. Milly and his team would have overheard what I'd told her too, although it was nothing I wasn't about to tell him, anyway. We just don't want him knowing about the hacker yet, because if he knows about that and turns out to be on the wrong side of this thing, then our last hope would be dashed. If we can't put a stop to the criminals, we could at least put a stop to the crime.

Next, I called Milly, who also answered after just one ring. 'Geez, seems like you and Shaz are really sweating on these phone calls.' I began.

'Yeah, well, our level of concern over here has certainly been rising. As has the body count.' he replied.

'What do you mean?' I asked. 'Jiang? Constable Wedge? Who? Who the hell else is dead.' I was still breathing a little heavily from my run across to the park. That feeling of being a little short of breath added to my exasperation at the news I was about to hear.

'Tell me, are those two amateur spooks still following you?' Asked Milly.

'Yeah.' I said. 'They're still conspicuously present. They didn't bother following me all the way to the park this time. Instead, they're just hanging out nearby on opposite sides of the street. But they're here.'

'Good.' he replied. 'I've got a team that's arriving in about two minutes to watch the watchers.'

'Are they suspected of having killed someone?' I asked.

'We don't know yet. The man we had following you is dead. That's all we know for sure. You're not beyond suspicion yourself as far as the Directorate is concerned. My money's on the others, of course.'

'Well, I sure as hell didn't do it.'

'I'm sure you didn't. The trouble is, someone did and not many people knew he was following you. He was last seen by a stationary surveillance unit outside your apartment this morning. They found him riding around in a trolley, his head leaning up against the wall in a side seat.'

I thought back to this morning and the overt male follower sitting down hard in the side seat on the trolley. That's when he must have done it.

'People don't just suddenly die very often, no matter what you've been told.' I said. 'Painful as it may be, I'd say you have a leak.'

'It appears that way.' agreed Milly coldly. 'It's harder to tell these days with surveillance so ever present. It's possible that someone else just had access to our systems and was monitoring our intel and processes. They could have found out we were watching you and needed an open window for themselves. The question is who? And what did they do in that window?...'

'What are you going to do now?' I asked.

'I've cut my team down to twelve people that I can personally vouch for and trust.' said Milly. 'I'm also only reporting directly to the deputy in charge of the DSSMD now, so the circle is small and tight.'

'Well, then I think you've done what you can for now. Listen, I want to help you out here because I don't want these bastards to get away with all this.' I said, speaking rapidly. 'Plus, it benefits us both. Thing is,

I'm on a time limit right now to access the OGT building and I need to get back up there. As I'm sure you may already be aware, I've begun arresting suspects in the case. I've started at the bottom, and plan on working my way up.'

'I actually haven't seen that yet.' said Milly. 'I was just in a meeting with the Deputy about adjusting the team and data access here to try and plug the leak.'

'Right.' I said. 'Well, I've arrested Detective Thise, who admitted to being a part of this crazy plot. At the moment she isn't telling me anymore than that and she isn't likely to for a good few hours at least. I am also in the process of arresting Matthias Schmidt from OGT, who only minutes ago admitted some level of collusion in the murder of Katie Hansley.'

'Really? What did he say?' asked Milly, sounding intrigued more than surprised.

'He accidentally suggested that if OGT had a dungeon, then Katie would still be alive.'

'Sure. That sounds like an admission…' replied Milly uncertainly. 'What did you mean you were in the process of arresting him?'

'I mean, he isn't in cuffs yet, though he is being held at the business end of an electro, and I expect him to be cuffed by the time I've finished questioning him.'

'Okay, what are you going to do with them after that?' He asked. 'Given what you know of Captain Ironie's actions, the cells at your station hardly seem secure.'

'That's where I was hoping you might come in.' I replied, adding a little sugar to my voice to sweeten the pitch.

As long as I'd known him, Milly has had an irritating habit he unconsciously enacts whenever he's stressed. He'd put the tip of his left thumb against the tip of his left middle finger and click the nail of his thumb up and down on the nail of his finger. I knew what I was asking him now was causing him stress, because I could hear the clicking clearly through the device's speaker.

'Oh, I didn't realise I was working for you, again.' he scorned with more than a little annoyance reverberating through.

'Hey, if you want to go it on your own, you best pull your new set of followers off me, or I'll arrest them too.' I fired back. 'You want me to do all the legwork for you whilst you use me as bait to flush out the perpetrators, I'll play ball. In return, I need you to commit that we can trust each other and work together on this, or we're all screwed.'

'Okay, okay, I get it. What do you need me to do?'

'I was hoping you might have some spare holding cells or a compound somewhere nearby where we could hold these prisoners for now. Like you said, I can't trust anyone at our station at the moment. We put them in there and someone will just let them go.'

'Alright fine, I've got something that'll do. I'll send a couple of my guys to grab them and take them to a little safe house we keep.' said Milly. 'I can only spare one agent to stay with them though.'

'That's very old school of you.' I said. 'Out of curiosity, why in this Global world would the DSSMD need safe houses?'

'For Old Thinkers.' He replied.

'Of course.' I said. 'We're supposed to be the danger and yet somehow, we're the one's endangered. Listen, when your guys get here, tell them to call Clubman in case I'm still caught up with Matthias or following down another lead in the building. I'll send you his details.'

'So, what's the rest of your plan?' He asked.

'Well, I was trying to uncover evidence, chase every lead and whittle my way down to the unquestionable answer, but people keep getting shot, killed, or violently beaten. So instead, I've decided to just keep arresting people until I either find the right one or I've arrested the whole damn lot of em…'

Milly might not have agreed with my plan of action, although under the circumstances, chose not to question it, possibly feeling at risk of losing a nail with the stress. His crew would be on the road within thirty minutes and ready to assist.

I ended the call at that and raced back to the OGT building with only ninety seconds to spare before my passcode for the lift expired. Thankfully, the automated concierge accepted the code without issue and the lift delivered me back to Level 7 as planned.

I was surprised that nobody had come down and confronted me, shot me or at least tried to shut down my investigation on the way. Damwell certainly wouldn't be happy that his partner had been shot, and I wondered how long Watcher was a going to be able to keep that a secret from the building's concierge services, or whether it was really doing that at all.

My mind engaged on that thought was then subsequently unprepared for what I found when I re-entered Katie's office. There, at the rear corner of the room, I saw Matthias sprawled and convulsing on the floor. 'What the hell happened?' I asked Clubman, who was yet to holster his weapon.

'He tried to make an escape.' he replied tensely. 'Got up to run for it, so I did what you said.'

On hearing this, the now recovering Detective Thise shot a look my way as if to suggest that wasn't quite the truth, and to be honest, I couldn't see a reason for her to lie. Having said that, I was hardly in a mood to believe her. She had just attempted to shoot me, after all.

'Why? Where was he going to go?' I asked.

'I don't know, he just said, "You can't keep me here." and got up to start running.'

'Didn't make it far.' I replied.

Looking down at him, it appeared to me as though he'd been shot whilst seated and convulsed himself off the chair. He wasn't collapsed in the middle of the floor or stretching out for the door, instead slumped back against the front of the chair I had earlier been seated in. His position mirrored Thise's, only his condition was much worse due to the more recent jolt of volts.

'He's going to be a little hard to question now, isn't he.' I said, allowing my frustration to show through. 'I suppose it's okay. Might give him some time to think about the level of honesty he's been providing. Won't it mate?!' I shouted down at his writhing form.

'I guess we're done here for now. All these convulsing's bodies are really starting to warm the room up, anyhow. Keep minding our prisoners for a moment please, Constable. I need to step next door to inspect the office our new friend has been using and see if there's anything of note there.'

As soon as I was out the door of Katie's office, I immediately sent a message to Milly. 'Do not call Clubman on arrival. Contact this number instead. Meet on the side street entrance to the basement off Short Street.'

Re-entering the office Matthias, Damwell, and Schmidt had been in when we'd arrived this morning, I was looking for two things. Anything useful for the case, and a way to contact the manager on duty for the cleaner's section downstairs. I needed someone to authorise me taking prisoners down via the service lifts. By doing so, I was hoping to avoid too many prying eyes, and I didn't think that asking another member of the team would help my cause. I also wanted to use the cleaners as an excuse to return here later and interview the friendly mood screen.

The room was no fuller than it had been two days ago when Shaz and I had conducted the initial interviews. Nevertheless, I figured there must be something in here that brought two certain colluders and the still questionable Damwell here. I started by looking at the desk in the centre of the room. As a cop, one of the frustrating things about this New Think world is that with very little paper in use, stumbling on secret documents requires a little more breaking through firewalls than breaking into buildings and draws. The only thing on the table was the desk device and I could see that Matthias had wisely locked his console. No doubt I wouldn't have been able to search it anyway due to the built-in user recognition security now standard on all devices.

After a cursory search of the desk and a brief scan of the room, I'd turned up nothing of use for the case. I did, however, remember that I already had the number of one of the cleaning managers, Carlos, who we'd met yesterday, and figured I'd give him a call.

'Cleaning Manger's office.' answered a voice.

'Hi, Carlos is it?' I asked.

'No, it's Johnny. Carlos is on tonight.' came the reply.

'Oh yeah, Johnny, it's Detective Johnson.' I said. 'I'm up on level 7, and I'm wondering if you can authorise myself and another officer to come down in the lifts with two prisoners? We need to escort them into a vehicle that's coming to collect them via the basement.'

'Prisoners? You've found the killers?' Asked Johnny.

'I've arrested two people that were intentionally perverting the course of justice, Johnny. Now, I'm sure you'd be willing to assist us with our ongoing investigation, wouldn't you?' The bold print between the lines was clear to Johnny, who was only too eager to help.

'Ah, yes, yes, of course.' he said sounding nervous.

'Excellent. Have you got that code for me?'

'Sure, just one second. JC23CE.' he read out moments later. 'That will give you lift authorisation to come to the basement and return to level 7 if you need.'

'Thanks. Oh, and there'll be no problem with there being four occupants.' I asked.

'No.' he said. 'One authorisation is all that's required.'

'Great, thank you.' I replied before hanging up.

When I returned to Katie's office, I saw Matthias had stopped convulsing. Which would have made the task of moving him easier had he been able to hold his bladder. The acrid smell was pungent to the nose, the stain on his pants and troubled look on his face almost made me feel sorry for him. Thise appeared to have recovered a little more, the stunned eyes having dissipated, though she still seemed drowsy and unfocussed. It's an after effect of the Electro's that tends to last several hours, keeping the person docile and easy to control.

'Okay.' I said to Clubman. 'You take Empher and I'll grab our incontinent friend. We're heading down to the basement via the service lift.'

'The basement?' said Clubman.

'Yeah, I think we have to go that way. I'm not keen on parading these two past the rest of the building and onto the street. The fewer people that know about this, the better. Our prisoners will be picked up downstairs and taken to a secure location so we can keep moving on the case. We need to strike while the iron's hot.'

'Right, that makes sense. I guess.' he said, bending down to reposition Empher so he could get under her arm and support her weight.

'Oh, by the way, did you end up getting hold of Wedge while you were outside? Is he the one coming to grab them?' He asked, a little too excitedly.

I didn't bother telling him I hadn't even tried to contact Wedge. Wherever he was, he would not be part of my plans moving forward. Few are.

'Ah, I don't think it'll be him picking them up.' I replied. 'I haven't spoken to Wedge. You'll just have to catch up with him later. Now come on, let's get moving. I want these two out of here and into a cell so they're all recovered and perked up for questioning later.'

'Don't we need a code to get down?' Asked Clubman, trying to stall. 'I don't want to have to deal with that Cam character again.'

'Already got one. Let's go.' I said.

In his crouched position, Clubman took a deep breath and sighed in defeat, before lifting Thise's arm over his shoulder, then raising her to a standing position. I did the same with Matthias, minus the sigh, and with encouragement, we slow walked our prisoners from the room.

They looked more like thunderbirds or malfunctioning anthropomorphised bots than adult humans, which is just what a good dose from an electro will do to you. For all my despair at the lack of real guns, these sure pack a punch without the death rate.

We managed the trip to the lifts more easily than expected, thankfully encountering no one on route, while doubtless being monitored by surveillance bots as soon as we left the room. Based on the ease of our movement, I could only assume that Watcher had taken control of them and again disabled the other surveillance screens in and around Katie's office, or else we might have been met by the unwelcome wagons at the lift. Then again, who knows what's waiting for us below.

When the lift doors opened at the basement, I was relieved to find just a couple of cleaners generally busying themselves with the restocking of their cleaning trollies. Shuffling out into the open space of the cavernous basement, I saw through his office window, that Johnny appeared to be working on something at his desk, his focus on the projection in front of him and not on the secretive movement of prisoners just outside.

We assisted our captives over to the right of the sliding door and sat them down on the raised concrete gutter to await their transport, which a check of my watch told me should be coming soon. It was now 10:11 AM, twenty-three minutes since I'd called Milly, meaning his team should be here in the next ten to fifteen.

Leaving the prisoners again under the watch of Clubman, I crossed the basement to Johnny's office.

'Hey Johnny.' I shouted.

'Detective?...' he replied cautiously. 'I see you've made some progress on the case. That's two down, I suppose.'

'Are you saying that because you know that's two down, or are you just being hopeful?' I asked.

'Oh, ah, I just assumed because they're in cuffs.'

'Sure.' I said. 'Listen, I've got transport meeting us at this door. They should be contacting me soon. Is there any way I can view what vehicles are approaching down that street without having the door open?'

'Yeah, of course.' he said, indicating a bank of monitors hidden behind the door on the wall to his right.

It was a good setup. I had to pull the door partway closed to get a view from my side of the desk. The monitors couldn't really be seen from outside the office, or even from the doorway, whereas from his seat Johnny would have a view of all the camera fields, plus the basement and roller door out his window.

'You mind if I join you behind the desk while I wait for the transports?' I asked.

'No, no problem.' said Johnny.

He looked nervous, and I felt for him. Like most people, he seemed unhappy in the world he lived, or certainly that part of it which I had observed, yet he was dutiful and no matter how joyless, he like the rest of us, just wanted to get through each day without issue. Toeing the line just to stay alive.

Standing behind Johnny, I could see his head and eyes cast downwards in the pose of a man trying to hide in plain sight. The top of his head shone brightly as it reflected the LED downlight above. His dark black horseshoe of hair, clear evidence of male pattern baldness, which further saddened the appearance of the man.

Looking up from him to the screens, I saw the one I wanted, second from the top, offering a clear view of the alley leading out to Short Street.

'I don't suppose you can control those cameras from here, can you?' I asked.

'Ah, well I can control the movement of three of them, just not the one watching the lifts.' he said, lifting his head and looking almost happy to be of service.

'Excellent. When I say so, I want you to turn the camera on the entry door away from that alley.' I instructed.

'Okay, I can do that. You mind if I ask what for?' queried Johnny.

'Because there are things I don't want seen or recorded.' I replied. 'Now, I don't mean to be rude, but I just need you to do it. It's in the interests of the safety and what little remains of personal autonomy for the people of this planet.'

Johnny complied without further comment, using a small console on his desk to select the appropriate cameras ready for adjustment, then returned his focus to what appeared to be next week's rosters, silently taping his holographic keyboard, editing numbers and names. After two minutes of watching empty cameras and daydreaming of a simpler role in a compliant life, reality rushed back in retaking pride of place in my mind. My device buzzed with a message advising that my prisoner transport was about to enter the street.

'Turn that camera away now, hard right, I want it staring at that fence!' I instructed Johnny.

'Okay.' He said, turning sharply away from his projection screen and immediately following my instruction.

'If anyone else monitoring these, calls you and tells you to fix it, including the automated control centre here, tell em Detective Johnson told you, to tell them, to fuck off! Now, I need you hang about here for me Johnny. I'm going to have to ask you some more questions as soon as I've despatched these prisoners.'

'Of course, Detective.' he said earnestly as I left the room.

As soon as I got over to Clubman and our prisoners, I hit the override button on the wall to raise the door. Usually, I'd a need chip authority to exit the building via this type of door, however as we found out yesterday, the scanner here's been moved and nobody seems interested in replacing it.

'You ready?' I asked Clubman, who was now largely supporting the weight of the still groggy Matthias.

'Yep, can't wait to ditch these two.' he replied. 'Matthias is starting to stink and I should tell you that while I agree that leaving them to sweat it out for a while might make them more talkative, I'd like to request they get a hose down before I have to see em again.'

As soon as the roller door hit its stops at the top of the guides, the back of a midnight-black prisoner transport truck with no rear windows pulled to a stop outside. Its diesel engine was running, the smell and heat of the exhaust a welcome reminder of old times. Within seconds, an agent appeared from either side of the cab, hand at the ready on their holstered SIG Sauer P226 pistols. The clips of their hip holsters were undone, the textured grips fully visible and freed for extraction. They were real weapons, with real lead projectiles, the likes of which are rarely seen these days, and I couldn't help being a little envious.

'You Detective Johnson?' asked the agent at the right of the truck in a gruff voice that matched the appearance.

'That's me.' I answered. 'Tell Milly thanks, by the way.'

At this, the agent produced a chip checker with bio-identification capability connected back to the Global Bio-Hub database. The device uses infrared laser technology to scan all identifiers from the chip implant, facial recognition, retina scan and other bio-security measurements, instantly confirming an identity match and any social discredits or flags. After quickly scanning the four of us, he seemed satisfied, nodding to his partner, now standing at the back of the truck. The partner then entered a time sensitive code into a security panel with his right hand whilst at the same time maintaining a retina scan. This dual key process is intended to avoid an agent being shot and having their head held up to the scanner whilst someone tries to type in the code at the same time. The system requires the code to be typed over a particular timeframe whilst the retina scan is maintained, and to date, no one has ever successfully broken into this type of lock. Within seconds, the doors opened, and the agent issued a command to start loading.

'Wait, Clubman, I'll go first.' I said. 'That way, I can help you with him. He's a damn sight heavier than Thise is.'

'Okay sure.' he replied, looking somewhat confused and alarmed by the presence of agents rather than police officers.

The agent who opened the door climbed in the back of the truck and took custody of Detective Thise, who was now fully ambulant if a little docile. He handed back my cuffs and used the sets welded solidly into the truck walls to cuff her wrists and feet. The agent then seated her on a bench that ran along the side and strapped her in with a six-point harness for good measure.

I turned and nodded to Clubman, who started shuffling forward with Matthias and his still limp body. Moving back to assist, I grabbed Matthias under his left arm and helped Clubman pass him up to the agent, who again handed back the cuffs and strapped him in.

The back of the truck was warm and smelled different to the old prisoner transports from my childhood. That pungent, hard plastic smell, mixed with vomit and urine, was replaced by a lavender scented air, no doubt to assist the Agents who these days have to actually enter the prisoner compartment in order to lock them in. The official line is that lavender is calming and sleep-inducing, and is therefore used to help keep prisoners under control. I say, whatever it's for, it's better.

'Okay, just one to go.' said the agent.

'Huh?' Said Clubman, who seemed to be in slow motion as he turned towards to me, eyes widening at the sight of the electro raising up to meet him.

The great thing about Electro's is their versatility, because they don't always have to be fired. The chamber can be locked, with the built in electrode probes pushed out of the barrel tip so the gun can be used as a stun gun, instead.

I'd moved so quickly and unexpectedly after releasing Matthias, that Clubman could do nothing about my attack. Pressing the electrodes into his side, I hit the trigger. 'Sorry friend.' I said as the highly charged volts travelled along the contact needles, meeting the resistance of his body. The shock nearly threw him up and into the rear of the prisoner transporter all by itself.

Releasing the trigger, I grabbed him under the arm to stop him from hitting the deck as his legs buckled under him. Then, with help from the agent, we lifted him into the truck and locked him in alongside the others. Thise, with all the energy she could muster, raised her eyebrows, but never muttered a word. She was either shocked that I'd turned on a friend, or impressed that I'd outed another.

'All done.' I said, before jumping down from the truck.

I spoke briefly to the agents, Ken and Travis, who provided me with the address of their previously secret hide out. Then, after signing the custody transfer screen, they were locked up and back on the road before I'd re-entered the basement.

I watched on as the truck moved away, smiling at the sound made by the smooth revving diesel and the small puff of smoke from the exhaust. Part of me couldn't help wondering if I'd just made a grave mistake. Could I trust Milly? Would I see the prisoners again? Who knew? There was nothing I could do about it now, so I put the thought to the back of my mind and refocused on the next task to hand.

The roller door had stayed open throughout the process of loading the now three prisoners into the back of the truck, and I was happy to note the security cameras stayed turned away as well.

Inside, no crowd had gathered to witness the incident. The cleaners clearly smart enough to know there are things that shouldn't be seen. Even if they are right in front of you. To be fair, not seeing what's happening right in front of you is a prerequisite for surviving this world, so they've all had plenty of practice.

I hit the door close override switch again and returned to Johnny's office.

'Everything okay in here?' I asked, opening it up for comment on what he might have seen.

For his part, Johnny was working or wisely pretending to, tapping away on his air keys and giving off the impression that he was actively avoiding the surveillance screens to his right, which except for the lifts were only displaying fences and basement walls.

'Um, yeah, nobody called while you were out there.' he said.

'And what about you, Johnny? Did you make a call while I was out there?' I asked, wanting to clarify and not willing to trust a soul. I hadn't meant it to sound as condescending as it did, the frustration of Clubman's turn clearly weighing on my mind.

'You know, just because I'm a cleaner that works in a basement, it doesn't make me stupid. And, because I'm a cleaner that works in the basement, I am when seen, looked down upon by those that work above me. I have no allegiance to them. None of us do.'

'What about when you're not seen?' I asked, switching gears to try and understand if there are things he gets away with simply because he can.

'Look, they don't even know I exist until they make a mess and need someone to clean or cover it up.'

'Sounds like there's a bit of animosity there, Johnny. Is OGT not the very embodiment of equality we've all been led to believe?'

'Ha! Believe it or not, no.' he said sarcastically. 'The Guides might claim that we're all equal members of an evolved Global society, but us cleaners are just as low on the totem pole as we ever were. Especially one's like me who grew up in the old world under communist rule. I thought escaping China for the free and wonderful west would be my emancipation from totalitarianism… only for the Guides to take over the world and introduce global totalitarian governance for all. Just like back home, we're told the limitations and mandatory adherence to the dictates are all for the good of the people, with each person's labour equal to and for the benefit of all others. Well, let me assure you, the only way I'm equal is in my right to a loss of privacy, autonomy, and independence. It seems equality cannot overcome authority, so in any hierarchal system where some people are required to manage others, and others required to manage the mangers and so on until you reach the top, the lines of separation will find their way back in… The idea of an equal world where we all work together for the greater good, is nothing more than a beautiful lie.'

Johnny's words struck a chord with me. Inconceivably (*at least to those of poor conception*), New Think never accounted for the very old problem of the historically lower classes feeling no connection to the upper classes they're now supposed to be equal to. History has many examples of the lower classes rebelling against their masters, should opportunity arise. With the wealthy being landowners and business owners, and the impoverished holding nothing of value, the large numbers of untethered poor hold no qualms about the loss of land and riches of the wealthy. They're busy just trying to survive. Why would anyone, given nothing by their masters, bother defending them against a foe who seeks only to take from the wealthy and keep for themselves? The poor are treated like a disease living upon a host, yet that host expects the poor to defend them if a threat should come their way.

I knew the point that Johnny was trying to make was this. The world had not changed for him. Not really. Not for the better. So while he might not quite be on my side, he's definitely not on theirs. It's no surprise, even here in the heart of the beast. Or perhaps especially here in the heart of the beast. The Global World isn't actually bursting with dedicated supporters of its wondrous cause. It's filled with subservient masses who abide the rules demanded by the extremist few who believe the manipulative lies of the powerful and hate anyone who doesn't. New Think's leaders are not beloved or admired, they're simply obeyed in the absence of an alternative option. The Guides are seen as one does a tormentor, who stands over them with a whip. Except that loyalty is not engendered by force, it can only be earned through excellent example, and kept by offering those you wish to follow you, the freedom to leave, and the impetus to want to stay.

'So, I guess what you're saying is you aren't working with the people upstairs, just for them.' I said.

'Not even that, Detective. I'm simply doing the job I'm required to do to in order to stay alive in this fucked up world. I work for OGT, I do what I have to do, and I take home my Global apportioned financial allotment at the end of each week, that's all.'

'Okay, I think we can see eye to eye here.' I said. 'Now, I need to ask you some questions about the case. It won't make this shitty world any better, but at least if you help me find out exactly who killed Katie and Chen, then we can work out why, and we might just stop the world from getting a whole lot shittier.'

'What makes you think I know who killed Katie or Chen?' he asked, crossing his arms defiantly.

'Well, you might not know you know. It happens all the time. You see something or someone at a certain time, doing certain things and think nothing of it. Until someone asks the right question, then Bob's your uncle.'

'What on earth does that mean?' He asked.

'That garage door with the broken chip scanner.' I said. 'What if the masters upstairs are aware of it and want it to stay broken for the same reason you do?'

'What, you think they're coming down and leaving from here as well?' Asked Johnny.

'You said most of the office cleaning is done after hours, right?'

'Yeah, that's right. They don't really like seeing us around while they're still here. They prefer us to be invisible.'

'Of course they do. And you have a cleaner assigned to each floor with a rostered cleaning time for each room on that floor?' I continued.

'Pretty much.' he said. 'Except where the office staff have requested a variation.'

'Right. That's what happened on the night Katie was murdered, wasn't it? Katie herself called down and asked for the time to be changed?' I asked, knowing that it was.

'Uh, yeah, that's right. Jiang was asked to come up earlier instead of his normal time.'

'After which, he went home sick?' I queried, attempting to both lead Jiang to my epiphany and confirm the details as I went.

'Yeah, that's right.' confirmed Johnny again, not quite picking up what I was putting down.

He sat at his desk, facing me directly over the holograph of his screen. The look on his face somewhere between defiant and nervous. Willing to help, while not wanting to be trapped or taken advantage of. I wanted to gain his trust because I needed his help on this and I also needed him to give me the information, willingly, which means I can't just go putting words in his mouth.

'Aside from the murder, did anything else odd happen that night?'

'I don't think so.' Replied Johnny, irritatingly.

'Okay, let's try changing tack. Would you say that you spend most shifts sitting in here behind your desk?'

'Yeah, I'm pretty much here all the time. This is where I'm meant to be. I'm a coordinator, a manager, not a spray and wipe guy.'

'So, if someone wanted to come in via that roller door so that their chips would not be registered, they'd have to make sure you weren't sitting here at the time, right?' I asked.

'That's true…' he said. 'You know, now that I think of it, Carlos was called up to level 10 on the night of Katie's murder. One of the cleaners reported tripping and rolling his ankle. Carlos had to go up to complete the injury report.'

I tried not to beam a smile too wide or fist pump as he finally caught my thread. 'How long was he gone?'

'Johnny tapped away on his air keys to check the log, before answering. About twenty-five to thirty minutes.'

'Seems like a long time, doesn't it?'

'Johnny tapped his keys some more and brought up a document. It's a long report.' he said, motioning for me to come around the desk and view the projection. 'He'd have to take pictures, get a statement of injury, conduct a first aid assessment of the injured person, and stay with them for a period of fifteen minutes after the assessment to make sure they show no signs of a head injury. It's OGT policy.'

'How convenient.' I said. 'Sounds like plenty of time for a group of people to make their way through the basement. So, who was the cleaner that injured themselves?'

There was a long pause again, during which Johnny stared at the document being projected in front of him. His mouth was open slightly, his eyes blinking slowly as realisation finally distilled into words. 'It was Chen….'

I didn't know exactly what name I had expected to hear. Suffice to say, I was distinctly un-shocked by this one. It was finally something that made some semblance of sense. A puzzle piece fitting neatly into place.

'The picture's becoming a little clearer here, Johnny. Now let's see if we can give it some colour. You mentioned earlier that the camera on the lifts always stays on the lifts, because you can't adjust that one like you can the others. Who has control over adjusting that camera?' I asked.

'Ah, well, nobody. I should be able to adjust that too. Except, the motor or the actuator for adjusting it must be broken or jammed up somehow.'

'So, why hasn't the camera been fixed? This place has an automated system, doesn't it? Wouldn't Cam, the auto-concierge, just book it in to be fixed after some sort of system check or something?'

'Well, the camera itself isn't broken, it just doesn't turn.' said Johnny. 'It's possible that the auto concierge that doubles as a sort of building maintenance manager is unaware of the fault too. Lots of things are automated here, but there are still some things that need to be reported manually. Certain people in the building also have system override authority, so even if the system tells them something is faulty and has to be fixed, they can deny that action from taking place.'

'Do you have that authority?' I asked.

'No. Only a select few, all well above me in the food chain, have that.'

'Is there a chance that someone could have turned the cameras all away from their intended surveillance point and not realised that one of these cameras didn't turn?'

'I suppose so.' said Johnny. 'Actually, the people with override authority can reposition the cameras remotely by simply logging into the building's surveillance system and entering an instruction to turn left or right, etc. If you were doing this immediately and observing the angles, you'd notice that the camera hadn't turned where you instructed it to. If you plan ahead, you can also set the camera movements on a timer to ensure they're looking the right way at the right time of day. Some areas are busy in one direction in the morning and the opposite in the evenings, so they move on a timed cycle. But, these are just service elevators, so there's really no need to turn that camera, anyway. Unless you're trying to hide something.'

'Wouldn't it make sense just to get more cameras, so you don't have to turn them?' I asked.

‘OGT might be the kings of surveillance, but they’re arrogant too. They figure with devices, chips, mood screens and everything else that’s spying on you, they don’t need that many cameras. Besides, it’s not like they really need evidential proof to determine that something has happened. They say it happened, it happened, there’s no argument.’

‘Do you think it’s possible that someone trying to set up an unseen entry and exit from the building could have preset timers for all the cameras down here to be turned away while they entered and exited without realising that the camera at the lifts never actually turned?’ I asked again. It’s a habit I developed in the army (*and learned from Austin Powers*). I’ll often ask the same question more than once when I don’t get the answer I need the first time. It’s incredible how often it works.

‘Yes, I suppose it’s possible. Probable even.’ He added, seeming to gain confidence in his conviction. ‘The camera at the lift is inside a housing, so it would be difficult to see what way it was facing.’

‘Excellent.’ I said. ‘Then who do I need to speak to in order to view the footage from those cameras the night Katie was killed?’

‘You’re speaking to him.’ said Johnny, smiling. He seemed more relaxed now. The stiffness of his shoulders gone, his blue polo shirt sitting more comfortably, with his head and neck upright and confident.

‘How is it you’re so low on the totem pole, and yet you’re allowed to review surveillance footage?’ I asked.

‘I can’t review all the cameras in the building. I’m not that special. On this floor, however, it’s my responsibility to be the human side of monitoring them and reviewing footage for any reports of theft or damage to deliveries that the cleaners might be suspected of. Like I said, we are beneath those who are above us. They don’t waste time with the issues of the less equal.’

‘Pull it up.’ I urged. ‘It’s time to find out exactly who was in that room.’

It didn’t take Johnny long to locate the data files from between 20:00 and 23:00 the night of Katie’s murder. A few taps of the keyboard, a couple of seconds scrolling, a click of the mouse, and he had them loaded up and ready to go.

‘It may be best if you don’t see these.’ I said. ‘You mind if I take over your office for fifteen minutes.’

‘No, you’re probably right.’ said Johnny. ‘It may be best I don’t know exactly who’s involved. I already assume they’re evil up there. I don’t need to see the proof.’

After Johnny left, I started the video, fast forwarding my way through the earlier portion, looking intently for anything that stood out, which nothing did. Luckily, we’d started to piece the timeline together with the events of that night, so when the recording reached around 20:35 I slowed the video to normal speed and eight minutes later at 20:43 the real show began. Carlos exited the office opposite the one I now sat in, heading for the break room before disappearing from view. About a minute later, he exited again, walking back to the office in a straight line, with no deviation or emotion on display. Thirty seconds later, Jiang came out of the break room, wiping food from his mouth as he went.

He appeared casual, unbothered, dressed neatly in his blue overalls and clearly unaware of the chain of events about to unfold that would change the course of his and many other's lives. Jiang remained visible on the cameras right up to the point he entered the lifts and disappeared upstairs. I kept watching the time tick by for 11 more minutes before he reappeared exiting the lifts and returned to the break room, presumably to finish his meal. Evidentially, he'd only taken half his break and in a New Think world, you always take your full break. There's nothing to be gained by working longer or harder. Same shit pay, same shit benefits.

I found it interesting he hadn't immediately gone home though, given what had occurred since. It wasn't until I re-watched the video of his return that I noted the stiffer, more nervous gait to his movement. He walked faster too, and with the distinct purpose of not only wanting but needing to get somewhere. As the tape kept rolling, I realised Jiang had only stayed in the lunchroom for a couple of minutes before exiting again with a bag over his shoulder and heading straight for Carlos's office. Not quite the break absorbing move I'd predicted.

There was no footage showing the discussion that took place in there. Needless to say, it was short. After five minutes, Jiang exited the office, heading directly for the roller door and into the alley. That was around 21:11 and it appeared to confirm that what we thought we knew about Jiang's movements was, in fact, the truth. After that, not much happened until 21:50, at which time, Carlos came out of the office with a clipboard in his hand, moving quickly towards the lift. If Johnny was telling the truth, then Carlos must have received the call from Chen and headed up to level 10.

At 21:52, the garage door began opening, with nobody and no vehicles visible on any of the cameras. Soon, three of the four cameras turned away in unison whilst the fourth seemed to vibrate for several seconds before ultimately remaining in place.

After three minutes of nothingness, displayed on all four of the cameras, a lying horde of twenty-two people entered the lift foyer, and in three lots, boarded a lift and disappeared upstairs. Fourteen minutes later, the first lift full of people returned to the basement, followed by two more. Then at 22:14, three of the four cameras turned back towards their ordinary focal points and the show was over. 'Gotcha!' I said out loud.

I watched the footage of people entering and exiting the lifts again two more times before being satisfied I'd identified them all. We now had recorded confirmation of each person entering the building just prior to the murder of Katie and exiting the building just after. I pulled the list from the chip register Empher had provided before being shot and arrested, ticking the names off against those identified from the footage. There were four people present on camera, who were conspicuously absent from her list. Captain Isabelle Ironie, Chief Brandy Blindspot, Detective Empher Thise and none other than the all-powerful Cheq Fencegap.

Having seen enough for now, I called Johnny back into the office and asked him to send me a copy of the file. I was planning to forward it to Milly and Shaz to bring them into the loop, and for posterity's sake, just in case I don't make it out of here.

'Is that all you need?' asked Johnny in the manner of a chemist who'd just scanned my Codral's and hoped I'd leave before he caught whatever I had.

He was standing awkwardly in the doorway on the other side of his own desk, while I remained sitting in his seat where I had been viewing the footage and enjoying the warmth of an electric heater.

'No, I'm afraid not Johnny. I am going to solve these murders, and I'm going to do it today! I know you have a job to do here, and my presence is a hindrance, but I don't think I have to remind you that two of your fellow employees, equal or otherwise, have been murdered, and that takes precedence.'

'Certainly, Detective. I didn't mean to be dismissive or rush you out. I'm just not sure what else I can provide.'

'Well, you're on a roll so far. Next, I need to see the footage from the night of Chen's murder. I have a strong feeling the murderer on that occasion came alone and from inside the building.'

'Wouldn't they have already reviewed that when the officers were here?' he asked.

'Perhaps.' I replied. 'Trouble is, I have no faith in whatever was seen, being accurately reported. So far, we've received not one piece of actionable evidence of the crimes here. Until tonight, that is. I say, let the hot hand roll!'

'Okay. I'll look it up and then leave again, shall I?' asked Johnny.

'You've got the rhythm of things now.' I said, not bothering to address the apparent annoyance of Johnny's comment. A few more taps on the air and he had retrieved the file I needed, ready to project.

After he dutifully left the room again, I began reviewing the footage from the night of Chen's murder and it wasn't long before a smile uncreased my lips when my eyes confirmed the theory would hold. Only minutes prior to the time of his shooting, the cameras turned just as I'd expected, except this time, only two of them moved, the third failing its task while the fourth remained fixed on the entry via the alley. I watched the lifts intently, waiting for what I knew must occur, surprised all the same, when not one, but two, people exited the doors. The first, quite clearly and brazenly brandishing a small Beretta 21A Bobcat, a weapon that fires a .22 calibre round matching both the murders here at OGT.

Sophia held the pistol comfortably, odd for an apparently hardcore New Thinker. Then again, they were never really anti-aggression, violence, or retribution. In fact, those three things were core to their mission statement and still are. Ostracise, destabilise, criminalise, and then exterminate Old Thinkers and anyone else that dare oppose their New World Order. By her side, none other than Captain Isabelle Ironie… leaving no doubt she's as crooked as they come…

'Johnny!' I yelled out, satisfied with what I'd seen and ready for him to forward a copy of the evidence.

Hearing no response, I headed out of the office to see where he'd gotten to. 'Johnny!' I yelled again.

My voice echoed off the solid concrete walls, yet nobody answered, and still nobody moved. I walked towards the lifts searching as I went and thinking that perhaps he'd gone to prep some trolleys or check his stock levels, finding only empty space surrounded by grey concrete and shiny blue and silver doors.

I stopped outside the lifts trying to extend my senses and scan my surrounds, when an odd feeling came over me. It was daytime, so I knew there wouldn't be many cleaners about, but right now there appeared to be none. The ordinarily quiet basement was flat out empty.

Starting from my head and moving down my arms and back, my skin crawled with that creepy, nervy feeling you get when you realise no one's there but you're not alone.

Then it happened, click, click, click, click… My head snapped in the direction of the lifts, where I immediately identified the noise. It was the very thing that had finally helped me progress the case. The lift camera was attempting to follow instructions and turn away from the doors.

I whirled back around to check the other two cameras inside the basement, both of them turning away in unison. My years of training kicked in again as I assessed my situation. I'm out in the open here, exposed. I could try surprising whoever was coming by taking up a position behind some cleaning trollies near the lifts, except the angles were bad, and with a solid wall at one end of the lift foyer, it would be more likely to give cover to those coming out while blocking my line of sight. Having just watched a replay of this very situation, it was possible there was more than one of them coming, and they could come down in separate lifts with two different and opposing arcs of fire, leaving me blind to at least one threat. Plus, if it was someone high up or with system access, they could've been watching me on the cameras right up to the point they turned. In fact, it's likely they did. This couldn't have been pre-planned. I'm not even meant to be here.

As I work through my evaluation process, it occurs to me that if someone was watching the cameras on their device, they would now have realised the lift camera didn't turn. If they didn't know there was footage of the killers travelling via the lifts before, they certainly do now.

'Shit, the footage of Chen's murderers.' I said aloud to myself. If I don't get a copy of that now, I may never get it. I ran back to Johnny's office, where the chip trackers would record my entry, as would the desk device. Another unavoidable gift to my attackers, pinpointing my location. At least they're harder to access remotely than the cameras they already have control of. Besides, if they were watching me or monitoring what we were looking at on Johnny's computer, then they'd already know I've seen what they've done. Plus, they'd know I was taking copies as evidence. I expect that's what drew their attention to begin with. Now I just have to make sure I send the second lot before they delete it or kill me.

Taking a seat at Johnny's console again, which thankfully had its bio-security measures paused so that I could view the projections, I realised the most immediate issue with my plan might just be me. I'm not remotely tech savvy, which is both impressive and a monumental hinderance in a Global world. Despite tech wizards always sprouting about how they're making life simpler, the tech they produce is generally superseded before they've even finished developing it and it's seldom simpler or easier to use than that which it replaced. Having said that, even I should be able to share or send a file to myself… that is, so long as I don't need to re-enter a passcode or find some sort of database to locate it.

I winced at the thought of accidentally clicking on the cross to close the projection, worrying that I'd never find the link that launched it. Luckily, the projection sprung back to life at my touch, the program paused exactly as I had left it. After closing the file, the process was as simple as advertised and I subsequently downloaded it, quickly hitting share to send it directly to my email, Cc'ing in Milly in case I never get an opportunity to forward it on.

POP! Went a loud noise, accompanying the instant disappearance of the projected screen and keyboard. It reminded me of an old glass fuse blowing. The ominous sign clearly being that they'd cut the power, meaning they were not only down here, they were ready to attack.

Fuck! Did the footage send or is it gone forever, I wonder for the shortest of seconds before another noise snaps me back. "scher-k" went the sound I immediately identified as a scuffed boot on the concrete floor of the basement. By the speed and loudness, I'm guessing whoever made it was attempting to move slowly, and still a little distant from the office where I sat. Perhaps ten to fifteen meters away. That could mean only one of two things. Either they aren't sure where I am, so they're slowly sweeping the area… Or the noise I heard is only the backup for someone who's already here…

Chapter 27

Peaceful violence

'When the shit hits the fan, rely on your training.' Said the voice in my head, its calming presence a remnant of my years of military training. The voice wasn't mine, nor the words, instead born of Army doctrine and repeated infinitum to imbed them deep in my mind. Their goal, that of instinctive obedience, desired of every soldier before me and every solider since. Don't think, act, on a predetermined set of instructions. Time is of the essence, but training keeps you alive.

First, where's the threat?

Seated at Johnny's desk, I take stock of what I know. Johnny's device is dead, the pop when the power cut out, seeming to fry its little brain, so it could monitor me no more. My own device was safely tucked inside its restrictive sleeve, rending me safe from that as well. That left only the chip reader on the office door (*supported by a backup battery, because surveillance never takes a holiday*) to confirm the obvious. They know where I am. What they don't know is that I know just who's after me.

Seconds before the device shut down, I saw on the screens to my right, two figures emerge from the lift. Neither of them glancing at the camera they must now realise captured the arrival of Chen's murderers.

Isabelle led the way with Sophia watching her six, covering the open expanse of basement to the right of the lift well. That end of the building held reasonable options for concealment, with a trolley-bay, freestanding supply cabinets and two small E-trucks parked at charging stations against the rear wall.

Also at that end, sits the large toilet and shower rooms where Chen's involvement in this nasty plot came to a sudden end. From there, moving around to the right, are the parking bays currently occupied by two company E's, the garage door in the centre of the far wall opposite the office, and on the other side of that, the noisy, hot, air-conditioning units that supply, treat and purify the buildings air. To the left of the lifts, runs a long concrete wall, initially formed by the outer part of the lift well itself, carrying on unbroken until it meets the two opposing offices of Johnny and Carlos. Past these offices lies the break room and kitchen, and past that, the open expanse of basement floor curves down and around to the left onto another small car park, with no other feature save the base of the lifts.

Here I sit, little piggy in the middle of my house made of concrete and glass, waiting for the big bad wolf to come along and eat me.

In the Old Think days of flash bangs and stun grenades, I'd be a goner. Flick one of those through the door, charge in, put two in my chest and one in the head for good measure, and that'd be all she wrote. Lucky for me, Sophia and Ironie are no tactical unit, and they don't have flash bangs. Nor do they have the ability to render me motionless via my chip… not anymore. That was trialled, with electric shocks or the release of a paralysing or deadly drug, that failed so often and killed so many it became useless as a deterrent. Being inserted with one of those chips was akin to putting a cyanide pill in your paracetamol bottle. It was going to kill you. It was only a matter of when.

Instead, they would have to use good old stealth, surprise, or speed to get me. The window to my right looking out on the basement floor would make it hard for Ironie and Sophia to sneak all the way up on me from that angle. They could try getting low, crawling under the window, and coming from a low trajectory at the doorway, except they'd have to know that I'm alert. After all, they cut the power to the office, not the whole basement, so that's not going to work. Trying to move around the office past me to come one from either side was nearly impossible, too. The wall behind me is solid concrete, so nothing doing there, and there's a window opposite the desk, so even if Johnny turned out to be a bad guy who'd been hiding out that way, I'd most likely see him before he ever got the jump.

For them, the best option was for one go under the window, ready to take the doorway, while the other takes a heavy object capable of smashing the glass. On a count, the rear person breaches the window, immediately following the projectile with the barrel of their gun, while simultaneously, the one at the door comes rushing through and blazes away. A surprise attack from two different angles is hard to cover, even if you do know it's coming.

Second, how do you counter it?

I think about my position in the room, rapidly identifying and discarding my options as they fail the test in my mind. I could crouch at the end of the desk to my left, giving me a view of both doorway and window, while leaving very little cover, save for a thin piece of plywood that forms both the end of, and support for, the table. I could position myself against the wall in front of the desk between the doorway and the monitors and try to draw them into the room, except then I'd risk giving them a shot from both sides with virtually no cover at all.

In the end, I take the one remaining option. I pick up Johnny's desk device, which appeared to be the only object in the room with any significant weight. After unplugging the charging cord, I move round the end of the table to my left, device in hand. I can't hear my would-be killers breathing or moving out there, the vibrating hum of the cooling units providing a sort of white noise cover in the concrete chamber. No matter. I've practiced this situation a thousand times before. There's no magic to it, no tricks. A good soldier is a well-trained soldier who knows how to pick their timing, control their breathing, and commit to the plan. Calmness is key.

Third, it's time to act.

I'd marked in my mind where I thought they'd been when I heard the scuff of the foot, my internal clock counting down ever since.

I wait a beat…2…3, then at the exact moment I think they're about to strike. 'NOW!' screams a voice in my head. I launch the projectile at the centre of the window looking out on the basement floor, shattering the glass, and creating an almighty crash!

As soon as I release the device, I'm on my way out the door, keeping low to the ground, my movements quick and controlled till I reach the point I'd selected about eight feet out from the doorway. My electro's held out in front at the ready, my hands relaxed to avoid jerking the weapon when I fire and costing precious time as I move swiftly out to my mark. Timing is everything and while it feels like forever, a split second after the window shatters, I'm right where I planned to be.

Out in the open now, I have to be careful not to get to target fixed, allowing my eyes to take in as much of my 180-degree view as I can. There's nothing to my left as I exit the door, but I clock two targets on my right, just as I'd expected. Both Ironie and Sophia were still moving backwards, reacting to the shattering of the window, their heads turning away from the doorway focussed on the exploding glass.

I steady myself, dropping my right knee to the ground to form a solid base to fire from. Bringing my left hand up steadily, controlling my breathing, I pause momentarily, iron sights aligned mid-exhale and gently squeeze the trigger, releasing my first electro round at the shocked and exposed Ironie. It strikes her in the upper breast plate on the right of her chest. An intentional shot to the right, wanting to avoid it landing over the heart and potentially inducing a cardiac arrest. I want to subdue, not kill.

As Isabelle rocked backwards, already off balance from her turn toward the shattered window and now with the jolt of the electro voltage pulsing through her, I shift my focus up and behind her to Sophia, who given her standing position back from the window was quicker to recover and raise her gun. She meant business too and clearly had training, the beretta out in front, her rear foot planted in a firing position. She had a look on her face somewhere between anger, determination, and shock.

Seeing me, she brought the weapon up in line with my head, finger inside the trigger guard and ready to fire. I hadn't quite adjusted my aim when a thumping thud combined with the crack of a pistol and the fizz of a hot lead pebble flew past my head… Shit… I took another beat, just breathing…2…3… then slowly got to my feet.

'Thanks!' I said, for the second time today, my heart racing with the buzz of nerves and fear that even thirty years of training can't dampen. 'I had her covered, you know.' I added, looking down at the now convulsing and probably unconscious Sophia. Blood oozed from the wound on her head and dripped down onto the grey concrete floor.

I walked over to check Ironie, confirming her vitals were strong. She'd automatically crumpled into the foetal position, her dark attractive features now hidden, the almond-shaped eyes and full curved lips contorted into the painful scowl of a gargoyle. After rolling her into the recovery position and gathering my spent round, I turned back to Sophia.

'You okay?' I asked Johnny, who, having struck Sophia from behind, was still standing there holding a large spanner and shaking.

'Boy, am I glad the cameras are turned away now.' I added, attempting to break through his shock. 'In this world, they'd just edit out the part where these two were trying to kill us and it'd be you and me in jail!'

It didn't work. He merely stood there, his mouth hanging open, eyes wide with fear and adrenaline pulsing through his veins, driving his heartbeat ever faster. I walked up to him and calmly took the spanner from his cold clammy hand, placing it off to the side of the shattered window.

As I bent to the concrete floor, a large shard of glass reflected back the image of a ruddy faced, intense looking man. I'd been shot at before, many times in fact, and the reality is, you're either able to cope with it, or you're not. You can be trained in tasks of skill and taught the depths of knowledge, but nerves and the fight-or-flight response are autonomic. Which is the same as saying automatic. You can't just tell yourself not to react. If you could, it wouldn't be a reaction.

Taking a moment to breathe and centre my thoughts, I focus my eyes on those staring back at me, assuring myself I'm ready to go again, before kicking back into gear.

Turning to Johnny, I help him over to the front of his office where the floor was clear of broken glass, and set him down, laying him out as straight and comfortably as I could. Despite the sweat on his brow, I know from years of first aid training that keeping him warm is imperative. Taking off my own jacket and placing it over his shoulders and chest, I then run to the kitchen and swipe my chip in order to get him a glass of water. He could speak, and so far as I could tell, had no other injuries of note, so I left him there, turning my attention back to the would-be attackers.

Now that Sophia had stopped convulsing from the effects of the electile lodged in her thigh, I checked her vitals, confirming she was, in fact, still breathing, albeit rapidly. Rolling her into the recovery position like her fellow attacker, then searching the pockets of her sliver/grey pant suit for any other weapons, I find the most dangerous of all. Her device. It's probably recorded and transmitted every moment of this violent attack, and I couldn't help wondering just who might've been listening.

While I stash it along with Ironie's device in a spare RFID bag, Johnny shows signs of a quick recovery, slowly sitting up and sliding back to lean against the wall.

'Why did they do that?' He asked, more as an externally expressed thought than an actual question.

'They think they're only doing what must be done.' I said. 'Actually, they think they're protecting the world. The latest in a long line of people willing to do harm in the name of a supposed greater good. Throughout history, people have gone to extremes to implement, enforce, or protect their beliefs. The idea of enacting them may seem very reasonable to begin with, until other people's non-belief or opposing ideals weaken their own, at which point they'll do whatever it takes to silence them. New Think's the ideology of today, Sophia and Isabelle its zealots, believing they're duty bound to protect it, no matter the cost.'

Johnny already knew this, of course, his question a rhetorical one, voiced out of frustration, not confusion. My answer, the expression of my own frustration and an attempt to reason the unreasonable.

As I stood in the aftermath, surveying the considerable destruction that lay before me, I knew there was only one thing left to do. To call my good friend Milly.

Chapter 28

New Think, in the clink

If there was one good thing about being attacked, it was the comfort that gave me about having earlier tazed someone I used to trust.

Constable Clubman was one of "them". There was no doubt in my mind now. He shot Matthias because he was concerned he'd fold and start talking. Matthias had already given away a certain amount of confirmation that he was complicit, if not outright guilty of involvement in the murder of Katie Hansley. I hadn't quite put it together at the time, but I now believe Cliff shot Empher, not so much to save me as to save the plan. I guess he must've been in the doorway a little while before the screen alerted me to his presence. He probably heard Empher admit to her involvement in the plot, then acted. Just another guardian of the cause, no doubt. A clean-up crew for a movement whose plumbing had sprung a leak.

Which means that all his fear and anger this morning was nothing more than an act designed to build a layer of cover and gain my trust. The question that needs answering is, who sent him and how has this person acquired so many police officers to guard their plan? Is it money? And if it is, what do they do with it in a world like this? You can't buy anything worth having. Even if they are excused the absurd restrictions of the Global Impact Score (*GIS*), which assigns a negative value for everything you buy and do, so that you can see your theoretical impact on the world, feel bad for existing, and worse for seeking to do so with some joy in the experience. You are then, of course, suitably punished for the very minimal and necessary purchases you are allowed to make by being banned from making any more. Until, that is, you take the necessary steps to reduce your GIS back down to a zeroed level. A goal achieved by paying more money to the same people you bought the products from to begin with, who themselves put it back in their pocket. An ingenious process, we're told, that supposedly benefits the global world. After which, you go to work and contribute more to the pockets of the same people you bought your products from, because not only are they global saviours, they're business elites, who've monopolised their field and are by some miracle of coincidence, best placed to determine how to save the globe and its inhabitants by using their products exactly how and when they tell us to. By which means, you shall reduce your burden on the earth to a level where you are permitted to burden it some more.

Still, I'd be surprised if the likes of Clubman, Ironie, or Empher were in it for the money, even if they could spend it outside the system. So, what then? There's no social ladders to climb these days, and no virtue gained from the depth of their commitment to the cause. Not now that it's compulsory. Besides which, as individual New Thinkers, I had never thought of any of them as extremists, likely as not to kill just for the principle of the thing. Sophia, I can see that way. She's the most openly committed to perpetual over-bearance and appears the most likely to be a martyr for greater good. Matthias not so much. I'm sure he'd do it for the money or the cause, but only so long as he was getting more than he gave.

Chief Blindspot, meanwhile, has never liked Sharon or I, Old Think or not. Regardless of which, I'd always considered her to be the type to ensure the principles that underpin the Globalist morals were adhered to, no matter the presence of an Old Thinker or a wavering comrade. Hell, she agreed to employ Sharon and I, knowing full well that we're unapologetically anti-Global, which in itself makes us a minority appointment of sorts. And anyway, despite generally hating us, the perception of tolerance and acceptance remains central to those who actually believe the Global ideals are genuine, and that we're all just part of the plan. Then again, maybe I'm wrong. Maybe I know nothing at all. Nothing I can prove yet, at any rate.

What I do know, and what I can prove, is exactly who was there on the nights the victims were murdered. A critical piece of evidence that places the suspects at the scene of the crime but fails to show who did the deed. It therefore seemed to me that the only way I was going to get to the bottom of this was to arrest the whole bloody lot of them. I just had to hope Milly's safe house was a freaking mansion, or at least has a bloody big dungeon.

I called him again, knowing he was the only one who could help me now. While I can't be certain that every other copper apart from Sharon and I are in on this, the fact is, they may as well be. Standing here in the middle of OGT's basement, I had about as many friends around me as I had in the world right now.

Johnny, having recovered from his shock, was slowly sweeping the shattered glass from the floor behind me. Sharon and Sophia were now both cuffed, and despite being in a daze, had recovered sufficiently for me to prop them up against the far wall, where they now sat, attempting to glare at me spitefully between waves of nausea and dizziness.

Of the three people here, I had two enemies and one friend. Outside of here, I had two friends and a whole lot of enemies.

'What the hell's happening over there?' Asked Milly, who had apparently become greeting averse.

'How are my first lot of prisoners doing?' I responded, dodging his question and levelling our cordiality at nil all.

'They're alive, sweating it out in the dark. Now answer my damn question!' He replied.

'Calm down, friend. I call bearing gifts. Well, more gifts. I take it you got my email with the surveillance footage?' I asked.

'No! What fucking surveillance footage?' he replied.

'You're kidding, right?' I almost shouted back. 'I nearly got killed trying to send that.'

'No Gary, I am not! If you had sent me some evidence of something tied to these crimes, I'd be far calmer about having several prisoners locked up in a safe house, without just cause. As it stands, I've got the head of DSSMD breathing down my neck. Apparently, he's taken a very personal interest in the outcome of this case. So no, I'm not fucking kidding. If I had some useful surveillance footage, I'd be showing it to him and crowing about the progress. In the meantime, I've been trying to prevent him from becoming aware that two x police officers and an OGT employee are currently under lock and guard without us having any understanding of why, they in particular, have been arrested and exactly what involvement they've had.'

'Shit!' I said. 'Hang on a second.'

Johnny was presently in the process of setting a target zone on his device to guide a robo-sweeper to the site of the glass he'd piled up. Designed for exactly this type of mess, they have the ability to clean up large chunks a normal vac couldn't handle. The units are about a meter tall and equally wide, with a rotating brush wheel capable of lifting and lowering to match the surface type, while a regular vac sits underneath at the rear of the unit to pick up the dust and shards.

'Hey Johnny!' I shouted, pulling the device away from my ear.

'Ah, yes, Detective?' He shouted back without looking up from his task.

'That surveillance footage we saw. Now that I smashed your desk device, will you still be able to access it somewhere else?'

'Ah, yeah. I can log into Carlos' office and access it from there.' he replied, looking up at me now, having finished setting the task. It pleased me to see colour returning to his face, replacing the fear and shock of earlier. Johnny was not a man I wanted to lose. For one thing, he was the only human ally I had in this building. Apart from which, he appeared to be the rarest of things these days, a selfless, decent man.

'Right. Good.' I said. 'Any reason the emails wouldn't have gotten through the first time?'

'Maybe.' he replied. 'All outgoing communications are flagged for review here, particularly if they have attachments. They first go through an automated scan. If the system doesn't confirm them as safe, then they are reviewed by a supervisor in the relevant section.'

'And who would the supervisor for these be?' I asked.

'That would be one of our resident moralist's. Probably Adam Abers.' He said with the "Oops" look of someone who should have known this and mentioned it earlier. It's possible the alert from the first email was the very reason we were attacked to begin with.

'Good.' I said. 'I'm going to be paying a visit to him soon. You catch that Milly?' I asked, returning the device to my ear.

'Yeah, he said, you smashed something important. I want that surveillance ASAP, Gary. And it had better make me feel a hell of a lot better.'

'You're going to have a whole lot more than that.' I said. 'That small team of yours. How many can you spare?'

'Why…?' he asked cautiously.

'Because I need a little help rounding up the suspects.'

Milly was slower to respond this time, caution clear in his voice when he did. 'How many are there?'

'Twenty two.' I said matter-of-factly. 'The good news is, I've already arrested five of them. So, only seventeen to go.'

'Jesus Christ, Gary! Do you really need to arrest twenty-two people? Are you sure you wouldn't be better off just locking them down at OGT…'

'No, you're quite right. There's probably a lot more than that. Unfortunately, there's only twenty-two that I can place at the scene of Katie's murder at this point. Two of those same twenty-two were at the scene of Chen's murder as well. And, to save us some time, I have both of them handcuffed and with me right now. I haven't quite worked out if any of this lot were involved in the attack on Sgt Ease and Detective Wilson yet, but I will. As for locking them down here, I considered that. Trouble is, they seem to know how to get in and out without being seen. Or so they thought.'

'So, who exactly are the latest two you've arrested?'

Milly's question was laced with concern, and rightly so. He clearly suspected I'd done something that would come back to bite, not just me, but him, which was very likely true. The fact is, I had out of necessity done the very thing I was specifically told not to do… this morning.

'Sophia from OGT… and Isabelle Ironic.' I replied.

There was a brief pause and a sharp inhalation on the other end of the line as Milly filled his lungs, ready to explode. 'I thought I made it very clear you were to stay away from Captain Ironie, on pain of death!!!' Screamed Milly.

'You did.' I replied calmly.

'Then what the fuck happened?!'

'I arrested Captain Ironie and Sophia after they saw your threat, and doubled down it, taking it upon themselves to personally try to inflict that pain of death upon me. When that happened, Captain Planet himself (*New Think's mascot by the way, much to the annoyance of several sexes... mother nature anyone?)* couldn't convince me to leave them be. You're lucky Sharon wasn't healthy enough to be here, or we'd need a casket, not a cell.'

'Christ!' He said. 'I don't suppose you can just let her go?'

I didn't bother answering Milly. There was no way I was going to do that, and I knew he didn't really expect I would.

'Then, what do you need?' He asked begrudgingly.

'As many agents as you can spare and as much room in a safe house or cells away from prying untrustworthy eyes. We need to arrest, then interrogate, all the suspects, gather evidence from the OGT surveillance systems and find out what on this hellish earth was so damn important about that program to warrant them acting this way.'

'Do we have evidence to support these arrests so that I can at least give my boss something to go off?' asked Milford desperately.

'Yes. Two of the three prisoners you already have, admitted to perverting the course of justice, and the other discharged his weapon to silence a suspect, also with the express intent of perverting the course of justice.'

'And they admitted that?' Asked Milly.

'No. But I'm sure he would have, if I hadn't zapped him.'

'And the rest?' He asked.

'We have the surveillance footage showing them heading up to Katie's office and entering just prior to her murder, then exiting the office and the building just after the fact. At the very least, every single one of them witnessed or took part in what I would at this point characterise as a premeditated and cult-like murder, then lied about it, not once, but twice, to two separate investigative teams.'

'Well, it's a shame we don't have the surveillance footage of the murder, too.' said Milly. 'A smoking gun, so to speak.'

'It's not just "so to speak" Milly. There's literally a smoking gun, and I'm almost certain I will have the footage of its lethal retort by tomorrow afternoon at the latest.'

'What?!' He said, more shocked than I'd expected. 'I thought all the surveillance in the room was compromised?'

'Yeah, well, we all thought that. Turns out that's not quite true. I think I have a way of getting it, except I can't tell you how or who will provide it yet. Let's just say there's always someone watching.'

'Yes, I know.' he replied dryly. 'As often as not, that someone is me.'

'On top of that, I'm confident I literally have the physical smoking gun.' I added. 'Sophia tried to shoot me with it today. She almost succeeded, too.'

Milly took a deep breath, then sighed, long and slow. 'Well, I've got four, two-person teams I can send your way. I'm pretty sure I can get a few prisoner transport vehicles for them to bring over as well. That should help you round up the crowd.'

'Great. Send them to the basement entry of the OGT building, same as last time. Most of our targets should still be here, so we can mount the operation from directly below them before anyone gets wind of what's going on. Do you still have an agent out the front?'

'Yeah, still there.' he said. 'Nothing much to report, so he tells me. Except that he's not alone, that is. Your other two friends are out there and we're yet to identify who they are or what group they belong to. All we know is their chips don't register.'

'Hmm, interesting. I wonder if they're part of a fourth or fifth party involved in this and whether they're investigating or perpetrating. Well, keep me abreast of that. Let me know if anything changes or if any of our targets exit the building. That'd be a tremendous help. I would try to tap into the building's surveillance system and monitor it myself… eh, we both know I'm not really capable of that.'

'Sure.' he said. 'You give the instructions and I'll coordinate the overall troop movements from here. Oh, and you'll have to take your device out of its protective sheath.' he added. 'If we're going to monitor and guide you, I'll need to know where exactly you are and what you're doing throughout the process.'

'There's no need to worry about that. It's going to be out for a while now. I want to make sure all the arrests are recorded for evidence and prosecution purposes.'

We wrapped up the conversation with Milly confirming he'd have all four units out to me within thirty minutes, leaving me just enough time to formulate an action plan for conducting the remaining arrests. After disengaging (*New Think term*) from the call, I immediately contacted Sharon to give her an update and see what she'd been up to whilst I was being shot at. I wanted to make sure the broader plan was coming together, and that we had all our ducks in a row.

'Shaz, you still alive?' I asked.

'Yeah, still kicking. Getting better by the minute, actually.' she said. 'Amazing what you can achieve when you find a few hours with nobody trying to kill you.'

'Makes you long for your library days, I suppose?' I replied.

'I'm always longing for my library days.' Said Shaz. 'Not least because it was a better world back then. If I needed to answer a historical question, or to do some research for school or work, all I had to do was look up the book and find the answers I sought. Better yet, they weren't re-edited or adjusted for ideological acceptance, or blocked out because you're not allowed to know, or constantly monitored and tracked. And I didn't need a bloody password. I suppose you did need a library card and the book would show against your name, but for all that, I could find whatever I wanted, in the same words and context as it was originally published.'

'Plus, people weren't trying to kill you.' I added.

'I dunno.' said Sharon. 'Law student looks up a book that the system says is in isle 6, section D, under "s" that they need to reference for their dissertation and that book isn't actually there… I might prefer if someone was trying to kill me. The righteous ranting of a would be lawyer is the most painful torture I've ever endured.'

'Funny you mention lawyers.' I quipped. 'I need to know if we can trust Susan Sly. I've started gathering evidence on these crimes and I'm hoping you and your geek friend are getting somewhere, too. Even if you're not, the next big step is to get Sly's thoughts on the case. We need to know if what we've got is going to be enough to support a successful public perception prosecution. Without that, we've got nothing. What do you think, can we trust her?'

'I hope so!' said Shaz. 'We haven't got any other options unless we recruit from another station and I don't see that going well. Speaking of my geek friend, he's been helping me a lot. In fact, he's working under my direct instruction now.'

I knew that Sharon's casual statement was, in fact, a veiled question, asking if I minded having him at my place, without explicitly having to say it. Millys team was listening, and while they would now know we were up to something, we could at least make it hard to know where.

'Always best to be direct with techs. They have a tendency to stray from the task otherwise.' I responded in the same veiled manner as Sharon. 'So, what about Sly?'

'Well, we should know if she's had any involvement in all of this soon. One of the first things I have our geek friend doing is to map the movements of all the officers from our station over the last 48 hours. That mapping will include Sly and all senior officers and should give us a better picture of whether any of them were at either OGT, the hospital, or Ease' place at the time of the attacks.'

'Sounds like a good starting point.' I said. 'One of the most important pieces of information to come out of that might be how often they're not tracked at all. Anyone that goes missing for more than five minutes should go straight to the top of your list.'

'That's actually how I plan to narrow the pool. I figure we can target the obvious and the unexplained first, then work our way outwards from there.'

'Sounds promising. Keep me updated with any standouts you find. Or if Sly starts to rise towards the top. Out of curiosity, am I on that list?' I asked.

'No. I didn't think that would be necessary. Should you be?'

'Put me on there.' I said. 'There're some gaps I'd like to fill. At the very least, I'd like to confirm that something really happened.'

'Done!' she said, after audibly making a note on her device. 'What's next for you, then?'

I was a little nervous about detailing my plan to Sharon. I trust her judgement, which is usually sound and well-grounded, apart from when an emotional element is involved, as there would be here. Plus, I hadn't actually consulted her before launching down my current path.

'Ah, yes, well, that's where your work and mine should come together nicely.' I said, trying to sound confident. 'I'm going to arrest every single person that was in the room during Katie's murder.'

The quiet pause that preceded Sharon's response was, ah, disquieting. 'Okay… is that the best way to do this?' She asked in the manner that only a woman can, casting an overwhelming shadow of doubt across my soul. It was the "I'm worried you might be going out on a limb here, but I want you to come to that conclusion yourself" tone that had been commonplace when I was married.

'I think it might be the only way to do it.' I replied instead.

'How many people is that?'

'Twenty two.' I answered sheepishly. 'It's worth noting I have already arrested five of them, so you know, only seventeen to go. Oh, and by the way, it turns out Clubman wasn't on our side. It seems he was only here to help protect the lie. I'm not sure why or what that means for the broader case, but he was also doing his best to protect me from the lie.'

'What do you mean?' asked Shaz.

'Well, he shot Detective Thise in order to stop her shooting me. An action only taken after she admitted to having been co-opted into the plot, without yet telling me how or why. She did tell me who, mind you. Our good friend, Captain Ironie, was behind the move.'

'No surprises there.' said Shaz.

'Clubman also shot Matthias after he too admitted to being involved in the plot, again without elaborating on the how's and why's. I'm pretty sure he only shot him to shut him up. Same goes for Thise.'

'Well, it has been eventful there, hasn't it!' She said, sounding slightly miffed.

'That's not all of it. I'll soon send you over some footage of the murderous horde entering a lift to head up to level 7 immediately prior to Katie's murder, then returning again right after. It's the first in a string of actual evidence I've finally pulled together.'

'Why didn't Damwell send that to the police techs before?'

'Damwell didn't find it. I did. I'd imagine he and his team weren't actually looking for it. In fact, I suspect they were under the impression that this couldn't possibly have existed because it was supposed to have been planned that way. Besides, evidence is the last thing they'd need to determine who's actually guilty here. Facts have a nasty way of derailing ideological crusades.'

'Well, I can't wait to see it. So, who else have you arrested?'

'Captain Ironie and Sophia from OGT.' I replied, talking quickly and hoping she didn't get too caught up on that first one.

'In my drug addled state, did I fail to notice you were missing both ear's this morning?' asked Sharon with eye of the storm calmness.

She was obviously baiting me with an ad absurdum question, in spite of which part of me wanted to answer yes, then chop my ears off to provide the evidence. 'I think you know I'm still fully eared.' I replied.

'Then why the hell did you arrest her?! I told you to leave Ironie to me!' she roared. 'That bitch tried to kill me at least once so far, and possibly twice. She was meant to be mine!'

'Well, actually, you and I are even on that front now. That's why I disregarded both Milly's and your warning and arrested her. Right after I shot her. Ironie and Sophia are something of a hit squad, it seems. They're also guilty of killing Chen, which I know for a fact, because there's footage of them both coming down in the lifts to the basement just prior to Chen's murder, guns drawn. And I mean guns. Sophia was carrying a Beretta 21a Bobcat, which, if you don't already know, fires a .22 round and matches the type of weapon we suspect was used to kill both Chen and Katie.'

I could actually hear the begrudgment of Sharon's mind as it worked to absorb what I'd said, knowing I had no other choice. At the end of which, a heavy sigh on her end, was a clear sign that knowing this didn't make her any happier. She could hardly be blamed for her anger. Poor thing was laid up at home because of these psychos, and in fairness, she had soundly recited her case for first dibs this morning and certainly had the worst of the treatment. Unfortunately, life rarely offers us the desired revenge we seek. Sometimes we just have to hope that justice will eventually be served.

'Sounds like we have our killers, then.' she said testily.

'Yes, I think we have the one that pulled the trigger. For Chen, at least. I can't really be sure if Sophia shot Katie, although it would appear to be consistent with what we know of her.'

'Do we really need to arrest everyone else then?' She asked.

Sharon, ever the voice of reason, had climbed down from her all too recent place on the ledge of retribution, to ensure that only reasonable measures were to be taken. As usual, her own internal moral compass, the one aligned with what we used to know was right and wrong, had kicked back in and the needle was turning south. Restraint is of course crucial to remaining on the good side of objective review, however, standing here at the coal face, I personally couldn't agree on this one. She didn't know all the names on this list yet and she still hadn't answered the what's, why's and how's about the program, so as far as I'm concerned, arresting all twenty-two of these nuts might not be reasonable enough.

'Hell yeah, we do!' I said. 'There's motive behind these murders and I can only assume that it's compelling and dangerous enough to require most of the local Police Service to protect it. We need to find out what the hell that motive is to ensure more people don't die for the cause. Every one of those twenty-two people were at the very least accomplices to murder, who knowingly and intentionally obstructed the course of justice and mislead a police investigation. They endangered the lives of several police officers, hospitalising two and, in addition to that, attempted to murder both you and I. Hell, these arrests might just be the tip of the iceberg.'

'Well, how are you going to arrest them all on your own, Gary?' Continued Sharon, now aggressively critiquing my plan.

'Milly is sending out some teams to assist. He's also providing an alternate location, or locations, to hold and interrogate them. They're on their way here now.'

'Okay, so we still trust "them", I suppose. What about me? What can I do from here? I told you I want in on this, Gary. I might be injured, but don't you dare minimise me or leave me out?'

'You're pivotal.' I cooed. 'You and your tech need to gather as much information on the movements of this group as you can, then start putting some storyline detail to your mapping. I'll send through some footage to add to it soon. And, if you can get a good enough view of Sly to trust her, then bring her into the loop, too. I want her involved in our interrogations to make sure we get what we need to bring these bastards to justice.'

'Okay. I suppose that's still important.' said Shaz.

'Great, I'll have my phone unsheathed from now on, so let me know straightaway if there're any updates from your end. And Shaz.'

'Yeah?'

'Don't let anyone else in the apartment. I'm trusting Milly because I have no other choice for now, but I don't know how high up this thing goes, or how deep its roots are. Keep your Electro close, and if you need it, there's a compartment in the bottom of that foot stool your leg is resting on. Let's just say that what you'll find there would leave a Sauer taste in your mouth. If it's you or them, don't hesitate, just shoot.'

I disconnected the call with Shaz and turned to check on the recovery of my latest arrestees. Captain Ironie was coming round. Sophia, on the other hand, likely had a concussion. We'd have to keep an eye on her and get a medic to check her out at the safe house. Her vitals are all there and her breathing's not laboured, but she's definitely still not with it.

I'd removed both their weapons into evidence bags, which I always keep a handful of in my jacket pocket. I'd also removed and bagged their devices before cuffing them both, so it's a good thing they aren't terribly conscious. New Thinkers don't cope well being separated from their electronic brains.

I picked up the bags currently stacked next to the girls, not really fearful they'd be strong enough to get to them, and not entirely sure they wouldn't either. I then headed to what was really Carlos' office, which, under my direction, Johnny had requisitioned.

'Johnny, how are you going logging into that computer?' I shouted as I entered the room.

'All done.' he said. 'I was just extending the time for the cameras to be averted to make sure they don't catch something we don't want them to see.'

'Okay, good. Where are your staff at right now?' I asked.

'There are only two on until 16:00 this afternoon.' he replied. 'They're both upstairs going through all the kitchenettes on every floor, cleaning and restocking them with the supplied of the privileged.'

'When are they due back down?'

Johnny checked his watch before responding, 'A bit over an hour from now.'

'Nice watch.' I commented, wandering over to get a look. 'I'm glad to see it's not an E-watch or satellite controlled.'

'That's actually why I wear it. It's over eighty years old and still keeps great time. My grandfather was a watchmaker. He showed me how to do a basic service on mechanical watches like this one. He gave me this Seiko Champion 850 as a present on his last birthday before he died. I've serviced it and worn it ever since. It reminds me of him. Of a world that was simpler, where people had at least some level of control over their lives. To most people it's just a watch. For me, the joy I take from winding it every morning… it makes me feel like I'm in control of my time… Makes all the difference in this world… You like watches?'

He asked his question with enthusiasm and genuine interest. The truth is, I do like watches. A lot, actually, and mostly for the same reasons he does. The incredible craftsmanship and extraordinary quality of watches made back in the early part of the 1900's is really something to behold. They were often made by hand turned machines and the human eye with nothing but the aid of a loupe. As technology and consumer access improved, so too did the volume of watches produced, along with their price tags. Sadly and in almost inverse quotas, as the watch making capacity increased, the number of tradesmen skilled in the craft decreased. With them went the soul of the industry.

'Love em.' I said, automatically glancing at my own and realising Milly's crews should be here any minute now.

'The DSSMD agents should be here imminently.' I said. 'If you're all ready to go in there, could you send that footage again for me? Same email group as last time would be great.'

'Sure.' said Johnny, obediently returning to the task.

I knew I hadn't been kind to Johnny. Treating him somewhat like his bosses here at OGT. Needing him for his services without paying him the respect or credit he deserved as an equal human being. I made a mental note to rectify this later, then reset my mind to the task at hand.

Right on cue, there was movement at the end of the street leading into the basement door. One after another, four prisoner transport trucks turned and backed down the street, the first edging in just under the door itself, the other three stopping at two meter intervals in front of that.

Just like the one that took Clubman and Thise, these trucks were diesel, same as the old days. That's not nostalgia or rebellion on behalf of the Defence Department, it's far more practical than that. You see, electric vehicles can be hacked and remotely controlled or shut down. Not good risks to carry in vehicles for which the entire purpose is transporting dangerous prisoners to and from lock up.

All eight cab doors opened shortly after the trucks had parked and soon there stood a team of nine DSSMD agents spread in a semi-circle to my front. After briefly introducing myself and attempting to memorise their names, I was handed a tactical earpiece so that all eleven of us could communicate in real time. The eleventh, being Milly back at their base, who would monitor and record each of the arrests as they occurred. In return, I split the team into four groups of two, with one spare, and provided each pair of agents with a small list of individuals to arrest, along with their floor and office location in the building. I had figured the best approach would be an all-out blitz, with every team moving in unison, hitting five targets at a time, to maximise efficiency and minimise the risk of alerting the others before their turn. A plan to which they agreed.

I had decided to operate alone, while agent Brown was tasked with remaining in the garage to guard the vehicles and existing prisoners. The other agent, already tasked with watching the front of the building for my movements, was co-opted into watching for any runners from the list as well.

'We all go at once, coordinated office entries on my countdown, five arrests at a time.' I said. 'When you make the arrest, remove their personal devices and bag them in an RFID bag, grab their desk devices and any other relevant documents or electronic storage you find and bring them down here. Load the prisoners in the van, wait for me, then we go again for the next five. When we're all done with the targets here, three of the vehicles can be taken to the safe house to place the prisoners into whatever we're using as cells. The fourth vehicle will have to accompany me to the police station where we'll have one more arrest to make.'

After loading Sophia and Ironie into the closest prisoner transporter and securing them in cuffs and seats, Johnny, under my instruction, told his cleaners to head for the kitchenette on whatever level they were on and wait there for approval to leave or continue their duties.

'Keep an eye on the cameras, Johnny. If you see anything unusual, let the agent down here know right away.' I directed.

Once all instructions were delivered, the team headed for the lifts to set about their tasks. As a unit, we moved smoothly, with the sharp focus and precision of highly trained agents of the Old Think world, who knew their task of the moment was more important than the perception of how they did it and to whom they paid respect in the process.

We split up, two agents per lift and within three minutes had been effectively deployed on the appropriate floors and staged at the doors outside our first target's offices.

I was nervous that after all this effort, they wouldn't even be here. That we'd burst into the rooms only to find them empty or worse yet, with cameras pointed right at the door, watching, while they laughed at us from some evil lair. Because of this fear, I'd had Johnny check the room occupancy log, an automatic monitoring program that's stated intent was to show if a room had been vacated for the day, so the cleaners knew whether it was free to clean. As with most technology, if it can be used for more than one purpose…well…

Happily, for me, all our targets were registered and present in their offices. Green light.

Each team completed a radio check-in outside their allocated target office. 'Team's Alpha, Bravo, Charlie, and Delta, you are cleared for take down.' I said in a low, firm voice that was smoothly and instantaneously transmitted to every earpiece on the freq.

As one, we launched.

After charging through the door of my target office, it was a relief not only to find Adam Abers sitting behind his desk, but to see the shocked look on his face at the harsh reality of my intrusion. It really made my day. Whether he thought I should be dead or not, didn't really matter. The fact he hadn't expected me to come into his office electro drawn and cuff him where he sat, was telling. Arrogance had clearly overcome diligence and the team at OGT had failed to use the information excesses at their disposal to confirm the success or failure of Sophia and Isabelle's earlier mission.

My transient joy, however, was quickly tempered by the importance of the additional task I need to complete with this arrest. In order to justify my current actions, I needed Adam to approve the release of the very surveillance footage that may ultimately land he and his fellow conspirators in the clink. Without it, these arrests are only being made on suspicion. Not a solid basis for an officer like me to rely on.

'Before we go, Adam, there's something important I need you to approve.' I said, bending down to speak directly into his bright red ear.

'Fuck you!' He shouted back forcefully.

'Wow, New Think never did get around to improving insults, did they?' I shot back.

Abers was handcuffed, on his knees, and leaning forward, his forehead supporting his full body weight against the wall behind his desk. I'd put him in a stress position while I attempted to use his computer to access the email files I needed approved.

With me working alone, I hadn't wanted to give him an opportunity to use the swivel or roller actions of his desk chair to mount some sort of attack and get away. In order to avoid the issue, I moved quickly once inside the door, Electro trained on Abers and shouting for him to put his hands behind his head.

'Stay in your seat and push yourself back from your desk until your chair is hard against the wall!' I shouted. 'Once you hit the wall, raise your feet off the floor!'

In his shock, he acted like a good soldier, displaying instinctive obedience and following my instructions to a T. As he did this, I rounded the desk and moved forward, pausing two paces back from his chair. 'Look straight ahead!' I demanded loudly, whilst firmly planting my left foot behind me for balance, then launching a fierce frontal kick to the broadside of his chair, sending him grunting and sprawling to the floor at the rear right-hand corner of his office.

The chair clattered onto the hard surface after spitting him out, his body weight spinning him slightly as he went, causing his shoulder and head to hit the floor first.

'How do I find emails awaiting your approval?' I asked again, this time from a position hunched over his desk, eyes fixed on the screen projection, while my well stressed captive fought the urge to give in to the pain. His feet were cuffed behind his back, along with his hands. The chain of the handcuffs looped through the leg cuffs so that at best he could tip himself on his side in order to become only mildly more comfortable than he is now. In truth, it would probably help him avoid the rapidly developing headache being caused by a combination of the weight on his head and neck, the overall discomfort of the position, and my screaming at him to tell me where to find my surveillance emails for approval.

To his credit, he told me to fuck off again. Part of me liked that, because it's an answer more akin to a stubborn Old Thinker than a whining weak-willed apologist New Thinker. The other part of me, however, wanted him to give me the damn answer so I could get on with arresting the others.

Standing up from behind the desk, I moved over to Abers and bent a knee into his back, adding nearly impossible strain to his head, neck and shoulders. 'Ahhhh, fuck!!!' He said grimacing loudly, almost mouthing the wall with the effort.

Thankfully, unlike Katie's office, Adam had no external windows through which my actions could be viewed. His office was smaller than Katies, no couch chairs in the corner, no mood panels graced the walls. Just light green concrete paint and charcoal black floors. After cuffing him, I'd taken the precaution of shutting the door to prevent his yelling (*or mine*) from alerting the other targets on our list. That left me free to keep berating him until I got my answers.

'The pain can stop Abers. All you have to do is tell me where to find the damn emails for approval!'

'Okay, okay, okay!' He screamed through gritted teeth. 'They're in my deleted files.'

'Then won't they be, you know, deleted?' I asked, not wanting to seem stupid, but genuinely unsure.

'No! Nothing's ever deleted!!' he replied, still with the strain of my knee in his back.

Three minutes later I had approved both surveillance footage emails and confirmed receipt on my own device, forwarding them immediately onto Milly and Shaz.

Teams Alpha and Charlie had already radioed in to confirm their targets had been arrested and secured downstairs.

'You need a hand, Detective Johnson?' asked one of the Charlie team agents.

'No, I'm fine.' I said. 'Just needed my mark to help me complete a task first. I'm on the move in thirty seconds.'

An hour later, we had arrested all but two of our targets. Each of them was present in their offices and suitably surprised at our intrusion. It almost looked like a roundup at a well-dressed border camp, down in the basement. Seventeen prisoners herded into the back of trucks and shackled to a seat, pleading their innocence whilst being told to shut up by agents who then closed the doors to cut the din.

The agents and I held a quick mid-op debrief, the consensus opinion being that arrogance was the clear driver behind their surprise. How could this possibly happen to them? They're too smart. So much smarter than all the other idiots in the world, clearly seeing themselves as some sort of untouchable Globalist royalty, never likely to be held to account for their actions. As though they thought that even with clear evidence of their involvement in murder, their lie should still be believed, because, you know, New Think.

'Okay Team, we've got two more targets.' I announced. 'Despite the OGT members being here when we started this, the big fish has gotten away for now. I wanted to be there personally for both these arrests however, in the interest of time, we may have to split into two teams to take the final marks. Chief Blindspot was to be the prize arrest of this operation, not only because of her position as my boss, but for the influence she has over the many officers that appear to have ignored the law and bent the knee to her will. Unfortunately, the chief will have to become an equal top prize. The other will be her literal partner in crime. Cheq Fencegap.'

I don't think there's any doubt that Blindspot's working for Cheq. He is one of the Guides after all, which incidentally makes arresting him quite a big deal. There's never been a Guide held accountable for anything before. Accused sure. Had overwhelming evidence presented against them, certainly. Actually, being held to account and forced to pay for their crimes, though. Definitely not…

'We'll have to adjust the plan here.' I continued. 'Alpha and Bravo, you go as a five-person team over to the police station and arrest Chief Blindspot. When you get there, ask for Detective Damwell. I have a feeling he'll be more than happy to lead you to the chief, and if you're lucky, he might even help you tighten the cuffs. Team Charlie and Delta, I'm going to ride with you. We're heading to that pantheon of New Think equality "The Philanthropic Ingestor" which is apparently where OGT's, no, the world's great saviour from viruses, both biological and software, has retired for lunch.'

'Chief Blindspot was certainly involved in whatever plot led to these murders. Members of her staff accompanied her to witness the first, take part in the second, and attempt at least two more. It was, however, under Cheq's direction that the program was being created. Moreover, it was for the protection of this program or an element of it that these murders have been carried out. There's something extraordinary behind this. Be careful, team. Trust no one! With present company excluded, on the basis that Milford personally vouched for you, and excluding my own partner who's nearly been murdered twice since we started this case, I'm yet to meet a single person who hasn't got some nefarious involvement in this plot.'

'Now, we need to roll out of here together and synchronise our arrests of these final two marks. I don't want to lose either one because they've been alerted to the arrest of the other… nod if you're with me!'

I looked around at the group with this statement still hanging in the air, eyeballing each of the agents to confirm their commitment to the task. They returned a steely gaze, almost robotic in its stillness and consistency, accompanied by the requested nod. None seemed fatigued or bothered by my comments, displaying nothing other than vigilant professionalism and a refreshing detachment from the politic of the task, instead, prepared to simply follow the instructions they were given.

'We roll in two minutes.' I added, signalling a wind up with my right finger pointed to the sky and a swirling flick of the wrist. 'I just need a quick word with Johnny before we go.'

Leaving the agents to do what agents do, check their gear, check the trucks, yell at the prisoners, and ready themselves to be ready, I headed into Carlo's office to find Johnny staring blankly at his floating screen.

'You okay here?' I asked.

'Yeah!' said Johnny, with the forced effort of someone startled out of deep reflection, blinking purposefully as he spoke.

'You did good today. You did the right thing.' I said. 'You're not questioning yourself, are you?'

'Yeah, no, I know.' he said. 'I'm not worried about going against New Think. I don't even really feel like I did. I just can't believe that it's come to this and that I still live in a world under complete control. I don't know whose greater good we all serve these days, or how this world is any better than it was thirty years ago… I thought I'd left behind this idea that we are all supposed to work together to strive for the greater good, smiling like we're told to, whilst we have nothing of our own to enjoy or be proud of… We can't strive to be better than we are, or stand up, or stand out, or be different from the "new normal." We can't choose where to live, what to eat, who to talk to, or what we say. We can't even choose what drugs and medical treatments are administered to our own bodies. We live only within the extreme inner limits set for us by those who believe they're smarter and know better than anyone else… And what's it all for? So everyone else can be just as miserable as us? Is that the beautiful, clean, Global dream? Is this the "saved" world we wanted to leave for our children and their children and all the generations that follow?…'

Johnny looked up at me now, a man caught between pain, self-pity and anger. The skin of his cheeks and the bald smooth patch on his head, turning red, his face scrunched as if trying to make sense of the nonsensical.

'When I left my despotic eastern nation for the freedom and opportunity of the west, I hadn't known that the western leaders were envious of the controlling single mindedness of the east. So much so that they copied the blueprint and doubled down. Sometimes I think I should have just stayed. Not that it would have mattered, because pretty soon, there became like here, anyway. The world got worse as it strived to be better, like a man drowning in quicksand. The harder he fights, the faster he drowns. Yet, despite it all, you can't say anything. With all the censorship and restraint on our lives, you can't even tell your friends that you're unhappy, that you feel oppressed, or that you want more freedom, more opportunity, more choice. You're seen as greedy, a bigot, a racist, when all you really want is to be happy and to stand on your own two feet. If you dare question any of the restrictions or rules imposed by the Guides, you're called a "conspiracy theorist", when at worst you're a "conspiracy realist", pointing out the reality of the Global conspiracy playing out all around us. If you dare stand up against them, they no longer call you names, they just kill you off to shut you up, forever… just like they did to Katie and Chen… No Detective, I don't doubt that I did the right thing today. I just doubt that it will do us any good.'

There was nothing I could add, no comfort I could offer. He was right. No matter how much evidence I have, I'm still pushing shit up hill to make it stick to anyone who makes a difference.

'They all count Johnny.' I said, despite myself. 'We might not win this one, but they'll know we're here and we're not beaten yet. The toll against this regime is mounting. Tell your guys they're free to go, but keep them out of the rooms we've cleared until I come back this evening. Take it easy Johnny.'

I left him to his thoughts and headed to the rear truck, where Agent Dent opened the door to let me in. Thirty seconds later, we were on the move as a convoy, Dent filling me in on discussions they'd had in my absence. Milly had spoken with the four teams and confirmed a second safe house to hold and interrogate half of our twenty-two prisoners. Luckily, it was right next door to the first.

We didn't have far to go for our next and last targets. The police station was only four blocks from the OGT building, so teams Alpha and Bravo peeled off to the right at the intersection of Justice Avenue and Branch Streets. Teams Charlie and Delta carried on with me in tow. We only had one block further to go before turning left onto Profit Drive. The Philanthropic Ingestor, or "The Fill" as it's commonly known, is situated about one hundred meters from the corner and takes up a substantial portion of the block. It's the gathering place for all those who have what nobody is supposed to have, who go where nobody is supposed to go, and do what nobody is supposed to do. Those who preach but do not practice the many commandments of New Think. If I was being exceptionally kind, I might suggest they needed all our money, all those possessions and freedoms for themselves, to show us the glutinous lifestyle from which they've saved us. I suppose they'd only keep doing it so as we don't forget. Of course, if I wasn't so kind, I might see Cheq Fencegap as a hypocritical fat prick who's greed and arrogance have killed many thousands of people by experimenting on them without their consent and lying openly about it, all while squeezing money out of us at the point of a needle… or a mouse… Ironic though, he doesn't care to use mice to test the contents of his needles… to be fair mice don't have any money, so they can't pay for the products they receive.

Turning onto the street, the opulence of The Fill is not immediately obvious, due to the building being set back from the street and somewhat hidden by a large squared ten story office block that sits on the corner. Behind that, the only other neighbouring building on the same side of the street is "Expressionless". A female oriented restaurant/club named for its Botox filled clientele. Just because everybody else gave up all that they had to save the world doesn't mean the wives of the rich and famous shouldn't look like porcelain dolls. Their faces semi-permanently set with the serious or startled expression expected of all Global Citizens when out in public.

Returning my focus back to our destination and the man we seek inside its white Greco-Roman walls, I wonder at the purpose of his coming here today. Is this just his daily lunch stop? The empire building elites wanting always to surround themselves with the lavish stylings of former empires gone by, along with their fellow conspirators. Or had he really come here to hide, already knowing he's a marked man.

There were two access points for the monstrously large club. An entry and an exit road from which he might escape. Team Charlie pulled up across the entryway, blocking any vehicles from entering or exiting that way. Team Delta and I did the same on the exit and immediately had two red jacketed valet's heading toward each vehicle to complain.

'We don't need any help parking these. Thanks anyway.' I said, jumping out of the vehicle and flashing my badge. The Valet's stopped in their tracks, instinctively respecting the authority of the badge and uniformed agents while unaccustomed to having their elite establishment raided.

Within ten seconds, the truck doors were shut and vehicles secured. Team Charlie moved up the smooth concrete driveway from the left and headed for the rear of the building. Team Delta and I headed for the front entry, where we pushed past the manager and greeter who'd come to the door in a vain effort to block our path. Electros and pistols did the talking, allowing us to enter unabated. Ironically, had the staff just stayed inside, the security requirements for admission could have made it very difficult for us to enter without shooting our way in. A scenario that might have allowed Cheq to remain safely ensconced until friends in high places came to his rescue.

Inside, The Fill is everything you'd expect in a club for elite old boys. A restaurant with a 3-hat chef, and carpeted flooring… You know the diners aren't checking menu prices, when the establishment's prepared to risk staining thick Egyptian carpets by putting them in the dining room. More dark, thick carpet adorned the bar and lounge area where beautiful brown leather club chairs abound. Linen covered drinks tables sit patiently awaiting the touch of crystal tumblers, while dim low hanging lights hover above each set. There are no easy clean surfaces and nothing purely functional in here. It's all about comfort, luxury, and, of course, sound absorbing materials.

Even within the sanctity of these four walls (*or however many there really are*), and with the impossibility of anyone from "out there" working their way up to join the club in here, information and gossip remain a keenly guarded commodity. In fact, more so now than ever. Broadly speaking, the term "information security" is nothing more than a catchphrase thrown about by the Guides and their mouthpiece media to scare people into paying for a concept that doesn't really exist. I mean, even if your internet security program protects you from some external hacker group, your information isn't safe. It's just more valuable. If they can't get it for free from you directly, then they have to pay for it from the security provider or directly from the Global Alliance themselves. In here, information security and secrecy are the key to power and control. Knowledge is leverage and leverage is power, so discussions are held in hushed tones, with trusted company and never written down for posterity or evidence.

As a trio, Delta team moved through the front of the club, which comprised a luxurious foyer, concierge desk, and cloak room with some short, wide, thickly carpeted corridors leading off to either side. The names on the doors were "DarkStone" and "CombiKnight", both the names of money management groups of the Uber wealthy, who under the guise of investment, created global monopolies allowing their investors to circumvent laws designed to defend against such an anti-competitive market control from ever taking place.

Unfortunately, they didn't just have a monopoly on some industries, they have a monopoly on all of them, and their governing bodies. No doubt these names emblazon the doors of overpriced conference rooms used for the clandestine meetings of those who control the actions and options for every aspect of our lives.

Whilst I covered the foyer, my team mates check the rooms, finding neither was presently occupied, nor set for an impending gathering, so they resealed the deadly chambers and we moved along.

Continuing through the building, we passed the sumptuous restaurant and classy front bar, then along a softly lit corridor where wall sconces alone played the part of flaming torches or candles of old. There was a strong smell of cigar smoke in the air, distinguished by its powerful acrid smell. It was hard to say how much smoke there was, or from what distance it travelled to activate our olfactory senses, but it sent me spinning back to my youth when smoking was the norm.

Before us at the end of the hall stood a set of mahogany wood panelled doors guarding entry to the club lounge. That most revered of spaces in civilised society, where the aristocratic and downtrodden alike would go to quietly reflect, or drink away the troubles of the day. There would, of course, be no downtrodden here. Weary perhaps, or ailing in health, but certainly not short the means for survival.

As a unit, the three of us came to a stop outside these doors. The pause not for dramatic effect on entrance, instead because our earpieces had come to life with the voice of Jerry from Charlie team. There'd been very few people in the restaurant or anywhere else in the club, and I wondered whether Cheq had been alerted to our presence and snuck out the back, somehow. Thankfully, Jerry's words gave relative certainty that this had not occurred.

'All clear down in the basement. Cheq's E is still here, so he can't be far away.' he reported. 'That chalky boned fuck couldn't possibly walk far, his legs would crumble.'

'Well, I'm pretty confident he's not in the club's gym or sauna either.' said Dent, one of the Delta team agents standing with me. 'Maybe the massage rooms.' he added, chuckling.

'I dunno D, does marshmallow need massage?' said Harman, the second member of Delta.

As much as I enjoyed the banter at the expense of the overly privileged Cheq, I couldn't bring myself to laugh or smile until we had him in our grasp. 'Okay team, we've got plenty of time for Cheq jokes later on. Let's bring him in first. Charlie, you sit tight down there.'

We eased through the double doors, which swung smoothly and soundlessly inwards. Inside, the lounge was only sparsely patronised, with just a few elite individuals doing what others can't. Sitting in the absurdly soft leather club chairs, smoking a big fat cigar. Smoking, of course, is outright banned now for reasons you could squeeze into just about every category for ideological change. It's hard to believe that even these people could justify continuing the habit behind closed doors, as anything other than overt hypocrisy and classism. No matter. There's no one to justify it to, anyway.

Scanning the room through the heavy haze of smoke, we see a group of three chairs all sat together at the rear corner of the space. Each was occupied by a stuffy old man sat in the manner of self-assured relaxation that only the wealthy can conjure. One of them was contributing to the haze with his own thick stogie, while the other two sat with a snifter of some deep golden coloured whiskey or scotch. If this was thirty years ago, it would be something top shelf and unattainable for the masses. However, with alcohol production having been banned, it need not be high quality to be unattainable these days, and it's anyone's guess as to how and where they get it. Perhaps from some great store of confiscated liquor saved from the incinerator and reserved only for them.

In the middle of the three sat Cheq. Slouching back in his club chair, his left knee resting on top of the right, in that seated pose of wealthy older men from the Old Think days that exudes arrogance and self-importance. He looked calm and relaxed, dressed in ivory slacks with expensive looking brown leather shoes. Ferragamo's most likely, or something similar. I probably haven't even heard of the brand, as fashion was never my thing. A plain, yet high-quality sweater covered what looked like a casual collared shirt, worn with no tie. The cap for this obnoxious human suit was the smile… no, smirk… and those dull eyes. Eyes that don't seem to see the true form of what's in front of them, noting only what it's worth and whether it can give back more than it takes, or serves the purpose of enforcing control.

Between the three of us and our target group, was no more than thirty meters of plush red carpet. Small groupings of club chairs sat comfortably spaced in threes and fours off to the left and right of the luxuriously wide aisle. Five other patrons spaced randomly around the room huffed cigar smoke casually, while a red-coated waiter stood discreetly off to the side, holding a tray with a clean crystal ashtray and a knurl patterned whiskey decanter. None paid us any mind.

For his part, Cheq seemed intently focussed on his whiskey, oblivious to those around him. Neither glancing up towards us, nor engaging with his friends. Despite that tunnel vision, he must have seen us coming. Three armed agents stalking towards him through the lounge of his private club was not something he could fail to notice. In spite of which, it didn't seem to bother him. It appeared rather like he'd expected we were coming and didn't care to try and avoid us.

'Cheq Fencegap, my name is…' I started, addressing our target directly before being cut off by the man himself.

'Detective Gary Johnson and you're here to arrest me.' finished Cheq.

'Yes.' I said, a little pissed at having my moment stolen. 'And how did you know that? Somebody tip you off?'

'I'm the head of OGT, Global's largest surveillance and software technology manufacturer. I don't need somebody to tip me off. I have so much technology to do that for me. Plus, you just walked through the most exclusive club on the Globe with two armed DSSMD agents. If you're not here to arrest me, then you could only be here to protect me. I am a Guide, after all.' When he finished his little speech, Cheq stood, thrusting his hands out in front of him.

Turning him around, I pulled his arms behind his back and cuffed him.

'I don't suppose you need me to read you your rights?' I asked.

'We haven't the time for that…' he replied arrogantly, without cracking his standing smirk. 'I've got a few more than most.'

I couldn't deny the moment of self-aware humour was a good one. Even if it didn't quite cut through the overly conceited persona. Still, credit where it's due. At least he knows what he is.

I glanced down at his companions, sat quietly in their seats. Neither looked at all concerned or surprised about his arrest. The man to our left continued smoking his seemingly endless cigar, intermittently holding it to his mouth with his right hand, or hanging his arm out over the edge of his seat. His mid forearm was supported by the soft leather arm of the chair, while sheets of cigar ash drifted slowly to the floor like volcano ash after an eruption. In his left hand, was his snifter of what I now saw was a single malt scotch "The Macallan" aged 25 years, or at least that's what the bottle on the side table said. Given that alcohol for drinking purposes has been banned for 20 years in the Global World, it's more than likely that this bottle is aged 45 to 50 years by now, and all the more mature for its age.

He too was dressed in expensive looking threads, a charcoal-coloured wool suit, expensive black shoes, and a blue tie with a thin gold hexagonal pattern on it. He also wore a Vacheron Constantin perpetual calendar watch, which if all the other signs hadn't already tallied, was undoubted proof that he was an old boy, of Old Think style, in an old boys club. The very antithesis of New Think. Funny how those with the most drive and influence in implementing and enforcing these Global ideals are the least aligned with them at the personal level. Far too restrictive on their sumptuous lifestyles, no doubt.

To the right of Cheq sat a man who I'd seen before but couldn't say I knew. He's one of those nobodies who's an influential somebody to those of wealth and power. His background was highly questionable. His parents, members of a group who believed in unbending ideals, under which they conducted a terrible assault on the world that until the introduction of New Think, humanity had tried hard to forget.

He was also the face of New Think's fundamental ideologies, and head of the Global Currency Confluence Coordination Consortium. The group of uber wealthy titans of industry who, along with a team of highly motivated strategists, influential members of popular culture, and media moguls, created the Global ideals we all must follow. After convincing his followers of the cause, they penetrated western societies with their enviro-socialist reforms, then indoctrinated the world to their ways.

This is a man who learned from the mistakes of his parents, not so that he could make up for them and avoid them in the future, rather, he learned how to control the minds of the masses and successfully implement the tenets of a single form global race in the image he desires.

Like his other seated friend, he offered nary a glance at me or the other two agents. It all seemed just par for the course to them. An understandable and expected action which must be allowed to run its course. The head of the GCCCC wore an expensive black Brioni wool suit and shiny black Berluti shoes, which I knew from the subtle labelling at cuff and sole. He too was clutching his glass of scotch as it rested on the side table next to him, while he looked at nothing in particular at all.

'You two have a fine day now.' I said, looking for a response that confirmed they were actually human. I didn't get one.

As we marched the smirking Cheq from the lounge, I looked back at the pair still seated there, never once turning to watch us or protest the arrest of their comrade. They just sat, smoking and drinking, comfortable in their world.

Chapter 29

Shaz hacks back

'Iman Ottahaker, at your service.' said a surprisingly old computer whiz.

He must have been in his mid to late fifties, at least. His appearance, like a wild-haired, bush cabin, doomsday prepper with glasses, left me half expecting there'd been an error in communication and for him to come in with an axe or a small tomahawk, ready to do an inefficient job of chopping down some trees, or possibly the legs of the apartment furniture. Gary didn't spend much time here, so it mightn't matter much if he did.

'Did you change your name to match your career?' I asked.

'What? No, mum named me. Why?' Iman replied, apparently oblivious to the irony. I could only assume that others thought it so obvious they'd never bothered to ask.

'Never mind, come in.' I said, having already used the police app on my device to scan him and match his chip and biometrics to his profile.

Finding someone to help Gaz and I infiltrate OGT wasn't easy, and Iman certainly wasn't what I had expected. But, as the well-worn saying goes, "they say he's the best". Well, not "they" they. I'd spoken to some old friends of mine from the library days (*who call themselves the Librarators by the way... I know, I know, it's terrible*) and told them straight out I was seeking a hacker to help us dig into OGT's systems and software programming. Like me, they still live in this new world, but have not, and will never forgive New Thinkers for what they did to books, libraries, or the open pursuit of knowledge and the free and fair access to it all. A few of the truly brave and dedicated have been waging a silent war against Global's barriers to literature, and that means finding ways to hack the system and recover as much of the deleted material as possible for the consumption of a secret society of readers. All this under the nose of the most intrusive surveillance-based regime in history.

'So, Iman, what do you need in order to get set up?' I asked.

'Nothing from you.' he replied. 'I just need to know what we're looking for and for you to point me in the right direction to find it. Oh, and maybe an outlet to plug my device into. This puppy sucks a bit of juice.'

'Right.' I said. 'Well, that shouldn't be a problem. Gary's almost never here, anyway.'

He set up his portable device, at the small study desk on the right-hand side of Gary's lounge room, removing the red and grey flanno from over his black t-shirt and hanging it over the back of the chair as he did.

His version, I suppose, of getting serious, or perhaps just getting comfortable and settling in.

I wasted no time, starting him working on tracking and mapping the movements of a curated list of police officers over the last 48 hours, as Gary had requested.

This was a breeze for Iman, who, with my access to the police database, made light work of the task. As he was about finish, Gary called, and amongst some disturbing and angering news, requested that he himself be added to the list of officer movements reviewed. Aside from a shocking number officers either involved in the plot or abandoning their duties altogether, the most concerning thing was the huge gaps in Gary's own tracking. Basically, when he wasn't with me or performing police duties, it's as if he wasn't being tracked at all.

The next step for Iman was the hard one. Gary had stopped back by OGT after arresting Cheq in order to pay a quick visit to Watcher. Watcher provided its identifier number and passcode, allowing us remote access to the OGT system, using it as an entry point. That meant getting in was going to be easy enough. Doing so undetected, on the other hand, and extracting the truly valuable and no doubt well-guarded information inside, was going to be a whole lot harder.

By Gary's account, it was going to be worth it, with plenty of bounty to find. Watcher supposedly has the surveillance footage of Katie's murder that we're still yet to see, as well as direct access to the program Katie had been working on. What we really need is for Iman to tell us what the hell the program does, and how.

After filling him in on the plan, he hooked up to the Global Network via an IP jumper program he had apparently written himself, which he assured me would never be tracked back to him or this apartment. It piggy backs off other people's IP addresses all around the globe, changing IP every thirty seconds, and all that, apparently, without affecting his ability to explore and work uninterrupted.

'That might stop them finding you.' I said, 'But can't they still work out that you've hacked their system and block your entry point?'

'Not the way I do it.' said Iman. 'They'll never even know I was there.'

'Well, how is that possible?' I asked, struggling to reconcile the concept of a shadowy, slick, master hacker with the flanno and t-shirt, fluffy headed man before me. 'With all the technology advancements that exist, and the level of invasiveness they maintain in our lives, just how the hell is that possible? I mean, they've mapped my whole body, they own my DNA sequence, track my every movement, implanted me with a chip that not only monitors and records my geo-location and time in and out of places but also my heart rate, blood count, BMI, and has the capacity to introduce small radio wave controlled behaviour modification pulses if I exceed their Global Impact Score limitations. Yet, here you are, saying that whilst our Global overlords can hack me, they can't stop you hacking them?'

'That's right!' said Iman, without a modicum of doubt. 'Kind of nice to know, isn't it?'

'Actually, it is.' I said, feeling a strong smile developing on my face. It was indeed nice to know that there remains a subversive sub-culture eroding away the footing of the powers that be. 'How do you do it?'

The widening eyes and smiling face of the expert engaged shone back at me. My mistake was genuine intrigue, my punishment would be knowledge I'd never want, nor understand.

'Well, I'll start by using Watcher as the entry point to the system and check out what kind of firewall and how many layers of security they have. See, I won't need to conduct a brute force attack because of Watcher, but in all likelihood, they'll have Trojan hack back bots that detect unusual activity on the system and imbed counter-surveillance trojans into data that's being stripped or downloaded.' started Iman, whose own mistake was to look up from his device and see my eyes glazing over. He rightly deduced that I might not be quite as absorbed in the detail as he was and mercifully adjusted course. 'Put it this way, did you ever see Seinfeld?' He asked.

'Yeah, I've seen em.' I said.

'Well, I've got the equivalent of a radar detector, detector, detector, detector.'

'Works for me!' I replied, relieved to have escaped the tech talk and eager to disengage.

Leaving Iman to his work, I set about following up on the other missing piece in all of this. Sergeant Ease. As far as I know, that poor fool's been left to rot in hospital. Who knows whether anyone's bothering to check up on him to ensure he's still alive.

It's true, he'd nearly got me killed, although I doubt that's his fault. He's also happens to be just as single-minded and dedicated to the cause of causes as any of his brethren. Still, despite all his flaws, he is a good person, and he deserves our help as much as anyone else.

The reality is, I hadn't picked Blindspot or Ironie as being in on this plot and certainly not Detective Thise. There's one thing I'm certain of, though. There's no way known they could have trusted Sgt Ease to be a part of this without him giving it away. Even if he is a true die-hard New Thinker, Sgt Ease believes that the goodness of the cause is enough on its own without the need for subversive programming, trickery, manipulation and certainly without murder.

I dialled the hospital and asked the electronic receptionist if Ease was still there and how he was doing.

'Sure, he's still here.' said the receptionist in its synthesised and soothing female voice. 'Actually, I'm surprised he hasn't had a visitor today. Up until this morning, there was someone with him or outside his door 24/7. There's been no one here since the last one left at 6am.'

It was terrifying to me that an AI enhanced computer system could use surveillance, both security and medical, to pick up these details and so accurately insert them in an ad hoc conversation. 'Oh.' I managed in response. 'Well, I'll see if I can get someone over there. How's he doing, by the way?'

'He's starting to show signs of coming round.' the voice replied. 'His vitals are stable. It's really up to him now.'

'Okay, thanks.' I said. 'We'll get someone there soon.'

I already had someone in mind for this task, so as soon as I hung up from the hospital I put a call into a good Ease minding candidate. Someone of relatively similar disposition. A believer like Adam, albeit with a little more power and gusto. Mostly importantly, one of the few who we could say with relative certainty had no suspicious activity noted from their surveillance history.

'Damwell, what are you up to at the moment?' I asked.

'Not much. Half the station seems to have gone missing, including my partner. No one's assigning cases, so if there are any, I ain't working on em, and the only person left on my bloody task force, is me. You or your illustrious partner wouldn't know anything about that, would you?'

'Yeah, I've got a hunch.' I replied. 'Listen, Gaz and I have some seriously mounting evidence against about half of OGT and an indeterminate, yet growing, number of police officers. So far, you haven't appeared directly on our list of suspects, but your partner certainly has.'

'Empher?' asked Brian, in the gentlest voice I'd ever heard him use.

'Yeah, well, don't feel too bad. We didn't have her on our list either… until she went to shoot Gaz during their chat at OGT.'

'What?! No way!' Said Damwell, returning to his usual arrogance at lightning speed. He stopped right there though, his regular hubris falling short and leaving him unable to mount a further defence of Thise or provide an explanation as to the impossibility of the accusation.

'Why did you two leave OGT to print a copy of a list that could easily be printed within that building?' I asked.

'We didn't walk back to the station just to print a sheet of paper!' he snapped. 'We were done at OGT. The only reason we hung around was because Gary demanded he meet with us there, individually. He also wanted a printout of names from the surveillance in Katie's room. Empher suggested we go back to the station to complete our case notes and log the evidence. I figured Gaz could talk to Matthias first and we could print off the list at the station while he did. I assumed he would call when he needed to see Empher anyway and she could take it with her when she went.'

'What happened while you were at the office?' I asked.

'Nothing!' said Damwell defensively. 'About five minutes after we got back, Empher stood up from her desk. Said that Gaz had messaged her, and she had to go. She printed off the list and then went back to OGT to meet him.'

'Why didn't you go back with her?' I asked.

'She told me not too.' replied Brian. 'Said I should keep digging and work out the next step in the case. She'd let me know if I needed to come back over.'

'Okay. Digging into what?' I pressed, keen to flesh out any major concerns his surveillance tracking had not.

'Well, the list to begin with. There were twenty-one names on that thing.'

'And do you know how many were on the list she gave to Gaz?'

'Twenty one, I'd assume. Given that's how many I just told you were on it!' said Brian, his overbearing personality creeping in once more.

'There were only eighteen names on that list by the time Empher handed it to Gary. She'd removed Captain Ironie and Chief Blindspot's names from it, trying to cover for them, which appears to be her key role in all of this. She also removed her own name…'

Damwell was quiet on the line. I could almost hear his mind ticking like a hot engine rapidly cooling in the garage. A realisation that he was in the dark and had been betrayed by his closest ally.

'Why did Ironie make you the head of the task force on this case?' I asked, trying to spur him towards the desired conclusion.

Despite my efforts, it was a further fifteen seconds before he eventually responded, doing so in the fashion of someone who's been made a fool of, having had the wool pulled over their eyes but whose vision is finally clearing. 'Well, I suppose the old adage is true. You keep your friends close, and your enemies closer.' He said with a sigh.

'Are you and Captain Ironie enemies?'

'I'm not sure. We're both New Thinker's, but we're not exactly friends.' said Damwell. 'No matter how much certain elements of the Global world try to water down biological certainties, I am still a man with all the original requisite parts to prove it, and frankly that doesn't sit too well with the captain.'

'That's too much information, Brian.'

'Oh great, another offence I'll have to do penance for.' he mumbled morosely.

'No need.' I countered. 'I'm not offended by the facts of life. I'm Old Think, remember. I just don't need the proof. I'll accept you at face value. Even so, I do get your point. Ironie really only believes and supports the things we are "supposed" to believe and support, and biological males are on the outs. So why the big show of support for you on this task force?'

'Like I said, to keep your enemies close, I guess.' he replied again. 'She brought me in without telling me what I was being brought into, pointed me towards the enemy outside the gate to make sure that's where I'd be looking and sent me on my way. The enemy of my enemy is my friend…'

'You sure you're not one of us?' I asked.

'Ha, yeah! But, some of the compulsory collective opinions are wearing a little thin on me. I've got the icicle tattoo. The stalactite that represents the fight to hang on to an earth cool enough that we might still survive and return to a simple cave person style of living where we reduce our impact on nature. Unfortunately, that ideal doesn't exactly gel with the high tech, endless surveillance world we live in. I'm one of them. It's just that this isn't the world I was trying to save.'

'So, I take it you also don't support murdering people to protect it, then?' I probed.

'I'm not a psychopath, Sharon. I went with the crowd to begin with because it was easier than trying to swim against the current. Plus, there was such a compelling case that I was the progeny and ongoing embodiment of a long line of evil. The slavery, the treatment of indigenous peoples, of different sexualities, crass consumerism and greedy environment destroying energy use. The only way to fight against it was to join the cause and do what the experts told us.'

'Well, whilst parts of those things might be true, Brian, they're a long way from being the whole truth.'

'Yeah, well, after all my penance and good doing, what I've realised is, I'm just a guy with a fairly pointless tattoo on his arm and a very restricted lifestyle. I've also realised what I'd already known before without being able to pin it down. That most of these issues had nothing to do with me. Not specifically. I got blamed, simply because I exist. Not that I could complain, of course. Others have had it worse for much longer. So, I had to be quiet, accept my guilt, and do my penance. Everybody else was doing it, because it was the "right thing" to do. Nobody wanted to stand out and be the one who wouldn't accept what "we all must accept." To say this wasn't right was tantamount to saying that everything that happened before, was. The message was so clear and consistent. Every news program, every paper, every magazine, social media, it all said the same thing. We're all guilty… The thing is, I don't think it really used to be like that. There were other things before, different opinions, different reasons. The actions taken weren't part of an evil plan, it was just the rudimentary phase of evolution where dominant strength beat considered thought. Need trumped equality. Survival, security, and longevity ruled over pure intellect. Now, measured by today's standards, no manner of historical limitations can qualify the actions. Not to the Globalists, anyway. We the people were always just pawns in someone else's game, and nothing has changed, no matter our efforts. Not the weather, not our health, and not the nature of humans. We've just lost the scope to understand our plight. So, to answer your question Shaz, no, I do not support murder. Not to protect an ideal that treats human beings like batteries. Just little stores of energy, necessary only to power the machine.'

I paused for a moment, feeling pity more than sympathy. I could see a man on his knees in the face of a foe he couldn't understand. Yet sadly, one he believed he could not survive without or see a way to overcome. 'I wonder if there's something you could do, Brian?' I asked. 'For you and for us. Something good, with a clear outcome and a sense of satisfaction at the end.'

'What's that?' he asked.

'Go to the hospital and look after Ease. No one's been with him all day. There's a good chance he'll wake up, and when he does, I'm betting he'd like to see a face he can trust. If he's okay to talk, I think he's going to have something important to tell us, too.'

'And what if he doesn't?' Asked Brian. 'What if he's stuck in some unconscious limbo forever?'

'Well, at least he'll have a friend to watch over him for a while.'

'Yeah… Yeah of course I'll go.' said Brian. 'Beats the hell out of sitting here, feeling miserable.'

As I was about to hang up, Brian spoke again. 'Wait, Shaz?'

'Yeah?'

'Thanks for listening. Thanks for believing me.' he said.

'No problems.' I replied. 'Keep your phone close and stay in touch.'

I felt the weight of Damwell's doubts and confusion. Almost like I had when the Globalists first took over. It's the feeling of disbelief, abandonment and anger all rolled into one. It's knowing that your opinion has value and that you should be entitled to it, but that nobody wants to hear it because it's not the one you're supposed to have. I sat silently for several minutes waiting for the feeling to pass, having long ago come to understand it and build up a resilience. It never really goes away. You just learn to live with it and hide the anger.

Once I had it under control again, I turned my attention back to Iman and the task at hand. 'How's the hack going?' I asked. 'No Trojan attacks yet?'

'Nope, it's all going rather smoothly.' said Iman, looking comfortable and focused at his console. He had the air of someone who is "in the zone," so to speak.

'I've connected with Watcher, reviewed its setup and meshed with the OGT security system. It seems that this Katie character had already set up Watcher as a safe portal into OGT. I've extracted Watchers recordings over the last week and I'm about to access what I assume is the main target here. It's a program code named "Pulchra Mendacium." Sounds Latin, which I don't speak, and I haven't looked it up yet.'

'You won't have to.' I replied.

'Why? What does it mean?' Asked Iman.

'The Beautiful Lie…'

Chapter 30

Gary, all alone with his friends

A less educated fool is far better able to handle the pressures of a world with less to do, less to understand, less to see and with far less thinking required to survive it. The highly educated struggle with a paucity of stimuli. Perhaps that's why those who rode the very tip of higher education and industrial success were the very same that set about dismantling democratic process and installing themselves as controllers of the world. They were bored.

Meanwhile, the rest of the world struggles to survive and wrestles with the basic questions life poses (*No. Not what is the meaning of life. Douglas Adams already answered that...*) like, "How the fuck will I get enough money to pay for my mortgage, the kids school and braces, put bread on the table and have a schooner (*of cola, of course)* down the local with Barry (*or perhaps Barryanna to modernise the question*)?"

The wealthy and highly educated elites, meanwhile, can only host so many garden parties and "events" for the benefit of this, and that, cause, before the virtues of token benevolence wear off. They seek to be part of something bigger, greater, more profound, and, most importantly, more memorable. They want to effect real change in the world. They want to "fix" the broken system, in the most literal way. Which is to say, they'll set it on a course from which it cannot be changed.

The orchestrators of New Think's conceptual plan determined that an imperfect world for all is better than a perfect world for some. They did, of course, assume that they fit neither the "all" or "some" categories, believing they stand apart from the rest, to set the course and guide us. Not to be beholden to the rules themselves. They're extraordinary, therefore they are not to be lumped in with the ordinary. Besides, only by their distance and differentiation could they keep a wholly objective view of how the rest should live. But, oh how the double standards sit an uneasy burden on the shoulders of the masses. We the people, the adult members of a population who daily slaved for the wealth of these elites, could see through their virtuous preaching for what it was, no more than a thin veil to cover their true intentions.

So, they simply bought up all they needed, including companies, industries, media and, most importantly, trusted scientists and doctors, then set about establishing fear amongst humanity. They targeted kids first, teaching them fear in schools. Fear of history, fear of their parents, fear of themselves, and most importantly, fear of the end of the world. Question everything, they said. Except us, you can trust us. Use what we teach you and the urgency of your fear to warn others, to demand change because we're headed off a cliff, and those doing the driving don't know how to brake. They're destroying the world, your world, and humanity with it. Coal, oil, gas, all of earths naturally stored energy sources should not be seen as the foundations that powered the explorations, drive for knowledge, and intellectual connections upon which we built the modern world, but the drug of our addiction that leads to our destruction.

A hard pill for the masses to swallow was during the complete demonisation of fossil fuels by early New Think extremists. In an effort to change the view of many who had long lived with petrol vehicles as relied upon and beloved members of their families, New Think tried to re-characterise Herbie the Love Bug as "Herbie, the Global Warming, Nature Destroying, Bastard."

They repainted it with a skull and crossbones on the bonnet and rivulets of blood running from the roof. Much to their dismay, the emo's quite liked the style, while some of the swinging New Thinkers thought driving one was a sort of ironic protest of the gluttony and ignorance of man. Sure, as protests go, it was convenient and comfortable, if not terribly overt or clear in its message delivery. But you know, you set that ironic "Oh look, I'm an earth hater driving a petrol car," look on your face, and watch them nod ironic agreement as you go by…

There were far too many pleasers back then. Populists and egotists taking the place of leaders without ever living up to the name. Leaders, make tough decisions to lead their people. Pleasers, make decisions that are popular in the moment, all in an effort to buy support for their leadership. Now, under the Global Guides, popularity trumps certainty or accuracy every time. People don't ask themselves, "Do I trust them?" They ask, "How many others trust them?"… Dissenting voices, no matter their qualification were a nuisance for both the pleasers and the globalists, seeking to fix the world in their desired image. So, dissenting voices were duly chased from the public eye, becoming ever more condemned for their very existence. In return, those voices became more aggressive and desperate for balanced opinion to be heard.

These attacks on free expression can be weathered only so long, before decency erodes, leaving exposed the unfettered desire to strike back at your oppressors. Standing up for what you believe, and fighting to achieve those outcomes, is honourable and necessary for balance and good to be maintained. Being consumed by that fight, and losing yourself within it, leaving you only the enemy of your enemy, may be equally as bad as doing nothing at all.

I was sitting in an Authorised Late Opener or ALO, as it is commonly known (*not a bar, but as close as you'll get in this world*) and thinking these thoughts. I'm not really sure why. Perhaps it's this case and the fear of what OGT's program is planned to achieve. Or perhaps it's just the morose, unrelenting misery of living in an oppressive world from which I cannot escape. I can't help wondering how things might've been different if only we'd fought back harder, earlier, rather than meekly letting our world and our right to live freely within in it be taken away.

Every week or two I wake from a nightmare filled with vivid memories and reminders, of which the cruellest part is surely, that to begin with, the world goes back to how it was. A land of opportunity. Imperfect, and in need of some work, and yet a place where everyone could choose their own path. Those paths might've started and ended in different places to others who shared the world. After all, equality of opportunity does not guarantee equality of outcome. Still, a crucial freedom that doesn't exist today. The ceiling was as high as you were willing to make it, the floor a little way below. Today the floor is right up under your feet, the ceiling heavy on your head, crushing you down to the acceptable height.

Anyways, I'm here to meet Milly in the flesh and get the lowdown on DSSMD's progress on the case and discuss what we'll need for an actual conviction. Susan Sly, the District Police Prosecutor, or DPP, will meet us here too. She's the expert on the latter point, though this'll be the first time she's actually looking to put away New Thinkers, who up until now were largely thought of as perfection in progress, incapable of committing violent crimes. I want her there for the interrogations, to oversee and ensure that we press the right buttons to squeeze out all the juice we need.

All our soon to be interviewees are currently stewing in their own skin, under lock, key, and guard, at the DSSMD safe houses. The key targets having been separated from the others to reduce any level of intimidation or coercion they may apply.

The safe houses themselves are made up of three Victorian style adjoining terraces situated at the end of a cul-de-sac facing back up the street, not four blocks from here on Eastmore Place. Whilst the three terraces are all adjoined and inter-accessible, they remain detached from the adjacent buildings, providing a good separation of sound and access. Inside, each has been modernised to the mundane minimalistic standards of New Think, replete with white painted walls, repressive lighting and strong physical security measures. There is, of course, not an air conditioner in sight, although each room has a raging hot radiator pipe running through it to heat the space.

At my request, Cheq was placed in the very smallest room we could find. Not because it would make him tell us what we need to hear, rather, to give him a taste of how he thinks we all should live. I asked Milly for approval to inject him with things I deemed in the interests of the greater good, whether he wanted them or not, but he said no, and

Sharon told me not to stoop to his level. Oh well, perhaps some tools to assist the interrogation instead.

A cool breeze tightens the skin of my face and I glance across the room to the front where none other than Detective Damwell was striding through the doorway. He wasn't invited to this meeting so his presence is out of place, though we are close to the hospital here and Shaz had filled me in on his agreeing to stay with Ease.

It's frigid cold outside tonight and despite being suitably dressed in a ribbed black Gore-Tex jacket in place of his usual suit, Damwell's fluorescent red cheeks outshone even the fiery red of his hair.

I'd set myself up in the left rear corner of the room, close to a speaker to distort any recording or listening devices. Between the door and I, sat four rows of old round wooden oak tables. To my left was a polished chestnut bar, serving only non-alcoholic drinks, and in the corner along the wall stood a small group of people playing E-darts and pool. 'Cows eye!' shouted one (*because equality knows no bounds*) as Damwell strutted by. Behind the bar were automated drinks machines filled with various sodas made with sustainably sourced ingredients, or so we're told, packets of lightly salted crickets, and frozen Almond Ice tubs in place of good fashioned old ice cream.

What the place lacked in spades, was a profundity of atmosphere, warmth or personality that might entice one to return time and again. An outcome of intention met, no doubt…

Damwell had made a beeline for the bar and ordered a coffee, which appeared nearly instantly as they always do these days, being machine made, and served by robot. I'd hoped he hadn't seen me when he entered, my wishes quickly dashed, when after picking up his coffee, he continued striding straight for me.

'What are you doing here Johnson, come to check up on me?' Asked Damwell, unzipping his jacket and sitting heavily in the seat across from mine.

'Do I need to?' I replied. I hadn't intended to say that. It certainly wasn't why I was here. There's just always high tension with us, and he set em up, so I knocked em down.

'I dunno. You've arrested half the station. Why not me, too?' said Brian, who was clearly intent on having it out here.

'You're not a suspect in this Brian, we've confirmed that. As far as I'm concerned, you've been used and lied to, just like me, just like Sharon, and just like Ease was.'

'Yeah well, just because we're in the same boat, doesn't make me feel any better about it.' he replied. 'Certainly doesn't make us friends, either.' Damwell's face was tense and verging on angry, as he said this. Like me, he didn't know who to trust and never wanted to be anyone's fool. 'So if you're not here for me, why are you here? What are you really up to?' He asked.

'I'm here to talk strategy for the next steps.' I said, shuffling to a more upright seating position.

'With who?!' said Damwell, looking wildly around the room, clearly on the edge of losing it. He was searching for someone or something that would satisfy his curiosity or make sense of my presence and tether him back to reality. For him, without something solid to hang onto, I was just another liar, like the rest.

'I'm meeting with an old friend from the DSSMD whose team is assisting with the investigation from a Global standpoint. Susan Sly will be here too. She, of course, will be prosecuting the case.'

'What about your partner? Where's she? Or did you arrest her as well?' he asked sarcastically.

'Shaz is working the case from another angle right now. Making quite a bit of progress, actually. That's how we know you're not involved in this…'

'So, what, you've been investigating me and I'm clear! Am I supposed to be happy about that, too?'

'Brian, we're investigating everybody with a connection to this case, including ourselves. Don't forget, Captain Ironie, who we know for damn sure is involved in the violence that's been carried out, put you and your partner, who is also involved by the way, in charge of a task force to look into these crimes. Now, when was that… oh that's right, yesterday! You might like to know that since then, both Ironie and Thise have tried to shoot me, so you'll have to excuse our intrusion on your privacy. Besides, I didn't think you'd mind, being a hard-core New Thinker and all. I thought you lot were all for all out surveillance and intrusion, all the time, in the name of "The Greater Good"…'

Damwell didn't react straight away. Instead, he sat there seething. Not looking at me, not looking away either. I guessed he was feeling what I'd felt every day of my life since I became consciously aware of the Global machine. Your blood boils at the thought of truth by decree, having to accept that all you know to be true in the world is no longer correct. Even if you know that it is. You can no longer take in raw information and formulate your own opinion. You have to go with the approved group opinion. You can't even go home and have some privacy to yourself to do the things that make you happy. You can only do the approved things, and they'd better not make you happy, what with the guilt and all, for the things that you didn't do, but that someone did, and you're you, not them, so you get the guilt. And if you do do anything, even if you don't enjoy it, like you shouldn't, it's gonna cost some more of your freedom. You owe the world and we all must pay.

It was a damn good thing I'd arrived early, and that my guests were running late, because after a few minutes, he was ready to go. And I don't mean leave.

'You know, you're such an arrogant prick, Gary! It's not just that you're Old Think, it's like you really believe there were no crimes of the past, and that people just got what they deserved.'

'That's bullshit!' I said. 'I just believe that guilt doesn't have to be shared or carried on forever. You can't be born guilty, and you can't change the past. Believe it or not, I think that all people have a place in this world. I just don't believe they all have to be the same or live under the complete control of a totalitarian regime like the Global Guides. I signed up and served thirty years in the Army, because I wanted to protect and serve all the people of my country, whether they liked each other or not.'

'I don't believe that for a minute!' Damwell shot back. 'You don't care about people that were native to a place, about what happened to them, about making that right. Fuck em, ay? Someone came along with bigger guns. They lost. They'll just have to deal with it. We don't need to do anything to make that right… As long as it isn't you, that's affected.'

'Fuck you, Damwell! I've never said terrible things didn't happen to people in the past. I've never said that people shouldn't be equal, either. But you can't undo the past by saying sorry to future generations and offering them advantages above and beyond everyone else in the present. That's not creating equality. That just ostracises people more than ever. Particularly if they don't want the plight of former generations to be highlighted over and over again, following them around like a dark cloud for the rest of their lives. Not to mention the historically significant horrors you yourself would commit by punishing all existing and future generations based on their genetic heritage alone. Equality is meant to be about treating everybody the same, and accepting people for who they are, not making compensation adjustments to bring people up or down to an arbitrary definition of equal, based on modern judgements of the past. What pisses you off, is that today you realised New Think is everything they claim Old Think was, only much, much, worse. You're not doing what must be done for a better world. I mean, hell, what's better? What have we improved? You're simply doing what you've been forced to do by violent, self-appointed dictators who deemed themselves best placed to determine how we all must live. Today you realised you were just another pawn in their game, small and expendable. Your own partner was playing you and you didn't even know it…'

At this, Damwell stood to leave. Not in defeat. Facts will never defeat the ideology of a true believer. He simply couldn't see the world my way. Once you catch the fear and join the crowd, there's almost no turning back. No matter how obvious it is that you should.

Breathing deeply, he leant forward, placing both palms on the table, hatred, embarrassment and confusion dripping off him. He moved his mouth as if to speak, paused, then turned to leave, saying nothing at all. He stormed to the front of the store, zipping his jacket angrily as he went, then just as he got to the door, it swung inwards, with Milly and Sly entering one after another. The silently steaming Damwell waited impatiently off to the side, then stormed off into the night, barging past Milly as he went.

Knowing the risk this might pose to the Global public, I pulled my device from its RFID cover, and made a quick call to Sharon before the others could get to the table.

'Hey, it's me.' I said when she answered. My eyes focussed on the two guests moving towards me, timing their progress in my mind and hoping I could finish what I had to say before they got here.

'Mmm, I gathered that when your name appeared on my screen.' she said.

'Sure, listen, I need you and your tech friend to keep tabs on Damwell for me. I'm concerned about him.'

'Gary, I've already checked him out. I told you he's clear.' Said Shaz. 'There's almost no way he could have been actively involved in any of this.'

'Yeah, that's not why I want him tracked.' I said. 'The place I'm meeting Sly and Milly is close to the hospital. He must have come in to grab a coffee, or he was tracking me and wanted to confront me or something. Either way, he was here, and we had a bit of a disagreement and he's now stormed off.'

'Well, that's not unusual.' said Shaz. 'I can't remember a time when you two didn't have some sort of disagreement.'

'That might be true, but this was different. We got into it about New Think control and all the officers involved around him. He usually gives as good as he gets, firing back at me as a selfish individual. This time, he kind of let me get under his skin. I'm hoping he's just going to brush it off and head back to stay with Ease. Still, it's worth keeping an eye on him and making sure he doesn't do something stupid instead.'

'Okay, no probs.' said Shaz. 'Although I've gotta tell you, I'm a little shocked too. I didn't know you had a heart in there. Where've you been hiding it?'

'It's only small, but it's there.' I said, unmoved by the slight. 'Listen, the others are here now. I gotta go. You take care of yourself and let me know if there's a problem with Brian.'

I hung up right as Milly and Sly arrived at my desk, both of them puffing slightly as if they'd walked quite a distance in order to arrive here. In unison they removed their coats, Milly's, a heavy looking, long black coat, under which he wore a well-cut black suit. Susan's, a similarly heavy red coat, which was infinitely more stylish, leaving just a form fitting black dress running to mid-thigh.

After hanging her jacket on the back of a chair, she placed her palms down on the table, leaning forward towards me, her delicate floral perfume dancing with my senses. 'Did you upset Detective Damwell?' she asked cheekily, in lieu of a greeting.

'Yes, I believe I did.' I responded. 'He took it well though, as I'm sure you saw.'

'Funny, I thought it was only me you pissed off like that.' added Milly.

'Please, sit down, attack my character in comfort.' I said, smiling warmly, while we chuckled collectively.

'I've gotta say, I love how consistent you are, Gary. I've never even met Mr Milford here, yet I already know that he's seen the same version of you as I have.'

'I am what I am, for better or worse. No point in trying to be something I'm not.' I replied.

'Susan, the man you entered with is Mr Milford Frantello. Not many people know his last name, mind you. Most only know him as Milford or Milly.'

Sly turned her dark featured face to appraise him as if noticing his physical presence for the first time. At 5' 11" he wasn't tall enough to be a dominant figure by height, though DSSMD agents do have that way of looking straight at you that makes you feel uncomfortable. At 98kg of solid muscle, he's the kind of guy whose never skipped leg day, or any other gym session for that matter. His deep black, military cut hairstyle, every inch the army poster boy, was broken only by his cobalt blue eyes, which he used to return the favour.

She has what was once termed a "Latino" or "Mexican" appearance, quite aptly, given she was in fact of Mexican heritage, although now, of course, a much-assimilated Global citizen. Her ebony hair and eyes with irises of the darkest brown, made for wide eyed and sultry features, juxtaposed beautifully against her light olive skin. She had a svelte frame, the product of regular exercise and a general lack of sustenance which completed the look and made for easy viewing.

'I see.' said Susan. 'And how did you two get to know each other so well?'

'That would be because Detective Johnson spent a decade yelling at me.' said Milly. 'To be fair, he was my sergeant or warrant officer in those days. Actually, the truth is, Gary's the reason I'm here right now. He taught me all about the power of following the process, and the need for patient diligence when completing a task. Never overlook the little things, hey Gaz.'

'Well, that's really the crux of why I asked you both here.' I replied, cutting the pleasantries short and launching straight into an opening statement. 'As of this evening, we've gathered all the surveillance footage we need to prove exactly who did what in relation to the murders of Katie and Chen, along with the assault on Sharon at the hospital. Oh, and indeed, the attempted murder of yours truly at OGT. Unfortunately, the earlier attack on Sharon and Ease at his house remains a mystery. We're also still working on the details of the OGT program and what about it could possibly be worth killing for, or co-opting half the local Police Service into the plot. What I really want out of tonight is to confirm what we need to do to make these crimes stick with the evidence we already have. Chances are, we're only going to get one shot at this before they shut up shop or roll out this program and shut us out forever. I'm going to break down the key details of the evidence, and I want for the two of you to help me work out what we need from tomorrow's interrogations to get us over the line.'

'Milly, I'm hoping you can clarify what the DSSMD is looking for, and Sly, I'll need you to tell me how the hell we get New Thinkers convicted. Most notably, a New Think Guide, in a New Think world. We're going to need the overwhelming support of popular public perception, with its power to sway the courts, in order to convict them for carrying out violent actions in the name of New Think. As you know, the public have historically looked the other way on the crimes of those they generally see as good, in order to protect the cause. They're certainly not willing to do that for Old Thinkers, but I digress.'

'Now, if it was just one or two people to interview, whose positions we fully understood, then the plan would be straightforward. With twenty-two of them, however, all playing various parts in this, it's going to be a delicate process to get the full story. If they're confident, they'll all just clam up and we'll end up with nothing. After all, they have the advantage of strength in numbers and unity of cause. That's not to mention that Captain Ironie, Detective Thise, Constable Clubman and Chief Blindspot are four of those twenty-two, so this isn't going to be a walk in the park. We're going to need to have a unity of our own.'

'Alright, well, don't keep us in suspense.' said Sly. 'Give us the lowdown on what really happened here.'

'Wait!' said Milly. 'I know we're near a speaker here, but the world's had noise cancelling headphones that can cut out noise above specific decibel levels for fifty years, not to mention hi-tech surveillance devices that could do it long before that. Then there's our chips and devices and the myriad other options available these days, half of which OGT themselves make. This speaker is not a sufficient deterrent to surveillance if some other non-friendly agency or officers are listening in.'

'Ah, well, my device is in a RFID bag. I assume yours are too?' I asked, looking around the table at two blank faced professionals who should know much better than this. From my inside left jacket pocket, I produced two spare RFID bags, placing one in front of each of my counterparts.

'Great, that covers the devices, but it still doesn't help with the other surveillance like bugs with decibel limiting and parabolic microphones.' continued Milly.

'Well, the parabolic mic's will be interfered with by the loudspeaker. As for the others, there's this.' I said, producing a Dead Zone Device I'd borrowed from Iman during my brief visit home. Interestingly, he'd had two, which left me impressed with both his preparedness and his lack of trust that the first one would just work. I found his wonderfully untrusting nature really endearing.

Dead Zone Devices, by the way, are the bee's knees of electromagnetic technology, even if they do leave your sperm with only XX chromosomes to work with. Strictly speaking, they're illegal, and non-strictly speaking, they're extremely illegal. In a world where all-invasive surveillance is supposedly your friend, a device that's capable of blocking, without destroying, both hard wired and wireless digital and surveillance equipment, audio and visual, within a specific radius is sure to be the enemy. The DZD emits a controlled broad spectrum omnidirectional electro-magnetic pulse, firing out to a pre-determined distance where it hits a laser dome barrier created by the very same unit. For good measure, it also jams all available communications and recording frequencies within its zone. In effect creating, the Dead Zone.

'Okay, I guess we're set then.' said Milly, eyeballing the 4cm by 4cm cube as I set it down upon the table. 'Remind me to ask you more questions about that thing later, by the way. Starting with, where did you get that?...'

'Sure, I'll make a note of that right now.' I said, drawing with my finger on the table. 'Now come on, it's time to focus. Sly, I'm going to lay this out in a bit of detail for your benefit. I know Milly's been following along on the case with "very" active surveillance, so most of what I'm about to say, he will already know. For you, on the other hand, I believe this is your first real exposure?'

'Basically, yeah.' said Sly. 'Blindspot briefly consulted me on setting up the taskforce. I also stood in the Hydrogen room, awkwardly, with all the other officers at the station and watched your three-way power struggle take place. Of course, a lot of that makes more sense now. Some sort of staged show, I suspect. Though, what for I still don't know.'

'Well, maybe you can tell us what the chief asked of you a bit later, but before we get to that, I think you're going to hear a lot of new information here. We might just work out what the song and dance about the taskforce was while we're at it. Right, here are the details in their raw form. Murder one. Katie Hansley was shot from the other side of her desk like she was an actor in a stage play. We know for certain there were twenty-one witnesses to her murder, all of whom lied about having been there and seen it.'

'Do you also know who shot her?' Asked a keenly interested Sly.

Milly leaned forward too, satisfying me he hadn't yet seen the footage Iman had pulled from Watcher. I looked back and forth at the genuine intrigue on their faces, taking the moment to ratchet up the suspense before finally answering.

'Cheq… Fencegap.' I said, pausing to study their faces and track the movement of their eyebrows bouncing off the roof. My ears rung loudly from the choired, 'WHAT's?!?!' In reply.

'Cowshit!' Said Milly after taking a moment to collect himself. 'The guy saves the world from disaster after disaster, then murders someone in cold blood over something she did to his computer program. I can't possibly believe that.'

'Why the FUCK would he need to do it?!' demanded sly with such zeal that my head instinctively snapped around to look at her.

'I'm afraid it's not Cowshit, Milly. And the why is exactly what we need to work out. We have the footage that clearly proves who pulled the trigger. He even gave a little speech before doing it. Told them all nobody was above the integrity of New Think and the pursuit of permanence. If the Global world had space for religion, I'd almost say he asked her to repent before he shot her as well. "Confess your sins, so that you can meet your maker pure and clear of conscience." were his words. I assume he was talking about whatever it was she did or was suspected of doing to the coding of that program. For her part, Katie didn't panic, plead, or even cry. She just stared at him and didn't say a damn thing. Never even flinched. Cheq didn't say anything else, either. He simply raised the .22 and put a round right in her head. Didn't rush, had no nerves, no guilt, he never even turned his head to see what his followers thought. Not that that would've been much.'

I shook my head as I recounted the story. The images playing over in my mind as I did, still fresh from my recent viewing. It made for brutal watching, leaving an image that'll stay with me for life.

'Sly, if we have evidence that clear, what else do we need?' I asked.

'Should be pretty simple in that case.' she replied, clearly a little rattled from what she'd heard. 'A confession from Cheq will wrap it up straight away. If we could prove motive, that'd make it all the stronger. In reality, though, the evidence should speak for itself if it's as straight forward as you say.'

'Okay, that's what we need and what we have. What do we not want? What could they do to hurt the case and damage the public's perception of their wrongdoing?' I asked.

'What if everybody else, as in all of the other twenty-one of them, testified that Cheq didn't do it, or he wasn't there?' Asked Milly.

'Hmmm, I suppose they could add some reasonable doubt if they suggested the footage was doctored, but that's Old Think law.' said Sly. 'New Think law is all based on popular perception and social conscience. A video showing a man murdering a woman in cold blood is not going to play well for Cheq. There are ways he could try to play it off, although I can't see them working, even for him. He's not likely to start a campaign of innocence by trying to develop a groundswell of public support. I mean, nobody knows he's involved yet. That'd be especially hard when we already have him in custody, anyway.'

'What about using public opinion and Confirmers (*who also act as deniers or deleters*) to discredit and block the video as being of Old Think disinformation origins?' I asked. 'Some sort of deep fake or edit to skew the narrative?'

'Well, that's a risk, especially with an Old Thinker as the lead detective and the accused being the head of OGT.' said Sly. 'Of course, on the flip side, it would be hugely embarrassing for the head of OGT and a New Think Guide no less, to be convincingly accused of murder by someone like you. His best bet, and I suspect the one that best supports the need for the other crimes tied to this case, is to block it entirely.'.

'What about the article that reporter published?' Asked Milly. 'Didn't you say Captain Ironie gave her the story?'

'I might have an answer for that.' I said. 'Shaz has been doing a little digging and hypothesising. We believe the group involved in Katie's murder suspected the final letter Katie was writing contained information about their goings on. We think they planned to release some accurate information from the earlier letters to try to flush out anyone that knew anything about the missing one. That's why the reward of GCC10,000 was there. If anybody came forward to either the journalist or the police, Ironie or Blindspot would find out and have them silenced.'

'What about Ease? Ironie and Blindspot already knew he had the first seven letters and there was nothing much in them. Why would they have him killed for the eighth, which I gather he knew nothing about?' Asked Milly, clearly not buying the current theory. 'Even if he knew something they didn't want him to know, surely they could have controlled him and kept him quiet? He wasn't exactly Mensa material, right?'

'That's true.' I replied. 'They might've just controlled him, but only so long as they knew what he knew first, without having to expose themselves. And that's assuming he hadn't just asked the wrong question or dug in the wrong field with Ironie and Blindspot watching. Right now, that's only a theory, so we're also exploring the possibility that some other element of the case may have led to that attack.'

'Okay. Be sure to keep us in the hypotheses loop then.' said Milly sounding a little annoyed.

'So, would it be fair to say that by and large, we agree a sound motive, or confession, should be sufficient to put Cheq behind bars?' I'd posed this question to the group, hoping to confirm a common position between people who're essentially uncommon of belief.

'Yep!' said Sly, confidently. 'We get one of those to go along with the footage and once this goes public, the outcry should put this one in the bag. Or cell, I guess.'

'Okay, what about Chen?' asked Milly. 'Are we even sure they were both connected?'

'Well, we don't have quite as much on Chen's murder. What we have got is pretty sound, though.' I said. 'I've got a statement from his supervisor at OGT that Chen, who was up on level 10 cleaning immediately prior to Katie's Murder, called his supervisor up from the basement level to assist him with an injury. Apparently, Chen had said he'd rolled his ankle. That cleared the way for the twenty-two person kill squad to come through the basement without anybody seeing them enter the service lifts, travel up to level 7, and into Katie's office.'

'How would getting this supervisor out of the way "clear the path" as you say? Aren't there chip scanners and cameras?' asked Sly.

'There are, or there should be, except they used an OGT surveillance app to turn the cameras away on the basement level and the chip scanner on the basement roller door hadn't been working for months.'

'So, what, we have no proof of how they entered the building or evidence to corroborate this supervisor's statement?'

'On the contrary.' I replied. 'I believe the group knew about the scanner issue and used it to their advantage to enter without it ever being logged. As for the service lifts, there are no chip scanners in there, because only the cleaners use them, so they felt it was a waste. The thing they didn't know, was the surveillance camera pointed at the basement lifts, is faulty. It makes a noise as if it's turning, but the camera doesn't actually move. So when they thought they'd diverted the camera to the safety of a concrete wall, all they'd really done was bounce it up and down a few times. We have clear footage of all twenty-two people entering the lifts only minutes after Chen's supervisor had gone up to assist with his rolled ankle, thus clearing the path for the group to enter. Rather strains credulity to think that was a coincidence, doesn't it?'

'So, what, Chen was in on it as some sort of patsy?' asked Sly.

'It would seem so. Whether he knew why he was doing it, we may never know for sure.'

'You think they trusted him to do what they asked on the night, then killed him to clean up the loose end that tied them back to the murder?' she asked.

'I suppose he could've pointed the finger at whomever pulled him in, even if he didn't know why.' said Milly.

'True.' I replied. 'It doesn't seem to be a particularly good reason to kill him, though. Surely, having already killed Katie, the threat itself should be real enough.'

'Perhaps they didn't want to pay him whatever they promised.' added sly, thoughtfully.

'We should know soon. Shaz is reviewing his accounts now. Notwithstanding, it doesn't make much sense they would have paid him anything at all. We live in a Global world where every single digi-cent you receive is tracked and programmed. Besides, even if Cheq set up some alternate profile for him to be able to double spend, the delivery drones would flag the high number of deliveries to his location. He'd never get away with it. Not for long, anyway. Plus, what the hell would you rent? A slop of ingredients masquerading as meat, a second small portion of vegetables that you don't have the energy supply to cook? You can't buy clothes without returning the ones you have. Money is worthless to the individual in this world. It doesn't buy power, it doesn't buy peace, and it doesn't enrich.'

'What then?' asked Sly.

'I have a feeling it's the same as all other New Think actions. Fear, coercion, and the lack of an alternative. I don't think he chose to do what he did, or to be involved. He simply did what he was told to, whether he liked it or not. As with all other "choices" these days, he then paid the consequences for his involuntary compliance.'

When I'd finished saying this, the three of us drifted into our own private thoughts. I looked at my two counterparts, who appeared to be grappling with the concept that their championed form of governance, the only governance option available to them anyhow, is a method of oppression and control used to force people to take the only path they can. It's hard for people to understand the concept of conspiracy in a world that trades in compliance alone. There's never anything to gain, and always everything to lose.

'Why don't I get us some drinks while you ponder the theory I've presented.' I said, trying to break the obvious tension that was building. 'Might help us get those thinking juices going.'

Sly now sat with her legs crossed, arms folded on the table and shoulders hunched over in a closed off position. For someone who was social by nature, in the digital sense at least, this was not the image of content. Adjacent to her, Milly had taken the seated stance of the tough and defiant man, knees spread in a V, leaning back, with arms folded across his chest, his chin and eyes lowered. I grimaced slightly, knowing that to upset my allies was to damage my cause.

Rather than waiting for a response that likely wouldn't come, I headed to the bar to fulfil my promise. Like all ALO's it was staffed by a humanoid robot with built-in glass buffer for that authentic bar tender feel. It also has a chip sensor and biometric scanner to identify and apply appropriate discredit to its patrons. The thing looked more like a skin-coloured C-3PO with a tin man belly for its ultrasonic cleaning tub than the fantastically humanised robots of terminator ilk. Nevertheless, it still felt like just another example of life imitating art, as if we're incapable of preventing the fiction of our past from becoming the reality of our future.

The one benefit of the Bot-tender over the old school human variety is their ability to catalogue the order of service for people standing at the bar. They're capable of determining the exact proximity and intent of those at or near the Bar and will only serve people in the correct order. If it'd been around, it certainly would've solved a lot of arguments back in the old days, although it's not really an issue now, given I'm the only person here.

Since alcoholic drinks were outlawed, bars are not exactly popular places to hang out and spend your GDC's. In person discussion groups, particularly those taking place at night, are strongly discouraged as they have the potential to breed misinformation (*because, of course, people get dumb and deceitful after dark*) and are generally considered as an intentional attempt to avoid surveillance, which puts at risk their pursuit of the greater good. However, because the Globalists like to gaslight people into believing they have freedom of choice, they've made it so it's not actually illegal to go to a bar or coffee shop to meet with people. It's just strongly discouraged. The Christmas tree of cameras at the entrance, several visible moralists outside, and the hefty Global-Discredit's levied against you merely for entering, are only there to keep you and the rest of the world safe. Fear, couched as safety, strikes again.

I returned to the table with three glasses of E-cola. Not to be confused with E. Coli the bacterium, nor is it a reference to electrons and carbonation or the electricity age in which we live. It's "Eco friendly-Cola". Like everything else these days, it's got to have a reference to some sort of environmental or social positivity. You can't just have a fucken drink.

'Oooh, E-Cola. I love this stuff.' said Sly, bouncing swiftly out of her mood. 'It makes me feel like I'm doing something good for the world, too.'

I smiled a broad flat smile and tried not to roll my eyes at the fact the Public Perception Prosecutor I'm relying on for advice, thinks drinking a cola that claims to be environmentally friendly (*without explaining how, mind you*), is actually doing good for the planet.

'Okay.' said Milly, taking up his drink with markedly less enthusiasm. 'So, let's say we accept that Chen was forced to take part in this plot on threat of a worse fate. An offer he couldn't refuse, so to speak. What made them need to follow through and actually kill him? Evidentially he did what they wanted him to. You have the evidence to prove that.'

'That's one of the things we'll need to find out tomorrow.' I said. 'My assumption is that Chen might not have realised why they wanted him as a decoy. Someone more equal than him asks him to take a dive, he does it no questions asked. He's got nothing to gain or lose by challenging them. Then, once he heard of Katie's murder, perhaps he planned to tell someone or do something about it. The one thing New Think can't surveil and control is the human spirit. Inside everyone one of us lies our own personal limit of compliance. What I might call the "Nope, don't give a fuck!" line, beyond which consequences and repercussions of action or inaction no longer matter. I'm going out on a limb to say he was killed for the same reason unwilling patsies have always been killed. Dead people don't talk.'

'So, we just have to hope that one of them gives it up and tells us what happened, having found their own internal line?' Asked Sly.

'Not quite. We also have footage of Sophia from OGT and our very own Captain Isabelle Ironie exiting the lift into the basement, Sophia with gun drawn, only two minutes prior to Chen's TOD. The Beretta Bobcat Sophia used to try and kill me is being checked out by forensics now. I suspect it will match both the murder of Chen and that of Katie.'

'Seems pretty strong. I still think we'll need to get a clearer picture of what turned Chen from co-conspirator to murder victim, though.' said Sly. 'We get that, we get public opinion on Chen's murder, and I think we're 2 for 2.'

'Okay, I like the sound of that. Next up is the attempted murder of yours truly, which I think should be pretty straightforward. We have surveillance footage of Sophia and Captain Ironie coming down together in the lifts, both exiting with guns drawn and heading towards the office where I sat. Combine that with the two eyewitness statements, my own and Johnny's, and the fact that they were caught red-handed with the guns, and are now both in custody having been arrested in the act, along with three recordings of the event via the unsheathed devices of Johnny and our two careless attackers, in addition to clear intent, with Sophia having fired a shot in anger before being shot and struck in the head herself, and I think it's a slam dunk.'

'You shot her in the head?' Asked a horrified looking Sly.

'No. I shot her in the thigh with an Electro. Johnny hit her in the head with a spanner, trying to save me. If he hadn't, I mightn't be here to tell the tale.'

'Oh, I see.' said Sly, slumping back in her chair, her expression shifting from one of horror to concern. 'I'm not entirely sure that's better, mind you.'

'It was better for me.' I replied. 'I was the victim in this.'

I saw the internal machinations of Sly's mind. She was fighting the modern mental battle of a New Thinker, who splits society into different categories, races, and sexes, when it suits them, in order to determine whether a would-be victim who successfully defends themselves, should now be seen as the aggressor in a fight they didn't pick, when their attacker fails to overwhelm them.

'Well, don't be so quick to assume it's in the bag. You being Old Think is going to make that hard despite all the evidence to support your story.' said Sly, reaching her conclusion. 'Fair or not, the Global world simply won't support the actions of Old Thinkers even if you were just protecting yourself. Especially an Old Think cop. No matter how much you've been persecuted, you'll never get the empathy of traditional minorities.'

'Hmmm, what a shame that fairness and truth couldn't survive the evolution of Global equality.' I said. 'It wasn't a "story" by the way, just a summary of the facts…'

'I guess we'll have to play up the angle that Johnny was the one under attack and you just happened to be in the way.' said Milly, with a smart-arse smile on his face and a quick upward flick of the eyebrows for emphasis.

'Yes, I suppose that would work.' I said, while biting my tongue. 'Sly, thoughts?' I asked, raising my own eyebrows as I cast a sidelong glance at my doubtful colleague.

'Works for me.' she replied. 'Poor New Think cleaning supervisor attacked by corrupt cop and deranged technology expert, after stumbling on surveillance footage of another crime. That one sells the message of the abused proletariat of old.'

'Then in really small print, we could put "Old Think cop caught in the firing line".' Added Milly, still smiling as he twisted the ideological knife.

'I know you're probably joking.' said Sly, 'But I think any mention of Gary might hurt the cause. If we want to succeed, we'll have to leave it at the cleaner. It's a stronger case.'

'Right, next up is the torture and attempted murder of Sgt Ease and the subsequent assault and attempted murder of Detective Sharon

Wilson. Followed, naturally, by a second attempted murder of Detective Sharon Wilson.'

'So, what do we have on this one?' asked Sly, sipping her E-Cola happily. She plucked a handful of shiny black hair that had fallen forward over her ear as she sipped, guiding it back into place with thumb and forefinger and watching me intently for my response as she did. To a casual observer, it might seem that she was just an interested bystander, rather than the primary prosecutor attempting to build evidence on one of the most important cases she'll ever try.

'Not a whole lot.' I said. 'We know that Ease was investigating Katie's murder for us, and that he uncovered the original seven letters the cleaners had taken for their reading practice. Shaz, I, and Captain Ironie had a brief catch up with Sgt Ease at his desk after the initial investigation of Katie's Murder. Ease seemed to be well aligned with what Ironie would have wanted at the time. His early hypothesis was that this crime was almost certainly Old on New. Then, once he'd read the letters, he was convinced of a different theory.'

'New on Old?' asked Milly.

'No.' I said. 'He thought it was Old on Old, because whilst he accepted Katie had turned herself Old Think through her readings, he couldn't believe a New Thinker would kill her in cold blood. He's the idealist's idealist, it seems. In spite of which, when the news article about the letters came out the next morning and Ease didn't show up to work the next day, we assumed he'd leaked the information himself and was hiding out somewhere to avoid the scrutiny. We didn't chase him straightaway because Chen had been murdered the same morning the story came out and we needed to keep the case moving. New Think or not, after 48 hours it gets a hell of a lot harder to solve a murder. When we finished at Chen's crime scene, Sharon decided to head to Adam's place and get the story straight. Thankfully, Ease had sent us copies of Katie's letters along with his report after his discussions with the cleaners at OGT. Without them, we wouldn't have known how accurate the news article was. Anyway, whoever attacked Ease managed to enter his building without being registered by the chip reader or being picked up by any other form of surveillance that we've found, including the old human eye. They bound ease, tortured him with an electro, which was probably his own service weapon, leaving no prints or DNA in the apartment and none of Ease's surveillance equipment captured or recorded a thing. Shaz said there were definitely people there when she found him, except she didn't get a look at them before they attacked her. They had to be pros, although strangely, they never took her service weapon off her, nor did they take Ease's with them when they left. That was a mistake on their part if they actually planned to kill them, because ultimately Sharon's electro is what saved their lives. They glued the windows and door shut, then set the gas on, after having lit a candle in the lounge room. Shaz managed to smash one window with her gun before succumbing to her injuries, in effect preventing a big bang and two assaults becoming murder. We have forensics looking into the candle and glue now. Aside from that, we have little else to go on.'

'The second attempt on Sharon at the hospital, on the other hand, is almost certainly the work of one, Captain Ironie. Sharon has a recording of the attack in which Ironie's voice has been positively identified, and prior to the attack Milly's team had been tracking the captain to one block away from the hospital. At that point, she sheathed herself, possibly with a Dissolution Suit, and disappeared from surveillance only minutes before the attack occurred. Afterwards, Ironie wasn't sighted at the station, or anywhere else as far as I know, until she came downstairs with Sophia to shoot me earlier today. We are also yet to find the Officer who had been stationed outside Sharon's room on protection detail, a task that Milly's team is working on now.'

'So, it sounds pretty straight forward regarding what happened to Sharon at the hospital and who the guilty party is.' said Sly. 'We may need some sort of confession, or to find the officer that was assigned to guard Sharon's room, to make it a slam dunk, but we already have her for today's shooting, so tacking on the crime of a high-ranking officer attempting to murder her underling who'd been lying helpless and injured in a hospital bed, should really help our public perception case for the guilty verdict. My only question here is, are we absolutely certain that the attempted murder of Sgt Ease is connected to the OGT murders?'

'Well, no, we aren't. However, it would have to be a phenomenal coincidence if it wasn't.' I answered. 'Particularly when you consider the second attempt on Shaz. Ironie tried to kill her in the hospital and then tried to kill me at OGT. There has to be a connection. What other reason would there be for our direct manager to deem Sharon's injured and unconscious state in hospital too great an opportunity to miss, before turning invisible and then injecting her with some sort of poison.'

'That's a strong point.' Said Sly, leaning forward to place her elbow on the table. The movement released another wave of her floral scent, which mixed well with the spices of a tofu curry, ordered by the only remaining patron not seated at this table.

'What about these letters?' Asked Milly. 'I haven't read them yet. Is there any value there?'

'Yeah, I'd like to get a copy of those too.' added Sly.

'You'll get them. I'll give you everything you need to help win public perception. Unfortunately, I didn't think there was much to them from my read. Essentially, they're an attempt by Katie to reconnect with her mother, who is a staunch Old Thinker. They started after Katie was assigned to this program, tasked with ensuring the perpetually enduring dominance of New Think. Katie is a highly trained psychologist who specialises in psychological programming, commonly called brainwashing or mind control. It's even more commonly used as the method of control for everybody in the Global World, via coercive advertising, structured media messaging, and manipulation of social media topics and trends, using suggestive wording to guide public opinion. Basically, Katie was another cog in the wheel of the Global Machine that starts with indoctrination in schools and carries on indefinitely through endless conscious and subconscious psycho-suggestive manipulation. I'm sure you're familiar with Katie's line of work Sly, given we use people with her skill set to garner successful Public Perception outcomes.'

'Yes. They are the underlying basis of a conviction, and will likely be the key to successfully prosecuting the crimes of this very case.' said Sly, with a tautness of attitude. It was clear she hadn't enjoyed this any more than my previous comments on New Think. Her already tight skinned face pulled even tighter as she pursed her full-bodied lips into an unintended pout.

'Well, as part of her research for the program, Katie had begun reading influential books from the Old Think era. She started with those that strongly aligned with the dominant mindset of the time, or at least New Thinks perception of it. It appears that through this research, some of the content had seeped into Katie's own conscious view of the world. The first book she read was on critical thinking, followed closely by books on individual freedoms and inalienable rights. She read both fiction and nonfiction books covering these topics, then books on democracy, fascism, communism, and authoritarianism, books about the world wars, and the cold wars, and before she knew it, she had a totally different view of the world that was. She learned that people fought, not because they liked fighting, but because they loved their way of life enough to go to war to protect it. The world of the past was imperfect, yet still open and packed with opportunity, competition, and individual choice. In the letters, you can see these concepts starting to impact her attempts to communicate with her mother. Rather than learning about the dangers of Old Think, identifying the triggers for that ideology and using the knowledge she gained to create psychological barriers to it, she began to believe those concepts had merit. Remember that she'd been alive before the Guides established the Global world. She was a kid, albeit one old enough to have memories of life back then stored in the back of her mind, just waiting for their moment to return to the fore.'

Again, my two friends were silent. Appearing introspective, or perhaps defensive, both with their heads down, contracting into themselves and trying not to absorb what I said. As if by doing so, they could protect themselves from the uncritical presentation of the abandoned thoughts I was projecting. Behind them, a passerby outside, a moralist no doubt, looked pointedly at our group through the window. Perhaps my anti-New Think sentiment had been powerful enough to set off his sixth sense as well.

'She never actually sent any of the letters.' I continued. 'They were written on paper so they couldn't be digitally monitored or traced, and she threw them out in her office waste bin, not quite willing to commit to her internal changes, or make them part of her external being. The cleaners, many of whom came from that part of the Global World once known as China, claim that they were keen to improve their mastery of Global, so they took the letters when they cleaned her office and used them to practice their reading.'

'Was there anything in them worth killing over? Anything that was dangerous enough to justify the actions of Mr Fencegap and Isabelle?' asked Sly hopefully, with sincere respect for the named, as if salvation would come for these people, confirming they only acted out of a desperate need to protect the world from evil. It's the hope of every committed New Thinker. A belief that extreme action is necessary and excusable in pursuit of the greater good. Or, in the old parlance, the end would justify the means.

'Not as far as I could tell.' I said.

'Well, there must be something in the eighth one!' added Milly, who was running on the same wavelength as Sly. 'Jiang cut the chip out of his arm and disappeared off the face of the planet with it. Nobody does that for no good reason.'

'That's the working theory.' I said. 'The missing letter could be why Ease was attacked, too. We think the attackers may believe that Jiang either gave Ease the letter, or someone at OGT suspected that Ease had it, so they came after him to destroy it, or to make sure he never spoke about it. We have no proof of that theory. What we have is footage of Sophia coming to Katie's office to speak to her about two hours prior to the murder. Sophia's story is that she'd gone to see Katie in the belief she was about to complete her conversion to Old Think and sabotage the OGT program. Sophia said she had tried to talk her out of it. Apparently, the two of them had been in some sort of relationship, or so Sophia tells us. Unfortunately for her, we've found nothing aside from Sophia's own statement to verify that. When the uniforms searched Katie's apartment, they found nothing that was identified as belonging to Sophia, nor did her chip or biometric markers show up on any of the mood screens or surveillance cameras in Katie's apartment or its immediate surrounds. Sophia had told us they'd been together for a while, but the relationship began to sour as Katie drifted away from the righteous path of the committed Globalist. She admits to being angry that someone charged with protecting the integrity and longevity of New Think would so easily defect to the very thing they were trying to protect against, though maintains her claims that she never acted on this anger. In the footage on the afternoon of Katie's murder, Sophia can be seen talking to Katie, or at her, at least. Near the end of the conversation, Katie's head turns an inch to the left as she appears to glance down at the corner of her desk. There, a letter can be seen sitting on the edge of the table. It's hard to tell from the footage if Sophia actually saw the letter. She left a few seconds later and didn't return until the whole crowd arrives together.'

'We now know that Jiang was called up to Katie's office shortly before 21:00, at which point she handed the letter directly to him, rather than hoping he'd fish it out of the trash. She obviously knew something bad was going to happen and wanted to make sure that whatever was in the letter got out to the right person, rather than being destroyed or confiscated by OGT. As you said Milly, whatever was in that letter appears to have been enough to send Jiang into permanent hiding and probably set this whole thing in motion.'

Throughout this story, I'd been mixing the truth with omissions and lies. For instance, I knew exactly where the eighth letter was. Sharon was sitting not far from it now, while she and Iman reviewed the OGT program searching for answers. Whether it started this whole debacle, I didn't yet know, and more to the point, I still didn't know who I could trust. I'm also yet to fully understand what Milly's bosses and their wider organisation plan to do with it. They are, after all, a secretive military arm of the Global Guides Alliance, with very close ties to the technology and software companies whose products they use, and for whom they use them. They are also under the direct control of senior Guides, of which, Cheq Fencegap is one.

Despite their apparent lack of familiarity, Milly and Sly shared a knowing glance at one another, perhaps suspecting that I'd withheld or amended the truth. Neither said a word to confirm my suspicions, Sly merely took another sip of E-cola and returned her attention to me.

'Well, we haven't got everything yet, but you seem to have a pretty good handle on this.' said Sly. 'Are you sure you really need our input?'

'Yes, I am. While your commitment to New Think might not be on the extreme end of the scale, you are both certified members of the club. I needed to make sure that what we have passes muster with the powers that be, and that we're digging in the right places, so to speak.'

Milly and Sly simply nodded in unison. I could tell from their reactions they weren't committed to this particular cause, like I was. They were here professionally because they had to be, although generally speaking they'd been conditioned to support those at which I was presently pointing the finger of blame. Or, perhaps the Dead-zone Device was effecting them too. Either way, Sly sipped her Cola again, adding no vocal response to her nod, whilst Milly mindlessly thumbed his sheathed device.

'Well, I guess that's it then. Milly, I know you'll be there tomorrow, but Sly, I want to know that you're going to be there too?' I asked assertively, trying to re-engage them.

'Sure, I can be there.' Said Sly. 'I'm just not sure what I bring to the party?'

'I need you there for two reasons. One is to help me out with the interrogations of the police officers to ensure they don't try to trip me up or stone wall me. I'm sure you'll have the right phrases and social perception offerings to get me through. The other is for Cheq Fencegap. I'm going to need New Think witnesses there to hear what he has to say when we squeeze him and verify the truth…'

Chapter 31

Break em down and build em up again

Wanting to protect your own national identity by reducing the number of foreign immigrants entering, has long been considered by New Thinkers as a racially motivated and hateful action. It's not, of course. Immigration policy restricting the number and type of immigrants a country will accept, is just how countries must and did ensure the security of their people. The aim was to protect employment opportunities, social wealth, and pride in a unified national identity. Doing so would ensure that political structures remain supportive of the nation's true foundational values and aren't diluted to unrecognisable homogeneous blobs of multiculturalism.

Those countries whose people are forced to give up the right to their own identity in order for an equal representation of others, are seldom peaceful and united. You need only look at world history to see that lines drawn arbitrarily on a map, forcing different ethnic groups to form a nation, solely because they share the same geographical space, whilst fundamentally different in nature, have never become a united form.

Democracy couldn't save them either. Forcing different ethnicities and religious belief systems into a western democratic form of governance is no better than leaving them to their pre-existing battles. The same troubles will ultimately occur. One group does not wish to be ruled by the other. And not wanting to bring this challenge to your own country, with its own established identity, which in the first place makes it a desirable place to emigrate, is not racist. It's the simple act of preventing the inevitable, protecting the freedom and peace of a nation to ensure the continuation of its establish norms.

Unfortunately, New Thinkers never really grasped that concept. Until they got into power, that is, and it was their norms they sought to protect…

The reality is, the Guides didn't really believe in the principles they espoused. They simply knew they couldn't attain the absolute level of authority needed without fostering, championing, and controlling them. The key was to disrupt the stable status quo. Change the voters, change the vote. To begin with, they used the effect of war and general political and ideological activities to drive global migration, which in turn, slowly diluted established strongholds of individualist freedoms, ideology and traditional "western thinking".

When the world wasn't changing fast enough, they started wars of their own, chose sides in pre-existing ones, funded one regime to topple another, foisted power on people friendly to their cause, until they weren't, then did it all over again. Combine their geopolitical medalling with indoctrination of the young at home and abroad, through political activism, controlled and funded by lobbyists, swapping money for favour no matter the cause, and before you know you it, you're really starting to influence the political views and societal actions across the world. Or at least agitate against the established ones. Whatever its origins, money talks. And talks and talks and talks. And as the world changed, lobbyists methods remained the same, just their audience became more willing. The more the world opened up as a purportedly free and equal place, the easier the manipulation of politics became.

The idea of sleeper agents and monetary manipulation of the past becomes unnecessary when western nations welcome with open arms, citizens from a foreign national power of alternate governance, which allows its people to leave for western democracies on the proviso that they maintain an allegiance to the mother country. This influx of foreigners still tied to the fortunes of their homeland, become dual nationals who vote for puppet politicians pulling the strings of favour for their country of origin, all in the name of global cooperation and the redistribution of wealth and power. In effect by allowing and championing immigration and multiculturalism, western nations encouraged and facilitated their own political and ideological demise. In many cases, with immigrants receiving monetary benefits of welfare systems on arrival in western countries, the citizens of those countries unwittingly paid them to do it.

This was no mistake on behalf of the Guides who'd pulled the strings and waited in the wings for their moment to strike. It was all a part of their plan. For individual rights, freedoms and nationalism to be defeated in free western countries, you either have to make people feel like they're bad and selfish for holding those beliefs, or fill the country with people who hold the beliefs you want them to. By those means, you can sway government and artificially change what can genuinely be justified as the will of the people.

All this brings me to the place I find myself now. Facing twenty two New Think killers, colluders and commanders. I'm seeking to bring about some sort of genuine justice, supported only by New Think officers, operating under New Think laws, in a New Think world, with all of them on both sides believing unquestionably that all New Think ideals, no matter how they came to be, or how damaging they are, are absolute, and unquestionably right. They've been told to fear the alternative and they damn well do… Whatever that might be, they will obediently set out to destroy it with the heat of a thousand suns and never allow the Global rule to be questioned. For their commitment is to the greater good, no matter the cost.

From this group of individuals united in fear, I must find a way to needle and prod their delicate emotions and bridge their deep detachment from reality, such that they feel the guilt of their crimes and admit what they saw and did. Which, by the way, is a heck of a challenge in itself, because I'll first need them to understand that what they did was wrong. The pièce de résistance will be getting them to explain, why.

Standing in the foyer of the middle safe house in the row of three, I take in my surrounds. Each house is connected by oversized doorways joining all three entrance foyers and thus allowing easy access for our detainees and guards from house to house. The buildings had been fitted with sound deadening materials, creating an obvious sort of silence. The kind you hear ringing all around you. The buildings are large by Global housing standards, though hardly palatial. Yet, even jammed to the gills with crooked cops and coders, there wasn't a sound from the prisoners and barely a scuffle from the agents posted nearby.

Milly was standing in the adjoining foyer to my right, quietly conversing with his specialist interrogator, Naomi, whom I hadn't met before. Frankly, I had no idea she was going to be a part of this, and it made me nervous to think about the risk a new member of the group might pose at this late stage. She wasn't part of the arrest team yesterday and Milly didn't mention her last night, either. Irrespective of which, she's here now, so I'll have to trust that she'll do the job and, more to the point, that she's on our side.

Like Milly, Naomi wore a dark suit and skinny tie, every bit the agents of old, in appearance, if not belief and attitude. Her mousy blonde hair was close cropped, falling to the right side just above the ear, shaved to only a few mm in length on the left. She wore a Sig on her left hip, a notable addition not present on Milly or I. Milly had removed his from its holster, and I, my Electro, for the purposes of a comfortable interrogation. Naomi's masculine look was softened by the fruity floral perfume she wore, which itself was a welcome relief from the slight musky heat of the buildings.

'Naomi, it's a pleasure to meet you.' I said. 'Do you mind if I steal Milly away for a minute?' As I said this, I placed a hand on Milly's left shoulder, turning him and cutting his connection with her, making clear that whilst I'd asked this as a polite question, I meant it as an authoritative instruction.

'To talk about me?' asked Naomi bluntly as we turned away.

'Yes.' I said over my shoulder, assuming that stating the blatantly obvious was better than attempting a pathetic lie.

'I'd expect nothing less.' she replied, although by now essentially talking to herself.

'What's the problem Gaz?' Asked Milly testily, straightening his suit jacket as he did.

'Did you two both get up on the wrong side of the bed, or what?' I shot back.

'Well, it is 03:30 in the morning, Gary.' he replied, trying not to crack a smile now. 'I've barely even been to bed. So, what's the problem here? Old Think misogyny shining through? Don't trust a woman to do the job? What?'

'On the contrary' I said. 'I'd have Sharon here in my place if she were healthy enough. Or my ex-wife. They'd all confess just to get her to stop talking. Women make excellent interrogators and investigators in my experience. My issue is not with her sex, it's that the circle of people I'm willing to trust on this case isn't large enough to make a circle. I want to know that she's here for the right reasons and that I can trust her. Where did she come from?'

'Look, she's not part of my personal inner circle, but I didn't get to choose my own interrogator. I was told by the Deputy of DSSMD that Naomi would be "available" to assist with these interrogations. I was also told how "lucky" that made me… So, congratulations. By extension, you're now lucky too.'

'Right. I see. So, where's she from?' I asked again, the hairs now standing up on the back of my neck. The only reason previously uninvolved agents get parachuted into a scenario like this, is if the brass aren't confident as to how it's going to pan out and want to add a little insurance to make sure it goes their way. Precisely what their way is, I'm still not sure.

'She's the DSSMD director's personal choice.' Said Milly again, in a hushed, conciliatory tone. 'Where exactly she's from and what she normally does, I couldn't bloody tell you.' He added, losing a little conciliation in the process.

'Great.' I said. 'There's no-one I trust less than the Guides… except perhaps Guide adjacent leaders of New Think organisations who are seeking to prove their worth to their revered overlords.'

'Yeah, yeah, I get it Gaz. But like I said, it's not my choice.'

'I want you in that room too, Milly. Not behind the glass.' I said. 'We need outcomes here and I need to know they're real outcomes I can trust, and that they're related to the crimes of the case, not some imagined crimes of Old Think origin, designed only to cast doubt on the perpetrators.'

'Don't worry, Gary, I want outcomes on this as much as you do. Real ones. I gotta impress the revered overlords too, you know… Look, for what it's worth, I've seen Naomi at work before. She's like a surgeon getting information out of people.'

‘A minute ago, you didn’t know what she did.’ I replied, growing more concerned by the second.

‘You know what I mean, Gary. I don’t know what section she works for, or her day-to-day duties, but I’ve seen her around and I know that she’s good. You’re just going to have to trust me on this cause she’s here now and we’re ready to go.’

‘Yeah. Righto.’ I said, taking a deep breath, knowing full well that he was right and there was nothing I could do. ‘Let’s scrub up and get to it. I’ve split the group in half, by the way. You will not find Cheq Fencegap or Captain Ironie on your list. I want them for myself. You do, however, have Sophia, Blindspot and Clubman and I expect you to give em hell. I also plan on saving Cheq till last, because I want to sweat him right to the end, so if you get anything I can use against him, or a series of confessions, just be sure to pass them on. I’m going to need maximum pressure in order to break him.’

With everything agreed, I turned on my heel and headed off to find Sly, while Milly and Naomi entered interrogation room number two and summoned their first victim.

May the truth prevail.

Chapter 32

Learn to rote

'Well, if it isn't my favourite Moralist.' I said, as Adam Abers was frog marched into makeshift interview room number 1. Brian, one of Milly's agents who took part in yesterday's spree of arrest's brought him in, seating him on the opposite side of the table and cuffing his arm to the metal chair.

'Is this some kind of Old Think joke?!' demanded a ruddy faced and saggy eyed Abers. The lack of his tailored silver jacket exposed his formerly crisp white shirt, now heavily creased with dust and dirt streaks, while fresh pit stains peaked out from under his arms accompanied by the requisite smell. He was also notably absent the lovely Panerai watch that I'd noticed when I'd first met him. Presumably, it had been removed to help disorient and confuse him.

'No.' I said. 'I've just got a lot of people to interview, and I prefer to start early and finish early, rather than start late, finish late. I like to walk in the evenings, you know.'

'Fuck you, you sadist prick!' He replied. 'This is a form of torture! You keep us locked up here, no air conditioning, no shower, no change of clothes, and then the minute we finally fall asleep, you drag us out to interrogate us. What sort of asshole are you?!'

'Well Adam, when Oscar Wilde said "Be yourself, everyone else is taken" he didn't say you had to be nice or easy to deal with. Of course, you've probably never heard of Oscar Wilde, have you? Shame, really, he was pretty progressive for his time. Not that you'd ever know. I'd wager you're not a reader. Anyone from that era was just an "Old Thinker" no matter who they were or what they did, right? You know what, don't bother answering that. Save your energy. There are far more important questions to come, and those are the ones you need to get right to reduce the time you'll spend in jail. Besides, I thought you'd enjoy the reduced drain on nature's resources that comes from denying twenty-two people all those evil creature comforts. You'll probably earn some Global Credits for your sacrifice.'

'I won't be spending a second in jail! I haven't done a damn thing wrong!' Retorted Abers, while simultaneously using the sleeve of his free arm to wipe sweat from his forehead.

'Ah, I see the problem here, Adam. I haven't laid out the crimes for which you will answer yet. Of course, being a moralist, you probably can't understand how anything you do could be considered a crime. Hear me out though, because I think I can bring you round. Let's start here. You were an accomplice in the premeditated murder of Katie Hansley.

You obstructed the course of justice by intentionally misleading a police investigation. You attempted to destroy evidence. And, in the case of your specific role as a moralist, you knowingly failed to prevent a violent crime and protect the integrity of New Think. Hell, you've brought New Think into disrepute! Or at least, you will have, once our DPPI (*District Public Perception Influencer*) releases the details of the case to the media to make the public aware of your failure to protect them.'

'What details?! You haven't got any evidence of my involvement in anything!' He spat.

'Oh contraire! We know all about your role at OGT and your position as an embedded Moralist within the organisation. We know that from your very own statement of three days ago. That gives us a nice clear picture of what standards you are expected to uphold. We also have video, with accompanying audio surveillance, of you and twenty-one other persons entering the OGT building the night of Katie's murder via the basement level roller door, then heading to the service elevators, riding up to level 7, and as a group watching on while our Global Guide and your OGT CEO, Cheq Fencegap, asked Katie to confess her sins and detail her actions in amending the program your project team had worked on. When she didn't, Cheq produced a .22 Beretta pistol and shot her dead, right there at her desk. You stood not two meters away, doing absolutely nothing to stop it, nothing about it after the fact, and when later questioned by police officers including myself, you claimed to have been home at the time of the murder with no knowledge of its occurrence.'

Abers sat quietly staring at me, hate filling his red eyes. He had the slight shake of a trapped animal, incapable of compromise or concession, fight or flight being the only responses that drive them, yet unable take either action.

I'd brought into the room with me a single glass of water. Not for him. I brought it for me. It was both an interrogation prop and a nourishment. I took a sip, calmly, confidently and happily, vocalising my satisfaction with an audible 'Ahhhh', then replaced the glass on the small wooden table that sat between us. Abers watched me enviously, swallowing hard. He watched the glass move through its full arc, his anger level appearing to rise again as he mentally added this slight to the list.

I was trying to use whatever I could to gain an advantage over my interogees, which meant maximising the effects of the tools at hand. Because the building in which we sit is a safe house and not a police station, the room's not quite set up as an interrogation room might ordinarily be. On any other day, this is a bedroom for those hiding out or under the protection of the Global Guides for some reason. With the little notice I gave them, only minimal adjustments could be made, which explains why there's still a heavy looking, black framed, steel fold up bed, standing folded against the wall to the right.

The lighting in the room was average at best with only one central LED down light, per Global regulations, making for a rather moody interview scenario. Abers and I both sat on basic and uncomfortable midnight coloured metal chairs, putting us in an equally uncomfortable position, so no advantage to be gained there. The place does have its upsides, mind you. For example, using DSSMD safe houses means we have an uninterrupted supply of power, so I don't have to worry about it cutting out on me mid interrogation.

There are also surveillance cameras in every room, the most disturbing of which being located in the mirrored cupboards at the hallway end of the bedrooms, which are not actually cupboards at all, but one way glass walls like you'd see in a regular interrogation room. The other side of that glass was a small cupboard sized space that backed onto the hallway, disingenuously appearing to be a closet from the hallway side.

Currently sat in that small space behind me, was Susan Sly, who, via an open comms app "Chatter" was providing me feedback and guidance about the interrogation, direct to my device. There was no need for me to type. The dialogue was being directly translated into sentences on the screen, right under today's Global message "Deviation is defiance, and defiance is dangerous". Abers chip, along with my own, provided a biometric signal which allowed the app to triangulate our voices and compare them to the biometric database to identify the speaker, turning words into text, which include context, inflection, and slang, personalised to each participant. From her surveillance booth, Sly can type or talk directly in reply and that reply will instantly display as a side note to the feed on my screen.

'So, what is it you want from me?' Asked Abers. 'You seem to think you already have it all.'

'Well, I'm not into wasting my time.' I replied, 'So, I'll be straight with you, Adam. What I need from you, is motive. We know what you did, and we know how you did it. What we don't know, is why.'

'You think I'm going to tell you why I did something I won't admit to having done?!' He shouted, his exhaustion and discomfort turning to anger.

'Yes. Even if you never admit involvement, I want you to at least shed some light on why these things happened… You do know why you were there, don't you?'

'Ah-hahaha, so, you've got nothing then.' He laughed manically. 'In a New Think world, if you can't convince the people there's a cause to follow or someone to hate, then you haven't got a bat's chance in a wind farm. I could shoot someone in the head, point blank, live on the Global news, and If I told them it was because they refused to recognise the validity of historical guilt, people would march to my location and launch a parade in my honour for doing what had to be done to promote and protect the Global agenda.' he continued before breaking into a chuckle again.

I'd expected nothing less than this from someone like Abers. Moralists are without exception, New Think extremists. Admitting some sort of guilt for an action carried out in the name of, or what they perceive to be, "the greater good", is something they simply won't do. I'm hoping to use that arrogant god complex to my advantage. If he believes there's nothing wrong with what was done, he might at least tell me why they did it, and explain the wondrous and righteous intent of his actions in the process.

'Okay, Adam, so you don't want to admit being a party to the murder of Katie Hansley. But you do admit she was murdered, right?' I asked.

'I don't admit to knowing how she was killed, at all.' said Abers.

'Well, the good news for me is that I already know you do know how she was murdered, and that you were unquestionably present at the time. What I am willing to hear is either yours or even the OGT approved perspective as to what drove that action. If, as you said, this was indeed a justified response, necessary for the protection of the New Think agenda, then surely you can detail that justification to me?'

Abers sat silently contemplating the question, though surely not pondering the truth. A moralist's mind, and the mind of all captive New Thinkers, is a complex web of victimhood and activist demands. Each new thought, considering both the means to overcoming some bias or destructive human trait, and the excuse or justification for their own horrible actions. I decided to try and press home an advantage to see if his current disrupted mental state might offer a weak spot. An entry point for my questions to break through.

'It was the program, wasn't it?' I asked. 'Katie began to believe there was merit in other ways of life, ideals, and methodology. She wasn't seeing an evil that had to be erased forever through psychological manipulation. Instead, she saw the endless tools of control and blatant lies about the need to blindly and unquestioningly follow the word of the Guides to save the world from an evil that didn't really exist. She started seeing the world as it really was in those books she'd been reading, and knowing the world as it is now, Katie could see what we'd become. That we've given up everything and saved nothing. All while demonising ordinary people just for wanting to be free to live their own lives. So, rather than completing her task and building psychological loops into the program, she did something else instead. Maybe she did the opposite of that… Except, you don't really know, do you?' I asked, pausing for an answer I knew wouldn't come.

'New Think or Old Think notwithstanding, Katie was a smart cookie. Not only do you not know what she did, you couldn't find it in the program no matter how hard you searched. You couldn't tell the difference between how it was, and how it is, although that probably says more about your skill than hers. Of course, that didn't matter much, did it? The most important thing for your lot was that you couldn't let an Old Thinker be seen to win. Even if you weren't sure exactly what it was, she was winning. And, if you can't beat her, you sure as hell couldn't let her live to tell the tale. A high-ranking member of the silver suited brigade defects to the other side right under your noses. Phaw, she has to be killed! Does that sound about right?' I pressed.

Abers just sat there, red with anger, his eyes awake now, focused and unwavering on some arbitrarily chosen spot on the table between us. Unconsciously, he rapidly bounced his left knee, the action, some sort of comfort or pressure release valve I couldn't allow.

"BANG!" I slammed the table with my right hand, causing the glass to jump along with Abers. 'Well? I've never met a moralist that didn't have an opinion they wouldn't share.'

Despite my attempt to disrupt his thoughts and draw him into an honest answer, his focus returned to that spot on the table, where it remained while he took a series of deep breaths to calm himself before finally responding.

'I am part of a project team, tasked with designing a program to protect the ideology of New Think, in perpetuity.' Began Abers. 'This program is being designed and implemented at the request of the New Think Guides, directly. The protection of the program's integrity is of the utmost importance and is the responsibility of every member of the team. They are to protect it with their lives if necessary, for the greater good of humanity is at stake.' Abers reeled off this statement like it was an advertising slogan. Spoken calmly and slowly despite his recent bout of anger, as if he was reading it from a teleprompter on the inside of his head.

'Protect it with their lives, aye?' I said. 'Is that what you believe Katie did? Gave up her life to protect the integrity of the program against her own personal swing towards Old Think?'

Abers paused a couple of beats, glancing at me briefly, before responding again. 'I am part of a project team, tasked with…'

Whilst Abers repeated his mantra verbatim, Sly sent me some thoughts via Chatter. 'He seems to have gone into some sort of premeditated story he's planning to hide behind.' she wrote, rather stating the obvious. 'Having said that, he's definitely rattled. Perhaps try one more time from another angle. If that doesn't work, we can sweat him a little longer and try again later. At the end of the day, we have the evidence of complicity, or at the very least, his failure to act. Moralists are both hated and feared as it is, even by New Thinkers. Should be easy to sell that to the people. He's a goner either way. Perhaps with a little more time in the sweatbox, he'll see that clearly.'

'Yes, I suppose so.' I typed while Abers took a breath. 'But, only so long as he actually believes he has something to fear from a conviction.'

I looked up from the device to my prisoner, now reciting his ode for the third time without any goading from me. His eyes remained fixed at that same point on the table that seemed to centre him for the endless repetition of his lines. 'If you're quite finished with your little spiel, Mr Abers, I have a few more questions for you.' I said.

While Abers appeared somewhat calmed by his repeated phrases, I was confident in gambling that, as a proud man, it would only take a little personal needling to get his blood boiling again.

'How do you think your moralist peers and supervisors at the Global Moralist Alliance (*GMA*) will handle your "failure" to uphold the Global standards?' I asked. 'I mean, I know bullying is no longer accepted… but, they may make an exception for you, given you have been rather pathetic. And I believe retribution is very popular in your guild.'

This seemed to break the spell. His eyes snapping up to meet my own, cutting short yet another recital. 'What failures?!' He replied defiantly.

'We've detailed those, Mr Abers. Are you suffering some sort of memory loss?' I fired back. 'I suppose that would explain your lack of action in Katie's office. Perhaps you simply forgot what you were supposed to do.'

Abers didn't respond at this slight, merely shaking his shoulders slightly and readying himself for another round of the ode.

'How about this one.' I shouted in an attempt to cut him off. 'You were an embedded moralist at OGT and yet you failed miserably to see or stop Katie from over accessing Old Think materials. Basically, you not only allowed her to turn Old Think, you actually stood by and watched while she brought those ideals back to life. So useless were you, in fact, that several other people in your team noticed and tried to stop her themselves. And what did you do? Nothing! The very foundations of New Think were not just being questioned but outright rejected by a card-carrying New Thinker, who knew damn well what she was doing, and you did nothing! This was your responsibility, Adam! Your territory! Your damn cause, and you did nothing! Goes against everything you just told me in your little spiel there. Come to think of it Adam, that confirms everything us Old Thinkers always thought about your kind. Weak! Pathetic! Utterly disillusioned fools! You and all your moralist mates are nothing but sulking, whining, spineless weaklings, who talk about defending the righteous ways of their superior ideals, and then when the heats on, you go to water. You're nothing but a coward. You didn't take her in for questioning, you didn't do what moralists are supposed to do, which is to alert "ICE" (*the Isolation, Coercion & Education team*) and have her taken in for "Treatment". You didn't alert the DSSMD that she may be an imminent threat to New Think. From what I can tell, you didn't even monitor her behaviour, or the quality of her work during the period that she was reading Old Think books. If you did, she would never have had to be shot at all. You just stood meekly by and let it happen. You watched her lose her faith, then let Cheq and Sophia do all the dirty work. Hell, OGT even had to call in the much-maligned Police Service to run interference and provide protection. Have you no pride? Do you really have nothing to say about any of this?'

Abers, now positively luminescent with rage, had shifted his focus from the safety of the table to the direct opposite of my own. Our eyes bore into one another, the weight of my words obviously straining his pride, though not enough to break him. Something was still holding his tongue. Something he was so committed to, or fearful of, that he would swallow his pride and shut his mouth in the face of withering criticism and taunts. He simply repeated his New Think mantra all over again…

'Okay then. If that's the way you want to play it, we have what we need. We've already started drafting our public perception case. We'll publish on the government streams first so that all your fellow moralists will see you've been discredited and shamed. Meanwhile, you can return to your little hovel until we need you again. Thanks for all your assistance, Adam. We really couldn't have done it without you.' I added winking at him, confident he knew I was a referring to his unwilling release of the damming surveillance footage during his arrest.

Abers looked at me, still red with rage, now almost with a hint of pity coming over his face. 'You have no idea what you're up against.' he said. He watched me as if waiting for some sort of response, right up until he was marched out of the room. 'It's stronger than we ever imagined.' he muttered to himself as he left.

One out, one in. After Abers, my next interrogee was a project assistant named Maleena. Maleena had seemed unremarkable in terms of her position on the team. Particularly because she was somewhat lower down the totem pole. To paraphrase Orwell, Maleena was less equal than her counterparts on this project. That, mind you, was the very reason I wanted to speak to her. Specifically, I wanted to speak to her after the Moralist, whose repercussions she no doubt fears, so that I offer him no scraps of repeated information from the others with which he could punish his colleagues.

When she entered the room, I saw Maleena was as physically bland as her status. So bland, in-fact, I couldn't recall having interviewed her the first time around. I know it sounds harsh, but the reality is she looked both common and forgettable all at once. She had shoulder length, straight, light brown hair, only notable now as it was heavily messed by a night of cramped, sweaty confinement. Her eyes were of a perfect scale to match the size and shape of her face. Not so that they were beautiful, just such that their evenness made them blend in to the blur of her nose and mouth. She wore a modest, simple, midnight coloured dress that ran to the top of her calves, apparently not being up to the standards of the silver suited mafia. The dress covered her shoulders, its mid length sleeve stopping halfway down her bicep. There was nothing wrong or unusual about the look, which is entirely my point. She simply didn't stand out in any way, whatsoever. As though, had she not been sitting right in front of me, and, had I not specifically sought to speak to her, I'd never have known she was there.

'So, Maleena, how are you enjoying the perks of criminal life thus far?' I asked, intentionally appearing disinterested as I turned my glass upon the table. I could see in those quiet brown eyes, her furrowed brow, and the slight oily shine of her skin that the stress of cramped confinement was leaving its mark. In the old days, long haul airline travel could cause this sensation, unclean, uncomfortable and un-free. Of course, that's not something most could relate to these days, because there are no long-haul passenger flights for the common Global citizen. Or any other flights, for that matter. Global Guides and what they term "The necessary few" are the only people allowed to fly. There are lots of reasons for that, not least of which is that they simply couldn't get the balance of weight, passenger space, and battery power right on Electronic Aircraft (*EA's*) of sufficient size to transport large groups of people. Not to mention that the time taken to recharge those batteries off the inefficient renewable power sources, made time between flights, and airport space unmanageable. There were attempts to use special paints to absorb the friction of air passing over the surface of the aircraft to recharge the battery as the plane flew, however, these were unreliable and extraordinarily expensive. They also worked in opposition to the laminar flow of air one seeks to create over the wing, to support the slippery, efficient progress of modern fixed-wing aircraft. That's not to mention that they don't want people to have the freedom of travel and see for themselves that the world outside their own Global city hasn't changed for the better or worse, despite all the sacrifice.

'I'm not a criminal.' replied Maleena, bringing me back from distraction. She looked at me hopefully, as if that statement alone might lead me to move along.

'That's funny.' I said, 'I have surveillance footage that says you are. But, if you really believe you've done nothing wrong, then what are you afraid of?' I asked.

Maleena's eyes had dropped to the centre of the table right where Abers' had been. Observing her form, I got the impression it wasn't me she feared, more likely what my questions might reveal. 'I will require an answer from you, Maleena.' I pushed after a full minute of silence.

'It's not you I'm afraid of.' she said, appearing to read my thoughts.

'Who then?' I asked. 'Who or what are you afraid of?'

'I… I can't say.' she replied, still focussed at that point on the table.

'Do you admit you entered the OGT building with twenty-one other people via the basement roller door, travelled up in the service lifts to level 7, before moving down to Katie Hansley's office, where you stood watching and listening as Cheq Fencegap questioned Katie about why she betrayed New Think, and how she altered the program to undermine the psychological traps that had been planned?'

Maleena looked at me again now, terror creeping into her eyes. 'Do you admit' I continued, 'that once Cheq realised Katie wasn't going to tell him what she'd done, he raised the pistol he'd been carrying in his hand and shot her point blank in the head, ending her life right then and there?'

I left the question hanging, like the reverberation of sound following the bang of a gunshot. Her breathing became jagged before finally she cracked. Maleena had raised her eyes from her safe place to hear the question before lowering them again, looking down at the table and feeling every word like a blow to the head. Tears streamed down her cheeks and a gentle sobbing bob took hold of her shoulders and torso.

'Answer… my damn… question!' I said forcefully, without resorting to shouting.

'Yes… Yes, I was there, I saw it.' said Maleena, collapsing under the pressure.

'You saw what?!' I asked, teetering on the edge of relief.

'What you said, everything. I was there, and I watched Cheq shoot Katie… I didn't know Katie was going to die, I swear… They just said I had to be part of the team and go along with whatever happened… They said that if I believed in protecting the environment, in protecting humanity… If I cared at all about the Global world, then I needed to keep my mouth shut, no matter what happened, no matter what you said, I just needed to stick to the script… just stick to the story and everything would be okay. They said it was for the greater good. Don't question it, just do the right thing. They said my life would be in danger if I said anything, or if I broke from the narrative… But, I never thought they were actually going to kill someone… New Think is supposed to be about saving the world, saving people, not destroying them… or killing them…'

After getting this out, Maleena broke into uncontrollable crying and childlike wails of despair. The cry of a terrified person who knows not where to turn. She raised her shaking hands, turning their clammy palms face up to catch her falling head.

I took a deep breath, frankly, feeling some relief, joy even, at finally having someone tell me the truth. Maleena had only admitted the occurrence of what I'd seen with my own eyes. Still, in a world like this, where New Thinkers could discredit the very air you breathe, simple confirmation of reality was a rare and beautiful thing. It had been days since we started investigating this, and that was the first time someone had plainly admitted that what we'd seen was real.

'Thank God!' Said Sly via Chatter, rather uncharacteristically for her. There is no God or religion anymore under New Think. You believe in the Guides and the ideology, nothing else…

Then it hit me. 'Did you say they told you to keep your mouth shut no matter what "I" said?' I asked, emphasising the pronoun that identified me, specifically.

'What?' Said Maleena, utterly engrossed in the task of emitting full bodied sobs and sniffs.

'Did they specifically say to keep your mouth shut, no matter what "I" said?' I repeated. 'As in me, specifically.' I clarified.

'Um, yes that's right.' said Maleena who had now strayed completely from the script she was meant to be following, and who appeared to have clearly not understood the significance of what she'd said.

Sly did though and sent me a Chatter message telling me to meet her in the hall. 'I'll give you a moment to gather yourself, Maleena. Fair warning, you should steel yourself while I'm out there, we're not done here yet.' I said, standing from my chair and heading out into the hall.

'You need to ask her who the hell told her that, and when!' said Sly without preamble. 'That's the hook right there! It'll help tie the crime and the underlying plot together and go towards pre-meditation and motive for continuing to commit other crimes in support of the original. Plus, it will answer the now intriguing, and terrifying, question as to why they thought, or worse yet, how they knew, that you in particular, of all the officers and detectives at our station, would be managing this case.'

'Well, I'd say they had a pretty good shot at getting the fix in. We already know Captain Ironie is deep into this thing, Chief Blindspot too, so perhaps the explanation is that simple.' I said. 'They knew that if anything happened here, I would be assigned to the case. The answer I want to hear is, why?'

'You might be right. Although that doesn't quite explain it.' said Sly. 'From Maleena's description, it seems as if "you" were always part of the plan. Crucial to it, in fact. As if they knew they were going to commit a crime that drew significant police attention, which might be why Ironie and Blindspot were drawn into the plans to begin with. Because you, you in particular, were always planned to be the detective that investigated it.'

Sly's assessment struck me. She was right. The fact that Ironie and Blindspot were involved, didn't fully explain why they had identified me as the police officer who would ask the questions she wasn't to answer. Did they think I wasn't a good enough cop to actually solve the case, so they planned to assign me, assuming that so long as they stuck to their story, I'd never get my man? Or, maybe they felt I was too good and wanted to discredit me somehow, or as an Old Thinker that no matter what I found I'd never be believed anyway… Or, perhaps it's something else, something worse, something more sinister…

I headed back to the makeshift interrogation room where Maleena was still sobbing, now more gently and controlled. She looked up briefly as I entered the room, her sad, wet, and puffy eyes lending sincerity to the emotion she was displaying.

'Just two or three more questions for now, Maleena.' I said, trying to keep her in a calm and pliable state. 'Firstly, who told you not to answer my questions honestly, or to keep your mouth shut, as it were?'

As soon as I said this, the fear flooded right back into her eyes, her mouth sagging open as she flitted between trying to stay silent and desperately wanting to release herself from the burden of the lie. As I watched her, realisation must have dawned that she'd given away far more than intended. Her mouth snapped shut, and she rapidly shook her head side to side like a child refusing to eat their peas.

'Come on Maleena, the cat's out of the bag now. We've arrested every one of your co-conspirators. There's no one to fear out there, because they're all in here, with you. Someone's going to crack, someone's going to give in and sell out the team in order to get a favourable Public Perception Trial (*PPT*). It may as well be you. Because, make no mistake about it, there's a whole lot of people going to jail for this.'

Maleena seemed to consider this for a moment before responding. 'It won't matter. It won't help. They're not all here, and you'll never get them all. It isn't possible. There isn't a building in the Global world that can house all of them.'

'How do you know that, Maleena? How do you know they're not all here?'

'Because it's far bigger than us.' she said. 'We are just one part of a much bigger plan. We were tasked with designing and writing the program and then with protecting its integrity. But it wasn't our idea. Not this teams, at least.'

'Then who's was it?' I asked evenly, trying to contain my excitement that more real information might finally be flowing my way.

'I don't know!' she replied, folding her arms in an attempt to be strong and instead coming across as comically ridiculous. What little makeup she had on was streaked now, giving her the look of a silent film character.

'Maleena, people who don't know anything have a lot of trouble gaining favour with both the Police Service and the public's perception. You need to start telling me what the hell is going on, and you need to do it right now!' I demanded, raising my voice and slamming my hand down on the table again. It hadn't worked with Adam. He'd expected a bit of noise. Maleena, on the other hand, is a whole different kettle of fish.

'You're not allowed to torture me, you know?…' she cried, with just a tad of defiance creeping in.

'Well, while I might not be the most enthralling conversationalist, I can assure you this is not torture. You don't want to know what real torture is like. Although, I suppose the general New Think mind fuck is a kind of torture of its own… Now answer the damn question!'

'Look, Matthias is our team leader. We get our directions from him. Except, he's not the real boss, he's just a people manager, an intermediate, who answers directly to… Cheq.'

The name came out as if it were an entity or a business, not a person.

'Yes, well, I assumed that.' I said. 'He certainly seemed to be the one calling the shots… and firing them.'

'No… I mean yes, I know that. But, what I mean is, he's one of "them." Not just one of the Guides, he's one of the "Inner Circle." They're a group so elite in status they sit above even the rest of the Guides. They decide what it's okay for us all to do… For all New Thinkers, all Global citizens. They decide what it's okay to think, to believe, to read, to see, to learn, to eat, everything. And they make those determinations not impulsively, but after careful coordination and planning, to ensure they align with their broader objective. Whilst the group that's at the very top might only be small, they aren't alone. They have people everywhere. Committed, loyal people who will do whatever it takes to plan, implement, and enforce their instructions… Or punish any failure to comply.'

'Okay, so if that's the case, why is Cheq Fencegap of the inner circle getting his hands dirty in this mess?' I asked.

'I don't know. That's what scares me so much. Whatever this is really about, it must be huge. Big enough that he can't trust the details to anyone else. A problem greater than the sum of its parts, so to speak.'

'You don't think it's about the program you were working on?' I asked.

'Well, yes, possibly. It's certainly something specific to this project, except I'm not quite sure why Katie's apparent defection was so much of an issue. She wasn't in charge of designing the whole program. She didn't have any actual oversight or control of the coding or final product, only the psychological channelling elements that guide people in specific New Think directions. Approved Decision Support is how we term it.'

'So, what are these New Think directions built into the program?' I asked. 'Are they new, New Think directions?'

'I really don't know.' She said, sounding scared again. 'Despite what you may think, we aren't all deliberately evil or "in on the plot," so to speak. I believe in what New Think stands for and I liked that OGT's technology and software could guide people towards it. That's why I wanted to join the company. Even so, when all is said and done, I'm just a project coordinator. A secretary of sorts, really. I had nothing to do with the actual detail of the program.'

'Well, you may say you're "just" a secretary, but I've known plenty of secretaries and project coordinators in my time, and they all knew more than anybody else on a project. Usually more than their boss, in fact.'

'I suppose I am privy to a lot of information.' she replied, allowing pride to briefly pierce the wall of sadness. 'That's why I was sworn to secrecy on pain of death. That's why I was there that night. They figured the best way to avoid people talking was to make them complicit in their despicable activities. Despite all that, I really don't know what the program was about or why people were being killed because of it. It was only meant to be an internet upgrade with some built-in features to strengthen the integration of progressive thought in society. That's what Katie was meant to be doing, just reviewing Old Think ideals and thought patterns and building in psychological barriers to prevent people following them. We would be guiding them away from evil.'

Maleena looked hopeful now, as if her clarifying explanations had cleared her conscience, giving confidence that her involvement was only as prescribed and that this should eradicate any guilt for her part in the horrors in which she participated. I wasn't buying that.

'One last question.' I said. 'When did Cheq and Matthias tell you not to answer my questions? When exactly?'

Maleena took a moment to think on this, her head tilting down in thoughtful repose. Her unremarkable eyes, however, looked up as if counting in her head. 'Um, six months ago, or thereabouts I suppose. It wasn't long before the project started. I was pulled into a room and told that this project was of the utmost importance and secrecy, and that compliance with the directions I was to be given was non-optional.'

'So before you even started working on this project, you were told it would lead you to a point that "I" meaning "me" personally, would bring you in for questioning and you would need to lie about it?' I asked, incredulously.

'Um, I suppose so, yes.' she replied sheepishly. Maleena was now affecting an innocent look, no doubt hoping to curate the mood here as one of shared concern with this most unusual of revelations as something for us both to ponder the meaning of. I still wasn't buying it.

'And that didn't seem odd to you?' I asked, with deep distrust of her affectation.

'It does now. I didn't really think about it then. I was scared by the threats about sticking to the narrative and what would happen if I didn't. There's even a specific set of phrases we're meant to use.'

'Who was in the room at that time you were told all this?'

'Only Matthias and Adam Abers.'

'So, they knew I would be involved in this too?'

'Yes, of course. They were the ones that told me.' she said, nodding to enhance the validity of her words.

'Then, would it be fair to assume that every person in here either received the same talk you did, or gave that talk?' I continued.

'Well, I didn't actually see it all happen, but if they were in Katie's office that night she was killed, then it's almost certain they were under the same obligations as me.'

'Thank you Maleena, you've been very helpful.' I said. 'Agents! You can take her back and bring in the next one.' I shouted.

Maleena stood and moved past me, leaving in her wake the smell of fear mixed with dead perfume and the distinct aroma of a hot night spent on a hard floor. As she moved towards the door, she asked the agents escorting her to pause a second. 'Detective?' she said.

'Yes?' I replied.

'Please don't tell them it was me that told you…'

I nodded and smiled comfortingly, the human side of me trying to calm her fear, while the cop inside me knew I'd do whatever it took to secure a conviction.

Once Maleena had been removed, I went out into the corridor to catch up with Sly while the next suspect was being retrieved. As I exited the door, I saw both Milly and Naomi holding a similar discussion to the one I was planning with Sly. She appeared behind me while I watched, neither of us quite able to make out what they were saying.

'How do you think they're going?' she asked.

'That's exactly what I was wondering. After that interview, I think I'll have to go over and ask.' As I said that, Milly, who'd been facing towards me, waved us over.

'You having any luck?' he asked.

'Not a lot.' I replied, keeping my cards close to my chest. 'We got confirmation of what we already knew, which frankly felt like quite an achievement. Trouble is, without anything else, I'm left holding the basket I came with. How about you?'

'Well, we got something new. Or at least we thought we did. Until we realised that all four interviewees we've seen were saying the exact same thing, verbatim.'

'Oh, right. Was it the bit about being part of a project team, working at the direct request of the Guides, protecting the integrity of New Think in perpetuity or some such thing?'

'Yes.' said Naomi, 'That's the one. Not quite in that order, but you're close enough to confirm that this is a dictate to be studied, committed to memory, then repeated upon questioning about these murders.'

'Not just the murders.' I said. 'That's what I found out. Whatever this thing is, they'd planned for it to end up here all along.'

'What do you mean?' asked Milly.

I decided to abandon my fears. After all, it's possible the people I stood here with already knew about the plot. And even if they didn't, telling them could hardly be worse than finding out I'm blindly following their pre-laid plan. 'I mean, they knew not only that they would be questioned by police but that "I" personally, would be the officer doing the questioning.'

'So, what, the murders, the attempted murders, all of this was just part of a plan to get you here?' asked Milly.

'Yes, apparently so.' I said, not yet knowing why or what else to say.

'To what end?' asked Naomi.

'That's what we need to find out!' I replied, allowing a little frustration to creep into my voice. 'We need to ascertain why they would do all of this. Why they'd kill their own people just to get me to ask them questions so they could lie to me with some predetermined message. It doesn't make any damn sense! Is this all some sort of sick game?'

I was already frustrated and suspicious of Naomi. For her to stand there and ask the bleeding obvious was a bridge too far. Sensing I might be about to snap, Sly placed her hand gently on my arm, giving me the "pity/pull your head in" combination look that only a woman can. That, accompanied by the calming persuasion of her perfumed aroma, calmed me down.

'I can't say that I've got an explanation to offer.' said Milly, placating me. 'What does seem clear is that we've got some new questions to ask. Did they say anything else?'

'Not really. Only confirmation that they were all in on it. Whatever "it" is.'

'I suppose we should get back to it then.' said Naomi shooting a look at Milly before checking her smart watch and setting off towards their interrogation room.

Sly and I moved back towards our own room, briefly comparing notes on what we'd heard so far. We agreed Maleena had certainly been helpful to a point, having confirmed the entire group was complicit and had been lying, even if she left us with more questions than she'd answered.

The next seven interogees came and went without sharing a single word I hadn't heard before. They didn't even change the order of them. Each one denied involvement, looked surprised, confused, then afraid when I explained we had audio-visual proof and corroborating statements confirming they'd conspired. Following which, and despite that revelation, each one repeated the pre-prepared phrase, evidentially not knowing, or unauthorised to say another word.

I soon began to realise it wasn't so much that they were intentionally lying or deceiving with the phrase. After all, in the Global world, you're always told what to think, how to act and what to do. They simply did what they were told on faith, believing they would never be led astray and hoping desperately that no matter what they saw or did, that it was, in fact, the right thing to do. How could they possibly do more? …

In a Global world, where the end always justifies the means, it's easy to fall into the trap of assuming that a failure to meet the end goal may bring into question the means. Not so. As far as New Thinkers are concerned, where the end can never be reached, or when reached, fails to justify the means, you simply write it off as having been worth the effort to at least disrupt the norm and prevent the continuation of the world as it was. Which was evil, of course. If the means simply extends the gap between the end and the norm, then all the better, and if it costs the many, to benefit the few, then that redistribution of wealth, from the many, topping up that of the few, is just fine, so long as the many are never allowed to disagree.

What New Thinkers are absolutely certain of, is that less many, and less few, is the ultimate goal and should there be nobody left to assess the means, then the end will have certainly been met.

Having now burned through most of the group, there were only two people left to interview. The big fish in my pond. I'd saved them til last, not because I expected them to give me the most information, I had actually hoped to garner something more useful from the earlier interviews that I could subsequently use against them. Unfortunately, all I really got were more unanswered questions. The reason I saved them til last was because Captain Ironie had been one of the most involved police officers of all, having assigned the case to Shaz and I, then mislead our efforts from the inside before attempting to kill us both. There's no doubt she had to be heavily involved in whatever this is, from both a planning and execution standpoint. She also had to be more than just some sort of overzealous security. Some patsy. From what I can tell, Isabelle Ironie intentionally messed with our heads, thoroughly enjoying it all the while. I still don't know what the plan was, or how much of what happened was actually part of that plan. What I do know, is how deceptive and manipulative she must have been throughout. Now I intend to find out why, and then make sure that Susan Sly helps me convince the public to punish her to the fullest extent.

Naturally, the Guides have the final say on everything, so this needs to be an impenetrable and overwhelmingly convincing narrative. One that the Guides themselves cannot control and twist to their own benefit. Especially for my final guest, Mr Cheq Fencegap. As a Guide and a member of the inner circle himself, I'm basically going to need an open and willing confession of guilt and wrongdoing. Without it, his money, his influence, and his all-powerful position will make it nearly impossible to achieve a just outcome.

I was standing in the interrogation room doorway, looking in at the empty room. The hallway behind me was empty too, Sly having gone to get a drink whilst the agents removed my latest interrogee and brought in Isabelle. I moved around the corner so that Ironie wouldn't see me before entering. I wanted her to feel as uncertain as possible about who was going to interrogate her and how much we already knew, right up until the point where I'm looking into her eyes. It mightn't be much, but if you've only one card to play and only one chance to play it, then you play the hand you've got or fold and watch the show. While I hid around the corner, another idea occurred to me.

'Shaz, how's it going with your tech wiz?' I asked when she answered my call on the fourth ring.

'Iman's doing a good job.' she said confidently. 'We've been working our way through the OGT program with the guidance of Watcher, and Iman is mapping it out as we go so that we can paint a clear picture of what it's meant to do, what changes Katie made, and when.'

'Didn't Watcher say he could tell us or show us, or whatever it is that computer personalities do, exactly what Katie did anyway?' I asked. 'It told me she programmed it to do just that.'

'Well, yes, that's true she did do that, and yes, Watcher has told us the changes that Katie made. The trouble is, they're coded changes, and they only make sense in the context of the program.'

'Oh, I see.' I said, though obviously I didn't. It was just more tech speak I didn't really understand.

'You and technology really don't get along, do you?' said Shaz, more a statement than a question.

'We're not so simpatico, no.' I replied. 'So, how long do you think until we know something of value?'

Sharon must have turned the phone away from her ear briefly to speak distantly to Iman before coming back to me. 'He says it could be a couple of days.'

'Days?!' I exclaimed. 'I was hoping to have something to use on these bastards right now.'

'This program is huge, Gaz. It's like an all of internet thing, apparently.' said Shaz, clearly reaching the limit of her own tech knowledge. 'Iman has to track and map Katie's changes in sequence in order to get the full picture. They appear to be very subtle from what we've seen so far. So subtle, in fact, that from what Iman says, if Watcher hadn't instructed him exactly where to look, he would never have found them at all.'

'Well, I guess that explains why the rest of the team resorted to having to confront Katie to ask her about it. It still won't explain why they murdered her until we get the full picture.'

'You're right, but there's nothing I can do about that. You're just going to have to wait. How're your interviews going anyway?' Asked Shaz.

'Not so well, to be honest. They all have some pre-rehearsed rote response they're sticking to despite our evidence to confirm what they did. Each of them says the same thing word for word. Something about being part of a team assigned to the protection of New Think ideology in perpetuity, blah, blah, blah.'

'Well, that's not really a surprise. That's essentially what they did when we initially interviewed them. Except, then it was a lie about how they hadn't been involved at all.'

'Yeah, except the big difference here is they'd always expected to give this phrase directly to "me".' I replied.

'Okay, I mean, you are on the case. Why wouldn't they expect that?'

'Because they were given this phrase and told they would need to stick to it when answering my questions, specifically, before they'd even started the project. That's over five months ago…'

On hearing this, Sharon went silent for a full minute, during which I heard Sly re-enter the closet viewing space and Captain Ironie shuffled into the makeshift interrogation room.

'WYA?' came an annoying shorthand message via Chatter.

'What?!' I typed in response to Sly, while waiting for Shaz to recover.

'Where You At?' Replied Sly using poor grammar if far more pleasing long hand. To be honest, I already knew what she meant by WYA. The ability to understand most modern shorthand is innate, although if you ask me, there are far too many bloody acronyms for all sorts of stupid phrases. Most of which don't make sense even when the full English, sorry, "Global" words are used. As an ex-military man, I believe acronyms are reserved for important messages that have to be delivered quickly and decisively. "Where are you" is not one of them. "Where You At" is just plain wrong… 'I'm around the corner, updating Sharon.' I typed.

Meanwhile, Shaz was still yet to speak in reply to my revelation. I could almost hear her shaking her head and rattling her brain trying to work out how it all fits together. 'I don't have any more answers yet, and I'm about to put the screws to our good friend, Captain Ironie.' I added, trying to hurry her along.

'Okay, be careful there Gaz.' She replied, having finally recovered her powers of speech. 'I don't know about you, but you're the only one I trust there. Just watch your back. You're obviously being set up for something.'

'Message received.' I replied. 'You stay alert too, Shaz. Listen, the door of my apartment has a wood texture look, which is misleading, because it's actually a hollow steel door in a steel frame. Lock those top and bottom latches and you should be able to sit tight for a fair while if anything happens.'

'Thanks, I'll do that.' she said. 'Oh, and Gaz, if it starts to get iffy in there, make an excuse and get the hell out. If we have to make a stand against these nut jobs, so be it, but I don't want to be stuck here on my own. I want you here by my side.'

'Roger that.' I replied, wondering if she just wanted to die with me, or had perhaps meant something she hadn't said. 'Oh, before I forget. The reason I called was to ask if you and Iman can stitch together some of the surveillance footage we have showing Ironie's involvement in the various crimes? Yours, mine and Chens ought to do it.'

'Sure, I can do that. Shouldn't take more than 10 minutes. Just do me a favour and make sure you record her response when she sees it. I want to know if that bitch is smiling or sad.'

Chapter 33

The Ironie of it all…

'Do you really think that you can get away with this?!' spat an angry Ironie as I entered the room. Her fierce eyes bore into me as she sat impatiently, somehow still managing to affect the demeanour of a pacing madman. Her normally straight black hair was wild and messy, her face sweaty and oily like the rest.

'Get away with what, exactly?' I asked, wondering if this was the point that I'd finally find out what I'm really being set up for.

'Are you fucking kidding me?! I'm your boss!' she yelled back.

'Were, my boss.' I corrected, before leaning back in my chair, folding my arms and smiling as a challenge to her temperament.

'You're right, you know.' said Ironie. 'Past tense is appropriate when your career is about to come to an end. As soon as I'm out of here, you won't be an officer anymore. You'll be a prisoner, instead! Worse yet, an Old Think prisoner, kept separate from the rest to avoid infecting the herd. Of course, there'll also be the New Think education camp that you'll get to attend… again. It'll be like you're a whole new man when you're done. Shame you won't live long enough to re-join our efforts to save the world. Still, at least you'll die knowing that the rest of us are out here enjoying the fruits of all our sacrifice and hard work.'

'Captain, are you trying to tell me you have been wrongly arrested? Accused of a crime, or in your case, crimes, you didn't commit?'

'Yes, obviously!' She replied.

'So, you don't believe you've committed any crimes?' I asked, no longer surprised at the arrogant indifference displayed by all but one of the prisoners and yet still feeling the need to really confirm they've understood what I asked.

'All I've done is my job, trying to support my officers and uphold New Think laws to protect the rights of the global citizens.' she answered, no doubt fully believing her own lies.

'Okay. Why don't we breakdown how you went about carrying out those duties you listed. Firstly, you assigned Detective Wilson and I to investigate the murder of Katie Hansley. A crime that you never intended us to solve… Not only that, it was a crime you knew had been planned from before OGT's project had even begun.'

'Lies!' shouted Ironie. But her eyes failed to deliver the same message. 'I want to see my Dis-Rep!' she demanded.

A Dis-Rep being a Dis-information Representative. They're like moralists who monitor the dissemination of information and ensure that it's accurate, factual and suitable for human consumption. Of course, what I mean by that, is that they ensure it's "New Think approved" and not considered offensive to New Thinkers. It has nothing to do with accuracy or facts. Each member of the Global World is assigned a Dis-Rep they can call upon to represent their concerns in scenarios such as this.

'That's a hard NO from me.' I replied.

'You can't do that!' she yelled, her face turning a crimson red. 'You can't deny me access to my Dis-Rep. You haven't got the right to just fill my head with your Old Think nonsense and lies.'

'I'm not filling your head with anything of the sort.' I replied. 'The information I'm going to share with you will be very recent indeed. I'm accusing you of committing violent crimes for which I have evidentiary proof.'

'Well, I'll need my Dis-Rep to review and verify the authenticity of that information.' said Ironie.

'Then you're in luck. Your Dis-Rep is Chief Blindspot, is it not?' I asked casually.

'Yes…' she replied warily, sitting up straighter as she did.

'Well, she's currently being interrogated in another room as a fellow prisoner of yours. So, you can rest assured that she too will hear the details of your criminal activities, along with her own, and be offered an opportunity to respond. As I'm sure you understand because you are, or were, a police officer, neither you nor Blindspot will be able to discredit the information. Facts are facts, and in this case, you are the criminals. You of all people know criminals don't get to decide guilt. That's up to public perception. Your very own ideology at work. How proud you must be.'

While I talked, my device buzzed on the table alerting me that Sharon had sent me the surveillance footage I'd requested. I could tell that Ironie was about to mount another counterattack of some sort, so I cut her off at the pass. 'I want you to watch something and tell me what you see.'

Placing my device down on the table between us and using the holographic projection function, I played the footage. Iman and Shaz had done a great job stitching it together. It was all about Ironie, following the chronological order of events in which she partook, like an evil chupacabra terrorising the village. They even included some footage of Ironie meeting the reporter to leak information about the letters. One look at her face told me it had the desired effect. When the recording finished, I didn't wait for her to think about it. I just ploughed on with my questions.

'What that didn't show is what part you played in the assault and torture of Sgt Ease and Detective Wilson at Ease's apartment. Although, I was thinking you might want to tell me about that yourself. Don't launch in too hastily mind you. I want you to tell me about each of your crimes in sequence. I want you to tell me again after watching yourself, a police captain, observe an innocent person being shot in the head point blank, leak case sensitive information to the media, attempt to murder Detective Wilson in the hospital, then attempt to murder me at OGT, just how it was that you were only supporting your Officers and upholding New Think laws…'

Ironie was gobsmacked. Her mouth fell open as she tried to comprehend what she had seen and what we obviously already knew. A small blue vein appeared, winding its way down the centre of her forehead. 'Where the hell did you get that?' She demanded.

'What are you, new?' I asked. 'Have you had your memory erased? This is the Global World, Isabelle. This is your world. There are surveillance cameras, mood screens, satellite drones, security drones, personal device cameras, chip scanners, you name it, it's watching you everywhere you go. Hell, there's barely a single object in the world that isn't actively spying on you and connected to the IOT. Why are you so surprised about this?' I asked.

'There were assurances… we… I… was told I would be protected.' she answered. 'That nobody would ever know I had anything to do with this. I was told you would suspect, but never actually know for sure.'

'You were told that I personally would suspect, never actually knowing for sure of your involvement?' I asked, growing ever more concerned about what my involvement in this was supposed to be.

'Yes.' she said, offering me another jolt of plain honesty pleasure.

'So, I take it you've given up the pretence of not being involved, or of knowing nothing about what's going on?' I continued.

'Yes.' said Ironie again, without elaborating.

'And you admit your crimes?' I continued, surprised at how easily and quickly she'd dropped her defences.

'No, I most certainly do not admit to any crimes.' She bristled.

'What?!' I blurted out, snapped back from my moment of joy, and struggling to grasp how the hell Ironie could admit all that she did, without accepting that her actions amounted to crimes.

'I committed no "crimes".' she said confidently, as if that clarified her position.

'Even though you do admit to doing all the things you just saw yourself do in the video?' I queried, wondering if I'd perhaps gone crazy.

'Yes, of course, except they aren't crimes.' she said stoically. 'Those are the actions of a Global patriot. I am a soldier for good, doing what must be done in the name of protecting our Global way of life.

Those deaths are just…. sacrifices for the greater good. Necessary culls of dangerous and weak-willed people, who were set to betray us and endanger the green planet we're fighting so hard to restore.'

I chose to let Ironie's insane belief that her violent and murderous actions were justified as being for "the greater good" slide for now. I'd heard this defence too many times before, and besides, it's public perception that decides what side of the line her actions fall. There were other questions that needed to be answered here.

'Isabelle, who was it that told you I'd be the person asking you questions? Was it Chief Blindspot?' I asked.

'No, Blindspot is just like me. A soldier in the fight to save the world.'

'Who then?' I pressed.

'Our lead Guide, Cheq.' she replied without hesitation. She'd said it as if I should already have known. As though, because she had always known that I was part of this plan, that I should have known that, too. Like we were all just actors in a stage show, obliged to play our assigned parts and hit our lines on cue.

'So, Cheq planned this whole thing more than six months ago, hey?' I asked.

'Yes, and recruited the team, too.' said Ironie, not missing a beat. 'Actually, that's the main reason you were promoted. You needed to be in a position to run the investigation.'

'What?!' I blurted, starting to feel myself on shaky ground. It's one thing to be the unwitting centrepiece of a plot. It's another entirely to find your whole life has been planned for you without your knowledge.

'That's right. I hadn't really wanted to promote you at all. Not because you're not capable as an officer, but merit is a thing of the past. Frankly, I didn't want to have two Old Think detectives on my team. Especially not a male one. Even more especially, not you!'

'Subtle.' I said. 'Though I suppose you lot never really did grasp the concept of that inclusivity you keep sprouting about.' Ironie simply rolled her eyes in response. See, New Thinkers truly believe that virtually everybody has been wronged and that those wrongs require restitution and quota-based inclusion in every role and every organisation in the world… Except of course traditional white males which they see as the very embodiment of all that is evil. Although to be fair, in Cheq's case, they might have a point.

'So why did I have to be a part of this? What was the ultimate goal here?' I asked.

'That "is" the ultimate goal here.' replied Ironie, again without explanation.

'Huh?! What sort of answer is that?' I asked, feeling my world starting to spin.

‘Your part in this is to try and work it out. To be here, right where you are.’ She continued, twisting the knife.

‘What about the murder?’ I asked. ‘Are you telling me that murder was just part of a plan to get me here and see if I could work out why? Like some sick game of guess who?’

‘If it went that way.’ She replied with casual indifference.

‘Is it safe to assume Katie wasn’t aware that that would be her part in this plot? Surely, she didn’t just go along with this?’

‘No, she was like you. Another unwitting player in the game.’

‘Game?! People died, Isabelle. This is no game. You do understand that, don’t you?’

Ironie had been playing with her hair, straightening it with the fingers of her free hand, the dark strands falling almost into place. She flicked her head to the right now, her hair arching out obediently before falling to rest behind her shoulder.

‘They betrayed New Think.’ she said, as if that explanation needed no embellishment. ‘That is what you might consider the crime of treason, which under Global law is punishable by death.’

‘So, this was all some big game to you? Some test to see if I could solve a New Think murder?’ I asked, still unsure of where to go here. Sly was no help, my device showing zero advice from her.

‘I guess so.’ said Ironie.

‘You guess so? How can you be so damn blasé?!’ I shouted, trying to snap her out of her calm indifference. ‘How can you be so cold and callus, simply watching on as someone is shot point blank, then try to kill your own subordinates? Was that all part of the plan?’

‘I was not privy to everything, Gary, only my part in it. That was to make sure that you were here and running the case. What happened outside of that was just variance that had to be managed. Decisions made, and actions taken, based on how things played out at the time.’

‘Oh right, of course. Managed. I can see how you’d justify that. Oh, I’m sorry Mr and Mrs Hansley, but your daughter is dead… what do you mean why? She was an issue that had to be managed, that’s why! … What about Sharon? Was she always part of this plan, too? Or just a variance that had to be managed?!’ I demanded.

‘Sharon wasn’t a part of the plan so far as I’m aware…’ said Ironie. ‘She wasn’t even your partner when it started.’ The pause in Isabelle’s answer told me she was trying not to say variance again.

‘What about Sgt Ease, who's currently comatose in a hospital?’ I continued, my anger now simmering. ‘I really believed you actually cared about him and Sharon after they were attacked. Turns out you probably arranged it.’

To this, Ironie offered no response at all, while her mood noticeably dimmed. ‘All these people, very nearly including myself, you condemned to death and injury, all in the name of some sick game you were playing at the behest of Cheq fucking Fencegap. Katie, Chen, Jiang, Ease, Sharon, me. You sucked us all into your sick game, then dispatched us when we displeased you.'

'Everyone has free will.' said Ironie. 'All of you were free and still you chose to be here.'

'In a roundabout way, Isabelle, that might be true. Except, none of us really "chose" to be here. Katie didn't choose to die, neither did Chen. Freedom is intrinsically linked to choice, because in order to be free, you must have the option to choose or not choose any given path or action. However, what you and your insane ideological leaders fail to understand, is that the presence of choice does not automatically mean the chooser is free.'

'New Think has done the world a favour by limiting your choices to only those that will benefit the world around you.' preached Ironie. 'We've edited the human way of life so that it's safe and good for everyone. Being free the way you see it is dangerous. Your type of freedom lacked fairness and protections for those that aren't as strong or numerous. Freedom had to be made fairer and easier for people to get it right. This little experiment just proves again that giving people freedom to make choices outside the safety net of New Think is as dangerous as it ever was.'

'Oh, that's what this was, huh? A little experiment to test our ability to handle a little freedom of choice?'

'Not exactly.' said Ironie. 'Although, choice certainly played a part. You Old Thinkers just never know what's good for you. It's nothing but selfish desire. You have to think about sacrificing for the greater good. Katie learned that lesson the hard way.'

'No, Katie was murdered!' I shouted. 'She didn't learn a lesson, and she certainly didn't choose to die. Cheq Fencegap shot her in the head. That's murder, plain and simple. Murder! You know what murder is, right? You're a fucking cop, or you were. You should damn well understand what it means to take someone's life against their will, and what it means to make a dangerous choice. Katie didn't make a dangerous choice. All she did was open her mind and hear an alternate point of view, and you killed her for it. You and your sick, single-minded cabal, of moral and ideological zealots, fucking murdered her!! And it wasn't for the greater good, it was just to silence an alternate view. It's basic New Think 101. Comply or die. Conform or cancel. Promote or perish. You're the most intolerant, anti-inclusive ideology I've ever heard of. I suppose I shouldn't be surprised though, should I. You've been doing it for years.'

Still, Ironie remained indifferent. Completely detached from the harm she'd done and would continue to do. Having satisfied herself with her hair, her attention turned to her nails, inspecting them, absent the tools for rectification work. The one on her right index finger was broken, no doubt an undesired effect of her side gig as a would be assassin. Watching this just made me angrier. I couldn't continue to let her coast through the interrogation, unaffected. I want answers and I want them now!

'What about Sgt Ease?' I asked again, unsatisfied with her earlier sidestep. 'What was his crime? He's one of you, is he not? Quite a committed one in my experience. A New Thinker's New Thinker. What incorrect choice did he make? Or was his violent torture and attempted murder all just part of the plan, too?'

'No.' replied Ironie, her voice softening and her eyes dropping from her hands to the table. 'To put it in words you'd understand, Ease fucked up. He saw something he wasn't meant to, and we couldn't have him talking about it.' Ironie wasn't so flippant now. It was clear that the actions taken against Ease were something she really hadn't wanted to do. It was also clear those actions were her's.

'That wasn't part of the plan then, hey? Another undesirable "variance" to be managed, I suppose… It's not all fun and games, is it. Not everyone was in on the plot. Not everyone saw this as being for the greater fucking good!'

'He was never meant to get hurt!' She said, emotion breaking through her voice. 'When the future of the world and all of humanity is at stake, it's all means necessary.'

'You'll have to forgive me, Isabelle. It was all just a game a minute ago. Now the end of the world's at stake. I can't see that at all.'

'Of course you can't. You can't see anything outside yourself.'

'Then help me, Isabelle. Help me understand. What did Sgt Ease see? What was it that wasn't meant to be a part of this experiment?' I probed.

Ironie sat silently, just swallowing and breathing, short, laboured breaths, the type that precedes an event you fear, or follows surviving the same. Still, they weren't accompanied by words, and there was no indication she might be building up to any sort of a share.

'Was it about the letters Katie had written? Was there something in those that put Ease's life at risk?'

'I'm hardly going to tell you that, am I…' she replied. 'The thing Ease was supposed to die to protect is not something I'm going to divulge to you here.'

'What if he wakes up and remembers while you're stuck in here?' I asked.

'He won't.' she said, definitively.

'And how can you be sure of that?'

'Because there are ways of being sure.' Ironie's tone as she said this was cold, spiteful, and laced with harmful intent.

Her comment sat uncomfortably in my mind, reverberating off the walls and jarring with the hope at which Sharon had hinted. I let it hang for now, willing myself to believe we could always come back to it later, if and when Ease comes round. As far as I know, his fallen angel, Detective Damwell, was there watching over him, anyway.

'One last question for you. How many police officers did you recruit to this cause?'

'I, didn't recruit any of them.' said Isabelle with what sounded like a measure of honesty. As if I had finally asked a question, she could answer truthfully.

'Okay, then. How many officers are in on this?' I asked, changing tact.

'As many as needed.'

'What do you mean by that?'

'I mean, that if another officer is needed, Cheq brings them in. It's as simple as that.'

'What, so every officer at our station, their loyalty is for sale, that easy?'

'Not every Officer.' she said, looking at me coldly. 'And we're not for sale. We're simply ready and willing to do whatever's necessary. It was only Blindspot and I to begin with. Everybody else, we just picked up along the way.'

'When was Clubman recruited?' I asked, exposing my own wound with the question. I hoped Clubman was someone I could have trusted, but in the end, he'd been like all the rest.

A wide smile spread across Ironie's face now as she looked up from her slumping posture, her eyes finally meeting mine. 'Ha, I bet that was a surprise for you.' she said, the gleeful cruelty clear in her voice. 'Don't feel too bad. He wasn't recruited by us until you recruited him yourself.'

'Well, he became a valuable asset to you pretty quickly then.' I replied. 'Kept others silent and I suspect he told you everything I knew.'

'Of course.' she said. 'Although, to be honest, you really didn't know that much. He was mostly just making sure you followed the path we'd laid for you.'

I shook my head. The interrogation was starting to go in circles. A gloating, goading conversation on the part of Captain Ironie. She seemed no less confident that she was still in control now than she had before we started. That tells me she got what she expected from me, and I got virtually nothing from her. Nothing aside from the confirmation of how few allies I have.

'Guards!' I shouted, deciding there was nothing else to be gained here. I took the clunk of Ironie's hand cuff against the table leg as some sort of consolation. At least she was keen to leave.

As Ironie was being escorted from the room, my device rang. It was Sharon, probably eager to find out how the interrogation went. Given how she currently feels about the captain, I imagine it would have been a much more physical encounter had she been here in my stead.

'Shaz, everything okay?' I answered, once Ironie had been removed. 'I didn't resort to torture, if that's what you were hoping to hear.'

'Shame.' said Sharon thoughtfully. 'And yes, we're fine, beavering away here. I've just had a call I think you'll be interested in.'

'Oh, do tell.' I replied. 'I'm learning all sorts of interesting things here already. Nothing helpful, mind you, but certainly interesting. Even so, I still have an appetite for more.'

'I should hope so. Detective Damwell just called from the hospital. Ease woke up, and he's singing like a canary!'

'Is that so?' I asked, my interest piqued, and a beaming smile spreading across my face. 'Fuck you, Isabelle! …'

'What?' Said Shaz.

'No. Nothing, never mind… So, he's actually awake, huh?'

'Yes, and I really think you need to hear what he has to say.'

'Okay, go ahead.' I said. 'I'll get them to hold off on bringing in the big dog. After all, anything I can use to pry open the mouths of this lot will be highly valuable.'

'Well, I think you need to hear it from him, directly.' she replied. 'Damwell is at the hospital with him now. Seems pretty shattered about it all. I'd recommend going to see them before you meet with Fencegap.'

'It's that big?' I was sitting bolt upright in my chair now and tapping my foot with nervous energy.

'Well, it explains the letters and why they were such a problem here. If you don't already know, it seems this was some sort of human psychological experiment. Some people were in on it, and some weren't. Their original plan got a little out of shape and they had to improvise on all sides, and it appears there are more sides than we knew, too.'

'Okay. I suppose I'd better get over to the hospital then. Cheq's the only one I've got left to interrogate here. If Adam's information is as powerful as you say, then maybe it will give us the leverage we need on Cheq.'

'Maybe. It'll certainly be something to think about. Oh, and take Sly with you. You'll want someone else to hear this and help you process it all. I only finished hearing it a minute ago and I know I'm going to need a debrief to work it through.'

'Alright, I'll grab Sly and get going.'

'Keep your wits about you.' warned Shaz. 'There's something particularly nasty going on here.'

'I will, thanks…Wait, Shaz?'

'Yeah?' she answered.

'What about the program? Is it just a dummy, some made up reason to validate this experiment? Or is it a legitimately heinous thing they're planning to roll out?'

'The program is real. I can assure you of that. It's the reason for the experiment. You'll understand more when you speak to Ease.' With that, she ended the call.

I was feeling a real mix of emotions now. On the one hand, I was happy Ironie had been wrong about Ease not waking up, let alone remembering anything. Whatever certainty she was so confident of hadn't come to fruition. At least not yet. Still, I felt as if, despite whatever progress I'd made today, I knew nothing at all and perhaps I never would. It's that feeling of loneliness you get sometimes. A despondence that sets in because you're the only one who doesn't know what everyone else knows. The incredulous looks you feel cast your way wherever you go. The butt of a joke that's about you, that no one ever lets you in on, as they smirk and chuckle about how you alone don't get it.

I stood from the cold metal chair and left the room, finding Sly waiting for me in the hallway.

'One more to go.' she said with the drained voice of someone whose long list of tick-a-box duties was finally nearing the end. Perhaps there was dread there, too. As a rusted on New Thinker, she must have immense respect for Cheq. Or fear, at least. He was the leader of their religion, after all. Now by my side, or perhaps more accurately, behind the glass, behind my back, she was about to accuse him of some horrible crimes.

'Yes, just one more, except not quite yet. He's going to have to wait a little longer, I'm afraid.'

'Why?' asked Sly.

'I just had a call from Shaz…' I said, pausing mid-sentence because the DSSMD agents were diligently bringing Cheq Fencegap around the corner.

'Sorry guys, he's going to have to wait. Put him back where he came from if you can. He's got another couple of hours to sweat it out. There's something we've gotta do before we get to him.'

Cheq had been blindfolded on route to the interrogation room. That was at the request of some of the agents who apparently feared his retribution. Despite this deficit, he'd instinctively looked up toward my voice on hearing he was being sent back. I saw a satisfying tensing of the shoulders, a sure sign of frustration. A little extra sweating in a small, isolated space wouldn't hurt our cause, either. Given the luxurious nature of his life compared to everyday Global citizens, I figured he could use a taste of the limitations the rest of us live with. Perhaps we should force feed him fake meat and bugs, seeing as he thinks they have all the benefits and joy of actual animal meat, without the farting. Personally, I'd take the farty cows, sheep, pigs, and chickens any day of the week. They only eat grass or other scrap vegetation, and their waste fertilises the soil for new plant life to grow, which in turn absorbs carbon dioxide from the atmosphere. So, they're truly part of nature's cycle. They also form part of the solution to the very problem that New Thinkers blame them for contributing to. But, of course, real animals also taste delicious and make people happy when they eat them, and New Think doesn't want people being happy or well nourished. Happy, nourished people don't stay afraid for long.

'So, what is it you were you saying?' Asked Sly after Cheq had been removed.

Well, I just had a call from Sharon to inform me that Sgt Ease has woken up. And, to use her words, "he's singing like a canary." I replied.

'That's great news!' said Sly, displaying genuine pleasure at Ease's positive turn. Her slightly too wide jaw extended even further to accommodate her beaming smile. I couldn't help wondering what sort of reaction Isabelle would've had in the same situation. Or will have, when she eventually finds out.

'Yes.' I said, 'For both Ease the person, and Ease the source of critical information for the case.'

'Oh right, sure.' said Sly, now seeing the other benefit and perhaps not so joyfully. 'So, what are we going to do now?'

'You and I are going to head to the hospital and listen to his song.'

Chapter 34

With conscious Ease

The safe houses are about 15 minutes from Mid-Town, where the "Central City Hospital - Brought to you by Global Pharmaceuticals" is situated. And yes, it is compulsory to say the second part of that title, as absurd as that may seem. The idea of free market competition and avoiding market monopolies to preserve competitive pricing, consumer options, and a fair opportunity for newcomers to enter the market are a thing of the past. The long past. As apparently, is the idea of going to the hospital for the treatment you need, at the time you need it.

While hospitals may never have been a real battleground for free market opportunity, they're now literally staffed by, and offer only, the products of their sponsor Pharma companies. Prescriptions are not so much based on medical need as sales quotas, with doctors acting more like cheesy second-hand car salesmen than medical professionals who've taken a Hippocratic oath, and who hold dear a heartfelt goal of practising medicine for the benefit of their patients. Hardly surprising, given the commercialisation of the world and the buy up of basically everything by investment mega groups. Besides which, in this Global world it's more important to appear to be doing the right thing, than it is to actually do it.

Apparently, the government agencies, whose express purpose it was to police and prevent monopolies from forming, had no problem with two or three investment groups owning the world. I suppose it's hard to avoid a conflict of interest when the theoretically independent industry watchdogs have their pay checks signed by the people they're supposed to be watching.

To be fair, the idea that the whole world could be completely controlled by a handful of self-righteous rich bastards with insatiable egos, is a challenge for most people. It all just seems so fantastical, so conspiratorial, and unbelievable. The truth is, nothing is harder to believe than the truth. Comfortable lies are far more palatable than horrifying realities.

Sly sat in the driver's seat, controlling (*if one could be said to do such a thing*) the police badged E that took us from the safe house to the hospital. After she'd programmed it to drop us at the entrance, then park itself in the nearest available spot, I found myself standing once again at the main nurse's station at the front entrance of the building. The bright white walls and myriad cameras made me feel the focus of something I was guilty of, though I wasn't sure what. Several other Global citizens sought the advice of Dr-E booths, with scanning lights tracing across their bodies at vertical and horizontal angles, ready to inform them of impending doom and medication deficits.

'We're looking for Sgt Adam Ease.' I advised the nurse, keenly aware of how lucky we were to find a human on duty. 'I believe he has now woken from his coma.'

'Yes, he's done very well.' said the nurse. 'I was just reading his file, actually. That's the only reason I'm in tonight, to maintain obs and make sure we don't lose him again. We weren't sure if he was going to pull through at the start.'

'Well, we're glad he did. Is he still in the same room?' I asked.

'Yes.' said the nurse, brushing the crumb of some artificially manufactured biscuit from the lapel of her blue uniform shirt. She signed us in, then Sly and I proceeded up the lifts and through the maze-like hallways to find our man.

When we got there, the door was open, and entering his room we saw that Ease had taken quite a beating. His bed sheet was folded down to just over his legs and waist. From the stomach up, he was black and blue, his face bruised and covered with cuts and burn marks, each of them dressed with the reddish yellow coloured disinfectant, while light gauze ran the length of his arms and over the larger part of his upper body.

'Christ… they did a number on him.' said Sly under her breath, tears forming in the deep dark wells of her eyes.

Detective Damwell was nowhere to be seen, but Ease seemed awake, if not alert, in his supine form. The top of the bed had been elevated to put him in a semi-upright position, while a drip and some sort of blood pressure monitor hung from the stand next to him, their connecting tubes attached to his hand and finger. A red buttoned morphine, or should I say "Global Pharmaceuticals Patented Pain Reduction Serum Self-Applicator" was positioned next to his head on the left.

'Hi there Sargent.' I said.

'Detective.' replied a wary, yet stronger sounding voice than I had expected. Ease winced audibly as he used his bandaged arms to prop himself up straighter, then opened his blood-shot eyes.

'How are you doing, Adam?' Asked Sly with a kindness, no, softness to her voice, that only a woman can make sincere.

Ease just smiled in reply, and it was strangely comforting to see. Truth is, despite our different ideologies, I do like the man. He believes unequivocally that doing the right thing is the right thing to do… at all times. He's one of those helpful to a fault types who would never intentionally do you wrong or lead you astray, and yet is utterly misguided, nonetheless.

'I'm glad to see you're awake.' I said. 'We were worried about you.' I didn't want to tell him that as a betting man I would've put money on him having been murdered, or at the very least, attacked again in here by those he held dearest. Not to mention that Ironie had all but confirmed it.

'Yeah, I spoke briefly to Sharon earlier when Brian called her.' said Ease. 'Damwell tells me she saved my life.'

'She did. Damn near lost her own in the process.' I replied.

'I heard. I'm sorry about that.' said Ease, typically feeling a responsibility for something he hadn't actually done. That's the New Thinker in him.

'It's not your fault, Sergeant. It was entirely out of your control. You were both victims, nothing more.'

'No, well I mean, it's certainly not something I wanted to happen, anyway.' he said.

'Are you up to talking to us about what happened to you? Shaz tells me you have quite a lot to say. Or would you prefer we wait for Detective Damwell to return?'

'Damwell's gone to get some things from my place. I'll be here for a few days yet, they reckon. My apartment has been released as a crime scene, hasn't it?' he asked.

'Yes, of course. The techs have finished gathering evidence, and it's been processed as a crime scene. Now it's just an apartment with a series of broken windows covered with tape. You never know, after this, The Global Council for Equitable Housing might even give you an upgrade for your suffering.' I said, laughing encouragingly.

'I don't think this compares to the suffering of others.' said Ease, rather deadpan. The response confirming his tormentors hadn't managed to change his general outlook or undermine his belief in societal categories of pain. There's no doubt that Ease really believes that even as the victim of torture and attempted murder, a real-world victim with all the scars to show for it, that those purporting to suffer from the locus of their identity are far more deserving of sympathy and support. Personally, I pine for a time of indifference and resilience. He probably doesn't know what the former means, but he was displaying the latter in spite of himself.

For New Thinkers, the concept of resilience is a term from a bygone era. No longer can one simply brush off a slight or offence, by being the bigger man and carrying on despite it all. For them, resilience was only a symptom or creation of a toxically masculine lifestyle… Now, dredging up and carrying with you forever, all the pain, heartache, and suffering, that either you or those from whom you derived life, ever experienced, is the supported, nay, championed norm. The perpetually offended are the model citizens of the new world. The wronged are always victims and victims need support. Big Global government can offer that support in exchange for eternal servitude.

'Right.' I said. 'Well, if Damwell is going to be a while, we can just wait around if that would make you more comfortable?'

'No, I'm okay to answer questions.' He said, making the effort to get his bloodshot eyes to meet my own. 'I'd prefer to get it out, anyway. Helps me feel confident that I've still got my faculties and my ability to think and remember, and you know, all the things that make me human… and a cop.'

'Okay, well, as long as you're comfortable. If it gets too much at any point, you just let me know.'

Ease nodded his approval for us to begin our questions. I took a couple of steps further into the room, standing now at the left corner of his bed as I look at him. Being this close, I can see the oozing of the wounds through the gauze coverings and worse yet, smell the mixture of disinfectant, bed sweat and the rubbery metallic odour of hospital equipment. Sly's perfume hung on the periphery of my olfactory sense, and I was glad for its presence.

'I suppose to start with, it would be great if you could recount for us the events that led to you being attacked. Once the story starts to unravel itself, we may have more specific questions, but for now we just want to understand what happened.'

'Well, it actually all started at the station. It was in the office, after I met with you, Shaz, and Captain Ironie. It was right after I gave you all a debrief on the letters Katie had written to her mother. When we had that little chat, it must have been the first time Captain Ironie had heard anything about those letters. Which should make sense, because you'd assume that Ironie had no prior knowledge of the case before Katie's murder. As far as you and I knew, this was just another case. Some random crime in Mid-Town's jurisdiction that we'd just commenced investigating… It's not. Turns out the captain was working with people from OGT in some sort of project security capacity and has a deep connection with what's going on there.'

'How do you know that?' I interrupted.

'That Captain Ironie was working with OGT?' Asked Ease, leaving me wondering, not for the first time, if there was a wily cop mind in there asking annoyingly simple questions in the pursuit of accuracy… or if he was just a little slow.

'Yes. How did you work that out? We didn't find out about her connection until yesterday.'

'Ah, well, I'll get to that, right now. That discovery was the double-edged sword that both brought me into the loop and put me in great danger. As I was saying, it was right after our meeting about the letters. Once you and Shaz left, Ironie cut a direct path to Chief Blindspot's office. Ordinarily I wouldn't think much of it, except she practically ran there, smoke pouring from her trail, shouldering the door open and slamming it behind her as she went. I was pretty curious about the reaction, so I pretended I needed the HD scanner, which, as you know, is located just outside Blindspot's window. The blinds were down, so I couldn't see in, but the windows looking out to the pigpen are thin, so I could still hear well enough.'

'As soon as she got in there, Ironie started talking fast and fearfully to Blindspot. Told her about the discovery of the letters and seemed very concerned about the one that was missing, that, as she put it, could very well "tell it all". Ironie actually said that if they'd known about the letters prior to getting rid of Katie, they would have interrogated her first to find out where they were and rounded up anyone who'd seen them.'

'Do you think you were you attacked because you'd seen those letters?' asked Sly.

'No, I don't think so. Too many people had seen them by then. Well, most of the letters, anyway. They were real scared about the eighth letter and what it might say about their plans, though. I was shocked to hear both Ironie and Blindspot openly discussing their direct involvement in Katie's murder, and what they would've done differently with prior knowledge of the letters. I've always looked up them as leaders and just generally as good committed New Thinkers, and here they were going against so much of what we stand for. Aside from the horror of hearing they were involved, I also found it very strange that they'd be so worried about the letters given they didn't seem to reveal anything much. All I'd seen was a New Think daughter attempting to reconnect and find common ground with their Old Think mother. Close family ties, especially ones that cross ideological spheres are undesirable, but that's hardly a good reason to worry about the content of these letters.'

'Okay, so you overheard Ironie and Blindspot talking about being involved. What happened next?' I asked.

'Well, then they talked about what they were going to do about it. How they could contain the problem and what to tell someone they referred to as "Saviour".'

'Saviour?' I asked with obvious disdain.

'Yeah, I never got to confirm exactly who that was, although I have my suspicions.'

'And they are?'

'Based on what Shaz said, my suspicions align with what you've since uncovered. It seems everybody was required to answer to the head of OGT, directly… Mr Cheq Fencegap.'

Saviour my arse, I thought. The only thing he's saved is a few of his rich prick friends from having to compete in a free society. I took a deep breath and glanced over at Sly, still seated in the corner and leaning forward on her elbows, a shocked look on her face. Why she was shocked, I wasn't sure. Perhaps at the horrific injuries Ease had received. Surely not by his story so far. He was basically confirming what we already knew.

'So, you think Cheq is this "Saviour"?' I asked.

'I believe so. It's him or some other unknown figure who sits atop this nasty tree. Isabelle and the chief sounded afraid of them, whoever they are.'

'Did you hear what they planned to do specifically?' Asked Sly.

'Yeah. They both went silent for nearly a full minute, and I started getting nervous standing there. I thought maybe they'd noticed me or something. Luckily, there weren't too many people in the pigpen, so nobody had pointed out the oddness of my being there so long without actually using the machine. When the silence broke, it was Blindspot who was speaking. She said, "Well, there's only one thing we can do, I suppose. Clean up this mess and tell Saviour he needs to wrap up the experiment. Speak to Sophia and arrange to take care of the guy that played distraction for us, then we need to find this letter, destroy it, and whoever took it. No mistakes this time. We need to find out everything they know before we get rid of them."

'Wow! Blindspot really said that?' said sly.

'I was shocked, too.' said Ease. 'So shocked in fact that I almost slipped off the edge of the scanner I'd been leaning on, and they weren't done yet. Ironie said, "What if one of these letters actually got through? What if the eighth letter isn't just missing but was actually taken to its intended recipient?". That seemed to make Blindspot angry. "Katie's mother cannot see that letter!" she said fiercely. That's when they decided to go to the press to see if they could flush out the missing letter, by letting whoever took it know they knew about it. I guess they figured it could scare them away from delivering it to Katie's mum if they thought they already knew about them. That way, if they couldn't get the letter, no one else would get it either.'

'This is all very interesting.' I chimed. 'It confirms they were heavily involved in the plot with some autonomy to make decisions. Even if those decisions were basically made out of fear. What I don't understand is why they would be so concerned about Katie's mum receiving the letter. What did they think was in it that was so damning? And what the hell was she going to do with it, anyway?'

'They didn't say, but I wondered the same thing. While I was wondering it, I failed to notice Captain Ironie quickly exit the chief's office and see me standing at the window listening. Ironie's eyebrows shot up in shock at the sight, but she didn't approach me straight away. She just paused briefly, looking at me with her mouth open, before snapping it shut, turning quickly away and walking toward her own office.'

'I immediately headed back to my desk and sat down, all nervous like. I could feel my body tingling and my heart racing. I even remember involuntarily checking my holster for my Electro. I hadn't sat for long before I decided I'd be best placed to get off the floor altogether and out of sight. So, I went down to see the Sci-Techs (*Science and Technology Investigators*) to check how they were going with the letters. Predictably, they hadn't finished yet, which I'd already known before I went down. They'd only had the letters for a few hours at that point. But because of what I had heard I needed somewhere to hide out and think. Somewhere not to be seen. I'd only been there a few minutes when an Urgent Alert popped up on my device, directing me to report to Chief Blindspot's office, immediately. If I was scared before, I was terrified now. They had to know what I'd just heard, or at the very least suspect it, and now they wanted to see me. Immediately. I considered taking off, and pretending I'd found a lead to follow, but who am I to do that. The boss called me to the office. I had to go.'

'When I got there, I winced looking at the spot where I'd been standing only minutes before and rather wished I'd never done it at all. The door was open, and once inside I saw that despite having raced off only minutes earlier, Captain Ironie had returned and was standing to the left of Chief Blindspot, making for quite an intimidating and united front. "Sgt Ease, I understand you've got sticky ears." said the chief as I approached the front of the desk. "Uh, yes, I suppose so." I responded. "I hadn't intended to offend. I was just concerned that something was wrong the way that the good captain had almost run to your office." When I said this, Chief Blindspot shot a dirty look at Captain Ironie, who in turn looked a little uneasy about it. "What exactly did you hear?" asked the chief not bothering with any sort of build up or pretence. "Ah, well, I overheard something about the letters and, ah, making sure that Katie's mum didn't receive them." I replied.'

'Rather than try to bring me in, or shut me down entirely, they simply played it off as my having overheard something I shouldn't have, which I might have misconstrued. Nothing other than the regular decision making process of management. Obviously, I wouldn't understand. They said that since the murder of Katie, OGT were worried that information about the program could leak to the public, so they were asked to keep a close eye on any sort of communication coming out and make sure that it didn't jeopardise the security of what they'd been working on. I knew this wasn't true. I'd heard exactly what they said, but figured it was best I didn't say so at the time.'

'Very wise.' I interjected. 'Well, kind of. I take it, they knew, you knew, more… you know, given you ended up here.'

'Actually, I'm not so sure.' said Ease. 'People's impression of me seems to be that I'm one of the common New Think sheep, not very bright or capable of individual thought. And, whilst that might be the popular perception, the truth is, I'm more than that. I fully believe in the principles and strive for the greater good, and yet I still try to think things out for myself. I wouldn't be much of a copper if I didn't.'

It pleased me to hear Ease say this. I'm certainly guilty of seeing him as a New Think sheep, thinking only the approved thoughts, taking only the approved actions. I still doubt he thinks very critically about the motives of the Guides or the Global mouthpiece media… though to be fair, he is a pretty good cop and capable of following simple logical patterns. Unfortunately, the rails beneath his trains of thought run right off a cliff just as they should be reaching the station, so that he often comes to illogical New Think biased conclusions, tied as they are, to some presupposed social recompense (*and seldom to reality*) perceived to be necessary by the socialist mindset. Even so, he managed to find out about the letters, who had them, and who had taken the missing and crucial one. So, peaks and troughs, right?

'Okay, what happened next?' I asked.

'They basically used my obedient, narrow-minded sheep status to sell their lie. I was more than a little sad to learn that my own bosses, who are both New Think Support Officers, in addition to being police officers, think so little of me. Anyway, they told me the reason they didn't want Katie's mum to see the letter was because she was an Old Thinker and couldn't be trusted with any sensitive information about the new OGT program. "Would Ms Hansley even understand it?" I'd asked the chief. "No, of course not. Old Thinkers don't get technology. That's why they can't exist in this new world." She replied. "Well, that and their absurd lack of social conscience. In spite of which, you never know what an Old Thinker is going to do with that kind of information". I knew this wasn't true. Katie had, by all accounts, been an intelligent person. I'm not suggesting her mother isn't an intelligent person too, but they hadn't spoken in years, and from the content of the previous letters, it seemed like Katie was merely trying to re-establish some sort of relationship with her mum. It didn't seem plausible to me that the first letter she'd actually sent, and the last letter before she died, would be about some technical aspect of a software program she was working on. Even if her mum did know what to do with that information, it would've been an odd letter to have sent. I'd also found it particularly strange, that Captain Ironie and Chief Blindspot, who only minutes earlier had known nothing of the existence of these letters, where now experts on their content and the risk of their exposure… And then there's the elephant in the room. Why was the Police Service being brought in to act as some sort of private security for a software program to begin with? More importantly, how on earth are they going to stay impartial in an investigation of OGT, for whom they are currently running security, whilst they also manage the officers tasked with investigating those same people. This was a conflict of interest of mammoth proportions, particularly when you consider their present goal appeared to be protecting OGT's program security rather than solving the cold-blooded murder of one of its employees. None of this made sense to me, so I decided that given one person involved in this was already dead, and I'd just overheard the planned threat to another by these two senior officers, that it would behoove me to stay quiet and do my questioning and investigation on the down low.'

Ease looked pretty impressed with himself at the use of the word "behoove" and frankly, I was too. He attempted a broad smile, which naturally turned to a grimace at the behest of the dark bruising and oozing wounds on his face, bringing them back into sharp focus. His already chubby cheeks were swollen, and when combined with the unfortunately thin look of his buzz cut blonde hair, he had the appearance of a talking pear. A dropped one.

'So, what happened next?' asked Sly, eagerly.

'I told them I understood what they were saying and asked if there was anything I could do to help. They said the best way I could help was by keeping my ear to the ground for the missing letter, and by making sure I kept an eye on The Sons of Old for anything you turned up that might put the program at risk. They didn't say any more about what I'd overheard, although they obviously knew I'd heard more than I let on. After that, I was free to leave the chief's office.'

'Despite my catch and release, I was still nervous, because I felt the issue hadn't really been dealt with. Of course, having feared a much worse fate, I was hardly going to argue with being set free. As I walked out the door, Chief Blindspot called out to me, "Sgt Ease. Remember. We should always put the integrity of New Think, first. It's for the Global Good!". A statement I agreed with in principle. Upholding New Thinks integrity is one of the foundations of the cause, and my guiding morals... It was just the way she said it. It sounded more like a threat than an affirmation of righteousness. It chilled me to the bone. I considered leaving the station right away to put some distance between us, more afraid now than I was before. Then I figured that just in case something did happen to me, I should make sure my report got done for you and Shaz. I knew I couldn't write what I'd heard. They'd be looking for that. But at least you'd have the letters to work from. Once I sent off the email with my report, I figured I'd best put some space between me and the issue by heading home for my second job. It was one of the two days a week I'm required in my virtual office anyhow, and it seemed like a good place to escape to.'

'When I got home, I was still feeling flustered, with a lot of nasty thoughts running through my head. Because of which, I didn't set my security system before entering the Alt-Verse, which I usually do straight away. As you might expect, once I enter, I'm entirely immersed in that world via my sensory and visual devices, no longer able to tell what's happening in the physical world around me.'

'Wait, I have a question.' said Sly. 'I know you have a duty to your second job in the virtual world, but given what you'd just overheard at the office and the fact that it had scared you, why did you log in at all?'

'That's a fair question.' said Ease. 'I did think about calling in sick and just continuing to dig into Katie's case. You know, try to run down the location of the letter and what might be in it. It's just that something was nagging at me about what they'd said in Blindspot's office. Something I couldn't let go. Why was Katie handwriting letters to her mother, anyway? There's no written mail anymore. They got rid of it because it was too hard to track and monitor. Unless they open and read every single letter that's sent, they've got no idea exactly what type of information is being exchanged.'

'As you know, when they banned written mail, they said it was for the good of the environment. Better to send electronic messages and emails, than cut down trees for the simple indulgence of writing or printing on them, then throwing them away. Which is ridiculous. Because even I understand devices aren't made out of thin air, and paper has been made from purpose grown trees, or recycled from previously discarded paper, for a lot of years now. Paper doesn't need to be charged, nor does it need electricity to save, store, or upload and read. Plus, Katie, a high-ranking New Thinker and psychologist, wasn't just printing a typed letter that she maybe could have emailed or something once she was ready to make contact. She was handwriting letters, which means they're personal or secretive, and she didn't want anyone apart from the recipient to see them. So why let the cleaners read them? And, without any option to post a letter, Katie must have known she or someone on her behalf, would need to either drop the letters off at her mother's apartment, or hand deliver them to her personally, at her home or place of work. There's no other way to get them there. I just felt there were a lot of unanswered questions about Katie's motives with these letters, and for that matter, about Katie's mum, too. So, I thought I'd use the freedom that my role in the Alt-Verse gives me to investigate some of those questions.'

'As a police chief in the VGW (*Virtual Global World*) or Alt-Verse, I can access every piece of information imaginable about anyone on the globe, whether it pertains to the Alt-Verse or the physical world. Once logged in, I can search anyone and view their Global Pass, which tells me where they shop, what they buy, what they eat, where they've been, who they associate with, all their personal details, their DNA sequence, allergies or other health conditions, their Global Impact Score, what they do for work, and any interactions with moralists or breaches of the law, both confirmed and suspected. With all that information at my fingertips, I figured it was worth checking out both Katie and her mum to see what sort of people they were, and why they hadn't talked for so long to begin with. Mostly, I wanted to see if I could find any valid reason Blindspot and Ironie would be so damn scared of Katie's mum receiving a letter from her daughter.'

'So, is that when you got attacked?' asked Sly, 'Whilst you were immersed in the Alt-Verse?'

'Well, yes.' said Ease, 'Although, not straight away. I managed to do some snooping first. Basically, as soon as I'd ported in, I checked with the Station that everything was okay, then headed straight for the GIS-Hub (*Global Impact Score - Hub*). That's where those with the requisite authority can literally, well, virtually, walk up to the hub, select a person and view their whole life. I looked into Katie's mum first, the original Ms Hansley, because I figured she was the one we knew the least about. I searched the GIS-Hub by first name, by last name, and both together, finding nothing at each attempt. And I don't just mean nothing of interest. I mean, I found nothing at all. It's as if she didn't exist. There was no GP (*Global Pass, what Old Think referred to as a Digital Identity*) to find. I know Old Thinker's spent a lot of time resisting Digital Identities, because they thought they would be used to track and control them… well, I suppose one could make a case… but in the end, nobody avoided it because you simply couldn't survive without it. You couldn't buy, sell, work or even get on a bus without it. Cash money was cancelled in the early days of the transition, around the same time that GP's were made mandatory. That meant that you couldn't do anything without GDC (*Global Digital Currency*) and given that to spend GDC you need verified GP & GIS confirmation, you can't do anything with GDC and no GP. So, I wondered, how on earth could someone survive for twenty-odd years, with no currency, and no identity in the Global World?'

'But, Shaz and I found her.' I said. 'We went to her place, we visited her in person, we know she exists.'

'Did you look up her GP to find the address?' Asked Ease.

'Well, I didn't. I just assumed Shaz did.' I replied.

'Nope, that's not possible, because she doesn't exist there. She didn't get the address from me, either.' said Ease confidently. 'It was on the letters that Katie wrote, but from what I recall, you'd already met with Katie's mum before I told you about them. I didn't bother looking into her profile at the time because I figured that you and Shaz were going to do it before you met her. Turns out, we all overlooked it.'

'So, what did you do next?' I asked. 'Did you get to do any digging on Katie?'

'Nope, I never got to search her profile at all. I couldn't get past the idea that Katie's mum didn't exist in the Digital World. The ability to track and access every detail of every person on the Globe is so much taken for granted these days, it's ubiquitous. So much so in fact, that in fifteen years as an officer I've never come across a single person, no matter how sinister or shadowy, that didn't have a detailed GP with a full BiPoGeFin (*Biological, Political, Geographical, Financial & Internet profile*). I'm sure some of them didn't realise they had one, but it was there. Not Ms Hansley. Not a trace.'

'Did you get attacked before you could do anything else?' Interrupted Sly again, clearly expecting that Ease's investigation must have come to an end at this roadblock and seemingly eager to find that point. I couldn't tell if she was in a rush to get at what she considered the juicy bit, or for the story to just hurry up and end.

'No.' replied Ease. 'I might be just a lowly Sargent here in Mid-Town city of the physical world. When I'm in the Alt-verse, however, I am the chief of my station. I know you two might not spend a lot of time in the Alt-Verse, but these days that makes you more and more the outsiders, and no longer the norm. I command quite a lot of power there and as far as police work goes, we are the busiest station on the digital spectrum. In fact, there's so much going on there I may end up having to perform my all-powerful role, from my living room storage closet, on a full-time basis. The crimes are real, and the lives, and jobs, and trade of goods on there, are the basis of what fuels the physical world now. It's no longer a fantasy game or a curiosity of the tech geek. The Alt-Verse IS the real world, and the physical world is simply there to support it.' he said, growing more enthusiastic by the minute.

'Yes, perhaps that's the modern view. Just don't go forgetting the physical world can survive without the digital, while the reverse of that is not true. Regardless of which, how did this all help with your investigation?' I asked.

Ease frowned at my derogation of his beloved world, made of bits, bites, and binary, then continued with his story, regardless.

'As I was saying, I command quite a bit of power there, and I happen to have some very capable allies. My role as chief requires me to have strong knowledge of the Global laws as they apply to the Alt-verse, which, by the way, is very similar to how they apply in the physical world. And, whilst I am capably proficient with technology, there are other members of my team infinitely more capable than I. In order to plumb the depths of the data system, I called upon my Master of Digital Surveillance and Programming, Jerry, to conduct a search for Ms Hansley. I gave him what I had to go on, which was the details of her physical address, name and assumed age. I also gave him the details of her familial relationship with Katie. If anyone could turn up a mountain of gold on such scant detail, he's the man that could. After half an hour of intense digging, Jerry had turned up an intimidatingly tall pile of nothing. Which was baffling, because I've seen the guy track a Smith, all the way back to the original one in England. Right on the point of giving up, he suggested we try reverse engineering our search and look for her through the bio-paternal data on Katie's GP, or via the Bio-Hub. As you know, to confirm the legitimacy of any registered human on the GP system, you need to provide a Bio-Hub link to their parents so that people can be tracked through their direct relations if needed for social categorisation, etc. We couldn't find Ms Hansley on her own until we searched Katie's DNA mapping. Then there she was… sort of.'

'What do you mean, sort of?' I asked.

'Well, her name appeared for the purposes of Bio-confirmation… and… that was it. The rest of her GP profile was locked somehow, not viewable at all. Now Jerry's a pretty smart cookie, not one to accept defeat, so he did some further digging in areas I'm not so sure he was supposed to dig. In fact, I'm halfway confident that was the real reason we were attacked. Anyway, he was able to view the firewall that was blocking her and said he'd never seen anything like it. Said that not only was he not sure how to crack it, but that he didn't even know what it was. As I'm sure you know, these tech guys don't like admitting there's someone smarter than them, so Jerry contacted a few of his old hacking buddies to ask about it. One of them used to work for the DSSMD's Bio-Security Division and told him he'd heard about an ultra-secret IOT (*Internet of Things*) research division within DSSMD that's title was cleverly disguised as a common place DSSMD job title, "HumInT". Normally the title refers to Human Intelligence which, as you well know, Gary, is the very basis of intelligence gathering. Its boots on the ground, eyes and ears on the target, old school style surveillance work. Except, in the context of this division, "HumInT" refers to something much more intrusive and disturbing. Human Integrated Technology. It's the bogeyman of Old Think fears about a New Think world, only it isn't a mythical evil. It's a very real and present, albeit secretive, wing of the DSSMD.'

'Human Integrated Technology. Isn't that what this is?' I said, holding up my chip.

'Yes, and no. Technically, it is, although the standard chip is pretty basic compared to what these guys look at. I'm talking about AI integrated humans, where the human brain itself is meshed with AI and used as a processing power source and filter for computer generated thoughts. Rather than computers assisting humans, they use the untapped power of the human brain to assist them.'

I was developing a twitch in my eye at the very thought of being tethered to a computer for its benefit. Ease was right, though. Being controlled by ideologically inept humans was one thing. Becoming the human version of an intel processor, to serve the desires of an artificial intelligence, was another entirely. I can just imagine some lonely Dell, using me to finally write that book they'd always dreamt about. Seeing my physical discomfort, Susan mercifully took up the reins.

'So, how did Jerry's friend know about it, if it's so secret?' Asked Sly.

'I asked the same question.' said Ease. 'Jerry just said he's a tech and tech's love to Bragg about what they do and how much they know. Especially top secret stuff.'

'You're saying this firewall that protects Ms Hansley's profile was set up as part of this HumInT section of DSSMD?' I asked.

'Apparently so. Having said that, there's no way of being sure without talking to someone in that division, or Ms Hansley directly. For now, it certainly seems that way. Unfortunately, we weren't able to find out before I was attacked. Even so, I would confidently say that whatever Ms Hansley does at HumInT, and whatever Katie does at OGT, they didn't want these two things coming together.'

As soon as I heard this, I had a whole new set of alarm bells going off in my head. My skin was crawling, and I instantly became acutely aware of all the surveillance devices in our immediate vicinity. When I heard a voice behind me, I nearly leapt through the roof!

'Gary, Susan, what are you two doing here?' asked Damwell, far too calmly for my liking.

'Jesus Brian! After what I just heard, I thought you were a hit squad coming up behind us.'

'A little jumpy aren't you, Gary.' he replied, quite enjoying the moment. He bustled past me with a bag of Adam's clothes, his fiery red hair looking more tussled than normal, key strands ordinarily combed neatly into place, falling free of their moorings. Clearly, he hadn't been back to his house since I'd seen him last night.

'Frankly, yes!' I said. 'Listen, we need to have a quick word outside. Drop Adam's gear there and leave your device here, too.' Brian looked at me questioningly until he saw me take my own device out and drop it on the plastic tray table they roll over you while you're seated partially upright in a hospital bed. He followed suit, then followed me outside. We left the brightly lit building, heading out into the cold cloudiness of the park across the street. It was one of those square little urban parks forced upon the city in a misguided effort to save the planet by meeting the arbitrarily chosen climate reduction targets. The official name for a park like this is a "Greenspace" while even New Thinkers refer to them by the more common nickname, "Nature Nook". It used to be an office building with a cafe underneath. Now it's a three tree park, with six surveillance cameras and one bench seat.

Thankfully, there weren't many people around, which there seldom are these days. This dearth of individuals, leaving several of the nearest cameras free to turn toward us, no doubt having already registered our presence via our chips and biometric image. I handed Ease an RFID case, which he took hesitatingly with a look of confusion.

'What the hell is this for? You told me to leave my device inside.' Said Brian.

I showed, rather than told him, by subtly wrapping the RFID sleeve over my chip. The action wouldn't stop the chip from picking up the vibrations of my voice, though I hoped it would at least reduce the likelihood of it hearing us clearly, therefore preventing any immediate transmission of our conversation to the likes of the DSSMD. Because the chips are subdermal, they aren't great at audio surveillance, although they are capable if the conversation is loud and close, or if they're able to connect to a better amplifier like a mobile device. They're auto programmed to check for audio surveillance quality, thus seeking the best available amplification in all potential surveillance scenarios, where information review by the relevant authorities may be required. Which, by the way, means all scenarios in which one might find themselves, from sitting on the couch watching TV alone, to your daily walk to work…

'Okay.' I said once I was certain Damwell had followed my lead. 'You've heard Sgt Ease's recount of what happened to him leading up to his attack?'

'Yeah, and what little he remembers during his attack.' he replied.

'Did you find the HumInT bit as deeply concerning as I did?'

'I got a little nervous when I heard that bit, sure.' said Damwell, clearly still uncertain of my motives here.

'Well I'm more than just nervous. I've got the DSSMD working with me on this case. They're currently guarding the prisoners and assisting with interviews as well. Plus, I've been told the DSSMD Director himself has taken a personal interest in the case, and wants to be kept abreast of everything that happens.'

'Well, that's not good!' said Brian emphatically. 'Do you trust the people working with you?'

A wave of paranoia washed over me as he said this, when right on cue, a middle-aged man carrying a black backpack by his hip turned down the footpath skirting the edge of the park. I was immediately reminded of the several loose ends we had yet to tie up during the investigation. Such as the two amateurish spooks who'd been following me around yesterday. I hadn't seen them since leaving the OGT building in the cab of a prisoner transporter, yet here one was, not ten meters away, glancing right at me as he walked casually by. Brian hadn't noticed him yet, not that he'd know who he was anyway, and I didn't want to send him running by drawing attention to him now.

In a low voice, that was really more of a loud whisper, I answered Brian's question. 'Yes, I suppose so. The people I worked with to make all the arrests, at least. Except there was someone new there today. Someone I'm suspicious of, simply for being there when they shouldn't. And I certainly don't trust the Director.'

Without ever questioning why, Brian mimicked my loud whisper, sensing, no doubt, the very real concern in my tone and timbre. 'Okay, so why are we sitting out here in the open?' He asked. 'Shouldn't we find somewhere more private to hold this conversation? It's not like they haven't got the resources to watch us.'

He was more right than he knew. The man with the backpack had paused two thirds of the way along the path, taking several steps onto the grass to take up a position against the trunk of a pine tree. Removing his device, he held it out in front of him, the apparent object of his attention, though hardly the broadsheet of old.

This time, I covered my mouth with my hand before answering. 'Because I didn't want anyone to hear or see me tell you to get Ease out of here. Today! Take these RFID slips and cover both yours and Eases' chips with them. The cameras will see you go but unless there's someone watching you directly, there won't be an automatic alert issued, which should give you some time to get him somewhere you can protect him.'

'Wouldn't they have set up automatic alerts to monitor him, anyway? I'm sure Ironie told me they had when she assigned me to the task force.'

'That's true, they did. Then Ironie attacked Sharon in this very hospital, with no flags raised, and from what she's told me during interrogation, they have a plan to silence Ease forever. "There are ways…" were her words. Hardly something they're going to want flagged and monitored.'

Damwell sat for a moment in silent contemplation, then nodded. 'Okay.' he said. 'What are you going to do?'

'I've still got the biggest fish of all to fry. After that, we plan to officially announce our case against the suspects, and Sly's gunna get us a public perception consensus. If I can get something tangible that explains why so many officers were involved, and what's really driving this plot, then I think with the surveillance footage we've got, and the anti-New Think actions the team took, we should have a slam dunk case.'

'What about the DSSMD involvement with Ease?' asked Damwell.

'We don't know for sure that the two are really connected. I mean, it doesn't look good, hence my concern. Even so, it's possible that when Ease and this Jerry guy started digging into HumInT, they set off some sort of watcher alert for them. That could be why they got attacked. Maybe it had nothing to do with the letters, or the case. It's hard to believe the two aren't related somehow, farfetched even. In spite of which, it is possible. Look, there's one guy I trust from the DSSMD that I can ask about all this. He might avoid the truth, but I'm sure he wouldn't lie to me or lure me into a trap. Not knowingly, anyway. If you can at least get Ease out of here, it'll make him harder to target or use as leverage against us. That'll give me a chance to find out if there's some secret DSSMD agents waiting to strike, or whether we've already arrested all the major threats.'

'Fair enough. Let's get moving.' said Damwell, standing from the bench, still holding the pouch over his arm. 'Oh, and watch your step. I have a feeling this all ties back to you somehow and that people are gunning for you. Even if we don't always see eye to eye, we are still brothers in arms.'

I smiled at the "brothers in arms" comment, a very un-New Think thing to say. He had to know that, and I appreciated it. 'You know, I kind of expected you to still be a little angry after our encounter last night.'

'Yeah, well, we are who we are. After Ease told me what happened to him and confirmed who was involved, I kind of saw it from your angle a bit. Whoever attacked Ease and Sharon didn't seem to care who they hurt or why. Maybe ideology isn't everything, so we've just gotta look after each other, no matter what we believe.'

When we crossed back to the hospital, my backpack carrying friend did nothing more than swivel slightly around the base of the tree in order to maintain a clear view. Whether his device was just a modern sort of cover, or rather overt surveillance, I wasn't sure. That he continued to hold it out in front as if his arms were locked like a selfie stick, would nonetheless guarantee whomever he worked for, knows precisely where we are.

After reaching Ease's room, we listened as he recounted the rest of his story. He'd waited for us apparently, in our absence engaging only in sympathetic small talk about his many injuries, with the now rather gloomy looking Sly. As Damwell had alluded to, the story from this point lacked a lot of detail. Basically, as you could guess from his earlier preamble, Ease had not only failed to secure his apartment, he also significantly dulled his senses with his Alt-Verse equipment, dragging his physical perception into the virtual world. His attackers simply cracked the door, walked up behind him, grabbed him by the arms and dragged him into his bedroom, where they sedated him with drugs before proceeding to torture him. Ease claimed to have remembered coming in and out of consciousness and little else. He couldn't remember anything he might have divulged or what questions they asked. The only thing he was certain of was that there were two males, and that they both wore balaclavas and gloves the whole time they were there. The next thing he knew for sure, it was today, and he was waking up in hospital.

After finishing up with Ease, we left Damwell to get on with what we'd discussed, while Sly and I headed to the E with a plan to return to the safe house and begin our final interrogation of Cheq. On the walk, I thought about what Ease had told us and what I'd said to Damwell, my own words ringing in my mind. It would be great to have something tangible aside from the surveillance footage to tie OGT to the police and establish that pre-existing relationship. It's all very well for the footage to prove police involvement in the murders, which I'm sure will gel with the general public perception. What would be even more powerful would be evidence that showed how and why the police were corrupted into Cheq's employ to begin with. The idea they were just protecting the ideology that underpinned the Global World didn't sit well. It's the police's job to enforce the law, not to simply murder those they think mightn't agree with it. It would also be good to find something solid that confirms whether the attack on Sgt Ease was purely related to the OGT stuff, or whether it was related to what Ease had stumbled on in the Digital Globe. Without that, those crimes will stay unsolved.

In my pondering, it occurred to me, that with Sharon injured, Detective Damwell walking away from the case after Thise was arrested, and the rest of the Police Service either being in on the crimes or without a supervisor to direct them, that besides the DSSMD going into Blindspot's office to arrest her, nobody had actually searched her's or Ironie's offices for any evidence. Even if it is a long shot that either had left a handwritten note admitting the OGT plot and how they came to be involved, it's always good practice to look, just in case. 'Sly, cancel the current trip.' I said, from the passenger seat of the E. 'We've got a new destination.'

Walking back into the station, I was surprised to see that most of the officers had continued to perform their regular duties without their two highest ranking members, or four of the eight total detectives assigned to the station, to guide them. To be fair, we aren't really that important to the daily operations or the assigning of tasks. Sharon and I especially. And, I suppose if I wasn't a detective and still in a uniform, I wouldn't have just sat at home either. The world doesn't stop needing to be policed simply because some senior officers have been playing both sides of the law. Even so, I felt the weight of this case hung heavily over us all. Like the world should be waiting on the outcome as if its future rested on the result… which it very well might. Nobody here stopped. Nobody else felt the weight and nobody agonised over the outcome. The world just went on. Indifferent, uncaring, and unaware.

Strangely annoyed by the undeterred stasis of the station's environment, I Strode through the pig pen with Susan diligently following me, under instruction to ensure a fair and legal search was conducted. As we passed by the noticeboard, I looked up at the signs which had been hastily made for Operation Ease. The short-lived and utterly undermined pretence of investigating a crime committed by the very people who launched the investigation, was a bold reminder not only of the hypocrisy and corruption of this case, but of the broader world we live in. The signs were suggestive, with a picture of Ease in hospital taking centre stage above a comical whodunnit line up of shadow outlined criminals, all of whom naturally resembled known Old Thinkers, endlessly condemned by the arbiters of the one set of global morals to which we must all agree and abide. The potential return of the beliefs and ideals of these shadow devils being the fear that fuels the Global commitment to the cause.

It's funny, I thought, entering Blindspot's office. It used to be that being "suggestive" was considered an action of concern. An unwanted coercive image, example or instruction, was seen as an infringement on someone's right to make a choice of their own free will, absent the perception or presence of force. Now, threatening suggestiveness is New Think SOP.

As if on cue, I spotted the official New Think word calendar on the chief's desk and headed across to take a look. Flicking through it to see if it held any notes of interest to the case, I found nothing other than the presence of thought guidance. Today's word was *"Reconciliation" e.g. To bring about a return of unduly taken things, by acknowledgment of negative actions past*, yesterday's word was *"Excessive" e.g. The greedy accumulation of more than one needs, such as material possessions, freedom, food or independence,* and before that it was *"Togetherness" e.g. we are all in this together, or 'stronger as one'* and rather oddly to my mind *'together we'll flatten the curve'*. Seemed like a pretty mundane and targeted set of words. Hardly surprising, given the producer of this daily propaganda tool.

I didn't look through each day specifically. I'd seen no obvious notes or circled dates to inspire a deeper look, and frankly, I'd have been surprised if there had been. It did, however, make me think of the importance of words, and how the new world has been manipulated with and without them. Especially without them. The removal of words from the public conscience to better control narratives and the minds of the Global population has been a machination of the Guides and Globalist governments for years. It was a tool of the New Think movement well before the official takeover began. People talked with excitement at the invention of new words, often overlooking the rapid degradation of the English (*now Global*) language by the modification of existing words, reducing them or assigning them a new meaning, often for the purpose of social engineering, such that a non-progressive word is given an entirely negative or derogatory context whenever it's used.

What many fail to notice until it's too late, is the outright removal of words that are no longer desirable for the public conscience. When New Think decides it doesn't want you talking or thinking about a subject, it modifies the words or meanings of words that support or refer to that subject and then removes the subject from the language all together. With the proliferation of predictive text and the Digital Global Pass, through which all communications and actions must travel, the unilateral control and power to remove undesirable language has become total and unquestionable. How can you raise a counterpoint or argue the validity of a subject if there are no words in the language with which to make your case? New Think changes the vocabulary available to the average person, and in doing so, restricts and controls their capacity to communicate with their peers. To a New Thinker, to speak a word that doesn't exist within the span of predictive text is simply the act of an old oppressor seeking to seem smarter than thou. The misleading lies of a bygone era. The more that time goes by, the fewer the people that know those words had ever existed to begin with…

Throughout history, words have had the power to create and destroy, and whomever had control of their meaning had control of the world. By the power of New Think, the Guides weaponised words such that their mere use overcame the hypocrisy of the actions of their user. New Think wanted to save the world from a supposed climate oblivion, so they weaponised words such as, climate, green, responsible, sustainable, change, and created new and dangerous phrases such as, climate action, net zero, carbon neutral, climate change, Global warming, and Carbon Footprint, to allow them to guilt the populace into living as starved hermits afraid to go outside for the damage their existence may cause. Meanwhile, uber wealthy globalists sprinkle a few of these words and phrases across the sentence they use to explain and promote the new venture they just planned and funded to conduct exploration and mining, in the previously pristine and untouched areas of Greenland, and wallah! Their new mining expedition is now their new *"Climate Action project, targeting the minerals needed to support positive change in the automotive and electronic industries! The goal is to achieve "our" net zero target and contribute to the global mission to combat Climate Change. Climate action is, of course, everyone's responsibility, and we're willing to take the lead and show the way for the sake of every Global citizen alive today, and for future generations of the Global world."* What hero's, taking on this brave and daunting venture and all for the greater good. Odd, how they fail to address the environmental impact to the previously untouched region, or that they expect to make a fifty to one profit on the minerals they mine, by using the taxed money from the hermitized global population to fund the project. Once they find the minerals, they'll charge the same people who funded the project a fortune to access the products they make with those minerals, because, naturally, they own it all. Before its mined, after its mined, and even after its refined and manufactured into a product. You, of course, will own nothing, and aren't you just happy about that?...

Sly, doing more participating than monitoring, brought me back from my daydreaming when she knocked over a stand-up device charger that was sitting on a side table at the rear of Blindspot's office, with the sweep of her hand.

'Shit, sorry!' She said. 'I didn't mean to disturb you from your... process.'

I looked up at her, my eyebrows raised, as she, in turn, looked questioningly back at me. Clearly, she was being facetious with her comment. Quite rightly too, as I was not at all focused on the task at hand. 'Right, sorry.' I said, gauging the situation. 'I drifted off for a minute there.'

'So, what are we actually looking for?' asked Sly.

'Um, anything that could help us, really. A record of communications, items of interest, ID passes, basically anything that might tie the chief to OGT. Outside of that, anything that looks unusual or out of place for the chief of a global police station to have in their office.'

'Well, to be honest, there's not much to see here at all, let alone any of that.' said Sly.

It was true. Since well before New Think entered the public consciousness, big business and government agencies had been under the control of the political and moral dictators of the workforce, known commonly as Human Resources, Human Services, People and Culture and later Employee Services. The de-personalisation of the workplace followed in stages, with each one chipping away at the personality and individuality of their employees, forcing them towards the status of a homogenised worker who represents the businesses ideals, whatever they are at that point in time, and nothing more. Human Resources banned family photos, posters with personal meaning, religious, political, or personal affirmations, or any other items that could be considered offensive by co-workers who did not have the same good fortune with family, might be unduly attracted or repulsed by them, or who might hold different beliefs.

Human Services replaced these personal items with generalised posters that demanded focus on safety, which by their mere presence seemed to replace the need to actually manage, monitor, or teach safe working practices to their employees. Managing and teaching safety costs far more than just hanging signs up that tell people to do it themselves. Plus, posters offer written and legal proof of the employer's application of their duty of care, and the employee's obligation to abide by it.

When HR became People and Culture, they upheld the removal of personal items, then took it a step further, removing any sense of belonging to the space their employees worked in, by scrapping assigned desks and making them all "hot desks". Turn up, grab a desk, work hard and safe, join the social group but share only the approved common thoughts, not your own, then get out and try not to trip on anything.

Rebranded as Employee Services, they determined that all employees must have a mental illness they were trying to hide from their fellow employees. This inspired the creation of endless awareness days, weeks, and months, designed to usher in the "silently suffering victim" culture they had to have embedded to ensure the success of future phases. ES also sent out employee engagement surveys with utterly non-specific and disengaging questions, in an effort to gauge whether people were happy in the sterile psych wards that formed their workplace. The ambiguity of the questions making clear that the answers weren't as important as your compliance with their request to respond.

Finally, when New Think entered the public realm, Equality, Engagement & Environment Coordinators took over and became a political tool embedded in big business, to enforce employment quotas, and demand the open support of the employed for their desired ideologies. EE&EC's pushed climate, race, sex and sexuality-based propaganda on its employees, demanded interaction on work based social media, so long as that interaction was aligned with the approved and unilaterally supported opinion of us all, and then set KPI's that we can only satisfy if we not only accept, but actively promote the socio-political issues, as every good and decent employee should in a Global World. How their actions actually supported the core role of the business, nobody knows, but that's hardly relevant, is it? …

Shit. I'd become distracted again, now blankly staring at Blindspot's inactive desk device. Meanwhile, Sly's eyebrows were beginning to mount an assault on her hairline, such was her incredulity at my shocking inability to remain present and focused on the task at hand. My own simmering discontent was bubbling up to sit just below the surface and I needed to keep it in check. 'Yes, yes, I know, I know.' I said without Sly having to verbalise her point.

'There's nothing here.' said Sly, repeating her earlier comment.

'Yeah, okay, you're right. Let's get out of here and see what's behind door number 2.'

Sly and I left the chief's office, shutting the door behind us and applying some good old-fashioned anti-tamper tape for good measure. Even though we didn't find anything this time, that doesn't mean there's nothing to find, and I wanted to know if seeing us come here made anyone worry enough to pay a visit themselves.

'Where on earth did you get that?' Asked Sly, a little sarcasm and disbelief sneaking into her voice.

'Found it in an old storeroom when I first joined the Service. I knew nobody else was going to use it, so I took it all home. I keep a roll in my work bag for times like this.'

'Times like this? Um, you do know that's what the chip detectors are for, on like, every single doorway, everywhere on the Globe?!' said Sly, sarcasm having found solid footing on her mood.

'I do, and I'm aware of their omnipresence. The thing is, if this case has taught me anything, it's that technology is only as trustworthy as the people who control it. When that turns out to be a singular group with a singular mindset, then the data it presents us can say whatever they want it to, and there're no guarantees it's telling the truth… You know, if you don't lower your eyebrows, they'll get stuck there.' I added while mimicking Sly's comical face.

'Oh, shut up.' she said, turning to follow me as we headed for our next destination.

This time, as we passed through the pig pen, we didn't go unnoticed. After watching us search and then tape up the door to the chief's office with magical tape that leaves physical evidence of tampering, the remaining officers present made no effort to hide their interest in what we were up to. Eight pairs of uniformed eyes followed our every step as we headed for the station abode of their other supervisor, one step down the ladder.

Entering Captain Ironie's office, we found it infinitely more occupied by stuff than Blindspot's had been. Nothing that was likely to be useful to the case, mind you, being mostly full of discarded examples of the Operation Ease taskforce posters. They aren't quite your old school thick cardboard or shiny glossed paper numbers. These are thin flexible screens, somewhere between a glossy poster, a computer monitor and an etch-a-sketch where electronic pictures can be downloaded and displayed on them, then drawn on or edited by hand. They're commonly used here for displaying the latest fad, or should I say "focus" of the Service. Amidst this pile of discards, we also discovered a basic notepad, and by basic I mean the old-style paper ones, not the electronic ones common today, along with a standard issue desktop device, a nameplate, half a pack of screen tacks, a poster pen and a pair of glasses that I'd never seen her wear.

There's no such thing as desk draws anymore, because as I've previously mentioned, they don't want you having any personal or territorial ties to a specific desk, and that applies to middle managers as well as us plebs. So despite both the chief and captain having their own offices, which in itself is a little unusual these days, offering far more privacy than you're supposed to have, there are still no draws.

'Well, there's fuck all here!' said Sly, dropping the sarcasm to return to the rather negative attitude she'd displayed ever since we got back to the station.

'There's these posters to check over and this notepad to review.' I replied. 'Perhaps you could start with the posters while I do the notepad.' I suggested encouragingly.

'Why? What's the point? What are you actually going to find here?' She snapped. 'What do you think, she's dumb enough to write "May 3rd: To Do List - Go to the killing of Katie Hansely as per Cheq Fencegap of OGT." in her notes there? Is one of the original drafts of these posters going to say "Operation Ease: Pretend to give a shit about the attack on Sgt Ease that we coordinated and carried out. Shhh, don't tell Gary"...'

When Sly drifted off on her sentence, tears were rolling down her cheeks. I knew why she was upset. That seemed pretty obvious. It was the issue we'd been dancing around since we'd started on this case. Hell, it's the same issue we dance around every day in the Global World. What I didn't know, was what to say. How am I supposed to comfort someone who's trying to process the violent hypocrisy of the ideology they support? Particularly when that ideology has always painted you as a wrongdoer, evil or ignorant.

'Look, we all know that not everyone is good.' I said. 'There are bad apples in every walk of life. I know as well as anyone that most people truly believe they're doing the good that the Guides tell them they are. These actions, this insane plot, whatever it really is, it shouldn't represent all the people of New Think. The people involved in this are just sick, and with your help, we're going to bring em down.'

I'd hoped my words seemed believable despite not believing them myself. Sly had taken a seat, flumped more accurately, onto a black cushioned, metal framed desk chair, and looked forlornly at the dark blue carpet tiles in front of her. If she was anything like me, she might be wondering, of all things, why they brought those back in vogue, though I doubt that's the focus of her attention. For my part, I leaned precariously against the flimsy internal office wall behind Ironie's desk, no doubt made of chipboard or MDF, as was the poster covered desk in front of me.

'It's more than that, Gary.' said Sly. 'I trusted these people. I looked up to them. It's not just that they've done wrong, it's that I feel like I've allowed it to happen somehow. Supported it even.'

'Did you know about what Blindspot and Ironie were involved in?' I asked.

'No! Why would you ask that?' She replied, seeming genuinely offended.

'Because if you didn't know, then you've got nothing to feel guilty about. Angry sure. Betrayed, definitely. Used, yep, they did that too. And, whilst I realise this might be a foreign concept these days, what with the collective guilt we're all supposed to carry forever, if you knew nothing and you're not involved, then you're not guilty. Look, you and I have always had an understanding. We know we come from different ideological standpoints, yet we don't let that impact our ability to work together, or dare I say, our friendship. In fact, I think we do what the world used to do so well. We know we don't agree on a lot of things, and yet we manage to get along and coexist in spite of it. Perhaps we even make each other stronger because of it. These people don't represent who you are. Don't let their actions define you or your way of life.'

I paused before continuing, hoping that what I'd said had been inspiring, therefore requiring some time to settle in. 'Now, what we do is, we find everything we can on them, punish them for what they've done and move on with our heads held high, knowing that no matter who does wrong or what ideology they believe in, that we punish them all the same.'

Sly looked at me tearfully and nodded. 'Okay, I've got the posters then…' She moved over to the spare desk where the bulk of them lay and lifted one dispassionately, still clearly burning from the betrayal of her people.

'Thanks, Susan. You know I need you on my side here. We're doing this together.'

'I think that's our saying, and it's, "…in this together".' said Sly without the slightest sign of humour.

Even now, I wait for the sarcastic grin or chuckle after this type of comment, which never comes. New Thinkers don't understand sarcasm and humour. They can't seem to compute that saying what you know is wrong to highlight the absurdity of something, can make you laugh. The incredible thing is, they still say it, they just don't laugh. They have irony instead. As far as they're concerned, when someone talks, it's either an attack, an affirmation, an apology for past wrongs, or something ironic. Usually a thinly masked insult of some sort. Nothing else exists in the sad, humourless, common isolation of their world.

'Righto.' I said. 'Well, let me know what you find.'

Flicking through Ironie's calendar, I found nothing more than the same irritating words and example sentences I'd already seen in Blindspot's office. There were no additional notes or circled dates. Not even a special day of the year or a birthday. The notebook was harder. There was a lot of writing, most of it in some sort of nonsensical shorthand I didn't understand. 'Hey Susan, does this make any sense to you?' I asked, showing her several pages of the notepad.

'No.' said a despondent Sly.

I thought about asking her if she was okay, which she clearly wasn't. But what would be the point, really? I figured I'd just get the "I'm fine" response that all women give when they're not fine, but don't want to talk to "you" about it. Usually because you're either the reason they're not fine, or because your lack of understanding and incorrect advice are now pushing them towards angry. 'Hmm, me neither.' I replied, instead.

I continued my review of the notepad, which had no dates written on the pages, and found on the third sheet from the back a circled note that read "*No contact, need FORGE*". Well, that is interesting, I thought. Dangerous too. I had heard whispers of a CIA or MI6 style clandestine group of trained killers that report directly to the senior Global Guides and carry out dirty deeds they deemed necessary for the greater good, but unsuitable for public consumption. Mostly because their actions are so very un-New Think, or at least unlike the New Think they want you to believe in. It's one of those myths that has an air of truth to it that nobody wants to admit, and everybody secretly believes, because you know that these things definitely existed in Old Think times and there's been too many TV shows with exactly this type of "fictional agency" for it not to be true.

The story goes, that as with all clandestine agencies, FORGE is an acronym. It stands for Forget or Regret Guides Emissary's. The theory is that if you're their mark, they'll either wipe your memory (*Forget*) or wipe you out (*Regret*) at the direction of the Guides. An emissary, by the way, is supposed to be a diplomatic representative on a special mission. I can only assume this is another case of that irony I mentioned earlier.

I chose not to inform Sly of this particular find and instead simply placed the notepad in an evidence bag and unlocked my device to fill out the Record of Evidence app. 'Can I swipe your chip?' I asked while she gently traced lines on the corner of the desk. 'I need you to sign as my witness for me to take Ironie's notepad into evidence.'

Sly didn't respond verbally. Instead, she gave me the reverse head nod of acknowledgment, normally reserved for the non-verbal hello you'd give to someone you see out in public at a short distance, who you know, but wish you didn't. She obliged me, swiping her chip with the device reader and allowing the biometric aspect of the program to scan her face to confirm she was a genuine physical witness. Good thing it didn't require an agreeable mood.

There was nothing else of interest or value on Ironie's desk. Taking a seat in her chair I observed the surrounds of the office, which with its thin white panelled walls, perspex window looking out to the pigpen and bland guest seating against the back wall, was the very embodiment of New Think, and for that matter, like every other government office I'd ever seen. Dreary, impersonal and inoffensive. Except for the Global Flag, which hung on a stand in the corner. It's a patchwork representing every minority group on the planet, with the very distinct exception of the one that was once the majority. All of them competing for space, control, recognition of pain suffered, and of course, the brightest, most prideful colours. It was not so much a symphony of patchwork as a cacophony of victims voices all trying to shout the loudest. I got a headache just looking at it. Not one of the represented groups could agree to be either top left, middle, or bottom right, so the Guides agreed that there should be innumerable versions with patches allowed in every different position. At public speeches given by the Guides Council, a veritable rolodex of flags had to be available to ensure that the displayed flag always had the patches in different positions to the previous speech, such that no favour was perceived to be shown to any one group.

Looking around to where we'd entered the office, I could see that Susan was already making a move towards the door. I hadn't actually confirmed we were finished yet, though it was clear we were. She hadn't looked at any of the posters, so I stood and ran an eye over them, finding nothing other than minor spelling mistakes or un-erasable E-pen marks as the cause of the many spares. Satisfied, I turned to see Sly standing in the doorway, leaning lightly against the frame. 'I know you said you were fine, but you sure don't seem fine.' I said.

'When did I say I was fine?' She asked pointedly.

'Oh, right.' I said. 'I had that conversation in my head.'

'What?!' she asked, straightening up and fixing me with a look, now more pissed off than un-fine.

'Um, never mind.' I mumbled. 'I'm just saying that you clearly look rattled and we are about to head back to the safe house and undertake probably the most important interview of our lives. Are you ready for this?'

'Yeah. I'm ready. Let's bury these pricks!'

Chapter 35

Time to pay the Cheq

Social media truly is the worst thing that ever happened to humanity. And the best thing that ever happened to globalist control. Nothing spreads faster and gathers more momentum than a one sentence message from an activist influencer, telling of the perceived oppression of a wronged and downtrodden person or group of people on any of the many social media platforms, all of which are ultimately the same.

Expectant scrollers are energised to act and create awareness of this heinous wrong, diligently sharing, angrily sun-facing, and commenting spitefully as a call to arms for all the other angry do-righters to see and join the cause. If you don't agree with the message, you're fair game to be tracked, attacked, shunned, shamed, and shut out of the world as we know it.

With that level of influence and control, the capacity to be judge, jury and executioner of Global morals, with only one opinion allowed to be seen, is child's play. You've got yourself a pretty captive audience of unidirectional thinkers to preach to, and built-in moderators to curate the responses and cull any opposition.

Cults used to escape to remote campsites to share their hatred of established societal norms. Now they manage their spiteful un-weaving of society's fabric from the comfort of their assigned Global homes and with the support of the Global flock around them. All New Think needs to do is make sure they control the person who writes that message.

It's not just social media, either. In order to diversify and meet the needs of all, or more accurately to ensure they spread the one true message to those of us not captivated by a 4-inch black hole you can hold in your hand, mainstream media companies were bought and paid for. So too were the newspapers, the magazines, internet search engines, the advertising companies and all the other message delivery and information sharing companies around the world. Sorry, the Globe.

Of course, just because these mainstream forms of media present their audience with more than a single sentence, doesn't mean they want to burden you with too much information. You surely haven't the time, and heaven forbid, you might develop a questioning mind. That's why the news shifted from simply reporting the facts of the events of the day, to telling us what to think about the events of the day, without all those mind-boggling facts, and… ugh, ugh, I can't even say it… context…

Still, people never do see the blatant message being delivered by their trusted news sources. Even when they keep telling us right there in the slogans *"keeping you informed on the important events, in your world" "delivering the important issues" "We'll tell you what you need to know"*. What you "need" to know. It's an interesting statement, isn't it? Did they ever ask you what you "wanted" to know, or what was actually "important" to you? If not, who decided? Who is it that determines what exactly "you need to know" and why? How are you to make an unbiased assessment of the world around you if some nameless, faceless person has already reviewed it all, edited it, and made an executive decision as to what you need to see and what's important to you?

Perhaps it isn't really what "YOU" need to know, after all. It's what "THEY" need you to know, and absolutely nothing else. If you cannot challenge the validity of their story, you can never prove them wrong, let alone find the truth. That's where internet search engines and the code that underwrites them come in. Which, given they either created or absorbed every one of them, is also where OGT comes in.

Because of the closed society the Global world lives in, it's actually harder to predict people's reactions to random or sudden stimuli these days because they are so seldom exposed to anything that isn't fully planned and controlled New Think propaganda. In fact, I try sometimes for a laugh to tell people things they wouldn't otherwise have heard just to see how they react. Inevitably they conduct an online search and wait for Globester, the largest, and therefore most trusted of the utterly corrupted search engines, to tell them I have indeed lied to them. Of course, Globester doesn't really know that I have lied. What it knows is that only things that have been created or approved by New Think are actually allowed on the internet and are therefore the truth. So, unlike the old days when search engines would just try to guess what you were searching for or simply bring up the most searched topics as alternate options for you to think about, it now tells you that you may have been a victim of misinformation or disinformation and requests the source of your query. Because of that, I also have to make sure the things I tell them aren't actually truths from Old Think, because anyone searching Old Think theories is flagged for much closer scrutiny, and depending on what exactly they search, they may get a visit from the nearest and most frightening New Think enforcers available, which is usually a Suppression Squad from DSSMD's Public Order and Safety Branch. Now, an Old Thinker might see the title "Suppression Squad" through a negative lens, as if they were coming to suppress you, when of course, all good New Thinkers know they're actually coming to suppress misinformation and in doing so ensure the safety of the Global world…

This afternoon, Cheq would not have the opportunity to search online for the truth, or have it pre-edited for him by anyone other than me. Nor will he be able to float comfortably on the safely curated cloud of New Thinks filters to protect him from that which might offend… Not that these truths would be there. Right now, he's the only one that knows them all, and I intend to extract them from him.

'Well, if it isn't Cheq Fencegap.' I said, entering the makeshift interrogation room in which Cheq already sat. I stood a while just inside the doorway, smiling smugly at the man. Not because I felt smug. I just wanted him to believe that I did. They say confidence is everything, or they used to, and I want him to believe I've got that and so much more. Now I think the saying is, "conformity is everything" or something like that, which isn't going to help me today.

'Did you forget I was here?' Asked Cheq from his sad, lonely seat in the centre of the room.

He was frustratingly calm, even if he did look rather childish, half slouched in the chair. I'd had the Agents remove the small table and replace the slightly more comfortable chair we were using for our other interogees because I wanted Cheq to be as uncomfortable as possible. I could see he clearly wasn't enjoying the experience. The hard metal of the new chair's square cornered frame was coated with a lacquered white paint which is the enemy of friction, making it very difficult to sit on without glacially sliding off and having to regularly correct your position. The absence of the table for support compounds the issue, and the thirty minutes I'd kept Cheq waiting here meant he'd already had to straighten himself on multiple occasions. Five so far, to be precise. I know, because I spent those thirty minutes in the viewing cupboard discussing tactics with Sly and observing our mark.

To be honest, I'm not sure whether I'm adding a non-violent stress element to the interrogation because it will help frustrate him and hopefully make him lash out with the truth, or whether I'm simply letting my pure hatred for the guy influence my process. Either way, he looked a little put out, which was helping my fake smug look take on an air of truth.

Looking him up and down, I tried to gauge the impact a night in solitary confinement had had on a man so used to luxury. His clothes looked satisfyingly dishevelled, his ivory slacks wrinkled and marked with smears of dust or dirt. His Ferragamo's had been removed at my request, again for the slip factor of his socks and also so he knew he wasn't in control of when he could leave. My favourite aspect of his current outlook, however, had to be the two-inch tear about six inches up from the bottom left corner of his obnoxious baby blue sweater. Yes, it's petty. So what? Suck shit, Mr Fencegap!

'No Cheq, I didn't forget. I knew very well where you were. I'm the reason you're here, remember… Well, you're the reason you're here. I'm just the one that brought you in. Of course, you knew that. Didn't you?' I asked with a heavy dose of sarcasm.

Cheq's head was turned down at an angle to the left, almost as if he were looking for the hole in his jumper, except that his eyes were shuffling back and forth like his mind couldn't cope with the question.

'Yes, of course I knew that, Detective. There isn't much I don't know.'

'Well, that's good to hear because I've got a lot of questions for you and I was really hoping you could answer them all. I'm relying on your memory of recent events and frankly, you're getting up there in years. Plus, from what I've heard, fake meat (*coincidentally also named BEEF, Bio-Ethically Engineered Food*) isn't so great for human health and may lead to cancer, mental decline, or Alzheimer's, as a result of the tumorous cells they're grown from and the chemicals used in the manufacturing process. Not something I would've thought was overly surprising, given you replaced an organic food source and part of the natural food chain, with a lab grown, chemically altered, faux meat (*or F-eat, which I think better describes the taste and texture of the substance*). Did you know that, Cheq? About BEEF?' I asked, not really expecting an answer, which was duly not received. After his lot banned the eating of meat under the grossly misguided concept that cows were a major contributor to rising temperatures or "Global Warming" fake meat became the cash cow (*pardon the pun*) for the Guides who invested in its creation. Unfortunately, it tasted more like the byproduct of cows eating grass, than grass-fed cows, if you catch my drift… Not that it bothered the likes of Cheq. For one thing, he didn't have to eat it. For another, he knew that every problem was a public problem, and all you had to do was work out how. Now, if only the thing was a crisis, the people would soon come around and eat it out of stoic duty. Trouble is, just how do you make meat a crisis? I mean, it's not like you can create or enhance the likelihood of livestock viruses that threaten the industry, and subsequently the supply of food required for humanities survival, from which you shore up the need for faux meat while simultaneously creating a new market for yourself by selling vaccines… (*wink, wink*).

Cheq Fencegap, by the way, was the major driver of this fake meat industry, and it was he that swung the scythe through real livestock farming, killing off the natural meat industry, along with animal farming and the livelihood of the farmers. Which makes him responsible for the loss of the most important and basic aspect of human life, going back thousands of years. That being, the ability for communities and societies to feed and sustain themselves by farming the food they need to survive.

The interesting thing is, fake meat was around long before Cheq used his money and cartel like influence over governments and independent advisory agencies to monopolise the industry. It hardly seemed an attractive investment at the time. As a free market alternative to the genuine article, it couldn't survive. Nobody wanted Pharma steaks, or Petrie dish patties, they wanted farmer steaks, instead. So, when Cheq got involved, he did what Cheq does best. He removed the competition.

He knew how to do it too, because he'd done it before with the computer and software industries many years prior, and for basically the same reason. At that time, computers and software offered the potential to improve the human existence by creating something we didn't already have. Filling a need that had yet to be filled. He'd had an idea. Unfortunately, so had everyone else. From there, technology moved at warp speed, with brilliant people creating things, followed by Cheq buying them out and shutting them down, so that his own creations were never surpassed.

This time, he told us he would save the world from the environmental impacts of farmed animals by killing them off and manufacturing artificial ones instead. This meant using factories, which require the power of electricity, produced by machines made of mined minerals and resources, while adding a significant drain to the power grid, increased logistical demands in order to move and store all the ingredients, apparatus, and disposable items required for the process. That's not to mention the huge, refrigerated warehouses, the masses of cleaning and production waste and the need to incinerate failed product, none of which comes without a "carbon footprint". Cows, meanwhile, just eat grass, powered by the sun, the rain and their own shit. Which in turn, fertilises the soil, helping it regrow so the cycle can repeat. Seems pretty, what's the word… sustainable. They fart though, as do most animals, and humans, and as we all know, because you simply must know this fact, methane is a greenhouse gas, and when the volume of methane a cow can produce is entered into the doom calculator, and multiplied by the number of cows required to feed the world, the calculator tells us the world will end. Kaboom!!! It's a shame there isn't a slot in the climate doom model for calculating the impact of the gases produced by rotting vegetation, including that which may come from vegetable and legume waste, which are of course the food sources upon which we are all supposed to survive. For that matter, there should be a spot to calculate the impact of the methane produced from the mouths of the talking heads of the doom cult, but I digress. Now we live in a world where the current zeitgeist supports the idea that factory meat is better for the environment, and nobody is allowed to question it. And, while we suffer through the unnatural factory food, getting further from nature and sicker in health, Cheq Fencegap's pockets swell along with his moral posturing, while the rest of ours shrink along with our place in the world.

'Are you actually going to ask me any relevant questions, Detective? I'd like to get home to my mansion, have a shower, then for dinner, a little foie gras from my personal farm. I like it thickly sliced and lightly pan fried. It's quite delicious.' He said, straightening himself in his chair for the sixth time. Despite his physical discomfort and a flicker of irritation, he seemed rather indifferent to the gravity of his current predicament. Frankly, he was bordering on smug, himself.

'Your personal farm used to be called America, didn't it?' I shot back. I was still standing, as I had been since entering the room, now recognising it was time to sit down and get serious. Picking up my own chair, which had been pushed back against the wall, I marched over to place it hard on the ground in front of Cheq. I sat, making sure that both my knees touched firmly against his, leaving us overly friendly, and unnecessarily close. Cheq, the notorious germaphobe, physically squirmed with discomfort and disgust at this human contact. 'What's wrong Cheq? Can't you see I'm ready to get started with my "relevant" questions now. That is what you asked for.'

'Ah, could you please move back a couple of feet?' he replied, attempting to be cordial, though clearly put out by the move. 'Frankly, I could hear you just fine where you were.'

'No. I'm happy here. And me, I don't hear so well.' I replied. 'Plus, I've seen some old footage of you being interrogated, in which it appeared to me like you struggled to understand the questions, or had difficulty with your memory, or perhaps a little of both. This way, I'll be nice and close so as I can assist with any clarification you might require.' Cheq was clearly unhappy at this outcome, which was all the more reason to stay right where I was.

'We're going to begin where my partner and I get drawn into your sordid world, and for your benefit, I'm going to get straight to the point. Why did you shoot Katie Hansley?' I asked.

The question was delivered blunt and hard from point blank range. Rather like his shot. I had decided while discussing the plan with Sly that this was exactly how I was going to play it. We figured I may need to verbally bludgeon the information out of him eventually, so why not start out that way and save some time.

Cheq looked at me before dropping his head and eyes to search the ground, or what he could see of it between our knees. His eyes flicked left to right as if scanning neatly listed narratives stored within his head and projected out in front of him when needed. After several seconds, his eyes paused on a spot between us, before he changed tack, shifting his position and looking up and to the right thoughtfully. To me, he seemed like an old computer running an MS Dos search command, attempting to execute the appropriate lie, the white dot blinking away patiently, while the processor worked to align it with the narrative he'd chosen before turning code into speech.

Still looking up, Cheq drew a deep breath, letting it out slowly, then turning his face towards me, he calmly answered 'Because I had to...'

It took everything I had to hide my shock at the honesty of this answer. My eyebrows and forehead fought a reverse tug-o-war, and by the smile on Cheq's face it was clear my forehead lost. It was my turn to take a deep breath now, and after regaining some composure, I was finally able to speak. 'Boy, that must be some damn good foie gras… Just to be clear, you are admitting to shooting Katie Hansley and killing her?' I asked, still in disbelief.

'Yes.' said Cheq. 'That's right.'

'And why did you have to? Kill her, that is?'

'Because she was going to ruin the experiment, and the experiment is of the utmost importance in ensuring New Think lasts forever.'

'I see.' I replied, for want of a better response. Questions such as "What bloody experiment?" ran through my mind, before I settled for finding out the "Why" first, figuring I could pursue the "What" later. 'Was it the letters? Is that what was going to ruin the experiment?'

'You know, you are quite an impressive investigator.' said Cheq facetiously, adding a mocking smile for surety.

'Well, you should have seen my ex-wife.' I replied, indulging his arrogance. 'She could track a Hollywood freckle from its very beginnings, right through to the demise of the star that bore it. You know, so long as they were in one of those bitchy wives shows she loved, and posted selfies on the regular.'

Cheq half smiled again, unwaveringly comfortable despite the scenario. 'Hmmm, we're better off without wives now, aren't we?'

'You are.' I replied. 'It must have been like looking in an evil, obnoxious mirror with her in the house. Luckily, you only see her at work these days. Now, let's get back to my question. Was it the letters? Is that why you killed Katie Hansley?' I asked again.

'Yes.' said Cheq flatly. 'She would still be alive if not for the letters. They were never part of the plan.'

'Did Katie know about the plan?'

'No, of course not. Katie knew about the project, not the experiment. Katie believed that the project was what we said it was.'

'And was the project just part of the experiment?' I pressed.

'Yes, and no. The project helped with the experiment and the experiment helped with the project.'

For someone supposedly keen to get home he was certainly slow walking his answers, leaving out any form of detail, even if they were admissive and succinct. Except for the odd glance, he still wasn't meeting my eyes, apparently content to look at the floor between our knees instead.

'Right, I see.' I said. 'So why were these letters so important again?'

'I just told you that. Because they were never part of the plan.' He snapped, raising his head, while still failing to have his eyes meet mine. 'Katie could have been giving away dangerous information to dangerous people, with or without forethought of intent.'

'Like who?' I asked, wondering who could be more dangerous than he.

'Like the cleaners for instance.' said Cheq. 'They could have passed that information on to others and before you know it, lots of people out there would have been fed dangerous misinformation, because of which, they'd be at risk of spreading it themselves. That's a crime, you know.'

'If you say so.' I replied. 'What I don't understand is why, if you were so concerned about the information getting out, didn't you just confiscate the letters rather than killing her?'

Cheq paused before answering, frustration clear on his face for the first time since the interview had begun. 'Because we didn't know she was writing them!'

His voice carried a little shake of anger as he said this, his face darkening in time with this emotion. I knew straight away that his reaction wasn't just that I had asked the question. He was angry that the answer was true. They really didn't know.

'Well, how is that possible in the middle of OGT headquarters?' I asked incredulously. 'How is that possible in this Global world of yours?'

'Because we didn't think she would be that stupid!' he replied.

'She outsmarted you. She couldn't have been "that" stupid.' I said. 'Unless that comment says more about you than her…'

'She didn't outsmart us for long.' He grumbled.

'Long enough to get her message out.' I chirped.

Cheq looked up at me, his eyes finally meeting mine and seemingly unsure whether I was telling the truth or not. His face was expressionless. 'Detective, I'm going to tell you everything you need to know about this case and when I'm done, I'm going home for a shower and a nice hot dinner. After that I'm going to go to bed. I've got a big day tomorrow and I have some rest to catch up on.'

'A big day?' I asked, trying not to laugh or scream at his casual arrogance.

'Yes.' he said. 'I'm launching our new program tomorrow. The project is complete now, the experiment a success.'

Despite our clash of knees, Cheq did his best to sit up straighter as he said this, as if to align his physical image with the professionalism of a completed project ready for public consumption.

'Oh, I see. It's that simple, is it? What do you think I am, some sort of priest? You confess your sins, I'll give you some Hail Mary's and send you on your way, so you can go back about your business and launch the program that's linked to the murder of at least two people, and the attempted murder of three others?'

'In a manner of speaking.' he replied, his chin raised with indifference. He smiled at me, evidently pleased at seeing something in my face he had all along wished to see. Exasperation perhaps. Truth is, people only ever really see what they want to see, regardless of what's actually in front of them. Especially people like him. It's even more likely that he only ever hears what he wants to hear, too.

'I suppose you'd better get started then.' I said coldly, throwing my hands out to the sides, palms up, to indicate the floor was his. 'I certainly can't commit to sending you home for dinner afterwards. Not now that you already confessed to the murder of Katie Hansley, which is just the cherry on top of an already very strong case for public prosecution (*funny how the term is the same, only nowadays, they don't bother waiting til you're in court to do it...)* against you. The thing you should note is, unlike your lot, I want to hear what you have to say first. I want to understand why. What was your motive? What were the letters about and why are they so damn important? Why was Sargent Ease attacked and tortured in his apartment? Why did you send Captain Ironie after my partner to finish her off in the hospital? What the hell was this experiment for and why do I appear to have been a part of it from the start? And lastly, who the hell has been following me all this time?'

'That's a lot of questions, Detective. I don't think I can answer all of them.' said Cheq.

'Why? Is your dinner getting cold?'

'No, my servants know not to begin until I'm on my way.' he replied matter-of-factly. 'The reason I can't answer them all is that not all of those things have to do with this experiment. I didn't send Captain Ironie after your partner. I have no reason to do so. Aside from the fact that she is your partner, Detective Wilson has nothing to do with my work here. I certainly didn't have anyone following you, either. Not anyone you wouldn't recognise, anyhow. Plus, as you said, this is OGT. I hardly need actual people to follow you… If you do find out though, I'd be interested to know those things too.'

'Sure thing.' I said, now growing a little irritated myself. 'I make it a habit to advise all the criminals involved in my cases as to the outcome of each of my lines of inquiry. I'll send you an email.'

'Actually, I'd prefer an encrypted text. Or, better yet, an in-person visit to my home.' said Cheq. 'I can guarantee us privacy there.'

'I wouldn't worry about that.' I retorted, 'There should be plenty of privacy in your jail cell. They still have internet access there, but no keyboard, so you only get to select from pre-programmed options to view. I'm sure one of them will be the latest news and you'll be able to see the outcome of our investigation on there. There'll be no need for me to visit or contact you, at all. Now, let's start with the first question. Why were you conducting this experiment to being with? What was the motive behind this?'

Cheq remained unfazed by my comments, projecting total confidence in a positive outcome for himself and zero doubt where his dinner would be served. This time when he spoke, it was as someone telling a story they knew well, not one they'd tried to stitch together from a series of lies or remember from a pre-rehearsed statement.

'When New Think united the Global world, we never had to take over land, or countries by force.' he started. 'The occupants simply gave it to us in order to be saved and join together as part of one united Global World, under one set of inspired leaders. They did this, not because it seemed like a good idea at the time, or on a whim as some reaction to a recent negative stimuli. The people handed over control and management because they wanted to. Because they knew it was the right thing to do. And the reason they knew it was the right thing to do… was because we told them it was. Anything else would be wrong. We'd been telling them for a long time, you see. For decades. Of course, most of them didn't actually know that. They thought it was their good idea. They thought they'd been watching the state of the world deteriorate in its current form to a point from which it could not recover. At least not under the corrupt solicitors and bean counters that made up the leadership of the world at that time. People joined online environmental action and awareness groups, believing they were supporting the causes of seemingly underfunded and unsupported scientists who were initially putting their careers on the line by risking speaking out against the likes of big energy and fuel companies. When their cause gained momentum, they thought they had helped share "the science" (*unquestionable, you know)* that proved beyond a doubt that what they believed was true. But again, they supported what we told them to support. They believed what we told them to believe. They cheered and marched and screamed like we told them to. Hell, they even follow the people online that we told them they should like to follow. Half of them aren't even people, just bots. Most of the others are not the people they appear to be either, merely paid lackeys doing as they're told, selling the opinions of their master. Truth is, there simply aren't that many good-looking shirtless men and bikini-clad women who are particularly knowledgeable about, or actually self-driven to "save the planet" in any capacity apart from on social media. Where, all they do is read a pre-written spiel which boils down to "just look at the science" and these horrific pictures… we need to save the planet. Needless to say, nobody ever really looks at the science, so it's immaterial whether it says that or not. Sometimes there isn't even any actual science to look at. As far as they're concerned, popular people have said it, and they must know, plus it must be true, because all those other people liked it, and a heap of them shared it, and it sounds like the right thing to do. Even if somebody wanted to challenge "the science" they couldn't. We control the entire flow of money in the scientific world. The publications, the institutions, the financing, all of it. If you cut the data in the right way, from the right angle, and exclude all those pesky inliers, it says exactly what we need it to say. Then, so long as long as you don't poke around too much, the science is sound and hey presto, we need to make a change to save the world.'

'The science?' I said. 'I've never heard a more absurd term in my life! The very creation of it would be baffling, if I hadn't long understood that in order to gain control of a subject, one must deride or eliminate any alternative to their own position. Nevertheless, the term "the science" is wholly unscientific given its use precludes any attempt to question or study a subject that "the science" has already interpreted. You use it in a way that makes it appear to standalone as a catalyst of truth. You present "the science" as some omnipotent entity. It makes no sense to anyone with half a brain. How can the presentation of one set of unquestioned and unquestionable data by any one person or group of people truly claim to be indisputable and all-encompassing? Particularly when it's being presented by parties with a vested interest in its being believed. If it cannot be questioned, then it can neither be proven nor disproven. Therefore, anyone who believes in this "science behind security glass" bullshit, is nothing but a captive of ideology. If you wish to be totalitarian about the determination and application of scientific outcomes, wouldn't it be clearer for those of us with a questioning mind, if our all-seeing, all-knowing overlords just used the old term "by decree" when you want to demand we follow a certain course of action or believe your lies? It'd be more accurate and make a hell of a lot more sense.'

'I suppose it would, to someone like you.' said Cheq, having calmly heard my retort. 'Someone whose mind was not captured by the persistent forces of persuasion and popularity. You don't feel the need to be one of the crowd, so you don't feel the need to take people or their statements at face value. You would question whatever we said until you were satisfied as to its truths or fictions.'

'No. I would know it was a lie as soon as you told me, because anything that cannot be tested or questioned is almost certainly false.' I replied.

'Most don't though.' continued Cheq, unfazed. 'Most people want to believe they are part of something good and honest. That their leaders are good and honest and care for the wellbeing of the people they govern. They also want to believe that their mere title gives them the access of a highly informed position, from which these leaders must surely be aware of all of the issues of the world. They have the benefit of direct access to "the science" and "the experts" to guide them, and if "the science" has spoken, and none of us are scientists, what reason, what right, do we have to doubt what we're told. So, with all but a few believing what we tell them to believe and, better yet, believing that they themselves decided to believe it, we say what we need to say, and people do what we need them to do. We can't be wrong if we're the only ones allowed to tell the story. What we say is the truth, because it cannot be disproven.'

'Of course you can be wrong!' I said. 'Reality pays no heed to ideology. The real world is unencumbered by a need to align with your narrative. It just is what it is. What you want the truth to be is no match for what outcome the world can deliver. Just because you say it, hell, just because people believe it, doesn't make what you say, true… What on earth has all this got to do with your experiment, anyway?'

'This.' said Cheq, opening his palms arrogantly, as if to present he and I and the current scenario we were in. 'This conversation is the very reason for it. People like you are the last remaining vestige of uncontrolled thought that exists outside of the Guides. The program we've developed is designed to fold you into the mass psychosis of New Think, without you ever knowing it happened. To your point about "the science" we couldn't very well know if it would work unless we tested it and it's no good testing it on existing New Thinkers who've already submitted to our will. We needed to be sure.'

'Well, isn't telling me about it a bit of an issue?' I asked, raising my left eyebrow unconsciously as I did.

'No. As I said, the program has completed its development and testing stages. I am, after all, going to present it to the world, tomorrow. I certainly wouldn't do that before it was ready.'

'So, are you saying that I am under the control of New Think, somehow? That I'm unknowingly following your desired path for me?'

'Well, aren't you?' asked Cheq.

'No!' I shouted. 'I've never even seen your program in action. I'm only aware of its existence in the context of this case. How could it possibly have affected me?'

'I didn't say that the program put you under its control or that you believed in New Think, just that you are under New Think control.' said Cheq. 'There's no mind control here, merely control of the environment in which your mind is allowed to operate.'

'I live in a world governed by your ideology, unable to live my old life, if that's what you mean.'

'Basically, yes.'

'Well, you hardly needed an experiment to confirm that… That's me and everybody else. It's just you and your old buddies at that club that have any semblance of a life outside of the devastating control of your regime. You live above us and the rest of us toil below as nothing more than pawns in the sick games you play with our lives.'

Cheq took a moment to shuffle back up his chair, arresting and correcting from his glacial slide and trying to use the move to reposition his knees to his favoured one leg over the other pose. Unfortunately for him, I had the inside ground on the physical battle, if not the verbal one, and I wasn't going to let him gain ground here. After an awkward moment where I physically blocked his lifted leg, he succumbed and continued on.

'Detective, the reason for the experiment was to test the ability of the program to meet the needs of each person, separately. All while ensuring they stay committed to their obligations to fight the ever-present emergencies we face, maintaining in perpetuity their willingness to sacrifice themselves for the greater good. You see, the incorporated Global World has been around for over twenty years now. Those old enough to remember its inception will know that warnings were issued about the end of the world, and promises made to change our way of life, in order to save planet earth and it's environment from us, and us from the unstable environment of the world. We were careful back then not to suggest that there would ever be an end to the threats we faced, or that the world would at some point actually be "saved". Even so, to keep this idea from people's minds, we were sure to renew the dangers and emergencies early and often. The new problem always blamed on the careless indifference of the past, renewing our need to condemn it, and our resolve to fight harder and sacrifice more and for the future of our children. Children, of course, we'd prefer they not have.'

'To keep the sheep in line, there is a novel and terrifying virus released every six months. Something that's crossed over from wild animals or evolved into the most virulent strain of an existing virus. Each time we tell the people these strains weren't a risk to us until we overstepped the mark, by destroying nature and forcing its inhabitants to live ever closer to us. Overpopulation and greed, the drivers for this encroachment leading to more and more viruses leaping across the species barrier. Nothing, mind you, to do with the extraordinary work we do in our laboratories, which are used to develop "the science" needed to fight these viruses and keep everybody safe from future events… That will occur in six months time.'

'Then the big one. Every unseasonable shower is Climate Change, or as I like to call it "Cha-Ching". Every earthquake, every land slide, every hurricane, Cha-Ching, Cha-Ching, Cha Ching. We hammer it home from every media source available. We create new statistical graphs to show how each and every warm day is unprecedented in its warmness. The world no longer has weather patterns or cycles over time, because they provide an inconvenient challenge for the statisticians. Hell, we even considered getting rid of the seasons all together and simply telling people they were just an invention of colonial control. Therefore, in a corrected world, free from colonisation, it was either a calm day or a CCRAPD Day (*Climate Change Resulting from Anthropologically Propagated Destruction*), the determination of which we would provide on the morning news. That basically meant any day that wasn't 21 degrees Celsius and sunny. Unfortunately, in testing, we found it freaked people the fuck out when summer and winter hit...'

'What!? You actually tested these ideas on people?' I asked.

In response, Cheq just looked at me blankly, waiting for me to accept that, of course they did. 'When insanity becomes the norm, medication is the world's candy, and reason and logic only barriers to its progress...' I mumbled under my breath.

Whether he'd heard me or not, Cheq continued merrily on his way. 'At some point, every person, no matter how committed to the cause, will wonder if we're really having a positive impact with these many heroic sacrifices. Is any of it worth it? I mean, just how many new novel viruses can really cross the species barrier when nobody is able to travel anymore. Especially when you consider that being surrounded by wind turbines, we don't see any wild animals in any of the Global cities around the world and nobody's allowed to leave those cities for the damage they might cause. Plus, since we "fixed" the African problem, there isn't a country in the world without stable governance (*we all have the same one you know*) reminding their people of what is needed, ensuring they are well medicated, up to date with their shots (*which nobody ever is, because there's always a countdown to the next obligatory dose. So, only in the split second before they withdraw the spent needle from your arm, are they satisfied you're "up to date".)* and aware that their problems and mistreatments of the past were only symptoms of the stupid old world. They no longer need to fight or fear for themselves or their country. They must now focus on the broader world and the greater good for us all.'

'Yes, thank God the Africans are finally on board with giving back to the rest of the world.' I said, tongue in cheek.

Cheq deadpanned me and continued without missing a beat. 'Now they get to work in the mines of their Global regions, bringing forth the minerals needed to support the world's technological saviours, while taking home enough GDC to live comfortably within the safety of the Global system.'

'I think you mean "confines of the Global System".' I replied. 'You're just the latest slave master on their continent, no different to the rest. You simply demand more obedience and put a limit on their dreams. Now, can we skip past all this propaganda and get to your point?'

‘Of course.’ said Cheq. ‘My point is this. Everybody eventually questions whether submitting to the Global need is worth it, and when it will all end. When will we cease to sacrifice for the greater good and just enjoy living in the world? Even those that continued watching the Bold and the Beautiful after the eighth time Ridge married Brooke would start to wonder whether this was really the right thing to do. The world hasn’t ended, the oceans haven’t boiled or flooded the earth. When will the job be done?’

‘So, we updated the program on which we all rely, redesigning it such that it will always lead people to see what they want to see in the world. The tricky bit was making sure that what they want to see, is what we wanted them to want to see. For a long time, we’ve tried to force everyone to see things the same way. With this program, we don’t have to. News will be tailored to the specific person or people watching or reading it. You will always get the sense that your viewpoint is being heard and understood, or at least that your view of the world hasn’t drastically changed. You will always believe that the work we are all doing is slowly turning the tide of the climate change and health crises, yet always with the threat of the latest danger, the new emergency and the overbearing issues of repentance and regret that can never be forgotten. The only constants from person to person will be the real world events of flooding and earthquakes and hurricanes, their every occurrence folding wonderfully into the mix.’

‘So, basically, you’re going to lie to everyone more efficiently, and on a much more personal level?’ I asked.

‘If you see it that way.’ said Cheq.

‘And how will your program be able to tailor the news, written, heard and socially shared to each and every person?’ I queried.

‘The whole world is digital now.’ he replied. ‘There is nothing you see or do that isn’t run by a software program and filtered through servers, algorithms and bots. We control literally everything. We know what people want to see and what they don’t want to see because we track, record, and assess every keystroke, every purchase, every eye movement, we hear every comment made, see every note written and all of that builds your profile. That’s not to mention the elephant in the room. Humans are far simpler than we’d like to think we are. There really aren’t that many variations of personality, or that many instinctively intelligent and genuinely individual people. People are taught and trained. Their environment and the information they are fed are what makes them who they are. It isn’t some spiritual magic, it’s the ingredients and the experience that sets the type. Once you realise that, it isn’t really so hard to meet the needs of all the world's people. Especially when you’ve told them what they needed beforehand.’

'What about me?' I asked. 'How could you possibly please someone like me? You said yourself that my mindset is different, unaffected by the need to be part of the herd. I'm not alone out here. There's still plenty of Old Thinkers around, even if nobody wants to admit it, and my needs haven't been met in over twenty years.'

'You're the easiest of all, as it turns out. The thing you want the least is to accept the New Think world as normal. It would be too final, the end of hope. What you fear most is the idea that you will one day cease to rail against New Think and be sucked into the endless vortex of progressive thinking, lost forever to the cause of causes. The best way to keep you happy, is to make sure that you're not. It isn't hard, either. You see corruption and coercion in everything, so everything is fuel for the fire. So long as you know the world around you is not as it seems, that it's not right and that everybody else has been fooled, then to you, the world is just as it should be. That, whether you admit it or not, is your happy place. As long as you're happy, you'll continue to colour between the lines, hating the world around you, all the while.'

'What a load of bullshit, you arrogant prick!' I exploded. 'Nobody wants to be angry all the time, knowing the world around them is corrupt, while watching their fellow humans being utterly controlled by your endless lies designed to feed your greed and give you the complete power that you desire to satisfy your god complex. You're a megalomaniac! An unmedicated loon! Part of a club of crazies who belonged in an asylum until you poisoned all the staff and took control. Credit where credit is due, though. You're a brilliant bunch of psychos. Once you escaped, you managed to convince previously sane people to join your insane causes. You played the long game knowing that you couldn't corrupt all the older generations who had seen and lived through this type of madness before. World wars were fought for freedoms and the integrity and rights for all individuals. Agreements were made and barriers put in place in an effort to ensure we never returned to those dark days. But, true evil senses opportunity and patiently awaits its moment. You knew from looking at history, from the rise and fall of every civilisation, idealist, and dictator, that time was the only real barrier to reaching your desired state of control. You used it wisely, too. Training new members to join the cause and act as agitators whilst specialising in key fields of education, medicine, politics, big business, and banking. Once they gained a foothold, they themselves started recruiting, using their recruits to spread the word. You're a pyramid scheme on steroids. Starting at the bottom and the top, infiltrating education systems, not just by filling front line roles, but by gaining control of the content of the curriculum so that all children were taught to see the world as New Think desired. Activism and disruption of the norm was the key. The stasis had to be broken, distrust had to be sown, doubt and fear in old world leadership, a loss of trust so deep that people would seek desperately for something constant, something solid, something to believe in and trust. Then, from the edge of despair at the fear and paranoia of impending doom that you created, you gave people a path to redemption, a branch to hold on to. Action would be taken, the world and its people saved, but only if you trust in the Guides. Follow obediently and we shall lead you to the promised land. You claimed to know what people wanted and needed, with any thought you didn't already place in their heads, stolen from them with your endless surveillance. Meanwhile, with the most virulent disease ever unleashed upon the planet, you kept the world captivated under your spell of fear and obedience. Yet, despite all your many avenues of indoctrination, influence, and control, targeted largely at convincing and training people to adopt New Think Ideals and policies on the individual level, only control of the collective power of social media platforms provided the ability to truly plug into a global psychosocial collective. Socialist media (*as it should really be known*) is not restricted by physical borders or local laws and policy. National governments of the old world tried to limit or control the content of socialist media to ensure it matched the legal and moral requirements of each individual nation. Trouble was, they didn't control all online content or the companies that host it, so these social media entities were essentially an alternative world, governed by and of themselves. National governments could not control the messages, the form or direction of global thought bubbles, or the narratives of global events and activist penetration of the norm. But, New Think could. You owned this new world, you created it and damned if you were going to let Old Think governments dictate terms in your world. This was the tool that infected the minds of the masses and in doing so, destroyed democracy and handed you the ability to mobilise, or as it turns out, demobilise the world.'

I paused for breath, letting my anger subside momentarily, taking the opportunity to glance at my device in search of support. It was strangely devoid of comment or advice from Sly on Chatter. Only an updated New Think banner hung across the app "United in diversity". I continued on, resolving that I'd do this alone if I had to.

'So, the motive for the program is simple then. The other members of your experiment were telling the truth, just not offering the detail. This is the final solution. A program to capture us all in an endless loop. A Groundhog Day of progressive ideals. Six more weeks of winter, every day of the week. Or Cha-Ching, Cha-Ching, Cha-Ching, in your words… It's funny, you know. Your program reminds me of something that happened when I was young. I was hiking up a mountain trail with my father, mother and sister, back when a traditional family was still a thing. I was maybe ten or eleven years old. The mountain wasn't especially high, though it was part of a long mountain range with a very long and winding path that led up to and around it. The trail started at a small, abandoned mine, several kilometres from the mountain's base, a great distance, or so it seemed to me at the time. The climb itself wasn't a hard one, no ropes or spiky shoes, just a long and gradual ascent along a rocky earthen path, cut into the luscious green forest of a temperate zone. There was to be a small lodge just shy of the summit, and that was our goal. I was afraid of heights, unlike the rest of my family, all of whom were moderately bold, so I said I wouldn't climb to the top. Instead, I would only hike to the lodge and wait within its safe and sheltering walls, while the others would make the summit, then return to the lodge to rest before heading home. At every bend in that track, I asked, "How far to the lodge?" only for my father to reply, "It's just around the next bend". At every new straight, I believed the next bend was my ultimate goal… I lost count of how many bends we must have turned, but we never did find that lodge… You know what the difference is between the nightmare you present and my day on that mountain, Cheq? It's that eventually I got to come down and do other things. You want people to walk those bends for all eternity, asking at every turn, How far to the lodge?'

'No.' said Cheq. 'I don't want them to ask at all. I want them to just keep walking, always knowing the lodge they seek is just around the next bend…'

We both sat silently a moment, contemplating the world as it was from our own viewpoint. Me, staring blankly at my device, waiting for support that wouldn't come. Cheq, searching the floor with his eyes, perhaps counting the seconds until I again broke the silence with my next question. 'So, you shot Katie, why?'

'Because she saw in those old books, the truth. That the world is not ending, because it has always been at risk from us and us from it.' said Cheq, already moving to the next wavelength as I had.

'We didn't need to give up our comfortable and convenient means of living, bend the knee to your will and wait for you to save us, did we?!' I said bitterly. 'We could have done a much better job of affecting positive change by simply reducing our technocratically driven consumerism, and the waste that goes with it. If it was people like you that were shut down, with your greed driven influence on the world, forcing advertising onto every square inch of every internet page and device screen, instead of the rest of us mere pawns, then we could have cleaned up the world and kept our lives to boot. Obviously, as an early convert New Thinker, Katie saw your lies because she was allowed to remember what the world used to be and compare it to how it is now. Was that her part in the experiment? Did you need her to actually build in psychological loops, or did you already have that covered?' I asked.

'Look at you, Detective, learning on the fly. I knew you were the right candidate for this experiment.' said Cheq pompously.

'You know, I never agreed to be a part of any experiment, Cheq.' I shot back. 'I never signed the New Think Global Dream Declaration, handing over my rights to bodily autonomy and free will, for the needs of the greater good.'

'Oh please, Detective. People have been experimented on against their will, and often entirely without their knowledge, for hundreds of years. It only became an issue when social media and the internet made information sharing instantaneous, with access available for all. We've experimented on countless people in dark corners of the globe, who, without reference, didn't realise that the things happening to them, which at the time they thought normal, were not actually that common, until the internet came along and pointed it out. That's why we took steps to ensure that people only saw what we wanted them to see. Not what someone else thought they should have the right to see. Besides, how are we supposed to understand the likely success of our endeavours if we aren't able to try them out in the real world on real people?'

'I don't know, maybe just don't experiment on people, period! And stop trying to find methods of controlling us!' I said angrily. 'Now answer my damn question!'

Cheq took a deep breath of frustration, as one does with a difficult child who refuses to let go of an unwanted question. He again attempted to shuffle his knees between mine as though he might make another run at crossing one leg up over the other, before giving in a second time and resettling himself all over again.

'Yes, we already had the program built.' he answered finally. 'There's no way I'd be able to launch it tomorrow if we hadn't. Katie did quite a good job of messing around with the version we used here. Unfortunately for her, and you no doubt, it was a dummy version, completely segregated from the real one that will go live tomorrow. As I have said, this was always just an experiment. Only two people on the project team actually knew that. One, obviously, was me. The other was a human control and monitoring tool, who, incidentally, I fear, came to have a genuine affection for one of our key trial subjects. Still, she did her job and confirmed for me the depth of the Old Think infection with her lover.'

'Sophia…' I said aloud, whilst my mind hummed through everything we had learned about Sophia in our investigation.

'Yes, she's one of yours, actually.' added Cheq casually. 'Well, not yours as such, although given you've teamed up with the DSSMD to affect your sweeping arrests, you're certainly working with her agency.'

I was shocked. Even though I'd expected there must be more to her background, I hadn't thought of this. The agents I'd been working with hadn't said a damn thing, and I didn't see any obvious signs of recognition. To be fair, she had just been hit with an electro, as well as being hit over the head, so she was hardly in a fit state to perform any notable ocular communication with them. Either way, if they knew her, they sure didn't say. I suppose it made sense, though. She did have a real gun, which only moments before this interview the lab had confirmed as the murder weapon of both Katie and Chen. Plus, aside from the blatant actions of Cheq in executing Katie, it was Sophia who'd done most of the dirty work.

'So, I take it you were in fact working with the DSSMD on this project, too?' I asked. 'Or did you just recruit Sophia as some sort of project security agent with an issued weapon and training?'

'Well, of course I'm working with them.' he answered. 'Although, it would be more accurate to say they are working with me. As an inner circle Global Guide, this project is an initiative I created for the purposes of increasing the security of the Global world, through psychological programming. The DSSMD's job is to protect New Think security and the global world from threats. Nobody belongs on this project more than they.'

'You know, for an organisation that's hell bent on using psychology to change people's minds, quite literally, you're sure using an awful lot of old school physical violence to get the job done.' I replied.

'We are in unprecedented times.' said Cheq, while smiling insincerely. 'A small amount of violence is necessary in the name of the greater good.'

'Unprecedented?! There couldn't be a greater precedent. All of history has set precedents for the use of violence to protect an ideal. You only have to look at the actions taken in the name of countless Old Think concepts. Every religion used it, every race of people seeking to expand, or to protect against rival cultures and ideals they saw as a threat, along with nations and empires who sought regional, resource, or trade dominance. The list of those that have used violence in the name of securing their way of life, spans the entire length and breadth of human history. The only thing that's "unprecedented" now, is the number of times that word is used to convince people to be afraid, or join "the effort" to protect against something they hope nobody remembers having happened numerous times before…'

Cheq again looked a little annoyed now. Clearly, he thought the level of control he'd had over this project, and his knowledge of the scenario would give him a dominant edge here. Sadly, Cheq had forgotten one thing. I was an Army man. Adapt and overcome was our motto. His knowledge of what had occurred, surprising or not, was exactly what I needed him to display. It's why we're here, after all. So he could cock and crow and confess his sins and tie the noose with which we would hang him.

'Why do you think you're so smart, so capable of seeing what others can't? What makes you think that you're right and everyone else is wrong?' asked Cheq, his annoyance slipping into anger. He sat forward a little, drawing our knees apart slightly, creating a physical separation to match our ideological positions.

'Oh, it's not that I'm smarter, Cheq, you know that. It's as you said, I'm less susceptible, so I never fell for your bullshit. When your evil empire took hold, it was at a time where paid agitators had created mass disruption in society. Not only with the viral response measures, designed to keep everyone apart, making them feel isolated and distrustful of those around them. You were also making significant ground in separating us into theoretical groups of different racial and sexual orientations. You could be a female in what was a man's world, a member of the alphabet group, of indigenous heritage in a now colonised region, or even of non-western heritage in a western country. And, in so being, you'd be assigned a position in any entity in the world on your newly introduced quota basis. It was the most heinous act of bigotry and segregation since slavery was first introduced. An act being carried out and championed by the very people who claimed to be trying to undo inequality and bring us all together. These actions were publicly accepted, not because they were good, and certainly not for "the greater good", but because the minority groups were supposed to be the ones who benefited. Or so it had seemed to many. The world had spent decades trying to make everybody equal no matter their religious beliefs, sexual orientation, background, or sex, and in the space of twelve months you tore that all apart and separated us into quota-based categories again. The only way to argue against it was to tell the truth, and to do so by the standards of the New Think's activist dictators, you were deemed racist, a committer of hate speech, hate crimes, or a denier of your own part in systemic hatred and oppression. Yet, to do the same thing as a member of one of the quota groups, was to speak your truth....'

'These days, the truth is this. To be white and of European decent, even if you are many generations down the line, was, and still is to be despised. If you are male and white, well why not just end it all now and do the world a favour... You used this sentiment to ostracise the masses, and those many hundreds of millions of people now had to make a choice. Do I hide amongst the activists, search my history and align with a minority, or simply be despised for who I am? Silently of course, because if you said what you really felt, you'd be met with spiteful, vicious replies to cancel you, telling you you're only getting the treatment that you or your ancestors used to give to the quota categories and you surely deserve it, you privileged piece of shit. That you might have grown up poor, respecting others and had to fight tooth and nail for everything you got, notwithstanding. You are what you see in the mirror, a criminal convicted by your birth, and should be treated as such for the rest of your despicable life. The steel bars and chains that held back the mistreated of the past were opened to release them and, before they could cool, were clamped shut on the new prisoners of society. I wonder how many who stand now on the steps of privilege, feel comfortable in their new position. Was this the equality they had strived for?...'

'The incredible thing is, these quota based hiring and positional allocation practices flew directly in the face of the anti-discrimination laws that existed at the time, which were intended to ban the practice of not hiring people based on their age, sex, religion, creed, colour, gender identity or expression. These quota based equality rules achieved the very opposite of equality, by enshrining discrimination into law. The only real equality they created was the equal opportunity to say "They didn't hire me because I'm *"insert category here"* … It was a time of incredible turmoil in the world and it created stress for everyone. Each of us trying to work out which way was forward, and how we could possibly adapt in this new, fast-paced, and ever-changing world, where you were convicted of crimes you never committed, yet couldn't deny without falling afoul of the moral standards. I was there, and I went through it all and survived with my own personality and beliefs intact. What's more, I still remember what real equality looks like. People must be equal in the face of opportunity, not in the distribution of jobs or assets and wealth. Meritocracy's drive opportunity, competition, invention, and growth. Your communist based ideals drive only obedience, suspicion, and suppression of talent, cruelling opportunity, lest anyone rise above.'

'So, Cheq, the difference between me and the rest is that I had always felt like an outsider. I had grown up in a poor multicultural area. I was small, short, and uncool. Therefore, an easy target to be bullied by people of all backgrounds. I was forced to learn things about the world that not everybody gets to know at that age, and some people never know at all. I learned to be cautious, distrusting, and self-reliant, physically, psychologically, and emotionally. I learned to prepare for a bad day, every day. I expected to have something uncomfortable or painful happen to me. I expected to be left out, teased, or abused, or all three. It became part of my daily preparations to check the mental fortifications of my mind before I ever left the house. When the changes came in the form of New Think, I didn't fear isolation from the masses because I had always been isolated and I learned to find comfort within those bounds. I didn't fear the moral reprisals of the do gooder movement, because I knew they didn't apply to me anymore than they did to anyone else. I knew who I was, so the colour of my skin, my background, and how I was subsequently to be seen by these new idealists didn't matter. I worked hard and diligently, and I was willing to stay in my established work role or do the things that others now shied away from, and I never expected to get rich in the process. The difference between me and the rest, Cheq… It's not intelligence. Its resilience, self-reliance, a natural scepticism, and an inextinguishable fire that burns with the hope of one day returning the world to a free and open society. I don't feel the need to be liked, as New Think sheep do. I'd far prefer to be ignored. That's what sets me and people like me apart. We don't demand that others look after us, we're happy to look after ourselves. All we need is the opportunity to do so.'

Silence followed. Cheq said nothing, just blankly staring at the floor between our knees again. His place of comfort, it seemed. Either he'd set me up to tell him about myself, something which he already knew, or he was simply playing another game with me. I wasn't sure which it was or what his goal could be. Either way, I had delivered him the truth. My truth, as the followers of New Think would put it. Now it was time to tie the facts of the case together and put this prick away. For good.

'Alright, we've established that you murdered Katie to prevent her from using her knowledge of your despicable program in some public way against OGT or the Guides Alliance. Seems weak to me, but I believe you're a control freak and don't want anybody out there telling the truth about what kind of monster you are. We now know what the program is about, too. Designed to destroy any chance of people being allowed to think for themselves, question the world around them, or hold any hope of a free, fair, and democratic future. Instead, locking them into an endless cycle of servitude and fear. But, there's still one thing I can't get my head around. Why would you shoot Katie knowing full well that doing so would bring the police in and end your little experiment?'

I had obviously worked out this was a calculated part of his plan. I'd learned as much when Ironie told me he'd earmarked me to be involved in his experiment even before I was a detective. What I couldn't understand, was aside from trying to prove that he could get away with whatever he liked, why was it that I had to be a part of his plan at all.

'Haven't we gone through this already?' He asked.

'Not to my satisfaction. You vaguely explained that I am different from all the others in your program, and that's why I'm here. 'This…' I said, opening my arms up to mirror Cheq's own earlier gesture, '… is apparently it, too. You and me, talking. Except it hardly makes sense, because you could have talked to me any time you liked. You are, after all, the grand pooh-bah of the Global Guides. It seems you can do virtually whatever you like, whenever you like. By the way, is it true you're the reason I got promoted to detective? Did I not earn that?'

'Oh, I'm sure you would have earned it at some point.' said Cheq condescendingly. 'Well, maybe not in this world. Still, a solid military man like you, with a naturally questioning mind, unbent to the will of the masses, certainly has the ability to perform the role.'

'You're obfuscating again.' I chirped.

'See, someone like Sgt Ease wouldn't even know that obfuscating was a word, let alone be able to use it in context.' said Cheq, enjoying himself. 'In case you didn't know, by the way, it has been removed from Global's dictionaries. We wouldn't want people knowing the word, watching the news, putting 2 and 2 together and actually coming up with 4.'

'Yes, well, be that as it may, I will need you to answer the question. Why would you plan to bring me into all this? Why did you want police involvement, my involvement?'

'Before I answer that. Do you have any other questions?' asked Cheq, instinctively checking for his watch, which had been taken from him. I checked my own as an automatic response, noting the time as 17:03.

'What?! Of course, I do.' I replied. 'We're far from done here. What do I have to say to make you understand that "I" will control the pace and length of this interrogation, and "I" will ask the questions in the order I see fit?!' I said, escalating my tone and shouting the last part of the sentence, drawing upon my military years to do so, authoritatively.

Cheq was visibly taken aback by the force of my message, his eyebrows raised, opening his ageing eyes wide, whilst his head jutted backwards as if forced to do so by the power of my words. Then, drawing upon his own past, he shifted back to a downward look of confusion, his eyes searching again, the bewildered man, unable to remember or understand what I was saying. I was growing tired of this act, having seen it several times already today, so I shouted again. 'Answer! My damn! Question!!!' After which, another sixty seconds of floor gazing passed, during which my fiery gaze bore into his forehead, mining for the truth at the back of his eyes, until he finally replied.

'Fine.' he said. 'Just know that this is the last answer I will give. I'll tell you what you need to know, and this time, when I'm done, I will be leaving.'

Cheq looked up at me for a response.

'I've already told you I will not be releasing you, Cheq. You will be held in custody awaiting the presentation of our case to the people of the Global world. Only then will you be released to face your public examination and trial, which will take place at a time of our choosing.'

'Well, I do so hate to disappoint you, Detective, but I will indeed be leaving after this. I won't face any public trial for my actions and even if I did, I certainly wouldn't be convicted of anything. My program will make sure of that. Do you really think I'd allow free will or objective reasoning to undermine my efforts to save the world? Public opinion, is my opinion…'

I was getting angry again, only this time I wasn't drawing on any teachings from my past… 'Well, if you're so confident of the outcome, then answer the damn question and get this over with!' I said, simmering with rage. Cheq raised his eyes to meet my own for only the second time today and we sat, staring directly at each other from a distance so close I could make out the layered cobweb patterns of the light grey iris of his eyes. They disgusted me, just as every other part of him does.

'The application of New Think controls is not always perfect.' he started, breaking the gaze. 'You go too hard on one aspect, you break the psychological spell and suddenly, the individual need outweighs the commitment to the common good. You go too soft and the stronger minded and the ignorant will simply ignore us and continue on their merry way. Ideals such as these require an extremely delicate balance in order for momentum to be maintained and controlled. Yin and Yang, good and bad, light and dark, they need each other in order to find a balancing point.'

'Trust exercises are predicated not on the ability to trust an individual, but rather to trust a process that requires there be an opposing force, which you cannot see or control, yet must nevertheless rely upon. In other words, if you fall backwards, you need someone with energy travelling in the opposite direction to save you. If they are supporting you by moving in the same direction as you are, you're only hitting the ground harder. So, whilst we want everyone rowing the same direction, so to speak, we still need a current running against us. We need the friction of the water, so people feel the strain of their efforts, knowing that if they ceased to row, they would be carried uncontrollably backwards. We need them to look out towards the banks and see that their efforts are progressive and slow. Because they are not experts on this river, they do not know where it ends. They see only the barren lifeless banks against which they appear to be moving, never knowing they are really anchored to the spot and that only the pictures we show them move.'

'You see, every aspect must be balanced. We need to stimulate and depress, to anger and calm, to create fear and then offer protection. They must know that there is risk and trust that we will save them from it. There must be those fears that they take at face value like Climate Change and its many predicted affects, and there must also be tangible things to fear… Things that they see and come up against, online, and on the streets. You mentioned that you're not the only Old Thinker in the world, Detective. Well, that's true. However, I assure you, you don't know the half of it. Most people are obedient because we tell them to be. We try to keep them balanced with fear of the danger they themselves pose to the world around them and the hereditary hate crimes for which they must bear the blame. We pit that against the good their sacrifices do the world, and the protection they offer their fellow man through obedient adherence to the requirements of each new medical and environmental emergency. Still, that all too human question mark hovers above their heads. If we're all following the rules and aligned in our commitment to the greater good, then why can't we have some more freedom and relief from restrictions and fear. Who is going to mis-inform us if the Old Thinkers die out. And surely they must. Those that were left grew old, and only "the truth" is now taught in schools, allowed in workplaces, and shared online. They expect progress and reward.'

'Our program will control the direction of their thoughts and the intensity of their emotions. Even so, without knowing people like you continue to exist, without seeing tangible evidence of your destructive efforts, your disobedience, your desire to return to the bad old ways, then you just become a myth. Myths don't exist in New Think. Unless you count anthropogenic climate change. We have no religion, no ethereal words, let alone beliefs. We believe only in a fear of the risks of destruction "the science" has proven inevitable. Our fears are of the tangible damage caused, and for anything that isn't tangible, we have adjusted people's understanding so that it is. Nevertheless, we need the threat of Old Thinkers to be visible and by their very existence to maintain the Global fear for the dangers they pose, and thus the commitment to the cause.'

'So, what are you saying? You encourage people like me to continue existing because we serve a purpose to keep people committed to your plan?' I asked.

'Yes, but it's much more than that. We breed and train them.'

This statement blew my mind! He said it so matter-of-factly, without emotion or the evil cackling laugh I would have expected to accompany such a revelation. He sat back now in his chair, transferring more of his weight onto my knees, though I felt it in my chest and temples.

'You breed them?!' I shouted. 'We're not dogs to be used as pets, or rats for your experiments!' I lifted my device from my lap, tapping madly at the screen, searching for words of shock or support that never came.

'No, of course not.' he said, now attempting the somewhat comforting tone reserved for those you consider an idiot, but to whom you must explain a topic you're sure they won't understand.

'Then what are you doing? Growing Old Thinkers in test tubes or barrels, and passing us down some laboratory conveyor belt, stamping us on the arse on the way out?'

'Not quite.' said Cheq, tolerating my response. 'Stamps rub off.'

'Wait, was Katie reading old dystopian novels when she turned? Is that what warned her of your very actions? I asked. Was that your test to see if she could pick up the thread between them and you? I mean, New Think has basically used those books as instruction manuals to guide the creation of the real-world nightmare we live in.'

'Certainly not. I wouldn't give her that poison.' said Cheq. 'I've read those books. Rubbish! All of them! 1984, Brave New World, Fahrenheit 451, Animal Farm, rubbish! They're so incomplete. The story never ends. The people lack direction and purpose. They follow without ever knowing where, or why. The message is so misguided. Free will cannot solve problems or get you where you're going. Free will creates problems and gets you lost. If correctly controlled, you can know how the story ends, you can dictate it, you can keep everyone safe by guiding them always in the right direction, to a satisfactory conclusion, with purpose and value. What you must understand is that the plan only works if you know where the endpoint is. I've built the endpoint, and I will guide everyone towards it.'

'You're delusional Cheq! Drunk on power! A narcissist with too much money and influence. You believe, arrogantly, that you're smarter and know better than everybody else about how they should, or in your case, "must" live their lives. What you clearly fail to see, is that there isn't supposed to be an end to the stories you so hate. Neither is New Think an end, or the means to it, for the people of earth. The only way a story can be eternally completed, brought to a definitive end, is if you destroy the world in which it exists… Well, I suppose I should give you some credit there. You're doing a far better job than those before you ever did. But you've misjudged the masses. Even those that follow your madness. Because, whilst people might want the story to end, they don't want their lives to end with it.'

'Whatever you may believe about New Think, Detective, dystopian, utopian, or otherwise, you are part of it too. You and all your people. You are the control group in this world. We don't breed you in test tubes or factories. We simply take children from mothers who suffer medical events during birth and raise them to contribute and have real purpose in this world.'

'Well, I wasn't one of them.' I spat. 'I wasn't born to a mother who died. I knew my mother. I had a childhood and a small part of adulthood before New Think ever took over. I was legitimately of the time. My thoughts were not curated, they evolved. I knew what the world was, and what it should be, and I know what horrible things you've done to it…'

'Yes, you're right.' said Cheq. 'That's exactly why we needed you.'

'What?!' I shouted.

'You're our source, our example for the others to live up to. Your anger, is their anger. It's your psychology, your mindset, your feelings, reactions and responses to stimuli in this New Think world that we monitor, and study, and distil into the lessons we teach our new Old Thinkers.'

'No. No, this still doesn't make sense…' I said, starting to lose the feeling of authority I had over this interrogation. It was now me who was searching the floor looking for answers I didn't have, in the face of information that I couldn't or didn't want to understand. 'I… I'm not part of New Think… I'm no template for your sick plans to program your human control group.'

'Oh, but you are, Gary.' said Cheq, now leaning forward towards me again. 'You are of the utmost importance to us. Once we lose you, we have only your surveillance history, your digital life and records upon which to model each new generation of Old Thinkers. I believe you know how our modelling has failed so far to predict accurate outcomes in this world.' he said smirking…

I was suffering a swirling sense of emotions that left me feeling light, as if I might tip over backwards as I lifted my head up towards the ceiling. My body took on the slight shake of anger that boils within you and ripples outward when you feel you're being played the fool, blatantly lied to, or downright used…

'I don't believe you, Cheq. This is just another one of your games.' I said without conviction.

'Of course you believe me.' he said. 'You might not know all the details, but you know that it's true. The same way that you will know this is true. In this experiment, you were a bargaining chip. A ransom of sorts.'

'What?' I asked, looking up from the ground. 'A bargaining chip for who? Who was being held to ransom, and how? Who could possibly be in a position for you to have to bargain with them? One of the other Guides? Is this all some stupid power struggle?'

'No, we Guides are all aligned in our cause and the actions required to achieve it. We'd never have gotten this far if we weren't.' Cheq smiled with what I can only describe as an evil intent. 'The struggle was with the lead psychologist on the Old Think program. She is the one who designs the methods of training and indoctrinating all the children from the day they're taken, right through to adulthood. There's also a team that monitors them throughout their lives and reports back to her. She's rather brilliant… Alas, she is also an Old Thinker at heart. You've met her, actually.'

'It's Katie's mother…' I said, feeling somehow as if I'd already known that. 'But, why…' I started.

'Oh, for the love of money, don't go rattling off a million questions again. We'll be here all day. Just give me a minute and I'll explain.'

'When New Think first emerged into the light, Jessica Hansley was a brilliant psychologist and the head of her department at the highly acclaimed Central University, the most prestigious psychology school in the old world. Jessica knew, long before most leaders of the old world, except those that were already involved, about what we were up to and what tools we were employing in our efforts to bend the minds of the populace to our will. She took an opposing stance and made it difficult for us in the early days, even warning some of those leaders about what we were doing and how to combat it. She also taught them about the mind control methods and the group psychologies we were using to recruit people to our cause. She taught them about the creation of mass detachment, and fear in society, and the links between global health emergencies, global environmental emergencies, the need for better security in technology, a global standardised programmable currency, single source of truth agencies controlling science from a centralised global governing body, and the global push for reconciliation and equality activism. She knew these were all tied together, and she knew we were using powerful human emotions as motivators to force people to accept the many fast-paced changes that occurred. Fear of others, fear of ourselves, fear of what we were doing to the world, to the future of our children, and deep remorse at how we unconsciously perpetuated the wrongs of our forebears. Fear of being left out or left behind. These were the levers we used to force people apart, separating them into categories by identity and guilt and forcing them to see the hate and division that goes along with that. Only by tearing them apart could we put them back together the way we needed. Our message was simple. We could only survive all this by working together and following the one ideology that seemed to understand and care. By accepting the one mindset that would unite us all despite our divisions. The New Think cause, under the guidance of aspirational activist leaders, was the personification of the answer they had all been searching for. New Think represented the hope and the opportunity to atone for the past and to right the ship for the future, together as one.'

'Jessica knew all this, and she knew how to break through the psychological wall we had built around the cause. Dr Hansley documented Old Think methods and fostered belief and unity, using powerful yet equally simple strategies of her own. Experiencing support of fellow non-believers, knowing that you are not alone with your views, gathering in person with large groups of your mindset, having uncensored spaces to share messages with those who also see through the ruse to the manipulation and the hollow pillars that support it. She knew this gave people strength and resolve to stand against the groundswell of New Think support.'

'She taught rebel groups how to fight back, how to counter recruit, and how, like a reformed smoker, an awoken New Think hypnotee could be a more powerful and driven soldier than all the rest. She knew many highly trained and qualified experts across medicine, science and law, who believed as she did, but feared the personal repercussions of standing up, or standing out, against the vicious social and societal backlash of New Think. She worked her magic and encouraged them to use their fields of expertise to provide genuine professional research papers, studies, insights and opinions that countered or explained the narrow view, the cherry-picked data and the ever-changing timelines and definitions of what was and what wasn't the truth.'

'Jessica had one weakness, though. For all that she knew about New Think, she refused to meet us on our level. She refused to do what would have to be done to stop us. She refused to fight dirty, instead believing that by fighting fair, the Old Think cause would not only be believable because it was based upon sound judgement, common sense, and real-world facts that were open to being reviewed and questioned, but that it would also be moral and fair.'

'Technology doesn't know fair. It's entire existence, the whole purpose of its design was to gain an advantage. We used technology to discredit any and all Old Thinkers, no matter their present or former status in their fields, and then to prevent them from ever returning, we simply blocked them out from popular public view. It's all very well to know the truth and have right on your side, yet it's useless if you can't spread the message.'

'We let them have some segmented sharing platforms that sprung up, ones that didn't advertise and were therefore only visited or searched for by people who already believed in what they would find there. This was a better tool of control than if we'd blocked them altogether. It allowed them to believe they were making a difference, sharing their message and having their voices heard. The reality was, the same small group of people were the only ones hearing that message repeated again and again in their own private echo chamber. They tried to march in public and "wake up" those sleep walking into New Think. That was no match for us. We simply used our media connections to discredit and label dangerous any gatherings big enough that they couldn't be ignored. Anything else we simply smothered with media blackouts and distractions of "new and terrifying evidence" that furthered the fear in society and deepened the desire to be sheltered from it.'

Cheq seemed almost wistful as he spoke, remembering with fondness a time where he led the drive to crush freedom and democracy. I didn't want him to enjoy this walk down memory lane, I wanted him to give me some answers.

'If she was such a formidable and intelligent resister, how did she end up working for you?' I asked, feeling more like a victim asking why this has happened to them, then a detective interrogating a suspect.

'Because even the most brilliant people overlook the simplest things.' said Cheq. 'She made a tactical error, left a weakness to be exploited… She kept sending her daughter to school…'

My eyes shot up, wide with anger, dragging my mind out of the depths of delirium with them. 'Listen, you prick! I don't think someone who claims to have humanity's best interests at heart in their supposed efforts to save the world, should look at a mother sending her daughter to school and see an enemy who's left an exploitable weakness exposed!' I seethed through clenched teeth.

'Well, in her defence, so did all the other parents.' he replied, either not quite seeing or otherwise indifferent to my point.

'And what about you, Cheq? Anything to say in your defence?' I asked.

'I don't need to say anything to defend my actions in the name of New Think. New Think won. Our strategies worked.'

'I mean, in defence of what you did to people and their families in order to win.' I growled, trying to clarify the personal nature of his horrible actions.

'That type of question is exactly why we won. Your type never understood the ruthless dedication to the cause that's needed to oust a sitting ideology and take control of the world. Full advantage must be taken wherever there's an opportunity, and each action must be seen through that lens right to the end…. no matter the cost.'

'To you, or to everyone else?' I shot back.

'I suffered too, Detective. It isn't always easy to deceive. But that doesn't mean it isn't necessary. Is a lie for the greater good even a lie? Surely it's just a tool of persuasion, if you have only the good of the lied to in mind. Therefore, that deception is an act of kindness.'

'So, what are you saying? It was an act of kindness to take Jessica Hansley's daughter from her and train her to be the very thing she fought against?' I asked, growing weary of his arrogant superiority and relativistic reasoning.

'Detective, part of the brilliance of New Think was that we didn't need to take children away from their parents in order to possess their minds and train them to change the course of history, reshaping the world into the image we wanted to see. Their parents dropped them off at school, willingly. Then, under our care, we moulded them into the leaders of today.'

'Over their years of schooling, parents battled to understand how their own children could see them as bad people, evil people, who lived in ignorant greed and destroyed the world. Their world. The world that was supposed to be left for them…'

'What a load of horseshit, Cheq! Stop pretending to be so virtuous! You didn't do the things you did for the betterment of humanity. You did them for the same old reasons people have always done them. Power, control, money. That's all there is.'

'That's all there was!' Said Cheq with all the excitement of a salesman about to throw in a set of steak knives.

'Oh, and what else is there now?'

'Hope, dreams, positive actions, and a united purpose to build a better world.' he said.

'That's bullshit! Or, cowshit in your words. Either way, it's your cowshit. You haven't been smoking your own merch have you? Boiling some of that poison you inject us with, and huffing the fumes? I mean, you do realise the hope, dreams, and positive actions that New Think pedal are all lies, right?'

'An Old Thinker would certainly say that.' he said dryly, trying on the usual New Think projection method, blaming those that oppose them for the things they themselves did… No matter how obvious and evidence based those actions are.

'Huh, maybe you've fallen victim to your own psychobabble brain washing bullshit, too. You've just been telling me all about it, after all. So, what happened next? You brainwashed Katie with New Think doctrine and verbiage at School, then what? Dr Hansley came begging for her daughter back and offered to join New Think in return?'

'Well, that wouldn't have been a very successful gambit, would it, given that Katie remained loyal to us right up until only weeks before she died.'

'You mean, before you murdered her.' I corrected.

'Of course.' he conceded with a shrug of the shoulders. 'Actually, Katie took to New Think like a duck to water. We were careful with her schooling, making sure she was placed into special classes where the indoctrination was a little more self-paced. She was a smart kid, even then. She had a psychologist's mindset, inquisitive and reasoning. We piled her up with literature by New Think authors, observing the world from the correct viewpoint, along with updated texts re-written to reflect the "progressive feelings, acknowledge all your flaws and demons" view of the world and its history. As she learned things that clashed with what her mother had told her, she would argue and search for evidence to support or refute the point, finding only what we wanted her to find. We took Katie from her mother, right from under her nose and by the time she realised, it was too late. The legal age for emancipation was lowered to 12 at that time. Of course, now there is no legal obligation of a parent to a child or rights of a parent over a child, at all. Back then there was, and at age 12, Katie, under our guidance, sought freedom from her mother and came to live at one of our OGT outreach safe houses, established for those seeking shelter from the tyranny of Old Think parents, unwilling to see the world the new way.'

'We knew that with our influence and ability to encourage children to turn against and separate from their parents, that there would be a need to house these kids somewhere where they could be with like-minded people their own age. Initially, we intended it as a way to keep these kids committed to the cause, rather than them having to face the struggles of the world and turning to violence or crime, or going back to their parents in order to just survive. In fact, that's how The Global Council for Equitable Housing got started. From the need that progressive separations between Old Think parents and New Think children created. These kids had no money to buy, therefore no power to establish their own way of life, a situation that had long forced progressive thinkers into the old tired system.'

'Mmmm.' I said, interrupting his roll. 'One of the many ways in which you crow-barred families apart so that they would come to rely on you as the new version of big government, for all their socioeconomic needs, rather than going back to their families, the tried and tested support network for CHILDREN!... You know, Cheq, for a long time, I didn't quite understand how the virus and the lockdowns tied into New Thinks plans. Why so harsh, why so long. Was it all about obedience and getting into the grooves of the endless "injection protection" propaganda? Then it hit me. It wasn't so much about creating a new cycle as it was about breaking an old one. You'd spent years filling kids minds with world changing propaganda in schools, then as soon as they finished, they'd go out, party every week, getting drunk, meeting partners, getting jobs, dealing with having to pay bills, experiencing real-life problems and realising that life's a bit more complex than you made it seem in your ideological teachings. They needed money. They needed somewhere to live. They needed to survive. They needed to pay their damn higher education debts. Fuck ideology, I've gotta do what I've gotta do to get by in this world.'

'So, in order to break the cycle, you designed a scenario where, for two years, you prevented them from being able to do all the things that broke the ideological spell. That was almost enough. There was just one more step to be sure of success. You decided to forgive the education debts of those who choose to continue in your ideology spewing institutions. Take the real-life bill pressure off so they could focus on the New Think concepts and how to disseminate them into the population more broadly, to foster and carry them through the rest of their lives. In doing so, you could finally get over the hump and have entire generations of people indoctrinated for life, not in debt, but indebted to New Think. They believe that life is far simpler than their parents had told them. All they needed to do was the "right thing" and open their minds to the new world. Their parents were just plain wrong. They couldn't see the world for what it was. Believe in New Think and New Think takes care of you.'

'The fact that their bills were being paid by millions of unwitting people, many of whom never had the opportunity to attend these prestigious schools and therefore had their earning capacity capped, was not a blip on the radar of the beneficiaries. Those that came before them knew, but what could they do with waves of freshly motivated and unencumbered extremists charging up behind them, demanding the world change to suit their entitled will.'

'Yes! Yes, brilliant, Detective.' said Cheq, clapping his chalky white hands softly together. 'I knew that someone like you, someone so strong of mind, could work it all out. That brings us back to Jessica. She taught people of the Old Think resistance about all this back then. We didn't allow her to distribute the information freely or easily, mind you. Only to those who already suspected that something was up, and that there was an all too consistent rote message being parroted around the globe about the virus, about the climate, about historic oppression that had to be undone across the many categories of sex, sexuality and race. Meanwhile, we fought harder, ever harder from every angle to reduce those numbers day by day.'

'With the support of our handouts, and free housing, otherwise ordinary people, appropriately indoctrinated of course, were becoming our willing and ferocious armies, spearheading our many converging causes.'

'Vegetarians and vegans used "the science" around climate change to gain an advantage over the meat industry, where messages of cruelty had previously failed. With restrictions on farming biting hard, bans on non-electric vehicles, and the intentionally limited E-charging infrastructure in the countryside, regular people could no longer take trips with the family to show the beauty of this once crucial farmland and see for themselves it was not as we said, instead believing only what they were told about the shocking climate damage these now greed driven establishments caused. Fresh waves of enraged and terrified citizens would join the cause, demanding to know why we would farm these harmful creatures in huge herds purely for the luxury of real meat. That farm animals provided natural wool and leather for clothing and furniture, that the dairy industry fed a huge percentage of the population, that their excrement was fertiliser for many foods including the vegetables we were now all to eat along with bugs and faux meat was not something we ever advertised. That vegetables and cotton require huge amounts of fertiliser and water in order to support the global population, or that many countries did not have the right climates, resources, or soils to achieve this, did not enter the equation.'

'Yes, I interjected. Your message was clear, the best way to save the environment is by killing all the animals and instead farming large resource heavy and inefficient fans and mirrors to fill the pockets of "environmentalist" investors like yourself, although certainly not the electricity needs of the globe. Killing off the meat industry did nothing to save the environment, but it sure helped eliminate the competition for your disgusting alternate food sources. Everybody used to know that natural was best, until you used the media and "the science" to kill off any belief in natural foods or immunity at all.'

'People ask, why would they do this if it wasn't true. That wouldn't make any sense. They're only following the science, and so on. But it does make sense when you consider the goals of New Think and the need to overcome people's actual memories of the world, the foods, and experiences they used to enjoy. You had to force non-believers to comply. Food shortages create hunger and hunger creates desperation and desperate people will do what they must to survive. That's why New Think had to gain control of the food and supply chains, which you did by hook or by crook. Those you couldn't buy, you starved of business by turning their customers away, poisoning their stock, destroying their buildings or creating emergencies that decimated their staff until they sold their business by force.'

'You knew if we could survive comfortably without you and your desired way for us to live, that there would be no impetus for us to listen and do as you instruct. If, however, the only way to survive is with your support and within your system, then we'd have no choice but to comply. Personally, I knew that the destruction of farming was the real beginning of the end for the way of life we had so fervently believed in. You know you've lost your way as a species when you're so well served you reject natural sources of food, because it's icky, and mean, to kill and eat them for survival. Once you'd convinced enough people to believe your lies and go down this path, you must have known the fight was over?'

'Almost.' said Cheq. 'Once we knew we had control of Jessica, that's when we knew the fight was over. Most of the world just wants to be liked and popular. Even if they do smell a rat, they'd rather go with the crowd right into the rat's lair than point it out and risk being ostracised from the group. Not Jessica. She knew that being outside the group was the only way to see where they were being led and by who, without being trampled or caught up in the fuss.'

'She didn't come to us begging for her daughter back. She knew that wouldn't stop anything or save anyone and her daughter saw her as a crazy deluded denier by then, anyhow. Katie had been fully converted and as a psychologist, Dr Hansley knew that bringing her back in this world, was nearly impossible. The pain of being rejected by her own daughter would be even worse.'

'Losing Katie changed her. Jessica went from being a rational non-violent resister, seeking to educate and shine a light on the methods of control being implemented. To an insurgent leader possessed with hate and driven by revenge. She no longer wanted to peacefully lobby for the rights of individuals, free speech, and freedom of information. She didn't have the technological reach to really take us on and get her message out, anyway. What she wanted was to destroy the enemy by violent force. So, she recruited an army to fight, rather than inform. Many of the Old Think leaders had always been willing to take up arms for the cause, believing it was the only way to freedom. With her calm and rational guidance, she had stayed their hands. No more.'

'Transformed, she encouraged and strategised their violent uprising. Their targets were simple, their heads highly priced. They wanted the people at the top of New Think's information, security and distribution channels. Those that controlled education, industry, and media messaging, especially.'

'They targeted media headquarters, internet sever farms, communications transmission hubs, as well as global banking headquarters and activist leaders. The attacks were effective, too.'

'By taking down security servers, they were able to hijack global search engines and redirect searches to alternate content, which they were uploading from their insurgent bases without the media content monitors or activist organisers being able to shut them down. Their attacks were timed to occur in multiple places at once, with old school mechanical and quartz watches rather than remotely controllable and trackable digital ones guiding their synchronised efforts. They gathered in person and only in small groups so as not to attract attention. They passed messages verbally, banning electronic devices of any kind. Basically, they went low tech, so even with the ever-expanding number of connected household items, street, building, satellite and drone cameras, we still had to be extraordinarily vigilant to catch them out in their planning phases.'

'They killed too, but only those that were in charge of content and messaging at the top of the agencies they attacked. For months, they wrought havoc on our plans. Our counterintelligence agencies were at pains to clean up and calm the masses in the aftermath of their attacks, let alone get ahead of them and shut them down. Misinformation, disinformation, and debunking agents were going into overdrive to eradicate and disprove the messages they were sharing. They had to be stopped. She, had to be stopped.'

'So, how did you stop her?' I asked.

'The only way we could. We baited them into attacking a live streamed meeting of ultra-progressive leaders. Using our operatives, we fed false information to some known Old Think feelers working for her, about the location of a critical New Think meeting. We said it was to be a forum to nominate members for the Global Council of Guides and that many of the expected nominees would be present. The event, we said, was to be live streamed online via an almost universal carrier-ship.'

'The beauty was that the meeting was indeed genuine, only the location was false. The event was being advertised all over the various media platforms we controlled, with the caveat that it was to be live streamed from a secret location to ensure the security of attendees. The address we fed to Jessica's followers was obscure enough to be believable and big enough to hold the promised event. We even held a legitimate clandestine gathering there. A watch party of "in the loop" but not "Guide material" New Thinkers attended and were, in fact, attacked. Of course, in reality, the real Guides appointed themselves and were safely ensconced elsewhere, because even a captive society couldn't be trusted to get the decision right.'

'What Katie's people didn't know, was the surrounding buildings were filled to the brim with heavily armed police and military personnel. As soon as they began their attack, we formed a ring around them and each and every one who was present was either captured or killed. Including some of our own, who saw what they shouldn't have seen.'

'Dr Hansely was smart enough not to attend the attack herself, but with the right motivation, we were able to coerce from our detainees, her location, and that of their small skilled cyber team. Within 24 hours we had shut down their communication hub and surrounded Jessica's base.'

'We didn't attack or kill her, obviously. That was never the plan. We could see how brilliant she was, how as one person she had managed to bring together and commit large swathes of people to either peacefully or violently, at her will, carry out the very actions that New Thinkers feared the most. Or at least the ones that we had trained them to fear at that point. They didn't follow public health advice, refusing masks and approved medicine alike. That made them public enemy number 1, seen to be endangering not only their own lives but those of the global community. How many co-morbid octogenarians would have to die before they were willing to enter the experiment and inject themselves and their children with our magic elixir.'

'They believed in fossil fuels and unapproved science. They ate meat, chanted for individual rights, doubted the validity of multitudes of non-genetic genders, and they refused to join the rest of society in its general fight for the greater good, instead choosing to fight for the individual good. She had, in fact, created the perfect cover for our lies.

These people she commanded whose opinions and way of life were not so long ago the accepted norm, had in response to our forced changes, become the very thing we needed most. They had personified the enemy of good and strengthened the public's resolve for change. For a New way of Thinking.'

'Anyone who had the power to do all that was someone worth having. We needed her. The trouble was she wasn't going to come over just because we heaped some praise upon her. We had to offer her something she cared about more than all the rest. More than revenge. Something she couldn't sacrifice, that she would rather conform to save, then deny out of spite. Sending myself or one of the other leaders in to see her ourselves and risk being her last hurrah wasn't going to win us the day. So, we sent in one of her own. Her 2IC Ryan, who'd led the charge the night they were captured.'

'We instructed Ryan to speak to her in the name of the greater good. Her greater good. We told him to propose that Jessica work with us in building an engineered and controlled Old Think Resistance to help sustain the global commitment to the cause and fulfil the role of inspiring the ever-present need for vigilance. We knew she wouldn't want to do it. No one fights that hard and gives up so much just to join the other side. So, to paraphrase an Old Think classic, "we made her an offer she couldn't refuse". She either came to work with us, or we'd kill her and her daughter.'

'And she accepted that?' I asked.

'Not at first.' said Cheq, coldly. 'Not until we shot Ryan in front of her… She was a fighter, but she had no other choice. She agreed to surrender and consider our terms. Told us we could kill her if we liked. It would be a kindness compared to being forced to live in this world. In the end, however, she couldn't bear to be the cause of her own daughter's death. The writing was on the wall for her organisation, anyway. We were in the process of dismantling every outpost they had. We dispatched officers to arrest anyone so much as subscribed to their sharing platforms. There was nothing left for her to lead, no army left to fight with.'

'That can't be it, the end of the fight. There are billions of people in the world, entire countries that rejected your cause. There must have been others like me.' I said. 'I didn't know of Dr Hansley, but I still had Old Think friends. We connected on various group chats, and followed high-ranking and trustworthy people across different fields of expertise, who could prove the supposedly settled science was wrong, or at the very least make well supported and evidence-based arguments against it and the policies and governance that followed.'

'Yes, of course.' said Cheq. 'There were lots of small groups who followed other individuals or connected with other small groups. People like you who opposed Global actions and knew what was really happening. It's just that they weren't really connected. Not like Jessica's group. They shared information but had no united purpose or legitimate call to action. You, for instance, were in the Army. You continued going to work every day and did your job and paid your taxes and, willing or not, contributed to the growth of the new Global World. You were willing to oppose, so long as you didn't sacrifice comfort and security. You went from protecting your sovereign country and all that you believed it stood for, to protecting the Global World without ever changing jobs. Sure, you complained about the changes, the loss of this, the lack of sense in that. In the end, though, you generally complied with the many limitations we placed upon you. You wouldn't mask and you didn't get the shot, actions which angered passionate New Thinkers, eager to be seen as committed do gooders following the rules. Regardless, you did no damage to our progress. You didn't unify like-minded souls or actively fight against us. Not like Jessica did.'

'One day, she called for us from lock up. Called for me, to be precise. Said she would take the offer and set up an Old Think school. If we wanted to keep Old Think alive, even as a ruse, it should be her that taught the people, so they at least got it right. So that the fear of Old Think would be believable, not just an image of itself. It would be her legacy, her way of still fighting, of keeping the flame of a free and democratic life burning, even if it was within the bounds of New Think control. She had one proviso. That we keep her daughter safe from harm, and if her daughter ever wanted to return to Old Think, that we allow her to come and join her mother at the school… At the time, it seemed quite reasonable. I certainly had no fear of that ever occurring. Katie was the most committed recruit we'd ever had. So, on that we agreed.'

'And yet, you not only failed to keep her safe, it was you, and you alone, that made her unsafe, by bringing her into a plot where you obviously intended to kill her. Then you followed through with that plan. Now she's dead. Why?' I pleaded. 'You still haven't told me why. Because she wanted to go back to her mother?'

'No. It was because she wasn't the only one that had a proviso for our deal.' said Cheq. 'Mine, was that we would leave Jessica largely to her own devices, provided she did not try to recruit outside of the subjects we gave her, and that she did not allow her subjects to circumvent the basic requirements of all Global citizens. Proper registration, must be chipped, must be capable of finding employment and minimally violent.'

'Minimally violent?' I asked, my head now swirling in a vortex of contradictions and subterfuge.

'Well, enough to make people fearful of them and what they stand for. But not enough to actually cause much damage.' said Cheq. ' Real, just not too real.'

'So after twenty-plus years, what was it that broke the pact? Jessica recruited a few ideological stragglers, so you killed Katie?' I asked.

'No… I'm Loathe to admit that Jessica Hansley had outsmarted us altogether. We don't yet know how. It seems that whether Katie consciously knew what she was doing or not, she had been some sort of sleeper agent since the very start. Evidently, Jessica had well known we were indoctrinating her daughter, and trained her to go along with the process to subvert our efforts from the inside. To answer your earlier question, that's why we ran this experiment. To see if it was true. We'd discovered there were triggers, stimuli that she had been trained to react to. Subconsciously, we believe. As it turns out, she had been subtly adjusting our New Think software and security programs for years. Probably her whole life.'

'Well, she can't have been too effective in her efforts.' I added. 'New Think remains utterly dominant.'

'Perhaps. Just not as much it should be. As I've said, people are easily controlled. Far more easily controlled than we think we are, and we have short memories, too. For example, you might be confronted with the same icon every day on your device, then in an update, we change that icon. You'll only realise that it's changed for the first couple of times before you become comfortable with the new look and forget all about it. A change in colour might be more noticeable, but the symbol of an icon you may never notice at all. Before long, you can't remember what it used to be, and in six months, whatever was there before may as well never have existed. If after six months we told you that the new symbol was the only symbol there'd ever been, not only would most fail to question it, they would emphatically agree, calling those that dispute it conspiracists, or deep fakers. Successful change management is all about making lots of tiny changes on a frequent basis so that you grow so comfortable with change, you never really notice it happening. Disruption becomes the norm.'

'The same goes for information, for words, for definitions, for all the details of the New Think policies, what we're targeting, why we're targeting it, and the guidance for what we should all be doing about the latest issue of the world. They are almost never the same today as they were yesterday, yet nobody ever knows because New Think doesn't want them to. Yesterday's definition or symbol disappears, replaced by today's, which, naturally, is the only one there's ever been.'

'This has been the norm for over twenty years now and should have been unknowingly accepted by every Global citizen in the world. However, our keystroke surveillance told us that, for some reason, people have been noticing things. They remember that something wasn't what we say it has always been. They remember promises yet to be delivered, rather than knowing those promises were never really made at all.'

'I remember those things.' I said.

'Yes, of course "you" do. The difference is you're supposed to. You were trained to. That's why you're here. You are "our" sleeper agent, trained by us to be an Old Think saboteur. You see, the truth, as hard as it might be to accept, is that you were trained by Dr Hansley to be an Old Think sustainer… and by us, to be a New Think spy.'

As Cheq spoke, he somehow used up all the oxygen in the room. It seemed to get smaller and smaller by the second, its bland white walls closing in around me. The dour, solitary downlight, felt now like the midday sun blasting down upon me. My urgent need to breathe deeply and refill the empty space in my lungs seemed impossible. Flickering black and white specks framed my eyes as the blood drained from my head, and I could feel myself turning pale. Eeeeeeeeee, the noise in my ear seemed to overwhelm everything for an eternity before the room snapped back into focus with a shake of my head.

'What?! I… how?!' I shouted with more power than I thought I could muster. 'You said I was a genuine Old Thinker. The last of my kind. The template for Dr Hansley to use for her school.'

'You were, you are.' he said. 'And don't you think we'd want to alter that template to match the history of Old Think we want the world to see… We hardly want the seeds of rebellion germinating in our purpose-built control group.'

I was stunned to silence yet again. Unable to move my mouth or utter a sound. I looked to my device for support. Chatter was still up and running, recording the words Cheq had spoken, their stark reality staring back at me from the screen. Where was Sly, why wasn't she providing me support or advice, or rushing in to revive me with an ice pack and some heavy medication, or better yet, a shot from my gin still to help regain my courage.

'You see Gary, it was you who told us about Katie.' Cheq continued. 'You alerted us to her deception. So, in the end, you only have yourself to blame for her murder, and ultimately, for the eradication of Old Think.'

'But, I didn't know Katie.' I said softly, finding my voice weak and uncertain now.

'You're right, you didn't.' confirmed Cheq. 'Jessica did, and you are her creation. You were her conduit to the world. And our conduit to her… Somehow, Katie knew you were a safe house of sorts, too. Or, thought you were, anyway. That's why the last letter she wrote was not to her mother, whom she knew her letters would never reach, but to you. Katie wasn't writing to tell you about the new software program. She was writing to tell you that the Old Think materials we'd let her read had awoken her from her unconscious state. She knew who and what she was, and she knew we knew. She knew she was being played and was trying to warn her mother, through you.'

'Now, exactly what the letter said, we do not know. The cleaners were most helpful, although unfortunately only one saw the final letter, and as you know he's disappeared. You see, we only got one thing from the surveillance footage in Katie's office, and that was the name of the addressee. Your name. So, as far as we're concerned, the circle is complete…'

I was still reeling from these revelations when the door behind me opened calmly and quietly. The light brush of air that swept over me was startlingly gentle, given the news I had just received. I'd half expected the door to burst open violently, followed by heavily armed Members of the GG (*Guides Guards*), a theorised and oft whispered secret security force designated to protect the Guides at all times, coming to deliver their own version of justice, or steal me away to some windowless cell. It didn't.

I turned in my chair to find one of the faceless men from The Philanthropic Ingestor standing there. Just one DSSMD agent stood by his side, an assault rifle at his chest, pointed down in the "ready to be ready" position of all well-trained soldiers and specialist police. Dressed in black coveralls, webbing vest and heavy black boots, his right wrist held the rear grip, his trigger finger outside the trigger guard and pointed downward in line with the rifle. The stick. Though for the life of me, I couldn't see a carrot.

The faceless man had no smile and no expression, whatsoever. He merely stood there dressed in his charcoal grey suit and fine, satin black leather shoes, looking casually across the room at Cheq. He nodded, and Cheq, still handcuffed, stood, his knees breaking contact with mine, before walking slowly toward the door. Cheq paused after two steps, turning briefly towards me and flipping an empty .22 shell casing he must have secreted away somewhere in his clothing. I caught it unconsciously, closing my hand around its form. 'Oh, I believe you were looking for this. It's Katie's.' He said, before turning and continuing on his way.

'Have my team prepare dinner, I'm starved.' he instructed the waiting men. Then he left without another word.

It took a moment for me to gather myself, my head still spinning, my body shaking with a mixture of anger and fear. I suddenly thought about Sly again and what she would think of the things we had heard. Did we still have a case? What do we do from here? Am I really what he says I am?…

Standing slowly and feeling unsteady, my vision seemed to swing inside my head, like one pass of a spinning weight turning on an insecurely mounted axle. I put my hand out and caught myself on the top of the chair behind me, taking a moment to run a mental scan of my body in case I'd been shot or poisoned without realising, my blood perhaps running down my torso and dripping from my knees to the floor.

After a full minute, I regained some semblance of balance and sanity. I hadn't been shot or poisoned. There was wetness at my knees, though nothing more than the sweat from my own ploy to discomfort Cheq, our knees having touched, our shared heat making me perspire.

The spinning slowed, and while I still felt leaden and confused, I knew I couldn't stand here all night. The world's greatest criminal had just admitted his guilt and walked out of my interrogation room of his own free will.

Taking a deep breath, I gathered myself, then set off out into the corridor at pace, stopping just outside the door.

It was empty, not a soul in sight, nor a sound to be heard.

Moving quickly to the cupboard viewing room, I thrust the doors open, expecting Sly to be slumped over in pity or pain, only to find an empty space. The small wooden board running horizontally across the one-way glass held nothing at all, the telescopic chair sitting motionless and cold. No Sly, no recording device, no nothing.

I slammed the doors shut, turning and rushing down the corridors, searching room after room to find them empty. Not a mattress or blanket in sight…

'Susan?!' I shouted desperately. 'Captain Ironie?!'

I was near to panic now, my mind frozen, my body moving a million miles an hour without direction. Heading back down the hallway, I bump into a thin wooden hall stand, catching sight of my pale reflection in its mirror as I jarred sideways from the impact and continued on by.

Breaking into a flat-out run now, I headed to the door at the front of the building and exited into a blinding light, stopping me dead in my tracks. My left arm raised instinctively to my forehead to shield my eyes and try to see what the hell was going on.

'Detective Johnson!' I heard a voice say, then… "Phump"… and the light went out.

Chapter 36

A beautiful nightmare or a terrifying dream…

Before New Think, technologies such as devices, gadgets, cameras, facial recognition, retina scanners, tracking devices, recording devices, and drones all seemed like exciting and desirable new toys. With the invention of every new gadget or thingumybob, we'd marvel at the progress, the ingenuity, the potential. Now they're just compulsory enforcers of totalitarian control. Virtually unavoidable non-human spies and information blockers that never tire and never forget. Even when you tell them to.

What they don't tell you, although everybody knows it, is that all screens, cameras, and recording devices are on and accessible at all times for surveillance purposes. They can track you, watch you, hear you, and if they want, they'll even communicate with you. Basically, whatever you think you're getting away with, someone somewhere is watching you.

Even if your camera isn't in a position to record you, someone else's probably is… Or the one on the street, or the one in your office, or the one in your lounge room, or the one in your bedroom, or the one hovering above you… and we just accept it all.

Why? Why would we just roll over and accept this? Our own governments, those that were once answerable to "we the people" treat us like a commodity. They owned, and then they sold us, and all our personal data, to the highest bidder. Sold us like digital slaves to private entities and organisations, who used that data to control us and take over the world. They tracked our every movement and action and scored us against a standard of their own design.

We were lambs to the slaughter, and yet, the most terrifying thing of all is how willingly, enthusiastically even, people marched into the arms of their masters. Not only allowing the huge infringements on their rights to privacy, freedom of movement, freedom of association and freedom of belief, but even accepting that their inalienable right to bodily autonomy was a selfish and anti-social freedom, only sought by the enemies of a safe global population. Never mind that whatever you put in your body is at best, only really able to protect you, the recipient.

Throughout history, you were never able to control the actions, desires, ingestibles or injectables used by those around you. Then New Think sought to change that. To standardise the human being. Demand a specific set of quality assurance guidelines for the global human factory. Fuck equality, we'll go one better and machine them to within a couple of thou of the acceptable standard. Nothing's more equal than that. Tell em it's not just for their safety, it's for the safety of everybody around them.

Tell em to do exactly what we say, when we say it, no matter if what we say today contradicts what we told you yesterday, we'll fix that. What we say is fact. Experts will confirm it and if they don't, they won't be experts anymore… We'll get rid of that pesky little scientifically proven concept called "natural immunity" too. It's a real party crasher at the Pharma bash. I mean, all these species surviving many thousands of years just because their bodies are capable of defending themselves with an (*use air quotes here*) "Immune system" is really getting in the way of people being willingly injected with all our laboratory goodness, at cost… So, we'll tell them there is no "immunity" … Conform or die, motherfuckers!

Incredible isn't it. That the argument in support of vaccination, *e.g. it will boost your immune system to help protect against infection and transmission by providing a copy of the virus for your body to practice on*, relies on the very same principle as prior infection providing your immune system with a blueprint for fighting future infection (*or, as it used to be known, natural immunity*).

In order to gain support for their money-making ventures, Pharma companies, made the argument that natural immunity is insufficient or ineffective. Which is the same as saying that having a natural blueprint of the actual virus is bad, but having an artificial blueprint of something they made similar to the virus is better? Well, I suppose they should know. After all, they did modify the original virus to create the problem before they workshopped that solution… as all good marketers should. It's like they say, never ask a question you don't already know the answer to… And what did we do? We just went along with it. Line up people. Don't question the logic, just line up with everyone else, and when you're finished at the front… rejoin the back of the queue, cause it's time to go-round again.

Now, I don't know "when" it started, but I'd wager I know "how" humanity lost sight of the line between fact and fiction. It was through the avoidance of offence and the pursuit of universal ease. Those were the conduits of convenient lies.

As with most concepts, they started small. Little inane tests to see how we'd react. Nobody batted an eyelid at the idea of almond milk or oat milk… If you've ever tried milking an almond, well… you're an idiot. What people are actually drinking is almond juice, or oat juice, which is only water with crushed almond oil or oats mixed in it, and I know what you're thinking… What?! Almond milk! Who gives a shit. That doesn't mean anything… Well, maybe. You might be right… or maybe that's whole point. It's just one convenient lie that was widely accepted without question. After all, we don't want to ostracise the non-milk drinkers, so juice becomes milk and milk is no longer only produced by mammals and other animals to feed their young. Milk is whatever we say it is, so long as we decide to use it for the same purpose that we used traditional milk.

Now, what was a fact, is no longer a fact, because it was inconvenient or exclusionary. We can't have that. Can't have facts that aren't inclusive. Plus, it's just one thing. Does it really matter?

Then, there's meat. Let's not call it meat anymore, we'll just call it protein. Not everyone eats meat, and we don't want them to feel left out. After all, when meat's alive it farts, and those farts are methane gas, and that methane gas contributes to global warming, and global warming is bad… So, maybe we'll just call meat, protein? I mean, meats are full of protein, anyway. And look! We've made these ultra-highly processed fake meats, to look, and (*not very convincingly*) taste like real meat. They're full of protein. So, meat is protein and protein is meat. And, if we get rid of real meat, we'll still have protein which is all that meat really is, in any case… Then, we won't be all mean and violent to the cows by eating them in the way the natural food chain and nature intended. Instead, we'll kill them off (*much kinder, obviously*) and that way they won't fart a hole through the ozone (*oh dear... or is methane the one that increases the parts per million in the atmosphere... no no, that's carbon... oh yes, that's right carbon... or is it Co2? Either way, it's that nasty little bugger that all lifeforms on earth are made of...).* Now, do you think we can get fake meat that moves around before we eat it? You know, like real meat. Maybe we could stick it on a drone, Uber-Meats style. That way we could get those carnivorous animals off the meat too…. I mean, onto the other meat… you know what I mean…

Anyway, isn't it all so exciting? We've now collectively come to the single-minded conclusion (*with which, nobody could disagree, because it's the "right" conclusion, and if you don't agree you're just a "denier" or a victim of "disinformation" anyhow.... duh!*) that there are too many of those bovine bastards and sheep on earth, ruining the planet and we need to get rid of them, like, ASAP! God, we're progressive! Oh, I mean, not like… God… you know. That's taking the lord's name in vain… well, not that he's a lord… religion's well… oh, um, or a he… I mean… ah… shit. Well, look at us, huh! Evolved, intelligent beings we are! … following our New masters every instruction as if this set of moral codes and ideals had been written down in a book for us… well, perhaps posted on Insta-Me, anyways… nobody else in history has thought of that…

Except, somehow we missed connecting all of this to the real problem on this planet… The same problem that requires us to produce so much energy, mine so many minerals, manufacture so many products, create so much waste, drive so many cars, clear so much land, operate so many ships, planes and trains, to catch so many fish, to suck so many straws, bag so many groceries, or milk so many cows (*or almonds*)… and it's so fucking obvious… there's too many racists on the planet…. no wait, that's not it… well, kind of… but not specifically limited to them…

Wait, I've got it. There's too many fucking people! … Or too many people fucking… whatever…. Why can't we talk about that one? It's not exclusive, racist (*though certain races do contribute more than others*), sexist, gender based, anti-religious or even anti-human. It's just a key link that ties most of the other problems in the world back to us. There's just too damn many of us. And it's not that the world can't support us, it's that we can't support ourselves…

How did we not notice this was happening? Why couldn't we see how we were being used. Consumers bred for the purpose of consuming. Readymade customers for a readymade market, to ensure the wealthy get wealthier and the poor stay gratefully poor. Keep em dumb, keep em busy, keep em dumb, keep em busy. Simple messages for simple minds, fast messages with fast conclusions. If I haven't got time to think about it, I haven't got time to wonder if it's true. It's devoid of fact or depth of content anyway, so…. oh look, a new message, be afraid, be afraid! Well, unless you take this, then you only need to be afraid of anyone who hasn't. What sort of crazy wouldn't be afraid? Don't they know there's something to fear? Look, here's the message, and again and again and again and again… on your tv, on your radio, on your phone, on your computer, on the billboards, in your mail… Oh, right, that's how…

All these people caught up in a world of lies they can't get out of. Maybe they don't want to get out of. To leave the lie is to have to face reality, and that's not convenient. Because, to face the lie is to acknowledge the things you did to sustain it and the damage that those things have done to others and the world around you. To live in the lie and be a part of it is to share the comfort of that burden with others, reaping the hollow benefits it may deliver. So, rather than face reality, people will instead do everything in their power to protect the lie. They'll kill to protect it, create all new lies to cover the last one, destroy careers, reputations, drag other people in and make them complicit. And if the lie is big enough, damaging enough, they'll just keep building layer upon layer on top until it's so deep that those outside it can never see in and those inside it can no longer see out. So, in order to be able to live with themselves, they do the only thing left to do. Make the lie true. Make it so there is no alternative, only the lie. And with no alternative, we can just lean on the deductions of Sherlock Holmes, "Once you eliminate the impossible, whatever remains, no matter how improbable, must be the truth."

New Think did their best to eliminate any alternative way of living or thinking (*including the actual truth*), keeping old books and even some Old Thinkers alive, allowing only for them to be seen as evil relics of the past to fear but not destroy, lest we forget. And, when that's not enough… when the threat of evil and the worlds impending demise starts to wear thin, because over time the curiosity of human nature forces the inquisitive or those with short attention spans to question why the threat is ever present, yet the end never arrives… what then?

Well. I suppose we look back angrily and evolve again. I mean, after all, at this stage in history, us, now, we know more than anyone ever has. We've moved forward in leaps and bounds, us developing technology and technology driving us to ever greater levels of knowledge sharing, problem solving and speed. Therefore, we couldn't possibly make the same mistakes that led us to the present. This broken world that needs our enlightened minds to fix it.

The world might be a few billion years old, and sure, it survived without us during huge volcanic eruptions, and ice ages and what not, but we're here now. Us. Modern intelligent humans are here to fix it all. We have after all, been recording the stuff that happens on earth, for like, at least a hundred years or so, and we totally would have seen the volcanic eruptions, or the ice ages coming and called a global emergency to put a stop to it all. Well, I mean, if it hadn't been too hot… or too cold… You know, for humans to actually inhabit the earth, that is. And, you know, if there were some water to drink and some wind turbines and batteries to power things that told us about those problems… And, like, someone maybe shared it, so it would go viral on ShareSpace…

See, the trouble is, we aren't really aware of all the stages of history, are we? The balance of the good and the bad. Sometimes good coming from bad and bad coming from good. Lessons learnt and forgotten only for the actions to be repeated again and again. The information is all there for us to learn from, but we haven't the time, or it might offend us, or, heaven forbid, we might realise we don't know much more now than we ever did. We just have fancier looking clothes, a penchant for eternal living and an obsession with carrying metals and chemicals around in our pockets… If they're ever out of our hands, that is. Funnily enough, we have since the Bronze Age carried metallic objects around with us in order to protect ourselves, or as a threat to others. We used to hit people over the head with them, but now they're just used to cancel them, instead… Eh, tomata, tomato…

And, I mean, "we" don't have to worry about all that history now, anyway. Someone important must know what happened before and they will raise awareness on ShareSpace to diligently steer us away from all the pitfalls of history. As long as we follow "the science" we'll all be okay. Meanwhile, we can watch promiscuous "ethno-sexuality quota'd" twenty somethings jaunting about poolside pretending to be "really" looking for love, all the while trying to out bitch, bastard, and backstory each other for social media attention and the advertising dollars those actions command.

We do know some history though, don't we! The bits we're reminded of. The bits we are supposed forever to be ashamed of. And whilst those things might very well appear bad or shameful to see, they are never viewed in the context of their time. Instead, framed in the light of modern understanding. That must be us exercising our enlightened minds. We look at history from our current perspective, whatever that may be, forcing pressure and judgement backwards on those that came before us.

What we should do is assess historical events by first understanding the period in which they occurred, accepting the general norms of the era, and only increasing the pressure of our judgement as we move forward with time. It is, after all, the order in which the events occurred and subsequent knowledge was gained. But we don't. We look back from our virtuous seat atop the towering pillars built by our forebears, judging them, demanding that their actions then, are seen through the lens of the now. Tearing down statues, decrying the formation of our nations and the very governance structure that gives us the freedom to decry it. Sadly, this isn't done so that we can avoid the pitfalls of the past. Instead, so that we can change how it's framed and recorded, in order to redefine our present, and reshape our future, by shifting the balance of power from those who had it, to those who never could.

This, they say, should bring about balance. This will finally be the levelling of all of humanity, the equality for which we've strived. Those who were downtrodden and mistreated should have the say now, and surely, knowing what life was like at the bottom, they should not want anyone to suffer like they did. Revenge would never cross their minds, punishing their oppressors would be abhorrent to those who simply want us all to live in harmony, with equal rights, and equal access for all. Except for those that should have more access, and more rights, and more benefits, because they didn't have those before… So, you know. That's equal. That's progress.

I have to wonder, though. Is the achievement of equality really the achievement of human perfection? Does this time in history represent the peak of humanity working together as one united body? After all, that is the promise of New Think.

Yet, somehow, in practice, it seems to be something different. Something else. In our endless drive to perfect the human race and control the world around us, we failed to create the supposed utopian dream. Instead, we simply repeated the work of Auguste Gaulin on a much grander scale, homogenising the human race into one faceless, right-less, obedient mass. We must all feel the pain of the oppressors, and the oppressed of our lineage, but never can we be an independent people or nation whose customs and actions diverge from the rest. We must respect people's differences so long as they are only token in nature, for we must also all conform to the one united Global World standard of human behaviour.

Surely this is not the answer to solving wrongs of the past or guaranteeing a peaceful future. Forcing people into a singular mould is no different than the Nazis or any other ethnic or religious cleansing. It might take a slightly different view of race and colour, but it's just as terrible and just as intolerant and just as destructive to the world around us. New think hasn't solved the world's problems, they've repeated the mistakes of history through greed, ignorance and hubris just as every group of leaders before them. The Guides are so deluded, blinded by their own self-importance, idealistic faith, and greed, that they've lost sight of people as individuals, seeing them only as pawns in their game of world domination. They've cancelled good advice and counsel in favour of hearing their own messages repeated back, ad nauseam, and created a world where no alternate opinion is ever allowed again.

New Think sold the world a beautiful dream, where we all live harmoniously as one united people striving for the same goals, all knowing the singular, unchallengeable truths that light the way. In reality, the Guides don't really seek equality or have any interest in saving the world and its people. They seek uniformity, and only for the purpose of control. If everyone is the same, with the same access to information, and the Guides control the information, then they control the world and all the people in it. If they control the world, they control its wealth and then the only question left to ask is, what now?

Once you've conquered the world as we know it, what then? A question that history has asked and answered time and time again, because nothing is really new. After the rise, comes the fall.

Greedy people will work together in seeking to gain control. Until, of course, they actually gain control. At which point they become the very things they sought to overcome and start tearing each other down again. Nobody is less trustworthy to a dictator than those that helped him reach the top. Hence, the fall.

Here in New Think, they're planning to avoid the fall. Not by ensuring they stand on solid ground, because their motives are so pure, or because they've truly created a utopian world. They're just building a false floor and telling us all there's nowhere else to go. Cheq Fencegap is the man at the top and he plans to leave no way back, no way down, and no way out, by using technology to permanently trap the minds of the masses in an endless loop of fear. Old Thinkers that never die out, with their insidious desires lurking always among the populace. Environmental emergencies that we can solve, only if we work together and give up the things that we once took for granted. All in the name of ensuring that future generations have somewhere beautiful to live. Oh, and of course health emergencies which are always tackled the same way. Lock down, separate, isolate, take your medicine, wear your mask and most importantly, follow, the, science. Generations of New Thinkers know nothing but this endless cycle of control and oppression, all in the name of the greater good.

So what would really happen if not everyone was fooled. What if there were just one or two minds out there that couldn't be tricked, trapped, or frightened into submission? What if they don't mind being alone in their thoughts and opinions? And, what if somewhere deep inside, there is always the same terrible question they ask themselves over and over again… Why?

In this world of obsequious human behaviour, how would we hold accountable the Guides, who control the minds of the people, even if a rare few did work it all out? When public opinion is the rule of the day and you already control the opinion of the public, then public opinion is just another weapon to wield at your will, the law, yours to apply as you see fit. How then, in a court where those very people judge the guilt of the accused, could justice ever be served?

Some people might argue that the laws have always been applied based on public opinion, which is true to a point. Although, past opinions were allowed to be formed by the individual, based on the impartial presentation of the facts. The law was blind, or at least it was intended to be. Judges were to apply it without bias or influence of current topics, events, or activism. The law should not be influenced by whims of public conscience as likely to change as the wind. The laws were set based upon an agreed standard and unencumbered by popular notions, are to be applied evenly and without prejudice.

Today, however, the meaning of the underlying laws and their application is constantly adjusted to suit the new and ever-changing mood of the public. Judges openly align their judgement with the swings of the public's moral compass, to appease the gods of the present, and apply the law as the public demands right here and now, rather than as it was written for all time. New Thinkers believe facts are only facts, truths only truths, if popular consensus says so at the time they choose to judge them. An old saying once went that, "An even keel keeps the ship steady, a loose keel leaves you at the mercy of the waves". Unfortunately, this makes no sense to New Thinkers who believe that the waves are only knocking the ship about because of the storm created by the wasteful ways of the Old Thinker… Remove the Old Thinker, calm the waves…

Wait! who's talking? Did I say that… or did someone say it to me?… What fucking waves?…

I woke with a start, although I'm not sure how I could have ever been asleep. I don't remember going to sleep… or… much of anything, really. The voice seemed so real. I felt like I was both listening and talking all at the same time.

Squinting in the bright light, I see that the blinds are open, and what appear to be early morning rays are streaming through and warming my face. My white ceiling remained darkened despite the light, so I know from the angle of the sun that it couldn't be late.

Tilting my head forward off the pillow with some small effort, I see that I'm still dressed in yesterday's clothes, so I can only assume I was dead tired when I got home. Which, by the way, is another event I don't remember.

What I do remember, is precisely how yesterday's interrogations ended. The sudden thought of which sent a lightning bolt of panic and confusion coursing through my body. Cheq's people just coming and clearing out the safe house like that, excusing Cheq from my custody and disappearing with everyone to who knows where.

Shit! I thought, jolting upright as I remembered Sharon and that computer guy, what was his name… Iman, had been in my house. I don't remember seeing them last night or speaking to them when I got home… or… getting home. Are they still here?

Throwing my feet over the side of the bed, I feel a wave of groggy nausea wash over me. The room spins a little, so I close my eyes, staying perched on the edge and waiting for my head to settle. In spite of my caution, I'm still a little dazed when I stand up, stumbling to the window and gripping the sill to steady myself.

After regaining a sense of stable horizon, I head out to the living room, only to find it empty of people or any other form of occupation by anyone other than me. No devices set up, no empty cups of coffee, no sheets on the couch, no nothing.

Finding my device on the coffee table in the living room, I key in my code to awaken it and below today's banner "*Safety at all costs*" I see 30 missed calls and 11 text messages. Plus, the battery is low, a most unusual occurrence for me.

Sitting on the couch, I rub my eyes, trying to clear my head, to think and gather myself. 'What the fuck happened?!' I wondered aloud. Why didn't I answer any of these calls? Why hadn't I plugged my device in to charge before I went to bed. It's my alarm for Cheq's sake, I said, trying out a new saying where I replace God, who no longer exists, with Cheq, who thinks he holds the same level of importance. I always plug my device in. In fact, it's the only mains connected outlet that's allowed to draw power in a residence at any time of day. Device charging is as critical to Global surveillance as it is to any of its citizens. It's the external drug they need us to need, and we need it whether they need us to or not.

As I sit pondering this unusual turn of events, my device begins vibrating for the 31st time, and the first I'm aware of having heard it.

'Shaz!' I answered enthusiastically. 'Are you okay?'

'AM I OKAY?!' she shrieked, so loud it caused me to pull the device away from my ear, a foot or so. 'You're the one that's been missing for two fucking days!'

'Two days! Wait, what?!' I said, pulling at my right earlobe and shaking my head to try and dispel the ringing from Sharon's explosive response.

'Yes, Gary!! Two fucking days!' She yelled again. 'Where the hell were you?'

'I just, I… I don't know.' I said.

'Well, where the hell are you now?' she asked, calming slightly with the knowledge that I was alive, her voice vibrating with a mixture of anxiety and anger.

'I'm at my place.' I replied. 'I only just woke up. I didn't really know what time it was or what was going on. Honestly, I figured I must've just blanked out after the interviews or something. Mind you, I also thought today was yesterday…'

Sharon was silent a moment, perhaps thinking through my story before responding. I took the opportunity to check my watch, which told me it was seven past seven in the morning.

'Listen, about the interviews.' she said, her voice wavering. 'What the fuck happened there? I hadn't heard from you since before you went to interview Cheq. I stayed at your place that night, because I figured you would come back to your own fucking apartment to tell me how it went, but I didn't hear a damn thing!' Sharon started to cry now, continuing to talk through it, the emotion clear in her voice as she posed the questions of a friend betrayed. 'So… What happened?! You just lost a day and a half, went walk about, what the fuck?!'

'I… I really don't know, Shaz.' I said again, realising I should feel terrible about whatever it was I'd been doing for the last two days. 'I'm sorry… I… I just can't remember anything yet.'

Another silence followed, filled only by Sharon's teary breathing as she tried to regain control and centre herself. I could hear background noise wherever she was, a phone ringing and the shuffling of people nearby.

'Well, stay at your place then.' she commanded, after finding her voice. 'I'm coming round.'

'How are you going to get here?' I asked, in a desperate attempt to add something useful to the conversation.

'I came into the station to log a few reports.' she replied. 'Saw Blindspot back in her office. Passed Captain Ironie in the entry foyer… dressed in uniform… just getting into work…'

Sharon left this statement hanging, buoyant with the bubbling gasses of pain and confusion, to which I didn't know how to respond.

'I'll bring you a coffee.' she said finally. 'Maybe that will kick your brain into gear. If you still have one, that is…'

After hanging up, I stood from the couch and walked around the apartment looking for clues as to what I might've been doing for the last two days, or how I'd gotten home, or where it was I'd been. Sadly, there was nothing to find, save for the fact I'd also forgotten to put my security system on when I got here.

That did get me thinking, though. There are so many forms of surveillance in the world surely one must have captured something. Hell, in my apartment alone there's got to be more than ten, and that's despite my actively trying to avoid them. You can't even buy a kettle or toaster these days that isn't tracking or recording you.

I went to my desk device, which had clearly been moved from its usual position, now slightly off angle from the wall. No doubt Iman or Shaz had adjusted it in the midst of their efforts to investigate the program we now know was a fake.

Using my remote access login, I brought up the Global Hub - Surveillance Suite, only accessible to police or governmental agencies. From here, I can access all the surveillance devices on the IOT (*Internet Of Things*) and hopefully begin piecing together my movements. Any Global citizen can view the surveillance recorded on the security systems at their assigned residence by logging into their Global Pass homepage, except that's as far as their access goes. They can't check their appliances, personal devices, chips, or any recordings from outside their homes. But I can.

I checked all my chip, personal and home devices, searching from the afternoon of the interviews until 6AM this morning, only to find that not a damn thing was registered.

Modern technology is as fallible as it ever was, prone to failure or system glitches, "Freezing" as it's commonly called. Normally if the system freezes, it freezes at a specific location before skipping to where it resolved itself, usually a loss of no more than a few seconds, a minute or two at worst. Any longer than that and it's flagged as a potentially deliberate attempt to avoid surveillance, a definite New Think no no. Yet somehow, my device and chip showed nothing at all. Not a single record of my movements, interactions or anything else from the time I finished the interview yesterday with Cheq fucking Fencegap, right up until I woke up this morning.

The strangest thing is, I remember the interview vividly. As if it had happened immediately prior to my waking up in bed. It crosses my mind that Sharon might just have been pulling my leg, a smile briefly creasing my face before the memory of her tearful emotion wiped it away. The only thing I know for sure is, whatever occurred between the end of that interrogation and now is missing from my mind. The question I have to try and answer is, is it a blank space, a black hole where nothing can be found, or just a locked door for which I need to find the key?…

I check my watch again, concentrating on the date this time, confirming as I do that today is indeed Saturday May 29th. The interrogations having taken place on Thursday the 27th…

Trying to think outside the box, I swivel in my chair, scanning the room for inspiration, wondering whether the site of some object or space might jog my memory and aid my search. The action wasn't fruitless, even if the outcome was undesirable, the bland white walls around me and unadorned coffee table leaving me with the dawning realisation that Cheq might well be right. It's not only the Sgt Ease's of this world whose apartments are sparsely decorated. None of us, myself included, has those things we feel define who we are anymore, extraneous to the needs of the day. Nicknacks, token reminders of fun times or experiences past, and certainly not valued possessions or heirlooms… misbegotten no doubt by the evils of one's ancestors … It's just as the bad man said, I'm more under their control than I'd been willing to admit.

Saying Cheq's name again brought him back into focus and, with no better option in mind, I tried searching for his device. There was no record, and no option to try an alternate search. I wondered how many automated alert flags, alarms more likely, were set off at the mere typing of his name in such a database. An escalation process would be underway as I sat here pondering the very thing. No matter, it could hardly put me in a worse position than I already am…

I searched each of the DSSMD agents from the case, or the ones I knew at least, each time coming up against the same barrier. No access and no alternate search options. If nothing else, I'd at least validated Sgt Ease's claims from prior to his attack.

That got me thinking about Jessica Hansley… so I searched her too… nothing… It was exactly as Ease had described. There was nothing to be found. Not even an empty profile. Just like the others, Jessica didn't exist. So much for all being in this together, or equal. It's one rule for the masses and one for the masters, same as every other authoritarian state there ever was.

Finally, I tried my apartments surveillance system, which I knew had been on the night I was taken, adjusting the search parameters to the day of the interrogations to see how far it went.

What a relief it was to find the cameras had actually worked at some point. From the recordings, I could see Shaz and Iman diligently working away on their devices, hour after hour, before a long discussion, with much screen pointing and nodding. The audio files were there too, though I wasn't listening to them, instead simply fast forwarding and searching… for me, basically. I had no doubt that Sharon was on my side and that she would have held Iman to account, so I wasn't expecting to see anything untoward from them. In fact, I trust Sharon so much I felt rather guilty just watching the tape. Not that it mattered. There was no grand scheme played out, nor through all that footage did I, or anyone else, ever appear.

Iman left around 10pm Thursday night, after which, Shaz could be seen multiple times attempting to make calls and looking frustrated at the lack of a response or appearance of my physical form. She wrote furious texts and clutched her head. She did a check of the place, looking out the windows and checking all the locks, before trying me one more time, then curling up on the couch for a restless sleep.

At 6am the next morning, she tried me again, before making a successful call to someone else who'd clearly answered, tidying the place, gathering her things and leaving.

Interestingly, the security system remained on after she left, right through until 04:32 this morning, with no sign of me at all… then it stopped. No audio. No video. No data.

I sat, still at my desk chair, pondering the implications in light of what Cheq had told me. The bit about me being a part of both New Think and Old Think. Nothing but a tool in their sick games, unconsciously doing the bidding of each in turn. Just whose pawn had I been these last two days. Did I go somewhere, or was I taken? And, if so, what happened whilst I was there?… What horrible secrets did I divulge or learn? The wellbeing of Jiang, who lived the very essence of the old US Postal Service's motto, letting nothing, not even risk of life and limb, stop him delivering his one and only letter, crossed my mind. Had I betrayed him? What had I really known about him, anyway?

Could Jessica Hansely have taken me so as to find out what happened in the case with her daughter or with Cheq. Maybe it was the DSSMD team. It's possible, no, probable it was them. They were the ones there with me. They take Cheq and the others out, then wait for me to exit, hit me with an electro or a nerve block via the chip, and down I'd go. Stuff me in a van and take me to their lab for poking and prodding or whatever it is they do. To learn something from me, or to force me to learn something from them? Was I unwittingly delivering a message or taking one? Would I ever consciously know?

Had anything I'd been told been true. Perhaps it was all a ruse by Cheq to disorient me and throw the investigation off course while he freed himself and his minions. Or was I simply seeking a more desirable narrative, a story with some sense, where none existed. I mean, it had to be him. It's always been him. Cheq and his army of useful idiots making his every whim a reality. And the more his words rung in my head, the more my being under their control made sense. It would certainly explain all those missing blocks of time. My abruptly ended call to Shaz from only days ago. That feeling of being followed, the cameras, all of it.

There was only one thing left to do, one thing still within my power, my last remaining lever on this stinking machine. The letter. It was the only thing I had, they didn't. I don't know if he was being honest or not, or whether he's ever been honest in his whole deceitful life, but the one thing Cheq said he didn't have, was that letter. Ironie and Blindspot had searched for it, feared it even. Jiang had risked his life to deliver it and Katie had died believing its content a worthy legacy. The only one who'd seen it was me and I didn't even know what it meant.

As evidenced by the recordings, my home surveillance system was off now, having either been shut off intentionally, or having conveniently run out of power at precisely the moment it would have been useful to be on. An event that itself is not impossible, although a little too convenient for me. Either way, I'm hardly going to turn it back on now, so that whomever has been watching and waiting for me to show my hand could continue to do so from wherever their lair might be. The system could still be remotely switched on, of course, each Global residence being fitted with a smart system by law, linking all IOT enabled devices and appliances to the Global hub for central control and monitoring. Even so, that risk of home surveillance was a risk I'd have to take.

Covering my mobile device with an RFID sleeve, despite no longer knowing whether it mattered, I headed to the small side table by my bed. It's an ordinary looking wooden side stand, dark mahogany in colour, around 80cm high and 60cm wide, with a small draw at the top and an ornate cabinet door taking up much of the space below. Despite its antique, pre-loved appearance from the era that shall not be named, this small side table actually contains a very heavy mechanical safe. It requires no electricity and there's no way to remotely hack it. If you want to crack this baby, you have to be here in person with some very heavy tools, or to the modernists delight, you'd need to know the code…

The safe inside is the height and width of an A3 piece of paper and only three inches deep, set as far back in the cabinet space as possible to maintain the deception. Whilst small, its size makes it less likely to be found and perfect for storing important paperwork, unapproved heirlooms such as jewellery or photographs, or perhaps even a gun. It would have been perfect for passports and money, back when they were tangible, physical items to hold. Now instead of dollars and cents and holographic booklets, we have bits and bytes, each of them programmed and tracked to the nth degree.

Right now, the safe only holds one thing. The eighth letter of Katie Hansley.

As I bend down to turn the mechanical dial and enter the unlock combination, the intercom for the door buzzes, startlingly me a little.

Shit! I thought. In my desperation to find out what had occurred, I forgot Sharon was on her way over. I closed the cupboard door and headed for the intercom to let her in. As I walked, I wondered if I might be better off not checking the letter until I'm alone again. They'd already done who knows what to me. I'd hate to think they might do the same to Shaz.

'Shaz, come on in.' I said, answering via my wall mounted intercom app in the lounge room. I could see her clearly on the intercam, the oh so cleverly named counterpart to the intercom. She stood with coffees held out in front, her eyes owllike and dour, the corners of her mouth tuned down in a frown. She looked roughly as she'd sounded on the phone. Unimpressed would be putting it mildly.

'Did you get taken again between my ringing the buzzer and your answering it?' she fired back snappily.

'Uh, please, come up.' I replied, ignoring the barb and pushing the button to unlock the door. I hadn't expected her to maintain her anger all the way here, though I probably should have after seeing footage of her waiting here nervously from Thursday night through Friday morning.

Thirty seconds later, she was at my door, coffees in hand. My entry cam alerted me, though I was already standing at the door and heard her arrive.

I opened it to find her standing there, unmoving. She wore one of her two approved outfits, this one her blue pants suit, slim fitting to match her fit physique. Her face looked tired, worn even from the stress of the previous week, while her fresh familiar perfume with its feminine rose and jasmine, combined with a light musky scent, gave me a strange kind of comfort. Her large green eyes held their owlish form, looking me up and down for a good ten seconds before she finally spoke.

'Well, I see you're still a complete prick.' she said, before jutting a hand out sharply for me to take a coffee. I took her comment as happy confirmation I was still in one piece… but I could be wrong.

'Ah, I see your arm seems a little better?' I asked, trying to lift the mood.

'No! That was my good one… not that YOU'D remember. You're welcome, by the way.' she snarled, before gingerly walking past me.

I closed the door and followed her down the hallway into the lounge room, where she plonked herself down in my favourite reclining chair. Given her current state and level of anger, I didn't alert her to this fact, which I'm sure she probably knew, choosing instead to sit on the less comfortable couch where I belong.

I handed her an RFID case, which she obligingly placed her device inside and sealed, before flashing me a "there you go, dickhead" smile, and placing it on the small metal drinks stand beside her.

'So, you got any answers for your whereabouts yet?' Asked Sharon bluntly.

'No, I can't say that I have I'm afraid. I've checked the surveillance for the apartment, which was on right up until 04:30 this morning, but there's no sign of me in it. Same goes for my chip and my device, both of which show no activity since walking out of the safe house yesterday after interrogating Cheq.'

'Oh.' said Shaz, for the first time appearing to consider that I might not be withholding anything from her intentionally.

There was something distracting about her form. A shadow or movement around her hip and thigh, shifting or changing slightly every few seconds or so.

'What's that in your pocket?' I asked.

'What?!' she said, looking down with concern. 'Oh, that's my News-Pad.'

Shaz pulled it from her pocket and threw it on the coffee table between us, where it automatically unfurled and continued flashing through the current headlines and stories, one of which was truly attention grabbing material.

'So, do you have any idea what happened with the case, at least? Why the hell all the people you arrested are now back at work like nothing's happened?'

'Um, not really.' I said distractedly. 'I'm still thrown by trying to work out where the hell I've been for the last day and a half. I haven't gotten to the others yet. Although, now you've said that, I know they're free.' I was still looking down at the epileptic News-Pad, trying to pick up the gist of a headline as it flicked past in sequence.

'Perhaps you went for a walk and just kept walking for a full day and a half because you weren't paying attention.' sniped Shaz, indignantly. 'You know, like how you're not paying attention, now!'

'Yes, right. Sorry.' I said. 'It's just there's a headline in the paper that's distracting me.'

'Oh yes. Do you mean the one about Cheq Fencegap being "free as a New Thinker" (*blatant oxymoron, but it is the approved term*) whilst out and about promoting the release of his despicable new mind control program to the tottering masses of gullible idiots?' Asked Shaz, clearly having had that round in the chamber and ready to fire long before she got here.

'The very same Cheq Fencegap (*let there not be another*) who two days ago was in the joint custody of the DSSMD and Global Police Service, accused of the crime of murder for which we have video evidence of him committing?' She continued, staring at me expectantly, as if waiting for me to provide a cogent answer for this abhorrent turn of events.

'Ah, yes. That would be the one.' I replied, feeling rather under attack from my supposed partner.

'Then what the fuck is going on?! Shouted Shaz, her arms shooting up and shaking about out of sheer frustration. 'How the hell did this happen? I nearly died on this fucking case. Twice!! We know exactly which arseholes did it, and they're walking around scot-free, anyway!' she seethed.

'I'm afraid we may need to work that out together.' I answered. 'But I don't want to put you in danger. Not again.'

'Why don't you start by telling me what happened in your interview with Cheq, and I'll decide if I'm in any danger.' she said, folding her arms across her chest defensively, a little wince of pain accompanying the movement.

'What happened was, Cheq openly admitted to murdering Katie as some sort of warning or retaliation against Katie's mum.' I replied.

'Katie's mum?! So she is involved in this?'

'Yep. Quite a bit, apparently. I assume Sgt Ease told you he was trying to look into her just before he was attacked, right?' I asked.

'Well, yeah, although I didn't think too much of it, given the footage we'd found on Cheq. I mean, it seemed like there was more to her than first thought, especially in light of the fact she doesn't show up on the Global Hub. Even so, I didn't quite see how it connected to any of this, aside from Katie being her daughter. I thought this was all about a new OGT mind control program.'

'It is.' I said. 'And it isn't. The program is real, but the project and the team at OGT, as we know them from the case, are all an elaborate ploy to draw out Katie's true allegiance. Except, only a few people knew that. Basically, the project was Cheq's ploy to flush out Katie as an Old Think sleeper agent of some sort. Apparently, she had been, or was at least suspected of, subtly altering New Think programs for years in order to reduce their capacity to control the minds of the people. The truly weak minded are gone, anyway. For the rest, however, the ability to think for themselves has apparently been kept on life support by Katie's meddling.'

'Why would she be doing that on behalf of Old Think?' asked Shaz.

'That's a good question.' I replied. 'And in response, I can only tell you what Cheq told me. Which is that Katie's mum runs an Old Think school of some sort, under New Think's guidance. She trains orphaned or perhaps more accurately "artfully estranged" children to become the necessary evil of the Global world. Unable to recruit for themselves and limited in their ability to raise any legitimate sort of Old Think rebellion, they are intended as an ever-present reminder of the tangible risk of the old ways returning. They are the shadows on a dark night. Something always to fear. A way of trapping people's minds in an eternal loop where the same threats to the world exist and the same Global sacrifices and vigilance are forever required in the name of the greater good.'

'It seems that despite New Thinks wishes and their apparent control of her daughter, Jessica had found a way to train Katie too. Knowing she'd be taken or planning it perhaps, she made her into a sleeper agent of sorts, presumably an unwitting one, carrying out subversive actions right at the heart of the beast. Until recently, that is, when Katie became aware of just who she was and started trying to contact her mother. More to the point, Cheq and OGT became aware of who Katie was, and used the cover of this new program to set a trap and draw out anyone else involved.'

'So, is the program actually real or not?' Asked Shaz. 'He's on the pad spruiking it, but that could be another ploy, who knows.'

'The program is real enough. Frighteningly so from what I understand of it. I was told by its head spruiker that it was designed to tailor your viewing of news, world events, threats, feel-good stories, shopping, entertainment options, even social media and search engine results, all to suit your personal perspective on the world. It's whole purpose is to keep you believing you need to remain in the safety of New Think's cocoon, that there's still so much to do and fear, but that the world is just what you expect it should be, so don't panic or give up either. All that, without you ever realising the world hasn't changed at all. It's quite brilliant, really. You always see what you want to see, both good and bad. The program provides the essential balance of New Think, something to fear and a goal to strive for. It's the carrot and the stick all wrapped up in a conveniently automated system that already runs your life. Nobody needs to do anything except keep their systems up to date and follow along with the script. What's truly terrifying is that even if people found out they were being controlled like this, half of them wouldn't care. As you know, New Thinkers love to be nestled in the breast of big government, preferring that someone arrange life for them, telling them what to think and do, so long as they're safe. As the saying goes, *Freedom is a small price to pay for safety*.'

Sharon appeared to be the distracted one now, deep in thought. She stared blankly down at the coffee table, as though retreating into her mind, the outer part of her body merely a shell that her subconscious brain instructed to remain in place.

'What are you thinking?' I asked.

Raising her head to look at me, she opened her mouth and closed it again, pausing for further reflection. 'Um, I'm just thinking through the case. Believe it or not, it makes more sense now.'

'Okay, tell me about that. What did you and Iman find?' I asked.

'Not a lot that stood out, unfortunately. Although, now that you've given me some detail, that makes more sense too. Iman was a real wiz breaking down the code. Especially after Watcher gave him some tips. Even so, he still couldn't see how Katie had altered the program. He found nothing in the week before her death, and nothing obvious before that, either.'

'Well, that's because she didn't get to make any actual changes. Not to the real program, at least.' I added.

'Right, well, whatever we had, Iman told me it looked quite similar to the current programs in use and those that have been introduced since New Think took control. The exception being that there are more AI loops built into this one. Apparently, there's some sort of re-write program that updates all user search history to a "today" format as well, so that yesterday never really existed, or at least not as you might remember it.'

'What does that mean?' I asked.

'I asked the same question.' said Shaz. 'Iman explained it like this. If you searched "*what is an apple*" yesterday and the answer came back *"It's a Pome Fruit, usually green or red with a core containing several seeds. Safe to eat for humans. Available in most stores."* Then as far the Global world is concerned, that would be true and the program would allow it. If however, overnight New Think decided they don't want you eating apples anymore and removed them from circulation, then the program would make it seem that they had never been available on shopping shelves and if you searched *"what is an apple"* again today, the definition would show, as it always has, *"It is a Pome Fruit, usually green or red with a core containing several seeds. Poisonous to humans, DO NOT EAT"*. It's an automated version of the Ministry of Truth from 1984.'

Sighing audibly, I gently placed my head in my hands. My last desperate hope that this was all just some sick joke evaporated at the sound of Sharon's words. I knew whatever happened now, the program would be out there soon, and it was going to do some damage.

'Are you okay? Was it something I said?' She asked.

'No, I'm not okay, and yes, it was something you said, but it's not at all your fault. It's just that what you described confirmed exactly what Cheq had told me.... What does this article about him say, anyway? Is there any truth to it?' I asked.

'Of course not.' said Shaz. 'Read it for yourself.'

I picked up the News-Pad and browsed the article.

You can't plan for the past and deliver the future. The saying goes "build it and they will come" not "they were here, let's build them something to have sat on." That's why OGT continues to look forward and strive for ever improved performance and service, while significantly reducing our environmental impact. Together, we take the long march toward our goal of saving our planet and stabilising the environment for future generations!

The "Global-Systems (G-Sys -9)" upgrade is the next great step in that mission, offering greater information security, enhanced Global Pass access, improved surveillance and tracking, faster browsing speed, and AI that tailors your experience to your specific needs, helping you see what you need to see, when you need to see it. Best of all, it has the smallest carbon footprint of any program OGT has ever produced!

G-Sys-9 will be released in full accordance with New Think's Consumer Rights And Protections (CRAP) guidelines and contrary to the misinformation being spread by tin foil hat wearing anti-chippers, we have not and will not make downloading of the update mandatory!

The upgrade will be available to all Global citizens this evening, Saturday 29th May, from 18:00 (G-Sys-8 will be disabled on Sunday 30th May at 09:00. No access to Global Hub or GDC's will be available without G-Sys-9 after this time...).

The brilliance of Cheq Fencegap is that he wears no mask. No disguise. He puts the mask on you, with its rose-coloured lenses, then calmly tells you just what he plans to do, slipping the real truth among the insignificant drivel and blatant lies, turning the handle and tightening the grip, while you smile and nod adoringly, seeing only what he wants you to see. Willingly, desperately, in fact, you hand over your hard-earned bits and bytes for a new set of mandatory cuffs. We are literally paying to be imprisoned. In a world that loves irony, it never ceases to amaze that these New Thinkers, these modern communists, champion the uber wealthy elites as their Guides, who in turn fund the fight for their causes, using them to monopolise global markets as they do.

Having finished reading, I placed the News-Pad back on the coffee table, along with my empty coffee. Sharon didn't ask for my thoughts, and I didn't offer any. We both know it was just a propaganda piece. They always are.

'So, we know what's happening with OGT and their program.' said Shaz, 'But what about all the suspects, what about our case? It can't just disappear. We know what was done and we can prove who did it.'

‘What case?’ I said. ‘I told you. Cheq admitted everything to me, then walked out under the protection of a faceless man and an armed DSSMD agent. They knew that by any standard, what he’d done was wrong, yet it didn’t matter. I, we, the Police Service, was not only powerless to stop it, we actively took part in its conveyance. The reasons for doing it are exactly what we think they are. In spite of which, nobody except for you or I is surprised or even cares. You see, early on in the interrogation with Cheq, he told me he would leave when he’d finished telling me what I needed to know and be home in time for dinner. Prior to that, Ironie had begrudgingly admitted her involvement, then stiffly disavowed any thought of her actions adding up to a crime. Quite frankly, I think even if we released every bit of surveillance footage we have and pursued the prosecution on our own, nobody would bat an eyelid. Not that we’d ever get that far without being locked up ourselves for crimes against New Think.’

‘So what, that’s it?’ She asked. ‘You’re giving up? We’re done? They all just get away with it like nothing ever happened?... Murders, assaults, imprisonment of society, does it all mean nothing? I mean, there must be something we can do. What did Sly say? Do we have any allies left in this world?’

‘I don’t know.’ I replied. ‘I never got a chance to speak to Sly. She had evidentially been removed from the building by the time I left. Hell, maybe she left of her own accord. Who knows what happened to her or why.’

‘What about your friend, Milly? You said you trusted him, and I trusted your faith. Have you heard from him? Can he help us?’

‘Unfortunately, I no longer know if that faith was well placed by you or me. I haven’t heard from him yet and there were no missed calls from him, so he clearly wasn’t worried about me. Whatever that means. Now that you mention it, though, I do need to speak to him and this seems as good a time as any to find out what he knows. Even if he isn’t on our side, we haven’t got much left to lose, and with a bit of luck he might be able to tell us where the hell I’ve been for the last day and a half.’

Shaz looked nervous, and I felt it. She was sitting forward now on the edge of her chair, her elbows resting hard on her knees, while she tapped an anxious tune with her empty coffee cup on her injured arm. Without conscious thought I had mirrored her pose, leaning forward myself, my own elbows resting on my knees, my still sheathed device held in hand. This was the last frontier for me. With the exception of Sharon, the loss of whom didn’t bear thinking about, Milford was the person I’d known the longest in this world, and the last friend whose trust I could least stand to lose. Sadly, I knew full well that knowing someone a long time does not preclude them from doing you harm or betraying your trust.

I removed my device from the protective cover and hit the dial icon for Milly's number. He answered after just two rings.

'Milly, you're alive.' I said, attempting joviality without much humour or conviction.

'Yes, good to hear that you are, too.' he answered, his voice laced with genuine concern.

'Listen, I have a couple of questions to ask you about the case and what's occurred since our interviews. I have Shaz here with me, too. You don't mind if she listens in, do you?' I asked.

'No. In fact, it's good that you're both there together, because I have some directives I need to pass on to both of you.' he said. 'These come directly from the head of the DSSMD and have been signed off by the Global Security Commissioner, which I'm sure I don't need to remind you is also the head of the Police Service.'

My device was already on speaker, so Shaz had heard this too. We looked at each other, concern and suspicion on both our faces.

'Okay…' I said hesitantly. 'We're listening.'

'Regarding your assignment on the investigation into Ms Katie Hansley's murder, and all other associated activities, you are hereby instructed to, stand, down. Now, this isn't written here, but I'm going to repeat that, because I know you struggle with instructions. Detective Johnson and Detective Wilson are both instructed to, STAND, DOWN. This case is to be closed effective immediately and marked NGP-BOTGG-Top Secret. The filing of this case will be handled personally by your station chief.'

NGP-BOTGG stands for "No Guilty Party - Benefit Of The Greater Good". Top Secret means what it always has, only these days, without express permission from the deputy of the DSSMD or higher, nobody is allowed to see that marking, anyway. That means that as unlikely as it may be in this world, there ain't a soul who's going to review these case files and determine that the outcome is in need of further review.

Even though I'd expected this outcome, knowing it couldn't possibly turn out any other way, I was still shocked at the finality of Milly's statement. The blows were mounting now, and I could feel them beating me down. Shaz looked shocked too, the wide expression on her face, telling. Still, she recovered quicker than I did and fired off her response.

'What?!' she exclaimed. 'There were two murders and at least three attempted murders and we can prove them all!' she shouted, unwilling to let go of the empirical truths she had observed.

'No! You can't! …' said Milly, leaving space for the gravity of his statement to sink in. 'All you can prove, is that extreme actions were taken to protect New Think and ensure the safety of the Global World. Cheq Fencegap is a hero, as are Sophia, Chief Blindspot and Captain Ironie.'

'Are you fucking kidding me?!' I blurted out from deep under the oppressive weight of his statements.

'No, I most certainly am not!' said Milly stubbornly, showing staunch commitment to following the directive he had received.

'Milly, they killed people.' I said, almost softly. 'You can still see that, can't you? You know this is wrong.'

'No, Gary. They took extreme actions to protect New Think and they will be pardoned for those actions.' He said again, wavering slightly the second time.

Surely he couldn't be comfortable with all this. This wasn't James Bond using his licence to kill in order to protect the world from evil, performing a necessary act of violence the likes of which the good people of the world need never become aware. This was the head of SPECTRE succeeding in killing the only people left that could stop him. Then, having those actions quietly covered up, leaving the world without protection and forever in their control.

The call fell silent, neither party happy with its progress thus far. Sharon, having ditched her coffee cup, now used her good hand to frantically twirl her hair, a look of intense anger on her face.

I stared at my device, watching the timer continue counting up the seconds of the call. The mindless automation of it calming me somehow.

On the line we heard a heavy sigh, then it was Milly again, who was next and last to speak.

'You will receive these instructions electronically within the next thirty minutes. You are not to pursue the case or any of the former suspects any further. Your fellow police officers whom you suspected of being involved, have or will return to work, and because of their brave efforts in going above and beyond to protect the Global World, they will all be receiving commendations for their actions. The Commissioner has deemed that you will both receive reprimands for blindly attempting to apply the law, without first considering these actions from the position of the Global greater good. As such, you will be required to undertake a New Think re-education course commencing tomorrow at the Mid-Town Centre for Global Re-Education. The head of the DSSMD and the Global Security Commissioner nonetheless thanks you for your efforts. End of directive.'

'Now, with that official bit out of the way, I will also unofficially tell you that the DSSMD is continuing to pursue the fugitive Jiang and the

8th letter he stole from OGT headquarters. If you happen to know of his whereabouts, or in the course of your investigation, came across anything that might assist, just be sure and let me know. It's important you understand that I cannot protect you if you're found to be withholding information from us.'

Milford let this statement hang in the ether a moment, then terminated the call without another word.

As soon as the counter stopped, I placed my device back in the RFID case and joined Sharon in an extended period of silent seething and reflection, during which we focussed intently on just how much we hated every word Milford had said. The silence wasn't so much deafening as it was definitive, in that we had certainly reached the end of the road.

After a good half hour of contemplation and introspection on this latest development, I had come to only one conclusion. I was pissed off! Really pissed off!

I wasn't overly bothered by the requirement to undergo New Think re-education. It was compulsory for known Old Thinkers to undertake the course yearly anyway, so both Sharon and I would just be plucking two carrots with one hand (*New Think saying, though still considered offensive to Pro-Rooters. Who aren't as fun as you'd think...).* Rather clever of them, really. The two weeks it takes to complete the course provides a nice time buffer between the disastrous end to the case, and Sharon and I having to re-enter the Station and interact with the criminals, who despite their crimes, will remain our colleges and bosses, now with bravery badges to boot.

Plus, as angry as I am at Cheq being pardoned for his crimes, I shouldn't be surprised. New Think laws are not blind and those that answer to them are not measured equally. Perhaps they never were blind, seeing only right and left as directed by their guardians. True justice cannot be delivered in a world like this. The old boys club hasn't disbanded, it just evolved with the times and got better at controlling the narrative.

'You want another coffee?' I asked the still silent Sharon. Her legs were curled up under her on the chair where she sat side on, unmoved since the call had ended. As I watched, she unfolded them, smoothing the material of her pant legs as she did, and swung around to a regular seated position.

'Not really.' she said bitterly. 'I could do with something to eat, though.'

Standing, she performed a well-rehearsed stretch, not unlike a cat who stands after a long slumber, and wandered languidly towards the kitchen.

‘Where are you going?’ I asked. ‘I don’t think I have much food. If you’re hungry, we may have to go out to get something. If they haven’t removed all our credits, that is.’

‘I’m just going to your fridge to collect the packet of mint slice biscuits I brought over… two days ago… They were intended as a celebration of our successful case.’ she said without added sarcasm, though its absence was clearly a trap.

Opening the fridge, she shouted back over her shoulder, ‘I guess the bickies will be equally good in consoling us as they would have been in celebrating success.’

From where I sat on the couch, I had a direct line of sight to the open and sparsely occupied fridge where Sharon stood. After removing the packet, the fridge door swung closed and when it did, a small green light on the handle blinked back on, indicating that this camera had resumed the operating mode, taking back control from the one mounted on the inner frame. Watching Sharon, biscuits in hand, heading back towards the lounge room, something occurred to me.

The fridge is on a separate system to the rest of the apartment. Powered by its own mini turbine, as required by the Treaty for Equitable And Sustainable Energy Distribution (*TEASED*). A treaty, of course, being between two parties, those being, we the Global citizens who need the energy to survive, and them, the government who’ll grudgingly supply it (*well, some of it*) at our expense.

The fridge is the one appliance accepted as necessary to keep running all day and night, because as far as the Guides are concerned, the waste from spoiled food is worse than the fact you need it to begin with.

Stupid as it may sound to someone who hasn’t lived in this world, fridges track our usage now. They independently go online to reorder approved staples or pre-selected food options and log the number of times the door is opened, registering and recording what is added or removed. They also record you using a movement sensor, which activates both audio and video monitoring. This surveillance footage is stored in a separate location to the rest, due to running off an independent power source. It would, you’d think, be possible to collate all that data in one location, however this is just another one of those times were logic and common sense (*Oops, that’s deadnaming, it’s now “common cause” there is no “sense” in this world*) were absent from the plan.

All fridge movement sensors are, at New Thinks insistence, extremely sensitive, because they don’t want to miss anything that occurs in the house from any angle which they may later want to review. Plus, heaps of shady shit gets stored in fridges and freezers, and lots of private discussions are held in a kitchen setting.

I leapt from my seat, grabbed my home device, and returned to the couch, where I logged into a special section of the Global

Surveillance Database, also located on the Global Hub. The GSD contains appliance specific surveillance not available to your average J-Public (*Joe was, of course, toxically masculine patriarchal hogwash and was thusly banned from use in Global slang*). I found my fridge, narrowed the search field from 04:00 today to the current time, hit the go button… and there it was. A data file, shockingly present, complete and ready to be viewed. That small gleaming camera icon, a beacon of hope for the truth.

By this time Sharon had returned from the kitchen plonking herself next to me on the couch in order to share her biscuits. She was now looking, as I was, intently, at the screen of my device.

'Is that from this morning?' she asked.

'Yeah.' I said, not knowing what else to say.

'Well, hit play, for fuck's sake!' She instructed, before eagerly biting into a biscuit.

I did. The vision kicked in with just a flicker past the doorway of the kitchen. That flicker, as it turned out, was my unconscious foot, poking out behind the elbow of a rather familiar looking man. He had been a figure on the periphery of my life for the last few days, though I knew not who he was. Last I saw him, he was still carrying his backpack and leaning on a tree. He was accompanied soon by my other foot, then my body, and that of a struggling woman whose elbows were hooked up under my armpits.

These two familiar strangers carried my limp, unconscious body through the doorway and across the living room, before disappearing into my bedroom, where I awoke only hours later.

Seconds after they vanished from view, a third figure entered the shot. It was a female figure, her body a shape I'm sure I'd seen before. I know her name, too… Dr Jessica Hansley.

'Place him on the bed and get that letter from the safe.' she shouted. 'The code is 20, 30, 24, 7.'

From go to whoa, it took a total of three minutes for Jessica's goons to enter my apartment, cart me through to the bedroom and exit again. Before leaving, she removed my device from a small bag she carried and placed it on the coffee table, turning to look directly at the camera, then walking casually out of the apartment, following behind her henchmen.

Sixty seconds later, the recording stopped.

For what seemed like the hundredth time today, Sharon and I sat silent, bemused by the footage we'd just seen.

A half-eaten biscuit hovered inches from Sharon's partially opened mouth, neither moving towards the other, her eyes still staring blankly where the image had been displayed.

I stood suddenly, the obvious striking me into action, and moved rapidly into the bedroom. I covered the distance from the couch in a mere second or two, instantly dropping to my knees and spinning the wheel like a madman, flinging open the safe door and revealing its contents.

The letter was gone. In its place, stood a simple, elegant note.

Now you know.

See you soon.

JH

The End

ABOUT THE AUTHOR

Born in Sydney, Australia, I grew up as an avid reader and began writing for my own pleasure while serving in the Australian Army. I have previously been an Army Aircraft Technician, a Workers Compensation / Life Insurance Claims Assessor, and planner/coordinator of freight trains operating across Australia.

This is my first novel, in what I plan to be a series based on these characters and concept. At the time of publishing, the second book in the Gaz and Shaz series is well underway.

Stay tuned for more…

Manufactured by Amazon.com.au
Sydney, New South Wales, Australia

16769002R00285